TELL ME NO SECRETS

Also by Joy Fielding

See Jane Run
The Best of Friends
The Transformation
Trance
Kiss Mommy Goodbye
The Other Woman
Life Penalty
The Deep End
Good Intentions

TELL ME NO SECRETS

Joy Fielding

HEADLINE

First published in Great Britain in 1993
By HEADLINE BOOK PUBLISHING PLC

10 9 8 7 6 5 4 3 2 1

British Library Cataloguing in Publication Data

Fielding, Joy
Tell Me No Secrets
I. Title
813.54 [F]

ISBN   0-7472-0797-6

Typeset by Avon Dataset Ltd, Bidford-on-Avon
Printed and bound in Great Britain by
Clays Ltd, St Ives PLC

HEADLINE BOOK PUBLISHING PLC
Headline House
79 Great Titchfield Street
London W1P 7FN

For Renee

ACKNOWLEDGEMENTS

I would like to thank the following people for the help, they gave me in the writing of this book: Neil Cohen, who provided me with a crash course in the law and generously gave of his time and expertise — he is not only a lawyer, but a poet as well; Dean Morask, Chief of The Criminal Prosecutions Bureau for Cook County, who took time from his busy schedule to grant me a prolonged interview and answer some pretty far-out questions; the Honourable Judge Earl Strayhorn, who allowed me into his courtroom and showed me how justice is best served.

I would also like to thank Julie Rickerd for knowing just the right things to say just when I needed to hear them.

My deepest gratitude and appreciation to all of you.

Chapter One

He was waiting for her when she got to work. Or so it seemed to
Jess, who spotted him immediately, standing motionless at the
corner of California Avenue and Twenty-Fifth Street. She felt
him watching her as she left the parking garage and hurried
across the street toward the Administration Building, his dark
eyes colder than the late October wind that played with his
straggly blond hair, his bare hands clenched into tight fists
outside the pockets of his well-worn brown leather jacket. Did
she know him?

His body shifted slightly as Jess drew closer, and she saw that
his mouth was twisted into an eerie little half-grin that pulled
at one side of his full lips, as if he knew something that she
didn't. It was a smile devoid of warmth, the smile of one who, as
a child, enjoyed pulling the wings off butterflies, she thought
with a shudder, ignoring the almost imperceptible nod of his
head that greeted her as their eyes connected. A smile full of
secrets, she understood, turning away quickly, and running up
the front steps, suddenly afraid.

Jess felt the man move into position behind her, knew
without looking that he was mounting the stairs after her, the
deliberateness of his steps vibrating throughout her body. She
reached the landing and pushed her shoulder against the heavy
glass revolving door, the stranger stopping at the top of the
steps, his face appearing and reappearing with each rotation of
the glass, the sly smile never leaving his lips.

I am Death, the smile whispered. *I have come for you.*

Jess heard a loud gasp escape her lips, understood from the
shuffling along the marble floor behind her that she had
attracted the attention of one of the security guards. She spun
around, watching the guard, whose name was Tony, approach

1

cautiously, his hand gravitating toward the holster of his gun. 'Something wrong?' he asked.

'I hope not,' Jess answered. 'There's a man out there who . . .' Who what? she demanded silently, staring deep into the guard's tired blue eyes. Who wants to come in out of the cold? Who has a creepy grin? Was that a crime now in Cook County? The guard looked past her toward the door, Jess slowly tracking his gaze. There was no one there.

'Looks like I'm seeing ghosts,' Jess said apologetically, wondering if this were true, grateful that whatever the young man was, he was gone.

'Well, it's the season for it,' the guard said, checking Jess's identification even though he knew who she was, waving her through the metal detector, as he'd been doing routinely every morning for the past four years.

Jess liked routine. Every morning she got up at 6:45, quickly showered and dressed in the clothes she had carefully laid out the night before, gobbled a piece of Pepperidge Farm frozen cake directly from the freezer, and was behind her desk within the hour, her calendar open to the day's events, her case files ready. If she was prosecuting a case, there would be details to go over with her assistants, strategies to devise, questions to formulate, answers to determine. (A good attorney never asked a question to which she didn't already know the answer.) If she was preparing for an upcoming trial, there would be information to gather, leads to run down, witnesses waiting upstairs to be interviewed, police officers to talk to, meetings to attend, timetables to coordinate. Everything according to schedule. Jess Koster didn't like surprises outside the courtroom any better than she liked them inside it.

After she had a full grasp of the day that lay ahead, she would sit back with a cup of black coffee and a jelly donut and study the morning paper, starting with the obituaries. She always checked the obituaries. *Ashcroft, Pauline, died suddenly in her home, in her 67th year; Barrett, Ronald, passed away after a lengthy illness, age 79; Black, Matthew, beloved husband and father, no age given, donations to be sent to the Heart and Stroke*

2

Foundation of America. Jess wasn't sure when she'd started making the obituaries part of her regular morning routine, and she wasn't sure why. It was an unusual habit for someone barely thirty years old, even for a prosecutor with the Cook County State's Attorney's Office in Chicago. 'Find anyone you know?' one of her partners once asked. Jess had shaken her head, no. There was never anyone she knew.

Was she searching for her mother, as her ex-husband had once suggested? Or was it her own name she expected to see?

The stranger with the unruly blond hair and evil grin pushed his way rudely into her mind's eye. *I am Death,* he teased, his voice bouncing off the bareness of the office walls. *I have come for you.*

Jess lowered the morning paper and let her eyes glance around the room. Three desks in varying degrees of scratched walnut sat at random angles against dull white walls. There were no framed pictures, no landscapes, no portraits, nothing but an old poster from Bye Bye Birdie haphazardly tacked onto the wall across from her desk by a few random pieces of yellowing scotch tape. Law books filled strictly utilitarian metal shelves. Everything looked as if it could be picked up and moved out with only a minute's notice. Which it could. Which it often was. Assistant State's Attorneys were rotated on a regular basis. It was never a good idea to get too comfortable.

Jess shared the office with Neil Strayhorn and Barbara Cohen, her second and third chair respectively, who would be arriving within the half hour. As first chair, it was up to Jess to make all major decisions as to how her office was run. There were 750 State's Attorneys in Cook County, over 200 of them in this building alone, eighteen attorneys to every wing, three attorneys to every room, each watched over by a wing supervisor. By eight-thirty, the labyrinth of offices that made up the eleventh and twelfth floors of the Administration Building would be as noisy as Wrigley Field, or so it often seemed to Jess, who usually relished these few moments of peace and quiet before everyone arrived.

Today was different. The young man had unnerved her,

thrown her off her usual rhythm. What about him was so familiar? she wondered. In truth, she hadn't gotten a good look at his face, hadn't seen much past the eerie grin, would never have been able to describe him for a police sketch artist, could never have picked him out of a line-up. He hadn't even spoken to her. So why was she obsessing on him?

Jess resumed her scanning of the obituaries: *Bederman, Marvin, 74, died peacefully in his sleep after a lengthy illness; Edwards, Sarah, taken in her 91st year . . .*

'You're here early.' The male voice travelled easily to her desk from the open doorway.

'I'm always here early,' Jess answered without looking up. No need to. If the heavy scent of Aramis cologne wasn't enough to give Greg Oliver away, the confident swagger in his voice would. It was an office cliché that Greg Oliver's winning record in the courtroom was surpassed only by his record in the bedroom, and for that reason, Jess had always made sure to keep her conversations with the forty-year-old prosecutor from the next office strictly professional. Her divorce from one lawyer had taught her that the last thing she ever wanted to do was get involved with another. 'Is there something I can do for you, Greg?'

Greg Oliver traversed the distance to her desk in three quick strides. 'Tell me what you're reading.' He leaned forward to peer over her shoulder. 'The obits? Christ, what some people won't do to get their name in print.'

Jess chuckled in spite of herself. 'Greg, I'm really busy . . .'

'I can see that.'

'No, really,' Jess told him, taking quick note of his conventionally handsome face, made memorable by the liquid chocolate of his eyes. 'I have to be in court at nine-thirty.'

He checked his watch. A Rolex. Gold. She'd heard rumors that he'd recently married money. 'You've got lots of time.'

'Time I need to get my thoughts in order.'

'I bet your thoughts are already in order,' he said, straightening up only to lean back against her desk, openly checking his reflection in the glass of the window behind her, his hand brushing against a stack of carefully organized paperwork. 'I bet your mind is as neat as your desk.' He laughed, the motion tugging at one corner of his mouth, reminding Jess instantly of the stranger with the ominous grin. 'Look at you,' Greg said, misreading her response. 'You're all uptight because I accidentally moved a couple of your papers.' He made a great show of straightening them, then whisked some imaginary dust from the ragged surface of her desk top. 'You don't like anybody touching your stuff, do you?' His fingers caressed the wood grain in small, increasingly suggestive circles. The effect was almost hypnotic. A snake charmer, Jess thought, wondering momentarily whether he was the charmer or the snake.

She smiled, amazed at the way her mind seemed to be working this morning, and stood up, moving purposefully toward the book shelves, though, in truth, she had no purpose in mind. 'I think you better go so I can get some work done. I'm delivering my closing argument this morning in the Erica Barnowski case and . . .'

'Erica Barnowski?' His eyes reflected the path of his thoughts. 'Oh, yes. The girl who says she was raped . . .'

'The *woman* who *was* raped,' Jess corrected.

His laugh invaded the space between them. 'Jesus Christ, Jess, she wasn't wearing panties! You think any jury in the land is going to convict a guy of raping some woman he meets in a bar when she wasn't wearing panties?' Greg Oliver looked toward the ceiling, then back at Jess, automatically smoothing back several hairs he'd displaced. 'I don't know, but her not wearing panties to a pick-up bar smacks of implied consent to me.'

'And a knife at her throat is your idea of foreplay?' Jess shook her head, more in sadness than disgust. Greg Oliver was notoriously accurate in his assessments. If she couldn't manage to persuade her fellow prosecutors that the man on trial was guilty, how could she hope to convince a jury?

'I don't see a panty line under that short skirt,' Greg Oliver was saying. 'Tell me, counsellor, you wearing panties?'

5

Jess's hands moved to the sides of the grey wool skirt that stopped at her knees. 'Cut it out, Greg,' she said simply.

The mischief in Greg Oliver's voice spread to his eyes. 'Tell me, counsellor, just what would it take to get into those panties?'

'Sorry, Greg,' Jess told him evenly, 'but I'm afraid there's only room in these panties for *one* asshole.'

The liquid chocolate of Greg Oliver's eyes hardened into brown ice, then immediately melted as the sound of his laughter once again filled the room. 'That's what I love about you, Jess. You're so damn feisty. You'll take anybody on.' He walked toward the door. 'I'll give you this much — if anybody can win this case, you can.'

'Thanks,' Jess said to the closing door. She walked to the window and stared absently out at the street eleven stories below. Large billboards shouted up at her: *Abogado*, they announced. Lawyer, in Spanish, followed by a name. A different name for every sign. Open 24 hours a day.

There were no other high buildings in the area. At fourteen stories tall, the Administration Building stuck out like the sore thumb it represented. The adjoining Court House was a mere seven stories high. Behind them stood the Cook County Jail, where accused murderers and other alleged criminals, who either couldn't make bail or were being held without bond, were kept until their cases came to court. Jess often thought of the area as a dark, evil place for dark, evil people.

I am Death, she heard the streets whisper. *I have come for you.*

She shook her head, glancing up at the sky, but even it was a dirty shade of grey, heavy with the threat of snow. Snow in October, Jess thought, unable to recall the last time it had snowed before Halloween. Despite the weather forecast, she hadn't worn boots. They leaked and had unsightly salt rings around the toes, like the age lines of a tree. Maybe she'd go out later and buy herself a new pair.

The phone rang. Barely past eight o'clock and already the phone was ringing. She picked it up before it had a chance to ring again. 'Jess Koster,' she said simply.

6

'Jess Koster, Maureen Peppler,' the voice said, with a girlish giggle. 'Am I interrupting anything?'

'Never,' Jess told her older sister, picturing the woman's crinkly smile and warm green eyes. 'I'm glad you called.' Jess had always likened Maureen to one of those delicate sketches of ballet dancers by Edgar Degas, all soft and fuzzy around the edges. Even her voice was soft. People often said the sisters looked alike. But while the two women shared basic variations of the same oval face, and were both tall and slender, there was nothing fuzzy around the edges about Jess. Her brown shoulder-length hair was darker than Maureen's, her eyes a more disturbing shade of green, her small-boned frame less curvaceous, more angular. It was as if the artist had drawn the same sketch twice, then rendered one in pastels, the other in oil. 'What's doing?' Jess asked. 'How are Tyler and the twins?'

'The twins are great. Tyler's still not thrilled. He keeps asking when we're sending them back. You didn't ask about Barry.'

Jess felt her jaw tighten. Maureen's husband, Barry, was a successful accountant, and the vanity license plates on his late-model Jaguar spelled EARND IT. Did she really need to know more? 'How is he?' she asked anyway.

'He's fine. Business is terrific despite the economy. Or maybe because of it. Anyway, he's very happy. We want you to come to dinner tomorrow night, and please don't tell me you already have a date.'

Jess almost laughed. When was the last time she'd had a date? When was the last time she'd been anywhere socially that wasn't connected, in some way, to the law? Where had she gotten the idea that only doctors were on call twenty-four hours a day? 'No, I don't have a date,' she answered.

'Good, then you'll come. I don't get to see nearly enough of you these days. I think I saw more of you when I was working.'

'So go back to work.'

'Not on your life. Anyway, tomorrow at six. Dad's coming.'

Jess smiled into the phone. 'See you tomorrow.' She replaced the receiver to the sound of a baby's distant cry. She pictured

7

Maureen running toward the sound, cooing over the cribs of her six-month-old twins, changing their diapers, seeing to their needs, while making sure that the three-year-old at her feet was getting the attention he craved. A far cry from the hallowed halls of Harvard Business School where she'd earned her MBA. Jess shrugged. We all make choices, she thought. Her sister had obviously made hers.

She sat back down at her desk, trying to concentrate on the morning that lay ahead, praying she would be able to prove Greg Oliver wrong. She knew that securing a conviction in this case would be next to impossible. She and her partner would have to be very convincing.

The State's Attorney's office always tried jury cases in pairs. Her second chair, Neil Strayhorn, was set to deliver the initial closing argument, recounting for the jury the straight, unpleasant facts of the case. This would be followed by the defense attorney's closing remarks, and then Jess would handle the rebuttal, a position that allowed ample room for creative moral indignation. 'Every day in the United States, 1,871 women are forcibly raped,' she began, rehearsing the words in the safety of her office. 'That translates to 1.3 rapes of adult women every minute and a staggering 683,000 rapes each year.' She took a deep breath, tossing the sentences over in her mind, like errant pieces of lettuce in a large unwieldy salad. She was still tossing them over when Barbara Cohen arrived some twenty minutes later.

'How's it going?' At five feet eleven inches, and with bright red hair that cascaded halfway down her back in frenzied ripples, Barbara Cohen often seemed the anthropomorphic version of a carrot. She was almost a head taller than Jess, and her long, skinny legs gave the impression that she was standing on stilts. No matter how bad Jess was feeling, just looking at the young woman who was her third chair always made her smile.

'Hanging in there.' Jess checked her watch. Unlike Greg Oliver's, it was a simple Timex with a plain black leather band.

8

'Listen, I'd like you and Neil to handle the Alvarez drug case when it comes to trial.'

The look on Barbara Cohen's face reflected a mixture of excitement and apprehension. 'I thought you wanted to take that one.'

'I can't. I'm swamped. Besides, you guys can handle it. I'll be here if you need any help.'

Barbara Cohen tried, and failed, to keep the smile that was spreading across her face from overtaking her more professional demeanor. 'Can I get you some coffee?' she asked.

'If I drink anymore coffee, I'll be excusing myself from the courtroom every five minutes to pee. Think that would win me any sympathy points with the jury?'

'I wouldn't count on it.'

'How could she not wear panties, for God's sake,' Jess muttered. 'At the very least, you'd think she'd worry about discharge.'

'You're so practical,' Barbara stated, and laughed, readying her cart with files for the judge's morning call.

Neil Strayhorn arrived a few minutes later with the news that he thought he was coming down with a cold, then went straight to his desk. Jess could see his lips moving, silently mouthing the words to his opening closing statement. All around her, the offices of the State's Attorneys for Cook County were coming to life, like a flower opening to the sun.

Jess was aware of each new arrival, of chairs being pushed back, pulled in, computers being activated, Fax machines delivering messages, phones ringing. She unconsciously monitored the arrival of each of the four secretaries who serviced the eighteen lawyers in the wing, was able to distinguish the heavy steps of Tom Olinsky, her trial supervisor, as he walked toward his office at the end of the long hall.

'Every day in the United States, 1,871 women are forcibly raped,' she began again, trying to refocus.

One of the secretaries, a pear-shaped black woman who could

9

have passed for either twenty or forty, stuck her head through the doorway, her long, dangly red earrings falling almost to her shoulders. 'Connie DeVuono's here,' she said, then took a step back, as if she half expected Jess to hurl something at her head.

'What do you mean she's here?'

'I mean she's outside the door. Apparently, she walked right past the receptionist. She says she has to talk to you.'

Jess scanned her appointment calendar. 'Our meeting isn't until four o'clock. Did you tell her I have to be in court in a few minutes?'

'I told her. She says she has to see you now. She's very upset.'

'That's not too surprising,' Jess said, picturing the middle-aged widow who'd been brutally beaten and raped by a man who'd subsequently threatened to kill her if she testified against him, an event that was scheduled for ten days from today. 'Take her to the conference room, will you, Sally? I'll be right there.'

'Do you want me to talk to her?' Barbara Cohen volunteered.

'No, I'll do it.'

'Think it could be trouble?' Neil Strayhorn asked as Jess stepped into the hall.

'What else?'

The conference room was a small, windowless office, taken up almost entirely by an old walnut table and eight low-backed, mismatched brown chairs. The walls were the same dull white as the rest of the rooms, the carpet a well-worn beige.

Connie DeVuono stood just inside the doorway. She seemed to have shrunk since the last time Jess saw her, and her black coat hung on her body as if on a coat rack. Her complexion was so white, it appeared tinged with green, and the bags under her eyes lay in soft, unflattering folds, sad testament to the fact that she probably hadn't slept in weeks. Only the dark eyes themselves radiated an angry energy, hinting at the beautiful woman Connie DeVuono had once been. 'I'm sorry to be disturbing you,' she began.

'It's just that we don't have a lot of time,' Jess said softly, afraid that if she spoke above a whisper, the woman might

10

shatter, like glass. 'I have to be in court in about half an hour.' Jess pulled out one of the small chairs for Connie to sit in. The woman needed no further encouragement. She collapsed, like an accordion, inside it. 'Are you all right? Would you like some coffee? Some water? Here, let me take your coat.'

Connie DeVuono waved away each suggestion with shaking hands. Jess noticed that her nails were bitten to the quick and her cuticles had been picked raw. 'I can't testify,' she said, looking away, her voice so low as to be almost inaudible.

Still, the words had the force of a shout. 'What?' Jess asked, though she'd heard every word.

'I said I can't testify.'

Jess lowered herself into one of the other chairs and leaned toward Connie DeVuono, so that their knees were touching. She reached for the woman's hands and cupped them inside her own. They were freezing. 'Connie,' she began slowly, trying to warm them, 'you're our whole case. If you don't testify, the man who attacked you goes free.'

'I know. I'm sorry.'

'You're sorry?'

'I can't go through with it. I can't. I can't.' She started crying.

Jess quickly drew a tissue from the pocket of her grey jacket and handed it to Connie, who ignored it. Her cries grew louder. Jess thought of her sister, the effortless way she seemed able to comfort her crying babies. Jess had no such talents. She could only sit by helplessly and watch.

'I know I'm letting you down,' Connie DeVuono continued, her shoulders shaking. 'I know I'm letting everybody down . . .'

'Don't worry about us,' Jess told her. 'Worry about you. Think about what that monster did to you.'

The woman's angry eyes bore deeply into her own. 'Do you think I could ever forget it?'

'Then you have to make sure he isn't in a position to do it again.'

'I can't testify. I just can't. I can't. I can't.'

'Okay, okay, calm down. It's okay. Try to stop crying.' Jess leaned back in her chair and tried to crawl inside Connie's

11

mind. Something had obviously happened since the last time they spoke. At each of their previous meetings, Connie, though frightened, had been adamant about testifying. The daughter of Italian immigrants, she had grown up in a household that believed fiercely in the American system of justice. Jess had been very impressed with that belief. After four years with the State's Attorney's Office, Jess thought it probably stronger than her own. 'Has something happened?' she asked, watching Connie's racking shoulders shudder to a halt.

'I have to think about my son,' Connie said forcefully. 'He's only eight years old. His father died of cancer two years ago. If something happens to me, then he has no one.'

'Nothing's going to happen to you.'

'My mother is too old to look after him. Her English is very poor. What will happen to Steffan if I die? Who will take care of him? Will you?'

Jess understood the question was rhetorical, but answered anyway. 'I'm afraid I'm not very good with men,' she said softly, hoping to elicit a smile, watching Connie DeVuono struggle to oblige.

'But, Connie, nothing is going to happen to you once we put Rick Ferguson behind bars.'

The very mention of the man's name caused Connie's body to visibly tremble. 'It was hard enough for Steffan to lose his father at so young an age. What could be worse than losing his mother too?'

Jess felt her eyes instantly well up with tears. She nodded. There could be nothing worse.

'Connie,' she began, surprised by the trembling in her voice, 'believe me, I hear what you're saying. I understand what you're going through. But what makes you think that if you don't testify, you'll be safe? Rick Ferguson already broke into your apartment once and raped you. He beat you so badly you could barely open your eyes for a month. He didn't know that your son wasn't home. He didn't care. What makes you think he won't try it again? Especially once he knows that he can get

12

away with it, because you're too frightened to stop him. What makes you think that the next time, he won't hurt your son too?'

'Not if I refuse to testify.'

'You don't know that.'

'I only know he said I'd never live to testify against him.'

'He made that threat months ago and it didn't stop you.' There was a moment's silence. 'What happened, Connie? What's frightening you? Has he contacted you in any way? Because if he has, we can have his bail revoked . . .'

'There's nothing you can do.'

'There's plenty we can do.'

Connie DeVuono reached inside her floppy black leather purse and pulled out a small white box.

'What's that?'

Connie DeVuono said nothing as she handed the box to Jess.

Jess opened it, gingerly working her way through layers of tissues, feeling something small and hard beneath her fingers.

'The box was in front of my door when I opened it this morning,' Connie said, watching as Jess pulled away the final tissue.

Jess felt her stomach lurch. The turtle that lay lifeless and exposed in her hands was missing its head and two of its feet.

'It was Steffan's,' Connie said, her voice flat. 'We came home a few nights ago and it wasn't in its tank. We couldn't understand how it could have gotten out. We looked everywhere.'

Instantly Jess understood Connie's terror. Three months ago, Rick Ferguson had broken into her apartment, raped her, sodomized her, beaten her, then threatened her life. Now, he was showing her how easy it would be to make good on his threats. He'd broken into her apartment again, as effortlessly as if he'd been handed the key. He'd killed and mutilated her child's pet. No one had seen him. No one had stopped him.

Jess rewrapped the dead turtle in its shroud of tissues and placed it back in its cardboard casket. 'Not that I think it'll do

13

any good, but I'd like to show this to forensics.' She walked to the door and quickly signalled for Sally. 'Get this over to forensics for me, will you?'

Sally took the box from Jess's hands as carefully as if she were handling a poisonous snake.

Suddenly Connie was on her feet. 'You know as well as I do you'll never be able to connect this to Rick Ferguson. He'll get away with it. He'll get away with everything.'

'Only if you let him.' Jess returned to Connie's side.

'What choice do I have?'

'A clear choice,' Jess told her, knowing she had only a few minutes left to change Connie's mind. 'You can refuse to testify, that way ensuring that Rick Ferguson walks away scot-free, that he never has to be held accountable for what he did to you, for what he's *still* doing to you.' She paused, giving her words time to register. 'Or you can go to court and make sure that that bastard gets what he deserves, that he gets put behind bars where he can't hurt you or anyone else for a very long time.' She waited, watching Connie's eyes flicker with indecision. 'Face it, Connie. If you don't testify against Rick Ferguson, you're not helping anyone, least of all yourself. You're only giving him permission to do it again.'

The words hung suspended in the space between them, like laundry someone had forgotten to take off the line. Jess held her breath, sensing Connie was on the verge of capitulating, afraid to do anything that might tip the delicate balance in the other direction. Another speech was already working its way to the tip of her tongue. There's an easy way to do this, it began, and there's a hard way. The easy way is that you agree to testify as planned. The hard way is that I'll have to force you to testify. I'll get the judge to issue a bench warrant for your arrest, force you to come to court, force you to take the stand. And if you still refuse to testify, the judge can, and will, hold you in contempt, send you to jail. Wouldn't that be a tragedy — you in jail and not the man who attacked you?

Jess waited, fully prepared to use these words if she had to, silently praying they wouldn't be necessary. 'Come on, Connie,'

14

she said, giving it one last try. 'You've fought back before. After your husband died, you didn't give up, you went to night school, you got a job so that you could provide for your son. You're a fighter, Connie. You've always been a fighter. Don't let Rick Ferguson take that away from you. Fight back, Connie. Fight back.'

Connie said nothing, but there was a slight stiffening of her back. Her shoulders lifted. Finally, she nodded.

Jess reached for Connie's hands. 'You'll testify?'

Connie's voice was a whisper. 'God help me.'

'We'll take all the help we can get.' Jess checked her watch, rose quickly to her feet. 'Come on, I'll walk you out.'

Neil and Barbara had already left for court, and Jess ushered Connie along the corridor of the State's Attorneys' offices, past the display of cut-off ties that lined one wall, symbolizing each prosecutor's first win before a jury. The halls were decorated in preparation for Halloween, large orange paper pumpkins and witches on broomsticks taped across the walls, like in a kindergarten class, Jess thought, accepting Greg Oliver's 'good luck' salutations, and proceeding through the reception area to the bank of elevators outside the glass doors. From the large window at the far end of the six elevators, the whole west side and northwest side of the city was visible. On a nice day, O'Hare Airport could be easily discerned. Even faraway Du Page County seemed within reach.

The women said nothing on the ride down to the main floor, knowing everything important had already been said. They exited the elevator and rounded the corner, pointedly ignoring the Victim-Witness Services Office with its large picture-laden poster proclaiming *We Remember You . . . In Loving Memory of . . .* and proceeded to the glassed-in, rectangular hallway that connected the administration building to the courthouse next door. 'Where are you parked?' Jess asked, about to guide Connie through the airport-like security to the outside.

'I took the bus,' Connie DeVuono began, then stopped abruptly, her hand lifting to her mouth. 'Oh, my God!'

15

'What? What's the matter?' Jess followed the woman's frightened gaze.

The man was standing at the opposite end of the corridor, leaning against the cold expanse of glass wall, his lean frame heavy with menace, his blunt features partially obscured by the thick mass of long, uncombed, dark blond hair that fell over the collar of his brown leather jacket. As his body swivelled slowly around to greet them, Jess watched the side of his lips twist into the same chilling grin that had greeted her arrival at work that morning.

I am Death, the grin said.

Jess shuddered, then tried to pretend it was from a gust of cold air that had sneaked into the lobby through the revolving doors.

Rick Ferguson, she realized.

'I want you to take a taxi,' Jess told Connie, seeing one pull up to drop somebody off, guiding Connie through the doors onto California Avenue, and thrusting ten dollars into her hand. 'I'll take care of Rick Ferguson.'

Connie said nothing. It was as if she had expended all her energy in Jess's office, and she simply had no more strength to argue. Tightly clutching the ten-dollar bill, she allowed Jess to put her in the cab, not bothering to look back as the car pulled away. Jess remained for a moment on the sidewalk, trying to still the loud thumping in her chest, then turned around and pushed her way back through the revolving doors.

He hadn't moved.

Jess strode toward him across the long corridor, the heels of her black pumps clicking on the hard granite floor, watching as Rick Ferguson's features snapped into sharper focus with each step. The vague generic menace he projected – white male, early twenties, five feet ten inches tall, 170 pounds, blond hair, brown eyes – became more concrete, individualized – shoulders that stooped slightly, unkempt hair pulled into a loose pony tail, deeply hooded cobra-like eyes, a nose that had been broken several times and never properly reset, and always that same unnerving grin.

'I'm warning you to stay away from my client,' Jess announced when she reached him, not giving him the chance to interrupt. 'If you show up within fifty yards of her again, even accidentally, if you try to speak to her or contact her in any way, if you leave any more gruesome little presents outside her door, I'll have your bail revoked and your ass in jail. Am I making myself clear?'

'You know,' he said, speaking very deliberately, as if he were in the middle of an entirely different conversation, 'it's not such a great idea to get on my bad side.'

Jess almost laughed. 'What's that supposed to mean?'

Rick Ferguson shifted his body weight from one foot to the other, then shrugged, managing to appear almost bored. He looked around, scratched at the side of his nose. 'It's just that people who annoy me have a way of . . . disappearing.'

Jess found herself taking an involuntary step back. A cold shiver, like a drill, snaked its way through her chest to her gut. She had to fight the sudden urge to throw up. When she spoke, her voice was hollow, lacking resonance. 'Are you threatening me?'

Rick Ferguson pushed his body away from the wall. His smile widened. *I am Death*, the smile said. *I have come for you.*

Then he walked away without a backward glance.

Chapter Two

'Every day in the United States, 1,871 women are forcibly raped,' Jess began, her eyes tracking the seven men and seven women who made up the two rows of twelve jurors and their two alternates sitting in courtroom 706 of the State Court House at 2600 California Avenue. 'That translates to 1.3 rapes of adult women every minute and a staggering 683,000 rapes each year.' She took a brief pause to let the sheer volume of her statistics sink in. 'Some are attacked in the streets; others are set on in their own homes. Some are raped by the proverbial stranger in a dark alley, far more by people they know: an angry ex-boyfriend, a once-trusted friend, a casual acquaintance. Perhaps, like Erica Barnowski,' she said, indicating the plaintiff with a nod of her head, 'by someone they met in a bar. The women, like the men who attack them, come in all shapes and sizes, all religious denominations and cultural backgrounds, all ages and colors. The only trait they have in common is their sex, which is very ironic when you think about it, because rape is not about sex. Rape is a crime of violence. It is not about passion, or even lust. It is about power. It is about domination and humiliation. It is about control. It is about the infliction of pain. It is an act of rage, an act of hate. It has nothing to do with sex. It only uses sex as its weapon of choice.'

Jess surveyed the majestic old courtroom, its high ceilings and large side windows, the dark panelling along the walls, the black marble framing its large wooden doors. A sign to the right of the judge proclaimed loudly over the rear door: Positively! NO VISITING in courtroom or cell block. To the left another sign declared: QUIET. No Smoking, Eating, Children, Talking.

The visitors' block, which contained eight rows of graffiti-

19

carved benches, was distinguished by an old black and white tile floor. Just like in the movies, Jess thought, grateful to have been assigned to Judge Harris's court for the past eighteen months instead of one of the newer, smaller courtrooms on the lower floors.

'The defense would have you believe otherwise,' Jess continued, making deliberate eye contact with each of the jurors, before gradually switching her focus to the defendant. The defendant, Douglas Phillips, white, ordinary, quite respectable-looking in his dark blue suit and quiet paisley tie, made a small pout with his lips before looking toward the brown-carpeted floor. 'The defense would have you believe that what happened between Douglas Phillips and Erica Barnowski was an act of consensual sex. They have told you that on the night of May the thirteenth, 1992, Douglas Phillips met Erica Barnowski in a singles' bar called the Red Rooster, and that he bought her several drinks. They have called several witnesses who testified seeing them together, drinking and laughing, and who have sworn that Erica Barnowski left the bar with Douglas Phillips of her own free will and by her own accord. Erica Barnowski, herself, admitted as much when she took the stand.

'But the defense would also have you believe that after they left the bar, what transpired was an act of runaway passion between two consenting adults. Douglas Phillips explains the bruises on the victim's legs and arms as the unfortunate byproduct of making love in a small, European car. He dismisses the victim's subsequent hysteria, witnessed by several people in the parking lot, and later observed by Dr. Robert Ives at Grant Hospital, as the ravings of an hysterical woman furious at being picked up and discarded, in his sensitive phrase, "like a piece of used Kleenex".'

Jess now devoted her full attention to Erica Barnowski, who sat beside Neil Strayhorn at the prosecutors' table, directly across from the jury box. The woman, 27 years old and very pale, very blonde, sat absolutely still in her high-backed brown leather chair. The only thing about her that moved was her bottom lip, which had been trembling throughout the trial, and which had occasionally made her testimony almost indecipherable. Still, there was little about the woman that was soft. The hair was too yellow, the eyes too small, the blouse too blue, too cheap. There was nothing to inspire pity, nothing, Jess knew, to trigger automatic compassion in the hearts of the jurors.

'He has a little more trouble explaining the cuts on her neck and throat,' Jess went on. 'He didn't mean to hurt her, he says. It was just a little knife, after all, barely four inches long. And he only brought it out when she started getting feisty. It even seemed to excite her, he told you. He thought she liked it. How was he supposed to know that she didn't? How was he supposed to figure out that she didn't want the same things he wanted? How was he supposed to know *what* she wanted? After all, hadn't she come to the Red Rooster looking for a man? Hadn't she let him buy her drinks? Hadn't she laughed at his jokes and let him kiss her? And don't forget, ladies and gentlemen, she wasn't wearing any panties!'

Jess took a deep breath, returning her gaze to the members of the jury, who were now hanging on her every word. 'The defense has made a big deal of the fact that when Erica Barnowski went to the Red Rooster that night, she wasn't wearing any underwear. An open invitation, they would have you believe. Implied consent. Any woman who goes to a pick-up bar and doesn't wear panties is obviously asking for whatever she gets. Consent before the fact. Erica Barnowski was looking for action, the defense tells you, and that's exactly what she got. Oh, she may have gotten a little more than she bargained for, but hey, she should have known better.

'Well, maybe she should have. Maybe going to a bar like the Red Rooster and leaving her panties at home wasn't the smartest thing Erica Barnowski could have done. But don't think for a moment that a lack of common sense on one person's part eliminates the need for common decency on another's. Don't believe for a second that Douglas Phillips got his signals crossed. Don't be hoodwinked into accepting that this man, who

21

repairs state-of-the-art computers for a living, who has no difficulty whatsoever decoding sophisticated software terminology, has trouble understanding the difference between a simple yes and no. What part of "no" is so difficult for a grown man to understand? No, quite simply, means no!

'And Erica Barnowski said no loud and clear, ladies and gentlemen. She not only *said* no, she *screamed* it. She screamed it so loud and so often that Douglas Phillips had to hold a knife to her throat to silence her.'

Jess found herself directing her remarks to a juror in the second row, a woman in her late fifties with auburn hair and strong, yet curiously delicate, features. There was something about the woman's face she found intriguing. She'd become aware of her early in the trial, and had occasionally found herself speaking almost exclusively to her. Maybe it was the intelligence that was obvious in her soft grey eyes. Maybe it was the way she tilted her head when trying to come to terms with a difficult point. Maybe it was simply the fact that she was better dressed than most of the jurors, several of whom wore blue jeans and baggy, ill-fitting sweaters. Or maybe it was just because Jess felt she was getting through to her, and that through her, she might be able to reach the others.

'Now, I don't claim to be an authority on men,' Jess stated, and heard her inner voice laugh, 'but I have a very hard time accepting that any man who has to hold a knife to a woman's jugular honestly believes she's consenting to intercourse.' Jess paused, choosing her next words very carefully. 'I suggest to you that, even in today's supposedly enlightened times, the double standard looms very large in Cook County. Large enough for the defense to try to convince you that the fact Erica Barnowski wasn't wearing panties that night is somehow more damning than the fact Douglas Phillips held a knife to her throat.'

Jess's eyes travelled slowly down the double row of jurors and two alternates, all of whom wore a red adhesive strip with white letters that said JUROR. 'Douglas Phillips claims he thought Erica Barnowski was consenting to sex,' she stated.

'Well, isn't it time we stopped looking at rape from the rapist's point of view? Isn't it time we stopped accepting what men are *thinking*, and started listening to what women are *saying*? Consent is not a unilateral concept, ladies and gentlemen. It cuts both ways, requires agreement from both parties. What happened between Erica Barnowski and Douglas Phillips on the night of May the thirteenth was decidedly *not* an act of consensual sex.

'Erica Barnowski might be guilty of an error in judgement,' Jess said simply in conclusion. 'Douglas Phillips is guilty of rape.'

She returned to her seat, gently patted Erica Barnowski's surprisingly warm hands. The young woman thanked her with a hint of a smile. 'Well done,' Neil Strayhorn whispered. No such acknowledgements were forthcoming from the defense table, where Douglas Phillips and his lawyer, Rosemary Michaud, stared resolutely ahead.

Rosemary Michaud was five years older than Jess but looked at least twice that. Her dark brown hair was pulled into a severe bun, and if she wore any make-up, it had been applied so subtly as to be invisible. Jess had always thought she resembled the stereotype of a maiden aunt, although this maiden aunt had been married three times and was rumored to be having an affair with a senior official in the police department. Still, in law, as in life, what was important wasn't the way things actually were, but the way they were *perceived* to be. Image, as the ads stated, was everything. And Rosemary Michaud looked like the kind of woman who would never defend a man if she truly believed him to be guilty of so vile an act as rape, or aggravated criminal sexual assault, as the state was now calling it. In her conservative blue suit and unadorned face, Rosemary Michaud looked as if the very idea of defending such a man would offend her to the bone. Douglas Phillips had been smart to hire her.

Rosemary Michaud's motives in accepting Douglas Phillips for a client were harder to fathom, although Jess well understood that it was not the lawyer's job to determine guilt or innocence. That was what the jury system was all about. How many times had she heard argued, had *herself* argued, that if lawyers started acting as judges and jurors, the entire system of justice would fall apart? The presumption of innocence, after all; everyone was entitled to the best possible defense.

Judge Earl Harris cleared his throat, signalling he was about to deliver his instructions to the jury. Judge Harris was a handsome man in his late sixties, his light black skin framed by a close-cropped halo of curly grey hair. There was a genuine kindness to his face, a softness to his dark eyes, that underlined his deep commitment to justice. 'Ladies and gentlemen of the jury,' he began, managing somehow to make even these words sound fresh, 'I want to thank you for the attention and respect you have shown this courtroom over the past several days. Cases like this one are never easy. Emotions run very high. But your duty as jurors is to keep your emotions out of the jury room, and concentrate on the facts.'

Jess, herself, concentrated less on the message being delivered than in how it was being received, her focus returning to the members of the jury, all of whom were leaning forward in their brown leather swivel chairs, listening attentively.

Which side's vision of the truth were they most likely to adopt as their own? she wondered, aware that juries were notoriously difficult to read, their verdicts almost impossible to predict. When she first came to work at the State's Attorney's office four years ago, she'd been surprised to discover how wrong she could be, and how often.

The woman juror with the intelligent eyes coughed into the palm of her hand. Jess knew that women jurors in a rape trial were often harder to win over than their male counterparts. Something to do with denial, she supposed. If they could convince themselves that what had happened was somehow the victim's fault, then they could assure themselves that they would never meet a similar fate. After all, *they* would never be so careless as to walk alone after dark, accept a ride with a casual acquaintance, pick up a man in a bar, *not wear any panties*. No, they were much too smart for that. They were too aware of the dangers. They would never be raped. They would simply never put themselves in so vulnerable a position.

The woman juror became aware of Jess's scrutiny, and twisted self-consciously in her seat. She drew her shoulders back and lifted herself just slightly out of her chair before settling in comfortably again, her eyes riveted on the judge's mouth. In profile, the woman seemed more formidable, her nose sharper, the shape of her face more convex. There was a familiarity about her that Jess hadn't noticed before: the way she occasionally tapped her lips with her finger; the way her neck arched forward on certain key phrases; the slant of her forehead; the thinness of her eyebrows. She reminded Jess of someone, Jess realized, drawing in an audible intake of air, trying to block out the thoughts that were taking shape in her mind, trying to banish the picture that was quickly developing. No, she wouldn't do this, Jess thought, scanning the courtroom, a dreaded tingling creeping in her arms and legs. She fought the urge to flee.

Calm down, she castigated herself silently, feeling her breathing constrict, her hands grow clammy, her underarms become moist. Why now? she wondered, fighting the growing panic, trying to will herself back to normalcy. Why was this happening now?

She forced her eyes back to the woman juror, who was leaning forward in her chair. As if aware of Jess's renewed interest and determined not to be intimidated by it, the woman turned to look her squarely in the eye.

Jess caught the woman's gaze with her own, held it suspended for an instant, then closed her eyes with relief. What had she been thinking of? she wondered, feeling the muscles in her back start to uncramp. What could have possibly triggered such an association? The woman looked like no one she knew, no one she had ever known. Certainly nothing at all like the woman she had fleetingly imagined her to be, Jess thought, feeling foolish and a bit ashamed.

No, nothing remotely like her mother at all.

Jess lowered her head so that her chin almost disappeared into the pink collar of her cotton blouse. It had been eight years since her mother disappeared. Eight years since her mother had left the house to keep a scheduled doctor's appointment and was never seen again. Eight years since the police gave up searching for her and declared her the probable victim of foul play.

In the first few days, months, even years after her mother disappeared, Jess had often thought she'd seen her mother's face in a crowd. It used to happen all the time: she'd be grocery shopping and her mother would be pushing an overflowing cart down the next aisle; she'd be at a baseball game when she'd hear her mother's distinctive voice cheering for the Cubs from her seat on the other side of Wrigley Field. Her mother was the woman behind the newspaper at the back of the bus, the woman in the front seat of the taxi going the other way, the woman struggling to catch up to her dog as they ran along the waterfront.

As the years progressed, the sightings had diminished in frequency. Still, for a long while, Jess had been the victim of nightmares and panic attacks, attacks that struck whenever, wherever, attacks so virulent they robbed her of all feeling in her limbs, all strength in her muscles. They would start with a mild tingling sensation in her arms and legs and develop into virtual paralysis as waves of nausea swept over her. They would end – sometimes in minutes, sometimes after hours – with her sitting powerless, overwhelmed, defeated, her body bathed in sweat.

Gradually, painfully, like someone learning to walk again after a stroke, Jess had regained her equilibrium, her confidence, her self-esteem. She had stopped expecting her mother to come walking through the front door, stopped jumping every time the phone rang, expecting the voice on the other end to be hers. The nightmares had stopped. The panic attacks had ceased. Jess had promised herself that she would never be that vulnerable, that powerless, again.

And now the familiar tingle had returned to her arms and legs.

Why now? Why today?

She knew why.

Rick Ferguson.

Jess watched him push through the doors of her memory, his cruel grin surrounding her like a noose around her neck. 'It's not such a great idea to get on my bad side,' she heard him say, his voice tight, his hands forming fists at his sides. 'People who annoy me have a way of . . . disappearing.'

Disappearing.

Like her mother.

Jess tried to refocus, concentrate all her attention on what Judge Earl Harris was saying. But Rick Ferguson kept positioning himself directly in front of the prosecutor's table, his brown eyes daring her to provoke him into action.

What was it about her and men with brown eyes? Jess wondered, a collage of brown-eyed images filling her brain: Rick Ferguson, Greg Oliver, her father, even her ex-husband.

The image of her ex-husband quickly relegated the others to the back corners of her mind. So typical of Don, she thought, to be so dominant, so overpowering, even when he wasn't there. Eleven years her senior, Don had been her mentor, her lover, her protector, her friend. *He won't give you room to grow*, her mother had cautioned when Jess first announced her intention to marry the brash bulldozer of a man who'd been her first year tutorial instructor. *Give yourself a chance*, she'd begged. *What's the rush?* But, like any rebellious daughter, the more her mother objected, the more determined Jess became, until her mother's opposition was the strongest bond between Jess and Don. They married soon after she disappeared.

Don immediately took charge. During their four years together, it was Don who picked the places they went, selected the apartment they lived in and the furniture they bought, decided who they saw, what they did, even what food she ate, what clothes she wore.

27

Perhaps it had been her fault. Perhaps that was what she'd wanted, needed, even begged for, in the years immediately following her mother's disappearance: the chance not to have to make any major decisions, to be taken care of, looked after, catered to. The chance to disappear herself, inside someone else.

In the beginning, Jess had made no objections to Don running her life. Didn't he know what was best for her? Didn't he have her best interests at heart? Wasn't he always there to wipe away her tears, nurse her through each crippling panic attack? How could she survive without him?

But increasingly, perhaps even unwittingly, Jess had struggled to reassert herself, picking fights, wearing colors she knew he despised, filling up on junk food before they were to go out to his favorite restaurant, refusing to see his friends, applying for a job at the State's Attorney's office instead of joining Don's firm, ultimately moving out.

Now she lived on the top floor of a three-storey brownstone in an old part of the city, instead of in the glassed-in penthouse of a downtown highrise, and she ordered pizza instead of room service, and her closest friend, outside of her sister, was a bright yellow canary named Fred. And if she was no longer the carefree spirit she'd been before her mother vanished, at least she was no longer the invalid she'd allowed herself to become during much of her marriage to Don.

'You are here to see that justice is done,' Judge Harris was concluding. 'It is only by your act of being fair and impartial, of refusing to be swayed by either sympathy for the victim or the accused, but by deciding the case strictly on facts, that you will turn this dark, dank, dreary building into a true, shining temple of justice.'

Jess had heard Judge Harris deliver this speech many times in the past, and it never failed to move her. She watched its effect on the jury. They filed out of the courtroom as if being guided by a shining star.

Erica Barnowski said nothing as the courtroom emptied out. Only after the defendant and his lawyer had left the room did she stand up and nod toward Jess. Neil Strayhorn explained that she would be contacted when the jury returned with a verdict, that it could be hours or possibly days, that she should keep herself available.

'I'll get in touch with you as soon as I hear anything,' Jess said instead of goodbye, watching the younger woman walk briskly down the hall toward the elevators. Unconsciously, her eyes drifted toward Erica Barnowski's full hips. ('I don't see a panty line,' she heard Greg Oliver repeat.) Roughly, she snapped her head back, then shook it, as if trying to clear her mind of all such unpleasant musings. 'You did a great job,' Jess told her second chair. 'You were clear; you were focused; you gave the jurors all the facts they needed to take with them into the jury room. Now, go get your cold some chicken soup,' she continued before Neil could reply. 'I think I'll grab some of that fresh October air.'

Jess opted for the stairs over the elevator, despite the seven flights. She could use the exercise. Maybe she'd take a long walk, buy those winter boots she needed. Maybe she'd even treat herself to a new pair of shoes.

Maybe she'd just grab a hot dog from the vendor at the curb, then go back upstairs to her office to wait out the verdict and start working on her next case, she decided, walking across the granite floor of the foyer.

The cold air hit her like a slap to the face. She hunched her shoulders up around her ears and pressed forward down the steps to the street, surreptitiously peeking toward the busy corner, assuring herself that Rick Ferguson was nowhere to be seen. 'A hot dog with everything on it,' she shouted with relief, watching as the vendor expertly tossed a giant kosher hot dog into a sesame seed bun and smothered it with ketchup, mustard and relish. 'That's great, thank you.' She deposited a fistful of change into his hand, then took a large bite.

'How many times do I have to tell you those things are deadly?' The voice, full, cheery, masculine, came from somewhere to her right. Jess turned toward the sound. 'They're solid fat. Absolutely lethal.'

29

Jess was tempted to rub her eyes in disbelief. 'My God, I was just thinking about you.'

'Good thoughts, I hope,' Don Shaw stated.

Jess stared at her ex-husband as if she couldn't quite decide if he were real or something her mind had conjured up to confuse her. He was such a remarkable presence, she thought, watching the rest of the street disappear into a soft blur around him. Although he was only of average height, everything about him seemed oversized: his hands; his chest; his voice; his eyes, their lashes the envy of all the women he met. What was he doing here? she wondered. She'd never run into him like this before, despite the fact they frequented the same turf. She hadn't spoken to him in months. And now she had only to think of him and he was here.

'You know I can't stand watching you eat this crap,' he was saying, grabbing the hot dog out of her hands and tossing it into a nearby trash bin.

'What are you doing?!'

'Come on, let me buy you some real food.'

'I can't believe you did that!' Jess signalled the vendor for another hot dog. 'Touch this one, you'll lose your hand,' she warned, only half in jest.

'One of these days you're going to wake up fat,' he cautioned, then smiled, the kind of loopy grin that made it impossible not to smile back.

Jess stuffed half the new hot dog into her mouth, thinking it wasn't as good as the first. 'So, how've you been?' she asked. 'What's this I hear about a new girlfriend?' She felt immediately self-conscious, whisked some imaginary crumbs off the front of her jacket.

'Who said anything about a girlfriend?' They started walking slowly toward twenty-sixth Street, falling into the casual rhythm of each other's steps, as if this impromptu walk had been carefully choreographed in advance. Around them swirled an indifferent chorus of police and pimps and drug dealers.

'Word gets around, counsellor,' she said, surprised to find that she was genuinely curious about the details of his new romance, perhaps even a little jealous. She'd never counted on him getting involved with anyone else. Don was her safety net, after all, the one she thought would always be there for her. 'What's her name? What's she like?'

'Her name is Trish,' he answered easily. 'She's very bright, very pretty, has very short, very blond hair, and a very wicked laugh.'

'That's a lot of verys.'

Don laughed, volunteering no further information.

'Is she a lawyer?'

'Not a chance.' He paused. 'And you? Seeing anyone special?'

'Just Fred,' she answered, gulping down the rest of her hot dog, crumpling its wrapper in the palm of her hand.

'You and that damn canary.' They reached the corner, waited while the light went from red to green. 'I have a confession to make,' he said, taking her elbow and guiding her across the street.

'You're getting married?' She was surprised by the urgency in the question she hadn't meant to ask.

'No,' he said lightly, but his voice betrayed him. It carried serious traces just beneath its surface, like a dangerous undertow beneath a deceptively smooth ocean. 'This is about Rick Ferguson.'

Jess stopped dead in the middle of the road, the hot dog wrapper dropping from her open palm. Surely she hadn't heard right. 'What?'

'Come on, Jess,' Don urged, tugging on her arm. 'You'll get us run over.'

She stopped again as soon as they reached the other side of the street. 'What do you know about Rick Ferguson?'

'He's my client.'

'What?'

'I didn't just run into you today, Jess,' Don told her sheepishly. 'I called your office. They said you were in court.'

'Since when have you been representing Rick Ferguson?'

'Since last week.'

'I don't believe it. Why?'

31

'Why? Because he hired me. What kind of a question is that?'

'Rick Ferguson is an animal. I can't believe you'd agree to represent him.'

'Jess,' Don said patiently, 'I'm a defense attorney. It's what I do.'

Jess nodded. While it was true that her ex-husband had built a very lucrative practice out of defending such low life, she would never understand how such a kind and thoughtful man could champion the rights of those whose thoughts precluded kindness, how a man of such fierce intelligence could use that intelligence on behalf of those who were merely fierce.

While she knew that Don had always been fascinated by the marginal elements of society, the years since their divorce had magnified this attraction. Increasingly he took on the kind of seemingly hopeless cases that other lawyers shunned. And won more often than not, she realized, not relishing the thought of facing her ex-husband in court. That had happened on two occasions in the last four years. He'd won both times.

'Jess, has it ever occurred to you that the man might be innocent?'

'The man, as you generously refer to him, has been positively identified by the woman he attacked.'

'And she couldn't be mistaken?'

'He broke into her apartment and beat her almost unconscious. Then he made her undress, one item at a time, nice and slow, so she had lots of time to get a good look at his face before he raped and sodomized her.'

'Rick Ferguson has an airtight alibi for the time of the attack,' Don reminded her.

Jess scoffed. 'I know – he was visiting his mother.'

'The woman put her house up as collateral for his bail. She's fully prepared to testify for him in court. Not to mention that there are thousands of men matching Rick Ferguson's description in this city. What makes you so sure Rick Ferguson is your man?'

'I'm sure.'

'Just like that?'

Jess told him about Rick Ferguson waiting for her when she arrived at work that morning and their subsequent altercation in the courthouse lobby.

'You're saying he threatened you?'

Jess saw Don struggling to stay neutral, to pretend she was just another Assistant State's Attorney, and not someone he obviously still cared deeply about. 'I'm saying I don't understand why you waste your precious talent on such obvious low-lifes,' she told him gently. 'Weren't you the one who told me that a lawyer's practice is ultimately a reflection of his own personality?'

He smiled. 'Nice to know you were listening.'

She reached over and kissed him lightly on the cheek. 'I better get back to work.'

'I take it that means you won't consider dropping the charges?' His statement curled into a question.

'Not a chance.'

He smiled sadly, taking her hand and walking her back toward the Administration Building, squeezing her thin fingers inside his massive palm before releasing her.

Watch to make sure I get inside safely, she urged silently as she raced up the concrete stairs.

But when she reached the top and turned around, he was already gone.

Chapter Three

The nightmare always started the same way: Jess was sitting in the sterile reception area of a doctor's office reading an old magazine while somewhere beside her a phone was ringing. 'It's your mother,' the doctor informed her, pulling a phone out of his large black doctor's bag and handing it over.

'Mother, where are you?' Jess asked. 'The doctor's waiting for you.'

'Meet me in the John Hancock Building in fifteen minutes. I'll explain everything when I see you.'

Suddenly Jess stood before a bank of elevators, but no matter how many times she pressed the call button, no elevator came. Locating the stairs, she raced down the seven flights only to find the door to the outside locked. She pushed; she pulled; she begged; she cried. The door wouldn't budge.

In the next instant, she was in front of the Art Institute on Michigan Avenue, the sun bouncing off the sidewalk into her eyes. 'Come inside,' an auburn-haired woman with grey eyes called from the top step of the impressive structure. 'The tour's about to begin, and you're keeping everybody waiting.'

'I really can't stay,' Jess told the crowd, whose faces were a blur of brown eyes and red mouths. The group paused for several minutes in front of Seurat's masterpiece, Sunday Afternoon in the Park.

'Let's play connect the dots,' Don called out, as Jess broke free and hurried outside in time to leap on board a bus that was pulling away. But the bus headed in the wrong direction and she ended up in Union Station. She hailed a cab, only to have the driver misunderstand her instructions and take her to Roosevelt Road.

He was waiting for her when she stepped out of the taxi, a

faceless figure all in black, standing perfectly still by the side of the road. Immediately, Jess tried to get back in the car, but the taxi had disappeared. Slowly, the figure in black advanced toward her.

Death, Jess understood, bolting for the open road. 'Help me!' she cried, the shadow of Death advancing effortlessly behind her as she raced up the steps of her parents' home. She pulled open the screen door, pushing it shut after her, desperately trying to secure the latch as Death's hand reached for the door, his face coming into clear view.

Rick Ferguson.

'No!' Jess screamed, lurching forward in her bed, her heart pounding, the bedding soaked in sweat.

No wonder he'd felt so familiar, she realized, drawing her knees to her chin and sobbing, her breath slamming against her lungs, as if someone were playing racquetball in her chest. A product of her darkest imaginings, he'd stepped, quite literally, out of her dreams and into her life. The nightmares that used to haunt her were back, and the figure had a name — Rick Ferguson.

Jess pushed away the wet sheets and struggled to her feet, only to feel her legs give way beneath her. She collapsed in a crumpled heap on the floor, trying to catch her breath, afraid she was going to throw up. 'Oh, God,' she muttered, addressing the panic as if it were a physical presence in the room. 'Please stop. Please go away.'

Jess stretched toward the white china lamp on the night table beside her bed and flipped on the light. The room snapped into focus: soft peaches mixed with delicate greys and blues, a double bed, a Drury rug, a white wicker chair over which hung her clothes for the next day, a chest of drawers, a small mirror, a poster by Niki de Saint Phalle, another by Henri Matisse. She tried to will herself back to normalcy by concentrating on the wood grain of the light oak floor, the stitching on the pale peach curtains, the white duvet, the expanse of high ceiling. One of the nice things about living in an old brownstone, she tried to remind herself, was the high ceilings. You didn't find that in modern glass highrises.

It wasn't working. Her heart continued to race as her breath curled into a tight little ball in the middle of her throat. Once again she forced herself to her feet, teetering on legs that threatened to send her sprawling, toward the tiny, purely functional bathroom that the landlord had laughingly described as ensuite when she'd moved in just after her divorce. She ran the tap and threw cold water across her face and shoulders, letting the water sneak down underneath her pink nightshirt and onto her breasts and belly.

She rested against the side of the tub and stared into the toilet bowl. There was nothing she hated worse than throwing up. Ever since she was a small child and had overdosed on red licorice sticks and banana splits at Allison Nichol's birthday party, she'd dreaded throwing up. Every night for years afterward, she'd gone to bed asking her mother, 'Will I be all right?' And every night her mother had answered patiently that yes, she'd be fine. 'Do you promise?' the child had persisted. 'I promise,' had come the immediate reply.

How ironic then that it had been the mother, and not the child, who'd been in danger.

And now the nightmare that had plagued her after her mother's disappearance was back, along with the shortness of breath, the trembling hands, the paralyzing, nameless dread that permeated every fiber in her body. It wasn't fair, Jess thought, leaning over the toilet bowl, gritting her teeth against the possibility of what might follow, clutching at the pain that stabbed repeatedly at her chest, like the dull blade of a long knife.

She could call Don, she thought, resting her cheek against the cool lid of the toilet. He always knew what to do. So many nights he'd held her trembling against him, his hands softly stroking the damp hair away from her forehead as he engulfed her inside his large arms, and assured her, as her mother had, that she would be all right. Yes, she could call Don. He'd help her. He'd know exactly what to do.

Jess pushed herself back toward the bedroom, perched precariously on the edge of her bed, and reached for the phone, then stopped. She knew all she had to do was phone Don and he would dash right over, leave whatever he was doing, whomever he was with, and race to her side, stay with her as long as she needed him. She knew Don still loved her, had never stopped. She knew that, and that was why she knew she couldn't call him.

He was involved with someone else now. Trish, she repeated, examining the name in her mind. Probably short for Patricia. Trish with the wicked laugh. The *very* wicked laugh, she heard him say, recalling the proud twinkle in his eyes. Had the possibility that she might be losing Don to another woman been enough to precipitate this anxiety attack?

The attack was over, she realized with a start. Her heart was no longer racing; her breathing had returned to normal; her body was no longer awash in perspiration. She fell back against her pillow, luxuriating in the sense of renewed well-being. Surprisingly, she discovered she was hungry.

Jess shuffled through the darkened hallway to the kitchen, heading directly for the freezer. She opened it, recoiling from the sudden flash of light, and drew out a box of frozen pizzas, quickly tearing at the cellophane around each individual pie and popping one stiff disk into the microwave oven that sat on the side counter. She pressed the necessary buttons and listened to the soft whir of the micro rays as they circled their frozen prey, careful not to stand directly in front of the oven.

Don had warned her against standing directly in its path when it was on. But surely these things are perfectly safe, she had argued. Why take chances? had come his instant rebuttal. He was probably right, she'd decided, adopting his precautions as her own. You never knew what harmful rays might be lurking about, just waiting for their chance to feast on larger game.

Jess watched the microwave silently ticking down its seconds, then defiantly thrust her body directly in its path.

'Come and get me,' she cried, then laughed again, feeling almost giddy. Was she really standing in her small galley kitchen at three o'clock in the morning challenging her microwave oven?

The timer beeped five times, announcing her pizza was ready, and Jess gently lifted the now hot piece of pie into her hands and carried it into the large combination living and dining area. She loved her apartment, had from the first moment she'd walked up the three flights to its door. It was old and full of interesting angles, the bay windows of its west wall looking out onto Orchard Street, only a block and a half away from where she'd lived as a child, and a far cry from the modern three-bedroom apartment on Lake Shore Drive she'd shared with Don.

It was the sharing part of her life she missed the most: having someone to talk to; to be with; to cuddle up next to at the end of the day. It had felt nice to share big ideas, small triumphs, needless worries. It had felt comforting to be part of a couple, safe to be part of *Jess and Don*.

Jess switched on the stereo that rested against the wall across from the old tie-dyed velvet sofa she'd found in a second-hand store on Armitage Avenue, and listened as the ineffably beautiful strains of César Franck's violin and piano concerto filled the room. Beside her, her canary, his cage covered for the night, started to sing. Jess sank into the soft swirls of her velvet sofa, listening to the sweet sounds, and eating her pizza in the dark.

'Ladies and gentlemen of the jury, have you reached your verdict?' the judge asked, and Jess felt a rush of adrenaline surge through her body. It had been nearly twenty-four hours since she had delivered her closing argument. The jury had deliberated for almost eight hours before deciding that no consensus was immediately forthcoming, and Judge Harris had impatiently ordered them to a hotel for the night, under careful instructions not to discuss the case with anybody. They had resumed their deliberations at nine o'clock this morning.

Surprisingly, an hour later, they were ready.

The jury foreman said yes, they had reached their verdict, and Judge Harris instructed the defendant to please rise. Jess listened, her breathing stilled, as the jury foreman intoned solemnly, 'We, the jury, find the defendant, Douglas Phillips . . . not guilty.'

Not guilty.

Jess felt a pin prick her side, sensed her body slowly losing air.

Not guilty.

'My God, they didn't believe me,' Erica Barnowski whispered beside her.

Not guilty.

Doug Phillips embraced his attorney. Rosemary Michaud gave Jess a discreet victory smile.

Not guilty.

'Damn it,' Neil Strayhorn said. 'I really thought we had a chance.'

Not guilty.

'What kind of justice is this?' Erica Barnowski demanded, her voice gaining strength through indignation. 'The man admitted holding a knife to my throat, for God's sake, and the jury says he isn't guilty?'

Jess could only nod. She'd been part of the justice system too long to harbor any delusions about its so-called justice. Guilt was a relative concept, a matter of ghosts and shadows. Like beauty, it was in the eye of the beholder. Like truth, it was subject to interpretation.

'What do I do now?' Erica Barnowski was asking. 'I lost my job, my boyfriend, my self-respect. What do I do now?' She didn't wait for an answer, fleeing the courtroom before Jess had time to think of a suitable response.

What could she have said? Don't worry, tomorrow is another day? Things will look brighter in the morning? It's always darkest before the dawn? How about, what goes around comes around? He'll get his? If it's meant to be, it's meant to be? Of course, there was always, tough luck, better luck next time, heaven helps those who help themselves. And for added comfort, give it time, you did the right thing, it only hurts for a little while, life goes on.

There it was in a nutshell, she thought: the wisdom of the ages condensed into three small words — life goes on.

Jess gathered her papers together, glancing over her shoulder as the defendant shook hands with each of the jurors in turn. The jury members carefully avoided making eye contact with her as they filed from the courtroom minutes later, the woman juror with the intelligent face and soft grey eyes being the only one to say goodbye to Jess. Jess nodded in return, curious as to what part this woman had played in the jury's final decision. Had she been convinced of Douglas Phillips's innocence all along, or had she been the reason for the lengthy deliberations, the final hold-out for a guilty verdict, giving in only when her obstinacy threatened to force a mistrial? Or had she sat there, impatiently tapping her foot, waiting for the others to come to their senses and see things her way?

Not guilty.

'Do you want to talk about it?' Neil asked.

Jess shook her head, not sure whether she was more angry or sad. Later there would be plenty of time to analyze and discuss whether they could have done things differently. Right now, there was nothing anyone could do. It was over. She couldn't change the outcome of the case any more than she could change the facts of the case, and the fact, as Greg Oliver had clearly stated the day before, was that no jury in the land was going to convict a man of rape when the woman wasn't wearing panties.

Jess knew she wasn't ready to return to the office. Quite apart from the unpleasant certainty of having to acknowledge Greg Oliver's superior savvy, she needed time alone to come to terms with the jury's decision, time to accept it before moving on, time to deal with her anger and frustration. With her loss. Time to get her mind ready for her next case.

Ultimately that was the biggest truth about the American justice system: one person's life was just another person's case.

Jess found herself on California Avenue with no clear

41

memory of having left the Court House. It was unlike her not to know exactly what she was doing, she thought, feeling the cold through her thin tweed jacket. The weather forecasters were still predicting the possibility of snow. Predicting a possibility, she repeated silently, thinking this an interesting concept. She bundled her jacket around her, and started walking. 'I might as well be naked,' she said out loud, knowing nobody would be paying attention. Just another casualty of the justice system, she thought, a sudden impulse guiding her aboard a number 60 bus, heading for downtown Chicago.

'What am I doing?' she muttered under her breath, taking a seat near the driver. It wasn't like her to act on impulse. Impulses were for those who lacked control over their lives, she thought, closing her eyes, the steady hum of the motor vibrating through her.

She wasn't sure how long the bus had been in motion before she reopened her eyes, or when she first realized that the woman juror with the auburn hair and soft grey eyes was sitting at the back of the bus. She was even less sure at what moment she decided to follow her. It was certainly nothing she had consciously planned. And yet, here she was, approximately half an hour later, exiting the bus several paces behind the woman, following her onto Michigan Avenue, trailing her from a distance of perhaps twenty feet. What on earth was she doing?

Several blocks down Michigan Avenue, the woman stopped to look in a jewelry store window and Jess did the same, gazing past the display of precious gems and gold bracelets, finding her shivering, quizzical reflection in the glass, as if her image were trying to figure out who she was. She'd never been into jewelry. The only jewelry she'd ever worn had been her simple gold wedding band. Don had given up buying her trinkets during their marriage when he found them inevitably consigned to the back of her dresser drawer. It just wasn't her style, she'd explained. She always felt like a little girl playing dress-up in her mother's things.

Her mother, she thought, realizing that the woman juror had

moved on. How could she have considered, even for an instant, that the woman looked anything like her mother? This woman was approximately five feet five inches tall and 140 pounds; in comparison, her mother had been almost four inches taller and ten pounds heavier. Not to mention the differences in the color of their eyes and hair, or in the amount of make-up they wore, Jess thought, confident that her mother would never have worn lipstick that pink or blush that obviously applied. Unlike her mother, this woman was clearly skittish and insecure, her heavy make-up a mask against time. No, there was nothing similar about the two women at all.

The woman juror stopped in front of another shop, and Jess found herself staring at an ugly assortment of leather bags and cases. Was the woman going to go inside the store? Buy herself a little treat? A reward for a job well done? Well, why not? Jess thought, turning her head discreetly away as the woman pushed open the door and headed for the center of the store.

Should she follow her inside? Jess wondered, thinking she could use a new briefcase. Hers was very old; Don had bought it for her when she graduated from law school and, unlike his jewelry purchases, he certainly couldn't complain about this gift's lack of use. The once shiny black leather had grown scratched and smudged, its stitching frayed, the zipper forever catching on some wayward threads. Maybe it was time to give it up, buy a new one. Sever her ties with the past once and for all.

The woman emerged from the store with only the brown handbag she'd been carrying when she went in. She gathered the collar of her dark green coat around her chin and stuffed her gloved hands inside her pockets. Jess found herself mimicking the woman's actions, following several paces behind.

They crossed the Chicago River, the Wrigley Building looming high on one side of the wide street, the Tribune Tower on the other. Downtown Chicago was a wealth of architectural splendors, boasting skyscrapers by the likes of Mies Van der Rohe, Helmut Jahn, and Bruce Graham. Jess had often contemplated taking a lecture cruise along Lake Michigan and the Chicago River. Somehow she'd never gotten around to it.

The woman continued for several more paces then stopped abruptly, spinning around. 'Why are you following me?' she demanded angrily, tapping impatient fingers against the sleeve of her coat, like a schoolteacher questioning an errant pupil.

Jess felt herself reduced in stature to that of a small child, terrified of getting her knuckles rapped. 'I'm sorry,' she stammered, wondering again what she was doing. 'I didn't mean to . . .'

'I saw you on the bus, but I didn't think anything of it,' the woman said, clearly flustered. 'Then I saw you by the jewelry store, but I thought, well, everybody has the right to look in the same window, I'm sure it's just a coincidence. But when you were still there when I came out of that leather goods store, I knew you had to be following me. Why? What do you want?'

'I don't want anything. Really, I wasn't following you.'

The woman's eyes narrowed, challenged her own.

'I . . . I'm not sure why I was following you,' Jess admitted after a pause. She couldn't remember a time she'd felt more foolish.

'It wasn't you, you know,' the woman began, relaxing slightly. 'If that's what you wanted to know. It wasn't anything you said or did.'

'I beg your pardon?'

'We thought you were wonderful,' she continued. 'The jury . . . we thought what you said about a lack of common sense not excusing a lack of common decency, well, we thought that was wonderful. We argued about it for a long time. Quite vehemently.'

'But you didn't accept it,' Jess stated, surprised by how eager she was to understand how the jury had arrived at its verdict.

The woman looked toward the sidewalk. 'It wasn't an easy decision. We did what we thought was right. We know that Mr Phillips was wrong in what he did, but, in the end, we decided that to put the man in prison for years, to make him lose his job and his livelihood . . . for an error in judgement, like you said . . .'

'I wasn't talking about the defendant's lack of judgement!' Jess heard the horror in her voice. How could they have misunderstood?

'Yes, we knew that,' the woman quickly explained. 'We just thought that it could apply to both sides.'

Wonderful, Jess thought, catching a gulp of cold air, finding it hard to appreciate the irony of the situation, harder still to exhale.

'We loved your little suits,' the woman continued, as if trying to cheer her up.

'My little suits?'

'Yes. The grey one in particular. One of the women said she was thinking of asking you where you bought it.'

'You were looking at my suit?'

'Appearances are very important,' the woman said. 'That's what I'm always telling my daughters. First impressions and all that.'

She reached out and patted Jess's hand. 'You make a very good impression, dear.'

Jess wasn't sure whether to curtsy or scream. She felt her heart starting to pound against the tweed fabric of her jacket.

'Anyway,' the woman was saying. 'You did a very good job.'

How could someone with such intelligent eyes be so stupid? Jess asked herself, finding it difficult to catch her breath.

'I really should get going,' the woman said, obviously uncomfortable with Jess's silence. She took a few steps, then stopped. 'Are you okay? You're looking a little pale.'

Jess tried to speak, could only nod, forcing her lips into what she hoped was a reassuring smile. The woman smiled in return, then walked briskly down the street, taking several quick peeks over her shoulder to where Jess remained standing. She probably wants to make sure I'm not following her, Jess thought, wondering again what had possessed her. What had she been doing trailing after this woman, for God's sake? What was she doing now?

Having a goddamn panic attack, she realized. 'Oh, God,' she moaned, fighting off the anxiety that was making her head too light to hold down even as it made her legs too heavy to lift. 'This is ridiculous. What am I going to do?'

Jess felt her eyes fill with tears, and brushed them angrily aside. 'I can't believe I'm crying in the middle of goddamn Michigan Avenue,' she berated herself. 'I can't believe I'm *talking to myself* in the middle of goddamn Michigan Avenue!' Unlike the drug pushers and crazies along California Avenue, the well-heeled shoppers along Michigan Avenue were much more likely to notice, although no more likely to do anything about it.

She forced her feet toward a nearby bus stop, leaned against its side. Even through her jacket, it felt cold against her skin. She wouldn't give in to this, she thought angrily. She would not let these stupid attacks get the better of her.

Think pleasant thoughts, she told herself. Think about getting a massage; think about a holiday in Hawaii; think about your baby nieces. She imagined their soft heads nestled against her cold cheeks, realized she was supposed to be at her sister's house for dinner at six o'clock.

How could she go to her sister's for dinner? What if she were still in the throes of an anxiety attack? What if she had another one in front of everybody? Did she really want to inflict her neuroses on those she loved most?

What's family for? Maureen would undoubtedly ask.

Jess felt the bile rise in her throat. God, was she going to throw up? Throw up in the middle of goddamn Michigan Avenue? She counted to ten, then twenty, swallowing rapidly, once, twice, three times, before the feeling finally disappeared. 'Take deep breaths,' Don used to tell her, so she did, filling her lungs with air, trying to keep from doubling over with the pain.

Nobody noticed her suffering. Pedestrians continued to file past, one even asked her the time. Not so different from California Avenue after all, she thought as a bus pulled to a halt in front of her and opened its doors, disgorging several people, who pushed past her as if she weren't there. The driver

46

waited several seconds for her to step in, shrugged his shoulders when she didn't, closed the doors and drove on. Jess felt the warm gust of dirty air from the bus's exhaust against her face as the bus departed. It filled her eyes and nostrils. She found it oddly soothing.

Soon, her breathing started to normalize. She felt the color returning to her cheeks, the paralysis beginning to lift. 'You're okay now,' she told herself, pushing one leg in front of the other, stepping gingerly off the curb, as if stepping into a too hot bath. 'You're okay now. It's over.'

The car came out of nowhere.

It happened so fast, was so unexpected, that, even as it was happening, Jess had the strange feeling it was happening to someone else. She was somewhere outside her body, watching the events alongside the half dozen spectators who quickly gathered at the scene. Jess felt a rush of air beside her, saw her body spinning like a top, took fleeting note of the white Chrysler as it disappeared around the corner. Only then did she return to the body kneeling on the side of the road. Only then did she feel the stinging at her knees and palms. Only then did she hear the voices.

'Are you all right?'

'My God, I thought you were a goner for sure.'

'He came this close! Missed you by not more than two inches!'

'I'm fine,' someone said, and Jess recognized the voice as her own. 'I guess I wasn't paying attention.' She wondered momentarily why she was accepting responsibility for something that was clearly not her fault. She'd almost been run down by a maniac in a white Chrysler who'd sped by and hadn't even bothered to stop; she'd bruised her hands and scraped her legs when she hit the pavement; her tweed jacket was streaked with grime; her panty hose were shredded at the knees. And she was feeling guilty about causing a scene. 'I must have been daydreaming,' she apologized, rising shakily to her feet. 'But it's okay now. I'll be fine.

'I'll be fine,' she repeated, limping toward the opposite corner and hailing a passing taxi, crawling inside. 'I'll be fine.'

Chapter Four

Jess pulled her red Mustang into the driveway of her sister's large, white, wood-frame house on Sheraton Road in Evanston at precisely three minutes before six o'clock. 'You'll be fine,' she told herself, turning off the ignition and gathering up the shopping bag containing wine and gifts from the seat beside her. 'Stay calm, stay cool, don't let Barry draw you into any silly arguments,' she continued, sliding out of the car and walking up the front walk to the large glass-panelled door. 'Everything will be fine.'

The door opened just as her hand reached for the bell.

'Jess,' Barry said, his voice blowing down the tree-lined street, like a gust of wind. Leaves swirled at her feet. 'Right on time, as always.'

'How are you, Barry?' Jess stepped into the large cream-colored marble foyer.

'Never better,' came the instant reply. Barry always said 'never better'. 'How about you?'

'I'm fine.' She took a deep breath, thrust the bottle of wine in his direction. 'It's from Chile. The man in the liquor store said it came highly recommended.'

Barry examined the label closely, clearly sceptical. 'Well, thank you, although I hope you won't mind if we save it for another time. I already have some expensive French on ice. Here, let me help you off with your coat.' He discarded the wine on the small antique table to the left of the front door, and started awkwardly pulling at her sleeve.

'It's okay, Barry. I think I can manage on my own.'

'Well, at least let me hang it up for you.'

Jess decided against playing tug-of-war with Barry for her coat. 'Is Maureen upstairs?'

49

'She's putting the twins to bed.' He hung her coat in the closet and led her toward the predominantly rose- and white-colored living room, accented by strong blocs of black: a black concert grand piano that took up much of the front part of the room, although nobody played; a black marble fireplace, in which a fire already roared.

'I'll go upstairs and say hello. I bought them something.' Jess indicated the Marshall Field's shopping bag in her hand.

'They'll be awake again in a few hours. You can give it to them then.'

'Jess, is that you?' Maureen called from upstairs.

'Coming right up,' Jess answered, her body gravitating toward the center hall.

'Don't you dare,' Maureen called back. 'I've just got everybody settled. Stay and talk to Barry. I'll be down in two minutes.'

'She'll be down in two minutes,' Barry parroted. 'So, what do you say? Think you can spend two minutes talking to your brother-in-law?'

Jess smiled, and sat down in one of two white wing chairs across from Barry, who perched on the edge of the rose-colored sofa, as if ready to hang on her every word. Ready to pounce, more likely, Jess thought, wondering why she and Barry had never been able to connect. What was it about the man that rubbed her the wrong way? she wondered, conscious of his clear blue eyes recording her every gesture. He wasn't ugly. He wasn't stupid. He wasn't overtly unpleasant.

Why could she only think of him in the negative? Surely there was more to the man than what he wasn't.

She had tried to like him. When he'd married her sister some six years ago, Jess had assumed she would like anyone who made her sister happy. She'd been wrong.

Maybe it was the sneaky way he tried to mask his receding hairline by combing his thinning hair from one side of his head to the other that bothered her. Or the fact that his nails were better manicured than her own, that he boasted of flossing his teeth after every meal. Maybe it was his habit of always wearing a shirt and tie, even under a casual cardigan sweater, like tonight.

More likely it was the thinly veiled chauvinism of his remarks, she decided, his casually dismissive ways, the fact that he could never admit he was wrong. Or maybe it was the fact that he had taken a bright young graduate of the Harvard Business School and turned her into Total Woman, someone who was so busy decorating their home and producing babies that she had no time to think about resuming her once promising career. What would their mother have thought?

'You look nice,' Barry told her. 'That's a lovely sweater. You should wear blue more often.'

'It's green.'

'Green? No, it's blue.'

Were they really arguing about the color of her sweater? 'Can we settle for turquoise?' she asked.

Barry looked sceptical, shook his head. 'It's blue,' he pronounced, looking toward the fire. Barry always lit a perfect fire.

Jess took a deep breath. 'So, Barry, how's business?'

He tossed aside her inquiry with a wave of his hand. 'You don't really want to hear about my business.'

'I don't?'

'Do you?'

'Barry, I asked you a simple question. If it's going to get too complicated, then . . .'

'Business is great. Terrific. Couldn't be better.'

'Good.'

'Not good.' He laughed. 'Great. Terrific. Couldn't be better.'

'Couldn't be better,' Jess repeated, looking toward the stairs. What was keeping her sister?

'Actually,' Barry was saying, 'I had quite a spectacular day today.'

'And what made it so spectacular?' Jess asked.

'I stole a very important client away from my former partner.' Barry chuckled. 'The son-of-a-bitch never saw it coming.'

'I thought you two were friends.'

'So did he.' The chuckle became a laugh. 'Guy thinks he can

screw me and get away with it.' He tapped his finger against the side of his head. 'I never forget. I get even.'

'You get even,' Jess repeated.

'Hey, I didn't do anything illegal.' He winked. 'By the way, some information about a new type of individual retirement account crossed my desk this afternoon. It's something I think you should take a look at. If you'd like, I could send the information on to you.

'Sure,' Jess said. 'That'd be great.'

'I think I'll mention it to your Dad as well.'

They both checked their watches. What was keeping her father? He knew how much she worried whenever he was late.

'How was *your* day?' Barry asked, managing to look as if he cared.

'Could have been better,' Jess replied sardonically, using Barry's words, not really surprised when he failed to notice. I lost a case I was desperate to win, I had an anxiety attack in the middle of Michigan Avenue, and I was almost killed by a hit-and-run driver, but hey, a woman said she liked my suit, so the day wasn't a total loss, she continued silently.

'I don't know how you stand it,' Barry was saying.

'Stand what?'

'Day after day of dealing with scum,' he said succinctly.

'I'm the one who gets to put the scum in jail,' she told him.

'When you win.'

'When I win,' she agreed sadly.

'I've got to hand it to you, Jess,' he said, jumping to his feet. 'I never thought you'd stick it out this long. What can I get you to drink?' He said the two sentences as if one naturally flowed from the other.

'What do you mean?'

'I mean, would you like some wine or something more substantial?'

'Why wouldn't you think I'd stick it out?' Jess asked, genuinely bewildered by his earlier remark.

He shook his head. 'I don't know. I guess I thought that you'd have opted for something more lucrative by now. I mean, with your grades, you could have gone anywhere you wanted.'

'I did.'

Jess saw the confusion settle behind Barry's eyes. Clearly, her career choices were beyond his comprehension. 'So, what can I get you to drink?' he asked again.

'A Coke would be great.'

There was a moment's silence. 'We stopped buying soft drinks,' he said. 'We figure if we don't keep soft drinks in the house, then Tyler won't be tempted. Besides, you're the only one who ever drinks them.'

It was Jess's turn to look confused.

There was a sudden cascade of footsteps down the stairs and through the hallway. Jess saw an explosion of dark hair, enormous blue eyes, and small hands waving frantically in the air. In the next instant, her three-year-old nephew was across the pink and white carpet and in her arms. 'Did you buy me a present?' he said instead of hello.

'Don't I always?' Jess reached beside her into the Marshall Field's bag, trying to avoid the realization that her nephew was wearing a shirt and tie, similar to his father's.

'Just a minute.' Barry's voice was swift, stern. 'We don't get any presents until we've said our proper hellos. Hello, Auntie Jess,' he coached.

Tyler said nothing. Ignoring the boy's father, Jess pulled a model airplane out of the bag, and deposited it in her nephew's waiting hands.

'Wow!' Tyler dropped off her lap onto the floor, studying the toy plane from all angles, whirling it through the air.

'What do we say?' Barry said, trying again, his voice tight. 'Don't we say, thank you, Auntie Jess?'

'It's okay, Barry,' Jess told him. 'He can thank me later.'

Barry looked as if the collar under his silk tie had suddenly shrunk two sizes. 'I don't appreciate your attempts to undermine my authority,' he pronounced.

'My attempts to what?' Jess asked. Surely, she must have misunderstood.

'You heard me. And don't give me that innocent look. You

know damn well what I'm talking about.'

Tyler ran happily between his father and his aunt, dipping his new plane between their hips and the floor, oblivious of the tension in the room.

Neither Barry nor Jess moved. Both stood in their respective positions, Barry by the sofa, Jess by her chair, as if waiting for something to happen, someone to interrupt.

'Isn't the doorbell supposed to ring now or something?' Jess asked, grateful when she saw Barry's jaw relax into a close approximation of a smile. If there was going to be an argument, and there was always an argument when she and Barry got together, it would not be her fault. She had promised herself that on the thirty-minute drive from her apartment to the upper class suburb.

'Oh, good,' Maureen said, suddenly appearing in the doorway. 'You two are getting along.'

Barry was immediately at his wife's side, kissing her cheek. 'Nothing to it,' he assured her.

Maureen gave her husband and sister one of her luminous smiles. Despite the fact that she had to be exhausted, she looked radiant in a crisp white shirt over black wool pants. Her figure was almost back to normal, Jess noticed, wondering if Barry had talked his wife into resuming her strict exercise routine. As if looking after a big house and three small children wasn't enough to keep her busy.

'You look wonderful,' Jess told her sister truthfully.

'And you look tired,' Maureen said, giving her sister a hug. 'You getting enough sleep?'

Jess shrugged, recalling her recent nightmare.

'Look what Auntie Jess gave me,' Tyler said from the floor, proudly brandishing his new airplane.

'Isn't that wonderful! I hope you said thank you.'

'Your sister doesn't believe in thank-yous,' Barry said, walking across the room to the wet bar and pouring himself a scotch and water. 'Can I get anybody anything?'

'Not for me,' Maureen said. 'That's a great sweater, Jess. You should wear blue more often. It's a great color for you.'

'It's green,' Barry corrected, lifting his eyebrows toward his sister-in-law. 'Isn't that what you said, Jess?'

'Oh, no, it's definitely blue,' Maureen said flatly. 'No question.'

'Are the twins asleep?' Jess asked.

'For the moment. But that never lasts very long.'

'I bought them a little something.'

'Oh, Jess, you don't have to buy them something every time you come over.'

'Of course I do. What are Aunties for?'

'Well, thank you.' Maureen took the Marshall Field's bag from Jess's hand and peeked inside.

'It's just some bibs. I thought they were kind of cute.'

'They're adorable.' Maureen held up the small white terry cloth bibs festooned with bright red apples and berries. 'Oh, look at these. Aren't they sweet, Barry?'

Jess didn't hear Barry's reply. Could this really be her sister? she was wondering, trying not to stare. Could they really have shared the same mother? Could the woman she'd watched graduate with honors from one of the top colleges in the land be so enthralled with a couple of five-dollar bibs from Marshall Field's? Could she really be proffering them forward for her husband's approval? From Summa Cum Laude to Stepford Wife?

'So, what happened in court today?' Maureen asked, as if sensing Jess's discomfort. 'You get a verdict?'

'The wrong one.'

'You were kind of expecting that, weren't you?' Maureen took Jess's hands and led her to the sofa, not relinquishing her hands even after they were both seated.

'I was hoping.'

'It must be tough.'

'So's your sister,' Barry said, taking a long sip of his drink, not releasing it from his lips until the glass was almost empty. 'Aren't you, Jess?'

'Something wrong with that?' Jess heard the dare escape her voice.

'Not as long as it's confined to the courtroom.'

Don't bite, she thought. Don't let him get to you. 'I see,' she said, despite her best efforts. 'It's okay to be strong when I'm fighting someone else's battles, just not my own.'

'Who says you always have to be fighting?'

'I don't think Jess is tough,' Maureen offered, her voice questioning.

'Tell me, Jess,' Barry asked, 'why is it that as soon as a woman gets a little power, she loses her sense of humor?'

'And why is it that whenever a man fails at being funny, he attacks a woman's sense of humor?' Jess shot back.

'There's a big difference between being strong and being tough,' Barry said, returning to his original point, and emphasizing it with a nod of his head, as if this were one of those constitutional truths supposed to be self-evident. 'A man can afford to be both; a woman can't.'

'Jess,' Maureen intervened softly, 'you know Barry's just teasing you.'

Jess jumped to her feet. 'Bullshit, he's teasing!'

Tyler's head snapped toward his aunt.

'Kindly watch your language in this house,' Barry admonished.

Jess felt the sting of his rebuke sharper than a slap across the face. She desperately hoped she wouldn't cry. 'So now we don't swear either, is that right?' she said, using her voice to keep the tears at bay. 'We don't drink Coke and we don't swear.'

Barry looked at his wife, his hands in the air, as if giving up.

'Jess, please,' Maureen implored, tugging on her sister's hand, trying to draw her back down on the couch.

'I just want to make sure I have all your husband's rules straight.' Jess glared at her brother-in-law, who was suddenly a poster boy for reason and calm. He'd gotten to her again, she realized, disgusted and ashamed of herself. 'I don't know how you do it,' she muttered dejectedly. 'It must take some special skill.'

'What are you fulminating about now?' Barry asked, a look of genuine puzzlement in his eyes.

'Fulminating?' Jess gasped, abandoning any further attempts at control. 'Fulminating?'

'Tyler,' Maureen began, rising and gently steering her son out of the room, 'why don't you take your new toy upstairs and play with it there?'

'I want to stay here,' the boy protested.

'Tyler, go play in your room until we call you for dinner,' his father instructed.

The boy jumped into immediate action.

'His master's voice,' Jess said as the youngster scampered up the stairs.

'Jess, please,' Maureen urged.

'I didn't start it.' Jess heard the hurt child in her voice, was angry and embarrassed that they could hear it too.

'It doesn't matter who started it,' Maureen was saying, speaking as if to two children, refusing to make eye contact with either of them. 'What matters is that it stops before it goes any further.'

'Consider it stopped.' Barry's voice filled the large room.

Jess said nothing.

'Jess?'

Jess nodded, her head swimming with anger and guilt. Guilt for her anger, anger for her guilt.

'So, what's next on the prosecutor's agenda?' Maureen's words were full of forced joviality, as if she were visiting a terminally ill patient in the hospital. Her normally soft voice was a shrill half octave higher than usual. She returned to the rose-colored sofa and patted the seat beside her with an intensity approaching desperation. Neither Jess nor Barry moved.

'A few drug charges I'm hoping we can plead out,' Jess told her, 'and I go to trial the week after next on another assault case. Oh, and I have a meeting on Monday with the lawyer who's representing that man who shot his estranged wife with a cross-bow.' Jess massaged the bridge of her nose, disturbed by

57

the matter-of-factness in her tone.

'With a cross-bow, my God!' Maureen shuddered. 'How barbaric.'

'You must have read about it in the paper a few months back. It made all the front pages.'

'Well, that explains why I missed it,' Maureen stated. 'I never read anything in the papers these days but the recipes.'

Jess struggled to keep her dismay from registering on her face, knew she was failing.

'It's just too depressing,' Maureen explained, her voice as much apology as explanation. 'And there's only so much time.' Her voice trailed off to a whisper.

'So, what special treat have you concocted for us for tonight?' Barry joined his wife on the couch, taking her hands in his.

Maureen took a deep breath, pulling her eyes away from Jess and staring straight ahead, as if she were reading from an imaginary blackboard. 'To start with, there's a mock turtle soup, followed by a honey-glazed chicken with sesame seeds, candied yams and grilled veggies, then a green salad with pecans and gorgonzola cheese, and finally, a pear mousse with raspberry sauce.'

'Sounds fabulous.' Barry gave his wife's hand an extra squeeze.

'Sounds like you've been cooking all week.'

'Sounds like much more work than it actually is,' Maureen said modestly.

'I don't know how you do it,' Jess said, sputtering over the 'how' when what she really wanted to say was 'why'.

'Actually, I find it very relaxing.'

'You should try it, Jess,' Barry said.

'You should stuff it, Barry,' Jess said in return.

Once again both Jess and Barry were on their feet. 'That's it,' he was saying. 'I've had enough.'

'You've had more than enough,' Jess told him. 'And for much too long. At my sister's expense.'

'Jess, you're wrong.'

'I'm not wrong, Maureen.' Jess began pacing the room.

58

'What's happened to you? You used to be this fabulous, smart woman who knew the morning paper backwards and forwards. Now, you only read recipes? For God's sake, you were on your way to a vice-presidency! Now you're on your way to the kitchen! This man has you up to your eyeballs in dirty dishes and dirty diapers and you're trying to convince me that you like it!'

'She doesn't have to convince you of anything,' Barry said angrily.

'I think my sister is perfectly capable of speaking for herself. Or is that another new rule around here? She only speaks through you.'

'You know what I think, Jess?' Barry asked, not waiting for an answer. 'I think you're jealous.'

'Jealous?'

'Yes, jealous. Because your sister has a husband and a family, and she's happy. And what have you got? A freezer full of frozen pizzas and a goddamn canary!'

'Next you'll tell me all I really need is a good fuck!'

'Jess!' Maureen looked toward the stairs, her eyes filling with tears.

'What you really need is a good spanking,' Barry said, walking to the piano by the large picture window, and slamming his knuckles against the keys. The sound, an unpleasant fistful of sharps and flats, swept through the house, like a sudden brushfire. From upstairs, the twins started to cry, first one, then the other.

Maureen lowered her head into her chest, crying into the crisp white collar of her blouse. Then without looking at either Jess or Barry, she bolted from the room.

'Dammit,' Jess whispered, her own eyes filling with tears.

'One day,' Barry said quietly, 'you'll go too far.'

'I know,' Jess said, her voice dripping sarcasm. 'You never forget. You get even.' In the next instant, she was on the stairs behind her sister. 'Maureen, please, wait. Let me talk to you.'

'There's nothing you can say,' Maureen told her, opening the door to the lilac- and white-papered nursery to the right of the

59

stairs. The smell of talcum powder immediately invaded Jess's nostrils, like a heavy narcotic. She hung back, newly dizzy and lightheaded, clinging to the doorway, watching as Maureen ministered to her infant daughters.

The cribs stood at right angles against the opposite wall, mobiles of tiny giraffes and teddy bears swirling gently above them. There was a large Bentwood rocking chair in the middle of the room and an overstuffed chair in bold white and purple stripes off to one side, as well as a changing table and a large flower-printed diaper pail. Maureen leaned over the cribs and cooed at her children, speaking over her shoulder at Jess with a gentle lilt in her voice that belied the strength of her words. 'I don't understand you, Jess. I really don't. You know Barry doesn't mean half of what he says. He just likes to give you a hard time. Why do you always have to rise to the bait?'

Jess shook her head. A million excuses fought their way to the tip of her tongue, but she swallowed them all, allowing only an apology to escape. 'I'm sorry. Really I am. I shouldn't have lost control like that. I don't know what happened,' she continued, when the apology didn't seem to suffice.

'Same thing that always happens when you and Barry get together. Only worse.'

'It's just that no matter how hard I try, he always finds a way to get to me.'

'You get to yourself.'

'Maybe.' Jess leaned against the doorway, listening to the babies settle down at the sound of their mother's voice. Maybe she should tell Maureen about Rick Ferguson's threat, and the nightmare and anxiety attacks that threat had subsequently unleashed. Maybe Maureen would cradle her in her arms and tell her that everything would be all right. How she needed to be held; how she longed to be comforted. 'I've had a really rotten day.'

'We all have rotten days. They don't give you the right to be mean and unpleasant.'

'I said I was sorry.'

Maureen lifted one of the twins out of her crib. 'Here, Carrie, go spit up on your mean Auntie Jessica.' She deposited the baby in Jess's arms.

Jess hugged the infant to her breast, feeling the softness of the baby's head against her lips, inhaling her sweet smell. If only she could go back, start all over again. There were so many things she'd do differently.

'Come to Mommy, Chloe.' Maureen lifted the second baby into her arms. 'Not everything has to be a confrontation,' she told Jess, rocking the baby gently back and forth.

'That's not what they taught us in law school.'

Maureen smiled, and Jess knew all was forgiven. Maureen had never been able to stay angry for long. She'd been like that since they were children, always eager to make things right, unlike Jess, who could nurse a grudge for days, a trait that drove their mother to distraction.

'Do you ever think . . .' Jess began, then hesitated, not sure whether to continue. She had never broached this subject with Maureen before.

'Do I ever think what?'

Jess began rocking the baby in her arms back and forth. 'Do you ever think you've seen Mommy?' she asked slowly.

A look of shock passed across Maureen's face. 'What?'

'Do you ever imagine that you've seen . . . Mother?' Jess repeated, straining for formality, avoiding her sister's incredulous gaze. 'You know, in a crowd. Or across the street.' Her voice trailed to a halt. Did she sound as ridiculous as she felt?

'Our mother is dead,' Maureen said firmly.

'I just meant . . .'

'Why are you doing this to yourself?'

'I'm not doing anything to myself.'

'Look at me, Jess,' Maureen ordered, and Jess reluctantly turned toward her sister's voice. The two women, each cradling an infant in her arms, stared into each other's green eyes from across the room. 'Our mother is dead,' Maureen repeated, as Jess felt her body grow numb.

They heard the doorbell ring. 'That's Daddy,' Jess said,

desperate to escape her sister's scrutiny.

Maureen's eyes refused to release her. 'Jess, I think you should talk to Stephanie Banack.'

Jess heard the front door open, listened as her father and Barry exchanged pleasantries in the front foyer. 'Stephanie Banack? Why would I want to talk to her? She's *your* friend.'

'She's also a therapist.'

'I don't need a therapist.'

'I think you do. Look, I'm going to write out her phone number before you go. I want you to call her.'

Jess was about to argue, but thought better of it when she heard her father's footsteps on the stairs.

'Well, look at this,' her father bellowed from the doorway. 'All my gorgeous girls together in one room.' He walked to Jess and engulfed her in his arms, kissing her cheek. 'How are you, doll?'

'I'm fine, Daddy,' Jess told him, and felt, for the first time that day, that maybe she was.

'And how's my other doll?' he asked Maureen, hugging her against him. 'And my little dolls?' he asked, drawing them all together. He lifted Chloe from her mother's arms, smothering her face with kisses. 'Oh you sweet thing. You sweet thing,' he chanted. 'I love you. Yes, I do.' He stopped, smiling at his own two daughters. 'I said that to a bigger girl last night,' he told them, then stood back and waited for their reaction.

'What did you say?' Maureen asked.

Jess said nothing. Maureen had taken the words right out of her mouth.

Chapter Five

Jess spent the first hour after she left her sister's house driving around the streets of Evanston trying not to think about the things her father had said at dinner. Naturally, she could think of nothing else.

'I said that to a bigger girl last night,' he'd announced, sounding so calm, so pleased, so sure of himself. As if falling in love was no big deal, as if he made that sort of declaration every day.

'Tell us all about her,' Maureen had urged at the dinner table, ladling out the mock turtle soup as Jess struggled to banish the image of a child's decapitated turtle from her mind. 'We want to hear absolutely everything. What's her name? What's she like? Where did you meet? When do *we* get to meet her?'

No, Jess thought. Don't say another word. Don't tell us a thing. Please, don't say anything.

'Her name is Sherry Hasek,' her father stated proudly. 'She's just a little bit of a thing. Not too tall, a little on the skinny side, dark hair, almost black. I think she colors it . . .'

Jess forced a spoonful of hot soup into her mouth, felt it numb the tip of her tongue, sear the roof of her mouth. Her mother had been tall, bosomy, her brown hair attractively sprinkled with grey. She'd always hated dyed black hair, said it looked so phony. Her father had agreed. Could he possibly have forgotten? she wondered, swallowing the urge to remind him, feeling the soup burn a path to her stomach. Pictures of headless turtles swam their way back up the path to her brain.

'We met at my life drawing class about six months ago,' he continued.

63

'Don't tell me she was a model.' Barry laughed into his soup.

'No, just a fellow student. Always liked to draw, never had the time. Like me.'

'Is she a widow?' Maureen asked. 'What's the matter, Jess? Don't you like the soup?'

She wasn't a widow. She was divorced. Had been for almost fifteen years. She was fifty-eight, the mother of three grown sons, and she worked in an antique store. She liked bright colors, dressed in long flowing skirts and Birkenstock sandals, and she had been the one to suggest coffee after class. Evidently she knew a good thing when she saw it. Art Koster was definitely a good thing.

Jess turned a corner and found herself back on Sheridan Road, stately homes to one side, Lake Michigan to the other. How long had she been circling the dark streets of Evanston? Long enough for it to have started raining, she realized, activating the car's windshield wipers, seeing one of them stick, drag itself across the car's window in what was obviously a Herculean effort. Rain then, not snow, she thought, not sure which she preferred. A fog was rolling in from the lake.

October was always the least dependable of months, she thought, full of ghosts and shadows.

People always raved about the glorious colors of autumn, the reds, oranges and yellows that disrupted, then replaced, the omnipresent green of summer. Jess had never shared their enthusiasm. For her, the change in colors meant only that the leaves were dying. And now, the trees were almost bare. What leaves were left were faded, shrivelled, drained of energy. Cruel reminders of their once buoyant selves. Like people abandoned in old age homes, death the only visitor they could rely on. Lonely people left too long without love.

Certainly her father deserved to find love, Jess thought, turning right and finding herself on a street she didn't recognize. She looked for a sign, didn't see one, turned left at the next corner. Still no street sign. What was the matter with people who lived in the suburbs? Didn't they want anyone to know where they were?

She'd always lived in the heart of the city, always in the same three-block radius, except during her marriage to Don. When she was little, and her father had worked as a buyer for a chain of women's clothing stores, they'd lived in a duplex on Howe Street. They'd moved when she was ten, her father then the successful manager of his own store, to a fully detached home on Burling Street, only a block away. Nothing fancy. Nothing particularly innovative or compelling in its architecture. Decidedly no Mies van der Rohe or Frank Lloyd Wright. It was just comfortable. The kind of house one felt good about coming home to. They'd loved it, planned on staying in it forever. And then one afternoon in August, her mother left for a doctor's appointment and never came back.

After that, everybody went their separate ways – Maureen back to Harvard, Jess back to law school and into marriage with Don, her father on increased buying trips to Europe. The once loved house sat empty. Eventually, her father worked up the necessary resolve to sell it. He could no longer bear to live in it alone.

And now her father had a new woman in his life.

It shouldn't have come as such a surprise, Jess realized, turning another corner and finding herself back on Sheraton Road. What was truly surprising was that he had waited eight long years. Women had always found him attractive. True, he was only average in appearance and his hairline had receded into nothingness, but there was still a twinkle in his brown eyes, and a ready laugh in his voice.

For a long while, there had been no laughter.

In the days, even months, after Laura Koster went missing, Art Koster had been the chief, and only, suspect in his wife's disappearance. Despite the fact he'd been out of town on a buying trip when she vanished, the police had refused to rule out his potential involvement. He could have hired someone, after all, they pointed out, delving into the couple's marriage, asking questions of neighbors and friends, probing into his business and financial affairs.

How had the couple been getting along? Did they argue? How

frequently? About money? The time he spent away from home? Other women?

Of course they argued, Art Koster had told them. Not often, but possibly more often than he realized. Not about anything important. Not about money. Not about his occasional business trips. Certainly not about other women. There were no other women, he told the police. He insisted on taking a polygraph test. Passed. The police seemed disappointed. Ultimately, they'd had no choice but to believe him.

There had never been any question as far as Jess was concerned. Her father was innocent. It was that simple. Whatever had happened to her mother, her father had had nothing to do with it.

It had taken Art Koster years to resume the rhythm of his daily life. For a time, he lost himself in his work. He drifted apart from old friends, then away. He rarely socialized, didn't date. He moved to an apartment on the waterfront, spent hours staring at Lake Michigan, seeing only Jess and Don and Maureen. Everyone coaxing everyone else. Come on, it'll be good for you. You need to get out. We need to see you. We're all we've got.

It was probably the combination of Maureen's marriage and Jess's divorce that brought Art Koster back to his normal pace. He'd been as upset by the news that Jess and Don were separating as he'd been by their engagement. Not that he didn't like Don. He did. Very much. He'd just wanted Jess to wait a little while. She was still so young. She was just starting law school. Don was eleven years her senior, already so well established. Jess needed time to be on her own, he'd told her, echoing her mother's sentiments, as he always did.

Still, he later confessed he'd been grateful that she'd had somewhere to turn after her mother vanished. It had taken some of the burden off him. And Don had taken good care of Art Koster's younger child. He was genuinely sorry when the marriage ended. Sorry, but supportive. As always. There for Jess when she needed him, resuming the fatherly role, taking her to dinner, the theater, the opera. Making sure she didn't hide out in her apartment, that she didn't bury herself in her work, as he had done. Trying to see that she ate properly. A losing battle.

And then Maureen had given birth to his first grandchild, and suddenly everything seemed to fall into place. Maybe it was just a question of time, Jess thought, continuing her drive north, away from the city, away from her problems. Not that time was the great healer that everyone promised. Just that time did indeed have a way of marching on. Ultimately you had no choice but to march with it. And now her father was in love.

The campus of Northwestern University appeared suddenly on her right. Jess passed the observatory with its giant telescope looking off into space, the frat houses, the drama building, the art center, the rain-soaked tennis courts. She continued past Lighthouse Beach, squinted past her defective windshield wiper at the old lighthouse that once warned sailors of dangerous rocks, then turned left on Central Street, driving the few blocks to Ridge Road, slowly ascending to the top of the steep incline, past the El stop, which Barry claimed was transporting crime back into the suburbs, past the hospital, past the Municipal Golf Course, over the bridge at the Chicago River, past Dyche Stadium, where the Northwestern University football team served as perennial losers to a variety of visiting teams, past the kosher hot dog outlet known as Custard's Last Stand, till she reached the Evanston Theaters, all in all a tour of less than a mile.

The street was crowded with parked cars. Jess had to circle the block before she found a parking spot. It was almost ten o'clock. The pizza parlor down the street was half empty, the ice cream store deserted. Not exactly a night for ice cream, she thought, recalling the taste of Maureen's exotic pear mousse with raspberry sauce.

No, she wouldn't think about Maureen, she decided, jumping out of her car and running toward the movie theater. She didn't know what movies were playing. She didn't care. Whatever was playing beat going home and having to deal with the revelations of this evening. Her sister's life was her own, as was her father's. She would have to let them live their lives as she had demanded the freedom to live hers.

'Which movie?' a young girl in a pink- and white-striped shirt and oddly angled red bow tie inquired as Jess pushed her money across the wicket.

Jess tried to focus on the list of films printed in white letters on the black slate behind the girl, but the names blurred, then ran together, disappearing before they reached her brain. 'Doesn't matter,' she told the girl. 'Whatever is starting next.'

'They've all already started.' The girl managed to look bored and confused at the same time.

'Well, then, you pick one. I'm having trouble . . .' She stopped, allowing the thought to dangle.

The girl shrugged, took the money, punched some figures into her cash register, and handed Jess a ticket. '*Hell Hounds*. Theater one, to your left,' she stated. 'It started ten minutes ago.'

There was no one waiting in the lobby to take Jess's ticket, no one to ensure she didn't wander into the wrong screening room, no one who cared what she did.

She opened the door to theater one and plunged into immediate, total darkness. Whatever was happening on the screen had to be happening in the dead of night. She couldn't see a thing.

Jess waited a few minutes for her eyes to adjust, was surprised by how little of the auditorium she could make out even after the screen filled with light. She proceeded slowly down the aisle, peering across rows of bodies, searching for a seat.

For a few minutes, it looked as if there weren't any. Sure, Jess thought, she sells me a ticket to the one movie that's all sold out. But then she saw it — a single seat in the middle of the fourth row from the front. Of course, it's Friday night, she reminded herself. Date night. Everybody a couple, she thought, carrying her aloneness like a bright neon sign as she tried to squeeze her legs between recalcitrant feet to get to the vacant seat.

'Will you sit down,' someone hissed from behind her, a command, not a question.

'Jeez, how long you gonna take, lady?'

'Excuse me,' Jess whispered, stepping over knees that refused to budge.

In the next instant, she was in her seat, afraid to take off her coat, lest she create a further disturbance. Around her, angry voices fluttered like autumn leaves, then settled into stillness.

On the screen, a young man, whose blue eyes were pierced through with fear, was fleeing an angry mob. The mob, individual faces contorted with rage, raised fists pummeling the air, was shouting obscenities at him, laughing when he tripped and fell, setting their snarling pit bulls after him. Seconds later, the dogs caught up with the hapless young man as he was clambering to his feet, and dragged him screaming back to the ground. Jess watched as a giant claw scratched across the young man's jugular, blood spurting from the wound to soak the screen. The audience cheered.

What on earth was she watching?

She closed her eyes, opened them again to see the same young man in bed with a beautiful woman whose curly blond hair draped teasingly along the tops of her bare breasts. Either a flashback or a very speedy recovery, Jess thought, watching their tongues disappear into each other's mouths.

Whatever happened to dialogue? she wondered. For as long as she'd been sitting here, nobody on the screen had said a word. They kissed, they killed, they fled, they fornicated. But nobody talked.

Maybe it was better that way, she decided. Think how much better off they'd all be if nobody ever said anything. It would certainly make her job as an Assistant State's Attorney a whole lot easier. She'd simply shoot the bad guys instead of trying to convince a peevish jury. As for family problems, a well-executed left hook to the jaw would put an end to her tiresome brother-in-law. Her father's disquieting announcement would be something she'd never have to hear.

Her father in love, she thought again, witnessing his image

jump onto the screen, suddenly larger than life, as he stepped into the young man's place, assumed his starring role. It was her father who now gathered the naked young woman into his arms, kissed her full on the lips, twisted her silky blond hair between his fingers. Jess tried to turn her head away, couldn't, sat transfixed, powerless, a prisoner to her own imaginings. She saw her father cup the young woman's face in his large hands, watching, with Jess, as her blond hair turned brown, dusted over with grey. Creases of wisdom appeared around the young woman's eyes and mouth. Her eyes deepened from light blue to navy to forest green. She turned and peered through the screen at Jess.

Her mother, Jess realized, as the woman's slow smile enveloped her. Her beautiful mother.

Jess leaned forward in her seat, her arms reaching around herself, holding her body tight.

And then another woman, smaller, thinner, her hair shoe polish black, dressed in flowing chiffon and Birkenstocks, dancing into the frame, into her father's arms, her father oblivious of his change in co-stars, her mother clinging precariously to the side of the screen, her image growing weaker, fading, disappearing.

Gone.

Jess gasped, her head dropping to her knees, clutching her stomach as if she'd been shot.

'What now?' someone muttered.

Jess tried to sit back up, aware of a tightening in her chest. She twisted her shoulders, arched her back, wondered if there was some subtle way she could unhook her bra, decided there wasn't. She felt hot, flushed, dizzy.

Well, of course she was dizzy. Of course she was hot. She was wearing her coat, for God's sake. The theater was crowded. They were packed in like sardines. Small wonder she could scarcely breathe. It was a miracle she hadn't already fainted. Jess threw her shoulders forward and pulled at her sleeves, wrenching the coat free of her arms as if it was on fire.

70

'For God's sake,' a voice beside her complained. 'Can't you sit still?'

'Sorry,' Jess whispered. She was still hot, flushed, dizzy. Taking off her coat had accomplished nothing. She began pulling at her sweater. Blue, green, turquoise — whatever color the damn thing was, it was too warm. It was choking her, denying her air. Why couldn't she breathe?

Jess looked around frantically for the exit sign, her head bouncing from her right to her left, her eyes darting in all directions simultaneously, her stomach pushing against her ribs. The turtle soup mocking me, she thought, pulling at the neck of her turtleneck sweater, picturing herself suddenly surrounded by a sea of headless turtles.

Was she going to be sick? Oh, no, please don't throw up. Please don't throw up. She looked back at the screen. The young man lay dead on the ground, his face so savaged by the dogs he was no longer recognizable. Barely human. The mob, satisfied, abandoned him to the deserted stretch of highway.

Had her mother met a similar fate? Savaged and abandoned on some desolate stretch of road?

Or was she sitting somewhere in a theater much like this one, watching some equally grotesque concoction and wondering if she could ever go home, if her daughters could ever forgive her for abandoning them?

'*I don't need this, Jess,*' she had shouted the morning of her disappearance. '*I don't need this from you!*'

Jess felt the bile rise in her throat. She tasted mock turtle soup mixed with honey-glazed chicken and Gorgonzola cheese. No, please don't throw up, she prayed, clenching her jaw, gritting her teeth.

Take deep breaths, she told herself, remembering Don's advice. Lots of deep breaths. From the diaphragm. In. Out. In. Out.

It wasn't working. Nothing was working. She felt the perspiration break out on her forehead, felt it trickle down the side of her face. She was going to be sick. She was going to throw up in the middle of a movie in the middle of a packed theater. No, please, she couldn't do that. She had to get out. She had to break free.

She jumped to her feet.

'Oh, no. Sit down, lady!'

'What the hell's going on?'

Jess grabbed for her coat, pushed her way through the row to the aisle, stepping on toes, knocking against the shoulders of the people in the row ahead, almost tripping over someone's damp umbrella. 'Excuse me,' she whispered.

'Ssh!'

'Don't come back!'

'Excuse me,' she repeated to no one in particular, racing for the lobby, gulping down the outside air. The girl behind the ticket window eyed her suspiciously, but said nothing. Jess ran along the street toward her car. It was still raining, now harder than before.

She fumbled through her purse for the car key, then fumbled with it again trying to put it in the lock. By the time she got behind the wheel, she was soaked through, her hair dripping into her eyes, her sweater clinging clammily to her body, like a cold sweat. She threw her coat into the back seat, then spread out across the front, letting the dampness cool her. She swallowed the cold night air, savouring it in her mouth as if it were a fine wine. She lay like this until, gradually, her breathing returned to normal.

The panic subsided, then died.

Jess sat up, quickly turned on the car's ignition. The windshield wipers shot immediately into action. Or, at least, one of them did. The other one merely sputtered into approximate position, then dragged itself along the window, like chalk across a blackboard. She'd definitely have to get it taken care of. She could barely see to drive.

She pulled the car out of her parking space onto the street, heading south on Central. She flipped on the radio, listened as Mariah Carey's high whine reverberated throughout the small car, ricocheting off the doors and windows. Something about feeling emotions. Jess wondered absently what else there was to feel.

She didn't see the white car until it was coming right at her. Instinctively, Jess swerved her car to the side of the road, the wheels losing their grip on the wet pavement, the car spinning to a halt as her foot frantically pumped the brake. 'Jesus Christ!' she shouted over Mariah Carey's oblivious pyrotechnics. 'You moron! You could have gotten us both killed!'

But the white car was long gone. She was screaming at air.

That was twice today she'd barely missed being demolished by a white car, the first a Chrysler, this one . . . she wasn't sure. Could have been a Chrysler, she supposed, trying to get a fix on the car's basic shape. But it had sped by too quickly, and it was raining and dark. And one of her windshield wipers didn't work. And what difference did it make anyway? It was probably her fault. She wasn't concentrating on what she was doing, where she was going. Too preoccupied with other things. Too preoccupied with not being preoccupied. About her sister. Her father. Her anxiety attacks.

Maybe she *should* give Maureen's friend, Stephanie Banack, a call. Jess felt in the pocket of her black slacks for the piece of paper on which her sister had written the therapist's address and phone number.

Jess recalled Stephanie Banack as a studious, no-frills type of woman whose shoulders stooped slightly forward and whose nose had always been too wide for the rest of her narrow face. Stephanie and her sister went all the way back to high school, and they still kept in frequent touch. Jess hadn't seen her in years, had forgotten she'd become a therapist, decided against seeing her now. She didn't need a therapist; she needed a good night's sleep.

Central Street became Sheraton Road, then eventually Lake Shore Drive. Jess started to relax, feeling better as she approached Lincoln Park, almost normal when she turned right onto North Avenue. Almost home, she thought, noting that the rain was turning to snow.

73

Home was the top floor of a three-story brownstone on Orchard Avenue, near Armitage. The old, increasingly gentrified area was lined with beautiful old houses, many of them semi-detached, most having undergone extensive renovations during the last decade. The homes were an eclectic bunch: some large, some tiny, some brick, others painted clapboard, a hodgepodge of shapes and styles, rental units next to single family dwellings, few with any front yard, fewer still with attached garages. Most residents, an equally eclectic mix, parked on the street, their parking permits prominently displayed on the dashboards of their cars.

The red brick façade of the house Jess lived in had been sandblasted over the summer and its wood shutters had received a fresh coat of shiny black paint. Jess felt good every time she saw the old house, knew how lucky she'd been to be able to rent its top floor. If only it had an elevator, she wished, though normally she thought nothing of the three flights of stairs. Tonight, however, her legs felt tired, as if she'd spent the last few hours jogging.

She hadn't jogged since her divorce. She and Don had regularly run the distance between the North Avenue and Oak Street beaches when they'd lived on Lake Shore Drive. But the jogging had been at Don's insistence, and she'd given it up as soon as she'd moved out, along with three balanced meals a day and eight hours sleep a night. It seemed she'd given up everything that was good for her. Including Don, she thought now, deciding that tonight was one of those nights when it would have been nice not to have to come home to an empty apartment.

Jess parked her old red Mustang behind the new metallic grey Lexus of the woman who lived across the street, and ran through the light drizzle – was it actually snow? – to the front door. She unlocked the door and stepped into the small foyer, switching on the light and relocking the door behind her. To her right was the closed door of the ground floor apartment. Directly ahead were three flights of dark red-carpeted stairs. Her hand tracing an invisible line along the side of the white wall, she began her ascent, hearing music emanating from the second floor apartment as she passed by.

She rarely saw the other tenants. Both were young urban professionals, like herself, one a twice-divorced architect with the city planning commission, the other a gay systems analyst. Whatever that was. Systems analyst was one of those jobs she would never understand, no matter how often and in how much detail it was explained to her.

The systems analyst was a jazz fan, and the plaintive wail of a saxophone accompanied her to her door. The hall light, which was on an automatic timer, turned off as she stretched her key toward the lock. Once inside, the saxophone's mournful sounds gave way to the happier song of her canary. 'Hello, Fred,' she called, closing the door and walking directly to the bird's cage, bringing her lips close to the slender bars. Like visiting a friend in prison, she thought. Behind her, the radio, which she left on all day along with the most of the lights, was playing an old Tom Jones tune. 'Why, why, why, Delilah . . .?' she sang along as she headed for the kitchen.

'Sorry I'm so late, Freddy. But trust me, you're lucky you stayed home.' Jess opened the freezer and pulled out a box of Pepperidge Farm vanilla cake, cutting herself a wide slice, then returning the box to the freezer, the cake already half-eaten by the time she shut the freezer door. 'My brother-in-law was in top form, and I got sucked in again,' Jess stated, returning to the living room. 'My father is in love, and I can't seem to be happy for him. It looks like it's actually starting to snow out there and I seem to be taking it as a personal affront. I think I'm having a nervous breakdown.' She swallowed the rest of the cake. 'What do you think, Fred? Think your mistress is going crazy?'

The canary flitted back and forth between his perches, ignoring her.

'Exactly right,' Jess said, approaching her large front window and staring down onto Orchard Street from behind antique lace curtains.

A white Chrysler was parked on the street directly across

from her house. Jess gasped, instantly retreating from the window and pressing her back against the wall. Another white Chrysler. Had it been there when she arrived?

'Stop being silly,' she said over the loud pounding of her heart, the canary bursting into a fresh round of song. 'There must be a million white Chryslers in this city.' Just because in the course of a single day, one had almost run her down, another had almost plowed into her car, and a third was now parked outside her apartment, that didn't necessarily add up to more than coincidence. Sure, and it never snowed before Halloween, she thought, reminding herself that she wasn't even sure that the car that had almost collided with her own in Evanston had been a Chrysler.

Jess edged back toward the window, peering out from behind the lace curtains. The white Chrysler was still there, a man sitting motionless behind the wheel, shadows from the street lights falling across his face. He was staring straight ahead, not looking in her direction. The darkness, the weather, and the distance combined to throw a scrim across his features. 'Rick Ferguson?' she asked out loud.

The sound of his name on her lips sent Jess scurrying out of the living room, down the hall, and into her bedroom. She threw open her closet door, falling to her hands and knees, and rifling through her seemingly endless supply of shoes, many still in their original boxes. 'Where the hell did I put it?' she demanded, getting off the floor, stretching for the top shelf where she kept still more shoes, old favorites not currently in fashion, but too precious to throw away. 'Where did I hide that damn gun?'

She ejected the boxes from the high shelf with one grand sweep of her hand, protecting her head as it rained shoes around her. 'Where is it?' she cried, spying something shiny and black beneath some crumpled white tissue paper.

A pair of black patent high-heeled shoes, she discovered, wondering what had ever possessed her to purchase shoes with four-inch heels. She'd worn them exactly once.

Jess finally discovered the small snub-nose revolver hidden

behind the enormous cloth flowers that adorned a pair of pewter pumps, the bullets painstakingly lodged inside the shoes' toes. Her hands shaking, Jess loaded six bullets into the barrel of the .38 caliber Smith and Wesson that Don had insisted she take with her when she moved out on her own. 'Call it my divorce present,' he'd told her, brooking no further discussion.

It had sat in the shoe box for four years. Would it still work? Jess thought, wondering if guns carried the same sort of 'Best if used before' warning that came with dairy products and other perishable items. She let the gun lead her back into the living room, tapping its short barrel against the light switch and throwing the room into darkness. The canary abruptly stopped singing.

Jess approached the window, the gun at her side. 'Just don't shoot yourself in the foot,' she cautioned, feeling as foolish as she did frightened, parting the lace curtains with trembling hands.

There was nothing there. No white Chrysler. No white car of any kind. Nothing white except the snow that was gradually peppering the grass and pavement. Nothing but a quiet residential street. Had there been a white car at all?

'Your mistress is definitely going crazy,' Jess told her canary, leaving the room in darkness. She covered the bird's cage with a dark green cloth and turned off the radio, carrying the gun back to her bedroom, freshly carpeted with shoes. Why couldn't she collect stamps? she wondered, surveying the mess. Stamps definitely took up less space, were less messy, less subject to the frivolous dictates of fashion. Certainly, nobody would have criticized Imelda Marcos for collecting three thousand pairs of stamps.

She was getting giddy, she realized, squatting on the floor and starting to tidy up. There was no way she'd be able to sleep when the floor of her bedroom looked like it could be declared a national disaster area. Assuming she could sleep at all.

'What a night!' she said, staring at the gun in her hand. Would she have actually been able to use it? She shrugged, grateful not to have been put to the test, and returned it to the shoe box behind the large cloth flowers of her old pewter pumps. Guns 'N' Roses, she thought, immediately lifting the gun back out.

Maybe it would be a better idea to hide it somewhere a little more accessible. Even if she wasn't ever going to use it. Just to make her feel better.

Opening the top drawer of her night table, Jess tucked the gun into the rear corner behind an old photograph album. 'Just for tonight,' she said out loud, picturing herself trying to outrun a pack of blood-thirsty pit bulls.

Just for tonight.

Chapter Six

Jess was the first of her party to arrive at Scoozi, located on Huron Street in River West. Unlike the small, dark bars along California Street, where Jess and her fellow prosecutors were more used to hanging out, Scoozi was an enormous old warehouse that had been converted into a restaurant and bar, with huge, high ceilings, and old Chicago-style windows lined with shelves of wine bottles. A giant Art-Deco chandelier hung down into the center of the ersatz Tuscany-style room. To the back sat a big clay pot filled with bright, artificial flowers, to the front an always crowded bar. The main floor of the restaurant was filled with well-lacquered wooden tables; to either side were raised decks with booths and still more tables. Jess estimated the large room could easily accommodate over three hundred people. Italian music played loudly from invisible speakers. All in all, the restaurant was the perfect choice for celebrating Leo Pameter's forty-first birthday.

Jess hadn't seen Leo Pameter in the year since he'd left the State's Attorney's Office to go into private practice. She was sure the only reason she'd been invited to his birthday celebration was because the entire eleventh and twelfth floors had been asked. She was less sure why she'd chosen to accept.

It was something to do, she supposed, smiling knowingly when the maître d' told her no one else from her party was here yet, asking if she'd like to wait at the bar. The bar was already crowded, despite the fact it was barely six o'clock. Jess checked her watch, more for something to do than for the information it could provide, and wondered again why she was here.

She was here, she told herself, because she'd always liked Leo Pameter, although they'd never had the time to get really close, and she'd been sorry to see him leave. Unlike many of the other

79

state prosecutors, Greg Oliver among them, Leo Pameter was soft-spoken and respectful, a calming influence on those around him, possibly because he never let his ambitions got the better of his good manners. Everyone liked him, which was one of the reasons everyone would be here tonight. Jess wondered how many people would show up if the birthday party were for her.

She grabbed a fistful of pretzels and some kind of cheese crackers in the shape of little fish, and stuffed them into her mouth, watching as several of the fish tumbled from her hand onto the front of her brown sweater.

'Let me get that for you,' a male voice said playfully from the seat beside her.

Jess quickly brought her hands to her chest. 'Thank you, I can do it myself.'

The young man had a thick neck, close-cropped blond hair, and a big barrel chest that stretched against the silk of his kelly green shirt. He looked like a football player.

'Are you a football player?' Jess asked without meaning to, picking the wayward fish off her sweater.

'Can I buy you a drink if I say yes?'

She smiled. He was kind of cute. 'I'm waiting for someone,' she told him, turning away. She had no room in her life for kind of cute.

What was the matter with her? she wondered, grabbing another handful of fish crackers. Everyone kept telling her what an attractive woman she was, how smart, how clever, how talented. She was young. She was healthy. She was unattached.

She hadn't had a date in months. Her sex life was non-existent. Her *life*, outside of the office, was non-existent. And here was this nice-looking guy, maybe a little big for her taste, but nice-looking nonetheless, and he was asking her if he could buy her a drink, and she was saying no. Was this what Nancy Reagan had in mind?

She turned back toward the would-be football player, but he was already engaged in conversation with a woman on his other side. That was quick, Jess thought, coughing into her hand so that no one could see her blush. What had she been thinking? Had she seriously considered letting some stranger in a bar pick her up because he was kind of cute and she was kind of lonely? 'Kind of stupid,' she muttered.

'Sorry?' the bartender asked, although it was hardly a question. 'Did you say you wanted something to drink?'

Jess stared into the bartender's somber blue eyes. 'I'll have a glass of white wine.' She took another handful of fish and stuffed them into her mouth.

'God, would you just look at the crap she eats.'

Jess spun round, spilling a small school of fish onto the lap of her brown skirt, jumping off the bar stool to her feet. 'Don! I don't believe this.' His arms quickly encircled her, drawing her into a warm, comforting embrace. She was disappointed when he pulled away after only several seconds.

'Once again, it's not quite the coincidence you think it is,' he explained. 'Leo and I went to law school together. Remember?'

'I'd forgotten,' Jess admitted. Or had she? Had she suspected Don might be here tonight? Was that at least part of the reason she had come? Was he the someone she'd told the would-be football player she was waiting for?

'I knew you'd be the first one here. Thought we'd come early to keep you company.'

We? The word fell, like a blunt instrument, on Jess's ears.

'Jess, this is Trish McMillan,' Don was saying. He pulled a pretty woman with short blond hair and a wide smile to his side. 'Trish, this is Jess.'

'Hi, Jess,' the woman said. 'It's nice to meet you. I've heard a lot about you.'

Jess muttered something inane, conscious of the woman's deep dimples, and the fact that her arm was round Don's waist.

'What are you drinking?' Don asked.

Jess reached behind her for her drink. 'White wine.' She took a long sip, tasted nothing.

Trish McMillan laughed, and Don beamed. Jess felt confused. She hadn't said anything funny. She surreptitiously checked her sweater to determine whether any stray fish might be

81

clinging to her breasts. There weren't any. Maybe Trish McMillan was just one of those sickeningly happy people who didn't need a reason to laugh out loud. Don had been right. Her laugh *was* wicked, as if she knew something the rest of the world didn't, as if she knew something that Jess didn't. Jess took another long sip of her drink.

'Two house wine,' Don told the bartender. 'You here alone?'

Jess shrugged. The question didn't require a response. Why had he asked?

'I haven't seen Leo since he left the department,' Jess said, feeling she had to say something.

'He's doing very well,' Don told her. 'He went with Remington, Faskin, as you know.' Remington, Faskin, Carter and Bloom was a small, but very prestigious, Chicago law firm. 'Seems very happy there.'

'What do *you* do?' Jess asked Trish McMillan, trying not to notice that her arm still encircled Don's waist.

'I'm a teacher.'

Jess nodded. Nothing too impressive about that.

'Well, not just a teacher,' Don embellished proudly. 'Trish teaches over at Children's Memorial Hospital. In the brain ward and dialysis unit.'

'I don't understand,' Jess said. 'What do you teach?'

'Everything,' Trish answered, laughing over the rapidly increasing din of the restaurant.

Jess thought: Everything. Of course.

'I teach kids in grades one through twelve, who are hooked up to dialysis machines and can't get to school, or kids who've had brain operations. The ones who are in hospital for the long haul.'

'Sounds very depressing.'

'It can be. But I try not to let it get me down.' She laughed again. Her eyes sparkled. Her dimples crinkled. Jess was having a hard time not hating her. Mother Teresa with short blond hair and a wicked laugh.

Jess took another sip of her drink, realized with some surprise that there was nothing left, signalled the bartender for another, insisted on paying for it herself.

'I understand you had a rather heated session this afternoon,' Don said.

'How'd you hear?'

'Word gets around.'

'Hal Bristol has a hell of a nerve trying to get me to go for involuntary manslaughter two weeks before the trial.' Jess heard the anger in her voice. She turned to Trish so suddenly, the woman jumped. 'Some bastard shoots his estranged wife through the heart with a crossbow, and his lawyer tries to convince me it was an accident!'

Trish McMillan said nothing. The pupils of her dark eyes grew larger.

'Bristol's claiming it was an accident?' Even Don sounded surprised.

'He says his client didn't mean to shoot her, only frighten her a little. And why not? I mean, she'd provoked the poor guy beyond reason. Right? What other options did he have but to buy a bow and arrow and shoot her down in the middle of a busy intersection?'

'Bristol was probably just trying to get you to settle for some middle ground.'

'There is no middle ground.'

Don smiled sadly. 'With you, there never is.' He hugged Trish McMillan closer to his side.

Jess finished her second glass of wine. 'I'm glad you're here,' she announced in as businesslike a tone as she could muster. 'I wanted to ask you something.'

'Shoot.'

Jess pictured herself behind the antique lace curtains of her apartment window, staring onto Orchard Street, gun in hand. She wished Don had chosen another word.

'What kind of car does Rick Ferguson drive?'

Don cupped his hand to his ear. 'Sorry. I didn't hear you.'

Jess raised her voice. 'Does Rick Ferguson drive a white Chrysler?'

Don made no effort to hide his obvious surprise. 'Why?'

'Does he?'

'I think so,' Don answered. 'I repeat, why?'

Jess felt her glass start to shake in her hand. She brought it to her lips, steadied it with her teeth.

There was a sudden explosion of sound, voices raised in greetings and congratulations, backs being slapped, hands being shaken, and in the next instant Jess found herself on one of the raised decks at the side of the room, another drink in hand, a party in full steam around her.

'I hear you really let old Bristol have it,' Greg Oliver was bellowing above the din.

Jess said nothing, searching through the crowd for Don, hearing Trish's wicked laugh mocking her from the far end of the deck.

'I guess word gets around,' she said, using Don's earlier phrase, catching sight of her ex-husband as he introduced his new lady to the rest of the gathering.

'So, what's the story? Are you going to settle for murder two? Save the taxpayer the expense of a hung jury?'

'I take it you don't think I'll get a conviction,' Jess stated, despair gnawing at the pit of her stomach. Did he always have to tell her what she didn't want to hear?

'For murder two, probably. Murder one? Never.'

Jess shook her head in disgust. 'The man murdered his wife in cold blood.'

'He was half out of his mind. His wife had been having an affair. She'd taunted him for weeks about his failings as a man. It got to be too much. They had a horrendous fight. She said she was leaving him, that he'd never see his kids again, that she'd take him for everything he owned. He just snapped.'

'The man was an abusive bully who couldn't stand the fact that his wife had finally worked up the courage to leave him,' Jess countered. 'Don't try to tell me this was a crime of passion. It was murder, pure and simple.'

'Not so pure,' Greg Oliver stated. 'Anything but simple.' He paused, possibly waiting for Jess to say something, continued when she didn't. 'She ridiculed his sexual prowess, remember.

A lot of male jurors are going to understand and sympathize with his response.'

'So, let me get this straight,' Jess said, finishing her drink and grabbing another from a passing waiter. 'You think it's acceptable for a man to kill his wife if she insults his precious manhood?'

'I think Bristol might be able to convince a jury of that, yes.'

Jess shook her head in disgust. 'What is it – open season on women?'

'Just warning you. I was right about the Barnowski case, remember.'

Jess scanned the room, hoping to find someone she could wave to, someone she could gravitate toward. Anyone. But there was no one. It seemed that everyone was either paired off or already engaged in pleasant conversation. No one even glanced her way.

It was her own fault, she realized. She didn't make friends easily. Never had. She was too serious, too intense. She frightened people, put them off. She had to work hard to establish friendships, harder to maintain them. She'd given up the pretense. She worked hard enough at the office.

'You're looking very delectable tonight,' Greg was saying, leaning closer, his lips brushing against the side of her hair.

Jess spun round, whisking her hair none too gently across Greg Oliver's cheek, seeing him wince. 'Where's your wife, Greg?' she asked, loud enough to be heard by those in the immediate vicinity. Then she turned and walked away, though she had no idea where she was headed.

She spent the next fifteen minutes in earnest conversation with one of the waiters. She couldn't make out most of what he was saying – the room was starting to sway slightly – but she managed to look interested and nod politely at appropriate intervals.

'Go easy on the drinks,' Don whispered, coming up behind her.

Jess stretched her head back against his chest. 'Where's Mother Teresa?' she asked.

'Who?'

'Teresa,' Jess repeated stubbornly.

'You mean Trish?'

'Trish, yes. Sorry.'

'She went to the washroom. Jess, why did you ask me about Rick Ferguson's car?'

Jess told him. About her narrow escape on Michigan Avenue, her near collision in Evanston, the white car waiting outside her apartment. Don's face registered interest, concern, then anger, in rapid succession. His response was characteristically direct.

'Did you get the license plate number?'

Jess was horrified to realize she hadn't even thought of it. 'It all happened so fast,' she said, the excuse sounding lame even to her ears.

'There are a lot of white Chryslers in Chicago,' Don told her, and she nodded. 'But I'll check it out, talk to my client. I can't believe he'd do anything so stupid so close to trial.'

'I hope you're right.'

Jess heard Trish's laugh, saw her arm snake round Don's waist, reclaim her territory. She turned away, watching the room spin to catch up. A young woman was striding purposefully across the floor toward the deck, a large portable cassette player in her hands. There was something off-kilter about her. She looked wrong, displaced. There was a kind of desperation to her heavy make-up, as if she were trying to hide who she really was. Her legs wobbled on a pair of too-high heels. Her trench coat was old and ill fitting. And something else, Jess thought, watching the young woman as she approached the birthday boy. She looked scared.

'Leo Pameter?' the girl asked, her voice that of a lost child.

Leo Pameter nodded warily.

The young woman, whose face was surrounded by a huge mass of unruly black curls, pushed a button on her tape cassette and suddenly the room reverberated to the traditional bump and grind music of a striptease show.

'Happy birthday, Leo Pameter!' the young girl shouted,

throwing off her trench coat and skipping around the deck in a white push-up bra and panties, complete with matching garter belt and stockings.

There were loud hoots from the men and embarrassed laughter from the women as the stripper shook her larger-than-life breasts in their direction before concentrating her energy on the hapless birthday boy.

'Jesus Christ,' Jess moaned, burying her eyes in her glass of wine.

'Those can't be real,' Trish exclaimed from somewhere beside her.

Jess looked up only when the music stopped. The young woman stood nude except for a G-string in front of Leo Pameter, who had the good grace to look embarrassed. She leaned over and planted a hot pink kiss on his forehead. 'From Greg Oliver,' she said, then quickly gathered up her things, threw her coat over her shoulders and fled to a smattering of self-conscious applause.

'How enlightened,' Jess muttered as Greg approached.

'It's you who have to lighten up, Jess.' Greg's eyes directly challenged hers. 'You have to learn to have fun, let yourself go, tell a few jokes.'

Jess downed the remainder of her drink, took a deep breath, and struggled to keep her eyes from crossing. 'Did you hear about the miracle baby that was born at Northwestern Memorial Hospital?' she asked, feeling all eyes turn toward her.

'Miracle baby?' Greg repeated, clearly wondering what this had to do with him.

'Yes,' Jess said loudly. 'It had brains *and* a penis!'

In the next instant, the room was spinning, and Jess was on the floor.

'Really, Don, this isn't necessary,' Jess was saying. 'I can take a cab.'

'Don't be silly. I'm not letting you go home alone.'

'What about Mother Teresa?'

'*Trish*,' Don emphasized, 'will meet me back at my apartment.'

'I'm sorry. I didn't mean to ruin your evening.'

'You aren't, and you didn't, so don't worry about it. Just get in the car.'

Jess crawled into the front seat of the black Mercedes, heard the car door shut after her. She leaned against the soft black leather, eyes closed, feeling Don assume his place behind the wheel, start the engine, pull away from the curb. 'I'm really sorry,' she began again, then stopped. He was right. She wasn't sorry.

No sooner had they started, but they stopped. She heard a car door open, then close. Now what? she thought, opening her eyes.

They were in front of her brownstone. Don came round to her side of the car, opened her door, and helped her out.

'That was fast,' she heard herself say, wondering how much time had elapsed.

'Think you can walk?' Don asked.

Jess said yes, though she wasn't at all sure. She leaned against Don, felt his arm slip round her waist, allowed him to guide her from the car toward the front door of the large house. 'I can do the rest on my own,' she told him, watching him search through her purse for her key.

'Sure you can. You don't mind if I just stand here and watch, do you?'

'Could you do me a favor?' she asked once they were inside the foyer, three flights of stairs stretching before her.

'You want me to leave?'

'I want you to carry me up.'

Don laughed, draping her left arm round his right shoulder and supporting her weight with his own. 'Jess, Jess, what am I going to do with you?'

'I bet you say that to all the girls,' she muttered as they began their slow climb.

'Only to girls named Jess.'

What on earth had possessed her to drink so much? Jess

wondered as she groped for the stairs. She wasn't a drinker, rarely had more than a single glass of wine. What was the matter with her? And why did she seem to be asking herself that question so often lately?

'You know,' Jess said, recalling the sneer in Greg Oliver's voice when he told her to lighten up, 'it's not that I don't like men. It's lawyers I have a problem with.'

'Are you trying to tell me something?' Don asked.

'And accountants,' Jess added.

They opted for silence the rest of the way. By the time they reached the top of the stairs, Jess felt as if she had conquered Mount Everest. Her legs were like jelly, her knees refusing to lock into place. Don continued propping her up as he twisted the key in the lock. Somewhere a phone was ringing.

'Is that your phone?' Don asked, pushing the door open. The ringing got louder, grew more urgent.

'Don't answer it,' Jess instructed her ex-husband, closing her eyes against the lights as he lowered her to the couch.

'Why not?' He looked toward the kitchen where the phone continued its insistent ring. 'It could be important.'

'It isn't.'

'You know who it is?'

'My father,' Jess told him. 'He's been trying to set up a good time for me to meet his new friend.' I've met enough new friends for one night, she thought, but didn't say.

'Your father has a girlfriend?'

'Well, I'd hardly call her a girl.' Jess curled up inside her sofa, drawing her knees against her chest. 'I'm an awful person,' she moaned into the velvet cushion. 'Why can't I just be happy for him?' The phone continued to ring, then suddenly, mercifully, stopped. She opened her eyes. Where was Don?

'Hello,' she heard him say from the kitchen, and for a minute, she thought maybe someone else had entered the apartment. 'I'm sorry,' he continued. 'I can't understand what you're saying. Can you speak slower?'

'I told you not to answer it,' Jess said, wobbling into the kitchen, holding her hand toward the telephone.

Don handed her the phone, his forehead creasing into a series of worried folds. 'It's a woman, but I can't make out a word she's saying. She has a very thick accent.'

Jess felt sobriety tugging at her consciousness. She didn't want to be sober, she thought, putting the phone to her ear, her mellowness seeping away from her, like a slow leak.

The woman's voice assaulted her ears before she had time to say hello. 'I'm sorry. What? Who is this?' Jess felt a terrible sinking feeling in the pit of her stomach. 'Mrs Gambala? Is this Mrs Gambala?'

'Who's Mrs Gambala?'

'Connie DeVuono's mother,' Jess whispered, her hand across the receiver. 'Mrs Gambala, you have to calm down. I can't understand you . . . What? What do you mean she didn't come home?'

Jess listened to the rest of what Mrs Gambala had to say in stunned silence. When she hung up the phone, her whole body was shaking. She turned to Don, watching his eyes narrow with unasked questions. 'Connie didn't pick up her son at her mother's house after work,' she said, dread audible in every word. 'She's disappeared.'

Chapter Seven

'I can't believe I was so stupid!'

'Jess . . .'

'So stupid, and so damned self-centered!'

'Self-centered? Jess, for God's sake, what are you talking about?'

'I just assumed he was talking about me.'

'Who? What are you talking about?'

'Rick Ferguson!'

'Rick Ferguson? Jess, slow down.' Don pushed some imaginary hairs away from his forehead, his expression hovering between curiosity and exasperation. 'What has Rick Ferguson got to do with this?'

'Come on, Don.' Jess made no attempt to hide her impatience with her ex-husband. 'You know as well as I do that Rick Ferguson is responsible for Connie DeVuono's disappearance. Don't try to tell me you don't. Don't play games with me. Not now. This isn't a courtroom.' Jess marched out of the kitchen into her living room, pacing restlessly in front of the bird cage, her canary hopping back and forth between perches, as if consciously mimicking her strides.

Don was right behind her, hands in the air, trying to get Jess to slow down. 'Jess, if you would just calm down for half a second.' He grabbed hold of her shoulders with both hands. 'If you would just stop moving for half a second.' The pressure of his palms forced her to a standstill. Don stared into her eyes until she had no choice but to look back. 'Now, can you tell me exactly what happened?'

'Rick Ferguson—' she began.

Immediately, he cut her off. 'Not what you *think* happened, what you *know* happened.'

Jess took a deep breath, shrugged her shoulders free of his strong grip. 'Connie DeVuono called her mother at approximately four-thirty this afternoon to say she was leaving work, she'd be there in twenty minutes to pick up her son, could she please have him dressed and ready to go. Her son has hockey practice every Monday at five-thirty, and it's always a bit of a rush.'

'Connie's mother looks after her son?'

Jess nodded. 'He goes to her house after school, waits there for Connie to pick him up when she's finished work. Connie always calls before she's leaving. Today, she called. But she never showed up.'

Don's eyes told Jess he expected more.

'That's it,' Jess said, hearing Don scoff, though in truth he made no sound.

'Okay. So, what we *know*,' Don emphasized, 'is that Connie DeVuono didn't pick her son up after work.'

'After she called and said she was on her way,' Jess reminded him.

'And we don't know whether or not anybody saw her leave work, or what kind of a mood she might have been in, or if she told anybody she had to stop off somewhere, or—'

'We don't know anything. The police won't officially start investigating until she's been missing for twenty-four hours. You know that.'

'We don't know if she was depressed or anxious,' Don continued.

'Of course she's depressed and anxious. She was raped. She was beaten. The man who attacked her convinced a judge he's a model citizen with deep roots in the community, the sole support for his aged mother, and other assorted crap, so they let him out on bail. Connie DeVuono's supposed to testify in court next week. And your client has threatened to kill her if she tries. You're damn right she's depressed and anxious! In fact, she's scared to death!' Jess heard the shrillness in her voice. Her canary started singing.

'Scared enough to just take off?' Don underlined the importance of his question with a furrowing of his brow.

Jess was about to answer, then stopped, swallowing her words before they could leave her mouth. She recalled the sight of Connie in her office the previous week, how frightened she'd been, how adamant that she wouldn't testify. Jess had convinced her otherwise. Persuaded her to go against her better judgement, to challenge her tormentor in a court of law.

Jess had to admit at least the possibility that Connie might have changed her mind again, decided she couldn't go through with testifying, that the risks were too great. She could easily have felt too embarrassed to inform Jess of her change of heart, too afraid Jess might be able to convince her otherwise, too guilty for being such a coward. So strange, Jess thought, how often it was the innocent who suffered the most guilt.

'She wouldn't leave her son,' Jess said quietly, the words half out of her mouth before she realized she was speaking.

'She probably just needs time to clear her head.'

'She wouldn't leave her son.'

'She's probably in a hotel somewhere. In a day or two, when she's calmed down, had a bit of a rest, decided what she wants to do, she'll call.'

'You're not hearing me.' Jess walked toward the window, stared out onto the street. Patches of snow lay across the grass and sidewalks, like torn doilies.

Don came up behind her, massaged the back of her neck with his strong hands. Suddenly he stopped, resting his palms on her shoulders. Jess could feel him thinking, formulating the words he wanted to say. 'Jess,' he began, speaking in slow, measured tones, 'not everyone who doesn't show up on time disappears for ever.'

Neither moved. In the background, Jess's canary hopped from perch to perch to the beat of an old Beatles melody. Jess tried to speak, couldn't for the sudden constriction in her chest. She finally managed to force the words out.

'This isn't about my mother,' she told him carefully.

93

Another silence.

'Isn't it?'

Jess maneuvered her body away from him, coming round to the front of the sofa, dropping lifelessly into its soft pillows, burying her face in her hands. Only her right foot betrayed her anxiety, twitching restlessly beneath her. She looked up only when she felt the cushion beside her sag, felt Don take her hands in his own.

'It's all my fault,' she began.

'Jess—'

'No, please don't try to tell me otherwise. It is my fault. I know it. I accept it. I'm the one who convinced her she had to testify when she really didn't want to; I'm the one who pressured her, who promised her everything would be all right. "Who will look after my son?" she asked me, and I made some silly joke, but she was serious. She knew that Rick Ferguson meant what he said.'

'Jess—'

'She knew he'd kill her if she didn't drop the charges.'

'Jess, you're really jumping the gun here. The woman's been missing less than six hours. We don't know that she's dead, for God's sake.'

'I was so proud of myself, too. So proud of my ability to turn things around, to convince this poor frightened woman that she had to testify, that she'd only be safe *if* she testified. Oh yes, I was very proud of myself. It's a big case for me, after all. Another potential winner for my files.'

'Jess, you did what anybody would do.'

'I did what any *prosecutor* would do! If I'd had an ounce of real compassion for that woman, I'd have told her to drop the charges and run. Jesus!' Jess jumped to her feet, though she had nowhere to go. 'I talked to that animal! I stood there in the lobby of the Administration Building and I warned him to keep away from Connie. And that bastard told me, told me right out, though I was too full of myself to really hear him, he told me that people who annoyed him had a way of disappearing. And I

94

assumed it was me he was threatening! Who else would he be threatening? Doesn't the universe revolve around Jess Koster?' She laughed, a harsh, cold sound that stuck in the air. 'Only it *wasn't* me he was talking about. It was Connie. And now she's gone. Disappeared. Just like he threatened.'

'Jess—'

'So don't you dare sit there and try to tell me that your client had nothing to do with her disappearance! Don't you dare try to convince me that Connie would leave her son, even for a day or two, because I know she wouldn't. We both know that Rick Ferguson is responsible for whatever's happened to Connie DeVuono. And we both know that, barring a miracle, she's already dead.'

'Jess—'

'Don't we both know that, Don? Don't we both know she's dead? We do. We know that. And we have to find her, Don.' Involuntary tears traced the length of Jess's cheeks. She wiped the back of her hand across her face, trying to rub them away, but the tears only came faster.

Don was on his feet beside her, but she moved quickly out of his reach. She didn't want to be comforted. She didn't deserve it.

'We have to find her body, Don,' Jess continued, starting to shake. 'Because if we don't, that little boy will spend the rest of his life wondering what happened to his mother. He will spend years searching through crowds for her, thinking he sees her, wondering what he did that was so awful she went away and never came home. And even when he's all grown up, and he rationally accepts the fact she's dead, he'll never quite believe it. A part of him will always wonder. He'll never know for sure. He'll never be able to put it behind him, to grieve for her the way he needs to grieve for her. The way he needs to grieve for himself.' She stopped, allowed Don to take her in his arms, hold her. 'There has to be a resolution, Don. There has to be.'

They stood that way for several minutes, so close their breath seemed to emanate from one body. It was Don who finally broke

95

the stillness. 'I miss her too,' he said quietly, and Jess knew he was talking about her mother.

'I thought it was supposed to get easier with time,' Jess said, allowing Don to guide her back to the sofa. She sat cradled in his arms as he gently rocked her to and fro.

'It only gets farther away,' he said simply.

She smiled sadly. 'I'm so tired.'

'Lay your head on my shoulder,' he said, and she did, grateful to be told what to do. 'Now close your eyes. Try to sleep.'

'I can't sleep.' She made a feeble attempt to get up. 'I should really go over to Mrs Gambala's.'

'Mrs Gambala will call you when she hears from Connie.' He pressed her head back against his shoulder. 'Ssh. Get some sleep.'

'What about your friend?'

'Trish is a big girl. She'll understand.'

'Yes, she's very understanding.' Jess heard the thinness in her voice, knew she was close to losing consciousness. Her eyes fluttered closed. She forced them open again. 'Probably because she works in a hospital.'

'Ssh.'

'She seemed like a very nice person.'

'She is.'

'I don't like her,' Jess said, closing her eyes and allowing them to stay shut.

'I know you don't.'

'I'm not a very nice person.'

'You never were,' he said, and Jess felt his smile against the side of her face.

She would have smiled in return, but she was having trouble controlling the muscles in her face. They were sinking toward her chin, giving in to the pull of gravity.

In the next second, she was asleep and a phone was ringing.

She opened her eyes to find she was in the sterile reception area of a doctor's office. 'The phone's for you,' the doctor said, producing a plain black phone from his bag. 'It's your mother.'

Jess took the phone. 'Mother, where are you?'

'There's been an accident,' her mother told her. 'I'm in the hospital.'

'The hospital?'

'I'm in the brain ward. They have me hooked up to all these machines.'

'I'll be right there.'

'Hurry. I can't wait for long.'

Jess was suddenly in front of Northwestern Memorial Hospital, lines of angry picketers blocking her way.

'What are you protesting?' Jess asked one of the nurses, a young woman with very short blond hair and dimples so deep they all but overwhelmed her face.

'Duplicity,' the woman said simply.

'I don't understand,' Jess muttered, transported in the next second to a busy nurses' station. Half a dozen young women in crisp white caps and garter belts and stockings stood behind the counter engaged in earnest conversation. No one looked her way. 'I'm here to see my mother,' Jess shouted.

'You just missed her,' one of the nurses said, though no lips moved.

'Where did she go?' Jess spun round, grabbing a passing orderly by the sleeve.

Greg Oliver's face glowered before her. 'Your mother is gone,' he told her. 'She disappeared.'

In the next instant, Jess was standing on the street in front of her parents' home. A white stretch limousine was idling on the corner. Jess watched as a man opened the car door and stepped onto the sidewalk. It was dark and Jess couldn't make out his face. But she could feel his long slow strides as he moved toward her, felt him mounting the front stairs after her, his hand reaching for her as she pulled open the door and slammed it shut. His face pressed heavily against the screen, his hideous grin seeping slowly through the wire mesh.

She screamed, her cried piercing the dimension between sleep and consciousness, waking Jess up with the sudden sharpness of an alarm clock. She jumped to her feet, flailing madly in the darkness. Where was she?

Don was immediately at her side. 'Jess, it's all right. It's all right. It was just a bad dream.'

It all came back to her: the party; the wine; Trish; Mrs Gambala; Don. 'You're still here,' she acknowledged gratefully, falling back into his arms, wiping the combination of sweat and tears from her cheeks, trying to still the frantic beating of her heart.

'Take deep breaths,' he advised, as if he could see the chaos growing inside her body. His voice was groggy, full of sleep. 'That's a girl. In, now out. Steady. That's right. You've got it.'

'It was the same dream I used to have,' she whispered. 'Remember? The one where Death is waiting for me.'

'You know I'd never let anyone hurt you,' he assured her, control returning to his voice. 'Everything's going to be all right. I promise.'

Just like her mother, she thought, settling comfortably into his arms.

Approximately half an hour later, he slipped his arm round her waist, and led her gingerly toward her bedroom. 'I think it's time to go to bed. Will you be all right if I leave you alone?'

Jess smiled weakly as Don tucked her, fully clothed, between the covers of her double bed. Part of her wanted him to stay; part of her wanted him to go, the way it always was when they were together. Would she ever figure out what she wanted? Would she ever grow up?

Without a mother, how could she?

'I'll be fine,' she assured him, as he bent over to kiss her forehead. 'Don?'

He didn't move.

'You're a nice man,' she told him.

He laughed. 'Think you'll remember that a few days from now?'

She was too tired to ask what he meant.

'You bastard!' she was screaming barely forty-eight hours later. 'You turd! You miserable piece of shit!'

'Jess, calm down!' Don was circling the oblong wooden table

backwards, trying to keep an arm's length from his angry ex-wife.

'I can't believe you'd pull a stunt like this!'

'Can you at least keep your voice down?'

'You shit! You creep! You . . . *shit*!'

'Yes, point taken, counsellor. Now, do you think you can calm down so that we can discuss this like the two rational attorneys-at-law we are?'

Jess folded her arms in front of her and stared at the blood-red concrete floor. They were in a small, windowless room on the second floor of the police station that serviced Chicago's downtown core. Recessed, high-wattage lights emanated from the dull, acoustic tile ceiling. A bench lay across one wall; a formica table was bolted into the floor on another, several uncomfortable chairs beside it. In the next room, which was smaller and even more claustrophobic, sat Rick Ferguson, sullen and silent. He hadn't said a word since the police had brought him in for questioning earlier that morning. When Jess had tried to question him, he'd yawned, then closed his eyes. He hadn't opened them even after they'd manacled his hands to the wall. He'd feigned indifference, then indignation, when they asked him what he'd done with Connie DeVuono. He'd looked interested in the proceedings only when his attorney, Don Shaw, arrived, apoplectic about what he deemed the deliberate abrogation of his client's rights, threatening to break down the door if he wasn't allowed in to confer with his client.

'You have no right to be here,' Jess told him, keeping her voice low and steady. 'I could report you to the attorney disciplinary committee.'

'If anybody's going to report anybody to the attorney disciplinary committee,' he shot back, 'it'll be me.'

'You?!' Jess was almost too flabbergasted to speak.

'You're the one who violated the canon of ethics,' he told her.

'What?!'

'You violated the canon of ethics, Jess,' Don repeated. 'You had no right to arrest my client. You certainly had no right to

99

try to question him without his attorney present.'

Jess struggled to keep her voice calm. 'Your client is not under arrest.'

'I see. He's sitting in a locked room manacled to the wall because he likes it. Is that what you're trying to tell me?'

'I don't have to tell you anything. I am perfectly within my rights here.'

'What about Rick Ferguson's rights? Or have you decided that because you don't like him, he doesn't have any?'

Jess clenched, then unclenched, her fist, grabbing the back of a chair to anchor herself, give her head time to clear, her thoughts a chance to settle. She glared at her ex-husband with barely concealed fury. He ignored the message in her eyes, continued his lecture.

'You have the police pick up my client at work; you don't read him his rights; you don't let him call his attorney. And it's not like you don't know he's got a lawyer. A lawyer who's already advised you that his client has nothing to say, that he's executing his legal right to remain silent. You already know that's the position we've taken. It's on the record. But it doesn't stop you from embarrassing him at work, dragging him down here, handcuffing him to the wall . . . Jess, for Christ's sake, was that really necessary?'

'I thought so. Your client is a dangerous man. He wasn't being very cooperative.'

'It's not his job to cooperate. It's *your* job to make sure he's treated fairly.'

'Did he treat Connie DeVuono fairly?'

'That's not the issue here, Jess,' Don reminded her.

'Did you treat *me* fairly?'

There was a moment's silence.

'You used me, Don.' Jess heard the combination of hurt and disbelief in her voice. 'How could you do that to me?'

'How could I do what? What is it you think I've done to you?' A look of genuine confusion filled Don's face.

Jess shook her head. Were they really having this conversation? 'You were with me the night Connie DeVuono

100

disappeared,' she began. 'You knew I suspected Rick Ferguson, that we were planning to pick him up.'

'I knew you suspected him. I had no idea you were planning to pick him up,' Don told her.

'What else would I be planning?'

'At the very least, I thought you might wait a few more days. Jess, it's been less than forty-eight hours since the woman disappeared.'

'You know as well as I do that she's not coming back,' Jess said.

'I know no such thing.'

'Oh, please! Don't insult my intelligence.'

'Don't insult mine,' Don parried. 'What do you expect me to do, Jess? Allow you free rein because you used to be my wife? Am I supposed to let my feelings for you override my responsibilities to my client? Am I?'

Jess said nothing. She looked toward the wall that separated the two small rooms. She'd seen the smirk on Rick Ferguson's face when she'd left the room to deal with Don. She knew he understood what was going on, that he was enjoying her discomfort.

'Now, either charge my client or release him.'

'Release him?! No way am I releasing him.'

'Then you're arresting him? On what grounds? On what evidence? You know you have absolutely nothing to link Rick Ferguson to Connie DeVuono's disappearance.'

Jess brought her hands to her lips, breathed deeply against her fingers. He was right, and she knew it. She had no hard evidence to justify holding him. 'For God's sake, Don, I don't want to arrest him. I just want to talk to him.'

'But my client doesn't want to talk to you.'

'He might if his lawyer would stop interfering.'

'You know I'm not going to do that, Jess.' It was Don's turn to take a deep breath. 'As far as I'm concerned, you've violated the fifth and sixth amendments guaranteeing the accused the right to counsel, and the accused the right to remain silent, under the fifth. I have every right to be here.'

Jess could scarcely believe what she was hearing. 'What are you trying to pull? You know the recent Supreme Court ruling as well as I do. The Miranda warning, the right to have an attorney present, they only apply the first time an arrest is made. They don't apply to a subsequent offense.'

'Maybe yes, maybe no. Maybe we should let the attorney disciplinary commission determine the propriety of your actions, and let a court of law decide what rights my client still has. If any. Let the courts decide whether the constitution is still alive and well in Cook County!'

'A truly bravura speech, counsellor,' Jess told him, impressed despite herself.

'In any event, Jess,' Don continued, his voice softening, 'you have to have probable cause to arrest my client. You simply haven't got it.' He paused. 'Now, is my client free to leave, or isn't he?'

Jess looked toward the wall separating the two interrogation rooms. Even through the locked door, she could feel the force of Rick Ferguson's contempt. 'How did you find out we'd picked him up?' She hoped the defeat wasn't too evident in her voice.

'His mother phoned my office. Apparently she called Rick at work, and his foreman told her what happened.'

Jess shook her head. Wasn't that always the way? It was probably the first time the woman had called her son at work in years, and it *would* be today. 'What, did she run out of booze?'

'I want to talk to my client, Jess,' Don said, ignoring her sarcasm. 'Now, are you going to let me talk to him or not?'

'If I let you talk to him, you'll tell him to keep quiet,' Jess acknowledged.

'And if you hold him, you have to let him have counsel.'

'Is this what they call a Catch-22?'

'It's what they call the law.'

'I don't need you to teach me the law,' Jess said bitterly, knowing it was futile to continue. She walked into the hall and knocked on the next door. It was opened almost immediately by a uniformed police officer. Jess and Don moved quickly inside. Another detective, wearing plain clothes and an expression of resignation, as if he had known what the outcome of her conference would be all along, stood against the far wall, sucking on the end of an unlit cigarette. Rick Ferguson, in black jeans and brown leather jacket, sat on a small wooden chair, his hands manacled to the wall behind him.

'Take those things off now,' Don commanded impatiently.

'I didn't say a thing, counsellor,' Ferguson told him, staring at Jess.

Jess signalled to the detective, who, in turn, nodded at the uniformed police officer. In the next instant, Rick Ferguson's hands were freed.

Rick Ferguson didn't rub his wrists, or jump to his feet as most prisoners would have done. Instead he rose slowly, almost casually, and stretched, as if he were in no hurry, like a cat awakened from a nap, as if he were thinking of sticking around. 'I told her I had nothing to say,' he repeated, staring at Jess. 'She didn't believe me.'

'Let's go, Rick,' Don advised from the doorway.

'Why is it you never believe me, huh, Jess?' Ferguson held on to the final s of her name, so that it emerged as a hiss.

'That's enough, Rick.' The edge to Don's voice was unmistakable.

'Almost made me miss Halloween,' he said, his lips stretching into the familiar, evil grin, his tongue flicking obscenely between his teeth. 'Trick or treat,' he said.

Without a word, Don brusquely steered his client out the door.

Jess heard the echo of Rick Ferguson's laugh long after he had left the room.

Chapter Eight

'I want him charged with murder,' Jess told her trial supervisor.

Tom Olinsky peered across his desk from behind small, circular, wire-rimmed glasses much too small for his round face. He was an enormous man, close to six feet six inches tall and at least two hundred and fifty pounds. As a result, he seemed to overpower almost everything that crossed his path. The granny glasses, a tribute to growing up in the sixties, while decidedly incongruous, humanized him, rendered him more accessible.

Jess fidgeted in the large leather wing chair across from Tom Olinsky's oversized desk. Like the man himself, all the furniture in the small office at the end of the hall was too big for its surroundings. Whenever Jess set foot in this office, she felt like Alice after eating the wrong mushroom. She felt diminished, insignificant, inadequate. She invariably compensated for these feelings by speaking louder, faster, and more often than was necessary.

'Jess . . .'

'I know what you've told me before,' she said stubbornly. 'That without a body—'

'Without a body, we'll be laughed right out of court.' Tom came around to the front of his desk, his wide girth threatening to squeeze Jess out of the room. 'Jess, I know you think this guy committed murder, and you're probably right. But we just don't have any evidence.'

'We know he raped and beat her.'

'Which was never proved in court.'

'Because he killed her before she could testify against him.'

'Prove it.'

Jess threw her head back, stared at the ceiling. Hadn't she

105

already had this conversation? 'Rick Ferguson threatened Connie, told her she'd never live to testify.'

'For which we have only her word.'

'What about what he said to me?' Jess asked. Too loud. Too desperate.

'Not strong enough.'

'Not strong enough? What do you mean, not strong enough?'

'It's just not strong enough,' Tom repeated, not bothering to embellish. 'We wouldn't get past a preliminary hearing. You know that as well as I do.'

'What about a grand jury?'

'Even a grand jury is going to want some proof the woman is dead!'

'There have been numerous instances of people being charged with murder without a body ever being recovered,' Jess reminded him stubbornly.

'And how many convictions?' Tom paused, leaned against his desk. Jess felt the wood groan. 'Jess, do I have to remind you that the man has an alibi for the time Connie DeVuono disappeared?'

'I know — his sainted mother!' Jess scoffed. 'He keeps her supplied with booze; she keeps him supplied with alibis.'

Tom returned to his side of the desk and lowered himself slowly into the oversized leather chair. He said nothing, his silence more intimidating than words.

'So, we just let him get away with it,' Jess said. 'Is that what you're telling me?' She threw her hands in the air, standing up and turning her head so that he wouldn't see the tears forming in her eyes.

'What's going on, Jess?' Tom asked as Jess walked toward the door.

She stopped, wiped at her eyes before turning to face him. 'What do you mean?'

'You're more involved in this case than you should be. Don't get me wrong,' he continued, without prompting. 'One of the things that makes you so special as a prosecutor is the empathy you seem to develop with most of the victims. It makes you see

106

things the rest of us sometimes miss, gives you an edge, makes you fight that much harder. But I'm sensing something more here. Am I right? And are you going to tell me what it is?'

Jess shrugged, trying desperately not to picture her mother's face. 'Maybe I just hate loose ends.' She tried to smile, failed. 'Or maybe I just like a good fight.'

'Even you have to have something to fight with,' Tom told her. 'We just don't have it here. A good defense lawyer — and your ex-husband is a very good defense lawyer — would make mincemeat out of us. We need evidence, Jess. We need a body.'

Jess recalled the image of Connie DeVuono, eyes ablaze, sitting across from her in the small conference room — 'Who will look after my son?' she'd demanded. 'Will you?' — and tried to imagine the woman lying lifeless and cold on some deserted stretch of road. The image came easier than Jess anticipated. It made her want to gag. Immediately, she clamped down on her jaw, gritting her teeth until they ached.

Jess said nothing, nodding her head in acknowledgement of the stated facts, and left her trial supervisor's office. The Halloween decorations along the corridors had been removed and replaced by an assortment of turkeys and pilgrims in anticipation of Thanksgiving. Jess returned to her office only long enough to pick up her coat and say goodbye to her cohorts, whose faces registered their surprise at seeing her leave so early, despite the fact it was after five o'clock.

Not that she wanted to leave work early. Not that she didn't have a lot to do. Not that she had any choice, she told herself. She'd given her word. After ten days of *I really can't, I'm up to my eyeballs*, Jess had finally given in to her sister's exhortations to meet Sherry Hasek, the new woman in their father's life. Dinner at seven. Bistro 110. *Yes, I'll be there. I promise.*

Her brother-in-law and her father's new love, all in one evening, two headaches for the price of one. 'Just what I need,' Jess moaned out loud, relieved at finding the elevator to herself. 'Just what I need to cap off the end of a perfect day.'

The elevator stopped at the next floor and a woman got on,

catching Jess in mid-sentence. Jess quickly twisted her mouth into a yawn.

'Long day?' the woman asked, and Jess almost laughed.

The day's events replayed quickly in her mind, like a video on fast forward. She saw herself standing in front of Judge Earl Harris, her ex-husband at her side, demanding his client's right to a speedy trial for assaulting Connie DeVuono. 'Justice delayed is justice denied,' he'd intoned.

She saw Rick Ferguson's mocking grin, heard her own weak response: 'Judge, we're forced to take a motion state because our witness isn't available for trial today.'

'What day do you want?' Judge Harris asked.

'Judge, give us thirty days,' Jess requested.

'Getting awfully close to Christmas,' the Judge reminded her.

'Yes, Your Honor.'

'Thirty days it is.'

'Sure hope the old lady shows up in thirty days,' Rick Ferguson said, not bothering to disguise the laughter in his voice. 'I hate to keep dragging my butt down here for nothing.'

Jess leaned back against the elevator wall, scoffed out loud, pretended to cough. 'You all right?' the woman beside her asked.

'Fine,' Jess said, recalling her later frustration with the auto body shop to which she'd taken her car first thing that morning. 'What do you mean, my car won't be ready by tonight? It's just a windshield wiper, for God's sake!' Now she'd have to take the El home, and it would be crowded and unpleasant, and she'd never get a seat. And she'd have to rush to make the restaurant by seven.

She could take a cab, she thought, knowing that no cabs would be waiting anywhere in the vicinity. Cabs hated coming even remotely near 26th Street and California, especially after dark. Of course she could have called for a taxi from her office, but that would have been too easy. Or she could have called Don. No, she'd never do that. She was angry with him, even furious. For what? For being objective? For believing there was a chance that Rick Ferguson might be innocent? For refusing to let his feelings for her trample over his client's rights? For being such a good lawyer? Yes, all those things, she realized.

So, she wasn't really fine, after all, Jess thought as the elevator stopped on the fourth floor to admit a bunch of tall, black men in an assortment of multi-colored wool hats. She was frustrated and fed-up and furious. 'Fuck it,' one of the tall, black men uttered as the elevator doors opened to the ground floor.

My sentiments exactly, Jess thought, tucking her purse underneath her coat as she hurried through the lobby toward the revolving doors.

It was very cold outside. Those fearless Chicago weather forecasters had predicted an unusually bitter November, and so far they'd been right. The possibility of lots of snow for December, they heralded. Jess still hadn't bought new winter boots.

She approached the bus stop at the corner, momentarily overwhelmed by what the darkness couldn't hide: the bag ladies, wearing their lives in layers against the cold; the crazies, raging against invisible demons, wandering around aimlessly, bottles in hand, no shoes on their feet; the kids, so stoned they didn't have either the energy or the inclination to pull the needles from their skinny arms; the pimps; the hookers; the dealers; the disenchanted. It was all there, Jess knew, and getting bigger every year. Like watching a cancer grow, she thought, grateful when a bus approached.

She rode the bus to California and Eighth, took the subway to State Street, transferred to the El, all with a minimum of fuss and bother. If Don could only see her now, Jess thought, and almost laughed. He'd have a fit. 'Are you nuts?' she could hear him yell. 'Don't you know how dangerous the El is, especially at night? What are you trying to prove?'

Just trying to get myself home, she answered silently, refusing to be intimidated by someone who wasn't there.

The El platform was crowded, littered, noisy. A youth bumped into Jess from behind, didn't bother with an 'excuse me' as he hurried past her. An elderly woman stepped on her toes as she edged in front of Jess, then glowered as if Jess owed *her* the apology. Black faces, brown faces, white faces. Cold faces, Jess thought, her mind painting everyone in winter blue. Bodies shivering against the night. Everyone just a little afraid of everyone else. Like watching a cancer grow, she thought again, seeing her mother's face suddenly appear in the front window of the approaching train.

The train stopped, and Jess felt herself being pushed toward its doors, barely conscious of her feet touching the ground. In the next instant, she was swept up and deposited into a cracked vinyl seat, squished between a large black man on her right and an elderly Mexican woman with a large shopping bag on her left. Across the crowded aisle sat a Filipina trying to keep a squirming white child on her lap. A whistle blew. The train lurched, then started. Torsos swayed to the rhythm of the moving train. Winter coats, like heavy curtains, fell across Jess's line of vision. Hot breath filled the air around her.

Jess closed her eyes, saw herself as a small child, holding on to her mother's hand as they stood on a platform waiting for the El. 'It's just a train, honey,' her mother had said, scooping the terrified youngster into her arms as the train barrelled toward them. 'You don't have to be afraid.'

Where was I when *you* were so afraid? Jess wondered now. Where was I when *you* needed me?

'*I don't need this from you, Jess!*' she heard her mother cry, tears streaking her beautiful face.

The train screeched to a halt at its next stop. Jess kept her eyes closed, heard the doors open, felt the exchange of passengers, the additional weight of more people pressing against her knees. The whistle sounded. The doors closed. The train began slowly resuming speed. Jess kept her eyes shut as the train raced through the center of the city.

She was remembering the morning of the day her mother disappeared.

It had been very hot, even for August, the temperature stretching toward ninety degrees before ten a.m. Jess had come down to the kitchen wearing shorts and an old T-shirt emblazoned with the head of Jerry Garcia. Her father was away on a buying trip. Maureen was at the library, preparing for her return to Harvard in the fall. Her mother was standing by the phone in the kitchen, dressed in a white linen dress, her make-up carefully applied, her hair neatly combed away from her face. She was obviously ready to go out. 'Where are you going?' Jess had asked.

Her mother's voice had emerged as if on pinpricks. 'Nowhere,' she'd said.

'Since when do you get so dressed up to go nowhere?'

The words reverberated to the rhythm of the train. *Since when do you get so dressed up to go nowhere? Since when do you get so dressed up to go nowhere? Since when do you get so dressed up to go nowhere?*

The train jerked, then twisted, and Jess felt someone fall across her knees. She opened her eyes, saw an elderly black woman struggling to regain her footing. 'I'm so sorry,' the woman said.

'Don't worry about it,' Jess told her, grabbing one of the woman's hands and trying to assist her, about to offer her her seat.

It was then that she saw him.

'My God!'

'Did I hurt you?' the old woman asked. 'I'm really sorry. The train jerked so suddenly, I lost my balance. Did I step on your foot?'

'I'm fine,' Jess whispered, pushing the words out of her mouth, staring past the woman at the sullen young man who stood several feet behind her, arms at his side, stubbornly refusing to hold onto anything, his defiance supporting him, holding him up.

Rick Ferguson stared back. Then he disappeared behind a wave of bodies.

Maybe she hadn't seen him at all, Jess thought, peering through the crowded car, trying to relocate him, recalling her experience with the white Chrysler in front of her brownstone. Maybe she hadn't seen anything. Maybe it was her imagination having cruel fun with her. Or maybe not.

Definitely not, Jess told herself, tired of pretending things were other than the way she knew them to be. She pushed herself to her feet. Immediately, her seat was occupied by someone else. She worked her way to the other side of the car.

He was backed against the door, wearing the same blue jeans and brown leather jacket he'd worn to court that morning, his long, dirty blond hair pulled back into a pony tail, his eyes an opaque brown that contained his entire past: the broken home; the abusive father; the alcoholic mother; the soul-destroying poverty; the frequent trouble with the law; the succession of back-breaking factory jobs; the frequent dismissals; the failed stream of relationships with women; the anger, the bitterness; the contempt. And always the smile, tight-lipped, joyless, *wrong*.

'Excuse me,' Jess whispered to a frail-looking gentleman blocking her path, and the man immediately backed out of her way. Rick Ferguson smiled as Jess stepped directly into his line of vision.

'Well, well,' he said. 'As I live and breathe.'

'Are you following me?' Jess demanded, her voice loud enough to be heard by everyone in the crowded car.

He laughed. 'Me? Following you? Why would I be doing that?'

'You tell me.'

'I don't have to tell you anything,' he said, looking over her head toward the window. 'My lawyer said so.'

The train slowed in preparation of its next stop.

'What are you doing on this train?' Jess persisted.

No answer.

'What are you doing on this train?' she said again.

He scratched the side of his nose. 'Takin' a ride.' His voice was lazy, as if the act of speaking was almost too great an effort.

'Where to?' Jess demanded.

He said nothing.

'What stop are you getting off at?'

He smiled. 'I haven't decided yet.'

'I want to know where you're going.'

'Maybe I'm going home.'

112

'Your mother lives on Aberdeen. That's the other way.'

'What if I'm not going to my mother's?'

'Then you're in violation of your bail. I can have you arrested.'

'The conditions of my bond state that I have to live with my mother while I'm out on bail. They don't say anything about what El trains I can, or can't, take,' he reminded her.

'What have you done with Connie DeVuono?' she asked, hoping to catch him off guard.

Rick Ferguson looked up toward the ceiling, as if he might actually be considering a response. 'Objection!' he suddenly taunted. 'I don't think my lawyer would approve of that question.'

The train lurched to a stop. Jess moved to secure her feet against the sudden motion, to reach for something to grab onto, but there was nothing, and she lost her balance, falling forward, crashing against Rick Ferguson's chest. He grabbed her, his hands gripping the sides of her arms so hard Jess could almost feel bruises starting to form.

'Let go of me,' Jess shouted. 'Let go of me this instant!'

Ferguson lifted his hands into the air. 'Hey, I was only trying to help.'

'I don't need your help.'

'You looked like you were headed for a rather nasty fall,' he said, straightening his jacket and shrugging his shoulders. 'And we wouldn't want anything to happen to you. Not now. Not when things are just starting to get interesting.'

'What does that mean?'

He laughed. 'Well, what do you know?' he said, looking past her again toward the window. 'This is my stop.' He pushed his way toward the door. 'See you around,' he said, sneaking through the doors of the train just as they were closing.

As the train pulled away from the station, Jess watched Rick Ferguson waving goodbye from the open platform.

She was sitting on the bed, naked, her clothes laid out carefully beside her, unable to move. She wasn't sure how long she'd been sitting like this, how much time had passed since she'd

113

emerged from her shower, how many minutes had elapsed since her legs had gone numb and her breathing had become labored and heavy. 'This is ridiculous,' Jess told herself. 'You can't do this. Everyone's expecting you. You'll be late. You can't do this.'

She couldn't do anything.

She couldn't move.

'Come on, Jess,' she said. 'Don't be silly. You have to get moving. You have to get dressed.' She looked at the black silk dress that lay beside her. 'Come on. You already know what you want to wear. All you have to do is put it on.'

She couldn't. Her hands refused to leave her lap.

The panic had started as a prickly feeling in her side as she stepped out of the shower. At first she'd tried rubbing it away with her towel, but it had quickly spread to her stomach and chest, then to her hands and feet. She became light-headed, lost the feeling in her legs, was forced to sit down. Soon, it hurt to breathe. It hurt to think.

Beside the bed, the phone began to ring.

Jess stared at the phone, unable to reach for the receiver. 'Please help me,' she whispered, her body shivering from the cold. 'Please, somebody, help me.'

The phone rang once, twice, three times . . . stopped at ten. Jess closed her eyes, swayed, felt her fear rising in her throat, like a mouthful of saliva. 'Please help me,' she cried again. 'Please help me.' She stared into the mirror across from her bed. A small, frightened child stared back. 'Please help me, Mommy,' the little girl wailed. 'Promise me I'll be all right.'

'Oh, God,' Jess moaned, doubling over, her forehead touching her knees. 'What's happening to me? What's happening to me?'

The phone began ringing again. Once, twice, three times.

'I have to answer it,' she said. 'I have to answer it.'

Jess forced herself back into an upright position, hearing her body crack, like a corpse stiff with rigor mortis. Four rings, five. 'I have to answer it.' She willed her hand toward the phone, watched it as if it belonged to someone else as it brought the receiver to her ear.

'Hello, Jess? Jess, are you there?' the voice demanded, not waiting for a hello.

'Maureen?' Jess expelled the word from her mouth in a desperate whisper.

'Jess, where have you been? And what are you doing at home? You're supposed to be here!' Maureen sounded vaguely frantic.

'What time is it?'

'It's almost eight o'clock. We've been waiting since seven. Everybody's starving, not to mention worried half to death. I've been calling and calling. What's going on? You're never late.' The sentences emerged almost as one.

'I just got home,' Jess lied, still unable to feel her legs.

'Well, get right over here.'

'I can't,' Jess told her.

'What?!'

'Please, Maureen. I just can't. I'm not feeling very well.'

'Jess, you promised.'

'I know, but—'

'No buts.'

'I can't. I just can't.'

'Jess—'

'Please tell Dad I'm really sorry, but I'll have to meet his lady another time.'

'Don't do this, Jess.'

'Honestly, Maureen, I think I'm coming down with something.'

She could hear her sister crying.

'Please don't cry, Maureen. This wasn't anything I planned. I have my dress laid out and everything. I just can't make it.'

There was a second's silence. 'Suit yourself,' her sister said. The line went dead in her hand.

'Shit!' Jess screamed, slamming the receiver back into its carriage, her crippling lethargy suddenly gone. She jumped to her feet. What the hell was going on? What was she doing to herself? To her family?

Didn't she hate it when people were late? Didn't she make a point of always being on time? Wasn't she always the first one to arrive? Eight o'clock, for God's sake! She'd been sitting on her bed for ninety minutes. Sitting naked, her clothes laid out beside her, unable to put them on, unable to move.

Ninety minutes. An hour and a half. The worst attack yet. Certainly the longest. What would happen if these attacks were to follow her to work, spill over into the courtroom, paralyze her during an important cross-examination? What would she do?

She couldn't take that chance. She couldn't let that happen. She had to do something. She had to do something now.

Jess walked to her closet, pulled out her black slacks and fished through the pockets, locating the slip of paper on which her sister had scrawled the phone number of her friend, Stephanie Banack.

'Stephanie Banack,' Jess read out loud, wondering whether the therapist could be of any help. 'Call her and find out.'

Jess punched in the appropriate buttons, suddenly remembering the lateness of the hour. 'You'll just get her answering machine.' Jess was debating whether or not to leave a message when the phone was answered on its first ring.

'Stephanie Banack,' the voice said instead of hello.

Jess was nonplussed. 'I'm sorry. Is this a recording?'

Stephanie Banack laughed. 'No, it's the real thing, I'm afraid. How can I help you?'

'It's Jess Koster,' Jess said. 'Maureen's sister.'

There was a second's silence. Then, 'How are you, Jess? Is everything all right?'

'Maureen's fine, if that's what you're asking. It's me,' she continued quickly, afraid that if she slowed down, she'd stop altogether. 'I was wondering if you might have some time to see me . . . soon.'

'I'll make time,' the therapist said. 'How about noon tomorrow?'

Jess hesitated, stammered. She hadn't been expecting such immediate action.

'Come on, Jess. I don't give up my lunch hour for just anybody.'

Jess nodded into the phone. 'Twelve o'clock,' she agreed. 'I'll be there.'

Chapter Nine

Stephanie Banack's office was located on Michigan Avenue in the core of the downtown shopping district. 'She's obviously doing very well for herself,' Jess whispered into her coat collar as she waited for an elevator to take her to the fourteenth floor. She hadn't seen Stephanie Banack in years, hadn't felt the slightest desire to see her, had never understood her sister's abiding friendship with the woman. But then there was much about Maureen that Jess didn't understand. Especially these days. But that was another matter. Something that had nothing to do with why she was here.

Why *was* she here?

Jess looked around the mirror-lined, black and white marble lobby, trying to come up with a suitable response. Immediately, she concluded there was none. She had no good reason to be here. She was wasting valuable time and energy on something that required neither. She checked her watch, noted that it was five minutes to twelve, that she still had time to call upstairs and cancel her appointment without seriously inconveniencing her sister's friend. The woman had said she was giving up her lunch hour to accommodate her. Now she wouldn't have to. She wouldn't be inconveniencing her at all: she'd be doing her a favour.

Jess was searching the mirrored walls for a phone when the elevator closest to her opened. It stood there empty and waiting. Well, it seemed to be saying, what are you going to do? There's no phone and I won't wait for ever. Shit or get off the pot, it hummed impatiently. What are you going to do?

'I guess I'm coming with you,' Jess answered, glad there was no one in the lobby to overhear her. 'I'm talking to elevators, and I have to ask what I'm doing here?' She stepped inside, the

117

elevator doors closing behind her.

The interior of the elevator was lined on three sides with the same mirrors as the lobby, and Jess discovered that, no matter how she turned her head, it was almost impossible to avoid her own reflection. Was this a deliberate ploy on the part of the therapists who occupied much of the building? Were they subtly forcing their reluctant patients to confront themselves? 'Give me a break,' Jess said out loud, refusing to be intimidated by her own image, staring past her worry-filled eyes, and securing her hair behind her ears.

The elevator doors opened on the fourteenth floor. Jess stayed pressed against the rear wall, feeling the elevator vibrate against her back, nudging her gently forward. First you won't come in; now you won't leave, it seemed to say. Jess defiantly pushed herself out into the hall, biting down hard on her tongue to keep from saying goodbye. 'You have now crossed the boundary from relative neurotic to total fruitcake,' she said, walking across the soft blue and grey carpeting to the appropriate door at the far end of the corridor. *Stephanie Banack*, the embossed gold lettering proclaimed across the dark oak, followed by an impressive number of degrees.

Too impressive, Jess thought, recalling the awkward teenager who'd often seemed glued to her sister's side, unable to imagine her as a woman capable of amassing so many initials after her name: BA; MSW; PhD. Obviously, the woman suffers from low self-esteem, Jess decided. All those expensive degrees to bolster her confidence, when a nose job was probably all she really needed.

Jess was reaching for the door knob when the door opened, and a young woman with a blond ponytail and deep purple eye shadow emerged. She smiled, the kind of loopy grin that went in all directions at once. 'Are you Jess Koster?' she asked.

Jess took a step back, silently debating whether or not to take ownership of her identity. She nodded without speaking.

'I'm Dr Banack's receptionist. Dr Banack is expecting you. You can go right in.'

118

She held the door open for Jess to enter, and Jess gamely stepped inside the office, holding her breath. All she had to do was wait a few seconds until she was sure the receptionist had gone, then she could leave. She'd find a pay phone somewhere on the street, call Stephanie Banack, BA, MSW, PhD, and tell her there was no need for a consultation after all. She didn't need anyone to tell her she was nuts; she'd figured it out all by herself. No need to waste time. No need to go hungry.

The reception area was pleasant enough, Jess observed, listening for the sound of an elevator door opening and closing down the hall. The walls and carpet were a soft shade of grey, the two tub chairs against one wall a pleasing mint green and grey stripe. There was a glass coffee table stacked with the latest in news and fashion magazines. The receptionist's desk was a light oak; the computer resting on it top of the line. Several posters by Calder and Miro hung on the walls, as well as a mirror next to a small closet. A large benjamin plant filled one corner. All in all, very warm and inviting. Even reassuring. You make a very good first impression, dear, she acknowledged silently, hearing the woman juror from the Erica Barnowski case whisper in her ear.

'I have to get out of here,' Jess told herself.

'Jess, is that you?' The voice coming from the inner office was clear, friendly, in command.

Jess said nothing, her eyes glued to the half-open door.

'Jess?'

Jess heard movement, felt Stephanie Banack's presence in the doorway even before she appeared.

'Jess?' Stephanie Banack asked tentatively, forcing Jess's eyes to her own.

'My God, you're beautiful,' Jess exclaimed, the words out of her mouth before she had a chance to consider them.

Stephanie laughed, a rich sound full of solid mental health, Jess thought, reaching forward to shake her outstretched hand.

'I guess you haven't seen me since I had my nose done.'

'You had your nose done?' Jess asked, striving for sincerity.

'And my hair lightened. Here, let me have your coat.'

119

Jess allowed Stephanie to help her off with her coat and hang it in the closet. She felt suddenly naked, despite the heavy wool of her black skirt and sweater.

The therapist motioned toward the inner office with a sweep of her hand. 'Let's go inside.'

The soft greys and greens of the reception area continued into the inner office, as did the posters and plants. A large oak desk, its top covered with numerous framed photographs of three grinning boys, sat against one wall, a paisley swivel chair in front of it. Light from the window cast an almost eerie glow on the series of framed degrees that hung on the opposite wall. But the room was dominated by the large grey leather recliner that sat at its center.

'It's been a long time since I've seen you,' Stephanie said. 'How've you been?'

'Fine.'

'Still with the State's Attorney's Office?'

'Yes.'

'You're happy there?'

'Very.'

'You're not on the witness stand, Jess. You don't have to confine your answers to one word.' Stephanie patted the high back of the grey leather chair as she walked toward her desk and sat down, immediately swivelling her chair in Jess's direction. 'Why don't you have a seat?'

Jess stubbornly remained standing, noting the proud thrust of Stephanie's shoulders, her effortlessly perfect posture, the warmth and directness of her smile. Surely Jess was in the wrong office. Or maybe she was in the right office but with the wrong therapist. The Stephanie Banack Jess had been expecting to see was stoop-shouldered and grim. She wore ill-fitting hand-me-downs, not sleek Armani pantsuits and stylish Maud Frizon shoes. This woman must be a *different* Stephanie Banack. It was not altogether outside the realm of possibility that there were two therapists named Stephanie Banack practising in downtown Chicago. Maybe they were *both* good friends of her sister. Or maybe this woman was an imposter, a patient who had murdered

120

the real Stephanie Banack and assumed her identity. Maybe Jess should get the hell out of here as quickly as possible.

Or maybe she should just check herself into the nearest psychiatric hospital. She was obviously certifiable, a definite wacko. Where were these crazy ideas coming from? 'This was probably a mistake,' she heard herself say, disassociating herself from even the sound of her own voice.

'What was?'

'My coming here.'

'What makes you say that?'

Jess shook her head, said nothing.

'Jess, you're already here. Why don't you sit down? You don't have to tell me anything you don't want to.'

Jess nodded, didn't move.

'When you phoned last night,' the therapist ventured, 'you sounded very distraught.'

'I was overreacting.'

'To what?'

Jess shrugged. 'I'm not sure.'

'You never struck me as the type who overreacts.'

'Maybe I never used to.'

'Maybe you aren't now.'

Jess took a few tentative steps forward, touched the soft leather of the high-backed reclining chair. 'Have you spoken to Maureen?'

'I usually speak to her every week or so.'

Jess hesitated. 'I guess what I really meant to ask was, has she spoken to you?'

The therapist cocked her head. Jess was reminded immediately of a friendly cocker spaniel. 'I'm not sure I understand the question.'

'About me,' Jess stated. 'Has she said anything to you about me?'

'She mentioned some weeks back that you might call,' Stephanie said simply. 'That you were having some problems.'

'Did she say what they were?'

'I don't think she knows.'

121

Jess came round to the front of the large recliner, slowly lowering herself into it, pushing against the back of the chair, feeling it surround her, like a cupped hand. The chair moved with her, a foot stool miraculously rising as the chair reclined. Jess lifted her feet, rested them on the much needed support. 'This chair's great.'

Stephanie nodded.

'So, tell me, what do you think of my sister these days?' Jess asked, deciding that since she was already sitting down, she might as well be friendly, make small talk. Play nice, as her mother used to say.

'I think she's wonderful. Motherhood suits her.'

'You think so?'

'You don't?'

'I think it's a bit of a waste.' Jess looked toward the window. 'Not that I think looking after children is a waste,' she clarified. 'Just that someone with Maureen's ability and brains, not to mention the job she gave up, well, it just seems like she should be doing something more with her life than diapering babies and catering to her husband's every whim.'

Stephanie leaned forward. 'You think that Maureen caters to Barry's every whim?'

'You don't?'

Stephanie smiled. 'That's my line.'

'I mean, it's not like my parents put her through all those years of school — and you know how much Harvard costs, even on a partial scholarship — only to see her throw it all away.'

'You think your father is disappointed?'

'I don't know.' Jess looked toward the floor. 'Probably not. He's thrilled about his grandchildren. Besides, even if he were disappointed, he'd never say anything.'

'What about your mother?'

Jess felt her back stiffen. 'What do you mean?'

'Well, you implied that your parents wouldn't be happy with the choices Maureen has made recently.'

'What I said was that I didn't think they'd put her through all

122

those years of school so that she could stay home and make babies.'

'How *do* you think your mother would feel?'

Jess turned her head to one side, pressed her chin toward her shoulder. 'She'd be furious.'

'What makes you say that?'

Jess felt her feet twitching impatiently on the footstool. 'Come on, Stephanie, you were always over at our house. You knew my mother. You knew how important it was to her that her girls get a good education, that they make something of their lives, that they learn to stand on their own two feet.'

'A woman ahead of her time. I remember.'

'Well then, you should know how she'd feel about what Maureen is doing.'

'How would she feel?'

Jess searched the air for the proper adjectives. 'Angry. Confused. Betrayed.'

'Is that how you feel?'

'I'm telling you how I think my mother would feel.'

'You don't think your mother wanted Maureen to have a family?'

'That's not what I'm saying.'

'What are you saying?'

Jess looked up at the ceiling, toward the window, at the series of framed degrees on the far wall, finally at the woman across from her. 'Look, you must remember how upset my mother was when I told her I was going to marry Don.'

'The circumstances were very different, Jess.'

'How? How were they different?'

'Well, for one thing, you were very young. Don was so much older than you. He was a practising attorney. You were just finishing your first year law school. I don't think it was marriage, per se, that your mother was objecting to, so much as the timing.'

Jess began chipping away at the clear polish of her fingernails. She said nothing.

'But Maureen had already finished her education,' Stephanie

123

continued. 'She was well established when she met and married Barry. I don't think your mother would have had any objections to her taking some time off to raise a family.'

'I'm not saying my mother wouldn't have wanted Maureen to marry and have children,' Jess stated, anger propelling her words. 'Why wouldn't she? My mother loved having children. She loved being married. She'd dedicated her life to being the best wife and mother anybody could hope for. But . . .'

'But what?'

'But she wanted more for her daughters,' Jess said. 'Is that so awful? Is there something wrong with that?'

'It depends on what the daughter wants for herself.'

Jess squeezed her upper lip between the fingers of her right hand, waiting till her heart stopped racing before trying to speak. 'Look, I didn't come here to talk about Maureen or my mother.'

'Why *did* you come?'

'I really don't know.'

There was a moment's silence. For the first time, Jess became aware of the clock on Stephanie's desk. She watched the minute hand jerk to its next stop. Another minute lost. Time passing, she thought, thinking of all the things she should be doing. She had an appointment with the Medical Examiner's Office at one-thirty, an interview with an eyewitness to the crossbow killing at three, a meeting with several police officers at four. She could have used this time to prepare. What was she doing wasting a precious hour here, accomplishing nothing?

'What were you doing when you called last night?' Stephanie asked.

'What do you mean, what was I doing?'

Stephanie looked confused. 'It's a pretty straightforward question, Jess. What were you doing immediately before you phoned me last night?'

'Nothing.'

'Nothing? And out of the blue you just decided, gee, I haven't seen Stephanie Banack in years. I think I'll give her a call?'

'Something like that.'

Another silence. 'Jess, I can't help you if you won't even give me a chance.'

Jess wanted to speak, couldn't.

'Why did you ask your sister for my number?'

'I didn't.'

'So she's the one who suggested that you call?'

Jess shrugged.

'Why is that?'

'You'll have to ask her.'

'Look, maybe the fact that I'm your sister's friend is what's getting in the way here. You must know that anything you say to me will be held in the strictest confidence. But maybe you'd prefer that I recommend someone else.'

'No,' Jess said quickly. 'It's not you. It's me.'

'Tell me about you,' Stephanie said gently.

'I've been having these anxiety attacks.'

'What do you mean by anxiety attacks?'

'Feelings of panic.'

'What happens when you get these feelings?'

Jess stared into her lap, saw the chips of her nail polish resting on the surface of her black skirt like sparkling sequins. 'Shortness of breath. Numbness. My legs won't move. They get tingly, weak. My head feels light, then heavy. My heart starts racing. My chest feels like someone's got me in a hammerlock. Paralysis. I literally can't move. I feel like I'm going to throw up.'

'How long have you been having these attacks?'

'They started again a few weeks ago.'

'Again?'

'What?'

Stephanie crossed, then uncrossed her legs. 'You said they started *again* a few weeks ago.'

'Did I?'

'Yes.'

'I guess that's what they call a Freudian slip.' Jess laughed bitterly. Was her subconscious so ready to reveal all her secrets?

'So these attacks aren't something new.' The comment was

more statement than question.

'No.' Jess paused, then pressed on. 'I had them after my mother disappeared. Almost every day for at least a year, then frequently for several years after that.'

'Then they stopped?'

'I hadn't had any attacks in about four years.'

'And now they've started again.'

Jess nodded. 'They've started happening with increasing frequency. Lasting longer. Getting worse.'

'And this started again, you said, a few weeks ago?'

'Yes.'

'What do you think triggered this latest round?'

'I'm not sure.'

'Is there some sort of pattern to the attacks?'

'What do you mean by pattern?'

Stephanie paused, rubbed her fingers against the side of her perfectly sculpted nose. 'Do they happen at any particular time of the day or night? Do they happen at work? When you're alone? In any particular place? Around specific people?'

Jess's mind raced through all the questions in turn. The attacks happened at all hours of the day or night. They happened at work, at her apartment, when she was alone, when she was walking along a busy street, when she was at the movies, when she was stepping out of the shower. 'There's no pattern,' she said hopelessly.

'Were you having an attack before you called last night?'

Jess nodded.

'What were you doing?'

Jess told her about getting ready to go out. 'I knew what I was going to wear,' Jess heard herself whisper. 'I had it all laid out and everything.'

'You were supposed to meet the new lady in your father's life?'

'Yes,' Jess admitted.

'I imagine that would be a fairly anxiety-provoking situation.'

'Well, it's not something I was exactly looking forward to,

126

which, I guess makes me a pretty horrible person.'

'Why do you say that?'

'Because I'm supposed to want my father to be happy.'

'And you don't?'

'I do!' Jess felt tears forming in her eyes. She struggled to contain them. 'That's what I don't understand. I *do* want him to be happy. Of course, I want him to be happy. What makes him happy should make me happy.'

'Why?'

'What?'

'Since when does what makes another person happy have to make us happy too? You're demanding a great deal of yourself, Jess. Maybe too much.'

'Maureen doesn't seem to be having any trouble with the situation. '

'Maureen isn't you.'

Jess sifted quickly through all that had been said. 'But it can't just be my father. The attacks started before I even knew that he was involved with anyone.'

'When exactly did they start?'

Jess thought back to the night she woke up to find her body shaking and her bed sheets soaking wet. 'I was in bed, asleep. I had a nightmare. It woke me up.'

'Do you remember what the nightmare was about?'

'My mother,' Jess said. 'I kept trying to reach her, but I couldn't.'

'Had you been thinking about your mother before you went to sleep?'

'I don't remember,' Jess lied. The whole day had been filled with thoughts of her mother. In fact, her first attack hadn't followed her nightmare at all. It had happened earlier in the day, in the courtroom during the Erica Barnowski rape trial, when she thought she recognized her mother behind a juror's face.

She didn't want to talk anymore about her mother.

'Look, I think I know why this is happening,' Jess announced. 'I think it has to do with a man I'm prosecuting.' She saw Rick

127

Ferguson's face in the reflection of the glass protecting Stephanie Banack's framed degrees. 'He's made some threats.'

'What kind of threats?'

People who annoy me have a way of disappearing...

Disappearing.

Like her mother.

I don't need this, Jess. I don't need this from you!

She didn't want to think about her mother.

'Look, I really don't think it's as important to know why these attacks are happening so much as what I can do to stop them.'

'I can give you some simple relaxation exercises to work on, some techniques that may take the edge off the attacks,' Stephanie told her, 'but I think that in order to really get rid of them, you have to deal with the underlying problems that are causing these attacks.'

'You're talking long-term therapy?'

'I'm talking some therapy, yes.'

'I don't need therapy. I just need to put this guy behind bars.'

'Why do I think it's not as simple as that?'

'Because that's how you've been trained to think. It's your job.' Jess checked her watch, though she already knew the time. 'And speaking of jobs, I have to get back to mine.' She pushed herself out of the comfortable recliner and walked briskly to the door of the reception room, as if responding to a silent fire drill.

'Jess, wait.'

Jess continued into the reception area without pausing, retrieving her coat from the closet and throwing it over her shoulders as she headed for the door to the hallway. 'It's been nice seeing you again, Stephanie. Take care of yourself.' She marched into the corridor and proceeded with purposeful strides toward the elevators.

'I'm here any time, Jess,' Stephanie called after her. 'All you have to do is call.'

Don't hold your breath, Jess wanted to reply, but didn't. She didn't have to. Her silence said it all.

Chapter Ten

'Can I help you?'

'I'm just looking, thank you.'

What was she doing now? Jess wondered, examining a pair of green suede Bruno Magli flats. What had possessed her to come into this store? The last thing she needed was another pair of shoes.

She checked her watch. Almost twelve-thirty. She had an appointment with the Chief Medical Examiner in one hour. The medical examiner's office was over on Harrison Street, a drive of at least twenty minutes, and she still didn't have her car back from the shop. They'd called first thing this morning; something about another minor, though very necessary, repair. She'd have to take a taxi.

'If you give me some idea of the type of shoe you have in mind,' the salesman persisted.

'I really don't have anything in mind,' Jess said curtly. The salesman, a short, middle-aged man with an ill-fitting brown toupee, bowed with exaggerated politeness and moved quickly toward a woman who was just coming in the door.

Jess let her eyes travel down a long table covered with an astonishing array of casual shoes in a variety of colorful suedes and leathers. She lifted a pair of mustard-yellow loafers into her palms and turned them over with her fingers. Nothing like a new pair of shoes to make the problems of the world disappear, she thought, stroking the soft suede. That was all the therapy she really needed. Certainly cheaper, she decided, staring at the price ticket stuck to the bottom of the heel. Ninety-nine dollars as opposed to . . .

As opposed to what?

She'd never even discussed price with Stephanie Banack,

129

never thought to inquire as to her hourly rate, walked out on the woman without so much as asking what she owed her. Not only did the woman not get lunch, she didn't get paid either. Two indignities for the price of one.

Jess returned the shoe to the table, shaking her head in dismay. It was one thing to be rude; it was something else to be presumptuous. She'd treated her sister's friend very badly. She'd have to apologize, maybe send the woman flowers and a brief thank you note. And say what? Thanks for the memories? Thanks for nothing? Thanks but no thanks?

'I think that in order to really get rid of your anxiety attacks,' she heard Stephanie Banack repeat, *'you have to deal with the underlying problems that are causing them.'*

There are no underlying problems, Jess insisted silently, approaching the next table, covered with more formal footwear, running her fingers across the toes of a series of black patent high-heeled shoes.

There was only one problem, and she knew exactly what that problem was.

Rick Ferguson.

Not that he was the first felon who had threatened her. Hate, abuse, intimidation – they were all part of her job description. For the last two years, she had received a Christmas card from a man she had successfully prosecuted and put away for ten years. He'd threatened to come after her as soon as he got out. The Christmas cards, innocuous as they appeared on the surface, were his not-so-subtle way of reminding her he hadn't forgotten.

In truth, such threats were rarely carried out. They were uttered; they were received; they were eventually forgotten. By both sides.

Rick Ferguson was different.

The man of her dreams, she thought ironically, recalling the nightmare that began with her frantically trying to find her mother and ended with her finding Death. Somehow Rick Ferguson had been able to reach into her most secret self, to accidentally trigger long-dormant feelings of guilt and anxiety.

Anxiety, yes, Jess acknowledged, lifting a shiny black shoe

into her hand, squeezing its toe so hard she felt the leather crack. Not guilt. What did she possibly have to feel guilty about? 'Don't be silly,' she muttered under her breath, again recalling Stephanie Banack's words. 'There *are* no underlying problems.' She began banging the sharp end of the high heel into the palm of her hand.

'Hey, be careful,' a voice called from somewhere beside her. A hand reached out and stopped the movement of her own. 'It's a shoe, not a hammer.'

Jess stared first into her bruised palm, then at the crumpled shoe in her other hand, and finally up at the man with light brown hair and worried brown eyes whose hand rested lightly on her arm. The tag pinned to his dark blue sports jacket identified him as Adam Stohn. White male, early to middle thirties, six feet tall, approximately one hundred and eighty pounds, she summed up silently, as if reading from a police report. 'I'm so sorry,' she began. 'Of course I'll pay for them.'

'I'm not worried about the shoe,' he said, gently lifting it from her hand and returning it to the table.

Jess watched it wobble, then fall over on its side, as if it had been shot. 'But I've ruined it.'

'Nothing a quick polish and a good shoe tree won't fix. What about your hand?'

Jess felt it throbbing, saw the round purple splotch that sat, like a discolored quarter, in the center of her palm. 'It'll be okay.'

'Looks like you might have broken a blood vessel.'

'I'll be fine. Really,' she assured him, understanding that he was genuinely concerned. Was the store liable?

'Can I get you a drink of water?'

Jess shook her head.

'How about a candy?' He pulled a red and white striped mint from his pocket.

Jess smiled. 'No, thank you.'

'How about a joke?'

'Do I look that desperate?' She sensed his reluctance to leave her to her own devices.

'You look like someone who could use a good joke.'

131

She nodded. 'You're right. Go ahead.'

'Clean or mildly risqué?'

Jess laughed. 'What the hell. Let's go for broke.'

'Mildly risqué, it is.' He paused. 'A man and woman are making love when they hear someone coming up the stairs and the woman cries, "My God, it's my husband!" Her lover immediately jumps out of the window into a clump of bushes. So, here's this guy, he's outside hiding in this sorry clump of bushes, he's naked, and he doesn't know what to do, and naturally, it starts raining. Suddenly, a bunch of joggers go jogging by, and the guy sees his chance, and leaps into the middle of the joggers, running along with them. After a few seconds, the jogger beside him looks over and says, "Excuse me, but do you mind if I ask you a question?" And the guy says, "Go ahead." And the jogger says, "Do you always jog naked?" And the guy says, "Always." And the jogger asks, "Do you always wear a condom when you jog?" And the guy says, "Only when it's raining." '

Jess found herself laughing out loud.

'That's better. Now, can I sell you a pair of shoes?'

Jess laughed even harder.

'That wasn't supposed to be funny. The funny part's over.'

'I'm sorry. Are you as good at selling shoes as you are at telling jokes?'

'Try me.'

Jess checked her watch. She still had a little time. Surely one pair of shoes wouldn't hurt. She probably owed the store that much, having murdered that poor black pump. Besides, she found herself curiously reluctant to leave. It had been a long time since a man had made her laugh out loud. She liked the sound. She liked the feeling. 'Actually, I could use a new pair of winter boots,' she said, remembering, relieved at finding a legitimate reason to stay.

'Right this way.' Adam Stohn directed her toward a display of leather and vinyl boots. 'Have a seat.'

Jess lowered herself into a small rust-colored chair, for the first time taking note of her surroundings. The store was very modern, all glass and chrome. Shoes were everywhere, on glass tables, on mirrored shelves, along the brown and gold carpeted floor, reflected in the high mirrored ceiling. She realized she'd shopped here several times before, though she had no memory of Adam Stohn.

'Are you new here?' she asked.

'I started this summer.'

'You like it?'

'Shoes are my life,' he said, his voice a sly smile. 'Now, what sort of boot can I show you?'

'I'm not sure. I hate to spend a lot of money on a leather boot that's only going to get ruined by the snow and salt.'

'So don't buy leather.'

'But I like some style. And I like my feet to be warm.'

'The lady wants style *and* warmth. I believe I have just what you need.'

'Is that so?'

'Have I ever lied to you?'

'Probably.'

He smiled. 'I see we have a cynic in our midst. Well then, allow me.' He reached over to a small display of sleek and shiny black boots. 'These are vinyl, fleece-lined, waterproof, absolutely no-maintenance winter boots. They are stylish; they are warm; they are guaranteed to withstand even the worst Chicago winter.' He handed Jess the boot.

'And they're very expensive,' Jess exclaimed, surprised at the two hundred dollar price tag. 'I can buy real leather for that price.'

'But you don't want real leather. You have to spray it; you have to take care of it. And real leather leaks and marks and does all the things you want to avoid. This boot,' he said, tapping its shiny side, 'you wear and forget about. It's indestructible.'

'You *are* as good at selling shoes as you are at telling jokes,' Jess said.

'Are you saying you'd like to try them on?'

'Size eight and a half,' Jess said.

'Be right back.'

Jess watched Adam Stohn disappear through a door at the back of the store. She liked the casual determination of his gait, the straightness of his shoulders. Confidence without arrogance, she thought, her eyes drifting back along the mirrored walls.

Was there no escape from one's own reflection? Were people really so interested in seeing themselves every second of the day? Jess caught the disappointed glare of the middle-aged salesman with the ill-fitting toupee in the glass. She closed her eyes. I know, she thought, responding to his silent admonishment, I'm shallow and easily swayed. A pretty face and a good joke get me every time.

'You're not going to believe this,' Adam Stohn said upon his return, his arms filled with two wide boxes, 'but I'm out of size eight and a half. I have a size eight and a size nine.'

She tried them. Predictably, the eight was too small, the nine too big.

'You're sure you have no eight and a halfs?'

'I looked everywhere.'

Jess shrugged, checked her watch, stood up. She couldn't afford to waste any more time.

'I can call one of our other stores,' Adam Stohn offered.

'All right,' Jess answered quickly. What was she doing?

He walked to the counter at the front of the store, picked up the black telephone, punched in some buttons, and spoke into the receiver, shaking his head, then repeating the process two more times. 'Can you believe it?' he asked upon his return. 'I called three stores. No one has size eight and a half. But,' he continued, his finger poking the air for emphasis, 'one store has several on order and will call me as soon as they come in. Would you like me to call you?'

'I beg your pardon?' Was he asking her out?

'When the boots come in, would you like me to call you?'

'Oh, oh, sure. Yes, please. That would be great.' Jess realized she was talking to cover her embarrassment. What had she been thinking of? Why had she thought he might be asking her

134

out? Because he'd offered her a candy and told her a joke about condoms? Because the idea appealed to her? Just because she thought he was attractive and charming, did that necessarily mean the reverse was true?

Don't be an idiot, Jess, she scolded herself, following him to the counter at the front of the store. The man was a shoe salesman, for God's sake. Hardly the world's prize catch.

Don't be such a snob, a little voice admonished. At least he's not a lawyer.

'Name?' he asked, reaching for a nearby pad and pencil.

'Jess Koster.'

'Phone number where you can be reached during the day?'

Jess gave him her number at work. 'Maybe I better give you my home number too,' she said, not believing the words coming out of her mouth.

'Sure.' He copied the numbers down as she recited them. 'My name is Adam Stohn.' He indicated the tag on his jacket, pronouncing the Stohn as Stone. 'It shouldn't be more than a week.'

'That's great. Hopefully, it won't snow before then.'

'It wouldn't dare.'

Jess smiled and waited for him to say more, but he didn't. Instead, he looked just past her to where a woman stood admiring a pair of tomato-red Charles Jourdan pumps. 'Thanks again,' she said on her way out, but he was already moving toward the other woman, and all Jess got was a perfunctory wave.

'I can't believe I did that,' Jess muttered as she slid into the back seat of a yellow taxi. Could she have been any more obvious? Why didn't she just wear a large sign round her neck that stated *Lonely and Deeply Disturbed*?

The cab reeked of cigarette smoke, although there was a large sign prominently displayed across the back of the front seat thanking people for not smoking. She gave the taxi driver the address of the Chief Medical Examiner on Harrison Street, and sank back into the scuffed and torn black vinyl seat. Probably what my new boots will look like by the end of the season, Jess thought, running her hand across the rough surface.

What had possessed her? That was twice in the last month she'd almost allowed a handsome stranger to pick her up. Had she learned absolutely nothing from the Erica Barnowski case? And this time the man in question hadn't even come on to her. He'd offered her a glass of water, a candy, and some amusing repartee, all in pursuit of a hoped-for commission. He'd been trying to get into her purse, not her pants, when he told the joke about the naked jogger. And she'd let him in without even a struggle, committing herself to the most expensive pair of rubber boots ever made. 'Not even leather,' she chastized herself, picking at a tear that sliced through the seat's cheap upholstery like a large, gaping wound.

'Sorry?' the cab driver said. 'You say something?'

'Nothing. Sorry,' Jess apologized in return, continuing silently. Just talking to myself again. Something I seem to be doing with alarming frequency these days.

Two hundred dollars for a pair of vinyl boots. Was she crazy?

Well, yes, actually, she thought. That fact had been pretty much established.

'Nice day,' Jess commented, struggling for normalcy.

'Sorry?'

'I said it's nice to see the sun again.'

The cab driver shrugged, said nothing. Jess rode the rest of the way to the Medical Examiner's Office in silence, punctuated only by the instructions and static coming over the driver's two-way radio.

The office of the Chief Medical Examiner was a nondescript three-story building on a block full of such structures. Jess paid the cab driver, exited the taxi, and walked briskly toward the entrance, gathering her coat tightly round her, preparing her body for the approaching chill.

Anderson, Michael, age 45, died suddenly as the result of a car accident, Jess recited in her mind, recalling the morning obituaries as she strode through the front lobby toward the glassed-in receptionist's corner. *Clemmons, Irene, died peacefully in her sleep in her 102nd year, remembered fondly by her fellow residents at the Whispering Pines Lodge. Lawson, David, age 33. He's gone on to other things. Mourned by his mother, his father, his sisters and his dog. In lieu of donations to your favorite charities, lots and lots of flowers would be gratefully appreciated.*

Why was it that some people barely made it past the first bloom of youth, when others hung on into their second century? Where was the fairness? she wondered, surprising herself. She thought she had given up on fairness a long time ago.

'I'm here to see Hilary Waugh,' she told the gum-chewing young woman behind the receptionist's window.

The woman, whose straight brown hair looked as if it could use a good washing, cracked her gum, and dialed the appropriate extension. 'She says you're early,' the receptionist informed Jess a few seconds later, her voice a rebuke. 'She'll be with you in a few minutes. If you want to have a seat . . .'

'Thank you.' Jess backed away from the small reception area toward a faded brown corduroy sofa that sat against one beige wall, but she didn't sit down. She could never sit down anywhere in this building. In fact, she could barely stand still. She hugged her arms round her, rubbed them in a vain effort to generate warmth.

Mateus, Jose, taken suddenly in his fifty-fourth year, survived by his mother, Alma, and his wife Rosa, and their two children, Paolo and Gino, Jess's memory recited. *Neilsen, Thomas, a retired civil servant, of a heart attack in his 77th year. Mr Neilsen is survived by his wife, Linda, his sons Peter and Henry, his daughters-in-law Rita and Susan, his grandchildren Lisa, Karen, Jonathan, Stephen, and Jeffrey. The family will be receiving visitors at J. Humphrey's Funeral Home all this week.*

Not like those unfortunates resting in Boot Hill, Jess thought, unwillingly conjuring up the image of that section of the morgue where rows of heavy grey metal drawers stored unidentified, unclaimed bodies. The only people who ever came to visit these lost souls were people like herself, people whose professional curiosity demanded their presence, if not their respect.

Doe, John, black male, suspected drug dealer, died of a gunshot wound to the head in his 22nd year; Doe, Jane, white female, suspected prostitute, suddenly in her 18th year, strangled and left for dead near the shore of the Chicago River; Doe, John, white male and probable pimp, dead of three stab wounds to the chest, age 19; Doe, Jane, black female, longtime crack addict, in her 28th year, beaten to death after being sexually assaulted. Doe, John—

'Jess?'

Jess's head snapped to the sound of her name.

'I'm sorry,' Hilary Waugh was saying, moving toward her. 'I didn't mean to startle you.'

Jess shook the outstretched hand. She never failed to be surprised by how fit and fresh the Chief Medical Examiner for Cook County always appeared, despite the unpleasantness and long hours of her job. Hilary Waugh had to be close to fifty, yet she had the skin of a woman half her age, and her posture, accentuated by her white lab coat, was impeccable. She wore her dark shoulder-length hair pulled back into a French braid, and her hazel eyes were framed by large glasses.

'Thank you for seeing me,' Jess said, following Hilary through the door that led from the lobby to the inner offices.

'Always a pleasure. What can I do for you?'

The long corridor was sterile and white and smelled faintly of formaldehyde, although Jess suspected any odors she was picking up were part of her overactive imagination. The morgue was in the basement, safely out of olfactory range.

'Have a seat,' Hilary said, stepping inside the tiny white cubby-hole that served as her office and motioning toward the empty chair across from her desk.

'If you don't mind, I'll stand.' Jess looked around the tiny cubicle that was the office of the Chief Medical Examiner of Cook County. It was sparsely furnished with an old metal desk and two chairs, one on either side of the desk, the deep wine of the seat covers fraying at the seams. File cabinets lined the walls, alongside precarious stacks of papers. A tall green plant flourished despite the fact that it was crammed into a corner and all but hidden by books. There was no window, fluorescent lighting taking the place of the sun. 'You obviously have a very green thumb,' Jess remarked.

'Oh, it's not real,' Hilary said, laughing. 'It's silk. Much less trouble that way. Much more pleasant. I see enough dead things as it is. Which is, I'm sure, the point of your visit.'

Jess cleared her throat. 'I'm looking for a woman, mid-forties, Italian-American, about five feet six inches tall, 135 pounds, maybe less. Actually, here,' Jess reached inside her purse, 'this is her picture.' She held out an old photo of Connie DeVuono standing with her arms proudly around her son, Steffan, then age 6. 'The picture's a few years old. She's lost some weight since then. Her hair's a bit shorter.'

The Chief Medical Examiner took the picture, spent several seconds looking at it. 'A very attractive woman. Who is she?'

'Her name is Connie DeVuono. She's been missing over two weeks.'

'This is the woman you called me about last week?' Hilary Waugh asked.

Jess nodded sheepishly. 'I'm sorry to be such a pest. It's just that I keep thinking of her little boy.'

'Looks just like his mother,' the Medical Examiner remarked as Jess reclaimed the photograph, carefully returning it to her purse.

'Yes. And it's very hard on him . . . not knowing exactly what happened to her.' Jess swallowed the catch in her throat.

'I'm sure it is. And I wish I could help.'

'No bodies matching Connie DeVuono's description have turned up?'

'At the moment we have three unidentified white females in Boot Hill. Two are teenagers, probably runaways. One died of a drug overdose; the other was raped and strangled.'

'And the third?'

'Just came in this morning. We haven't run any tests yet. But the state of decomposition indicates she's only been dead a few days.'

'It's possible,' Jess stated quickly, although she found it highly unlikely. Rick Ferguson would hardly have been foolhardy enough to kidnap Connie, then wait several weeks before killing her. 'About how old is she? *Was* she?' Jess corrected, hearing the word *decomposition* ricochet inside her brain.

'Impossible to say at the moment. She was beaten beyond all recognition.'

Jess felt her stomach turn over. She fought to stay steady. 'But you don't think it's Connie deVuono.'

'The woman on the table downstairs has blond hair and is approximately five feet nine inches tall. I'd say that eliminates her as the woman you're looking for. Are you sure you wouldn't like to sit down?'

'No, I really should get going,' Jess said, taking several tentative steps to the office door. Hilary pushed back her chair, rose to her feet. 'No, you don't have to get up,' Jess told her, not sure whether she was relieved or disappointed that the unidentified woman wasn't Connie DeVuono. 'Will you call me if anything . . .' She stopped, unable to complete the sentence.

'I'll call you if anyone even remotely resembling Connie DeVuono turns up.'

Jess stepped into the hall, hesitated, then turned back to Hilary. 'I'm going to get hold of Connie's dental records, have them sent over here,' she said, thinking of the woman lying downstairs. *Beaten beyond all recognition.* 'Just so you'll have them on hand if . . .' She stopped, cleared her throat, started again. 'It might speed things up a bit.'

'That would be very helpful,' Hilary agreed. 'Assuming we find her body.'

Assuming we find her body. The words followed Jess down the corridor and into the lobby. *Assuming we find her body.* She pushed open the door to the outside, and ran down the steps to the street. She threw her head back and inhaled a deep breath of fresh air, feeling the cold sun warm on her face.

Assuming we find her body, she thought.

Chapter Eleven

'Four hundred and eleven dollars?!' Jess yelled. 'Are you crazy?'

The young black man behind the high white counter remained calm, his face impassive. He was obviously used to such outbursts. 'The bill is carefully itemized. If you'd care to take another look—'

'I've looked. I still don't understand what could possibly have cost over four hundred dollars!' Jess realized that her voice was becoming dangerously shrill, that the other patrons of the auto body shop where she had taken her car to be serviced almost three weeks ago were staring at her.

'There was a lot that had to be done,' the young man reminded her.

'There was a windshield wiper!'

'Both wipers, actually,' the man, whose name tag identified him as Robert, stated. 'You recall we phoned you, told you that both would have to be replaced, along with the catalytic converter and the alternator,' Robert expanded patiently. 'Your car hadn't been serviced in some time.'

'There was never any need.'

'Yes, well, you were very lucky. The problem with these old cars is that they require a lot of maintenance . . .'

'Three weeks' worth?'

'We had to order the parts. There was some delay in getting them in.'

'And what's all this?' Jess said, desperately pointing to a host of other items at the bottom of the list.

'Winterizing, tune-up, valve changes. Actually, you got off pretty cheaply, considering.'

'That's it!' Jess exploded. 'I want to talk to the manager.'

141

Jess looked helplessly from side to side. A middle-aged man waiting at the next counter turned quickly away; a young woman giggled; an elderly woman waiting beside her husband raised her fist to her breast in a covert salute.

'He's not in yet,' Robert explained as Jess checked the large clock on the wall. 7:55, it read.

Normally, she'd have been in her office ten minutes ago. She'd be going over her calendar, making her notes, deciding on what more had to be done in preparation for her day in court. Now, instead of rehearsing her opening statement for the most high-profile murder case of her career, she was arguing with somebody named Robert about her car.

'Look, I really don't have time for this. What if I simply refuse to pay?'

'Then you don't get your car back,' Robert said, equally simply.

Jess stared into the black and white tile mosaic of the floor. 'You know, of course, that you won't be seeing my business again.'

Robert barely suppressed a smile.

'Can I give you a check?'

'Cash or charge only.'

'Naturally.' Jess pulled out her wallet and handed over her charge card, thinking that what was probably even more remarkable than the number of the murders that occurred every year in Chicago was the fact that there weren't more.

'Ladies and gentlemen of the jury,' Jess began, her eyes making brief contact with each of the eight women and six men who made up the jury and their alternates in what the press was calling the Crossbow murder trial, 'on June the second of this year, Terry Wales, the defendant, shot his wife through the heart with a steel-tipped arrow from a crossbow, in the middle of the intersection at Grand Avenue and State Street. No one here disputes that. It is a fact, pure and simple.

'The defense will try to convince you that nothing about this case is simple, that there is little that is pure,' she said,

142

borrowing Greg Oliver's clever phrase. 'But facts are facts, ladies and gentlemen, and the fact is that Nina Wales, a lovely and intelligent woman of 38, was mercilessly shot down, in a most cruel and horrible way, by the brutal husband she had recently worked up the courage to leave.'

Jess backed away slightly from the jury box, drawing the jurors' eyes toward the defendant, Terry Wales, a relatively innocuous, even mousey-looking man of forty. His frame was slender and wiry, his complexion pale, his thinning hair a colorless blond. It was his lawyer, Hal Bristol, a dark-haired beefy man of maybe sixty, to whom all eyes were naturally drawn. Terry Wales sat beside him looking meek and overwhelmed, his face a mask of bewilderment, as if he couldn't believe the words he was hearing, or the predicament he found himself in.

Perhaps he couldn't, Jess thought, her eyes drawn to the Bible Terry Wales twisted nervously in his hands. Criminals, like teenagers, thought they were invincible. No matter how great their crime, no-matter how obvious their motives, no matter how clear the crumbs of the trail they left behind, they never actually thought they'd be caught. They always believed they would get away with it. And sometimes they did. Sometimes all it took was the help of a well-trained lawyer and a well-thumbed copy of the New Testament. Would the jury fall for such a cheap bit of theatrics? Jess wondered, cynically.

'Don't be fooled by the carefully coached picture of pious innocence and regret you see before you, ladies and gentlemen,' Jess admonished, momentarily veering away from her planned speech, watching as Hal Bristol shook his head. 'Don't be tricked into thinking that just because a man clutches a Bible, he understands what's inside it. Or even cares.

'Where was his Bible when Terry Wales regularly battered his wife over the course of their eleven-year marriage? Where was it when he threatened to kill her if she tried to leave? Where was it when he bought a crossbow the day before the killing? Where was the Bible Terry Wales is clutching in his hand when he took that crossbow and used it to shoot down his

143

wife as she emerged from a taxi on her way to see her lawyer? That Bible was nowhere in sight, ladies and gentlemen. Terry Wales had no use for Bibles then. Only now. And only because you're watching him.'

Jess returned to her prepared script. 'The defense will try to tell you that the cold-blooded, premeditated murder of Nina Wales was, in fact, a crime of passion. Yes, they will concede, Terry Wales did purchase the crossbow and arrow; yes, he did shoot his wife. But don't you understand? He didn't really mean to hurt her. He only wanted to scare her. He loved her, they'll try to convince you. He loved her, and she was leaving him. He'd tried reasoning with her; he'd cajoled; he'd begged; he'd pleaded. He'd even threatened. He was a man in pain, a man in turmoil. He was beside himself with grief over the thought of losing his wife.

'They will also try to convince you that Nina Wales was not entirely without blame in her own demise. She was cheating on her husband, they'll assert, although for that we have only the word of the man who killed her.

'They will tell you that Nina Wales taunted her husband about his failings as a lover, that she ridiculed his manhood, baited him relentlessly for his failure to satisfy her voracious needs.

'Finally, the defense will tell you that Nina Wales not only threatened to leave her husband, she threatened to take him for everything he owned, that she threatened to take his children away, turn them against him for ever, leave him with nothing, not even his self-respect.

'And still he loved her, they will tell you. Still he pleaded with her to stay. And still she refused.

'I ask you,' Jess said simply, her eyes travelling across the double rows of jurors, 'what's a man supposed to do? What other choice did Terry Wales have but to kill her?'

Jess paused, giving her words time to sink in, turning in a small circle, taking in the room at a single glance. She saw Judge Harris, whose face registered the same interested yet impassive look it always did during a trial; she saw the prosecutor's table where Neil Strayhorn sat hunched forward in his seat, his head nodding silent encouragement; she saw the crowded rows of spectators, the reporters scribbling notes, the television news artists sketching hurried portraits of the accused.

She saw Rick Ferguson.

He was sitting in the second row from the back of the courtroom, in the third seat in from the center aisle, his hair hanging long behind his ears, his eyes staring straight ahead, his odious Cheshire cat grin firmly in place. Quickly, Jess looked away, her heart pounding.

What was he doing here? What was he trying to prove? That he could intimidate her? That he could harass her at will? That he wouldn't be controlled, couldn't be stopped?

Don't lose it, Jess told herself. Concentrate. Concentrate on the speech you're giving to the jury. Don't let one killer prevent you from bringing another killer to justice. Deal with Terry Wales now, and with Rick Ferguson later.

Jess turned back toward the jury, saw that they were anxiously waiting for her to continue. 'Take a good look at the defendant, ladies and gentlemen,' Jess instructed, again veering from her prepared text. 'He doesn't took like a cold-blooded killer, does he? Actually, he looks pretty harmless. Mild, maybe even a little meek. Pretty skinny for a guy who regularly beat his wife, you're probably thinking. But once again, ladies and gentlemen, don't be fooled by appearances.

'The fact is, and the prosecution will always be bringing you back to the facts of this case, the fact is that Terry Wales has a black belt in karate; the fact is that we have hospital records that will show a history of broken bones and bruises inflicted on Nina Wales by her husband over the years. The fact is that Terry Wales was a wife-beater.

'Let me ask you something, ladies and gentlemen of the jury,' Jess continued, resolutely confining her gaze to the jury box. 'Is it reasonable to expect us to believe that Terry Wales shot his wife in a fit of passion when they hadn't seen each other in several days? Is it reasonable to expect us to believe that there was no premeditation involved even though Terry Wales purchased the murder weapon the day before he shot his wife down? That there was no preconceived plan? That there was no expectation that when he fired the steel-tipped arrow into his wife's chest that she might die?

'Because that's exactly what defines an act of first-degree murder,' Jess explained, feeling Rick Ferguson's eyes burrowing into the back of her head. She spoke with deliberate slowness, making sure the jury heard and appreciated every word, reciting the statute from memory. ' "If the murder was committed in a cold, calculated and premeditated manner pursuant to a preconceived plan, scheme or design to take a human life by unlawful means, and the conduct of the defendant created a reasonable expectation that the death of a human being would result therefrom." That is the definition of murder in the first degree.

'The defense would have you believe that Terry Wales, thoroughly emasculated by his wife, yet distraught at the thought of losing her, was only trying to frighten her when he aimed that crossbow at her heart. They want you to believe that he was actually aiming for her leg. They would have you believe that Terry Wales, an already broken man, "snapped" after his wife taunted him once too often, that he was only trying to shake her up a little when he fired that crossbow into the middle of a busy intersection, that Terry Wales is as much a victim in this case as his wife.

'Don't be fooled, ladies and gentlemen. Nina Wales is the victim here. Nina Wales is dead. Terry Wales is very much alive.'

Jess pushed herself away from the jury box, forced her eyes back to the spectators' benches. Rick Ferguson smiled back from his seat in the second to last row.

'The prosecution will prove,' Jess stated firmly, turning back to the jury, 'that Terry Wales regularly beat his wife. We will prove that he threatened, on more than one occasion, to kill her if she ever tried to leave him. We will prove that after Nina Wales did just that, after she worked up the courage to take her children and run, Terry Wales purchased a crossbow in his local sporting goods store. We will prove that he used that crossbow to shoot Nina Wales through the heart as if she were a deer in a forest.

'He didn't care about her suffering; he *wanted* her to suffer. There was no compassion here, ladies and gentlemen. And this was no crime of passion. This was murder, pure and simple. Murder beyond a reasonable doubt. Murder in the first degree. Thank you.'

Jess smiled sadly at the eight women and six men. Three were black, two of Spanish extraction, one Asian, the rest white. Most were middle-aged. Only two were in their twenties. One woman was perhaps sixty. All looked solemn, prepared to do their duty.

'Mr. Bristol,' Judge Harris was saying as Jess returned to the prosecutor's table.

Hal Bristol was speaking even before he got to his feet, his voice booming across the courtroom, grabbing the jurors by their collective throat. 'Ladies and gentlemen of the jury, Terry Wales is not an educated man. He's a salesman, like some of you. He sells household appliances. He's very good at it, and he makes a good living. He's not a rich man, by any means. But he *is* a proud man.

'Like you, he's had to tighten his belt in these recessionary times. Not so many people out there buying. Especially high ticket items, like appliances. Not as many new homes going up. Not as many people needing new stoves and microwave ovens. Commissions are scarce. We're living in uneasy times. Not a lot to count on.'

Jess sat back in her chair. So this was to be the defense's approach. The killer as someone we could all identify with. The killer we could understand because his reflection mirrors our own. The killer as Everyman.

'Terry Wales thought he could count on his wife. He married her eleven years ago with the understanding that both would continue to work for several years before they started a family. But Nina Wales had a different understanding. After they got married, she decided she wanted children right away. She didn't want to wait. She'd continue to work, she assured him. She certainly had no intention of giving up her job. But soon after their first child was born, Nina Wales quit work. She wanted to be a full-time mother, and how could my client argue with that, especially when she quickly became pregnant again?

'But Nina Wales wasn't an easy woman to satisfy. No matter how much she had, no matter how much her husband could comfortably provide her with, Nina Wales was a woman who always wanted more. So, of course, there were fights over the years. There were occasionally even violent fights. Terry Wales is certainly not proud of his part in them. But spousal violence can happen in the best of marriages – and does. Especially when times get tough.

'Now I don't believe in blaming the victim,' Hal Bristol intoned, and Jess had to admire that the words escaped his mouth without the slightest trace of irony, 'but we all know it takes two to tango. My client is not a violent man. He had to be pushed pretty hard to react in a violent fashion.

'And Nina Wales knew just what buttons to push.'

Jess let her eyes drift toward the rear of the courtroom, feeling the bile rise in her throat. Was that what Rick Ferguson was doing here? Pushing her buttons?

Rick Ferguson stared straight ahead, seemingly mesmerized by what the defense attorney was saying. Occasionally he nodded his head in agreement. One Everyman killer to another. Damn him, Jess thought. Why was he here?

'Nina Wales was an expert at pushing buttons,' Hal Bristol continued. 'She constantly chided her husband over his sagging commissions; she berated him for failing to provide her with greater creature comforts. We have witnesses who will testify to hearing Nina Wales publicly embarrass her husband on more than one occasion. Facts, as the prosecution told you. Not just the word of the defendant. And we have witnesses who will testify that Nina Wales threatened, again on more than one occasion, to take her children and disappear, leaving him with nothing.

'Terry Wales is a proud man, ladies and gentlemen, although his wife made him feel as if there was little to be proud of. And nothing was sacred. Even their sex life became a target for public consumption and ridicule. Nina Wales made fun of her husband's performance in bed, and taunted him at every opportunity about his failure to satisfy her. She even told him she'd taken a lover, and although this may not have been true, Terry Wales believed her.

'Then she left, refused to let her husband even speak to his children. She informed him she was seeing a lawyer, was preparing to take him for everything he had, for everything he'd worked for all his life. Terry Wales was distraught. Destroyed. He was no longer thinking either clearly or rationally. He was desperate. And desperate men, in desperate times, sometimes do desperate things.

'So, he bought a crossbow. A crossbow, ladies and gentlemen. Not a gun, even though he holds several marksman's degrees. Even though a gun, for someone planning to murder his wife, would have been the more logical weapon of choice, much easier to use, more difficult to trace, far more likely to result in the death of the victim.

'No, Terry Wales bought a crossbow. An instrument that was far more likely to create a stir than it was to cause serious harm.

'Which was exactly what he meant to do.

'Terry Wales wanted to scare his wife. He didn't want to kill her.

'If you were planning to murder someone, ladies and gentlemen of the jury, would you choose a weapon as old-fashioned and conspicuous as a crossbow? Would you commit that murder in the middle of the day, in the middle of a busy downtown intersection, with at least half a dozen witnesses to identify you? Would you sit down on the sidewalk afterward, sobbing, and wait for the police? Do these sound like the actions of a rational man, a man who the prosecution claims callously and deliberately plotted the cold-blooded murder of his wife?'

Hal Bristol strode across the courtroom to the prosecutor's

149

table. 'The defense and the prosecution are in agreement on one thing,' he said, looking directly at Jess. 'My client *is* responsible for the death of his wife.' He paused, striding purposefully back toward the jury box. 'But it is our contention that Terry Wales never meant to kill his wife, that his only intention was to frighten her, bring her back to her senses, bring her back to their home. However misguided, however irrational those intentions may have been, they do not constitute cold, calculated, and premeditated murder.

'During the course of this trial, I'd like you to put yourself in Terry Wales's shoes. We all have our breaking point, ladies and gentlemen. Terry Wales reached his.' Hal Bristol paused dramatically before concluding. 'What would it take to reach yours?'

Jess pictured herself standing in front of the ivory lace curtains of her living room, staring out at the street below, gun in hand. Would she actually have been able to use it? We all have our breaking point, ladies and gentlemen, she thought, turning toward the back of the courtroom, seeing Rick Ferguson pop a piece of gum into his mouth and start to chew.

'Is the prosecution ready to proceed?' Judge Harris asked.

'The prosecution requests a ten-minute recess,' Jess said quickly.

'We will recess for ten minutes,' Judge Harris agreed.

'What's up, Jess?' Neil Strayhorn asked, obviously caught off guard.

But Jess was already on her way toward the back of the courtroom. If she expected Rick Ferguson to jump to his feet, he didn't. In fact, he didn't even look her way, forcing her to speak over the heads of the two people next to him. 'There's an easy way to do this,' she began, 'and a hard way.'

Still, he didn't look at her.

'The easy way is that you stand up and walk out of here now of your own volition,' she continued, unprompted.

'And the hard way?' he asked, eyes focused on the empty Judge's chair.

'I'll call the bailiff, and have you thrown out.'

Rick Ferguson stood up, shuffled past the two men beside him to where Jess stood. 'I just wanted to see what I might have been up against if that old lady hadn't disappeared the way she did,' he said, lowering his eyes to hers. 'Tell me, counsellor, you as good in bed as you are in court?'

'Bailiff!' Jess called loudly.

'Hey, the easy way, remember?' Rick Ferguson turned and walked from the room.

Jess was still shaking ten minutes later when the Judge called the court to order.

An armed Sheriff's deputy escorted Jess to the parking garage across from the Administration Building at almost seven o'clock that night.

She had spent the two hours after court was dismissed conferring with Neil and Barbara about the day's events and tomorrow's strategy, and trying to reach her ex-husband, but his office said he'd been out all afternoon and they weren't sure what time he'd be back. ('Jess, is that you?' the polite voice had inquired as she was about to hang up. 'Haven't heard from you in a long time. Why don't you try him at home later? You still have the number?')

'I'm on level three,' Jess told the deputy. Fully armed Sheriff's deputies always escorted prosecutors to their cars after dark.

'Finally got your car back,' the young man said, his blond hair peeking out from beneath his dark blue cap, his hand near his holster as he led Jess through the outdoor parking lot to the multi-storied garage. Jess told him the sad saga of her red Mustang as they waited for the elevator to arrive.

'At least they washed it,' Jess said as the elevator doors opened and they stepped inside.

'Something good comes from everything, I guess,' the deputy told her philosophically, and Jess nodded, though she was far from sure she agreed. 'God, what's that smell?' he said, as they stepped out at the third level. 'Stinks like an outhouse up here.'

Jess grimaced, the unpleasant odor filling her nostrils and

throat, making her want to gag. She motioned to where she'd parked her car, not wanting to open her mouth, in case whatever was in the air settled on her tongue.

'Jesus, it's getting worse.'

They turned the corner.

'My God,' the guard exclaimed, automatically pulling his gun from the holster and spinning round.

'There's nobody here,' Jess said, surprisingly calm, staring at her car. 'He's long gone.'

'Don't tell me this is your car,' the guard stated, though Jess was sure he already knew the answer. 'Jesus, what sick bastard would do something like this?'

Jess stared at her Mustang, which only this morning had been freshly washed and as good as new. Now it stood, smeared from top to bottom with what was unmistakably excrement, its windows streaked, its new windshield wipers broken and twisting out from the middle of large clumps of feces. Jess felt her eyes sting, and covered her nose and mouth, turning away.

The guard was already on his walkie-talkie, radioing for help. Jess returned to the elevator and sank down onto the cement floor beside it. 'Shit,' she muttered, thinking her choice of expletives remarkably apt, dissolving into peals of helpless laughter. She could laugh or she could cry, she decided.

She'd save the crying for later.

Chapter Twelve

'Walter! Walter, for God's sake, you left the front door unlocked again!' Jess pounded on the door to the second-floor apartment of the three-story brownstone, wondering whether she could be heard over Miles Davis's trumpet.

'Hold your horses, I'm coming,' came the darkly masculine voice from inside. An instant later, the door opened, and the short, roundish systems analyst who was her downstairs neighbor stood before her, wearing a green silk bathrobe and sipping a glass of red wine. He examined her quickly from head to toe. 'Jess, you're beautiful. And you're hysterical. Would you like to come in for a drink?'

'I'd like you to make sure you keep the front door locked,' Jess told him, in no mood for anything as civil as a glass of red wine.

'Oh, did I forget to lock it again?' Walter Fraser appeared resolutely nonchalant. 'I was bringing in the groceries, and I had to keep making trips to the car. It was just easier to leave the door unlocked.'

'Easier, and a lot more dangerous.'

'Bad day, huh?' Walter asked.

'Just keep it locked,' Jess said again, heading up the last flight of stairs to her apartment.

The phone started ringing as soon as she opened her door. What now? she wondered, knocking against the side of the bird cage as she hurried into the kitchen to answer it, hearing the canary chirp in frightened protest. 'Sorry, Fred,' she called, frantically grabbing for the phone . 'Hello.' Her voice was a shout.

'Ouch! Somebody's not happy.'

'Don, is that you?'

'My office said you've been trying to reach me. Something wrong?'

153

'Nothing that seeing your client in the electric chair wouldn't cure.'

'I assume we're talking about Rick Ferguson,' Don said calmly.

'Excellent assumption. How about this one? Your client shows up in my courtroom today and several hours later my car, which I've just spent over four hundred dollars repairing, turns up covered in shit. What assumptions would you make there?'

'Hold on a minute. You're saying that your car was literally covered in . . .?'

'Excrement, probably human. At least that's what the cops think it is. They've taken samples for analysis, and they're trying to dust the car for prints. Not that that will accomplish a hell of a lot. I'm sure rubber gloves were the order of the day.'

'Jesus Christ,' Don muttered.

'Just tell your client that if he ever sets foot in my courtroom again, I'll have him arrested. I don't care what for.'

'I've already warned him to stay the hell away from you.'

'Just keep him away from my courtroom.'

'You won't see him there again.'

Jess could hear the confusion in her ex-husband's voice, despite his even tone. She knew he was fighting to keep a safe distance between his professional and personal lives, that she was making it next to impossible for him.

'Look,' he said, after a long pause, 'it's almost nine o'clock. Knowing you, you haven't eaten.'

'I'm not very hungry.'

'You need to eat. Come on. I can be there in twenty minutes. We'll go out, grab a steak.'

'Don, I just spent two hours with a car that looks like a shit sandwich. I don't have much of an appetite.' She felt him smile. 'I'm sorry. Another time?'

'Anytime. Get some sleep.'

'Thanks.'

'Oh, and Jess.'

'Yes?'

'The state of Illinois doesn't execute criminals in the electric chair anymore. I believe lethal injections are the order of the day.'

She laughed. 'Thanks for the update.'

They hung up without saying goodbye.

Almost immediately, Jess felt her stomach growl. 'Great. Perfect timing.' Jess looked at the phone, decided against calling Don back. She was too tired, too aggravated, too fed-up to go out. She'd only drag Don down. Besides, why eat steak when she had nice, hard, frozen pizzas right in her very own freezer?

She removed two from their cellophane wrappers and popped them into the microwave, then grabbed a can of Coke from the fridge and pulled open its metal tab, taking a long sip directly from the can. More gas that way, she thought, taking another sip, thinking of her brother-in-law, his new no soft drinks rule. ('I think you're jealous,' Barry had said. 'Because your sister has a husband and a family, and she's happy. And what have you got? A freezer full of frozen pizzas and a goddamn canary!')

Was he right? Was she jealous of her sister's happiness? Could she possibly be so petty?

For the first time in years, Maureen hadn't invited her over for Thanksgiving dinner. She'd said something about having dinner with Barry's parents for a change, but probably she was just fed up. They were all fed up. Even her father had stopped suggesting opportune times for her to meet his new love. He appreciated how busy she was these days, he'd told her, citing all the publicity surrounding her current case. He'd wait for the trial to be over.

What was she doing to her father? Was she jealous of his happiness too? Did she want everyone who loved her to live the same sort of isolated lonely life she'd designed for herself? Could she believe her father's interest in another woman was somehow a betrayal of her mother, even now, after all these years?

Jess buried her head in her hands. No, she realized slowly. It was more that by allowing himself to love another woman, her father was, in some symbolic, but very real way signing her mother's death certificate.

Jess lifted her head from her hands, stared up at the ceiling, tears falling the length of her cheeks. Could it be that she still half expected her mother to come walking back into their lives? Is that what she was waiting for, hoping for, longing for? Even now, after eight years? Was she still waiting for her mother to appear on her doorstep, sweep her faithful daughter into her arms, smother her face with kisses, tell her all was forgiven, that she wasn't responsible for her disappearance, that she'd been found not guilty.

Was she still waiting for her moment of absolution? Could her life not proceed without it?

The microwave oven beeped to announce that dinner was ready, and Jess snapped back to reality, carefully lifting the two steaming pizzas onto a blue-flowered plate. She carried the plate and the can of Coke into the living room and sat down on the sofa, aware for the first time of the sixties music emanating from the radio. *Monday, Monday*, the Mamas and the Papas sang in harmony, and Jess shrugged. Monday, Monday was right! What a day.

'And how was your day, Freddy?' she asked her canary, blowing across the tops of the pizzas, trying to cool them down. 'Better than mine, I hope.' She took an enormous bite from one piece, pulling almost all of the top coating of cheese into her mouth.

The phone rang.

Jess shoved the piece of pizza to the left side of her mouth with her tongue. 'Hello.'

'Is this Jess Koster?'

The man's voice was only vaguely familiar.

'Who's calling?' Jess asked, her body poised, on alert.

'Adam Stohn.'

'Adam Stohn?'

'From Shoe-Inn. The boots you ordered — they came in late this afternoon. I tried to call you at work. They said you were in court. You didn't tell me you were a lawyer.'

156

Jess felt her heart start to race, the pizza stick to the side of her mouth. 'I didn't get a message.'

'I didn't leave one.'

Silence.

'So, my boots are in,' Jess said after what felt like an eternity.

'You can pick them up any time.'

'That's great. Thank you for letting me know.'

'Or I could drop them by,' he volunteered.

'What?'

'Save you the trip down. You could just give me a check, made out to Shoe-Inn, of course.'

'When?'

'I could come by now, if that's convenient.'

'Now?' *What? When? Now?* Jess heard herself repeat. When had she turned into such a sparkling conversationalist?

'They're calling for snow tomorrow.'

'Are they?'

'Actually, I haven't had dinner yet. How about you? Feel like splitting a pizza?'

Jess promptly spat the half-chewed lump of cheese still in her mouth onto the plate. 'That sounds great.'

'Good. Why don't you tell me where you live?'

'Why don't we just meet somewhere?' Jess suggested in return.

'Name the place.'

Jess named a small Italian restaurant on Armitage Avenue, within easy walking distance.

'Fifteen minutes?'

'See you there.'

'You're early,' he said, sliding into the red vinyl booth at the back of the small family-operated restaurant. He wore blue jeans and a black bomber jacket over a grey turtleneck.

'I'm always early. Bad habit,' she told him, studying his face, thinking him better-looking than she remembered. Was he having similar thoughts about her? She wished now that she'd changed into something more interesting than a plain black

157

sweater and pants. Probably a touch more make-up wouldn't have hurt either. All she'd done was splash some cold water on her face, brushed her teeth, applied a little lipstick, and dashed out of the house.

'Hello, Signorina,' the middle-aged proprietress greeted Jess, laying two stained paper menus on the table. 'Nice to see you again.'

'Nice to see you,' Jess agreed, smiling at the dark-haired, moon-faced woman. 'Carla makes the best pizzas in the world.'

'In the DePaul area anyway,' Carla qualified. 'Can I bring you a carafe of Chianti while you look over the menu?'

'Sounds good,' Adam said, taking a quick glance at the items listed.

'I already know what I want,' Jess said eagerly. 'I'll have the special pizza. It's my all-time favorite thing to eat in the entire world.'

'In that case, make it a large,' Adam said quickly. 'We'll share.' Carla retrieved the menus from the table and headed for the kitchen. 'Incidentally, your boots are in the car. Don't let me forget to give them to you.'

'Don't let me forget to write you a check.

'God, the pressure.' He laughed. 'I take it you come here often.'

'I live just down the street. And I'm not much of a cook,' Jess added.

'I would guess that you don't have a lot of time for cooking.'

'I don't, but I wouldn't anyway.'

He looked surprised. 'A matter of principle?'

'We lawyers do have them,' she said and smiled.

'There was never a doubt in my mind.'

'My mother used to cook all the time,' Jess explained. 'She hated it, so she never taught us how. Maybe she figured if my sister and I didn't know how to cook, we'd never get trapped into doing it.'

'Interesting theory.'

'Not that it worked.'

He looked puzzled.

'My sister has lately turned into Julia Child.'

'And you don't approve?'

'I'd rather not talk about my sister.'

Carla returned with the carafe of Chianti and two wineglasses. 'I was reading about that crossbow killer in the paper tonight,' Carla said, pouring some dark red wine into each glass. 'They mentioned your name and everything. Very impressive.'

Jess smiled. 'Winning would be impressive.'

Carla made a dismissive gesture with her hands. 'No question. You win. No question.' She rubbed her hands against the hospital green apron that stretched across her ample bosom, then made her way to the front of the restaurant. There were five booths and perhaps ten tables crowded into the small room, about half of them currently occupied. The walls were covered with bright, hand-painted scenes of Italy. Plastic grapes hung at irregular intervals from the ceiling.

'So I'm having dinner with a celebrity,' Adam stated, lifting his glass to hers in a toast.

'Just an over-worked, underpaid prosecutor, I'm afraid.' They clicked glasses. 'Health and wealth, as my brother-in-law would say.'

'To your imminent victory.'

'I'll drink to that.' They did. 'So, what about you? How long have you been selling shoes?'

'At Shoe-Inn, since the summer. Before that, for about a year.'

'And before that?'

'Odd jobs. This and that. Itinerant salesman. You know.'

'My father was a salesman.'

'Oh?'

'Then he owned his own store. A couple, actually. Now, he's retired.'

'And driving your mother crazy?'

Jess took a long sip of her drink. 'My mother's dead.'

Jess watched Adam's jaw drop. 'Oh, sorry. That was a bit clumsy. When did she die?'

'Eight years ago. I'm sorry — would you mind if we talked about something else?'

'Anything you want.'

'Tell me more about you. Are you from Chicago?'

'Springfield.'

'I've never been to Springfield.'

'Pretty city.'

'Why'd you leave?'

'Time for a change.' He shrugged. 'And you? Chicago born and bred?'

She nodded.

'No desire to try somewhere else?'

'I'm pretty much of a homebody.'

'You went to law school here?'

'Northwestern.'

'From which you graduated in the top third of your class?' he guessed.

'I stood fourth.'

He smiled into his glass. 'And from there you turned down all offers of lucrative private practice to become an overworked, underpaid prosecutor in the State's Attorney's office.'

'I didn't want to find myself in the litigation department of some big firm, where the only litigation I'd ever see was a war of memos crossing my desk. Besides, the State's Attorney was one of my law professors and he ran for office and was elected, and he hired me. The only question he asked me was whether or not I'd be able to ask for the death penalty.'

'You obviously gave him the right answer.'

Jess laughed. 'They don't want any liberals in the State's Attorney's office.'

'So what's it like there?'

'Honestly?'

'Only if you insist.'

She laughed. 'I love it. At least I do now. In the beginning, it was pretty dry. They started me out in traffic court. That's not wildly exciting, but you have to pay your dues, I guess. I was there for about a year, then I went into the First Municipal

Division, which prosecutes misdemeanors, anything from property damage to aggravated assault. Those are pretty much bench trials, only a few actual jury trials, the sort of stuff that's always serious to the victims, but not to anybody else. Does that sound callous?'

'I'd imagine you'd have to develop a pretty hard shell working in the State's Attorney's office.'

The image of a headless turtle popped itself into Jess's line of vision. 'I stayed at First Municipal Division for another year,' Jess said, speaking quickly. 'Then I went to Felony Review. That was a lot more interesting.'

'What made it more interesting?'

'It involves real investigative work, getting out there and talking to the victims and the witnesses. You work pretty closely with the police. You see, what most people don't realize is that the cops can't actually charge anyone. Only the State can bring charges. The cops investigate, but it's the Assistant State's Attorney who decides whether to approve the charges and put the case into the system.'

'Your first taste of real power.'

Jess took another long sip of her wine. 'My brother-in-law claims that when a woman gets a little power, she loses her sense of humor.'

'Hey, you laughed at my condom joke.'

'Actually, I have a joke for you,' Jess said, hurriedly trying to organize her thoughts. 'One of the secretaries at work told it to me.' She paused, trying to recall the exact phrasing. 'What do you get when you have a hundred rabbits in a row, and suddenly ninety-nine of them take one step back?'

'I don't know. What do you get?'

'A receding *hare*line!' Jess laughed, then stopped abruptly. 'That was terrible. That was a terrible joke.' She shook her head in disbelief. 'I can't believe I told you that joke.'

'It was a totally terrific joke, told with great flourish, I might add,' Adam said, chuckling quietly. 'Next time you see your brother-in-law, tell him he's full of shit.'

Jess pictured first her brother-in-law, then her shit-covered automobile. 'Could we talk about something else, do you think?'

'So you stayed in Felony Review for another year,' he said without missing a beat.

'Seven months.'

'Then on to the Trial section?'

Jess looked surprised. 'How'd you know that?'

'What else is left?' he asked simply.

'Each courtroom has three assistant State's Attorneys assigned to one particular judge, usually for about a year, maybe more. The most senior of those assistants is called the first chair. That's me.' Jess paused, finished the wine in her glass. 'How'd we get on to all this?'

'I believe I asked what it was like in the State's Attorney's office.'

'Well, you can't say I didn't tell you.' Jess looked toward her lap. 'Sorry, I didn't mean to get carried away. I guess it's pretty dry.'

'Not at all.' He poured more wine into her glass. 'Tell me more.'

Jess lifted the glass to her mouth, grateful to have something to do with her hands, breathing in the heavy aroma of the wine, trying to see beyond the warm brown of Adam's eyes. She wondered if he was as interested in the details of her career as he seemed. She wondered what he was really doing here. She wondered what *she* was doing here. 'Well,' she hesitated before continuing, 'I'm responsible for everything that goes on in that courtroom. I prosecute the major cases. I decide what cases to let my second and third chair try. I'm sort of the teacher, or the guidance counsellor, if you will. And I'm the one who takes the heat if they mess up. If something goes wrong in my courtroom, I'm the one responsible.'

'And how many cases do you prosecute in any given year?'

'Anywhere from twelve to twenty. That's in front of a jury. The majority of cases are disposed of through bench trials or plea negotiations.' She laughed. 'It gets very hectic at this time of year. There's usually a race to see which judge can dispose of

162

the most number of cases before Christmas.'

The pizza arrived, steaming and hot, its four different cheeses spilling over the sides of the aluminum pan, a variety of vegetables and sausages spread across its face. 'Looks fabulous,' Adam remarked, cutting a piece for each of them and smiling as Jess immediately lifted her piece into her hands and stuffed the end into her mouth.

Adam laughed. 'You look just like a little kid.'

'I'm sorry. I should have warned you. I'm a total slob when I eat. I have no shame.'

'It's a pleasure to watch you.'

'I could never understand how people can eat pizza with a knife and fork,' she continued, then stopped short, a long string of cheese stretching between her mouth and plate. 'Now you're going to tell me that you always use a knife and fork, right?'

'I wouldn't dare.' Adam lifted his piece of pizza into his large hands and carried it to his mouth.

'It's wonderful, isn't it?'

'Wonderful,' he agreed, his eyes never leaving hers. 'So, tell me more about Jess Koster, assistant State's Attorney.'

'I think I've probably said more than enough. Don't all the books advise women to let men do the talking? You know, find out what his interests are? Fake interest in same?' She paused, the pizza in her hand suspended in mid-air. 'Or is that what you're doing with me?'

'You don't think you're interesting?'

'Just because I find the law fascinating doesn't mean everybody else will.'

'What is it about the law that fascinates you?'

Jess lowered her pizza to her plate, giving serious thought to his question, choosing her words carefully. 'I guess that it's so complicated. I mean, most people like to think of the criminal justice system as a fight between right and wrong, good and evil, the whole truth and nothing but. But it isn't like that at all. It's not black and white. It's varying shades of grey. Both sides subvert the truth, try to use it to their own advantage. A good attorney will always put a "spin" on a bad act, so that it doesn't come out sounding so bad.'

'Lawyers as spin doctors?'

Jess nodded. 'The sad truth is that truth is almost irrelevant in a court of law.' She shrugged. 'Sometimes it's easy for lawyers to lose sight of basic moral and ethical considerations.'

'What's the difference?'

'Morality is internal,' Jess said simply. 'Ethics are defined by a professional code of responsibility. Did that sound as hopelessly pompous as I think it did?'

'It sounded charming.'

'Charming? I sounded charming?' Jess laughed.

'That surprises you?'

'Charming is rarely a word I hear used to describe me,' she answered honestly.

'What words do you hear?'

'Oh . . . intense, serious, intense, dedicated, intense. I hear a lot of intense.'

'Which is probably what makes you such a good prosecutor.'

'Who said I was any good?'

'Asked she who stood fourth in her graduating class.'

Jess smiled self-consciously. 'I'm not sure one thing has anything to do with the other. I mean, you can memorize precedents and procedures, you can study the law books backwards and forwards, but you really have to have a *feeling* for what the law is. It's a little like love, I guess.' She looked away. 'A matter of ghosts and shadows.'

'Interesting analogy,' Adam commented. 'I take it you're divorced.'

Jess reached for her wine glass, lifted it to her mouth, then lowered it without taking a drink. 'Interesting assumption.'

'Two interesting people,' Adam told her, once again clicking his glass against hers. 'How long were you married?'

'Four years.'

'And how long have you been divorced?'

'Four years.'

'Nice symmetry.'

'And you?'

164

'Married six years, divorced three.'

'Any children?'

He finished his wine, poured the rest of the bottle into his glass, and shook his head.

'Are you sure?' Jess asked, and laughed. 'That was a very pregnant pause.'

'No children,' he repeated. 'And you?'

'No.'

'Too busy?'

'Too much of a child myself, I guess.'

'I doubt that,' he told her. 'You look as if you have a very old soul.'

Jess disguised her sudden discomfort with nervous laughter. 'I guess I need more sleep.'

'You don't need a thing. You're very beautiful,' he said, suddenly focusing all his attention on his pizza.

Jess did the same. For several awkward seconds, nobody spoke.

'I didn't mean to embarrass you,' he said, still concentrating on his plate.

'I'm not embarrassed,' Jess said, not sure what she was.

'So, did your being a prosecutor have anything to do with your divorce?' Adam asked, suddenly shifting gears.

'I'm sorry?'

'Well, being a trial lawyer is a little like being a racehorse, I suspect. You're trained to be a thoroughbred. You hear the bell, you come out running. You've got a big ego, which you need because it's always on the line. And the worst thing is losing. When you're in the middle of a trial, I would think it's very hard to just turn all that off. Basically you're married to the trial for its duration. Am I wrong?'

Jess shook her head. 'You're not wrong.'

'What did your husband do?' Adam cut them each another slice of pizza.

Jess smiled. 'He's a lawyer.'

'I rest my case.'

Jess laughed. 'What about your ex-wife?'

'She's an interior decorator. Last I heard she'd remarried.'
Adam took a deep breath, lifted his hands into the air, as if to
indicate he'd exhausted himself on the subject. 'Anyway,
enough about past lives. Time to move on.'

'That was quick.'

'Nothing much to tell.'

'You don't like talking about yourself much, do you?'

'No more than you do.'

Jess was incredulous. 'What do you mean? I've been talking
about myself since I got here.'

'You've been talking about the law. Whenever the questions
get more personal, you clam up as tightly as if you were a
hostile witness on the stand.'

'I'll make you a deal,' Jess said, surprised to find herself so
transparent. 'I won't tell you my secrets if you don't tell me
yours.'

Adam smiled, his brown eyes impenetrable. 'Tell me no
secrets, I'll tell you no lies.'

There was a long pause.

'Sounds good,' Jess said.

'For me too.'

They resumed eating, finishing off the rest of the pizza in
silence.

'Why did you call me tonight?' Jess asked, pushing away her
empty plate.

'I wanted to see you,' he answered. 'Why did you accept?'

'I guess I wanted to see you too.'

They smiled at each other across the table.

'So, what's an ambitious lawyer like you doing out with a
simple shoe salesman like me?' He signalled for the check.

'I get the feeling there's nothing simple about you.'

'That's because you're a lawyer. You're always looking for
things that aren't there.'

Jess laughed. 'And I hear it's going to snow tomorrow. I could
use a new pair of winter boots.'

'I have just the thing in the back seat of my car. Can I offer
you a ride home?'

166

Jess hesitated, wondered what was she afraid of?

Carla approached with the bill. 'So, how was everything? You like the pizza?' she inquired of Adam.

'Without doubt, the best pizza in the De Paul area.'

Jess watched Adam take a twenty-dollar bill from his pocket, thought of offering to split the cost of the dinner, then thought better of the idea. Next time, she decided, dinner would be on her.

If there was a next time.

Jess was sleeping, the kind of deep, dreamless, luxurious sleep that had eluded her for weeks. Suddenly, she was awake, her body upright, her hands shooting forward, as if she were falling through the air. All around bells were ringing, alarms were going off.

It was the phone, she realized, reaching across the bed and lifting the receiver cautiously to her ear. The illuminated dial of her digital clock announced it was 3 a.m. No good news ever came at three o'clock in the morning, she knew. Only death and despair thought nothing of waking people up in the middle of the night.

'Hello,' she said, her voice alert and in control, as if she'd been waiting for the phone to ring.

She expected to hear the police on the other end, or possibly the office of the Medical Examiner. But there was only silence.

'Hello?' she repeated. 'Hello? Hello?'

No answer. Not even the courtesy of some token heavy breathing.

She hung up, her head falling back onto her pillow with a gentle thud. Just a stupid nuisance call, she thought, refusing to consider other possibilities. 'Go back to sleep,' she muttered. But sleep had deserted her, and she lay awake, watching as snow silently cascaded outside her bedroom window, until it was time to get up.

Chapter Thirteen

'So, all in all, how would you say it went today?' Jess looked across her desk at Neil Strayhorn and Barbara Cohen, both of whom were fighting off various stages of cold and flu bugs. Neil's cold had been dragging on for so long now, the Kleenex that moved continually between his hand and his long, aquiline nose seemed a permanent fixture. Barbara's red-rimmed eyes were the consistency of runny eggs, threatening to spill over onto her flushed cheeks. Jess swivelled her chair toward the window, concentrating on the mixture of snow and rain that cut diagonally through the dark sky.

'I thought it went pretty well,' Neil said, his voice wandering helplessly through congested nasal passages. 'We made some important points.'

'Such as?' Jess nodded toward Barbara Cohen.

'Ellie Lupino testified that she'd heard Terry Wales threaten to kill his wife if she ever tried to leave him.' Barbara coughed, had to clear her throat in order to continue. 'She swore that Nina Wales wasn't having an affair.'

'She swore that, *to the best of her knowledge*, Nina Wales wasn't having an affair,' Jess clarified.

'She was Nina's best friend for almost ten years. Nina told her everything,' Neil offered. 'Surely that will carry a lot of weight with the jury.'

'Ellie Lupino also admitted that she heard Nina Wales publicly disparage her husband's performance in bed on more than one occasion, that she threatened to take him for everything he had,' Jess reminded them.

'So?' Barbara asked, the word triggering a minor coughing spasm.

'So, that goes to the heart of the defense's case. If they can

169

convince the jury that Nina Wales provoked her husband into an uncontrollable fury—'

'... then she was responsible for her own murder!' Barbara sneezed in indignation.

'Then at best we're looking at murder two.'

'So what if Nina Wales taunted her husband with the fact he was lousy in bed? So what if she threatened to leave him? He beat her with his *fists*. Words were the only weapon that she had!' Barbara Cohen clutched at her chest, stubbornly swallowing another coughing fit, which made her sound as if she was choking.

'We have motive, we have malice aforethought, we have cold, calculated premeditation,' Neil rhymed off, punctuating his sentence with a loud blowing of his nose.

'The whole question is one of provocation,' Jess reiterated over the growing cacophony of bronchial histrionics. 'There was a recent case in Michigan where a jury found the husband of a judge guilty only of manslaughter when he killed his estranged wife in her own courtroom. The jury found that the break-up provoked him to kill her. In another case in New York City, a Chinese-American was put on probation, *on probation*, after he bludgeoned his wife to death with a hammer. The wife had been unfaithful, and the judge ruled that because of the husband's cultural background, the infidelity constituted provocation.' She took a deep breath, trying not to inhale the germs lingering almost visibly in the air. 'The only question those jurors are going to be asking themselves is whether, under similar circumstances, they might be capable of the same thing.'

'So what are you saying?' Barbara asked, a lone tear escaping her watery eyes.

'I'm saying that it all boils down to how well Terry Wales performs on the witness stand,' Jess told them. 'I'm saying that we better know everything Terry Wales is going to say to that jury before he does, and not only be ready to call him on it, but to tear him to shreds. I'm saying that it's not going to be easy to win this case. I'm saying that you guys better get out of here and get into bed.'

Neil sneezed three times in rapid succession.

'Bless you,' Jess said automatically.

'You don't have to say bless you when someone has a cold,' Barbara informed her. 'That's what my mother always says,' she explained sheepishly, heading for the door.

'I thought Judge Harris was looking a little rough around the edges today,' Neil said, right behind her.

'Probably too much Thanksgiving turkey,' Jess said, closing the door after them, collapsing into the nearest chair, feeling a nervous tickle at the back of her throat. 'Oh no,' she said, 'don't you get sick now. You do not have time to get sick. Tickle, be gone,' she ordered, returning to her own seat behind her desk, peering over the notes she'd made in court that afternoon, glancing menacingly at the phone.

So what if a week had passed and Adam hadn't called? Had she really expected him to? Their evening together had ended on a very businesslike note — he'd handed over the boots, she'd handed over the check. He'd deposited her in front of her brownstone without so much as a peck on the cheek. She hadn't invited him in; he hadn't asked. They'd said goodbye. No 'Can I see you again?' No 'I'll call you.' Nothing. So why had she been expecting more?

Had she really thought he might call, suggest they spend Thanksgiving together? Two virtual strangers sharing turkey and cranberry sauce? The assistant State's Attorney from Cook County and the shoe salesman from Springfield! What bothered her more? The fact he was a shoe salesman or the fact he hadn't called?

She'd ended up having Thanksgiving dinner with the gay systems analyst from the apartment downstairs, and eight of his friends, pretending she wasn't listening through the ceiling for her phone to ring. After a few glasses of wine, she'd immersed herself in Charlie Parker and Jerry Mulligan, and joined the others in giving thanks for their good fortune at being together, for their sheer good luck at being alive, when so many of their friends had perished.

She drank too much and Walter had to escort her back

upstairs. At least she hadn't had to drive home, she thought now.

She lowered her head into her hands, thinking of her car, vandalized beyond all recognition. A gift from her parents after her acceptance into Northwestern University, it had withstood law school, marriage, divorce, and four years with the State's Attorney's Office.

Only it couldn't withstand this last assault to its dignity. It couldn't withstand Rick Ferguson.

Jess hadn't immediately noticed the slashed tires, hadn't absorbed the gutted upholstery, or the brake pedal ripped from the floor. It was days before she learned the full extent of the damage. A total write-off, of course. No point in trying to put the pieces back together again. Much too difficult. Much too expensive, even with insurance. She was already out over four hundred dollars.

They hadn't found any prints, nothing to link Rick Ferguson to the murder of her car. So, he'd shown up in her courtroom that very day. So what? Nobody had seen him in the parking garage. Nobody had seen him anywhere near her car. Nobody ever saw him anywhere. People disappeared; property was destroyed; Rick Ferguson went on smiling.

Jess picked up the phone and called the office of the Medical Examiner. 'Good, you're still there,' she said when she heard Hilary Waugh's voice.

'Just getting ready to leave,' the woman told her. Jess understood that what she was really saying was, it's late, let's make this quick.

'I take it no one's come in resembling Connie DeVuono,' Jess began, as if Connie might still be alive, as if she had somehow wandered into the office of the Chief Medical Examiner of her own accord.

'No one.'

'You got the dental records I sent over?'

'I got them. They're here, ready and waiting.'

'That should speed things up.'

'Yes, it should. I really have to get going now, Jess. I'm not feeling so hot. I think I might be coming down with something.'

'Welcome to the club,' Jess said, wishing Hilary Waugh a speedy recovery. She replaced the receiver, then immediately picked it up again, needing to hear a friendly voice. She hadn't heard from her sister since before Thanksgiving. It wasn't like Maureen not to call, no matter how busy she was. Jess hoped she was well, that she hadn't been felled by the flu bug that seemed to be sweeping through the city.

'Hello.' The smile in Maureen's voice was audible. Jess felt instantly reassured.

'How are you?' Jess asked.

'I'm fine,' Maureen answered, the smile quickly fading, leaving her voice cold, matter-of-fact. 'Tyler's got the sniffles, but the rest of us are okay. How are you?'

'I'm okay. How was Thanksgiving dinner?'

'Great. Barry's mother's a gourmet cook. But you're not really interested in that.' There was an uncomfortable pause. 'So, you've been busy, as usual?'

'Well, this is a real heater case I'm trying.'

'Heater case?'

'Lots of publicity. I'm sure you've been reading about it.' Jess stopped when she remembered that Maureen didn't read the front pages anymore.

'Actually, yes, I have been following it. I guess it's quite a coup for you to have a case this big.'

'Only if I win it.'

There was silence.

'I haven't heard from you in a while,' Jess ventured, suddenly aware that it had always been her sister who'd made sure they kept in frequent touch.

'I thought that was how you wanted it.'

'How I wanted it? Why would you say that?'

'Oh, I don't know. Maybe because you're always so busy. Too busy to meet Dad's friend, anyway. Too busy to make dinner at Bistro 110. Too busy to keep your appointment with Stephanie Banack.'

'I kept my appointment.'

'Technically, yes, I guess you did. Look, Jess, I'm really not interested in pursuing this. I can appreciate that you're busy. Believe me, I do understand something about what that's like. But don't try to tell me that you're so busy you don't have any time for your family. Don't insult my intelligence that way. If you don't want to be part of this family, that's up to you. I guess I'm going to have to accept it.'

'It's not that I don't want to be with you, Maureen.'

'It's that you don't want to be with my husband.'

'We just don't get along. It happens. It's not the end of the world.'

'And Dad? How long are you going to keep shutting him out?'

'I'm not shutting him out.'

'No. Just the woman he loves.'

'Don't you think you're being overly dramatic?'

'I think Dad's going to marry this woman, Jess.'

Another silence. 'Did he say that?'

'He didn't have to.'

'Well, I'll worry about that when the time comes.'

'Why do you have to worry about it at all?' Maureen demanded. 'Why can't you just be happy for him? Why can't you at least pay him the courtesy of meeting her?'

Jess stared out the window into the encroaching night. It wasn't quite six o'clock and already so dark. 'I better go, let you get dinner ready.'

'Sure. It's what I do best.'

'Maureen—'

'Bye, Jess. Keep in touch.'

The phone went dead before Jess had a chance to say goodbye. 'Great. Just great.' She returned the phone to its carriage, thought of calling her father, decided against it. She could only bear the sound of so much disappointment.

What was she doing to her family? Why couldn't she just reconcile herself to the fact that her brother-in-law was an ass, her sister was Total Woman, her father was in love? When had she grown so intolerant, so inflexible? Did everyone have to live their lives according to her dictates? Was she doing such a great job with her own life?

The door to her office opened. Greg Oliver stood on the other side. The pungently sweet odor of Aramis raced toward her desk.

Just what she needed, Jess thought, acknowledging his presence with a sigh that stretched to the tips of her toes.

'Why aren't I surprised to find you here,' he stated rather than asked.

'Maybe because you heard me talking on the phone?'

'Was that you whining?'

Jess exhaled another deep breath of air. 'That was me.'

'Sounds like you could use a drink.'

'I just need a good night's sleep.'

'That too can be arranged.' He winked.

Jess rolled her eyes, stood up. 'How's the O'Malley trial coming along?'

'In the bag. Should be wrapped up by the end of the week. And the famous crossbow avenger?'

'Hopefully, it'll be in the jury's hands by Friday.'

'I heard they offered to make a deal.'

'Murder two, ten years in prison? Possibility of parole in four? Some deal.'

'You really think the jury's decision will be any different?'

'I can dream,' Jess told him.

Greg Oliver's sly grin curved toward a genuine smile. 'Come on, I'll drive you home.'

'No, thank you.'

'Don't be silly, Jess. Your car is dead and buried; you're never going to find a cab; you call for one now, you'll be here another hour at least, and I'm offering you a ride to wherever you want to go: Vegas, Miami Beach, Graceland?'

Jess hesitated. She knew he was right — a cab would take for ever to get here at this hour. And after her last excursion, she refused to take the El. She could call Don, even though she hadn't heard from him since she'd turned down his offer to spend Thanksgiving with him and Mother Teresa. No, she couldn't call Don. It wouldn't be right. He was her ex-husband, not her chauffeur.

'All right,' Jess agreed. 'But right home.'

'Whatever you say. I'm here to take the lady wherever she wants to go.'

Greg Oliver's black Porsche pulled to a halt outside Jess's three-story brownstone. He turned the engine off. The loud rock music which had accompanied them on the drive, mercifully making conversation all but impossible, came to an abrupt stop. 'So, this is where you live.'

'This is it.' Jess reached for the door handle, eager to escape the smell of his cologne. 'Thanks, Greg. I really appreciate the ride.'

'Aren't you going to invite me in?'

'No,' Jess said simply.

'Come on, Jess. You wouldn't let me buy you a drink. The least you can do is offer me something for my long trip home.'

'Greg, I'm tired; I have an itchy throat; and I have a date,' she added, the lie settling on her tongue like a bitter pill.

'It's half past six; take two aspirin; and you haven't had a date in fifty years. I'm coming up.' In the next instant, he was out of the car.

Jess threw her head back against the dark leather seat. What had she expected? She opened the car door, lifting both legs to the sidewalk simultaneously, and boosting herself out of the car's low frame with her hands.

'You did that very well,' Greg commented. 'A lot of women don't know how to get out of these cars properly. They throw one leg out at a time.' He laughed. 'Of course, it's a lot more fun that way for those on the sidewalk.'

'Greg,' Jess began, walking quickly ahead of him toward her front door, 'I'm not inviting you up.'

'You can't mean that,' he persisted. 'Come on, Jess. All I want is one little drink. What are you so afraid of? What is it you think I'm going to do?'

Jess stopped at her front door, fishing in her purse for her key. Why hadn't she thought to get it ready earlier?

'You think I'm going to come on to you? Is that it?'

'Isn't it?'

'Shit, Jess, I'm a happily married man. My wife just bought me a Porsche. Why would I come on to a woman who obviously hates my guts?'

'Because she's there?' Jess located her key and unlocked the door.

'You're funny,' he said, pushing the door open and stepping into the foyer. 'That's why I put up with all your crap. Come on, Jess. We're colleagues, and I like to think we could be friends. Is that so awful?' He knelt down suddenly, scooping up some letters that lay on the floor under the mail slot, casually rifling through them. 'Your mail.' He deposited the letters in her waiting hand.

'One drink,' Jess told him, too tired to argue further.

He followed her up the three flights of stairs, like a dog at her heels. 'Trust you to live on the top floor,' he said as they reached the door to her apartment.

She unlocked the door. Greg was inside almost before she was.

'You leave the radio on all day?' he asked, his dark brown eyes quickly assessing, then dismissing, the contents of her living room.

'For the bird.' Jess threw her purse and the mail on the sofa, silently debating whether or not to remove her coat and boots. Although it was her apartment, she didn't want to do anything that might encourage Greg to prolong his visit.

Greg Oliver cautiously approached the bird cage, peered through the bars. 'Male or female?'

'Male.'

'How do you know? You look up its feathers?'

Jess walked to the kitchen, located a few beers toward the

back of the fridge, and uncapped one, returning with it to the living room. Greg had already made himself at home on her sofa, his coat thrown across the dining room table, his tie loosened, his shoes off. 'Don't get comfortable,' Jess warned, handing him the beer.

'Don't get cranky,' he countered, patting the seat beside him. 'Come on, sit down.'

Jess hung her coat in the hall closet, leaving her boots on, and quickly took stock of the situation. She'd allowed a man she could barely tolerate, a man obviously on the make, to drive her home. That man was currently sitting on her living room sofa, drinking the beer she'd handed him herself. She was a smart woman, she thought, hearing herself scoff. How had she managed to put herself in this position?

'Listen, Greg,' she told him, walking back toward the sofa, 'just so we set the record straight: I don't want to create a scene; I don't want to make it impossible for us to work in the same department; I don't want to make your life − or mine − any more difficult than it already is.'

'Is there a point to this speech?' he asked, taking a long sip of his beer directly from the bottle.

Jess realized she'd forgotten to give him a glass. 'The point is that I'm very uncomfortable with your being here.'

'You'd be a lot more comfortable if you'd sit down.' Again, he patted the seat beside him. Jess watched her mail bounce toward the next cushion.

'I have no intention of going to bed with you,' Jess said, deciding the direct approach was probably best.

'Who said anything about going to bed with me?' Greg Oliver managed to looked both surprised and offended.

'Just so we understand each other.'

'We do,' he said, though his eyes said otherwise.

Jess sat down on the arm of the sofa. 'Good, because I'm really not in the mood for anything as tacky as date rape. I know the system sucks and even if I weren't too embarrassed to report it, you'd probably get away with it. So I want you to know that I have a loaded gun in the end table beside my bed, and if you so much as lay a hand on me, I'll blow your fucking head off.' She smiled sweetly, watching Greg Oliver's mouth drop into the vicinity of his knees. 'I just wanted to set the record straight.'

Greg sat for several seconds in stunned silence. 'This is a joke, right?'

'No joke. You want to see the gun?'

'Jesus, Jess, no wonder you haven't had a date in fifty years!'

'Drink up and go home, Greg. Your wife is waiting.' She stood up and walked toward the door.

'Why the hell did you invite me up here?' His voice radiated righteous indignation.

Jess could only shrug. Why was she surprised? 'I'm too old for this,' she muttered.

'You're constipated, is what you are,' Greg told her, reaching for his coat. 'Constipated and uptight and what the boys in the school yard used to call a real tease.'

'I'm a tease?' Jess couldn't disguise the fury in her voice.

'If the shoe fits,' he said, impatiently stuffing his feet inside his Gucci loafers. He thrust the beer bottle in the direction of her chest. Jess grabbed for it, the cold liquid splashing across her white blouse. 'Thanks for the hospitality,' he said, already at the door, slamming it shut after him.

'That was cute,' Jess said, watching her canary flit from perch to perch. 'Real cute.' She rubbed her forehead, wondering at what point exactly she had started losing control of her life. She, who meticulously hung each item of clothing in her closet according to color, who carefully placed her freshly laundered panties beneath those not yet worn, who made lists for everything from important appointments to when it was time to wash her hair, and then carefully crossed each item off that list as each was accomplished. When had she lost control of her life?

She walked back to the sofa, leafed through her mail. The heavy scent of Greg's cologne still clung to the cushion where he'd been sitting. Jess took the letters to the window, opening the window slightly to allow a breath of fresh night air inside. The antique lace curtains swelled in gentle surprise.

179

The mail consisted mostly of bills. A few more requests than usual for donations, not unexpected at this time of year. A notice about Individual Retirement Accounts. Jess looked each over hurriedly, then tossed them aside, concentrating on the stained white envelope that remained. No return address. Her name printed in awkward scrawl, as if by a child. Maybe an early Christmas card from her nephew, Tyler. No stamp. Obviously hand delivered. She tore it open, extricated the single blank sheet of discolored paper from inside, turned it over in her hands, then lifted it gingerly to her nose.

The stale smell of urine mingled with the scent of Greg's cologne.

Jess quickly stuffed the paper back inside the envelope, letting it fall, watching as the breeze carried it, dipping and turning like an expert dance partner, to the floor. It landed silently, effortlessly. She watched as little black specs tumbled from the envelope, like ashes from a lit cigarette, almost disappearing into the hardwood floor.

Slowly, she knelt down, brushing what appeared to be short, wiry black threads into the palm of her hand. Hair, she realized with growing revulsion. Pubic hair. Immediately she swept the hairs back into the envelope.

Pubic hair and urine.

Charming.

There was a knock at her door.

'Oh, great,' she whispered, rising to her feet, closing the window. Pubic hair, urine, and Greg Oliver. What more could a girl want? 'Go home, Greg,' she called sharply.

'Do I have to go home if my name is Adam?'

Jess dropped the offending letter onto her dining room table, not sure she had heard correctly. 'Adam?'

'I see you're wearing your new boots,' he said as she opened the door. 'Were you expecting me?'

'How did you get in?' Jess asked, angry and more than a little embarrassed by how glad she was to see him.

'The front door was open.'

'Open?'

180

He shrugged. 'Maybe Greg didn't close it properly on his way out.' He leaned against the doorway. 'Get your coat.'

'My coat?'

'I thought we could grab a bite to eat, maybe take in a movie.'

'And if I'm too tired?'

'Then tell me to go home, Adam.'

Jess stared at Adam Stohn, his brown hair falling carelessly across his forehead, his posture maddeningly self-assured, his face as unreadable as a suspect in a police line-up. 'I'll get my coat,' she said.

Chapter Fourteen

They went to a revival of *Casablanca*, despite the fact that each had seen the movie several times on television. They sat near the back and, at Jess's insistence, on an aisle. They said little on the short drive to the movie, nothing at all once seated, and only a few words as they walked to the restaurant afterwards. They never touched.

The restaurant, located on North Lincoln Avenue, was small, dark, and noisy, specializing in roast beef. They sat at a tiny table for two near the back, and only after they had given their orders to the waiter, who wore a thin gold earring through his nose, did they make a few tentative stabs at conversation.

'I read somewhere,' Jess said, 'that when they started filming *Casablanca*, they didn't have a finished script, and the actors were never sure who they were or what they were supposed to be doing. Poor Ingrid Bergman apparently kept asking the director who it was she was supposed to be in love with.'

Adam laughed. 'Seems hard to believe.'

Silence. Adam's eyes drifted toward the deep wine-colored walls. Jess grabbed a warm roll from the bread basket, tore it in half, stuffed it into her mouth.

'You have a good appetite,' he commented, although his eyes were still directed elsewhere.

'I've always been a good eater.'

'Mother tell you to eat everything on your plate?'

'She didn't have to.' Jess swallowed, tore off another piece of the roll.

'You must have a high metabolic rate.'

'I find that frequent hysteria helps keep the pounds off,' Jess told him, popping the bread into her mouth, wondering why they were so ill at ease with each other. They'd had better rapport when they were virtual strangers. Instead of relaxing more with one another, each fresh exposure produced only greater stiffness, as if they were succumbing to an emotional rigor mortis. Probably self-inflicted.

'I don't like the word "hysterical",' he said, after a long pause.

'What's not to like?'

'It has such a negative connotation,' he explained. 'I prefer "high energy".'

'You think they're the same thing?'

'Two sides of the same equation.'

Jess thought it over. 'I don't know. All I know is that ever since I was a little girl, people have been telling me to relax.'

'Which only reinforced this negative image you have of yourself as an hysterical person.' He finally looked her square in the face. Jess was startled by the sudden intensity of his gaze. 'When people tell you to relax, it usually means *they're* the ones having problems with your high energy, not you. But they've made *you* feel guilty. Neat, huh?'

'Another of your interesting theories.'

'I'm an interesting guy, remember?' He grabbed a breadstick, bit off its end.

'So what are you doing selling shoes?'

He laughed. 'Does that bother you, that I sell shoes?'

'Why would it bother me?'

'The fact is that I like selling shoes,' he said, pushing back his chair, extending his legs their full length alongside the table. 'I go to work at ten o'clock every morning. I leave at six. Except Thursdays. On Thursdays, I come in at one, go home at nine. No taking my work home with me. No hours of preparation for the next day. No hassles. No responsibility. I come in; I sell shoes; I go home. Vini; vidi; vinci. Or whatever.'

'But it must be very frustrating for you if someone takes up hours of your time, then leaves with only one pair of shoes or, worse, none at all.'

'Doesn't bother me.'

'Aren't you on commission?'

'Part salary, part commission, yes.'

'Then your livelihood is affected.'

He shrugged, straightened up in his chair. 'I'm a good salesman.'

Jess felt her feet warm in her new winter boots. 'Well, I can certainly attest to that.' She was gratified when he smiled. 'What about intellectually?'

He seemed puzzled. 'What do you mean?'

'You're obviously a very smart man, Mr Stohn. It can't be very intellectually stimulating doing what you do all day.'

'On the contrary. I meet all sorts of bright, interesting people, doing what I do all day. They give me all the intellectual stimulation I require at this point in my life.'

'What exactly *is* this point in your life?'

He shrugged, 'Haven't a clue.'

'Where did you go to school?'

'Springfield.'

'I meant college.'

'Who says I went to college?'

'I do.'

He smiled, an obvious strain. 'Loyola University.'

'You graduated from Loyola University, and now you're selling shoes?'

'Is that a crime in Cook County?'

Jess felt her cheeks flush. 'I'm sorry. I must sound very presumptuous.'

'You sound like a prosecutor.'

'Ouch.'

'Tell me about the crossbow killer,' he said, suddenly changing topics.

'What?'

'I've been following your exploits in the paper this past week.'

'And what do you think?'

'I think you're going to win.'

She laughed, an open, happy sound, feeling strangely grateful for his vote of confidence.

'Are you going to ask for the death penalty?'

'If I get the chance,' Jess said simply.

185

'And how is the state killing people these days?'

The waiter appeared with two glasses of red Burgundy.

'Lethal injection.' Jess quickly raised her glass to her lips.

'I think I might let that breathe for a few minutes,' the waiter cautioned.

Jess obediently lowered the glass to the table. She found the unintentional combination of wine breathing and lethal injections ironically compelling.

'So, lethal injections, is it? Disposable needles for disposable people. I guess there's a certain justice in that.'

'I wouldn't waste too many tears on the likes of Terry Wales,' Jess told him.

'No sympathy for the criminal underclass at all?'

'None whatsoever.'

'Let me guess, your parents were lifelong Republicans.'

'Are you opposed to the death penalty?' Jess asked, not sure whether she had the strength to engage in a long debate over the pros and cons of capital punishment.

There was silence.

'I think some people deserve to die,' he said finally.

'You sound like you have someone particular in mind.'

He laughed, though the sound was hollow. 'No, no one.'

'Actually, my father is a registered Democrat,' Jess told him after another long pause.

Adam brought his glass of wine to his nose and inhaled, though he didn't drink. 'That's right, you told me your mother passed away.'

'There's a park near here,' Jess said, speaking almost to herself. 'Oz Park. My mother used to push me there in my carriage when I was a baby.'

'How did your mother die?' he asked.

'Cancer,' Jess said quickly, gulping at her wine.

Adam looked surprised, then dismayed. 'You're lying. Why?'

The glass in Jess's hand started to shake, several drops of red wine spilling over onto the thick white tablecloth, like drops of blood. 'Who says I'm lying?'

'It's written all over your face. If you'd been hooked up to a lie

186

detector, the needle would have been all over the page.'

'You should never take a lie detector test,' Jess told him, steadying her glass on the table with both hands, grateful for the digression.

'I shouldn't?'

'They're way too unreliable. A guilty person can beat them, and an innocent person can fail. If you're innocent and you *fail* the test, it's assumed you're guilty. If you're innocent and you *pass* the test, it still doesn't eliminate you as a suspect. So you have nothing to gain and everything to lose by taking the test — that's if you're innocent.'

'And if I'm guilty?' he asked.

'Then you might as well give it a shot.' Jess patted her lips with her napkin, although they were dry. 'Of course, we're very big on lie detector tests at the prosecutor's office, so you didn't hear any of this from me.'

'Any of what?' Adam asked, and Jess smiled. 'Why won't you tell me what happened to your mother?'

Her smile immediately vanished. 'I thought we had a deal.'

'A deal?'

'No secrets, no lies. Remember?'

'Is there something secret about the way your mother died?'

'Just that it's a long story. I'd rather not get into it.'

'Then we don't get into it.'

The waiter approached with their dinners. 'Careful, the plates are hot,' he cautioned.

'Looks good,' Jess said, surveying the prime cut of rare roast beef, swimming in its own dark juices.

'Butter on your baked potato?' the waiter asked.

'And sour cream,' Jess told him. 'Lots.'

'The same,' Adam agreed, watching as Jess cut into her roast beef. 'I like a woman who eats,' he said, and laughed.

They ate for several minutes in silence.

'What was your wife like?' Jess asked, digging into her baked potato.

'Always on a diet.'

'Was she overweight?'

'I didn't think so.' He cut a large piece of meat, stuffed it into his mouth. 'Of course, what I thought didn't count for very much.'

'Doesn't sound like you're on very friendly terms.'

'One of the main reasons we got divorced.'

'I'm friends with my ex-husband,' Jess offered.

Adam looked skeptical.

'We are. Very good friends, as a matter of fact.'

'Is this the famous Greg? As in "Go home, Greg"?'

Jess laughed. 'No. Greg Oliver is a fellow prosecutor. He gave me a ride home.'

'You don't drive?'

'My car had a slight accident.'

A hint of worry fell across Adam's eyes.

'I wasn't in it at the time.'

He looked relieved. 'Well, that's good. What kind of accident?'

Jess shook her head. 'I'd rather not talk about it.'

'We're rapidly running out of things to talk about,' he said.

'What do you mean?'

'Well, you don't want to talk about your car or your mother or your sister or your brother-in-law, and I can't remember, was your father off limits as well?'

'I get the point.'

'Let's see. The ex-husband was relatively safe. Maybe we should stick with him. What's his name?'

'Don. Don Shaw.'

'And he's a lawyer, and you're great buddies.'

'We're friends.'

'So, why the divorce?'

'It's complicated.'

'And you'd rather not talk about it?'

'Why did *you* get divorced?' Jess asked in return.

'Equally complicated.'

'What's her name?'

'Susan.'

'And she's remarried and a decorator and she lives in Springfield.'

188

'And we're starting to cover familiar territory.' He paused. 'Is this it? We get no further than surfaces?'

'You have something against surfaces? I thought that's why you liked selling shoes.'

'Surfaces it is. So, tell me, Jess Koster, what's your lucky number?'

Jess laughed, took another bite of her roast beef, chewed it well.

'I'm serious,' Adam said. 'If we're going to stick with surfaces, I want them all covered. Lucky number?'

'I don't think I have one.'

'Pick a number from one to ten.'

'All right — four,' she said impulsively.

'Why four?'

Jess giggled, feeling like a small child. 'I guess because it's my nephew's favorite number. He likes it because it's Big Bird's favorite. Big Bird is a character on *Sesame Street*.'

'I know who Big Bird is.'

'Shoe salesmen watch *Sesame Street*?'

'Shoe salesmen are an unpredictable lot. Favorite color?'

'I've never really given it much thought.'

'Think about it now.'

Jess lowered her fork to her plate, looked around the dark room for clues. 'I'm not sure. Grey, I guess.'

'Grey?' He looked stunned.

'Something wrong with grey?'

'Jess, nobody's favorite color is grey!'

'Oh? Well, it's mine. And yours?'

'Red.'

'I'm not surprised.'

'Why not? Why aren't you surprised?'

'Well, red's a strong color. Forceful. Dynamic. Outgoing.'

'And you think that describes my personality?'

'Doesn't it?'

'Do you think grey describes yours?'

'This is getting more complicated than my divorce,' Jess said, and they both laughed.

'What about favorite song?'

'I don't have one. Honestly.'

'Nothing that you turn up the volume for when it comes on the radio?'

'Well, I like that aria from the opera *Turandot*. You know, the one where the tenor is out in the garden by himself.'

'I'm afraid I'm very ignorant when it comes to opera.'

'Knows *Sesame Street*, but not opera,' Jess mused aloud. 'And what else do you like?'

'I like my job,' she told him, aware how adept he was at turning the discussion away from himself. 'And I like to read when I have the time.'

'What do you like to read?'

'Novels.'

'What kind?'

'Murder mysteries mostly. Agatha Christie, Ed McBain, people like that.'

'What else do you like to do?'

'I like jigsaw puzzles. And I like to take long walks by the water. And I like to buy shoes.'

'For which I am eternally grateful,' he conceded, laughter in his eyes. 'And you like movies.'

'And I like movies.'

'And you like an aisle seat.'

'Yes.'

'Why?'

'Why?' Jess repeated, trying to hide her sudden discomfort. 'Why does anybody like an aisle seat? More room, I guess.'

'The needle just went off the page again,' Adam said.

'What?'

'The lie detector. You failed.'

'Why would I lie about liking an aisle seat?'

'You didn't lie about liking an aisle seat; you lied about why you like it. And I don't know why you'd lie. You tell me.'

'This is silly.'

'So aisle seats join the list of forbidden topics.'

'There's nothing to say about them.'

'Tell me why you insisted that you sit on an aisle.'

'I didn't insist.'

His mouth formed a boyish pout. 'Did too.'

'Did not.'

They both laughed, although a certain amount of tension remained.

'I don't think I like being called a liar,' Jess said, fussing with the napkin on her lap, watching it fall to the floor.

'I really wasn't trying to insult you.'

'A lawyer's good word, after all, is the only currency she has.' Jess bent over to retrieve her napkin.

'You're not in court now, Jess,' Adam told her. 'And you're not on trial. I'm sorry if I've overstepped in any way.'

'If I tell you,' Jess said suddenly, surprising them both, 'you'll think I'm a total wacko.'

'I already think you're a total wacko,' Adam said. 'I mean, come on, Jess, anybody who's favorite color is grey . . .'

'I was afraid I'd be sick,' Jess said.

'Sick? As in throw up?'

'I know it sounds silly.'

'Were you feeling queasy?'

'No. I felt fine.'

'But you were afraid you'd throw up if you didn't sit on the aisle?'

'Don't ask me why.'

'Have you *ever* thrown up when you didn't have an aisle seat?' he asked, logically.

'No,' she admitted.

'Then why think you might start now?'

He waited. She said nothing.

'Do I make you that nervous?'

'You don't make me nervous at all,' she lied, then immediately backtracked. 'Well, no, actually, you do make me a little nervous, but you had nothing to do with my thinking I might throw up.'

'I don't understand. '

'Neither do I. Can we talk about something else?' She lowered her head guiltily, another topic eliminated. 'It's just that it doesn't really seem like the right thing to be discussing when we're trying to eat dinner.'

'Let me see if I have this straight,' he said, ignoring her plea. 'You like an aisle seat because you think if you sit, say, in the middle of the theater, you might throw up, even though you've never thrown up in a movie theater before. Right?'

'Right.'

'How long have you had this phobia?'

'Who said I have a phobia?'

'What would you call it?'

'Define phobia,' she instructed.

'An irrational fear,' he suggested. 'A fear that has no basis in reality.'

Jess listened, absorbing his words like a sponge. 'Okay, I have a phobia.'

'What other phobias do you have — claustro, agora, arachna?'

She shook her head. 'None.'

'Other people are afraid of heights or spiders; you're afraid of throwing up in a movie theater if you don't have an aisle seat.'

'I know it's ridiculous.'

'It isn't ridiculous at all.'

'It isn't?'

'It's just not the whole story.'

'Still think I'm holding out on you?' Jess asked, hearing the quiver in her voice.

'What are you really afraid of, Jess?'

Jess pushed away her plate, fighting the urge to flee, her appetite gone. She forced herself to stay in her seat. 'I get these panic attacks,' she said quietly, after a long pause. 'I used to get them a lot a number of years ago. Eventually, they went away. A little while ago, they started coming back.'

'Any reason?'

'Could be any number of things,' Jess said, wondering whether her half-truth would send the needle of the invisible lie detector machine to which she was connected into orbit. 'My heart starts to pound. I get short of breath. I can't move. I feel

192

sick to my stomach. I try to fight it.'

'Why?'

'Why? What do you mean?'

'Why fight it? Does it do any good?'

Jess conceded that it didn't. 'What am I *supposed* to do?'

'Why not just go with the attacks?'

'Go with them? I don't understand.'

'It's simple. Instead of wasting all that energy trying to fight the anxiety, why not just give in to it? Go with the flow, as they say. Look, you're in the theater,' he continued, obviously sensing her confusion, 'and you feel one of these attacks coming on, instead of holding your breath or counting to ten or jumping up from your seat, whatever it is you do, just go with the panic, give in to the feeling. What's the worst that can happen?'

'I'll be sick.'

'So, you'll be sick.'

'What?'

'You'll throw up. So what?'

'I hate throwing up.'

'That's not what you're afraid of.'

'It isn't?'

'No.'

Jess looked around impatiently. 'You're right. Actually what I'm afraid of is not getting any work done tonight if I stay out much longer. I'm afraid I won't get enough sleep if I stay out too late, and I'll come down with this cold I've been fighting, and be a disaster in court tomorrow. I'm afraid I'll lose this case and a cold-blooded killer will walk away with less than five years in jail. I'm afraid I really have to get going.' She checked her watch for emphasis, half rose in her seat. Once again, her napkin fell to the floor.

'I think you're afraid of death,' Adam said.

Jess froze. 'What?'

'I think what you're afraid of is death,' he repeated as she slowly lowered herself back into her seat. 'That's all most phobias come down to, in the end. A fear of death.' He paused. 'And, in your case, the fear is probably justifiable.'

'What do you mean?' How many times tonight had she asked that question?

'Well, I imagine you receive your fair share of threats from people you've put away. You probably get hate mail, obscene phone calls, standard stuff. You deal with death every day. With brutality and murder and man's inhumanity to man.'

'More usually man's inhumanity to women,' Jess qualified, wondering how he knew about all this 'standard stuff'.

'It's only natural for you to be afraid.'

Jess reached down to scoop up her napkin, tossing it carelessly over her plate, like a sheet over a corpse, she thought, watching the brown juices seep through the white cloth. 'Maybe you're right. Maybe that's what it all boils down to.'

Adam smiled. 'So, I make you nervous, do I?'

'A little,' she said. 'Actually, a lot.'

'Why?'

'Because I don't know what you're thinking,' she said truthfully.

His smile turned shy, circumspect. 'Isn't it more interesting that way?'

Jess said nothing. 'I really should get going,' she said finally. 'I have a lot to do to get ready for tomorrow. I probably shouldn't have gone out at all tonight.' Why was she babbling?

'I'll take you home,' he said. But all Jess could hear was, 'I think what you're afraid of is death.'

Chapter Fifteen

The following Saturday Jess enrolled in a self-defense course.

The week had been a strange one. Tuesday saw the wrap-up of the prosecution's case against Terry Wales. A succession of witnesses — police officers, medical authorities, psychologists, eyewitnesses, friends and relatives of the deceased — had all testified. They had proved beyond a reasonable doubt that Terry Wales had murdered his wife. The only question remaining, the stubborn question that had been there from the beginning, was one of degree. Would Terry Wales be able to convince the jury that it had all been a tragic mistake?

He'd certainly made a successful start. Terry Wales had taken the stand Wednesday morning in his own defense, and answered his lawyer's careful questions slowly and thoughtfully. Yes, he had a temper. Yes, he and his wife had engaged in occasionally violent arguments. Yes, he had once broken her nose, and blackened her eyes. And yes, he had threatened to kill her if she tried to leave him.

But no, he never really meant it. No, he never meant to hurt her. No, he was not some unfeeling, cold-blooded killer.

He loved his wife, he'd said, his pale blue eyes focused on the jurors. He'd always loved her. Even when she verbally abused him in front of his friends. Even when she flew at him from across the room, determined to scratch his eyes out, forcing him to fight back in self-defense. Even when she threatened to take him for everything he had. Even when she threatened to turn his own children against him.

He'd only meant to scare her when he fired that arrow into the busy intersection. He'd had no idea his aim would prove so deadly. If he'd wanted to kill her, he would have used a gun. He had several, was an expert shot, whereas he hadn't fired a bow and arrow since he was a kid at camp.

Terry Wales finished the day in tears, his voice hoarse, his skin mottled and pale. His lawyer had to help him from the stand.

Jess and her two partners had stayed up half that night reviewing the testimony of each witness, poring over the police reports, searching for anything they might have overlooked, anything that might help in Jess's cross-examination of Terry Wales the next morning. After Neil and Barbara went home, sneezing and wheezing their way down the hall, Jess had stayed up the rest of the night, returning to her apartment at six the next morning only to shower and change her clothes before heading right back to her office.

She appeared in court on Thursday to find Judge Harris recessing the case till the following Monday. The defendant, it appeared, wasn't feeling too well, and the defense had requested a postponement of several days. Judge Harris coughed his agreement, and court was dismissed. Jess spent most of the day talking to police detectives, encouraging them to use this delay to ferret out additional evidence that might benefit the prosecution's case.

Friday saw the arrival of her annual Christmas card from the Federal Penitentiary. WISHING YOU ALL THE BEST FOR THE HOLIDAY SEASON, it read in letters of bright gold decorated with sprigs of holly. *Thinking of you*, it said at the bottom, as if from a close friend, followed by the simple signature, *Jack*.

Jack had murdered his girlfriend in a drunken argument over where he'd put his car keys. Jess had sent him to prison for twelve years. Jack swore he'd come visit her when he got out, thank her in person for her generosity.

Thinking of you. Thinking of you.

Jess had spent the rest of Friday researching self-defense classes in the city, found one on Clybourn Avenue, not too far from where she lived and right on a subway line. Two hours on Saturday afternoon for three consecutive weeks, the delicate Asian voice on the telephone informed her. One hundred and eighty dollars for the course. Something called Wen-Do. She'd be there, Jess told the woman, recalling what Adam had said. Was it really death she was afraid of? she wondered, unwittingly conjuring up her mother's face, hearing her mother assure her she would be all right.

Thinking of you. Thinking of you.

And then it was Saturday, cloudless, sunny and cold.

The classes were held in an old two-storey building. WEN-DO, the sign proclaimed in black letters almost as large as the structure itself.

'Please to give me your coat, then please to put this on and please to go inside,' the young Oriental woman behind the reception counter instructed, as Jess exchanged her long winter coat for a short, dark blue cotton robe and matching sash. Jess was wearing a loose sweatshirt and pants, as she had been advised over the telephone. They were grey, she noted, suppressing a smile, her favorite color. 'You are early,' the young woman giggled, her high black ponytail bouncing with the gentle movement of her shoulders. 'Nobody else here yet.'

Jess smiled and half bowed, not sure of the proper protocol. The young woman waved her toward a curtain to her right, and Jess, bowing again, stepped through.

The room she stepped into was twice as long as it was wide, and empty except for a series of dark green mats stacked in one corner of the well-scuffed wood-planked floor. Jess caught her reflection in the wall of mirrors that ran along the left side of the room, lending it a depth it didn't have. She looked ridiculous, she thought, a cultural hybrid in her American sweats and Oriental robe. She shrugged, pulling back her hair and securing it with a wide elastic band.

What was she doing here? What exactly was it she hoped to learn? Did she really think she could protect herself from . . . from what? From the elements? From the inevitable?

She heard a shuffle behind her, turned to see a woman with a noticeable limp emerge from between the green flowered curtains. 'Hi,' said the woman, who was probably the same age as Jess. 'I'm Vasiliki. Call me Vas, it's easier.'

197

'Jess Koster,' Jess said, stepping forward to shake the woman's hand. 'Vasiliki is a very interesting name.'

'It's Greek,' the woman said, checking out her reflection in the mirrored wall. She was tall and big-boned, her dark hair framing her olive complexion and ending bluntly at her square jaw. Aside from her limp, she looked quite formidable. 'I was attacked over a year ago by a gang of thirteen-year-old boys. Thirteen years old! Can you believe it?' Her tone indicated that she couldn't. 'They were after my purse. I said, "Go ahead, take it. There's nothing in it." So they took it, and when they saw I only had ten dollars, 'cause I never carry around much cash, they started beating me, shoved me to the ground, kicked me so hard, they broke my knee cap. I'm lucky to be walking at all. I decided as soon as my therapy was over, I was enrolling in a self-defense course. Next time anybody comes at me, I'm going to be ready.' She laughed bitterly. 'Of course, it's a bit like locking the barn door after the horse has escaped.' She tied an extra knot in the sash at her waist.

Jess shook her head. Juvenile crime had reached epidemic proportions in the city of Chicago. A whole new building was being erected to deal with these violent young offenders. As if a building could do any good.

'What about you? What brought you here?' Vas was asking.

Fear of the unknown, fear of the known, Jess answered silently. 'I'm not sure,' she said out loud. 'I just thought it was probably a good idea that I learn how to defend myself.'

'Well, you're smart. I tell you, it isn't easy being a woman these days.'

Jess nodded, wishing there was a place to sit down.

Again the curtains parted, and two black women stepped inside, their eyes warily scanning the room.

'I'm Vasiliki. Call me Vas,' Vas stated, nodding in their direction. 'This is Jess.'

'Maryellen,' the older and lighter-skinned of the two women said. 'This is my daughter, Ayisha.'

Jess estimated Ayisha's age as seventeen, her mother closer to forty. Both were very pretty, although a faded purple bruise was visible under the mother's right eye.

'I think it's neat, you taking this course together,' Vas was saying as the curtains parted again and another woman, short, plump and middle-aged, her hair noticeably salted with grey, entered the room, tugging nervously at her blue robe. 'Vasiliki, call me Vas,' Vas was already saying. 'This is Jess, Maryellen, and Ayisha.'

'Catarina Santos,' the woman said, her voice tentative, as if she wasn't sure.

'Well, we're a regular little United Nations,' Vas quipped.

'Here to learn the ancient Oriental art of Wen-Do,' Jess added.

'Oh, there's nothing ancient about it,' Vas corrected. 'Wen-Do was developed only twenty years ago by a couple in, of all places, Toronto, Canada. Can you beat that?'

'We're learning a martial arts system developed in Canada?' Jess asked incredulously.

'Apparently it combines physical techniques drawn from both karate and aikido. Anybody know what aikido is?' Vas asked. Nobody did.

'Wen-Do's guiding ideas are awareness, avoidance and action,' Vas continued, then laughed self-consciously. 'I memorized the brochure.'

'I'm all for action,' Ayisha mumbled as Catarina shrank back against the mirrored wall.

Once more the curtains parted and a young man with a dark pompadour and a healthy strut approached the loose circle of women. He was short and the muscles of his well-sculpted arms could be discerned even beneath his blue robe. His face was well scrubbed and boyish, a small scar, probably the result of a childhood case of chicken pox, sat in the bridge of his nose beside his right eyebrow. 'Good afternoon,' he said, speaking clearly from his diaphragm. 'I'm Dominic, your instructor.'

'Funny,' Vas whispered to Jess, 'he doesn't look Wen-Doish.'

'How many of you think you could fend off an attacker?' he asked, hands on his hips, chin thrust forward.

The women hung back, said nothing.

199

Dominic slowly sauntered toward Maryellen and her daughter, Ayisha. 'What about you, Mama? Think you could break an attacker's nose if he went after your daughter?'

'He'd be lucky to get away with his head still attached,' Maryellen said forcefully.

'Well, the experience of Wen-Do,' he said, 'is realizing that you are as valuable as any child in your life that you love. Valuable,' he continued, pausing carefully for effect, 'but not vulnerable. At least not as vulnerable as before. You may be weaker than your potential attackers,' he said, backing away from Maryellen and addressing each of the women in turn, 'but you are not all-weak and your attackers are not all-powerful. It's important that you don't think of your attackers as huge, impenetrable hulks, but think of them instead as a collection of vulnerable targets. And remember,' he said, looking directly at Jess, 'anger works a lot better than pleading in most cases. So don't be afraid to get angry.'

Jess felt her knees trembling, was grateful when he turned away, concentrated on someone else. Jess surveyed the faces of the different women, the mini United Nations, as Vas had accurately described them, so representative of all the changes that had occurred in the city in the last twenty years. So different from the Chicago of her childhood, she thought, escaping momentarily into the lily whiteness of her past, being pulled back into the present by the force of Dominic's voice.

'You have to learn to trust your sense of danger,' he was saying. 'Even if you're not exactly sure what you're afraid of, even if you don't know what's making you nervous, even if you're afraid of embarrassing a man who may or may not be a threat to you, the best thing you can do is remove yourself from the situation as quickly as you can. Denial can be very costly. Trust your instincts,' he said. 'And get out as fast as you can.'

If you can, Jess added silently.

'Running away is what works best most often for women,' Dominic concluded simply. 'Okay, line up.'

The women exchanged nervous glances, shuffled warily into a straight line. 'Up against the wall, motherfuckers,' Vas

200

whispered to Jess, then giggled like a small child.

'Give yourself plenty of room. That's right. Spread out a little bit. We're gonna be moving around a lot here in a few minutes. Roll your shoulders back. Loosen up. That's right. Swing your arms. Get nice and relaxed.'

Jess swung her arms from side to side and up and down. She rotated her shoulders backwards, then forwards. She rolled her neck from side to side, heard it crack.

'Don't forget to breathe,' Dominic instructed, and Jess gratefully expelled a deep breath of air. 'Okay, straighten up. Now pay close attention. The first line of defense is called *kiyi*.'

'Did he say kiwi?' Vas asked, and Jess had to bite down on her tongue to keep from laughing.

'*Kiyi* is a great yell, a roar from the diaphragm. *Hohh!*' he shouted, and the women flinched. '*Hohh!*' he yelled again. '*Hohh!*'

Ho, ho, ho, Jess thought.

'The purpose of *kiyi*,' he explained, 'is to wipe out the picture the attacker has of you as being quiet and vulnerable. It also helps ensure that you don't freeze up with fear. *Hohh!*' he shouted yet again, and the women jumped back in alarm. 'Also, it has the element of surprise. Surprise can be a very useful weapon.' He smiled. 'Now, you try it.'

Nobody moved. After several seconds, Ayisha and then Vas started to giggle. Jess wasn't sure whether she wanted to laugh or cry. How could she trust her instincts, she wondered, when she wasn't even sure what her instincts were.

'Let's hear it!' Dominic encouraged. '*Hohh!*'

Another second of silence, then a weak, tentative 'Hohh!' from Maryellen.

'Not "hohh", *hohh!*' Dominic emphasized. 'This is not the time and place to be polite. We want to scare our attacker, not encourage him. Now, come on, let me hear you. *Hohh!*'

'Hohh!' Jess ventured meekly, feeling totally ridiculous. Similar sad sounds echoed throughout the room.

'Come on!' Dominic urged, clenching his fists for emphasis. 'You're women now, not ladies. Let me hear you get angry. Let me hear you make a lot of noise. I know you can do it. I was raised with four sisters. Don't tell me you don't know how to yell.' He approached Maryellen. 'Come on, Mama. There's a man attacking your daughter.'

'*Hohh!*' screamed Maryellen.

'That's more like it.'

'*Hohh!*' Maryellen continued. '*Hohh! Hohh!*' She smiled. 'Hey, I'm starting to like this.'

'Feels good to assert yourself, doesn't it?' Dominic asked, and Maryellen nodded. 'What about the rest of you? Let's hear you put that would-be attacker on the alert.'

'Hohh!' the voices began, still tentative, then louder, gaining strength, '*Hohh! Hohh!*'

Jess tried to join in, but even when she opened her mouth, no sound emerged. What was the matter with her? Since when had she been afraid of asserting herself?

Think anger, she told herself. Think about your car. Think about Terry Wales. Think about Erica Barnowski. Think about Greg Oliver. Think about your brother-in-law. Think about Connie DeVuono. Think about Rick Ferguson.

Think about your mother.

'*Hohh!*' Jess screamed into the suddenly silent room. '*Hohh!*'

'Perfection,' Dominic enthused, clapping his hands. 'I knew you had it in you.'

'Well done,' Vas told her, squeezing her hand.

'Now, if *kiyi* doesn't frighten off a potential attacker, you've got to learn to use whatever weapons are around, starting with your hands, your feet, elbows, shoulders, fingernails. Fingernails are good, so any of you who bite your nails, stop right now. The eyes, ears and nose are among the targets.' Dominic made his fist into a hook, his fingers like talons. 'Eagle claws through the attacker's eyes,' he said, demonstrating. 'Zipper punch to the nose, using those bony knuckles. Hammer fist down on the nose.' Again he illustrated. The women watched with something approaching awe. 'I'm gonna show you how to do all that later,' he told them. 'Believe me, it's not hard. The important thing is not to expect that you're going to be able to match your force against your attacker's, which just isn't going to happen. Instead, what you've got to do is learn to use the attacker's force against him.'

'I don't understand,' Jess said, surprised she had spoken.

'Good. Speak up loud and clear when you don't understand something. Speak up loud and clear even when you do.' He smiled. 'And don't forget to breathe.'

Jess gratefully expelled another deep breath of air.

'That's right, from the diaphragm. You gotta remember to breathe or you're gonna run out of steam pretty fast. Anybody here who smokes, you should give it up. Breathe deeply instead. That's all you're really doing when you smoke anyway. Breathing deeply in and out. You just gotta learn to do it without the cigarette. What is it you don't understand?' he asked Jess, returning abruptly to her question.

'You said we have to use the attacker's force against him. I don't understand what you mean.'

'Okay, let me explain.' He paused for a minute, his eyes narrowing in thought. 'Use the image of circularity,' he began, drawing a circle in the air with his index finger. 'If someone pulls you toward him, instead of resisting and pulling back, which is what we tend to do in that sort of situation, use that attacker's force to be pulled into his body, and then strike when you get there.'

He grabbed Jess's arm. Instinctively, she pulled back.

'No,' he said. 'Exactly wrong.'

'But you told us to trust our instincts.'

'Trust your instincts when they *warn* you of danger. Remember that recognizing danger and getting away as fast as you can always comes first. But when you're already *in* danger, then it's a different story. Your instincts can mislead you. You have to educate your instincts. Now, come here, I'm going to use you to illustrate what I mean.'

Jess reluctantly stepped forward.

'I'm going to pull you toward me, and I want you to resist, the way you did before.' Dominic suddenly lunged forward, his hand clamping down on Jess's wrist, pulling her toward him.

Her adrenaline immediately in overdrive, Jess pulled back, trying to steady her feet against the wood floor, to gain some traction. She was no pushover, she decided, feeling the tugging at her arm, the pain shooting its way to her elbow. She pulled back harder, her breathing becoming shallow.

In the next instant, she was on the floor and Dominic was looming over her.

'What happened?' she panted, not sure how she had gone from two feet on the floor to flat on her back in less than a second.

Dominic helped her to her feet. 'Now, let's try it the other way. Don't fight me. Don't put up any resistance. Let my force pull you close to me. Then use that momentum to push me away.'

Again Jess braced herself. Again Dominic's hand encircled her wrist. But this time, instead of resisting, instead of struggling, she allowed herself to be pulled toward him. Only when she felt their bodies connect did she suddenly use the full force of her weight to push into him, throwing him off balance, and sending him upended to the floor.

'Way to go, Jess!' Vas cheered.

'That's it, girl, you did it,' chimed in Maryellen.

'Awesome,' Ayisha agreed.

Catarina nodded shyly.

Dominic slowly rose to his feet. 'I think you understand now,' he said, dusting himself off.

Jess smiled. '*Hohh!*' she said.

'Hohh, hohh, hohh!' Jess whispered to herself, emerging from the subway near the Magnificent Mile. She felt stronger than she had in weeks, maybe months. Empowered. Good about herself. 'Hohh!' she laughed, drawing her coat tight around her, walking toward Michigan Avenue.

Who said she had to wait for Adam to phone her? This was the nineties, after all. Women didn't sit around waiting for guys to call. They picked up the phone and did the dialing themselves. Besides, it was Saturday, she had no plans for the evening, and

Adam would probably be delighted to see her take the initiative. 'Hohh!' she said, more loudly than she had intended, catching the nervous attention of a passer-by.

The woman picked up her speed. That's right, lady, Jess told her silently. Your instincts tell you danger, get away fast. 'Hohh!' she said again, almost singing, approaching the front window of Shoe-Inn and peering inside.

'Is Adam Stohn here today?' she asked the salesman in the ill-fitting toupee who ran to greet her as soon as she stepped through the front door.

The salesman's eyes narrowed until they all but disappeared. Did he remember her from their last encounter?

'He's with a customer.' His chin directed Jess to the rear of the store.

Adam was standing beside a young woman, his hands full of shoes, her face full of laughter. Jess approached quietly, not wanting to disturb him in the middle of a sale.

'So, you don't like any of these shoes. Well, let me see. Can I interest you in a glass of water instead?' Adam was saying.

The young woman laughed, her long blond hair falling across her carefully rouged cheek as she shook her head.

'How about a candy?'

Jess watched Adam reach into his jacket pocket for a red- and white-striped mint, saw the young woman consider it before refusing the offer.

'How about a joke? You look like a woman who appreciates a good joke.'

Jess felt tears sting her eyes, and quickly backed away, deciding not to hang around for the punch line. She was the joke, after all.

'Did you find him?' the salesman with the ill-fitting toupee asked as she strode toward the front of the store.

'I'll speak to him later. Thank you,' Jess said, wondering what she was thanking him for. Women were so quick to say thank you, to be grateful. 'I'm sorry,' she said, stepping out of another woman's way, the other woman also apologizing. And what are we all so sorry about?

205

Damn it, she thought, feeling embarrassed and confused. What had possessed her to come here? Why did she think that just because she was feeling good and wanted to share that feeling with somebody, that Adam would be interested in fulfilling that role? So what if she felt empowered? So what if she'd learned to turn her fist into an eagle's claw? Who cared whether she could execute a zipper punch to the nose? Why would he be interested in *kiyi*? He was interested in selling shoes, in earning his commission. Why had she thought she was any different from any of the other hundreds of women whose feet he fondled in any given week? And why was she so disappointed?

'Hohh!' she said, standing alone in front of the store. But her heart wasn't in it, and the word fell to the sidewalk, to be trampled on by a parade of passing feet.

'Well, hi, stranger,' Don was saying, his voice an oasis, even over the phone. 'This is a pleasant surprise. I was beginning to think you were still mad at me.'

'Why would I be mad at you?' Jess pulled the door of the public phone booth closed.

'You tell me. All I know is you've barely said two words to me since our little disagreement at the police station.'

'Sure I have.'

'All right, maybe two words, both of them no: when I asked you over for Thanksgiving, and another time when I invited you out for a steak dinner.'

'Which is exactly why I'm calling,' Jess began, grateful to have been handed such a convenient segue. 'I'm downtown, and I haven't had a good steak in ages, and I thought maybe if you weren't doing anything tonight . . .' Her voice trailed off, leaving only silence. 'You're busy,' Jess said quickly.

'God, Jess,' Don said, his voice an apology, 'any other time, you know I'd jump at the chance, but—'

'But it's Saturday night and Mother Teresa is waiting.'

Another silence. 'Actually Trish is out of town this weekend,'

206

Don said easily. 'So I accepted an offer to have dinner over at John McMaster's. You remember John.'

'Of course.' John McMaster was one of Don's partners. 'Say hello for me.'

'I'd invite you—'

'I wouldn't go.'

'But you wouldn't go.'

Jess laughed, finding it suddenly hard to catch her breath. Did she really expect her ex-husband to be waiting by the phone every time she felt lonely or depressed and in need of a little friendly support?

'I have a great idea,' he was saying.

'What's your great idea?' Jess felt she was choking, that no air was reaching her lungs. She pulled at the folding door of the phone booth, but it refused to open.

'Why don't I drop over tomorrow morning with some bagels and cream cheese, and you can make me some coffee and tell me who died.'

Jess struggled with the door to the phone booth, numbness teasing at her fingers. She couldn't breathe. If she didn't get out of this damn phone booth soon, she would faint, possibly suffocate. She had to get out. She had to get some air.

'Jess? Jess, are you there? That was a joke. Don't you read the obituaries any more?'

'I really have to go now, Don.' Jess pounded against the door with her fist.

'How does ten a.m. sound?'

'Fine. Sounds great.'

'See you tomorrow morning.'

Jess dropped the phone, letting it dangle from its long cord, watching it sway back and forth as if the victim of a lynching, all the while pushing and pulling at the door of the phone booth in a desperate effort to free herself. 'Goddamn it, let me out of here!' she screamed.

Suddenly the door opened. A grey-haired old lady, not more than five feet tall, stood on the other side, her deeply veined hands clutching the side of the door. 'These things can be tricky sometimes,' she said with an indulgent smile before shuffling on down the street.

Jess shot out of the phone booth, sweat streaming down her face, despite the near freezing temperatures. 'How could I do that?' she whispered into her numbed hands. 'I forgot everything I learned today. How am I going to defend myself against anybody when I can't even get out of a goddamn phone booth?'

It was several minutes before the numbness left her hands, and she was able to hail a cab to take her home.

Chapter Sixteen

Dinner consisted of Stouffer's macaroni and cheese, two pieces of Pepperidge Farm frozen vanilla cake with strawberry icing, and a large bottle of Coca-Cola. 'Nothing like a good dinner,' Jess muttered to her canary as she returned her empty plates to the kitchen, depositing them in the sink, too tired to stack them in the dishwasher.

She shuffled back into the living room, her slippered feet too weary to lift themselves off the floor, reminding Jess of the old woman who had freed her from the phone booth that afternoon. 'She'd probably do better against an attacker than I would,' Jess said, debating whether to continue with the self-defense course for the rest of its two-week duration. 'I might as well. I paid for it,' she conceded, turning off her stereo and covering the bird's cage for the night. She turned off the light and shuffled toward her bedroom, pulling off her grey sweatshirt as she walked, and discarding it and her sweatpants in the laundry hamper, although she had no idea when she'd actually get around to washing them. She'd made it a habit lately to buy only clothes whose labels proclaimed DRY CLEAN ONLY. More expensive, maybe, but much less time-consuming.

She pulled a long, pink- and white-flowered flannelette nightgown over her head, then carefully laid out her clothes for the following day: a pair of blue jeans, a red turtleneck sweater, heavy red socks, and fresh underwear. Just waiting for her to climb inside. Her sneakers sat on the floor by the chair, ready for her to step into. All was right with the world, she thought, slouching toward the bathroom to wash her face and brush her teeth. She couldn't wait to get into bed.

It was barely nine o'clock, she realized with some surprise as she turned off the bedroom lamp and crawled in between the covers. She should probably be doing some work in preparation for the resumption of the Terry Wales trial on Monday, but her eyes were already closing. It had been a long day, and an exhausting one. She'd been disappointed by two men in one afternoon. She'd found power, only to lose it. That was enough to wear anybody out.

'Good night, Moon,' she whispered, recalling the children's book of that name she'd bought for her nephew, listening to vague noises from the apartment downstairs. Walter must be having another party, Jess thought, as she drifted off to sleep.

In her dream, she was facing a jury wearing only her pink and white flannelette night-gown and her tatty pink slippers.

'We love your pyjamas,' one of the female jurors told her, reaching across the jury box to stroke the soft arm of Jess's night-gown. But her hand was an eagle's claw and it ripped through the material as easily as sharp scissors through paper, drawing blood.

'Let me take care of that,' Don offered, vaulting over the defense table and reaching for her bleeding arm.

Jess allowed him to draw her close, feeling their bodies connect, then suddenly pushed her full weight against him, throwing him off balance and to the floor.

Judge Harris banged his displeasure with his gavel. 'Order in the court,' he demanded in Adam Stohn's voice. 'Order in the court.' Then, 'Jess, are you there? Jess? Jess?'

Jess sat up in bed, not fully awake, foolishly grateful to find herself in her bedroom and not in court. Trust me, she thought, clutching at pieces of her dream even as the dream evaporated, to rebuff the one person trying to help.

'Jess,' the voice from her dream continued, 'Jess, are you there?'

The banging of the gavel continued. Only not a gavel, but someone knocking on the door to her apartment, Jess realized, coming fully awake and reaching across her bed to the night table. She pulled open the drawer and reached inside for her gun, alarmed, even as she lifted the gun into her hands, at how easily she did so.

'Who's there?' she called back, sliding into her slippers and steadying the gun as she walked to the door, the floor vibrating beneath her feet from the loud music below.

'It's Adam,' came the response from the other side.

'What are you doing here?' Jess asked without opening the door.

'I wanted to see you.'

'Haven't you ever heard of the telephone?'

'I've seen enough telephones,' he said, and laughed. 'I wanted to see you. It was an impulse thing.'

'How did you get in the house?'

'The front door was open. There's quite a party going on downstairs. Look, I really hate yelling through the door this way. Are you going to let me in?'

'It's late.'

'Jess, if you've got someone else there . . .'

She opened the door. 'There's no one else here.' Jess motioned him inside with a wave of her gun.

'Jesus Christ, is that thing real?'

Jess nodded, thinking he looked wonderful, wondering if she looked as ridiculous as she felt in her pink- and white-flowered flannelette night-gown, fuzzy pink slippers and Smith & Wesson revolver. 'I'm wary of late-night visitors,' she told him.

'Late? Jess, it's ten-thirty.'

'Ten-thirty?'

'You could get a peephole for that door, you know. Or a chain.' He stared nervously at the gun. 'Think you could put that away now?' He took off his jacket, threw it over the arm of the sofa, as if, now that he was here, he intended to stay, and stood before her in a rumpled white sweater and pressed black jeans. It was only then she noticed the bottle of red wine in his hands. 'Tell you what,' he continued, 'you get rid of the gun; I'll open the wine.'

Jess nodded, not sure what else to do. She moved, as if on

automatic pilot, back to her bedroom, returned the gun to its drawer in the night table, and retrieved a pink quilted bathrobe from her closet. By the time she returned to the living room, Adam had opened the wine and poured them each a glass.

'Chateauneuf du Pape,' he said, depositing a glass in her right hand and guiding her toward the sofa. 'What shall we drink to?' he asked as they sat down, their knees touching briefly before Jess pulled away, tucking her legs beneath her.

Jess recalled her brother-in-law's favorite toast. 'Health and wealth?' she offered.

'How about to good times?'

'I'm all for good times.'

They clicked glasses, inhaled the aroma, then raised their glasses to their lips, though neither drank.

'It's nice to see you,' Adam said.

Jess concentrated on his lips, aware of a slight trace of alcohol already on his breath, and wondered where he'd been before he arrived on her doorstep. Out with the customer she'd seen him with this afternoon? Had their date ended early, leaving him with nothing but time and a bottle of wine on his hands?

Jess found herself getting angrier with each new thought. Now that she was fully awake, she was less charmed by his spontaneity than she was angered by his presumptuousness. What was he doing knocking on her door after ten o'clock on a Saturday night and scaring her half to death? Did he really think he could ignore her all week, then show up unannounced any time he felt like it? Did he assume she would just let him in, drink his wine, then take him gratefully into her bed? He was lucky she hadn't shot him!

'What are you doing here?' Jess asked, surprising them both with the suddenness of her question.

Adam took a long sip of his drink, playing with it in his mouth for several seconds before swallowing it. 'Why do you think I'm here?'

'I don't know. That's why I asked.'

He took another drink, this time throwing the liquid against the back of his mouth as if it were a shot of whiskey. 'I wanted to see you,' he said, though his eyes looked just past her, refusing to focus.

'When did you decide that?'

Adam fidgeted on the sofa, took another long sip of his drink, refilled his glass to the top, in no rush to answer her question. 'I don't understand.'

'At what time did you decide you wanted to see me?' Jess probed, impatient now. 'Two o'clock this afternoon? Four? Seven? Ten?'

'What is this, Jess? An interrogation?'

'Why didn't you phone first?'

'I already told you. It was an impulse.'

'And you're just an impulsive kind of guy.'

'Sometimes. Yes. I guess so.'

'Are you married?'

'What?'

'Are you married?' Jess repeated, seeing the situation clearly for the first time, wondering why she hadn't realized it before. 'Simple enough question. Requiring only a simple yes or no answer.'

'What makes you think I'm married?'

'Are you married? Yes or no?'

'The witness will please answer the question,' Adam said, sarcastically.

'Are you married?' Jess said again.

'No,' Adam proclaimed loudly. 'Of course I'm not married.'

'You're divorced.'

'I'm divorced.'

'From Susan.'

'Yes, from Susan.'

'Who lives in Springfield.'

'Who lives on Mars, for all I care.' He finished the wine remaining in his glass in one gulp.

'Then why don't you ever call? Why do you just show up on

213

my doorstep at all hours of the night?'

'Jess, for Christ's sake, it's ten-thirty!'

'You've already made your commission,' she said, still smarting from the little scene she'd witnessed in the shoe store that afternoon, her cheeks flushing with embarrassment. Had the toupeed salesman told Adam of her visit? 'What are you doing here?'

'You think I'm trying to sell you another pair of boots?'

'I'm not sure what you're trying to sell me.'

He poured himself more wine, drank it down in two gulps, then emptied what remained of the bottle into his glass. 'I'm not married, Jess. Honest.'

There was a long pause. Jess stared into her lap, her anger spent, more relieved than she cared to acknowledge.

'Did we just have our first fight?' he asked.

'I don't know you well enough to fight with you,' Jess answered.

'You know me as well as necessary.' He finished the wine, stared dumbfounded into the bottom of his empty glass, as if just realizing he'd drunk almost an entire bottle of wine in less than ten minutes.

'Necessary for me or for you?'

'I just don't like to plan things too far in advance.'

Jess laughed.

'What's funny?' he asked.

'I plan everything.'

'And just what does planning everything accomplish?' He leaned back against the sofa, shaking his shoes from his feet, lifting his legs off the floor, and casually stretching them across Jess's lap.

'It gives me an illusion of control, I guess,' Jess answered, feeling his weight across her thighs. Her body tensed, then relaxed, welcoming the contact. It had been so long since she'd been with a man, so long since she'd allowed herself the pleasure of a man's caress. Had he been right in his assumptions after all?

214

'And this illusion of control is important to you?' he was saying.

'It's all I've got.'

Adam leaned his head against the pillow, adjusted his hips so that he was almost lying down. 'I think I may have had too much to drink.'

'I think you're right.' There was a long pause. 'Why did you come here, Adam?'

'I don't know,' he said, his eyes closing, his words heavy, unwilling. 'I guess I shouldn't have.'

Don't say that, Jess said silently. 'Maybe you should go,' she said out loud, fighting the urge to cradle him in her arms. 'I better call you a cab. You're in no shape to drive.'

'Ten minutes' sleep is all I need.'

'Adam, I'm going to call for a taxi.' Jess tried lifting his legs, but they were like dead weights. 'If you'll just shift your feet a bit.'

He did, drawing his knees toward his chest in a semi-fetal position, turning fully on his side. If anything, he felt even heavier than before.

'Great,' Jess said, tickling the bottoms of his feet, trying to get him to move. But her fingers generated no response at all. 'Adam, I can't sit here like this all night,' she said, finding herself close to tears. 'No, this is silly!' she exclaimed. 'I will not be a prisoner in my own apartment. I will not spend the night sitting on my sofa with some comatose drunk sprawled across my lap. I need my sleep. I need to get to bed. *Hohh!*' she shouted, but Adam didn't move.

With renewed determination, Jess tugged at Adam's feet, managing, after a few minutes, to lift them just high enough so that she could slide out from under. Adam's feet returned to the sofa with a gentle plop.

Jess stood over him for several minutes, watching him sleep. 'Adam, you can't stay here,' she whispered, then louder, 'Adam, I'm going to call for a taxi.'

And tell them what? That you have a man passed out on your

215

sofa and you want someone to pick him up and carry him down three flights of stairs, and then take him home, except that you have no idea where he lives? Oh yes, right. They'll fight over that fare.

Face it, Jess, she told herself, covering him with his jacket. Adam Stohn isn't going anywhere. At least not tonight.

She studied his face, all traces of turmoil hidden by the peaceful mask of sleep. What secrets was he hiding? she wondered, brushing some hair away from his eyes, her fingers tingling at the contact. How many lies had he told her?

Jess tiptoed away from the sofa, wondering whether she was doing the right thing in letting him stay. Would she wake up in the middle of the night to find him looming over her with her gun in his hand? Was he some psychotic sociopath on the lookout for lonely prosecuting attorneys?

She was almost too tired to care.

Trust your instincts, Jess heard her Wen-Do instructor repeat as she crawled back into bed. Trust your instincts.

But just in case her instincts were wrong, she removed the gun from the top drawer of her end table and tucked it carefully underneath her mattress before allowing herself the luxury of sleep.

She awoke the next morning to find him staring at her from her bedroom door.

'Do you always lay out your clothes so neatly?' he was asking. 'Even on a Sunday?'

'How long have you been standing there?' she asked, ignoring his question, sitting up in bed, gathering her duvet around her.

'Not long. A few minutes, maybe.'

Jess looked toward her clock. 'Nine-thirty!' she gasped.

'Shouldn't drink so much,' he said and smiled sheepishly.

'I can't believe I slept till nine-thirty!'

'You were obviously exhausted.'

'I have so much to do.'

'First things first,' he said. 'Breakfast is ready.'

'You made breakfast?'

216

He leaned against the doorway. 'It wasn't easy. You weren't lying when you said you don't cook. I had to run out and buy some eggs and vegetables.'

'How'd you get back in?'

'I borrowed your key,' he said simply.

'You went into my purse?'

'I put it back.' He approached her bed, held out his hand. 'Come on, I've been slaving over a hot stove all morning.'

Jess threw back her covers and stepped out of bed, ignoring the offer of his hand, not sure she liked the idea of his having gone into her purse. 'Let me just wash my face and brush my teeth.'

'Later.' He grabbed her hand, pulled her through the hallway to the dining area. The table was set, orange juice already poured into glasses.

'I see you found everything.' So, he'd been through her kitchen cupboards as well.

'You don't have any dishes that match,' he said and laughed. 'You're a strange woman, Jess Koster. Interesting, but strange.'

'I could say the same about you.'

He smiled, cryptically. 'I'm not really that interesting.'

It was her turn to laugh. Jess felt herself relax instantly with the sound. If he was some psychotic sociopath who was going to kill her, he'd obviously decided to do it after breakfast, so she might as well enjoy the meal he'd prepared. Trust her instincts. 'What's on the menu?' she asked, her stomach rumbling at the thought of a half-decent breakfast.

'The best Western omelet in the De Paul area,' he answered, sliding one of two perfectly shaped omelets onto her plate, the other onto his, garnishing each with a sprig of parsley.

'You even got parsley. I'm really impressed.'

'That was the general idea. Don't let it get cold,' he said, pouring her a cup of coffee. 'Cream? Sugar?'

'Black.'

'Eat up.'

'It looks wonderful. I can't believe you did all this.'

217

'It was the least I could do after the way I behaved last night.'

'You didn't do anything last night.'

'Precisely. I finally get to spend the night with a beautiful woman, and what do I do? I drink myself into a stupor and pass out on her sofa.'

Jess ran a self-conscious hand through her tangled hair.

'No, don't do that,' he said, bringing her hand back to the table with his own. 'You look lovely.'

Jess slid her hand away from his, poked at her omelet with her fork.

'So, what's the verdict?' He waited while she took her first mouthful of food.

'Fabulous,' Jess said, enthusiastically. 'Definitely the best omelet in the DePaul area.'

They ate for several minutes in silence.

'I took the cover off the bird cage,' Adam said, 'and I brought in your morning paper. It's on the sofa.'

Jess looked from the bird cage to the sofa. 'Thanks.' She paused. 'Anything else you did that I should know about?'

He leaned across the dark mahogany table and kissed her. 'Not yet.'

Jess didn't move as Adam leaned forward to kiss her again. Her lips were tingling; her heart was pounding. She felt like a teenager. She felt like a blushing bride. She felt like an idiot.

Was she really such a pushover? Were a glass of orange juice, a cup of coffee, and a Western omelet all that was necessary to get into her heart and into her bed?

And now he was kissing her lips, her cheeks, her neck, back to her lips. His arms wrapped around her, pulled her against him. How long had it been, she wondered, since a man had kissed her in this way? Since *she* had kissed a man in this way?

'I shouldn't be doing this,' she said, as his kisses became deeper, as her kisses responded in kind. 'I have so much work to do to be ready for tomorrow.'

'You'll do it,' he assured her, burying his lips in her hair.

'Most murder trials only last a week to ten days,' she

whispered, trying to talk herself out of her ardor, 'but the defendant got sick . . .'

Adam covered her mouth with his own, his hands reaching for her breasts.

She tried to protest, but a grunt of pleasure was the only sound that emerged.

'Murders are actually among the easiest cases to try,' she continued stubbornly, wondering which was stranger — what she was doing or what she was saying. 'Except when they involve the death penalty, as this one does . . .'

Again he silenced her with his mouth. This time she surrendered to the almost unbearably pleasant sensation of his lips on hers, his hands on her body.

Suddenly, a buzzer sounded. It beeped once, then again.

'What's that!' Adam asked between kisses.

'The intercom,' Jess answered, wondering who it could be. 'Someone's downstairs.'

'They'll go away.'

The buzzer sounded again, three times in rapid succession. Who was it? Jess wondered. Now, of all times. Ten o'clock on a Sunday morning!

'My God!' Jess said, pulling out of Adam's embrace. 'It's my ex-husband! I forgot all about him. He said he'd drop by this morning.'

'He's as good as his word,' Adam said as the buzzer sounded again.

Jess went quickly to the intercom by the door and spoke into it.

'Don?'

'Your bagels have arrived.' His voice filled the apartment.

'This should be interesting,' Adam said, grabbing his coffee mug and flopping down on the living room sofa, obviously enjoying the situation.

'Oh God,' Jess whispered, hearing Don's footsteps on the stairs and opening the door before he could knock. 'Hi, Don.'

He was wearing a heavy parka over dark green corduroy

pants, his arms filled by two large bags of bagels.

'It's freezing out there,' he remarked. 'What kept you? Don't tell me you were still asleep!' He took two steps inside the apartment, then froze at the sight of Adam on the sofa. 'Sorry,' he said immediately, confusion evident in his face as he extended his hand toward Adam. 'I'm Don Shaw, an old friend.'

'Adam Stohn,' Adam replied, shaking Don's hand. 'A new one.'

There was silence. No one seemed to breathe.

'There's coffee,' Jess offered.

Don looked toward the dining room table. 'Looks like you've already eaten.'

'Jess forgot to tell me you were dropping by,' Adam explained, his voice a smile. 'I'd be happy to whip up another omelet.'

'Thank you, but maybe some other time.'

'Let me hang up your coat.' Jess held out her arms.

Don dropped the bags of bagels into them. 'No. I think I'll get going. I just wanted to get these to you.' He headed for the door. 'You should probably put them in the freezer.'

The phone rang.

'Busy place,' Adam said.

'Don, wait a minute. Please,' Jess urged. Don waited by the door while Jess went to the kitchen to answer the phone. When she came back a minute later, she was pale and shaking, her cheeks streaked with tears. Both men moved instantly toward her. 'That was the Medical Examiner's office,' she said quietly. 'They found Connie DeVuono.'

'What? Where? When?' Don asked, the words emerging like pellets from a gun.

'In Skokie Lagoons. An ice fisherman stumbled across her body late yesterday afternoon and called the police. They brought it to Harrison Street by ambulance.'

'They're sure it's her?'

'Dental records don't lie.' A cry caught in Jess's throat. 'She'd been strangled with a piece of wire rope, so tight she was almost decapitated. Apparently, the body was quite well preserved because of the cold.'

'I'm so sorry, Jess,' Don told her, drawing her into his arms.

Jess cried softly against his shoulder. 'I have to go see Connie's mother. I have to tell her.'

'The police can do that.'

'No,' Jess said quickly, seeing Adam tiptoe toward the door, his jacket over his arm. 'I have to do it. Jesus, Don, what can I say to her? What can I say to her little boy?'

'You'll think of just the right words, Jess.'

Jess said nothing as Adam opened the door and threw her a delicate kiss good-bye. The door closed softly after him.

'Where does Connie's mother live?' Don asked. If he was aware of Adam's departure, he said nothing.

'Miller Street. I have the exact address written down somewhere.' Jess wiped the tears away from her eyes.

'Go take a shower and get dressed. I'll drive you over.'

'No, Don, you don't have to do that.'

'Jess, you don't have a car, and there's no way I'm letting you go through this alone. Now, please, don't argue with me on this one.'

Jess reached over and stroked her ex-husband's cheek. 'Thank you,' she said.

Chapter Seventeen

'Are you all right?' he was asking.

'No.'

Jess was crying. She'd started the minute she heard the Medical Examiner's voice, and hadn't stopped. Couldn't. Even in the shower, her tears hadn't abated. She'd cried as she slipped into her jeans and red sweater, cried as she slid into the front seat of Don's Mercedes, cried as they pulled up in front of Mrs Gambala's modest duplex in Little Italy.

'You have to stop crying,' Don had urged gently. 'Otherwise she'll know before you even open your mouth.'

'She'll know anyway,' Jess had told him. And she had been right.

The front door had opened before Jess reached the top step of the elaborate little red brick porch. Mrs Gambala stood in the doorway, a small woman dressed from head to toe in black, her grandson peeking out warily from behind her ample hips. 'They found her,' Mrs Gambala said, accepting the truth even as she shook her head from side to side in denial.

'Yes,' Jess had admitted, her voice catching, unable to continue.

Steffan had taken one look at Jess, one look at his grandmother, then raced up the narrow staircase to his room, his door slamming in painful protest.

They'd gone inside where Jess had explained the details to Mrs Gambala, promising to tell her everything as soon as the coroner's report came in, assuring her that the man responsible would be quickly apprehended and brought to trial. She stared at Don, as if daring him to contradict her.

'Are you going to issue a warrant for Rick Ferguson's arrest?' Don had asked as they were returning to the car.

There was nothing Jess wanted to do more, but she knew that until she learned the details of the way Connie DeVuono died, she was smarter to hold off. She had to know exactly what, if any, physical evidence there was to link Rick Ferguson to Connie's death. 'Not yet. Are you going to call him?'

'What reason would I have for calling him if you're not going to arrest him?' he'd asked in exaggerated innocence. 'Besides, it's Sunday. I don't work on Sundays.'

'Thank you,' Jess told him, then started crying again.

'Are you all right?' he was asking now.

'No,' she said, folding her top lip under the bottom in an effort to stop them from quivering.

Don reached across the front seat and took her hands in his. 'What are you thinking about?'

'I'm thinking about how Mrs Gambala keeps all her furniture covered in plastic wrap,' Jess told him, releasing a deep breath of air.

Don laughed, clearly surprised. 'You don't see much of that any more,' he agreed.

'Connie told me about it once. She said that Steffan didn't like waiting for her at his grandmother's house because she kept all the furniture in plastic and there wasn't anywhere comfortable to sit down.' A sob caught in Jess's throat. 'And now, that's where he'll grow up. In a house full of plastic covers.'

'In a house full of love, Jess,' Don reminded her. 'His grandmother loves him. She'll take good care of him.'

'Connie said her mother was too old to look after him, that her English was poor.'

'So, he'll teach her English, and she'll teach him Italian. Jess,' Don said, giving her hands an extra squeeze, 'you can't worry about everything. You can't absorb everyone else's pain. You have to pick and choose, or you'll make yourself nuts.'

'I always thought it would be better to know,' Jess confided, after a long pause. 'I always thought it would be better, no matter how awful, to know the truth, for there to be a

224

resolution. Now, I'm not so sure. At least before today, there was hope. Even if it was false hope, maybe that's better than no hope at all.'

'You're talking about your mother,' Don said quietly.

'All these years I thought that if only I'd known one way or the other what happened to her, then I could get on with my life.'

'You *have* gotten on with your life.'

'No, I haven't. Not really.' She looked out the car window, noticed for the first time that they were travelling east on I-94.

'Jess, what are you talking about? Look at all you've accomplished.'

'I know what I've accomplished. That's not what I mean,' she told him.

'Tell me what you mean,' he directed gently.

'I mean that eight years ago, I got stuck. And no matter what I've done, no matter what I've accomplished, emotionally, I'm still stuck back on the day my mother disappeared.'

'And you think that if you'd known what happened to her, that if someone much like yourself had approached you then and given you the same sort of news you delivered to Connie's son today, you would have been better off?'

'I don't know. But at least I would have been able to deal with it once and for all. I would have been able to grieve. I would have been able to go on.'

'Then you've answered your own question,' he told her.

'I guess I have.' Jess wiped the tears away from her eyes, rubbed at her nose with the backs of her fingers, stared out the side window of the car. 'Where are we going?'

'Union Pier.'

'Union Pier?' Jess immediately conjured up the image of the small lakeshore community approximately seventy miles outside Chicago where Don maintained a weekend retreat. 'Don, I can't. I have to get ready for court tomorrow.'

'You haven't seen the place in a long time,' he reminded her. 'I've made some changes, incorporated some of the ideas you

225

once suggested. Come on, I promise to have you back by five o'clock. You know you aren't going to be able to think clearly before then anyway.'

'I don't know.'

'Give yourself a break, Jess. We both know you're as prepared for tomorrow as anyone could possibly be.'

They continued in silence, Jess following the scenery, watching as the few drops of rain that had started falling turned gradually to snow. Buildings gave way to open fields. They took the Union Pier exit, continued east toward Lake Michigan. *Elsinor Dude Ranch*, a large wooden sign announced over an arched wrought-iron gate. *Horse trails and Lessons. Inquire inside. Driving range*, another sign proclaimed half a mile down the road, oblivious to the fact it was the wrong season for golf. Jess remembered her father teasing her mother about teaching her to play golf after he retired.

Union Pier Gun Club, another large wood sign stated, as they continued east, the snow becoming heavier, more insistent. Jess sat up straight in her seat, all her senses on instant alert.

'What's the matter?' Don asked.

'Since when did they have a gun club out here?' Jess asked.

'Since for ever,' Don reminded her. 'Why? You feel like working off some frustration? Although I'm pretty sure you have to be a member,' he continued when she failed to respond.

'Do they have an archery range?'

'What?'

'An archery range,' Jess repeated, not exactly sure where her thoughts were headed.

'I wouldn't think so. Why the sudden interest in archery?' He stopped abruptly. 'The crossbow killer?' he asked.

'Terry Wales swore on the stand that he hadn't fired a bow and arrow since he was a kid in camp. What if I can prove he did?'

'Then I'd say you have a clear shot at murder one.'

'Can I use your phone?'

'The whole point of this trip was for you to relax.'

'This *is* how I relax. Please.'

226

Don lifted the car phone off its receiver, handed it to Jess. She quickly dialed Neil Strayhorn at home.

'Neil, I want you to find out about all the archery clubs within a two-hour drive of Chicago,' she said without unnecessary preliminaries.

'Jess?' Neil's voice filled the car over the speaker phone.

'I want to know if Terry Wales is a member of any of them, if he's even been near an archery range in the last thirty years. Detective Mansfield can probably help. There can't be that many archery clubs around. Tell him we need the information by tomorrow morning. I'll call you later.' She hung up before he could object or ask questions.

'You're a hard taskmaster,' Don told her, turning left onto Smith Road.

'I had a good teacher,' Jess reminded him, bracing herself as the car bounced along the unpaved, bumpy, one-lane road.

Summer cottages lined the secluded route. Despite the fact that the homes along the Bluff had roughly quadrupled their value in the last decade, the residents obviously considered repairing the potholes in the road a low priority. Jess held tightly to the door handle as the car bounced toward Don's pinewood cottage, finding it increasingly difficult to see out the front window.

'It looks so forbidding,' Jess said, as snow swirled everywhere around them.

'I'll light a fire, open a bottle of wine, it won't look so bad.'

'It's really starting to snow.'

'I'll race you to the front door,' Don said, and Jess was off and running.

'I'd forgotten how beautiful it is here.' Jess stood by the large glass window that made up the back wall of the cottage and stared through the snow at the small garden she had planted herself many years ago. The Bluff stood just beyond, a series of steps carved right into its steep side, leading down to the lake. Large spruce trees lined the borders of Don's property, separating him from his neighbors on either side, guarding his

227

privacy. Behind her, a fire roared in the large brick fireplace. Don sat on the white shag rug between the fireplace and one of two old-style colonial chesterfields, the remains of the picnic lunch he'd prepared spread out before him.

'We miss you,' Don said quietly. 'The garden and I. Do you remember when you planted those shrubs?'

'Of course I do. It was just after we got married. We argued about what kind of bushes would grow the fastest, be the prettiest.'

'We didn't argue.'

'All right, we *discussed*.'

'And then we compromised.'

'We did it your way,' Jess said, and laughed. 'This was a nice idea, coming here. Thank you for thinking of it.' She returned to the white shag rug, lowered herself to the floor, leaned back against the brown- and ochre-striped sofa.

'We had a lot of nice times here,' he said, his voice steeped in nostalgia.

'Yes, we did,' she said. 'I think I liked May the best, when everything was just starting to bud, and I knew I had the whole summer to look forward to. By the time June came around, I was already starting to worry that summer would be over soon and winter would be coming.'

'And I always liked winter best because I knew that no matter how cold it got outside, I could come up here and build a fire and make a picnic lunch, and be warm and happy. What more could anyone ask for than to be warm and happy?'

'Sounds so simple.'

'It doesn't have to be difficult.'

'Do you bring Trish here often?' she asked.

'Not often.'

'Why not?'

'I'm not sure.'

'Are you in love with her?' Jess asked.

'I'm not sure,' Don said again. 'What about you?'

'I'm definitely not in love with her.'

228

Don smiled. 'You know what I mean. You gave me quite a surprise this morning.'

'It wasn't the way it looked,' Jess said quickly.

'How did it look?'

'I guess like we'd spent the night together.'

'You didn't?'

'Well, in a manner of speaking, I guess we did. Adam had a little too much to drink and passed out on my couch.'

'Charming.'

'He's really a very nice man.'

'I'm sure he is, or you wouldn't be interested in him.'

'I'm not sure I am. Interested in him.' Jess wondered if she was protesting too much.

'How long have you known him?'

'Not long. Maybe a month,' she said. Maybe less, she thought.

'But he obviously feels comfortable enough to pass out on your couch. And you obviously feel comfortable enough to let him.'

'What choice did I have?'

'I couldn't answer that.'

'Neither can I,' Jess admitted.

'What does he do?'

Jess could hear the strain in Don's voice from trying to sound casual, and was touched by it. 'He's a salesman.'

'A salesman?' He didn't bother to hide his surprise. 'What does he sell?'

'Shoes.' Jess cleared her throat. 'Don't be a snob, Don,' she said quickly. 'There's nothing wrong with selling shoes. My father started out as a salesman, you know.'

'Adam Stohn seems a little old to be starting out,' Don said.

'He likes what he does.'

'So much that he has to drink himself into a drunken stupor and pass out?'

'I don't know that one thing has anything to do with the other.'

'Why do *you* think it happened?'

229

'Objection. Calls for a conclusion.'

'Objection overruled. Witness will answer the question.'

'I'm not in love,' Jess stated.

'The witness may step down,' Don said, and Jess bowed her head in gratitude.

'So, what's it like these days in the prestigious law firm of Rogers, Donaldson, Baker and Shaw?' she asked, picturing Adam Stohn as he waved good-bye to her from the doorway of her apartment that morning.

'It's all right.'

'You don't sound very enthusiastic.'

'The place has changed.'

'Really? How?'

'Well, when I first came on board, there were only ten of us,' he explained. 'Now, there are over two hundred. That's quite a change right there.'

'But you always wanted the firm to grow, to be the biggest and the best,' she reminded him.

'The best, yes. Not necessarily the biggest.'

'So bigger isn't necessarily better?'

'That's right. Haven't Masters and Johnson taught you anything?'

She laughed. 'Did you know they got divorced?'

'Masters and Johnson?'

'Shocking, isn't it?' Jess, wondering how they got on to the subject of sex, stared out the window at the steady downfall of heavy snow.

'So, aside from the size, what else about your firm aren't you happy with?'

'Everything's far more dollar orientated than it used to be, which I guess is only natural these days,' he began. 'Nobody really cares about anything except getting their dockets out. I think the personality of the firm has changed over the years. Not for the better.'

Jess smiled. What he was really saying was that the firm no longer reflected his own strong personality, the way it had in the beginning, when he was one of ten, not two hundred.

'So, how would you change things?'

Don lowered his chin against his chest, the way he did whenever he was giving a matter serious thought. 'I don't think they *can* be changed. The firm's too big. It's a law unto itself. The only way to change it would be to leave it.'

'Are you prepared to do that?'

'I've been thinking about it.'

'What would you do?'

'Start up again,' he said, his voice warming to the idea. 'Take a few of the top guns with me, recruit a few others. Form a small firm in a family neighborhood, you know the kind, with interior brick walls and plants hanging from stucco ceilings. A couple of secretaries, a couple of bathrooms, one small kitchen at the back. You interested?'

'What?'

'I may have just talked myself into a very interesting idea. What about it, Jess? How does Shaw and Koster sound to you?'

Jess laughed, but only because she wasn't sure what else to do.

'Think about it.' Don stood up and walked to the window. 'It doesn't look like we're going to be able to get out of here this afternoon.'

'What?' Jess was instantly on her feet behind him.

'The snow's not letting up at all. If anything, it looks like it's getting worse. The wind's picking up. I'd hate to get caught in a white-out on the highway.'

'But I have to get back.'

'I'll get you back. Just not this afternoon. We may have to wait until after dinner.' He walked toward the large open pine kitchen to his left and opened the freezer. 'I'll defrost a couple of steaks, open up another bottle of wine, and call the highway patrol, find out how bad weather conditions are on the roads. Jess, stop worrying,' he told her. 'Even if worst comes to worst and we can't get out of here tonight, I'll have you back in time for court in the morning, I promise. Even if I have to carry you back on snowshoes. Okay? Does that set your mind at rest?'

'Not really,' she told him.

'That's my girl,' he said.

Jess spent the rest of the afternoon on the phone.

The Medical Examiner had nothing new to report. The autopsy on Connie DeVuono hadn't been completed; it would be a few days until they could interpret all their findings.

Neil Strayhorn had contacted Barbara Cohen and Detective Mansfield. They had managed to find the names of two archery clubs in the Chicago area and another four within a hundred-mile radius of the city. The police were already on their way to question the management. Luckily, all the clubs were open on Sundays, although two had closed early because of the storm, and couldn't be reached. Messages had been left on their answering tapes to call the police first thing in the morning. Neil would call her as soon as they had any news.

Jess went over in her mind the list of questions she had prepared for Terry Wales. Don was right, she acknowledged, watching him as he busied himself in the kitchen preparing dinner. She was as ready as she was ever going to be. She didn't need her notes. She'd already memorized her questions and the likely responses they'd elicit. The only thing that she had to do now was show up in court on time.

'The radio just said they expect the snow to stop by midnight,' Don told her, depositing a glass of red wine in her hand before she could protest the news. 'I say we stay here overnight, get a good night's sleep, and head back around six. That way we're in the city by seven-thirty at the latest, and you still have plenty of time to get ready for court.'

'Don, I can't.'

'Jess, I don't think we have any choice.'

'But what if the snow doesn't stop by midnight? What if we can't leave here in the morning?'

'Then Neil will ask for a continuance,' Don said simply. 'Jess, the weather isn't your fault.'

'And if we leave now?'

'Then we'll probably spend the night in a snowbank. But if that's what you want, I'm willing to gamble.'

232

Jess stared out the back window at a blizzard in full rage. She had to acknowledge the insanity of trying to go anywhere in weather like this. 'How soon till dinner?' she asked.

'That was Detective Mansfield,' Jess said, pushing the phone off the white shag rug, absently watching the flames as they danced, like cobras ready to strike, in the fireplace. 'None of the four archery clubs they were able to contact has any record of Terry Wales being a member.'

'Did they show his picture around?'

Jess nodded. 'No one knew him.'

'That still leaves a couple of places, doesn't it?'

'Two. But we can't reach them till morning.'

'Then there's nothing to do but get a good night's sleep tonight.' Don, sitting beside Jess on the floor, reached over to twist the long wire cord of the telephone around his fingers, returning the phone to the small pine table between the two couches.

Jess followed the motion of his hands, mesmerized by the slow, circular movement. When she spoke, her voice was equally slow, as if emerging from a deep trance. 'Did I tell you that the coroner said the wire was twisted around Connie's neck so tightly she was almost decapitated?'

'Try not to think about that now, Jess,' Don said, wrapping his arms around her. 'Come on, you've had a good dinner and some excellent wine, and now isn't the time to—'

'It's my fault,' she told him, feeling the wire as it sliced its way into Connie's throat.

'Your fault? Jess, what are you talking about?'

'If I hadn't convinced Connie that she had to testify, she'd still be alive.'

'Jess, that's ridiculous. You can't know that. You can't blame yourself.'

'It must have been so awful,' Jess continued, a shudder racing through her body, pushing her tighter into Don's arms, 'feeling that wire cutting into her neck, knowing she was going to die.'

'Jesus, Jess.'

Jess's eyes overflowed with tears, spilled down across her cheeks. Don quickly moved to brush them aside, first with his fingers, then his lips.

'It's all right, baby,' he was saying. 'Everything will be okay. You'll see. Everything will be all right.'

His lips felt gentle, soothing against her skin as he traced the line of her tears from her cheeks to the sides of her mouth, then followed the tears as they ran between her lips, his mouth softly covering her own.

Jess closed her eyes, picturing Adam as he'd reached across her dining room table to kiss her, felt herself respond, knowing she was responding to the wrong man, but unable to stop herself.

It had been so long, she thought, her arms moving to encircle Adam's waist even as Don's hands disappeared under her red sweater, tugged at the zipper of her jeans. It was Adam's caresses she experienced as Don's weight fell across her, Adam whose fingers and mouth knowingly brought her to a gentle climax even before he penetrated her.

'I love you, Jess,' she heard Adam say, but when she opened her eyes, it was Don she saw.

Chapter Eighteen

The dream began as it always did, in the waiting room of the doctor's office, the doctor handing her a phone, telling her her mother was on the line.

'I'm starring in a movie,' her mother told her. 'I want you to come and see me. I'll leave tickets at the box office.'

'I'll be there,' Jess assured her, arriving at the theater within seconds, asking for her tickets from the gum-chewing ticket taker.

'No one left any tickets for you,' the girl told her. 'And we're all sold out.'

'Are you looking for a ticket?' Mrs Gambala asked. 'I can't go. My daughter swallowed a turtle and she died, so I have an extra ticket.'

The theater was dark, the movie about to start. Jess located an empty seat on an aisle, sat down, waited. 'I found a lump in my breast,' her mother was saying as Jess looked toward the screen. But a huge pillar totally obstructed her view. No matter how frantically she tried, how stubbornly she persisted, Jess couldn't see round it.

'It's my fault,' she whispered to Judge Harris, who was sitting beside her. 'If I'd gone to the doctor with her that afternoon like I promised, she wouldn't have disappeared.'

In the next instant she was on the street, about to climb the front steps of her parents' house, when a white car pulled up at the corner and a man got out and started walking toward her, his face in shadows, his arms outstretched. He was right behind her as she raced up the stairs and tore open the door, her fingers frantically searching for the lock. But the lock was broken. She felt the tug at the screen door, felt her fingers losing their grip, knew that Death was only inches away.

Jess sat up with a start, her entire body bathed in sweat, her breath coming in painful, uneven gasps.

It took her a moment to assess where she was. 'Oh, God,' she moaned, seeing Don sleeping peacefully beside her on the white shag rug, the remains of the once grand fire flickering meekly behind the black wire mesh screen. 'Oh, God,' she whispered again, throwing off the blanket he had obviously covered them with. She gathered her clothes around her, wondering how she could have allowed what had happened between her and Don.

'I love you,' she could still hear him say.

I love you too, she wanted to tell him now, but she couldn't, because she didn't, not in the same way he loved her. She'd used him, used his feelings for her, his deep commitment to her, used the love he felt for her, the love he'd always felt for her. For what? So that she could feel better for a few minutes? Feel less alone? Less frightened? So that she could hurt him all over again? Disappoint him anew? The way she always hurt and disappointed everyone who'd ever loved her.

Her hands shaking, she slipped into her panties and bra, shivering now, straining to breathe, as if a giant boa constrictor had wrapped itself round her and was slowly tightening its coils. She staggered to her feet, pulling her sweater over her head, trying desperately to get warm.

Falling back onto the chesterfield behind her, she brought her knees to her chest and hugged them, an uncomfortable numbness seeping through her body. 'No,' she cried softly, not wanting to wake Don, selfishly wishing that he would awake on his own and surround her with his arms, make her demons go away.

Take deep breaths, she told herself, as the invisible snake continued its deadly embrace, extending its wide coils from her toes to her neck, cutting off all hope of air. She stared into the snake's cold eyes, saw its jaws open in eager anticipation, felt a final squeeze at her ribcage.

'No,' she gasped, fighting to keep from throwing up, struggling

236

with her imaginary tormentor. 'No!'

And suddenly she saw Adam's face, and heard his voice. 'Don't fight it,' he was telling her. 'The next time you have one of these attacks, just go with it. Let yourself go.'

What did he mean?

'What's the worst thing that can happen?' he'd asked.

'I'll throw up,' she'd answered.

'So, you'll throw up.'

I'm afraid, she thought now.

'I think what you're afraid of is death.'

Help me. Please help me.

'Go with the flow,' he was saying. Don't fight it. Just go with it.'

The same advice, Jess realized, as her self-defense instructor had given her.

When faced with an attacker, don't fight him, go with him.

Strike when you get there.

'Go with it,' she repeated over and over. 'Go with it. Don't fight it. Go with it.'

What's the worst that can happen?

So you'll throw up.

So you'll die.

She almost laughed.

Jess stopped fighting, letting the panic fill her body. She closed her eyes against the dizziness that enveloped her, threatened to send her sprawling to the floor. She felt light-headed and sick to her stomach, sure that at any second she would lose consciousness.

But she didn't lose consciousness.

She didn't die.

She wasn't even going to throw up, she realized with growing amazement, feeling a loosening at her chest, the giant snake slowly losing interest and slithering away. A few minutes later, the numbness vanished and her breathing returned to normal. She was all right. She hadn't died. Nothing had happened to her at all.

She'd gone with her panic, flowed with her anxiety, and

nothing of any consequence had happened to her. She hadn't thrown up all over herself. She wasn't paralyzed. She wasn't dead.

She'd won.

Jess sat for several minutes on the striped couch without moving, savoring her victory. 'It's over,' she whispered, feeling suddenly confident and happy, wanting to wake Don, tell him the news.

Except she knew it wasn't Don she wanted to tell.

Jess pushed herself to her feet and rummaged gently under the blanket for her socks. She found them, put them on, then quickly slid into her jeans. She walked to the window and stared out through the darkness at the Bluff beyond.

'Jess?' Don's voice was full of sleep.

'It's stopped snowing,' she told him.

'You're dressed.' He propped himself up on one elbow, and reached across the rug for his watch.

'I was cold.'

'I would have warmed you.'

'I know,' she told him, an unmistakable note of melancholy creeping into her voice. 'Don . . .'

'You don't have to say anything, Jess.' He slipped the watch over his wrist, snapped it shut, massaged the back of his neck. 'I know you don't have the same feelings for me that I have for you.' He tried to smile, almost succeeded. 'If you want, we'll just pretend that last night never happened.'

'The last thing I ever wanted to do was hurt you again.'

'You haven't. Honestly, Jess. I'm a big boy. I can deal with last night if you can.' He paused, checked the time. 'It's only four o'clock. Why don't you try to sleep for a few more hours?'

'I wouldn't be able to sleep.'

He nodded. 'Do you want me to make you a cup of coffee?'

'How about I make you one back at my apartment?'

'Are you saying you want to leave now?'

'Would you mind very much?'

'Would it matter?'

Jess knelt on the rug beside her ex-husband, and gently stroked his cheek, feeling the early morning stubble. 'I *do* love you,' she said.

'I know that,' he told her, placing his hand over one of hers. 'I'm just waiting for *you* to figure it out.'

It was almost seven o'clock in the morning before they arrived back in the city. The drive home was slow and treacherous. A couple of times, they'd slid on a hidden patch of ice and almost veered into a ditch. But Don hadn't panicked. He'd merely gripped the wheel tighter and continued resolutely on, although it often felt to Jess as if she could have walked back to Chicago faster.

She was on the phone the instant she arrived back in her apartment.

'Anything?' she asked Neil instead of hello.

'Jess, it's seven o'clock in the morning,' he reminded her. 'The clubs don't even open till ten.'

Jess replaced the receiver, watched Don as he tidied up the remains of the breakfast Adam had prepared for her yesterday. Was it really only yesterday? Jess wondered, thinking it felt like so long ago. 'You don't have to do that,' Jess said, taking the dish Don was washing out of his hand and laying it on the kitchen counter.

'Yes, I do. There isn't a clean dish in the place.' He lifted it off the counter and ran it under the tap.

'There's coffee,' Jess said, shaking the coffee pot. 'I can just pop a couple of mugs in the microwave.'

Don took the coffee pot out of Jess's hands and poured its muddy brown contents down the sink. 'You and your microwave,' he said. 'Now get out of here. *I'll* make the coffee; *you* take a shower.'

Jess walked into the living room. 'Hello, Fred,' she said, bringing her nose up against the narrow bars of his cage. 'How are you doing, fella? I'm sorry I didn't come home last night to cover you up. Did you miss me?'

The bird hopped from perch to perch, oblivious to her concern.

'Why don't you get a dog or a cat?' Don called from the kitchen.

239

'That thing doesn't care whether you're here or not.'

'I like Fred. He's low-maintenance,' she said, thinking of the black vinyl boots she had purchased from Adam. Definitely a worthwhile investment, she thought now, seeing them by the front door, the snow melting off their toes onto the hardwood floor. No salt rings. No water marks. Satisfaction guaranteed or your money back.

She thought about Adam, wondered what he was doing now, where he'd gone after he left her apartment. What he'd made of the morning's confusing events. What he'd say if he knew about last night.

Jess shook her head as she headed down the hall toward her bedroom, trying to shake loose such disconcerting thoughts. She'd started the day by almost making love to one man, and ended it by making love to another. One was little more than a stranger, a man she knew virtually nothing about; the other was her ex-husband, about whom she knew virtually everything. One was here now, was always here when she needed him; the other dropped by whenever he felt the urge.

Was that what she found so appealing about Adam Stohn? she wondered. The fact that she was never sure from one moment to the next when, or even if, she might see him again?

The room was as she'd left it, the bed unmade. Jess hated unmade beds, the way she hated anything left unfinished. She quickly set about making it, fluffing the pillows and tucking in the sheets. Then she went into the bathroom and ran the shower, pulling off her sweater and jeans, tucking them neatly in the closet, selecting her grey suit and pink blouse for today's appearance in court, laying them neatly across the white wicker chair.

She pulled a pair of skin-colored pantihose from the top drawer of her dresser, along with a fresh pink lace bra and panties, laying them carefully on top of her suit, about to discard the underwear she had on when she noticed a rip in the crotch of the pink lace panties. 'Great. How did that happen?' she asked, examining the uneven tear that split the crotch of her panties from seam to seam.

She tossed them into the waste paper basket, retrieved another pair from the top drawer, casually looking them over, her eyes quickly fixating on the jagged tear at the crotch. 'My God, what's going on here?' With growing panic, Jess examined all her underwear, discovering all her panties had been slashed in exactly the same way. 'My God! Oh, my God!'

'Jess?' Don called from the other room. 'What are you muttering about?'

'Don!' she cried, unable to say anything else. 'Don! Don!'

He was instantly at her side. 'What is it? What's the matter?'

Wordlessly, she handed him her torn underwear.

'I don't understand.'

'They're ripped! They're all ripped!' She scrunched the delicate fabric of the panties in her hand between trembling fingers.

He looked as confused as Jess felt. 'Your panties are ripped . . . ?'

'*All* my panties are ripped,' she said, finally finding her voice. 'Every last one of them. Look. It's like they've been slashed with a knife.'

'Jess, that's crazy. They must have gotten torn in the washing machine.'

'I wash them by hand,' Jess snapped, losing patience. 'Rick Ferguson's been here, Don. Rick Ferguson did this. He's been here. He's been in my things.'

It was Don's turn to lose patience. 'Jess, I can understand your being upset, but don't you think you're flying a little fast and loose with the assumptions here?'

'Who else could it be, Don? Who else *would* it be? It has to be Rick Ferguson. Who else could get in here as easily as if he had a key?' She broke off abruptly.

'What?' Don asked.

Adam had borrowed her key, she thought. Borrowed it when he went out to buy groceries while she'd been asleep. Had he had another key made? Had he used it to get back into her apartment when she was away?

'It had to be Rick Ferguson,' Jess continued, immediately pushing aside such unpleasant thoughts. 'He broke into Connie's apartment without any problem. Now, he's broken into mine.'

'We don't know who broke into Connie's apartment,' Don reminded her.

'How can you keep defending him?' Jess demanded.

'I'm not defending him. I'm just trying to get you to be reasonable.'

'He used to work in a locksmith's shop!'

'A summer job. When he was a teenager, for God's sake.'

'It explains how he's able to get into apartments without any sign of forced entry.'

'It explains nothing. Jess,' Don persisted. 'Anyone could get into this apartment without much trouble.'

'What are you talking about?'

He led her back toward the front door. 'Look at this lock. It's useless. I could pick it open with my credit card. Why don't you have a dead bolt, for God's sake? Or a chain?'

Hadn't Adam asked her almost the same thing? Why don't you get a peephole? Or a chain? he'd asked as she stood before him, gun in hand.

Her gun! Jess thought, almost knocking Don over as she raced back toward her bedroom. Had whoever broke into her apartment and slashed her underwear also stolen her gun?

'Jess, for God's sake, what are you doing now?' Don called after her.

The goddamn gun, she thought, pulling at the bedcovers she had recently tucked in. Had he stolen her gun?

The gun was exactly where she'd left it. She pulled it out from underneath the mattress with a deep sigh of relief.

'Jesus Christ, Jess! Is that loaded?'

She nodded.

'You're sleeping with a loaded gun under your mattress? Are you trying to kill yourself? What if you moved funny and the damn thing went off? Are you nuts?'

'Please stop yelling at me, Don. It's not helping.'

'What the hell are you doing sleeping with a loaded gun under your mattress?'

'I usually keep it in the drawer.' She indicated the night table with a nod of her head.

'Why?'

'Why? You're the one who gave me the damn thing in the first place. You're the one who insisted I have it.'

'And you're the one who insisted she'd never use it. Would you put the damn thing away before you shoot somebody!'

Jess deposited the gun gently in the top drawer of her night table. 'I've been threatened,' she reminded him, closing the drawer. 'My car's been vandalized and destroyed. I've received strange letters in the mail.'

'Letters? What kind of letters?'

'Well, just one letter,' she qualified. 'Soaked in urine, full of pubic hair clippings.'

'Jesus, Jess. When was this? Did you tell the police?'

'Of course I told them. There's nothing they can do. There's no way of proving who sent the letter. Just like there'll be no way of proving who slashed my panties or broke into my apartment. Just like they couldn't prove who broke into Connie's apartment, or who killed and mutilated her son's pet turtle.'

'Jess, we don't know that there's any connection between the break-ins at Connie's place and yours. We don't even know that there was a break-in here,' he said.

'What does that mean?' Jess asked, anger swelling her throat, making it hard to speak.

'Who is this Adam Stohn anyway, Jess?'

'What?' Had he been able to reach inside her brain, read her most secret thoughts? Tell me no secrets, I'll tell you no lies, she thought.

'Adam Stohn,' Don repeated. 'The man who passed out on your sofa Saturday night. The man who was making you breakfast Sunday morning. The man who could easily have gone through your things while you were sleeping, maybe had a little fun with one of your kitchen knives.'

'That's ridiculous,' Jess protested, trying not to remember he'd also gone into her purse, borrowed her key.

243

'He's the wild card here, Jess. Just who is this man?'

'I already told you. He's a guy I met, a salesman.'

'A shoe salesman, yes, I know. Who introduced you?'

'No one,' Jess admitted. 'I met him at the shoe store.'

'You met him at the store? Are you saying you picked him up when you went to buy shoes?'

'It's legal, Don. I didn't do anything wrong.'

'Not wrong, maybe. But certainly stupid.'

'I'm not a little kid, Don.'

'Then stop acting like one.'

'Thank you. This is just what I needed this morning. A lecture on dating by my ex-husband.'

'I'm not trying to lecture you, goddamn it. I'm trying to protect you!'

'That's not your job!' she reminded him. 'Your job is defending men like Rick Ferguson. Remember?'

Don slumped down on the bed. 'This is getting us nowhere.'

'Agreed.' Jess plopped down on the bed beside him, several pairs of panties scattering to the floor. 'It's so hot in here,' she said, realizing she was still in her underwear. 'Jesus Christ, the shower!'

She hurried into the bathroom, steam rushing to escape the small room as she fought her way through the rush of hot water to turn off the taps. She returned to the bedroom, sweat pouring off her face, her hair wet and dripping into her eyes, her shoulders slumped forward in defeat. 'How am I supposed to go to court looking like this?' she asked, near tears.

'It's not even seven-thirty,' Don told her gently, 'so you still have lots of time. Now, first things first. The first thing we're going to do is call the police.'

'Don, I don't have time to deal with the police now.'

'You can tell them what happened over the phone. If they think it's necessary, they can come over later and dust for prints.'

'That won't do any good.'

'No, I don't think it will. But you have to report the incident anyway, you know that. Get it on the record. Including your suspicions about Rick Ferguson.'

'Which you don't share.'

'Which I *do* share.'

'You do?'

'Of course I do. I'm not a complete idiot, even where you're concerned. But suspicions are one thing, assumptions are another.' He underlined his words with a nod of his head. 'The second thing I want you to do,' he continued, 'is take your shower and get dressed. Forget the underwear for the time being. I'll call my secretary and have her drop something off for you before you go to court.'

'You don't have to do that.'

'As soon as you're dressed, I want you to pack a suitcase. You're moving into my apartment until this whole thing gets straightened out.'

'Don, I can't move into your apartment.'

'Why not?'

'Because this is where I live. Because all my things are here. Because of Fred. Because . . . I just can't.'

'Bring your things. Bring Fred. Bring whatever, *whoever*, you want. Separate bedrooms,' he told her. 'I won't come anywhere near you, Jess, if that's the way you want it. I just want you safe.'

'I know you do. And I love you for it. But I just can't,' she said.

'Okay, then, at the very least, I want that lock replaced,' he told her, obviously recognizing there was nothing to be gained by continuing the argument. 'I want a deadbolt and a chain installed.'

'Fine.'

'I'll arrange for it this morning.'

'Don, you don't have to arrange everything. I can do it.'

'Really? When? When you're in court? How about while you're cross-examining Terry Wales?'

'Later. When I get home.'

'Not later. This morning. I'll have my secretary come over, stay with the locksmith.'

'Is this the same secretary who's bringing me my underwear?'

'Things are a little slow at the office.'

'Sure they are.'

'Lastly,' he continued, 'I want you to consider a bodyguard.'

'A what? For whom?'

'For Santa Claus. Who do you think, Jess? For you!'

'I don't need a bodyguard.'

'Someone just broke into your apartment and slashed your underwear, probably the same someone who destroyed your car and sent you a urine-soaked letter in the mail. And you don't think you need protection?'

'I can't be guarded twenty-four hours a day indefinitely. What kind of life is that?'

'Nobody said anything about indefinitely. A few weeks, then we'll see.'

'That's silly. Why can't we just hire a detective to keep tabs on Rick Ferguson instead?'

'Agreed,' he said quickly. 'I'll take care of it this morning.'

'What? Wait a minute, I'm having trouble keeping track here. How can you do that? Is it ethical? Hiring a detective to spy on your own client?'

'I almost hired one after your car was destroyed. I should have, dammit, then maybe this wouldn't have happened. Anyway, if he's innocent, he has nothing to worry about.'

'That's my line.'

'Jess, I love you. I'm not going to take a chance on anything happening to you.'

'But won't it be expensive, hiring a detective?' she asked, steering the conversation away from the personal.

'Consider it my Christmas present. Will you do that for me?' he asked, and Jess marvelled at how he could make it sound as if she'd be doing him the favor by accepting his generous offer.

'Thank you,' she said.

'I'll tell you one thing,' he told her solemnly. 'If it *is* Rick Ferguson who's been harassing you, then client or no client, I'll shoot the bastard myself.'

Chapter Nineteen

'Could you state your full name for the jury, please?'

'Terrence Matthew Wales.'

Jess rose from her seat behind the prosecutor's table and approached the witness stand, eyes fastened on the defendant. Terry Wales stared back steadily, even respectfully. His hands were folded in his lap, his posture bent slightly forward, as if he didn't want to miss a word she might say. The impression he created, in his dark grey suit that curiously complemented her own, was that of a man who had tried all his life to do the right thing, that he was as sorry and surprised as anyone for the way things had worked out.

'You live at twenty-four twenty-seven Kinzie Street in Chicago?'

'Yes.'

'And you've lived there for six years?'

'That's correct.'

'And before that you lived at sixteen Vernon Park Place?'

He nodded.

'I'm afraid the court stenographer requires a yes or no, Mr. Wales.'

'Yes,' he said quickly.

'Why did you move?' Jess asked.

'I beg your pardon?'

'Why did you move?' Jess repeated.

Terry Wales shrugged. 'Why does anybody move?'

Jess smiled, kept her voice light. 'I'm not interested in why anybody moves, Mr Wales. I'm interested in why *you* moved.'

'We needed a bigger house.'

'You needed more space? More bedrooms?'

Terry Wales coughed into the palm of his hand. 'When we moved to the house on Vernon Park Place, we only had one

247

child. By the time we moved to Kinzie, we had two.'

'Yes, you already stated your wife was in a hurry to have children. Tell me, Mr Wales, how many bedrooms did the house on Vernon Park Place have?'

'Three.'

'And the house on Kinzie Street?'

'Three,' he said quietly.

'Sorry, did you say three?'

'Yes.'

'Oh, the same number of bedrooms. Then I guess it was the house in general that was bigger.'

'Yes.'

'It was three square feet bigger,' Jess told him matter-of-factly.

'What?'

'The house on Kinzie Street was three square feet bigger than the house on Vernon Park Place. Approximately this size,' she explained, pacing out a three-foot square in front of the jury.

'Objection, Your Honor,' Hal Bristol called from his seat at the defence table. 'Relevance?'

'I'm getting to that, Your Honor.'

'Get there fast,' Judge Harris instructed.

'Isn't it true, Mr Wales, that the reason you left your house on Vernon Park Place was because of repeated complaints about your conduct by your neighbors to the police?' Jess asked quickly, her adrenaline pumping.

'No, that's not true.'

'Isn't it true that the neighbors reported you to the police on several occasions because they feared for your wife's safety?'

'We had one neighbor who called the police every time I played the stereo too loud.'

'Which just happened to coincide with every time you beat your wife,' Jess stated, looking at the jury.

'Objection!' Hal Bristol was on his feet.

'Sustained.'

'The police were called to your house on Vernon Park Place the night of 3 August 1984,' Jess began, reading from her notes, though she knew the dates by heart, 'the night of 7 September 1984, and again the nights of 22 November 1984, and 4 January 1985. Is that correct?'

'I don't remember the exact dates.'

'It's all on file, Mr Wales. Do you dispute any of it?'

He shook his head, then answered, looking toward the court stenographer. 'No.'

'On each of those occasions when the police were called, your wife showed obvious signs of beatings. Once she even had to be hospitalized.'

'I've already testified that our fights often got out of hand, that I'm not proud of my part in them.'

'Out of hand?' Jess said. 'More like out of *fist*. Your fist.'

'Objection!'

'Sustained.'

Jess walked to the prosecutor's table, exchanged one police report for another. 'This report states that on the night of 4 January 1985, the night your wife was hospitalized, Nina Wales had bruises to over forty per cent of her body and was bleeding internally, that her nose and two ribs were broken, and that both eyes were blackened. You, on the other hand, had several scratch marks on your face, and one large bruise on your shin. That doesn't sound like a very fair fight, Mr Wales.'

'Objection, Your Honor. Is there a question here?'

'Isn't it true that your wife had recently given birth to your second child?'

'Yes.'

'A little girl?'

'Rebecca, yes.'

'How old was she on the night of 4 January 1985?'

Terry Wales hesitated.

'Surely you remember your daughter's birthday, Mr Wales,' Jess prodded.

'She was born on December 2nd.'

'December 2nd, 1984? Just four weeks before the fight that put your wife in the hospital?'

'That's right.'

'So, that would mean that all these other attacks—'

'Objection!'

'All these other *incidents,*' Jess corrected, '3 August 1984, 7 September 1984, 22 November 1984, they all occurred while your wife was pregnant. Is that correct?'

Terry Wales dropped his head toward his chest. 'Yes,' he whispered. 'But it isn't as one-sided as you make it out to be.'

'Oh, I know that, Mr Wales,' Jess told him. 'Who among us could forget that bruise on your shin?'

Hal Bristol was on his feet again, his eyes rolling toward the ceiling. 'Objection, Your Honor.'

'Withdrawn,' Jess said, retrieving yet another police report from Neil Strayhorn's outstretched hand, then returning to the witness stand. 'Jumping ahead a few years, if we could, to the night of 25 February 1988, you put your wife in the hospital again, didn't you?'

'My wife had gone out and left the kids alone. When she came back home, it was obvious to me she'd been drinking. Something inside me just snapped.'

'No, Mr Wales, it was something in your wife that got snapped,' Jess immediately corrected. 'Specifically her right wrist.'

'She'd left the kids alone. God knows what could have happened to them.'

'Are there any witnesses to the fact that she left the children alone, Mr Wales?' Jess asked.

'I came home and found them.'

'Was anyone with you?'

'No.'

'So we have only your word that your wife went out and left the children by themselves?'

'Yes.'

'Well, I don't know why we wouldn't believe you,' Jess stated, bracing herself for the objection she knew would follow.

'Ms Koster,' Judge Harris warned, 'can we please skip the sarcasm and get on with it.'

'I'm sorry, Your Honor,' Jess said, smoothing her skirt,

suddenly reminded of the new underwear Don's secretary had brought over just prior to the start of court. The events of the morning, of the day before, crowded into her mind. The discovery of Connie's body, the break-in at her apartment, the destruction of her underwear all swirled in her brain, fuelled her anger, propelled the words out of her mouth. 'What about the nights of 17 October 1990, 14 March 1991, 10 November 1991, 20 January 1992?'

'Objection, Your Honor,' Hal Bristol said. 'The witness has already admitted his part in these domestic disputes.'

'Overruled. The witness will answer the question.'

'The police were called to your house on each of those occasions, Mr Wales,' Jess reminded him. 'Do you remember that?'

'I don't remember specific dates.'

'And your wife ended up in the hospital on two of these occasions.'

'I believe we both ended up in the hospital.'

'Yes, I see that on the night of 10 November 1991, you were treated at St Luke's for a bloody nose and then released. Your wife, on the other hand, stayed on till morning. I guess she just needed a good night's sleep.'

'Ms Koster.' Judge Harris warned.

'Sorry, Your Honor. Now, Mr Wales, you told the jury that the reason for most of these fights was because you were provoked.'

'That's right.'

'It doesn't take much to provoke you, does it, Mr Wales?'

'Objection.'

'I'll rephrase that, Your Honor. Would you say you have a quick temper, Mr Wales?'

'These last few years have been difficult ones in the retail business. They took their toll. On occasion, I was unable to control my temper.'

'On many occasions, it would seem. Including long before we entered into these tough economic times. I mean, 1984 and 1985 were pretty good years, businesswise, weren't they?'

'Businesswise, yes.'

'I see you posted record commissions those years, Mr Wales,' Jess stated, again exchanging one piece of paper for another.

'I worked very hard.'

'I'm sure you did. And you were amply rewarded. And yet, police records show you beat your wife. So it would appear that your temper really didn't have anything to do with how well you were doing at work. Wouldn't you agree?'

Terry Wales took several seconds before answering. 'No matter how well I was doing, it wasn't enough for Nina. She was constantly complaining that I wasn't making enough money, even before the recession hit. These last few years have been hell.'

'Your income took a substantial drop?'

'Yes.'

'And your wife resented the fact there was less money coming in?'

'Very much.'

'I see. How exactly did your drop in income affect the household, Mr Wales?'

'Well, the same way everybody else has been affected, I guess,' Terry Wales answered carefully, glancing at his attorney. 'We had to cut down on entertaining, eating out, buying clothes. Stuff like that.'

'Stuff that affected your wife,' Jess stated.

'That affected all of us.'

'How did it affect you, Mr Wales?'

'I don't understand.'

'Objection. The witness has already answered the question.'

'Get to the point here, Ms Koster,' Judge Harris advised.

'You were the sole supporter of your family, isn't that right? I mean, you made quite a point earlier of telling us that it was your wife who insisted she give up her job.'

'She wanted to stay home with the children. I respected that decision.'

'So, the only money Nina Wales had access to was the money that you gave her.'

'As far as I know.'

'How much money did you give her every week, Mr Wales?'

'As much as she needed.'

'About how much was that?'

'I'm not sure. Enough for groceries and other essentials.'

'Fifty dollars? A hundred? Two hundred?'

'Closer to a hundred.'

'A hundred dollars a week for groceries and other essentials for a family of four. Your wife must have been a very careful shopper.'

'We had no choice. There was simply no money to spare.'

'You belong to the Eden Rock Golf Club, do you not, Mr Wales?'

A slight pause. 'Yes.'

'How much are the yearly dues?'

'I'm not sure.'

'Would you like me to tell you?'

'I think they're just slightly over a thousand dollars,' he answered quickly.

'Eleven hundred and fifty dollars, to be exact. Did you give that up?'

'No.'

'And the Elmwood Gun Club. You're a member there as well, aren't you?'

'Yes.'

'How much are the yearly dues there?'

'About five hundred dollars.'

'Did you give that up?'

'No. But I paid out a lot of money to join those clubs in the first place. It would have meant losing my initial investment.'

'It would have meant a saving of over fifteen hundred dollars a year.'

'Look, I know it was selfish, but I worked hard; I needed some sort of outlet.'

'Do you belong to any other clubs, Mr Wales?' Jess asked and held her breath. She was still waiting for this morning's police report to come in.

'No,' came the immediate reply.

'You don't belong to any other sports clubs?'

Jess watched for a look of hesitation in Terry Wales's eyes, but there was none. 'No,' he said clearly.

Jess nodded, looking toward the rear of the courtroom. Where was Barbara Cohen? Surely they must have heard from the police by now.

'Let's go back to the night of 20 January 1992,' Jess stated, 'the last time police were called to your house to investigate a domestic dispute.' She waited a few seconds to allow the jury to adjust to her change in topics. 'You testified that was the night your wife first told you she had a lover.'

'That's right.'

'How exactly did that come about?'

'I don't understand.'

'When did she tell you? At dinner? When you were watching television? When you were in bed?'

'It was after we'd gone to bed.'

'Please go on, Mr Wales.'

'We'd just finished making love. I reached over to take her in my arms.' His voice cracked. 'I just wanted to hold her. I . . . I know I wasn't always the best husband, but I loved her, I really did, and I wanted everything to be all right between us.' Tears filled his eyes. 'Anyway, I reached for her, but she pulled away. I told her that I loved her, and she started to laugh. She told me I didn't know what love meant, that I didn't know what *making* love meant. That I didn't know how to make love. That I was a joke. That I had no idea what it took to satisfy a woman, to satisfy her. And then she told me that it didn't matter, because she'd found someone who *did* know how to satisfy her. That she had a lover, someone she'd been seeing for months. That he was a *real* man, a man who knew how to satisfy a woman. That maybe one night she'd let me watch them together so that I could learn a thing or two.' Again his voice cracked. 'That's when I lost it.'

'And you beat her.'

'And I hit her,' Terry Wales qualified. 'And she started

254

pounding on me, scratching at me, telling me over and over again what a loser I was.'

'And so you hit her, over and over again,' Jess said, using his words.

'I'm not proud of myself.'

'So you've said. Tell me, Mr Wales, what was your wife's lover's name?'

'I don't know. She didn't say.'

'What did he do for a living?'

'I don't know.'

'Do you know how old he was, how tall? Whether or not he was married?'

'No.'

'Did you have any suspicions as to who it might be? A friend, perhaps?'

'I don't know who her lover was. It wasn't the sort of thing she would confide in me.'

'And yet she *did* tell you she had a lover. An interesting thing to confide in an often abusive husband, wouldn't you say?'

'Objection, Your Honor.'

'Sustained.'

'Did anyone else hear your wife confess to having a lover?'

'Of course not. We were in bed.'

'Did she ever talk about him when you had company?'

'No. Only when we were alone.'

'And since her friends have already testified that she never confided any such news to them,' Jess went on, 'it seems that once again we have only your word.'

Terry Wales said nothing.

'So, your wife told you she had a lover; you beat her to a bloody pulp, and the neighbors called the police,' Jess summarized, feeling Hal Bristol object even before the word was out of his mouth.

'Your wife *did* end up in the hospital that night, didn't she?' Jess said, rephrasing her question.

'Yes.'

'How long after that did your wife tell you she was leaving you?'

'She was always threatening to leave me, to take my kids away from me, to take me for everything I had.'

'When did you know she meant it?' Jess asked.

Terry Wales took a deep breath. 'The end of May.'

'You've testified that your wife told you that she'd consulted a lawyer and was moving out.'

'That's correct.'

'You testified that you begged and pleaded with her to change her mind.'

'That's right.'

'Why?'

'I don't understand.'

'You've told us that your wife told you she'd taken a lover, that she repeatedly called your manhood into question, told you you were a lousy lover, a lousy husband, a lousy provider, that she made your life a living hell. Why would you beg and plead with her to stay?'

Terry Wales shook his head. 'I don't know. I guess that, despite everything we did to each other, I still believed in the sanctity of marriage.'

'Till death do you part,' Jess stated sardonically. 'Is that the general idea?'

'Objection, Your Honor. Really.'

Judge Harris waved away the objection with an impatient hand.

'I never meant to kill my wife,' Terry Wales said directly to the jury.

'No, you were just trying to get her attention,' Jess said, watching the rear door of the courtroom open, and Barbara Cohen walk through. Even from a distance of thirty feet, Jess could see the glint in her assistant's eye. 'Your Honor, may I have a minute?'

Judge Harris nodded and Jess strode to the prosecutor's table.

'What've we got?' she asked, taking the report from Barbara's hands, and quickly scanning the pages.

256

'I'd say just what we need,' Barbara Cohen answered, not even trying to suppress her smile.

Jess had to bite down on her lower lip to keep from laughing out loud. She spun round, then held back, careful not to appear too eager. Move in slowly, she told herself, as she inched forward. Then move in for the kill. 'So, you were distraught and emasculated and desperate, is that right?' she asked the defendant.

'Yes,' he admitted.

'And you decided you wanted to do something that would shake your wife up, make her come to her senses.'

'Yes.'

'So you went out and you purchased a crossbow.'

'Yes.'

'A weapon you hadn't shot since you were a kid in camp, is that right?'

'Yes.'

'What camp was that?'

'Sorry?'

'What was the name of the camp you went to where you first learned to shoot a bow and arrow?'

Terry Wales looked toward his lawyer, but Hal Bristol's subtle nod directed him to answer the question. 'I believe it was Camp New Moon.'

'How many years did you attend Camp New Moon?' Jess asked.

'Three, I believe.'

'And they taught you how to shoot a bow and arrow?'

'It was one of the activities offered.'

'And you won several medals, did you not?'

'That was almost thirty years ago.'

'But you did win several medals?'

Terry Wales laughed. 'They gave medals to all the kids.'

'Your Honor, would you please instruct the witness to answer the question,' Jess asked.

'A simple yes or no will suffice, Mr Wales,' Judge Harris told the defendant.

Terry Wales lowered his head. 'Yes.'

'Thank you,' Jess said, and smiled. 'And until you fatally shot your wife through the heart on June the second of this year, it had been almost thirty years since you'd fired a bow and arrow?'

'Twenty-five or thirty,' Terry Wales qualified.

Jess checked the folder in her hand. 'Mr Wales, have you ever heard of the Aurora County Bowmen?'

'I'm sorry, the what?' Terry Wales asked, a slight flush blotching his cheeks.

'The Aurora County Bowmen,' Jess repeated. 'It's an archery club located about forty-five miles southwest of Chicago. Do you know it?'

'No.'

'According to the brochure I have, it's a non-profit organization formed in 1962 with the purpose of providing facilities where archers can pursue their sport. "No matter what area of archery your interest lies in",' Jess continued reading, '"be it hunting, competitive target or pleasure shooting, using the longbow, recurve, compound or *crossbow*, the Aurora County Bowmen offers ideal facilities for practising throughout the year."'

Hal Bristol was on his feet and moving toward the Judge's bench. 'Objection, Your Honor. My client has already stated he has no knowledge of this club.'

'Interesting,' Jess said immediately, 'since club records show Terry Wales has been a member there for the past eight years.' Jess held up a faxed copy of the club membership. 'We'd like this entered as State's Exhibit F, Your Honor.'

Jess handed the records to Judge Harris who looked them over before passing them down to Hal Bristol's waiting fist. Hal Bristol scanned the evidence, nodded angrily, then returned to his seat, glaring openly at his client.

'Do you remember the club now, Mr Wales?' Jess asked pointedly.

'I joined the club eight years ago and hardly ever used it,' Terry Wales explained. 'Frankly, I'd forgotten all about it.'

'Oh, but they didn't forget you, Mr Wales.' Jess was careful to keep the gloat out of her voice. 'We have a signed affidavit from a Mr Glen Hallam, who's in charge of the equipment at Aurora County Bowmen. The police showed him your picture this morning, and he remembers you very well. Says you've been a regular there for years, although, oddly enough, he hasn't seen you since the spring. I wonder why that is,' Jess mused, offering the statement as State's Exhibit G. 'He says you're quite a shot, Mr Wales. Bull's-eye nearly every time.'

A collective gasp emanated from the jury box. Hal Bristol looked toward his lap. Terry Wales said nothing.

Bull's-eye, Jess thought.

Chapter Twenty

'I understand you pulled off quite a coup in court today,' Greg
Oliver greeted Jess as she walked past his office at the end of
the day.

'She was brilliant,' Neil Strayhorn exclaimed, a step behind
Jess, Barbara Cohen at his side. 'She laid her trap, then stood
back and let the defendant strut inside and slam the door
behind him.'

'The case isn't over yet,' Jess reminded them, unwilling
to rejoice too early. They still had other witnesses to
cross-examine, final arguments to deliver, and the unpredicta-
bility of the jury to contend with. One could never get too
cocky.

'My favorite moment,' Neil was saying as they settled in
behind their desks, 'was when you asked him if he'd ever heard
of the Aurora County Bowmen.'

'And he didn't move,' Barbara continued, 'but you could see
his cheeks kind of sink in.'

Jess permitted herself a loud, raucous laugh. That had been
her favorite moment too.

'Well, well, the ice maiden cracks.' Greg leaned in from the
doorway, one hand on either side of the frame.

'What can we do for you, Greg?' Jess felt her good mood about
to evaporate.

Greg ambled toward Jess's desk, shaking a loosely clenched
fist, as if he were about to toss a dice. 'I've got a present for you.'

'A present for me,' Jess repeated dully.

'Something you need. Very badly.' His voice all but spun with
innuendo.

'Is it bigger than a breadbox?' Neil asked.

'I could really use a breadbox,' Barbara stated.

Jess looked Greg coolly in the eye and waited. She said nothing.

'No guesses?' he asked.

'No patience,' Jess told him, gathering up her things. 'Look, Greg, I want to get a bit more work done here, then I'm going home. It's been a very long day.'

'Need a ride?' Greg's lips curved into a wavy line, like a small, thin snake.

'I've already offered to drive Jess home,' Neil said quickly, and Jess smiled gratefully.

'But I've got what you need,' Greg persisted, opening his fist and dropping a set of keys onto the desk in front of Jess. 'The keys to Madame's apartment.'

Jess reached for the new set of keys, the stale scent of Greg's cologne bouncing off the shiny metal. 'How did you get these?'

'Some woman delivered them this afternoon. Kind of cute actually, except that her thighs were in two different time zones.'

'You're a class act,' Barbara told him.

'Hey, I'm the sensitive new man of the nineties.' He sauntered back to the door, his fingers waving good-bye, then disappeared down the hall.

'Where's my crossbow?' Barbara asked.

'They're never around when you need them.' Jess glanced over the list of witnesses who would be testifying the next day, and jotted down a few notes before feeling her eyes cross with fatigue. 'How're things coming on the Alvarez case?'

'Examination for discovery is coming up next week,' Barbara told her. 'I'm almost finished taking depositions, and it doesn't look like McCauliff is in the mood to bargain.'

'McCauliff loves nothing better than the sound of his own voice echoing in a crowded courtroom. Be careful. He'll try to intimidate you by using lots of big words nobody understands,' Jess warned them. 'Think you can handle him?'

'I've got my dictionary ready,' Neil told her, and smiled.

Jess tried to smile back, but her mouth was too tired to cooperate, and she managed only a slight twitch. 'That's it for me, gang. I'm gonna call it a day.'

Barbara checked her watch. 'You feeling all right?'

'I'm exhausted.'

'Don't get sick on us now,' Barbara pleaded. 'We're entering the home stretch.'

'I don't have time to get sick,' Jess agreed.

'Come on, you heard me tell Oliver I was driving you home,' Neil volunteered.

'Don't be silly, Neil. It's way out of your way.'

'You trying to make a liar out of me?'

'When are you going to give in and buy a new car?' Barbara asked.

Jess pictured her once proud red Mustang, battered and broken, covered in excrement. 'As soon as I get Rick Ferguson behind bars,' she said.

The phone was ringing when she got to her apartment. 'Just a minute,' she called out, fiddling unsuccessfully with her new key, twisting it in the lock. 'Damn it, come on. Turn, for God's sake.'

The phone continued to ring, the key still refusing to connect properly. Had Greg Oliver given her the wrong set of keys? she wondered, then asked herself whether such an error would have been deliberate or accidental. Or maybe the fault lay with Don's secretary. Maybe she'd mixed up Jess's keys with her own. Or possibly the locksmith had made the mistake. Maybe the keys were defective. Maybe she'd never get inside her apartment. Maybe she'd grow old and die right here in her hallway without ever seeing the inside of her apartment again.

Maybe if she just calmed down and stopped trying so hard.

The key turned in the lock. The door opened. The phone stopped ringing.

'At least you're inside,' Jess said, acknowledging her canary with a wave of her fingers, uncomfortably bringing Greg Oliver to mind. She set her briefcase down, pulled off her boots, and rifled through the mail she'd carried upstairs in her coat pocket. Nothing interesting, she thought gratefully, tossing both the letters and her coat across the sofa. 'So, Fred, I had quite a day today. A woman I hardly know bought me some new panties, and I got new keys, and look here, brand new locks.' She walked back to the door, locking and unlocking it several times until she felt the key turn easily, playing with the deadbolt as if it were a shiny new toy. 'And I was positively amazing in court,' she continued. 'Let me tell you about how my brilliant hunch paid off.'

She stopped.

'This is pathetic,' she said out loud. 'I'm talking to a goddamn canary.' She walked into the kitchen, looked toward the phone. 'Ring, damn you.'

The phone was stubbornly silent. This is silly, Jess thought, impatiently grabbing the phone from its receiver. The phone works both ways. Who said she had to wait until someone called her?

Except who would she call? She didn't really have any friends outside of the office. Judging from the lack of jazz riffs emanating from the apartment below, Walter Fraser wasn't home. She had no idea where to reach Adam. She was afraid to call her father. Her sister was barely speaking to her.

She could call Don, she thought, *should* call Don, share with him the news of her day, thank him for insisting that she come with him to Union Pier yesterday. If she hadn't, she would never have seen the sign for the Union Pier Gun Club, would never have thought to seek out archery clubs in the Chicago area, would never have had the chance to shine so brilliantly in court today. Not to mention, she should thank him for everything else he had done for her – the new underwear, new locks, new set of keys.

Which was precisely why she didn't want to call him, she understood. Like a spoiled child who has received too much and is in danger of being overwhelmed, she was tired of saying thank you, weary of being grateful. She couldn't share the news of her triumph in court today with Don without sharing at least part of the credit, and she wasn't ready to do that. 'You're getting very selfish in your old age,' she admonished herself aloud, then thought she was probably no more selfish now than she'd always been. 'What witnesses from the past could we dredge up to testify against you?' she asked, the image of her mother's tear-streaked face filling her mind before she had a chance to block it.

'The hell with this nonsense,' Jess growled, quickly dialing her sister's number in Evanston, waiting while it rang six times. 'I'm probably taking her away from the babies,' she muttered, debating whether or not to hang up when a strange voice answered the phone.

The voice was somewhere between a croak and a rasp, unidentifiable as to gender. 'Hello?' it said painfully.

'Who is this?' Jess asked in return. 'Maureen, is that you?'

'It's Barry,' the voice whispered.

'Barry! What's the matter?'

'Terrible cold,' Barry said, pushing the words out of his mouth with obvious effort. 'Laryngitis.'

'My God. Do you feel as bad as you sound?'

'Worse. The doctor put me on antibiotics. Maureen just went to the drugstore to pick up the prescription.'

'So, now she has four children to look after, not three,' Jess said without thinking.

There was a moment's silence.

'I'm sorry,' Jess apologized quickly. Hadn't she intended this call as a conciliatory gesture? 'I didn't mean to say that.'

'You just can't help yourself, can you?' Barry asked hoarsely.

'I said I was sorry.'

Another long pause. The sound of an almost other-worldly voice. Slow. Deliberate. 'Did you get my letter?'

Jess froze. The image of a urine-soaked piece of paper pushed itself in front of her eyes and under her nose. 'What letter?' Jess asked, hearing a baby cry in the distance.

'Shit, they're waking up,' Barry exclaimed, his voice surprisingly close to normal. 'I've got to go, Jess. We'll have to talk about this some other time. I'll tell Maureen you called. Always a pleasure talking to you.'

A busy signal assaulted her ears. Jess quickly hung up the

phone, then didn't move. Could she really be thinking what she was thinking? Could her brother-in-law, *her sister's husband*, for God's sake, father of her nephew and twin nieces, a respected *accountant,* of all things, could he really be the person responsible for that disgusting letter she'd received in the mail?

Certainly, he disliked her. They'd been at each other's throats almost since the wedding. She didn't like his values; he didn't like her attitude. He thought she was spoiled and humorless and deliberately provocative; she found him small-minded, controlling, and vengeful. She'd accused him of undermining her sister's autonomy; he'd accused her of undermining his parental authority. *One of these days, Jess, you'll go too far,* he'd told her that night at dinner. Had that been a threat or simply an acknowledgment of the way things were? She remembered how Barry had gloated about stealing a client away from his former partner and supposed friend. *I never forget*, he'd boasted. *I get even.*

Was the urine-soaked letter Barry's way of getting even? Had he sent her clippings of his public hair in order to prove some perverse point? Had she alienated him to such a loathsome degree?

How *many* men had she managed to alienate in her young life?

Jess massaged the bridge of her nose. The list of candidates was endless. Even after she eliminated all the men she'd helped send to prison, there were the countless number of other men she'd prosecuted, defence lawyers she'd offended, fellow workers she'd tangled with, potential suitors she'd scorned. Even her relatives weren't immune to her peculiar charm. Any one of a hundred men could have sent her that letter. She'd made enough enemies to keep the post office busy for weeks.

A buzzer sounded. Jess immediately picked up the phone, realizing as soon as she heard the busy signal that it wasn't the phone at all, but someone at the downstairs door. She approached the intercom by the front door cautiously, wondering who was there, not sure whether she wanted to find out.

'Who is it?' she asked.

'Adam,' came the simple response.

She buzzed him up. Seconds later, he was outside her door.

'I tried to phone,' he said as soon as he saw her. 'First, no one answered; then the line was busy. Are you going to invite me in?'

He's the wild card here, Jess. Just who is this man? she heard Don say.

'You must have been very close by.' Jess stood in the doorway, blocking his entrance. 'I wasn't on the phone that long.'

'I was around the corner.'

'Delivering shoes?'

'Waiting for you. Are you going to invite me in?' he asked again.

He's the wild card here, Jess.

Her mind raced back to when she'd first met Adam Stohn. The vandalization of her car, the urine-soaked letter, the torn underwear, all had taken place since their first meeting. Adam Stohn knew where she worked. He knew where she lived. He'd even spent the night on her sofa.

All right, so he'd had the opportunity to do these things, Jess acknowledged silently, losing herself momentarily in the soft stillness of his brown eyes. But what possible motive could he have for wanting to terrorize her?

Her mind rifled through old mental files. Was it possible she'd prosecuted him once? Sent him to prison? Maybe he was the brother of someone she'd sent to jail. Or the friend. Maybe he was someone's hired gun.

Or maybe he was the reincarnation of Al Capone, she scoffed. Maybe she could spend the rest of her life questioning the motives of every man who showed her even the most casual of interest. He doesn't want to kill you, for God's sake, she thought, stepping back and letting Adam inside her apartment.

267

He wants to get you into bed.

'I was curious about what happened yesterday,' he told her, taking off his jacket and throwing it over her coat, as if their coats were lovers.

Jess told him about having to break the news of Connie DeVuono's death to her mother and son, and about today's triumph in court. She left out that in between the two events she'd spent the night with her ex-husband.

'He's still in love with you, you know,' Adam said, twisting the dials on her stereo until he found a country music station. Garth Brooks was singing cheerfully about his father shooting and killing his mother in a jealous rage.

'Who?' Jess asked, knowing full well whom he meant.

'The bagel man,' Adam told her, pacing restlessly about her apartment, lifting the bag of bagels from the dining room table and holding them up. 'You forgot to put these in the freezer.'

'Oh, damn. They'll be hard as rocks.'

Adam redeposited the bag on the table, walked slowly back toward her. 'How do you feel?'

'Me? A little tired, I guess.'

'How do you feel about your ex-husband?' he qualified.

'I told you, we're friends.' Jess ached to sit down, was afraid to.

'I think there's more to it than that.'

'Then you're wrong.'

'I called you last night, Jess,' he told her, very close now. 'I called you till quite late. I think it was three in the morning when I finally gave up and went to sleep.'

'I wasn't aware I had to answer to you.'

Adam stopped, took two steps back, hands in the air. 'You're right. I have no business asking you these questions.'

'Why are you?'

'I'm not sure.' He looked as puzzled as she felt. 'I guess I just want to know where I stand. If you're still involved with your ex-husband, just say the word. I'm out of here.'

'I'm not involved,' Jess said quickly.

'And the bagel man?'

'He understands how I feel.'

'But he's hoping to change your mind.'

'He's involved with someone else.'

'Unless you change your mind.'

'I won't.'

They stared at each other for several seconds without speaking.

He's the wild card here, Jess.

In the next second, they were in each other's arms, his hands in her hair, her lips on his.

Just who is this man?

His hands reached down, drew her hips toward his, his lips moving down her neck.

Who is this Adam Stohn anyway, Jess? she heard Don ask again, feeling her ex-husband still inside her. How could she have let last night happen? How could she allow one man to make love to her one night, and another the next? Wasn't this the nineties? The age of AIDS? Wasn't promiscuity an outdated relic of more innocent times?

She almost laughed at the correlation of promiscuity with innocence. She was a lawyer all right, she thought. She could put a spin on anything.

'I can't do this,' she said quickly, pulling out of the embrace.

'Can't do what?' His voice sounded almost as hoarse as Barry's.

'I'm just not ready for this yet,' she told him, searching the room for invisible, disapproving eyes. 'I don't even know where you live.'

'You want to know where I live? I live on Sheffield,' he said quickly. 'A one-bedroom apartment. A five-minute walk from Wrigley Field.'

And suddenly they were laughing, great wondrous whoops of laughter straight from the gut. Jess felt the tension of the last few days break up and dissolve. She laughed for the sheer joy of it, for the miraculous release it provided. She laughed so hard her stomach ached and tears spilled from her eyes. Adam quickly kissed the tears away.

269

'No,' she said, pulling just out of his reach. 'I really can't. I need time to think.'

'How much time?'

'I could think over dinner,' she heard herself say.

He was already at the door. 'Where would you like to go?'

Again they were laughing; this time so hard Jess could barely stand up. 'How about I just make us something here?'

'I didn't think you cooked.'

'Follow me,' she told him, laughing her way toward the dining area, where she picked up the bag of bagels and carried it into the kitchen. 'One or two?' she asked, popping open the door of the microwave oven.

He held up two fingers. 'I'll open the wine.'

'I don't think there is any,' she said sheepishly.

'No wine?'

She opened the fridge. 'And no pop either.'

'No wine?' he said again.

'We can have water.'

'Bread and water,' he mused. 'Where'd you learn your culinary skills? The federal penitentiary?'

Jess stopped laughing. 'Have you ever been to prison?' she asked.

He looked startled, then amused. 'What kind of question is that?'

'Just trying to make conversation.'

'This is your idea of small talk?'

'You didn't answer me.'

'I didn't think you were serious.'

'I'm not,' Jess said quickly, putting four bagels on a plate and sticking them in the microwave.

'I've never been to prison, Jess,' Adam told her.

She shrugged, as if the matter were of absolutely no consequence. 'Not even to visit a friend?' The forced note of casualness sounded jarring even to her own ears.

'You think I consort with convicted felons? Jess, what am I doing here?'

'You tell me,' Jess said, but Adam's only answer was a smile.

'So you were an only child,' Jess said as they sat on the floor in front of the sofa finishing their dinner.

'A very spoiled only child,' he elaborated.

'My sister always says that children aren't apples — they don't spoil.'

'What else does your sister say?'

'That you can't spoil a child with too much love.'

'She sounds like a very good mother.'

'I think she is.'

'You sound surprised.'

'It's just not what I expected from her, that's all.'

'What did you expect from her?'

'I'm not sure. A brilliant career, I guess.'

'Maybe she thought she'd leave that to you.'

'Maybe,' Jess agreed, wondering how the conversation always reverted back to her. 'You and your wife never wanted children?'

'We wanted them,' he said. 'It just never worked out.'

Jess understood from the way his voice dropped that it was a topic he didn't wish to pursue. She finished the last of her bagel, lifted the glass of water to her lips.

'What was your mother like?' he asked suddenly.

'What?' Jess's hand started to shake, the water spilling from the glass onto the floor. She scrambled to her feet. 'Oh my God.'

His hand was immediately on her arm, gently pulling her back down. 'Relax, Jess, it's only water.' He used his napkin to wipe up the spill. 'What's the matter?'

'Nothing's the matter.'

'Then why are you shaking?'

'I'm not shaking.'

'What did your mother do to you?'

'What do you mean, what did she do?' Jess snapped angrily. 'She didn't do anything. What are you talking about?'

'Why won't you talk about her?'

'Why should I?'

'Because you don't want to,' he said evenly. 'Because you're afraid to.'

'Another one of my phobias?' Jess asked sarcastically.

'You tell me.'

'Anybody ever tell you you'd make a good lawyer?'

'What happened to your mother, Jess?'

Jess closed her eyes, saw her mother standing before her in the kitchen of their home, tears falling down her cheeks. I *don't need this, Jess, she was saying I don't need this from you.* Jess quickly opened her eyes. 'She disappeared,' she said finally.

'Disappeared?'

'She'd found a small lump in her breast, and she was pretty scared. She called the doctor, and he said he'd see her that afternoon. But she never showed up for her appointment. Nobody ever saw her again.'

'Then it's possible she's alive?'

'No, it's not possible,' Jess snapped. 'It's not possible.'

He reached for her, but she pulled away from his reach.

'She wouldn't abandon us just because she was scared,' Jess continued, speaking from somewhere deep inside her. 'I mean, even if she was scared, and I know she was, that doesn't mean she'd run out on us. She wasn't the kind of woman who would just walk out on her husband and daughters because she couldn't face reality. No matter how scared she was. No matter how angry.'

'Angry?'

'I didn't mean angry.'

'You said it.'

'I didn't mean it.'

'What was she angry about, Jess?'

'She wasn't angry.'

'She was angry at you, wasn't she?'

Jess looked toward the window. Her mother's tear-streaked face stared back at her through the antique lace curtains. *I don't need this, Jess. I don't need this from you.*

'I came downstairs and found her all dressed up,' Jess began.

272

'I asked her where she was going, and at first she wouldn't tell me. But eventually it came out that she'd found this lump in her breast, and she was going to see her doctor that afternoon.' Jess tried to laugh, but the laugh stuck in her throat, like a piece of bagel she could neither swallow nor cough up. 'It was just like my mother to get all dressed up in the morning when she didn't have to be somewhere till late in the afternoon.'

'Kind of like someone who selects the clothes she's going to wear the next day the night before.'

Jess ignored the implication. 'She asked me if I'd go with her to the doctor. I said, sure. But then we got into an argument. A typical mother-daughter kind of thing. She thought I was being headstrong. I thought she was being overprotective. I told her to stay out of my life. She told me not to bother taking her to the doctor's. I said, have it your way, and slammed out of the house. By the time I got back, she'd already left.'

'And you blame yourself for what happened.' It was more statement than question.

Jess pushed herself to her feet, walked to the bird's cage with exaggerated strides. 'Hi, Fred, how're you doing?'

'Fred's doing great,' Adam told her, coming up behind her. 'I'm not so sure about his owner. That's a shitload of guilt you've been carrying around all these years.'

'Hey, whatever happened to our pact?' Jess asked, swiping at her tears, refusing to look at him, concentrating all her attention on the small yellow bird. 'No secrets, no lies, remember?' She made awkward chirping noises against the side of the cage.

'Do you ever let him out?' Adam asked.

'You're not supposed to let canaries out of their cages,' Jess said loudly, hoping to still the shaking in her body with the sound of her voice. 'They're not like parakeets. Parakeets are domestic birds. Canaries are wild. They aren't meant to be let out of their cages.'

'So you never have to worry about him flying away,' Adam said softly.

This time the implication was too blatant to ignore. Jess spun

273

round angrily. 'The bird is a pet, not a metaphor.'

'Jess—'

'Just when did you give up psychiatry for selling shoes?' she demanded bitterly. 'Who the hell are you, Adam Stohn?'

They stood facing one another, Jess shaking, Adam absolutely still.

'Do you want me to go?' he asked.

No, she thought. 'Yes,' she said.

He walked slowly to the door.

'Adam,' she called, and he stopped, his hand on the doorknob. 'I think it's probably a good idea if you don't come back.'

For an instant she thought he might turn round, take her into his arms, confess all. But he didn't, and in the next instant, he was gone and she was alone in a room full of ghosts and shadows.

Chapter Twenty-One

By the end of the week, the Medical Examiner's report on Connie DeVuono was in and the jury in the Terry Wales murder trial was out.

Connie DeVuono had been raped, then beaten and strangled with a piece of thin magnetic wire that had sliced through her jugular and almost severed her head from her body. Forensics had determined that the wire that caused her death was identical to wire found in the factory that employed Rick Ferguson. A warrant had just been issued for Rick Ferguson's arrest.

'How long do you think the jury will be out?' Barbara Cohen was asking when the phone rang on Jess's desk.

'You know better than that,' Jess told her, reaching for the phone. 'Could be hours. Could be days.'

Barbara checked her watch. 'It's already been over twenty-four hours.'

Jess shrugged, as anxious as her assistant but reluctant to admit it. She picked up the phone, brought the receiver to her ear. 'Jess Koster.'

'He's disappeared,' Don said instead of hello.

Jess felt her stomach lurch. She didn't have to ask who Don was talking about. 'When?'

'Probably sometime in the middle of the night. My guy just called. He's been watching the house all night and when he didn't see Ferguson leave for work this morning at the usual time, he got suspicious, waited awhile, finally did some snooping around. He could see Ferguson's mother either asleep or passed out in bed; Ferguson was nowhere to be seen. My guy called the warehouse, and sure enough, Ferguson hasn't shown up. It looks like he picked up on the tail, figured the police were about to arrest him, and climbed out one of the back windows while it was still dark.'

'The irony is that the police *were* about to arrest him,' Jess admitted. 'We issued a warrant this morning.'

Don's tone became instantly businesslike, no longer the concerned ex-husband but the ultimate professional, carefully attuned to the rights of his client. 'What've you got?' he asked.

'The wire used to kill Connie DeVuono was the same kind of wire found in the warehouse that employs Rick Ferguson.'

'What else?'

'What else do I need?'

'More than that.'

'Not to bring him in.'

'Any prints?'

'No,' Jess admitted.

'Just a flimsy piece of wire?'

'Strong enough to kill Connie DeVuono,' Jess told him. 'Strong enough to convict your client.'

There was a slight pause. 'Okay, Jess, I don't want to get into all this now. We can talk about the case against my client as soon as the police bring him in. In the meantime, I've asked my guy to keep an eye on you.'

'What? Don, I told you I don't want a baby-sitter.'

'*I* want,' Don insisted. 'Indulge me, Jess. Just for a day or two. It won't kill you.'

'And Rick Ferguson might?'

His sigh echoed against her ear. 'You won't even know you're being watched.'

'Rick Ferguson knew.'

'Just do this for me, will you?'

'Any ideas where your client went?'

'None.'

'I better go,' Jess told him, already thinking ahead to what she would tell the police.

'I take it the jury's still out in the Crossbow case?'

'Over twenty-four hours.'

'Word on the street says your closing argument was a classic.'

276

'Juries are notably impervious to classics,' Jess said, anxious now to get off the phone.

'I'll call you later.'

Jess hung up without saying goodbye.

'Detective Mansfield just called,' Neil told her. 'Apparently Rick Ferguson's skipped. They're issuing an APB for his arrest.'

The phone rang on Jess's desk.

'Looks like it's going to be one of those days,' Barbara said. 'You want me to get that?'

Jess shook her head, answered the phone. 'Jess Koster.'

'Jess, it's Maureen. Is it a bad time?'

Jess felt her shoulders slump. 'Well, it's not the best.' She could almost see the disappointment in her sister's face. It seeped into the air around her, like an invisible, poison gas. 'I can spare a few minutes.'

'Barry just told me this morning that you called on Monday,' Maureen apologized. 'I'm so sorry.'

'Why should you apologize for Barry's mistakes?'

There was silence.

'Sorry,' Jess said quickly. Couldn't she ever leave well enough alone?

'He's been so sick all week. He could hardly think straight, he was so stuffed up. The doctor was afraid it might be pneumonia, but whatever it was, the antibiotics killed it. He went back to work this morning.'

'I'm glad to hear he's feeling better.' Jess immediately pictured the urine-soaked letter filled with pubic hair she had received in the mail, wondering again whether Barry could have sent it.

'Anyway, he just remembered about your phone call as he was walking out the door this morning. I almost killed him.'

'A lot of killing going on in your house these days,' Jess remarked absently.

'What?'

'So, how've *you* been?'

'Me? I don't have time to get sick,' Maureen said, sounding

277

very much like her younger sister. 'Anyway, I know how busy you are, and how you don't like to be interrupted at work, but I didn't want you to think I was ignoring your phone call. I'm really so glad that you phoned . . .' Her voice threatened to dissolve into tears.

'How's Dad?' Jess asked, realizing she hadn't spoken to her father in weeks, feeling the familiar pattern of guilt and anger. Guilt that she hadn't spoken to him, anger for her guilt.

'He's really happy, Jess.'

'I'm glad.'

'Sherry's very good for him. She makes him laugh, keeps him on his toes. They're coming for dinner next Friday night. We're going to put up the Christmas tree and decorate the house and everything.' She paused. 'Would you like to join us?'

Jess closed her eyes. How long could she go on hurting the very people who meant the most to her? 'Sure,' she said.

'Sure?'

'Sounds great.'

'Great?' Maureen repeated, as if she needed the confirmation of her own voice to accept what she was hearing. 'Yea,' she agreed, 'it will be great. We've missed you. Tyler hasn't stopped playing with that toy airplane you bought him. And you won't believe how much the twins have grown.'

Jess laughed. 'Really, Maureen, it hasn't been that long.'

'Almost two months,' Maureen reminded her, catching Jess off guard. Had two months really elapsed since the last time she'd seen her family?

'I better go now,' Jess told her.

'Oh, sure. You must be swamped. I heard on the news that the jury in that Crossbow killing thing retired yesterday. Any word?'

'None yet.'

'Good luck.'

'Thanks.'

'See you next week,' Maureen said.

'See you next week,' Jess agreed.

'Something wrong?' Barbara asked as Jess replaced the receiver.

Jess shook her head, pretended to be studying a file on her desk. Almost two months! she thought. Two months since her last visit to her sister's house. Two months since she'd hugged her nephew and cradled her infant nieces in her arms. Two months since she'd seen her father.

How could she have let that happen? Weren't they all she had left? What was the matter with her? Was she so self-centered, so self-absorbed, that she couldn't see past her own narrow little world? Was she so used to dealing with scum that she no longer knew how to act around decent people who loved her, whose only crime was in wanting to live their lives as they saw fit? Wasn't that all she'd ever wanted − no, demanded − for herself?

Wasn't that exactly what she'd been fighting about with her mother on the day her mother disappeared?

Jess threw her head back, feeling the muscles in her shoulders cramp. Why couldn't she stop obsessing on her mother? Why was she still a prisoner of something that had happened eight long years ago? Why did everything ultimately have to hark back to the day her mother had vanished?

Damn Adam Stohn, she thought, the cramping in her shoulders spreading to the other muscles in her back. He was responsible for her current malaise. He'd gotten her to open up, to talk about her mother. He'd unleashed all the anguish and the sadness and the guilt she'd been suppressing for so long.

It wasn't Adam's fault, she knew. He couldn't have known the emotional minefield he was walking into when he'd asked his simple questions, the raw nerves he was exposing. You can't put a band-aid on a cancer, she thought, and expect it to heal. Pull the band-aid off after years of benign neglect, and you had a full-scale malignancy raging out of control.

No wonder he hadn't wanted to stick around, that he'd been in such a hurry to leave. 'Do you want me to go?' he asked, and she'd said, 'I think it's probably a good idea if you don't come back.' And that was that, she thought now, remembering that she'd also once told him that a lawyer's good word was the only currency she had.

He was only being as good as her word.

'Damn you, Adam Stohn,' she whispered.

'Did you say something?' Barbara asked, looking up from her desk.

Jess shook her head, an acute sense of unease creeping into her chest, toying with her breathing, playing havoc with her equilibrium. She felt dizzy, light-headed, as if she might topple from her chair. Oh no, she thought, automatically stiffening, the world around her disappearing into a cloud of anxiety. Don't fight it, she told herself quickly. Go with it. Go with it. What's the worst that can happen? So you fall off your chair. So you land on your ass. So you throw up? So what?

Slowly, she released the air in her lungs and floated into the center of the large, miasmal mist. Almost immediately, it began evaporating around her. Her dizziness subsided and her breathing returned to normal, the muscles in her shoulders relaxing, surrendering their tension. Familiar sounds filtered to her ears − the hum of the fax machine, the clicking of computer keys, the ringing of the telephone.

Jess watched Neil walk over and pick up the phone on her desk. How long had it been ringing? 'Neil Strayhorn,' he pronounced clearly, his eyes locked on Jess. 'They are? Now?'

Jess took a deep breath, rose quickly to her feet. She didn't have to ask. The jury was in.

'Ladies and gentlemen of the jury, have you reached your verdict?'

Jess felt the familiar surge of adrenaline race through her body, though she was holding her breath. She both loved and hated this moment. Loved it for its drama, its suspense, the knowledge that victory or defeat was just a word away. Hated it for the same reasons. Hated it because she hated to lose. Hated it because, in the end, winning or losing was really what it was all about. One lawyer's truth against another's, justice relegated to the role of hapless observer. No such thing as the whole truth.

The foreman cleared his throat, checked the paper in his hand before speaking, as if he might have forgotten the decision the jury had reached, as if he wanted to make absolutely sure what it said. 'We, the jury,' he began, then cleared his throat again, 'find the defendant, Terry Wales, guilty of murder in the first degree.'

Immediately the courtroom erupted. Reporters ran from the room; briefcases snapped shut; friends and relatives of the deceased hugged each other in tearful abandon. Judge Harris thanked, then dismissed the jurors. Jess embraced her partners, accepted their congratulations, caught the look of resignation in Hal Bristol's eyes, the sneer of scorn on the defendant's lips as he was led away.

Outside the courtroom, the reporters thronged around her, pushing microphones up against her mouth, waving notebooks in front of her face. 'Were you surprised at the verdict? Did you expect to win? How do you feel?' they asked as cameras clicked and flash strobes exploded.

'We have great faith in this country's jury system,' Jess told the reporters, walking toward the elevators. 'We never doubted the outcome for a minute.'

'Are you going to ask for the death penalty?' someone called out.

'You bet,' Jess answered, pressing the button for the elevator, hearing Hal Bristol tell another reporter he intended to appeal.

'How does it feel to win this case?' a woman shouted from the back of the throng.

Jess knew she should remind the reporters that what was important here wasn't winning but the truth, that a guilty man had been convicted of a heinous crime, that justice had been served. She smiled widely. 'It feels great,' she said.

'Hey, was that your picture I saw in the paper this morning?' Vasiliki watched as Jess pulled her hair into a ponytail in front of the long mirror of the Wen-Do instruction hall.

'That was me,' Jess acknowledged shyly, her head still thumping from too many beers at Jean's Restaurant the night before. Normally she didn't frequent Jean's after work, unlike many of the prosecuting attorneys to whom Jean's was a second home. But everyone kept telling her a celebration was in order, and in truth, she'd felt like a nice long pat on the back.

She'd called her father right after she got back to her office, but he wasn't home, phoned her sister, but she was busy with the babies and had time for only the briefest of congratulations.

She'd called Don, told him of her victory, heard him mumble his apologies about not being able to take her out for a celebration dinner, something about a prior commitment. A prior commitment named Trish, Jess thought but didn't say, wondering what she expected from the man.

Then she'd done something she'd never done before, never permitted herself the luxury of doing before: she'd gone into the washroom, locked herself in a cubicle, closed her eyes, and just stood there. 'I won,' she'd said softly, allowing the ghost of her mother to pull her into a proud embrace.

The celebration at Jean's lasted until the early hours of the morning. Her trial supervisor, Tom Olinsky, had driven her home, walking her right to her door and making sure she got inside safely. Jess never saw the man Don had hired to watch out for her, but she knew he was there, and was grateful in spite of herself.

She'd fallen into a deep sleep, hadn't even heard her alarm clock go off, and was almost late for her self-defense class, arriving just seconds before everyone else, her hair not even brushed.

And now here she stood, her stomach empty and her head pounding, and she was expected to yell and execute eagle claws and zipper punches and hammer fists. 'Use those bony knuckles!' she could hear Dominic shouting even before he entered the room.

'You didn't tell us you were some hot-shot district attorney,' Vasiliki scolded as the other women circled round her.

'State's attorney,' Jess corrected automatically.

'Whatever, you're a celebrity!'

Jess smiled, uncomfortable with her new status. The other women stared at her with open curiosity.

'I read you're gonna ask for the death penalty,' Maryellen said. 'Think you'll get it?'

'I'm keeping my fingers crossed.'

'I don't believe in the death penalty,' Ayisha stated.

'She's young,' her mother whispered.

The curtains parted and Dominic entered the room. 'Good afternoon, everybody. Are you ready to kick ass?'

The women responded with a variety of grunts and raised hammer fists.

'Good. Let's all spread out now. Give yourselves lots of room. That's right. Now, what's the first line of defense?'

'*Kiyi,*' Vasiliki shouted.

'*Kiyi,* that's right. And what is *kiyi*?' Dominic stared directly at Jess.

'It's a cry,' she began.

'Not a cry. A great yell,' he corrected. 'A roar.'

'A roar,' Jess repeated.

'Women cry too easily. They don't roar nearly enough,' he instructed. 'Now, what is *kiyi*?'

'A roar,' Jess responded, the word reverberating against her brain.

'So, Jess, let me hear you roar,' Dominic instructed.

'Just me?' Jess asked.

'These women probably aren't gonna be with you when someone tries to grab you off the street,' he told her.

'You don't seem to have any trouble roaring in the courtroom,' Vasiliki reminded her slyly.

'Come on,' Dominic ordered. 'I'm coming at you. I'm big and I'm dangerous and I want your ass.'

'Hohh!' Jess yelled.

'Louder.'

'Hohh!'

'You can do better than that.'

'*Hohh!*' Jess roared.

'That's better. Now I'm having second thoughts about messing with you. What about you?' Dominic turned his attention to Catarina.

Jess smiled, pushing her shoulders back proudly, listening to the sound of women roaring.

'Okay, let's see those eagle claws through the attacker's eyes,' Dominic told them, once again starting with Jess. 'That's right. A little more defined,' he told her, fitting his fingers over hers, shaping them into an eagle's talon. 'Now, go for my eyes.'

'I can't.'

'If you don't, I'll cut you into little pieces,' he warned. 'Come on. Go for my eyes.'

Jess lunged at her instructor's eyes, watching with relief as he ducked out of her way.

'Not bad. But don't worry about me. I can take care of myself. Try it again.'

She did.

'Better. Next,' he continued, again working his way down the line.

They worked on their eagle claws and zipper punches and hammer fists until they were fluid motions. 'Don't be afraid to drive the bone from your attacker's nose right up into his brain.'

'In that case,' Vasiliki quipped, 'shouldn't we be aiming for below the belt?'

The women laughed.

'Hey, why is it that women don't have any brains?' Vasiliki asked teasingly, her hands on her wide hips.

'Why?' Jess asked, giggling already.

'Because we don't have penises to keep them in!'

The women hooted.

'I got another one,' Vasiliki continued quickly. 'Why can't men ever tell when women have orgasms?'

'Why?' they all asked.

'Because they're never there!'

The women roared.

'Ouch!' their instructor yelled. 'That's enough. I give up. You got me, ladies. I'm a dead man. You can put away those hammer fists. You don't need 'em.'

'What's that small piece of flesh at the end of a penis?' Vasiliki whispered to Jess as the women rearranged themselves in a straight line.

Jess shrugged her shoulders.

'A man!' Vasiliki shouted.

'Okay, okay,' Dominic said, 'let's start putting some of that hostility and aggression to good use, shall we?' He paused to make sure he had their undivided attention. 'Now, I'm gonna teach you some other moves that are designed to help you fend off an attacker. Say you're walking home alone, and some guy grabs you from behind. Or some guy lurches out of the bushes and grabs you. What's the first thing you do?'

'Kiyi!' Maryellen answered.

'*Hohh!*' her daughter said at the same time.

'Good,' Dominic told them. 'Start screaming! Anything that's gonna get attention. Doesn't have to be "Hohh!" but it does have to be loud. Now, what happens if he's got his hand round your mouth, or a knife at your throat? You're not gonna scream. What are you gonna do?'

'Faint,' Catarina said.

'No, you're not gonna faint,' Dominic assured her. 'You're gonna . . . what?'

'Go with him,' Jess stated. 'Don't resist. Use the attacker's force against him.'

'Good. Okay, let's try a few moves.' He motioned to Jess. 'I'm gonna grab you and I want you to pretend to go with me.' He reached out and grabbed Jess's hand, pulling her toward him in slow motion. 'Come with me, that's right. Okay, now you're here, push hard against me. That's right. Use my own weight against me. Use the force of my pulling you in to push me off. Push. Good.' He let go of Jess's hand. 'Once you've got the bastard off balance, remember to use whatever weapon is at hand, including your feet. Kick, bite, gouge, trip. We've gone over some of the things you can do with your hands. Now here's some moves you can do with your feet.'

285

Jess watched carefully while Dominic executed a few choice maneuvers.

'What about flips? Can we flip 'em into the air?' Vasiliki asked.

They learned flips, how to use their shoulders to lead the attack, carry the weight. At the end of almost two hours, the women were breathing hard and fighting harder.

'Okay, let's see you put this together,' Dominic told them. 'Divide up into twos. Vas, you and Maryellen pair up; Ayisha, go with Catarina. You,' he said, pointing at Jess, 'come with me.'

Jess took several tentative steps toward Dominic. Suddenly he reached out and grabbed her, pulling her toward him. *'Hohh!'* she screamed loudly, hearing the word fill the room, as she instinctively pulled back. Damn, she thought, how many times did she have to be told? Go with him. Don't resist. Go with him.

She allowed herself to be pulled forward, fell against him, then pushed her full weight into him, quickly using her feet to trip him and her shoulder to upend him before falling with him to the ground.

She'd done it, she thought triumphantly. She'd gone with her attacker, used his superior strength against him, flipped him flat on his rear end, proved she wasn't so vulnerable after all. She threw her head back and laughed out loud.

Suddenly she felt a tapping at her forehead, turned to see Dominic smiling at her, the index and middle fingers of his right hand pressed against her temple like the barrel of a gun. His thumb snapped down, then up, as if pulling an imaginary trigger. 'Bang,' he said calmly. 'You're dead.'

Chapter Twenty-Two

'Goddamn, son-of-a-bitch.' Jess was still muttering as she walked along Willow Street. What the hell was she doing wasting her time, her Saturday afternoons, for God's sake, one of the very few free afternoons she had, for God's sake, trying to learn how to defend herself, pretending she was invulnerable, for God's sake, when in truth, she was no match for anyone really determined to do her harm. A well-timed 'Hohh!' wouldn't do much good against a crossbow; an eagle's claw to the eyes was no match for a bullet to the brain.

Here she'd been roaring away, feeling invincible, in control, all-powerful, and all it took was a couple of fingers to rip her illusions into pathetic shreds. There was no such thing as control. She was as vulnerable as anyone else.

Next week, Dominic had assured them, next week he'd show them how to disarm a knife-wielding or gun-toting attacker. Great, Jess thought now, crossing the road. Something to look forward to.

She saw him as soon as she turned the corner onto Orchard Street. He was coming down her front steps, the collar of his bomber jacket turned up against the cold. She stopped, not sure whether to continue or whether to turn on her heels and run as fast as she could in the other direction. Recognizing danger and getting away from it came first on the list of priorities, she had been taught. Running was what worked most often for most women.

She didn't run. She just stood there, stood waiting in the middle of the sidewalk until he turned and saw her, stood there while he walked toward her, stood there as he reached for her, drew her into his arms.

'We need to talk,' Adam said.

287

* * *

'I grew up in Springfield,' he was saying, leaning across the small table of the Italian restaurant they had gone to their first evening together. It was still early. The restaurant was almost empty. Carla hovered nearby, although she made no move to approach them, as if she understood there were things that needed to be said before anyone could even think of food. 'I think I already told you that I'm an only child,' Adam continued. 'My family is quite well off. My father is a psychiatrist,' he said, and laughed softly, 'so you weren't so far off the mark when you asked me when I'd given up psychiatry for selling shoes. I guess some things are in the genes.

'My mother is an art consultant. She has a thriving little business she runs out of their home. A very large home, I might add, filled with expensive antiques and modern paintings. I grew up with the best of everything. I learned to expect the best of everything. I thought I was entitled to the best of everything.'

He stopped. Jess watched his hands fold and unfold on the top of the table. 'Things always came pretty easily for me: school, grades, girls. Everything I wanted, I more or less got. And for a long time I wanted a girl named Susan Cunningham. She was pretty and popular and as spoiled as I was. Her father is H. R. Cunningham, if you know anything about the construction business.'

Jess shook her head, focusing on his mouth as he spoke.

'Anyway, I wanted her, I set my sights on her, and I married her. Needless to say, since we are now divorced, it was not a marriage made in heaven. We didn't have a thing in common except we both liked looking in the mirror. What can I say? We were two very self-absorbed people who thought everything we did and said deserved a round of applause. When we didn't get it, we pouted and argued and generally made life miserable for one another.

'The only thing we did right was Beth.'

Jess looked from his mouth to his eyes, but Adam quickly looked away. 'Beth?'

'Our daughter.'

'You have a daughter? You said—'

'I know what I said. It wasn't the truth.'

'Go on,' Jess directed softly, holding her breath.

'Beth was born a few years after we got married, and she was the sweetest little thing you ever saw. She looked like a china doll, one of those porcelain figurines that are so beautiful and so delicate you're almost afraid to touch them. Here,' he said, shaking hands fumbling for the wallet in his pocket, removing a small color photograph of a blond, smiling, little girl in a white dress with bright red smocking across the top.

'She's lovely,' Jess agreed, trying to still his hand with her own.

'She's dead,' Adam said, returning the picture to his wallet, stuffing the wallet back into the pocket of his jeans.

'What?! My God! How? When?'

Adam looked across the table at Jess, but his eyes were unfocused and Jess knew he didn't see her. When he spoke again, his voice was strained, distant, as if he was speaking to her from some faraway place. 'She was six years old. My marriage was pretty much over. Susan claimed I was married to my work, I claimed she was married to hers. We both claimed that neither one of us spent enough time with our daughter. We were both right.

'Anyway, my father could see what was going on and he suggested counselling, and we tried it for awhile, but our hearts weren't really in it. Her parents could see what was going on too, but their approach was a little different. Instead of therapy, they bought us a cruise to the Bahamas. They thought that if we could just spend a few weeks alone together, maybe we could sort through our differences. They offered to take care of Beth. We said okay, what the hell, why not?

'Beth didn't want us to go. Kids sense when things aren't right, and I guess she was afraid that if we left, one of us might not come back, I don't know.' He stared toward the door, saying nothing for several seconds. 'Anyway, she started having tantrums, stomach aches, that sort of thing. The morning we were leaving, she complained about a stiff neck. We didn't pay too much attention. She'd been complaining about one thing or another for several days. We just figured it was her way of trying to get us to stay home. We took her temperature, but she didn't have a fever, and Susan's parents assured us that they'd take good care of her, whisk her off to the doctor at the first sign of any real problems. So we left on our cruise.

'That night she developed a slight fever. Susan's parents called the doctor who told them to give Beth a couple of Children's Tylenol and bring her to his office in the morning if she wasn't any better. By the middle of the night, her fever had spiked to almost a hundred and five and she was delirious. My father-in-law bundled her up and took her to the hospital, but it was too late. She was dead before morning.

'Meningitis,' Adam said, answering the question in Jess's eyes.

'My God, how awful.'

'They called us on the ship, arranged for us to get home, but of course there was no home. The only thing that had been keeping us together was gone. We tried grief counselling, but we were far too angry with each other for it to work. Basically, we didn't want it to work. We wanted to blame each other. We wanted what happened to be somebody's fault.

'I thought of suing the doctor, but we had no case. I even thought of suing my in-laws. Instead, I sued for divorce. And then I ran. Gave up my job, gave up my home, gave up everything. What does anything mean anyway when you lose a child? So I took off. Came to the big city. Got a job selling men's ties at Carson, Pirie, Scott and Company. Then I discovered women's shoes and the rest is history.'

He looked from Jess to the door to the table and back to Jess. 'I met a lot of women but I stayed clear of any involvements. I flirted; I played games; I sold lots of shoes. But no way would you catch me drifting into another relationship. No sir. Who needs that kind of heartache?

'And then you walked into the store, and you were banging the heel of that shoe into the palm of your hand so hard it was only a matter of time before one or the other broke. And I looked at you, and I looked into your eyes, and I thought, this person is as wounded inside as I am.'

Jess felt tears fill her eyes and looked briefly away.

'I wasn't going to call you,' he continued, his voice drawing her eyes back to his. 'The last thing I was looking for was to get involved in somebody else's problems, although, who knows, maybe that's exactly what I was looking for. At least that's what my father would probably say. Maybe it was just time, I don't know. But when those damn boots came in, I knew I had to see you again. And so I called and asked you out, although I kept telling myself it would be a one-shot deal. I certainly had no intention of calling you again.

'But I kept finding myself at your door.

'And all this past week, I've been thinking about you, and that even though you told me not to come back, that I had to see you, and I haven't sold a single goddamn pair of shoes . . .'

Jess found herself laughing and crying at the same time. 'And your parents?' she asked.

'I haven't seen them since I left Springfield.'

'That must be very hard on you.'

He looked surprised. 'Most people would have said hard on *them*, but yes, it's been hard on me too,' he admitted.

'Then why do it?'

'I guess I just haven't been ready to face them,' he said. 'I speak to them occasionally. They're trying to understand, give me the time and space I need, but, you're right, I guess it doesn't make much sense anymore. Just that you get into patterns. Dangerous patterns sometimes.'

'You didn't sell shoes back in Springfield, did you?' she asked, knowing the answer but asking anyway.

He shook his head.

'What did you do?'

'You don't want to know.'

'I have this awful feeling I already do,' she stated. 'You're a lawyer, aren't you?'

He nodded guiltily. 'I wanted to tell you, but I kept thinking that since I wasn't going to call you again, what difference did it make?'

'And here I went on and on about the law, about how the legal system works.'

'I loved it. It was like a refresher course. It made me realize how much I've missed the practise of law. Your enthusiasm is contagious. And you're a great teacher.'

'I feel like such an idiot.'

'I'm the only idiot at this table,' he corrected her.

'What kind of law did you practice?' She started laughing even before she heard his answer.

'Criminal,' came the expected response.

'Of course.'

Jess rubbed her forehead, thinking she should have run when she had the chance.

'I really never intended to lie to you,' he reiterated. 'I just never thought it would get this far.'

'How far is it?' Jess asked.

'Far enough for me to know I didn't want to lose you. Far enough for me to think you deserved to know the truth. Far enough for me to think I'm falling in love,' he said softly.

'Tell me about your daughter,' Jess said, reaching across the table and taking his hands in hers.

'What can I say?' he asked, his voice shaking.

'Tell me some of the nice things you remember.'

There was a long pause. Carla approached, then caught the look in Jess's eye, and backed away.

'I remember when she was four years old, and she was all excited because it was her birthday the next day,' Adam began. 'Susan had bought her a new party dress and she couldn't wait to wear it. She'd invited a bunch of kids over for a party, and we'd arranged for a magician and all that stuff you do at kids' parties. Anyway, we went to bed, I'm sound asleep, and all of a sudden I felt this gentle tap on my arm, and I opened my eyes, and there was Beth standing there looking at me. And I said, "What is it, sweetie?" And she said in this very excited little voice, "It's my birthday." And I said, "Yes it is, but go back to bed now, honey, it's three o'clock in the morning." And she said, "Oh, I thought it was time to get up. I got all dressed and everything." And there she was, she'd put on her party dress all by herself, and her shoes and her white frilly socks, and she was standing there all ready to go at three o'clock in the morning, and I remember thinking how wonderful it was to be that excited about something. And I got up and I walked her back to her room, and she got back into her pyjamas, and I tucked her into bed, and she fell right off to sleep.'

'I love that story,' Jess told him.

Adam smiled, tears forming in the corners of his eyes. 'One time at nursery school, she must have been all of three, she told me there was this little boy who was bothering her in class, that he was calling her names and she didn't like it. So I asked her what names the little boy was calling her, and she said, in this sweet, innocent little voice, "He calls me a fucker and a sucker."'

Jess burst out laughing.

'Yes, that was my reaction too, I'm afraid,' Adam said, laughing now as well. 'And of course that only encouraged her. And she looked at me with those enormous brown eyes and said, "Will you come to school with me today, Daddy? Will you tell him not to call me a fucker and a sucker again?"'

'And did you?'

'I told her I was sure she could handle the little bugger all by herself. And I guess she must have, because we never heard about him again.'

'You sound like you were a good daddy.'

'I like to think I was.'

'Were you a good lawyer?' Jess asked after a pause.

'Springfield's finest.'

'Ever think of going back to it?'

'To Springfield, never.'

'To the law.'

He paused, signalled for Carla, who hesitated, then approached cautiously. 'We'll have the special pizza and two glasses of Chianti, please.'

Carla nodded her approval, then left without speaking. 'You didn't answer my question,' Jess reminded him.

'Do I ever think about going back to the law?' he repeated, measuring out each word. 'Yes, I think about it.'

'Would you do it?'

'I don't know. Maybe. My knees are getting a little tired of the shoe business. Maybe if an inspiring case came along, I might be persuaded. Who knows?'

Carla brought their drinks to the table. Jess immediately lifted her glass in the air, clicking it against Adam's.

'To sweet memories,' she said.

'To sweet memories,' he agreed.

As soon as they got to her apartment, she knew something was wrong.

Jess stood frozen outside her door, waiting, listening.

'What's the matter?' Adam asked.

'Can you hear that?' she asked.

'I hear your radio, if that's what you mean. Don't you usually leave it on for the bird?'

'Not that loud.'

Adam said nothing as Jess twisted her key in the lock, gently pushing open the door.

'My God, it's freezing in here,' Jess exclaimed immediately, seeing her antique ivory lace curtains billowing into the air.

'Did you leave the window open?'

'No,' Jess said, hurrying toward the window and bringing it quickly shut. The curtains collapsed around her, covering her face like a shroud, as the music swelled. Opera, she realized, shaking off the curtains as she would a giant spider's web, and rushing to the stereo, turning the music down. *Carmen*. The March of the Toreadors.

'Maybe we should call the police,' Adam was saying.

Jess spun round on the heels of her boots. Except for the open window and the stereo, nothing appeared to have been touched. 'Nothing seems to be missing.' She started toward her bedroom.

'Don't go down there, Jess,' Adam warned.

Jess stopped, turning toward him. 'Why not?'

'Because you don't know what, or who, might be waiting for you,' he reminded her. 'Christ, Jess, you, of all people, should know better. What's the first thing the police advise when you think your place has been burglarized? They tell you not to go inside,' he continued without waiting for her response. 'And why do they tell you that?'

'Because whoever broke in might still be there,' Jess answered quietly.

'Let's get out of here and call the police,' he said again.

Jess took two steps toward him, then stopped dead. 'My God!'

Adam spun round, then back to Jess. 'What? What's the matter?'

'Fred,' she said, her voice shaking, her hand pointing toward the bird cage.

For an instant, Adam looked confused, unable to focus.

'He's gone,' Jess shouted, running to the bird cage, peering in through the bars, checking the inside to make sure the small canary wasn't hidden underneath the paper that lined the bottom. But the bird was definitely gone. 'Somebody opened the cage door and let him out,' Jess cried. 'He must have flown out the window.'

Even as she spoke, Jess realized the unlikelihood of the canary having successfully navigated its way through the billowing curtains without someone's firm hand to guide it, the virtual certainty of its having frozen to death once tossed into the hostile night. Tears once again filled her eyes and she started to cry. 'Why would anyone do that? Who would want to hurt a poor little bird?' Jess moaned into Adam's arms, the unwanted image of a small boy's mutilated pet turtle appearing before her eyes.

They called the police from Walter Fraser's apartment, waited there while the police looked through her apartment.

'They won't find anyone,' Jess said as Walter fixed her a cup of tea, and insisted that she drink it. 'He's long gone.'

'You sound like you know who it is,' Adam commented.

'I do,' Jess nodded, telling them briefly about Rick Ferguson. 'Did you hear anyone go up the stairs, Walter?' Jess asked. 'Or see anyone suspicious?'

'Just your friend here,' Walter remarked, winking at Adam, fitting his round body into a green velvet tub chair.

Jess looked toward Adam.

'He was pacing around outside,' Walter continued. 'Waiting for you, I guess.'

'What about the music?' Adam asked quickly. 'Do you know what time the volume went up?'

'Well, I was out most of the afternoon,' Walter told them, his eyes tracing back through the events of his day, 'and when I came home, the music was already blaring. I thought it was unusual, but then I thought, who am I to complain? Besides, it was Placido Domingo, so it wasn't exactly hard to take.'

'You didn't hear anyone walking around upstairs?' Jess asked.

'If I did, I guess I assumed it was you.' He tapped her hand reassuringly. 'Drink your tea.'

The police asked the same questions, received the same answers. They'd found no one in Jess's apartment. Nothing in the other rooms appeared to have been touched.

'You're sure you didn't leave the window open yourself?' one of the officers, a young woman with short red hair and a razed complexion, inquired, pad and pencil ready to jot down Jess's response.

'I'm very sure.'

'And the stereo and the bird cage, there isn't a chance—'

'No chance,' Jess replied testily.

'We can send someone over to dust for prints,' the older male officer, whose name was Frank Metula, offered.

'Don't bother, Frank,' Jess told him, thinking him greyer than the last time she'd seen him. 'He didn't leave any prints.' Jess told them of her suspicions, that there was already a warrant out for Rick Ferguson's arrest.

'Would you like an officer to watch the house tonight?' Frank asked.

'There's already somebody keeping an eye on me,' Jess told

them. 'A detective my ex-husband hired.'

'He's been watching the house?' Adam asked.

'No, unfortunately. He's been following me, so he wouldn't have seen anything.'

'We'll drive by every half-hour or so anyway,' Frank Metula volunteered.

'He won't be back,' Jess told them. 'At least not tonight.'

'I'll stay with her,' Adam said, his voice brooking no arguments.

'That gun in the night table by your bed,' the female officer remarked, 'I assume you have a license for it?'

Jess said nothing as the young woman followed her older partner out the door.

She lay on top of her bed, wrapped in Adam's arms.

Several times, she drifted off to sleep, wandering in and out of strange, unsettling dreams where everything was larger than life and nothing was as it seemed. The dreams would disappear as soon as she opened her eyes. Each time she moved, she felt Adam's arms tighten around her.

After the police left, she and Adam had returned to her apartment, stumbling toward her bedroom, collapsing on top of the bed, fully clothed. There'd been no fumbling for buttons, no attempt at romance. They'd simply lain there in each other's arms, Jess occasionally closing her eyes, opening them to find Adam watching her.

'What?' she asked now, sitting up, rubbing at the sleep in her eyes, brushing some hair away from her face with her hands.

'I was thinking how beautiful you are,' he said, and Jess almost laughed.

'I have no make-up on,' Jess told him. 'I've been wearing the same sweats all day, and I've been crying half the night. How can you say I'm beautiful?'

'How can you think you're not?' he asked in return, gently massaging the muscles in her back.

Jess arched her back, pressed against his hands. 'I keep hearing those damn toreadors marching through my brain,' she said, referring to the music that had been playing when they'd first come home. 'It's funny, I never really liked *Carmen*.'

'No?'

'Another uppity woman doesn't respond the way a man wants, so he kills her. I get enough of that at work.'

Adam's expert fingers worked their way into her sore muscles. 'Try not to think about any of that now. Just relax. Try to get some sleep.'

'Actually, I'm hungry,' Jess said, surprising herself. 'I can't believe how no matter what happens, I'm always hungry.'

'Want me to fix you one of my special omelets?'

'Too much trouble. How about I just pop a few frozen pizzas in the microwave?'

'Sounds wonderful.

She pushed herself out of bed and shuffled toward the kitchen, hearing her mother call after her to pick up her feet when she walked. Adam was right behind her as she opened the freezer door and pulled out the package of frozen pizzas.

'Just one for me,' he said.

Jess placed three small frozen pizzas on a plate, feeling Adam's arms encircle her waist. She fell back gently against his chest, letting his weight support her, confident he wouldn't let go. She felt his lips in her hair, on her neck, the side of her cheek. Slowly, reluctantly, she pulled out of his embrace, carried the plate of pizzas to the microwave oven, pulled open its door.

Immediately, she felt a giant wave of revulsion sweep through her body, filling her stomach and threatening to drown her from within. She brought her hand to her mouth, gasping in silent horror at what she saw.

The small canary lay stiff on its side, its spindly feet extended straight ahead, its yellow feathers charred and blackened, its eyes glassy in death.

'Oh, my God,' Jess sobbed, falling backward, her body caving forward, nausea causing her head to spin and her legs to wobble.

'What is it?' Adam asked, rushing to catch her before she fell.

Jess opened her mouth to speak, but no words came. In the next instant, she was vomiting all over the floor.

Chapter Twenty-Three

She woke up to the smell of fresh coffee.

Adam was sitting at the foot of her bed, extending a full mug of black coffee toward her. 'I wasn't sure if you'd feel like eating,' he said, shrugging apologetically, 'so I didn't make anything.'

Jess took the mug from his hand, downed a long sip of coffee, swishing it gently against the sides of her mouth, trying to rid herself of the unpleasant taste that still lingered. She vaguely remembered Adam washing her off, getting her out of her wet clothes and into her night-gown, insisting she lie down, tucking her into bed.

'How do you feel?' he asked.

'Like I've been hit by a train,' Jess said. 'Like someone's knocked the stuffing right out of me.'

'Someone did,' he reminded her.

'Oh God,' Jess moaned. 'My poor Fred.' A sob caught in her throat, as she watched her hands start to shake. Adam reached over to steady them with his own, lifting the coffee mug from her grasp and placing it on the night table beside her. 'That was some night,' Jess remarked, and almost laughed. 'I mean, when was the last time you had an evening like last night? You take a woman to dinner, and next thing you know, you're being interviewed by the police and scraping roasted canaries out of microwave ovens.' Jess bit back a fresh onslaught of tears. 'Not to mention your date throws up all over you.'

'Actually, you missed me,' he said softly.

'Really? You must have been the only thing I missed.'

'Just about.'

'Oh God, the thought of cleaning up that mess . . .'

'It's already done.'

299

Jess stared at him with a gratitude that was almost palpable. 'And Fred?' she whispered.

'He's taken care of,' Adam said simply.

Jess said nothing for several seconds, her sniffling the only sound in the still apartment. 'I'm a real treat,' she said finally, swiping at her tears with the back of her hand. 'Stick with me.'

'I intend to,' Adam said, leaning forward, kissing Jess gently on the lips.

Jess pulled back self-consciously, hiding her mouth behind her hands. 'I should take a shower, brush my teeth.'

He backed away. 'I'll see what I can rustle up for breakfast. Think you could eat anything?'

'I'm ashamed to say, yes.'

He smiled. 'You see, it wasn't so bad after all, was it?'

'What?'

'Throwing up. The very thing you feared the most. You did it — spectacularly, I might add — and you lived to tell the tale.'

'I still hated it.'

'But you survived it.'

'Temporarily.'

'Go take your shower. You'll feel a lot better.' He kissed the tip of her nose, then left the room.

Jess sat for several minutes in bed, staring toward the window, imagining the cold air pressing its face against the pane, like a small child eager to come inside where it was warm. It looked to be a beautiful day, she thought, clear and sunny, only a hint of wind rattling the bare upper branches of the trees. She wondered what fresh terrors the cold sun was hiding. Look at me too long, it seemed to say as she approached her bedroom window, and you'll go blind. Get too close and I'll reduce you to a pile of ashes. '*Hohh!*' she barked, but the sun held fast, undaunted.

She'd never realized before how quiet her apartment was without the subtle song of her canary. That song had always been there, she realized, heading into her bathroom, starting the shower, slipping out of her clothes. Such a gentle sound, she thought, closing the bathroom door, hearing Adam busy in the

300

kitchen, stepping inside the tub, pulling the shower curtain closed. So soothing, so constant, so life-affirming.

Now silenced.

'Goddamn you, Rick Ferguson,' she whispered.

He was getting closer, cleverly orchestrating his every move in order to achieve the maximum effect, Jess realized, positioning herself directly under the hot spray of the shower. Exactly what he'd done with Connie DeVuono. The effortless, unseen break-ins, the mounting campaign of terror, the sadistic slaying of innocent pets, scaring the hapless woman half to death before moving in to finish her off. So, he was still pulling the wings off butterflies, Jess thought, recalling the smile that had sent shivers through her body the first time she'd seen him. The smile had said it all.

'*Hohh!*' Jess cried, spinning round quickly, her fingers twisting into sharp claws, slicing through the steam. Her heel slipped on the bottom of the tub. She skidded, lost her balance, fell forward, her arms shooting forward, the wrist of her left hand smacking sharply against the tile wall, her right hand grabbing for the clear plastic shower curtain, pulling on it, hearing it snap, break away from its hooks, then miraculously holding, supporting her weight, permitting her to regain her footing. 'Goddamn it,' she said, throwing her head back, her wet hair whipping against the top of her spine, taking several deep breaths, filling her lungs with hot air.

She reached for the soap, rubbing it harshly across her body and into her hair. She didn't have the patience for shampoo. Soap would do just as well, she thought, feeling the lather growing between her fingers as she worked it into her hair, suddenly reminded of the shower scene from Alfred Hitchcock's *Psycho*.

In her mind she watched a hapless Janet Leigh begin her innocent ablutions, saw the bathroom door creak slowly open, the strange shadowy figure approach, the large butcher's knife rise into the air as the shower curtains were pulled open, the knife coming down against the screaming woman's flesh, again and again and again.

301

'Jesus Christ,' Jess exclaimed loudly, impatiently rinsing the soap out of her hair. 'Are you trying to do Rick Ferguson's job for him? What's the matter with you?'

And then she heard the bathroom door open and saw Rick Ferguson walk through.

Jess held her breath, trying to force a scream from her mouth, to make any kind of sound at all. *Hohh!* she thought wildly, but no sound emerged. Rick Ferguson stood watching her for several seconds from the doorway as Jess reached over and twisted the shower taps to Off. The water trickled to a stop. And suddenly he was striding toward the tub, his arms extended, reaching for the curtain. Where was Adam? Jess wondered, fumbling for whatever weapons were at hand, seizing on the soap, preparing to hurl it at Rick Ferguson's head. How had he gotten inside? What had he done to Adam?

Hands grabbed the shower curtain, pushed it aside. Jess lunged forward. '*Hohh!*' she cried loudly, hurling the soap at her attacker's head. He flinched, fell backward against the sink, his hands raised to protect his face.

'Jesus Christ, Jess,' she heard him yell. 'Are you nuts? Are you trying to kill me?'

Jess stared at the man cowering in front of her. 'Don?' she asked meekly.

'Jess, are you all right?' Adam called, racing into the room.

'I'm not sure,' Jess told him honestly. 'What are you doing here, Don? You scared the life out of me.'

'I scared you?' Don demanded. 'I almost had a heart attack, for God's sake.'

'I told you to wait until she had finished her shower,' Adam said, not doing a very good job of hiding his growing smile.

'What are you doing here?' Jess asked again.

Don looked from Jess to Adam and then back to Jess. 'Can I talk to you for a few minutes alone?'

Jess pushed some wet hairs away from her forehead, realizing suddenly that she was standing naked in front of two men, one of whom was her ex-husband, the other her would-be lover.

302

'Could somebody please hand me a towel,' she asked, trying to sound casual.

Adam immediately wrapped her in a large peach-colored bath towel, helping her out of the tub and onto the bathmat. Jess found herself squeezed between the two men, not sure how she wound up in situations like this one, wondering whether it was all another of her silly dreams. The small bathroom, barely big enough for one, was threatening to explode with three.

'It's okay, Adam,' Jess assured him.

Adam looked toward Don, then gave the smile that had been playing with the corners of his mouth full rein. 'We have to stop meeting like this,' he told Don before leaving the room.

'What's going on, Don?' she asked.

'Suppose you tell me.'

'You're the one who barged into my bathroom,' she reminded him.

'I didn't barge in. I called your name a couple of times. I thought I heard you say something. I assumed you said to come in. So I did. Next thing I know I'm getting beaned with a bar of soap.'

'I thought you were Rick Ferguson.'

'Rick Ferguson?'

'My imagination's in overdrive these days,' she told him. 'Do you mind if we go into the bedroom. I'm feeling a little ridiculous talking to you dressed in a towel.'

'Jess, we used to be married, remember?'

'You still haven't told me what you're doing here.'

Jess walked past him into her bedroom, pulling on her housecoat and using the towel to dry her hair.

'I was worried about you,' he said. 'The guy I hired to watch you said there was some excitement here with the police.'

'That was last night.'

'I didn't get home till this morning,' he admitted sheepishly.

Jess looked at him with mock reproach. In truth, she felt enormous relief.

'I came right over. Your boyfriend,' he said, almost choking on the words, 'let me in. He said you were in the shower, but—'

'But you wanted to see for yourself. Well, you certainly did.'

'What happened last night?' Don asked.

Jess told him about returning home, meeting Adam outside, finding the window in her apartment open, the bird missing. About waking up in the night hungry, deciding on a snack, opening the door to the microwave oven, finding her dead canary inside.

'Jesus, Jess. I'm so sorry.'

Jess wiped away a few stray tears, amazed at her seemingly endless supply. 'He was such a sweet little bird. He just liked to sit in his cage and sing all day. What kind of sick mind . . . ?'

'There are a lot of sick people out there,' Don said sadly.

'One in particular.'

'I have something to tell you,' Don stated. 'Something that should put your mind at rest. If that's possible.'

'What's that?'

'Rick Ferguson walked into the police station at eight o'clock this morning and turned himself in.'

'What?' Jess ran immediately to her closet, started fumbling for some clothes.

'He claims he had no idea the police were looking for him. He'd been with a woman he'd met.'

'Sure he was. He just doesn't happen to remember her name.'

'I don't think he asked.'

Jess pulled on some underwear, followed quickly by her jeans and a heavy blue sweater. 'How long have you known about this?'

Jess noted the sadness that registered in Don's eyes. 'There were two messages on my service when I got home this morning,' he said evenly. 'One concerned you and what went on here last night; the other was from Rick Ferguson, telling me he'd been home, talked to his mother, found out the police were looking for him, and that he was headed for the station to turn himself in. I'm on my way down there now. I think I might be able to persuade him it's in his best interests to cooperate with the State's Attorney's office.'

304

'Good. I'm going with you.' Jess pulled her wet hair into a ponytail.

'What about Chef Boyardee?'

Jess looked through the bedroom wall toward the kitchen. 'Breakfast will have to wait till I get back.'

'You're going to leave the man alone in your apartment?' Don's voice was incredulous. 'Jess, need I remind you that the last time he was here, you woke up to find all your panties slashed to ribbons.'

'Don, don't be ridiculous.'

'Was it just a coincidence that he turned up here last night, Jess?' Don asked, impatiently. 'Hasn't it even occurred to you that it might have been Adam who broke into your apartment? That it might have been Adam who killed your canary? You caught him leaving the scene, for God's sake!'

'I didn't catch him,' Jess protested, her voice hollow. 'He was here looking for me. He hadn't been upstairs.'

'Says who?'

'He does,' Jess stammered.

'And you believe everything he tells you? You don't even admit the possibility that he might be lying?'

'Tell me no secrets, I'll tell you no lies,' Jess said quietly, not realizing she was speaking out loud.

'What?'

Jess snapped back into the present. 'It doesn't make sense, Don. Why would Adam be doing these things? What motive could he possibly have?'

'I have no idea. I only know that ever since you met this guy, a lot of strange things have been happening to you. Strange and dangerous.'

'But Adam has no reason to hurt me.'

The look on Don's face changed from concern to sadness. 'Are you falling in love with him, Jess?' he asked.

Jess released a deep sigh. 'I don't know.'

'Jesus, Jess, he's a shoe salesman, for God's sake. What are you doing with this guy?'

'He isn't a shoe salesman,' Jess said quietly.

305

'What?'

'Well, he is, I guess,' Jess corrected herself. 'Not that it matters.'

'What are you trying to say, Jess?'

'He's a lawyer.'

'What?'

'He's a lawyer.'

'A lawyer,' Don repeated.

'Something happened. He got disillusioned, so he gave it up . . .'

'And found fulfillment selling shoes, is that what you're seriously trying to tell me?'

'It's a very long story.'

'And a very tall one. Jess, are you so enamored of this guy that you can't recognize a crock of shit when it hits you in the face.'

'It's very complicated.'

'Only lies are complicated,' Don told her. 'The truth is usually very simple.'

Jess looked from the floor to the ceiling, then over to the window, anywhere but at her ex-husband, refusing to consider the possibility he might be right.

'You know I only want what's best for you, don't you?' Don was saying.

Jess nodded, tears returning to her eyes. She brushed them angrily away.

'That's all I've ever wanted,' he added quietly.

Jess nodded. 'We should get over to the station,' she said. 'I have a few questions I want to ask your client.'

Rick Ferguson was slumped into the same chair, in the same interrogation room, in almost the same position, as when Jess had questioned him the last time. Two plain clothes detectives sat off to one corner. For an instant, Jess felt as if she'd never left.

He was wearing the same brown leather jacket, the same blue jeans, the same spike-toed black boots. The same superior attitude clung to his posture. As soon as Jess walked in the room, he stiffened, following her movement with his hooded, cobra-like eyes. Slowly, he uncoiled his body, as if preparing to strike. Then immediately, he relaxed, opening his legs wide, as if deliberately exposing the bulge at his crotch. 'I like your hair,' he drawled at Jess, scratching lazily at the inside of his high. 'Wet suits you. I'll have to remember that.'

'Shut up, Rick,' Don ordered, following Jess into the room. 'And sit up straight in the chair.'

Rick Ferguson pushed his body up into something vaguely resembling a sitting position though he kept his legs wide apart. His long hair hung loose to his shoulders. Absently, he reached up to flick it behind his ears. Jess noted the presence of an earring in his left ear.

'Is that new?' she asked, pointing to the small gold loop.

'How observant you are, Jess,' Ferguson remarked. 'Yes, it's new. I also got a new tattoo. The scales of justice.' He laughed. 'On my ass. Want to see it?'

'Cut the shit, Rick,' Don told him succinctly.

Ferguson looked surprised. 'Hey, what are you getting so bent out of shape about? You're *my* lawyer, remember?'

'Not if you keep this up.'

'Hey, man, what's going on here?' His eyes travelled rapidly between Don and Jess. 'You got something going with the pretty prosecuting attorney?'

'You said you'd answer a few of Ms Koster's questions,' Don said, his voice sharp. 'I'll tell you if there's anything I think you shouldn't answer.'

'Hey, my life's an open book. Fire away, counsellor.'

'Did you kill Connie DeVuono?' Jess asked immediately.

'No.'

'Where were you on the day she disappeared?'

'What day was that?'

She gave him the exact date and appproximate time.

He shrugged. 'I think I was home with my mother that afternoon. She hadn't been feeling too well.'

'You work where?'

307

'You know where.'
'Answer the question.'
'Ask me nicely.'
Jess glanced at her ex-husband.
'Answer the question, Rick. You agreed to cooperate.'
'She doesn't have to be rude.' Rick Ferguson's hand rubbed at the crotch of his jeans.
'You work at the Ace Magnetic Wire Factory, is that correct?'
'Bingo.'
'Can you describe your job for me, Mr Ferguson?'
'Mr Ferguson?' he repeated, sitting up tall. 'I think I like the way you say that.'
'Tell her what you do, Rick,' Don advised.
'She knows what I do. Let her tell me.'
'You operate a forklift that transfers spools of wire from the warehouse down to the dock, is that right?'
'That's right.'
'Before that, you were a press man, someone who presses out the wire.'
'Right again. You've obviously done your homework, Jess. I had no idea you were so interested in me.'
'What do you make of the fact that the wire you take down to the dock every day is the same wire that was used to kill Connie DeVuono?'
'Don't answer that,' Don said quickly.
Rick Ferguson said nothing.
'Where have you been the last few days?'
'Nowhere special.'
'Can you be more specific?'
'Not really.'
'Why did you sneak out of the house in the middle of the night?'
'I never snuck out of the house.'
'Your house was being watched. You were seen entering it on the night of 9 December. You were not seen leaving. You didn't show up for work the next morning.'
'I took a few days' sick leave. I'm entitled. And hey, if you

308

didn't see me walk out of my front door, that's your fault, not mine.'

'You didn't run off?'

'If I'd run off, why would I have come back? Why would I voluntarily turn myself in?'

'You tell me.'

'There's nothing to tell. I didn't run off. Hey, as soon as I heard you guys were looking for me, I rushed right over. I had no reason to run away. You got nothing on me.'

'On the contrary, Mr Ferguson,' Jess told him, 'I have motive, I have opportunity, I have access to the murder weapon.'

Rick Ferguson shrugged. 'You got nothing,' he repeated.

'You never answered my questions about where you've been the past several days.'

'Yes, I did. It just wasn't the answer you wanted to hear.'

'What about yesterday?'

'What about it?'

'Where were you yesterday? Surely, you can remember that far back?'

'I can remember. I just don't see where it's any of your business.' He looked at his lawyer. 'What's where I was yesterday got to do with why I'm being arrested?'

'Answer the question,' Don told him, and Jess thanked him with an almost imperceptible nod of her head.

'I was with a girl I met.'

'What's her name?'

'Melanie,' he said.

'Last name?'

'I never asked for her last name.'

'Where does she live?'

'I have no idea. We went to a motel.'

'Which motel?'

'The one that was closest.'

Jess looked from the blood-red concrete floor to the acoustic tile ceiling in exasperation. 'In other words, you can't prove where you were yesterday.'

'Why should I have to?' Again, Rick Ferguson turned to Don,

309

his eyes squinting into a question. 'What does where I was yesterday have to do with this DeVuono dame's murder?'

'Ms Koster's apartment was broken into sometime between two in the afternoon and seven in the evening yesterday,' Don told him.

'Gee, that's too bad,' Rick Ferguson said, his voice a smile. 'Anything missing?'

Jess pictured the open window and empty bird cage that greeted her upon her return to her apartment. 'You tell me,' she said, her voice flat, void of emotion.

'What — you think I did it?' A look of reproach filled Rick Ferguson's face.

'Did you?' Jess asked.

'I already told you. I was with a girl named Melanie.'

'We have witnesses who can place you at the scene,' Jess lied, wondering whether Don would object, grateful when he didn't.

'Then your witnesses are mistaken,' Rick said calmly. 'Why would I want to break into your apartment? That wouldn't be very smart.'

'Nobody claimed you were very smart,' Jess told him.

Rick Ferguson clutched at his chest. 'Ouch! You sure know how to hurt a guy, Jess.' He winked. 'Maybe some day I can return the favor.'

'Rick,' Don said before Jess could respond, 'have you ever met a man named Adam Stohn?'

Jess's head snapped toward her ex-husband.

'What's that name again?' Rick Ferguson was asking.

'Adam Stohn,' Don repeated.

Jess turned her attention back to Rick Ferguson, reluctantly waiting for his reply.

'Is he one of your supposed witnesses?' Rick Ferguson asked, then shook his head. 'I'm afraid the name doesn't ring a bell.' He smiled. 'But then, you know how I am with names.'

'This is getting us nowhere,' Jess said impatiently. 'You're saying you know absolutely nothing about Connie DeVuono's murder? Is that what you're telling us?'

'That's what I'm telling you.'

'You've just been playing games with us,' Jess said angrily.

'I've just been telling you the truth.'

'In that case,' Jess told him, 'consider yourself under arrest for the murder of Connie DeVuono.' She turned and strode briskly from the room.

Don was right behind her. 'Jess, wait a minute, for Christ's sake. Think about what you're doing.' The officers in the outer area looked discreetly away.

'There's nothing to think about.'

'You don't have a case, Jess.'

'Stop telling me I don't have a case. I have motive. I have opportunity. I have the murder weapon. What more do I need?'

'Some fingerprints on the murder weapon would be nice. Some hard DNA evidence linking Connie DeVuono to my client, which I know you don't have. A few witnesses who might have seen my client and the victim together around the time she disappeared, which you also don't have. A bridge between the dead body and Rick Ferguson, Jess, something to connect the two.'

'I'll connect them.'

'I wish you luck.'

'I'll see you in court.'

Chapter Twenty-Four

Jess was arguing with her trial supervisor right up to the moment of Rick Ferguson's preliminary hearing the following Friday.

'I still think it was a mistake not to take this before the Grand Jury,' Jess told Tom Olinsky as she walked beside him through the mistletoe-laden corridors, paying scant attention to the Christmas and Channukah decorations that covered the walls.

'And I told you that we don't have a strong enough case to take before the Grand Jury.'

Tom Olinsky walked very quickly for such a big man, Jess thought, having to take very long strides just to keep up.

'Your ex-husband has already hit us with a motion *in limine*.'

'Damn him,' Jess muttered, still smarting over Don's move to limit the state's introduction of evidence.

'He's just doing his job, Jess.'

'And I'm trying to do mine.'

They pushed their way through a reception area that was all but overwhelmed by a huge, tinsel-draped, popcorn-swaddled Christmas tree, into the exterior hall, heading toward the elevators.

'A Grand Jury would have rubber-stamped the indictment,' Jess continued. 'We'd have a trial date set by now.' Jess also wouldn't have had to face her ex-husband in court so early, she admitted to herself, since the defense wasn't present at Grand Jury proceedings, and no cross-examination of witnesses was allowed. The prosecution simply presented its case to the twenty-three members of the Grand Jury and asked them to find a 'true bill', which held the defendant over for trial.

When a case was shaky, and everyone but Jess seemed to agree this case was shaky, the prosecutor's office usually went

313

the route of a preliminary hearing. That way, the onus was on the judge, and not the State's Attorney, to decide whether there was sufficient evidence to hold a person over for trial. It was a very political decision, Jess recognized, a way to get the case out of the system. The State's Attorney's office didn't like to prosecute a case when there was a good chance the state might lose. A preliminary hearing let the prosecutor's office off the hook by forcing the judge to decide whether or not there was probable cause to hold a person over for trial. The whole procedure could take as little as twenty minutes.

Jess was reminded of Don's longstanding advice to think of the criminal justice system as a game: in a preliminary hearing the state put forth its evidence in as general terms as possible, careful to reveal the least amount of evidence in hand, just enough to produce a finding of probable cause; the defense, meanwhile, tried to uncover as much information about the prosecution's case as possible.

If the prosecutor's office was successful, an arraignment would follow three weeks after the preliminary hearing, wherein the accused would appear before the Chief Judge for the criminal division of the circuit court of Cook County to hear the charges read aloud. According to the unwritten rules of the game, this right was usually waived by the defense counsel, and the accused then entered a plea of either guilty or not-guilty.

The accused *always* pleaded not guilty, Jess acknowledged, following Tom Olinsky into the elevator, suppressing a smile as the three people who were already inside took a giant collective step back to give him room.

The Chief Judge then used a computer to randomly assign which judge would try the case. A court date was selected, and the case now became one of approximately 300 cases on a judge's call. Murder cases generally took anywhere from a few months to a year to hit court, and this was where the game started to get really interesting.

The state could no longer be coy with its evidence. It was obliged to reveal the full extent of its case against the defendant. This was done through a series of 'discoveries'. Any evidence that would be helpful to the accused, all police reports, experts' statements, documents, photos, names and addresses of witnesses, prior convictions, and so on, would have to be handed over to the defense. The defense, in turn, was obligated to disclose its own list of witnesses, along with whatever medical and scientific reports it planned to introduce into evidence, and to reveal its main strategy of defense, be it alibi, consent, self-defense, or varying degrees of insanity.

If the defendant was denied bail, the state had 120 days to bring him to trial, if this was the defendant's wish. It always was. If the accused was out on bond, the state had 160 days to bring him to trial, if the defendant so demanded. He almost never did.

Even if the accused wanted to go to trial right away, the lawyer would need time to review all the state's evidence. Still, part of the poker game on the part of the defense was to keep the demand for trial running. That tended to unnerve the state, occasionally forcing the prosecutor's office to trial before it was ready. Justice delayed, after all, was justice denied.

If after 160 days the prosecution still wasn't ready, the defense could bring a speedy trial discharge motion before the judge and have the case thrown out of court. This was the worst thing that could happen to an assistant state's attorney, Jess knew, stepping off the elevator at the ground floor ahead of Tom Olinsky, although he quickly passed her as they marched through the corridor that connected the Administration building to the Court House.

But all that was later, Jess reminded herself, her heels clicking along the granite floor. First she had to make it through the preliminary hearing.

The preliminary hearing was being held in one of the smaller, more modern courtrooms on the second floor. 'Let's take the stairs,' Tom Olinsky suggested, walking between the tall, brown, Doric-style pillars, past the bank of ten elevators, to the stairwell. For a man of his girth, he was amazingly spry, Jess thought, thinking she would be exhausted before she even set foot in the courtroom.

Jess smelled the food emanating from the various lunch rooms on the first floor as they made their way up the stairs, and she wondered if Don and Rick Ferguson were having coffee in the room reserved for defendants and their lawyers, the room that the State's Attorney's office not so affectionately referred to as the gang-bangers' lounge.

She hadn't seen Don all week, hadn't even spoken to him since he'd filed his motion *in limine*. She knew, as even Adam had reminded her, that her ex-husband was only doing his job, but it made her furious anyway. Did he have to be so damn *good* at his job?

As for Adam, she hadn't seen him all week either, although she'd spoken to him every night over the phone. He was in Springfield, visiting his parents for the first time in almost three years. He'd be back in Chicago tomorrow. Meanwhile, he called every night at ten o'clock to wish her a good night's sleep. And to tell her he loved her.

Jess hadn't yet spoken of her feelings. She wasn't sure quite what they were. Certainly she was attracted to him; certainly she liked him enormously; certainly she understood the pain he'd been through. Did she love him? She didn't know. She was afraid to let herself go enough to find out.

Go with it, she heard distant voices murmur. Go with it. Go with it.

Maybe after the preliminary hearing was over. Maybe after she'd succeeded in getting Rick Ferguson bound over for trial, she could let go of the nagging doubts about Adam that Don had planted in her brain, concentrate on letting whatever was developing between them progress naturally.

Trust your instincts, the voices purred. Trust your instincts.

'After you,' Tom Olinsky said, pulling open the door and allowing Jess to step inside first. An odd time for chivalry, Jess thought, looking around the circular, windowless courtroom.

The courtrooms on the second, third and fourth floors reminded Jess of small spaceships. Once inside the outer doors, one found oneself in a sparse, predominantly grey, glass-enclosed space, where spectators waited in a semi-circular area on the other side of the glass from the actual proceedings. The judge's bench was directly opposite the outer doors, the jury box either to the judge's left or right, depending on the courtroom. In this courtroom, the jury box, which would remain empty during the preliminary hearing, was to the judge's left, and Jess's right.

After four o'clock in the afternoon, these courts handled nothing but drug cases. They were always busy.

The various clerks were likewise busy at their stations as Jess and Tom Olinsky stepped up to the prosecutor's table where Neil Strayhorn was already settled in. Jess deposited her briefcase on the floor, perusing the room to see whether any of her witnesses had yet arrived.

'No one's here,' Neil told her.

'You checked with the police to make sure they got their notification of trial?' Tom Olinsky asked, sitting down beside Neil, his wide hips spilling over the sides of the wooden chair.

'At 7:45 this morning,' Jess answered, wondering why he was asking her such a basic question. Obviously she had checked with the police to make sure they'd be here. She'd also called the crime lab to go over the analysis of the physical evidence in the case, and conferred with Hilary Waugh about the questions she'd be asking her on the stand. Connie's mother, Mrs Gambala, would also be testifying, along with one of Connie's co-workers and Connie's closest friend.

They would corroborate the state's contention that Connie was deathly afraid of Rick Ferguson because of threats he'd made against her life if she proceeded with the assault charges against him, thereby providing the state with the motive for the murder.

'Tom, you don't have to stay,' Jess told her trial supervisor. 'Neil and I will be fine.'

'I want to see how this one goes down,' he said, leaning back into the chair, his weight lifting its front legs off the floor.

Jess smiled, realizing she was grateful for his show of support. He'd given her a hard time all week, fretted openly that he thought the state's case too circumstantial, but in the end he'd gone along with her intense desire to proceed.

'I have a feeling this one's looking for you,' Tom said as the door to the courtroom opened and an older woman, dressed all in black, tentatively poked her head inside.

'Mrs Gambala,' Jess said warmly, approaching her and taking hold of both her hands. 'Thank you for coming.'

'We put that monster away?' Mrs Gambala said, her statement curling into a question.

'We'll put that monster away,' Jess assured her. 'You remember my associate, Neil Strayhorn. And this is Tom Olinsky, my trial supervisor. Tom, this is Connie's mother, Mrs Gambala.'

'Hello, Mrs Gambala,' he said, slowly rising to his feet. 'Hopefully, we'll have you out of here pretty quickly.'

'You see that justice is done,' Mrs Gambala said in return.

'You'll have to wait outside until you're called as a witness,' Jess explained, leading her back into the hallway. 'You can sit here.'

Jess pointed to a bench along the wall. The older woman remained on her feet. 'You understand what I'm going to ask you on the stand? You're comfortable with the questions I'm going to ask?'

Mrs Gambala nodded. 'I tell the truth. Connie, she was terrified of that man. He threatened to kill her.'

'Good. Now, don't worry. If you don't understand a question, or you don't understand anything that's going on, anything the defense attorney asks you, just say so. Take all the time you need.'

'We put that monster away,' Mrs Gambala said again, walking toward the window at the end of the corridor, staring out at the cold grey day.

The other witnesses arrived soon after. Jess spoke briefly with the police and the forensics expert, thanked Connie's friend and her co-worker for being so prompt. She guided them toward the bench and told them they would be called shortly. Then she returned to the courtroom.

The spectator section was filling up, mostly lawyers and their clients awaiting their turn before the judge. Don and Rick Ferguson had yet to arrive. Was it possible that Don was planning some last minute pyrotechnics?

The court clerk loudly cleared his throat before calling the court to order and introducing Judge Caroline McMahon. Caroline McMahon was a woman in her early forties, whose round face belied her angular frame. She had short dark hair and a pale complexion that blushed deep red whenever she lost her patience, a not infrequent occurrence.

Don pushed through the doors of the courtroom with appropriate dramatic flourish just as the clerk was reading Rick Ferguson's name aloud.

'Here, Your Honor,' Don said loudly, leading his client to the defense table.

'Is the defense ready?' Caroline McMahon asked, a trace of sarcasm evident in her voice as she peered over her reading glasses at the tardy attorney for the defense.

'Yes, Your Honor.'

'And the state?'

'The state is ready, Your Honor,' Jess answered, almost eagerly.

'I'm going to reserve judgement on your motion, Mr Shaw,' Caroline McMahon announced immediately, 'until I see where the prosecution's case is going. Ms Koster, you may proceed.'

'Thank you, Your Honor,' Jess stated, walking toward the empty witness stand. 'The state calls Detective George Farquharson.'

Detective George Farquharson, tall and fair-skinned and balding, marched through the outer doors of the court, through the already crowded spectator section, through the glass doors that split the courtroom in half, to the stand. He was duly sworn in and seated, stating his name and rank clearly and loudly, a man obviously comfortable with himself and the job he was about to do.

'On the afternoon of 5 December,' Jess began, 'did you have occasion to investigate the death of Connie DeVuono?'

'I did.'

'Can you tell us about it?'

'My partner and I drove out to Skokie Lagoons in response to a telephone call from a Mr Henry Sullivan, who'd been ice-fishing and come across Mrs DeVuono's body. It was obvious as soon as we saw the body that she'd been murdered.'

'How was it obvious?'

'The piece of wire was still wrapped round her neck,' Detective Farquharson answered.

'And what did you do after you saw the body, Detective Farquharson?'

'We cordoned off the area and called the Medical Examiner's office. Then the body was placed in an ambulance and sent over to Harrison Street.'

'Thank you, Detective.'

Don rose briefly. 'Did you find any evidence at the scene, Detective Farquharson, other than the wire round Mrs DeVuono's neck?'

'No.'

'No footprints? No cigarette butts? No clothing?'

'No, sir.'

'So there was nothing at the scene linking my client to the deceased?'

'No, sir.'

'Thank you.' Don returned to his seat.

'You may step down, Detective Farquharson,' Judge McMahon told him.

'The state calls Dr Hilary Waugh.'

Hilary Waugh wore a royal blue pantsuit and a simple strand of pearls, her dark hair pulled into her trademark French braid.

'Dr Waugh,' Jess said, as Hilary Waugh settled into the witness stand, 'what were the results of the post-mortem on Connie DeVuono?'

'We found that Connie DeVuono died of asphyxiation as the result of being strangled with a piece of magnetic wire. The wire also severed her jugular, but that was after death.'

'Was there evidence Connie DeVuono had been beaten?'

'Yes. Her left wrist had been broken as well as several ribs, and her jaw had been dislocated.'

'Was there evidence of sexual assault?'

'Yes. The body was nude, and the vagina showed signs of trauma.'

'How long had Mrs DeVuono been dead before she was found, Doctor?'

'Approximately six weeks. We identified her through her dental records.'

'Thank you.

'Was there any sperm found in the vagina?' Don asked, quickly jumping to his feet.

'We found no traces.'

'Any bite marks?'

'Just from animals.'

'Any traces of blood that weren't Connie DeVuono's?'

'No.'

'Traces of saliva?'

'None that we could find at this time. Mrs DeVuono had been dead for about six weeks and was in a state of advanced decomposition.'

'Yet, due to the severe cold, the decomposition hadn't advanced as much as it would normally. Isn't that correct?'

'Yes.'

'And yet you found no blood samples, no teeth marks other than animal, no saliva traces, nothing of any real significance. Certainly nothing that would help you identify the perpetrator of this crime.'

'No,' the doctor admitted.

'Thank you, Doctor.'

'The state calls Dr Rudy Wang,' Jess said immediately following Hilary Waugh's exit from the stand.

An expert in forensics, Dr Wang was short, grey-haired, and, despite his Oriental-sounding name, of Polish extraction. He wore a brown pinstripe suit and a worried expression that made him look as if he had forgotten to wear his glasses.

'Dr Wang, did you have a chance to examine the wire that

was used to strangle Connie DeVuono?' Jess asked, approaching the witness stand.

'Yes, I did.'

'Could you describe it, please?'

'It was a magnetic wire, steel-grey, eighteen inches long and approximately a quarter of an inch round. Very strong, very sturdy.'

'You also examined a similar piece of wire taken from the Ace Magnetic Wire Factory where the defendant works, did you not?'

'I did. They were identical.'

'Thank you, Dr Wang.'

Don was on his feet and in front of the witness before Jess had a chance to return to her table. 'Dr Wang, were there any fingerprints on the wire that was found round Connie DeVuono's neck?'

'No.'

'Partial prints? Anything?'

'No. Nothing.'

'And how common would you say this type of wire is?'

Rudy Wang shrugged. 'Pretty common, I guess.'

'You could buy it in any hardware store?'

'You might be able to find it in a hardware store, yes.'

'Thank you.'

'You may step down,' the judge directed.

Don smiled over at Jess before returning to his seat.

'I hate it when defense lawyers look so happy,' Tom Olinsky whispered to Jess.

'The state calls Mrs Rosaria Gambala,' Jess said loudly, anger gripping her hands, twisting them into tight fists.

Mrs Gambala, in a long-sleeved black sweater over a long black skirt, ambled slowly from the back of the courtroom toward the witness stand, swaying from side to side as she walked, as if she was in danger of tipping over. She steadied herself against the front of the witness stand as she was sworn in, her dark eyes nervously scanning the room, stumbling when she saw the defendant. A muffled cry escaped her lips.

'Are you okay, Mrs Gambala?' Jess asked. 'Do you need a glass of water?'

'I'm okay,' the woman said, her voice surprisingly strong.

'Can you state your relation to the deceased?' Jess asked.

'I'm her mother,' the older woman answered, speaking of her daughter in the present tense.

'And when did you first report your daughter missing, Mrs Gambala?'

'On 29 October 1992, when she didn't pick up Steffan after work.'

'Steffan being her son?'

'Yes. My grandson. He comes to my house after school, till Connie is finished working. She always calls before she leaves work.'

'And on the afternoon of 29 October, your daughter called and said she was on her way, but then she never showed up, is that right?'

'I called the police. They say I have to wait twenty-four hours. I call you. You no home.'

'Why did you call me, Mrs Gambala?'

'Because you were her lawyer. You were supposed to help her. You knew her life was in danger. You knew about the threats he made.' She pointed an accusatory finger at Rick Ferguson.

'Objection!' Don called out. 'Hearsay.'

'This is a preliminary hearing,' Jess reminded her ex-husband. 'Hearsay is admissible.'

'I'm going to allow it,' the judge ruled. 'Proceed, Ms Koster.'

Jess returned her attention to Rosaria Gambala. 'Rick Ferguson made threats against your daughter's life?'

'Yes. She was so afraid of him. He say he's going to kill her.'

'Objection,' Don called again. 'Your Honor, can we approach the bench?'

The two lawyers moved directly toward the judge.

'Your Honor, I believe now would be a good time to rule on my motion to limit the evidence introduced in this case on the

323

grounds that almost all the evidence against my client is hearsay, and highly prejudicial,' Don began, taking the initiative.

'Which is perfectly admissible in a preliminary hearing,' Jess said again.

'Your Honor, there is no direct evidence that my client ever threatened Connie DeVuono.'

'The state will call two more witnesses in addition to Mrs Gambala who will testify that Connie was scared to death of the defendant, that he threatened to kill her if she proceeded with her plans to testify against him in court.'

'Your Honor, such hearsay evidence is not only prejudicial, but irrelevant.'

'Irrelevant?' Jess asked, hearing her voice bounce off the surrounding glass. 'It goes to motive, Your Honor. Connie DeVuono had accused Rick Ferguson of raping and beating her—'

'Something that was never proved in a court of law,' Don reminded her.

'Because Connie DeVuono never made it to court. She was murdered before she could testify.'

'Your Honor,' Don argued, 'my client has always claimed to be innocent in the attack on Mrs DeVuono. In fact, he has an airtight alibi for the time of the alleged attack.'

'I will call several police officers to testify that Connie DeVuono positively identified Rick Ferguson as the man who beat and raped her,' Jess offered.

'Hearsay, Your Honor,' Don stated flatly. 'And since Connie DeVuono didn't say anything to the police about Rick Ferguson until three days after she was attacked, her statement cannot be classified an "excited utterance", and therefore is not an exception to the hearsay rule. The only person, Your Honor, who can identify my client as her assailant, who can testify that he threatened her life, is dead. Since it was never proved that my client had anything to do with the attack on Mrs DeVuono, I must ask that you disallow the introduction of such highly inflammatory and prejudicial evidence against my client.'

'Your Honor,' Jess stated quickly, 'the state contends that this evidence, while admittedly hearsay, is definitely probative. It goes to the heart of the state's case against Mr Ferguson.'

'The fact is that the state has nothing that links my client to the dead woman except a series of unsubstantiated, second-hand claims.'

'Judge McMahon,' Jess said, noting the judge's cheeks were now brushed with broad strokes of crimson, 'the state intends to call Connie's best friend and a co-worker to the stand. Both women will testify that Connie DeVuono was terrified of Rick Ferguson, that she told them he'd threatened to kill her if she testified against him.'

'Your Honor, we're just going round in circles here.' Don raised his arms in exasperation.

'What is going on?' Mrs Gambala cried from the witness stand. 'I don't understand.'

Caroline McMahon looked sympathetically toward the older woman leaning forward in the witness stand. 'You may step down, Mrs Gambala,' she told her softly, the color in her cheeks deepening.

'I don't understand,' Mrs Gambala repeated.

'It's okay,' Jess told her, helping her down from the stand. 'You did very well, Mrs Gambala.'

'You don't need to ask me any more questions?'

'Not at the moment.'

'That man doesn't have to ask me questions?' She pointed a trembling finger at Don.

'No,' Jess said quietly, noting the look of defeat on Tom Olinsky's face as Neil Strayhorn led Mrs Gambala out into the hall.

'I'm prepared to rule on your motion now, Mr Shaw,' the judge stated.

Don and Jess drew closer to the bench.

'I'm inclined to side with the defense on this one, Ms Koster,' she began.

'But, Your Honor—'

'The prejudicial effect of the evidence clearly outweighs its probative value, and I will prohibit the state from introducing this evidence at trial.'

'But without this evidence, Your Honor, our hands are tied. The state can't prove motive. We simply don't have a case.'

'I'm inclined to agree,' the judge stated. 'Are you prepared to bring a motion to dismiss?'

Jess looked from the judge to her ex-husband. To his credit, he refrained from visibly gloating.

'It's your move,' he told her.

The next minute, all charges against Rick Ferguson were dismissed.

'How could you do it?' Jess demanded angrily of her ex-husband as she paced back and forth in front of him in the now empty corridor outside the courtroom. Tom Olinsky had gone back to the office; Neil was at the other end of the long hall trying to explain to Mrs Gambala and the other two witnesses exactly what had transpired, why Rick Ferguson would not be charged with murder. 'How could you let that killer walk free?'

'You didn't have a case, Jess.'

'You know he killed her. You know he's guilty!'

'Since when did that count for anything in a court of law?' Don demanded, then immediately softened. 'Look, Jess, I know how much you want Rick Ferguson to be guilty. I know how badly you want him behind bars. Frankly, I'd feel better about him behind bars too, at least until we figure out who's been terrorizing you. But I'm not at all convinced it's Rick Ferguson we have to worry about, and I can't abandon my professional obligation to my client because I happen to be in love with you.' He stopped, his eyes searching hers for a trace of understanding. Stubbornly, Jess refused to comply. 'Look, let's call a truce,' he offered. 'Let me take you out for dinner.'

'I don't think that would be a very good idea under the circumstances.'

'Come on, Jess,' he urged, 'you can't take these things personally.'

'Well, I do. Sorry if that disappoints you.'

'You never disappoint me.'

Jess felt the crest of her anger ebbing. What was the point in being mad at Don when the person she was really angry with was herself? 'I can't tonight, Don. I've already made plans,' she said.

'Adam?'

'My sister,' she said. 'And my brother-in-law. And my father. And his new love. A fitting end to a perfect day. I'll talk to you soon.' She spun round on her heels, found herself face to face with Rick Ferguson. 'Jesus Christ!'

'No,' he said. 'Just me.' He smiled. 'I was hoping we could go out and celebrate,' he said to Don, speaking over Jess's head.

'I'm afraid I can't make it,' Don said coldly.

'Oh, that's too bad.' Rick said, his smile belying his words. 'How about you, Jess? I could show you a real good time.'

'You won't show her so much as your shadow. Ever again,' Don stated. 'Is that clear?'

Rick Ferguson fell back, his hand on his heart, as if he'd been mortally wounded.

'You're a tough man, Mr Shaw,' he said, quickly straightening up, 'but hell, if that's the way you want it, that's the way you'll have it. I'm just feeling so good right now, I wanted to spread some of that good feeling around.'

'Go home, Rick,' Don said. He grabbed Rick roughly by the elbow and guided him toward the elevators, one obligingly opening as they neared. But just as they were about to step inside, Rick Ferguson scrambled free of his lawyer's grasp and darted back toward Jess.

Jess held her breath as he approached, determined to stand her ground. Surely he wouldn't do anything to hurt her now, not here in the Court House, not with his lawyer fast approaching.

327

'Want to know how good I feel, counsellor?' he was asking, staring directly into Jess's eyes and speaking so quietly that only she could hear. 'I feel just like the cat who swallowed the canary.'

For a second, Jess couldn't find her voice, could barely find her breath. 'You bastard,' she whispered.

'You bet,' Rick Ferguson told her. 'And don't worry,' he added, seconds before Don wrestled him to the floor. 'You won't even see my shadow.'

Chapter Twenty-Five

Jess drove her rental car to Evanston, pulling into her sister's driveway at five minutes to six o'clock. Her father's blue Buick was already in the driveway. 'Great,' she whispered, wishing she'd had time for at least one drink before she had to meet the new recruit. 'Now just stay calm. Smile. Look happy.'

She repeated these simple phrases to herself until they became meaningless, and she went on to new ones. 'Be nice. Be gracious. Don't fight.'

'Don't fight,' she said again, nodding her head up and down until it felt in danger of dropping off trying to work up the necessary courage to get out of the car. 'Be nice.' The front doored open and Barry appeared, motioning for her to come inside with a giant sweep of his hands. Could her brother-in law really have sent her that awful letter?

Don't be ridiculous, she said to herself, careful not to let her lips move. Barry didn't send you that letter. Rick Ferguson sent you it.

Now you're *really* being ridiculous, another voice argued. Rick Ferguson didn't do anything. He isn't guilty, remember? There's simply no hard evidence linking him to any wrongdoing of any kind. You did not prove him guilty. Therefore, he is innocent.

Innocent and out there just waiting for you, she thought, opening her car door, stepping out, then slamming it shut, refusing to be intimidated. Tomorrow she'd attend her final class in self-defense, learn how to disarm a would-be attacker. She doubted Rick Ferguson would do anything before then. That would be too obvious, even for him. If anything happened to her, he'd be the immediate suspect.

Big deal, Jess thought, realizing she had forgotten to bring either a bottle of wine or gifts for the kids. Rick Ferguson had been the immediate, and *only*, suspect in the murder of Connie DeVuono. That had seemed obvious enough too. And yet, the state hadn't been able to produce enough evidence to bring him to trial. Undoubtedly, he'd be just as clever in dispatching her. She'd probably just disappear one day, never to be seen or heard from again.

Like mother, like daughter, she thought, finding a curious comfort in the irony of the situation, as if fate had brought her full circle. She saw her father appear in the doorway behind his son-in-law, and was, for the first time, grateful that he had a new woman in his life. It would make it easier for him when the inevitable happened.

'Christ, Jess,' Barry called out. 'Could you walk any slower? Get the hell in here. It's freezing.'

As if to underline his point, the wind blew an extra gust of cold air in from the water, shaking the bare branches of the trees. Jess noted the blue lights that were laced through the small evergreen shrubs against the front of the house, wondered if they'd turned blue from the cold. They looked mournful, sad. A circular green paper wreath decorated with a bright red bow hung in the middle of the doorway.

'Tyler made it in nursery school,' Barry said proudly as Jess maneuvered her way up the poorly shovelled front steps, feeling as if lead weights had been attached to her ankles. 'Where'd you get the car?'

'I rented it this afternoon,' Jess explained, stepping inside and allowing her father to take her in his arms. 'Hi, Daddy.'

'Hi, sweetheart. Let me look at you.' He pushed her an arm's length away, careful not to let go of his hold on her, then drew her back into his embrace. 'You look wonderful.'

'What kind of car is that?' Barry was asking.

'A Toyota,' Jess said of the small red car she had newly leased, strangely grateful to have something so mundane to talk about.

'Shouldn't be driving Japanese cars,' Barry scolded, helping her off with her coat and hanging it in the closet. Jess caught

330

sight of a black mink coat she knew wasn't her sister's, and wondered fleetingly how mink meshed with Birkenstock sandals. 'The American car industry needs all the support it can get.'

'Which explains your Jaguar,' Jess said, dropping her purse to the floor.

'My next car will be American,' Barry assured her. 'I was thinking of a Cadillac.'

'Cadillac's a good car,' Art Koster said, the look in his eyes imploring Jess to leave it at that.

Jess nodded. 'I'm sorry I've been so busy lately, Daddy,' she apologized, delaying her entry into the main part of the house.

'I understand, sweetie,' her father told her, and Jess could see from the compassion that shaped his soft brown eyes that he did.

'I'm so sorry if I hurt you,' she whispered. 'You know it's the last thing I'd ever want to do.'

'I know that. And it's unimportant. No harm done. You're here now.'

'I'm sorry I forgot to bring anything for anyone,' Jess apologized again, seeing Maureen appear in the foyer holding one of the twins, Tyler wrapped, as tight as cellophane, around her legs. The entire Peppler clan, Jess noted, was dressed in festive red and green. Maureen and the baby were wearing almost identical red velvet dresses; Tyler and his father wore dark green trousers, matching red cardigans and wide murky-green ties. They looked as if they had just stepped off the front of a greeting card. Jess felt distinctly out of place in her black and white argyle sweater and plain black slacks.

'I'm so glad you could make it,' Maureen said, tears in the corners of her eyes. 'I was afraid you might call at the last minute and—' She broke off abruptly. 'Come on inside.'

Art Koster put his arm round his younger daughter and brought her into the living room. The first thing Jess noticed was the enormous Scottish pine Christmas tree that stood in front of the grand piano, waiting to be adorned. The next thing she saw was the Madonna figure sitting next to it on the rose-

331

colored sofa holding a baby in a red velvet dress.

'Sherry,' her father said, leading Jess to the sofa, 'this is my younger daughter, Jess. Jess, this is Sherry Hasek.'

'Hello, Jess,' the woman said, handing the baby to Jess's father as she stood to shake Jess's hand. She was as slim as her father had described and even shorter than Jess had imagined. Her black hair looked surprisingly natural, and was pulled back into a jewelled clasp at the nape of her neck. A large black onyx heart hung from a long gold chain round her neck. She wore a simple white silk blouse and charcoal-grey pants over solid black leather shoes. No Birkenstocks anywhere in sight. Her handshake was firm, though her hands were ice cold, despite the fire roaring in the fireplace.

She's as nervous as I am, Jess thought, telling herself not to cry as she shook the woman's hand. 'I'm sorry it's taken so long for me to meet you,' Jess told her sincerely.

'These things happen,' Sherry Hasek said.

'What can I get you to drink?' Barry asked. 'Wine? Beer? *Coca-Cola*?' he asked pointedly.

'Can I have a Coke?' Tyler asked immediately.

'You can have milk,' Maureen answered.

'I'll have some wine,' Jess said, lifting the baby from her sister's arms, thinking her sister was right — the twins really had grown in the last two months. 'Hello, you sweet little thing. How are you doing?'

The baby stared at her as if she were a creature from outer space, her eyes crossing as she tried to focus on Jess's nose.

'They're really something, aren't they?' Barry said proudly, pouring Jess a glass of white wine and holding it toward her. 'I'll take Chloe,' he said, exchanging the glass of wine for his infant daughter.

'I always wanted twins,' Sherry said. 'And girls. Instead I got three boys. One at a time.'

'My friends all say that boys are more trouble when they're young,' Maureen said, sitting down, a baby in her arms, a small boy clinging to her knees, 'but girls are worse when they hit their teens.'

332

'What about it, Art?' Barry asked. 'How were your girls as teenagers?'

Art Koster laughed. 'My girls were always perfect,' he said graciously, as Jess fought down the image of her mother's tearful face.

I don't need this, Jess. I don't need this from you.

'I don't think we were perfect,' Jess said, quickly raising her glass to her mouth. 'Cheers, everyone.' She took a long sip, then another.

'Health and wealth,' Barry toasted.

Jess tried to concentrate on Sherry Hasek's oval face. Her eyes were dark and wide apart, but the rest of her features were curiously crowded together, as if there wasn't quite enough room on her face for everything. When she became animated, her mouth seemed to jump all over the place. And she talked with her hands, using her long, manicured fingers for emphasis, creating the impression of an alert, if cluttered, mind.

Not at all like her Mother, Jess thought, superimposing her mother's wider face over that of Sherry Hasek, recalling her mother's blue-green eyes, her soft skin, the nose in perfect proportion to the mouth, her cheekbones high and prominent. It was a face that created the illusion of calm, made those around her feel safe and secure. There had been something so soothing about the delicate balance of her features, as if the serenity she projected was the result of a deep inner peace.

Her mother had always been that way, Jess realized, so comfortable with herself that she had effortlessly been able to make those around her feel comfortable too. She rarely lost her temper, almost never yelled. Yet there was never any question as to how she felt about something. She was never coy, had no patience for second-guessing. She said what she felt and expected the same courtesy from others. She treated everyone with respect, Jess thought now, seeing her mother's face streaked with tears, even when those around her were undeserving of that respect.

'Earth to Jess,' she heard Barry say. 'Come in, Jess. Come in.'

Jess felt the glass of wine slipping through her fingers, and squeezed it tightly before it could fall to the floor, feeling the fragile glass crack and collapse inside her fingers, her hand becoming sticky and wet. She looked down to see her blood mingling with the white of the wine to create a delicate rosé, her ears suddenly open to the sounds of horror and concern that were filling the room.

'Mommy!' Tyler cried.

'My God, Jess, your hand!'

'How the hell did you do that?' Barry rushed a napkin under her hand before she could drip blood on the carpet.

One of the babies started crying.

'I'm all right,' Jess heard herself say, though in truth she still wasn't sure what had happened, and therefore couldn't decide whether she was all right or not.

'That's quite a grip you've got there,' her father was saying, gently opening her fist to examine her injured hand, carefully extricating two small triangles of glass, softly wiping the blood away with his white linen handkerchief.

'My eagle's claw,' Jess said.

'Your what?' Barry asked, patting the carpet down with a bit of soda water.

'I've been taking self-defense classes,' Jess muttered, wondering if she was really having this conversation.

'And they're teaching you how to protect yourself from a glass of white wine?' Barry asked.

'I'll get some antiseptic cream for that,' Maureen said, efficiently depositing both babies into Jolly Jumpers that stood side by side near the doorway. The twins bounced happily as their mother left the room, Tyler, still crying, clinging to his mother's feet.

'I'm really sorry,' Jess said.

'Why?' Sherry asked. 'Did you do it on purpose?'

Jess smiled gratefully. 'It hurts like hell.'

'I'm sure it does.' Sherry examined the small cuts that mingled with the natural lines of Jess's hand. 'You have a good strong life line,' she observed in passing.

'What the hell were you thinking about?' Barry asked, getting to his feet as his wife re-entered the room.

'I thought you didn't allow swearing in the house,' Jess reminded him.

'Here, let me rub some of this on.' Maureen rubbed the soothing salve into her palm before Jess could protest. 'And I brought some gauze.'

'I don't need gauze.'

'Keep your hand above your head,' Barry instructed.

'Really, Barry, the cuts aren't that deep.'

'Maybe we should call a doctor,' Maureen said. 'Just to be on the safe side.'

At the mention of the word 'doctor', Tyler started to wail.

'It's all right, Tyler,' Maureen assured him, reaching down to scoop the frightened child into her arms. 'The doctor's not for you.' She turned to Jess. 'He hates doctors because the last time he was sick, you know, when everybody had colds, the doctor stuck that thing down his throat to have a look, and it made Tyler gag. He just hates throwing up.'

Jess laughed and Tyler cried louder. 'I'm sorry, sweetie,' she said, bending down to her nephew's height while keeping her arm raised, allowing Sherry to wrap the gauze round her injured hand. 'I wasn't laughing at you. It's just that I know exactly how you feel. I don't like throwing up either.'

'Who does?!' Barry asked, reaching for the phone on an end table beside the sofa. 'What about it, Jess? Is medical attention required?'

'Not for me.' She let her father lead her to the sofa where he carefully positioned her between himself and his new love. 'I'm tough. Remember?' But if Barry recalled the details of their last argument, he gave no such acknowledgement.

'Did they ever find out who trashed your car?' Maureen asked.

Jess shook her head, feeling Rick Ferguson's eerie presence in the room, like the ghost of Christmas Past. She shooed it away with the sound of her voice. 'So, I understand you're quite an artist,' she said to the woman sitting beside her.

335

Sherry laughed. It was a charming laugh, like wind chimes in a warm breeze. Jess heard her mother's more raucous laughter in the distance. 'I just play around really, although I've always had a very deep love of art,' Sherry explained, looking over at Jess's father for approval, something Jess's mother would never have done, Jess thought.

'Is that art or Art?' he asked playfully.

Again Sherry laughed. 'Both, I guess.'

'Do you prefer oils or pastels?' Jess asked, not caring one way or the other, but anxious to get away from the subject of love.

'I'm better with pastels. Your father prefers oils.'

Jess winced. Her mother would never have presumed to speak for her father. And did this woman really feel it necessary to inform her of her own father's preferences?

'Sherry's being overly modest,' her father said, presuming now to speak for Sherry. Were all people in love guilty of such presumption? Jess wondered. 'She's quite a talented artist.'

'Well,' Sherry demurred. 'I'm not too bad at still-life.'

'Her peaches are terrific,' Art stated with a wink.

'Art!' Sherry laughed, reaching across Jess to mockingly slap Art Koster's hand. Jess felt vaguely sick. 'Your father is better at the nudes.'

'Figures,' said Barry.

'I keep offering to paint her picture,' Art said, smiling at Sherry as if Jess wasn't sitting between them. 'But she says she's holding out for Jeffrey Koons.'

Again the sound of wind chimes in the air. Jess supposed she should know who Jeffrey Koons was, but she didn't, although she laughed anyway, as if she did.

Jess wondered what her mother would make of this pleasant little family scene: Maureen standing beside Barry, his arm draped across her shoulder, her own arms wrapped round her son; Jess snuggled on the sofa between her father and the woman he wanted to paint in the nude; the twins bouncing in their Jolly Jumpers, their saucer-like eyes keeping a guarded eye out for their mother. That's right, Jess thought, watching them gently bounce up and down, like human yo-yos, their bootied toes barely touching the floor. Keep an eye on your mother, she warned them silently. Watch out that she doesn't disappear.

'Earth to Jess,' she heard again. 'Earth to Jess. Come in, Jess.'

'Sorry,' Jess said quickly, catching the look of annoyance in Barry's eyes, as if her inattentiveness was somehow a reflection on his abilities as a host. 'Were you saying something?'

'Sherry asked you if you liked to paint.'

'Oh. Sorry. I didn't hear you.'

'That much was obvious,' Barry said, as Jess caught the worried look that suddenly clouded Maureen's eyes.

'It's not important,' Sherry immediately qualified. 'I was just making conversation.'

'Actually I don't know whether I like painting or not,' Jess answered. 'I haven't done it since I was a child.'

'Remember the time you got a hold of those crayons and you drew all over the walls of the living room,' Maureen said, 'and Mom got so mad because they'd just been freshly painted.'

'I don't remember that.'

'I don't think I'll ever forget it,' Maureen said. 'It was the loudest I think I ever heard Mom yell.'

'She didn't yell.'

'She did that day. You could hear her for blocks.'

'She never yelled,' Jess insisted.

'I thought you said you didn't even remember the incident,' Barry reminded her.

'I think I can remember my own mother.'

'I remember lots of times she yelled,' Maureen said.

Jess shrugged, trying to disguise her growing anger. 'Never at me.'

'Always at you.'

Jess stood up, walked to the Christmas tree, her hand throbbing. 'When are we going to decorate this thing?'

'We thought right after dinner,' Barry said.

'You never knew when to let go of things,' Maureen

continued, as if there had been no interruption. 'You always had to have the last word.' She laughed. 'I remember Mom saying that she always loved having you around because it was so nice living with someone who knew everything.'

Everyone laughed. Jess was beginning to hate the sound of wind chimes.

'My boys were like that,' Sherry agreed. 'Each one thought he had all the answers. When they were seventeen, they thought I was the stupidest person on earth. By the time they were twenty-one, they couldn't believe how smart I'd gotten.'

Again, everyone laughed.

'Actually, we had a few very rough years,' Sherry confided. 'Especially just after their father left. Not that he was around that much to begin with. But his leaving kind of made it official, and the boys did a lot of acting out. They were rude and rebellious, and no matter what I said or did, it wasn't right. We always seemed to be fighting about something. I'd turn around, and there I'd be in the middle of a confrontation, and I could never quite figure out how I got there. They said I was too strict, too old-fashioned, too naive. Anything I could be, I was too much of it. It seemed we were always at each other's throats. And then, suddenly they were all grown up, and I found that I was still relatively in one piece. They went off to college, eventually all moved out on their own. I bought a dog. He loves me unconditionally. He sits by the door and waits for me whenever I go out. When I get home, he smothers me with kisses, he's so glad to see me. He doesn't argue with me; he doesn't talk back; he thinks I'm the most wonderful thing on earth. He's the child I always wanted.'

Art hooted with delight.

'Maybe we should get a dog,' Barry said, winking at his wife.

'I think every mother probably goes through periods where she wonders why she bothered,' Maureen said.

Once again, Jess saw her mother's face. *I don't need this, Jess. I don't need this from you.*

'I mean, God knows I adore my children,' Maureen continued, 'but there are moments—'

'When you wish you were back at work?' Jess asked, watching Barry's shoulders stiffen.

'When I wish it were a little *quieter*,' Maureen told her.

'Maybe we *should* get a dog,' Barry said.

'Oh great,' Jess exclaimed. 'Something else for Maureen to take care of.'

'Jess,' Maureen warned.

'Sherry's dog is the cutest little thing,' Art Koster said quickly. 'A toy poodle. Beautiful red coat, a very unusual color for a poodle. When she first told me she had a poodle, I thought, oh no, I can't get involved with a woman who could love a dog like that. I mean, poodles are such a cliché.'

'And then he met Casey,' Sherry interjected.

'And then I met Casey.'

'And it was love at first sight.'

'Well, more like love at first walk,' Art Koster qualified. 'I took the damn pooch out for a walk one afternoon, and I couldn't believe how absolutely everyone we passed came over to pet the damn thing. I never saw so many smiles on so many people in one afternoon in my life. It made me happy just to be part of it. And of course poodles are very smart. Sherry says that when it comes to dogs and intelligence, there's poodles and then there's everything else.'

Jess could barely believe her ears. Was her father really engaged in an avid discussion about a toy poodle?

'Jess was always an animal lover,' her father was saying.

'Really? Do you have any pets?' Sherry asked.

'No,' Jess said.

'She has a canary,' Maureen answered at almost the same moment.

'No,' Jess said again.

'What happened to Fred?' Maureen asked.

'He died. Last week.'

'Fred died?' Maureen repeated. 'I'm so sorry. Had he been sick?'

'How would you know whether or not a canary was sick?' Barry scoffed.

'Don't talk to her in that tone,' Jess said sharply.

'I beg your pardon?' There was more surprise than anger in Barry's voice.

'What tone?' Maureen asked.

'Are the boys coming home for Christmas this year?' Art Koster asked suddenly. For a minute, nobody seemed to know what he was talking about.

'Yes,' Sherry answered, snapping to attention, her voice a touch too loud, a shade too enthusiastic. 'At least, that's the latest word. But you never know what they could decide at the last minute.'

'Where are your boys now?' Jess asked, allowing herself to be drawn back into the conversation. Smile, she thought through tightly gritted teeth. Be nice. Be gracious. Don't fight.

'Warren is a gym teacher at a high school in Rockford. Colin is at the New York Film School; he wants to be a director. And Michael is at Wharton. He's my entrepreneur.'

'Three very bright young men,' Jess's father said proudly.

'Maureen has an MBA from Harvard,' Jess said, her resolve of only seconds ago crumbling.

'Have you met them yet, Dad?' Maureen asked, as if Jess hadn't spoken.

'Not yet,' her father answered.

'I was hoping I could persuade you all to come for Christmas dinner at my place this year,' Sherry proposed. 'That way I could introduce you.'

'Sounds great,' Maureen said immediately.

'Count *us* in,' Barry said, pointedly. 'What about you, Jess?'

'Sounds fine,' Jess concurred, straining for sincerity. Smile, she thought. Be nice. Don't fight. Stay calm. 'Speaking of dinner . . .'

'Ready whenever you are,' Maureen said.

Jess found herself staring at the woman who was poised to take her mother's place. 'Ready or not,' she said.

Chapter Twenty-Six

'This roast is delicious,' Sherry Hasek was saying, delicately patting at the sides of her mouth with her rose-colored napkin. 'It's so rare these days that I eat red meat. I've forgotten what a treat it is.'

'I've tried to wean Maureen away from red meat,' Barry said, 'but she says she was raised on mother's milk and good old-fashioned Chicago roast beef, so what are you going to do?'

'Enjoy it,' Art said.

'I think as long as you don't overdo things, you're okay,' Sherry said. 'Everything in moderation, isn't that what they say?'

'They say so many things,' Maureen continued, 'it's hard to keep track. One minute we're supposed to avoid red meat; the next minute they tell us it's good for us. They keep warning us of the dangers of alcohol, then they tell us a glass of red wine a day prevents heart attacks. Something's good for you one day, bad for you the next. Right now, fiber is in, fat is out. Next year, it'll probably be the reverse.'

'To moderation,' her father toasted, lifting his glass of red wine into the air.

'Health and wealth,' Barry said.

'I was reading an article in the doctor's office the other day,' Art Koster began. 'It was an old magazine, and the reporter was asking this celebrity he was profiling, I didn't know who she was, he asked her to name her favorite drink and state three reasons why she liked it. It's a game. Why don't we try it?'

'My favorite drink?' Barry mused. 'It would have to be red wine. It's tasty; it smells wonderful; and it's intoxicating.'

'I like orange juice,' Maureen followed. 'It's healthy; it's

341

invigorating; and it's refreshing.'

'Sherry?' Art asked.

'I'd have to say champagne,' she answered. 'It's fun; it suggests celebration; and I like the bubbles.'

'Jess?' Barry asked.

'What?'

'It's your turn.'

'Did you say you'd been to the doctor?' Jess asked her father.

'Haven't you been listening?' Barry asked.

Jess ignored her brother-in-law. 'What's wrong, Dad? Haven't you been feeling well?'

'I'm fine,' her father stated. 'It was just my annual check-up.'

Where are you going? Jess asked her mother.

Nowhere, she answered.

Since when do you get so dressed up to go nowhere?

'So, what's your answer?' Barry prodded.

'My answer to what?'

Barry shook his head. 'Really, Jess, I don't know why you bother accepting our dinner invitations if you're not going to take part in the conversations.'

'Barry, please,' Maureen pleaded softly.

'What's your favorite drink?' Art repeated 'And the three reasons why.'

'This is the conversation we're having?' Jess asked.

'It's a game,' Sherry said pleasantly.

'I don't know,' Jess said finally. 'Black coffee, I guess.' She noticed they were all waiting for her to continue. 'Why? Because it wakes me up in the mornings; it's slightly bitter; and it's good to the last drop.' She shrugged, hoping she had fulfilled all expectations.

'Dad?' Maureen asked.

'Beer,' he told them. 'It's simple; it's straightforward; it makes me feel good.'

'So what does it all mean?' Maureen wondered.

'Well,' Art said with appropriate flourish, 'the drink represents sex. In my case, I like it because it's simple, straightforward, and makes me feel good.'

Everyone struggled to remember their three reasons for liking the drink each had selected, laughter breaking out as each realized what had been said.

'So you think sex is tasty, intoxicating and smells wonderful,' Maureen reminded her husband. 'I think I'm flattered.'

'I think I'm lucky,' he answered, looking over at Jess. 'Slightly bitter, huh?'

Jess said nothing. Be nice, she thought. Try to smile. Be gracious. Don't fight.

'And you like the bubbles,' Art said, snuggling up to Sherry.

Jess wondered what her mother would have said. White wine maybe, because it was clear, direct, and to the point. Or maybe cream soda because it was sweet, pretty, and laced with nostalgia. Or maybe even milk, for the same reasons her father liked beer.

'Earth to Jess,' Barry was saying again. 'Earth to Jess. Come in, Jess.'

'The first time was cute, Barry,' Jess said, more sharply than she'd intended. 'Now it's merely tiresome.'

'So is your behaviour. I'm just trying to figure out whether you're simply preoccupied or whether you're being deliberately rude.'

'Barry . . .' Maureen warned.

'Why on earth would I be deliberately rude?' Jess demanded.

'You tell me. I don't profess to have any understanding into what you're all about.'

'Is that so?'

'Jess . . .' her father said.

'I'd say we understand each other pretty well, Barry,' Jess told him, her patience evaporated. 'We hate each other's guts. That's pretty clear, isn't it?'

Barry looked stunned, as if he'd just been slapped across the face. 'I don't hate you, Jess.'

'Oh, really? What about that charming little letter you sent me? Was that a token of your affection?'

'Letter?' Maureen asked. 'What letter?'

Jess bit down on her tongue, tried to stop herself from saying anything further. But it was too late. The words were already pouring out of her mouth. 'Your husband sent me a urine-soaked sample of his esteem, along with the clippings of his pubic hair.'

'What? What are you talking about?' everyone seemed to demand at once.

'Have you flipped out altogether?' Barry was yelling. 'What are you saying, for Christ's sake?'

What *was* she saying? Jess wondered suddenly, aware that their yelling had triggered a fresh onslaught of tears in the twins. Did she really believe that Barry had sent her that letter? 'Are you saying it wasn't you?'

'I'm saying I haven't got the foggiest notion what the hell you're talking about.'

'You're swearing again,' Jess said.

Barry sputtered something unintelligible in response.

'I got an anonymous letter in the mail last month,' Jess expanded. 'It was filled with strands of pubic hair and soaked in urine. When I spoke to you on the phone a little while later, you asked me if I'd gotten your letter. Are you denying it?'

'Of course I'm denying it! The only thing I ever sent you in the mail was a notice about Investment Retirement Accounts.'

Jess vaguely recalled tearing open a letter, seeing something about a registered retirement savings plan, tossing it away without much thought. My God, was that what he'd been talking about on the phone that day? 'That's what you sent me?'

'I'm an accountant, for God's sake,' he told her. 'What else would I send you?'

Jess felt the room starting to spin. What was the matter with her? How could she have accused her own brother-in-law of such a depraved act? Even if she'd believed it, how could she have said it out loud? In the man's own home? At his dinner table? In front of his family?

Her sister was voicing the same sentiments. 'I can't believe you'd say these things!' she was crying, holding her son in her arms. 'I can't believe you'd even think them.'

'I'm sorry,' Jess said helplessly, Tyler wailing at the sight of his mother's tears. The twins shrieked in their Jolly Jumpers.

'Children, can we just calm down,' Art Koster urged, speaking to the grown-ups.

'It's just that Barry and I had just had that big argument,' Jess tried to explain, 'and I knew how angry he was, how he liked to get even, and then I got this letter in the mail, and soon after that, I spoke to Barry and he asked me if I'd gotten his letter . . .'

'So you concluded he was the one responsible! That he could have such a sick, perverted mind. That I could have married such a disgusting individual!'

'You had nothing to do with it. Maureen, this isn't about you.'

'Isn't it?' Maureen demanded. 'When you attack my husband, you attack me too.'

'Don't be silly,' Jess argued.

The twins cried louder; Tyler squirmed out of his mother's arms and ran upstairs.

'You haven't given him a chance from the day we got married,' Maureen yelled, her free arms waving frantically in the air.

'That's not true,' Jess countered. 'I liked him fine until he turned you into Donna Reed.'

'Donna Reed!' Maureen gasped.

'How could you let him do it?' Jess demanded, deciding that now that she was in it, she might as well go all the way. 'How could you give up everything and let him turn you into Superwife?'

'Why don't I take the twins upstairs?' Sherry offered, deftly lifting the girls from their Jolly Jumpers and carrying them upstairs, one under each arm.

'Children, why don't we stop this now before we say things we'll regret,' Art said, then sighed, as if acknowledging it was already too late for that.

'Just what is it exactly that you think I've given up?' Maureen demanded. 'My job? I can always get another job. My education? I'll always have that. Can't you get it through that thick head of yours that I am doing exactly what I want to do? That it was *my* decision, not Barry's, *mine,* to stay home and be with my children while they were young. I respect *your* choices, Jess, even if I don't always agree with them. Can't you respect mine? What is so wrong with what I'm doing?'

'What's wrong with it?' Jess heard herself say. 'Don't you realize that your whole life is a repudiation of everything our mother taught us?'

'What?' Maureen looked as if she had been struck by lightning.

'For God's sake, Jess,' her father said, 'what on earth are you talking about?'

'Our mother raised us to be independent women with lives of our own,' Jess argued. 'The last thing she would have wanted was for Maureen to be trapped in a marriage where she wasn't permitted room to grow.'

Maureen's eyes glowed with red-hot fury. 'How dare you criticize me. How dare you presume to know anything about my marriage. How dare you drag our mother into it! *You* were the one, *not me,*' she continued, 'who was always fighting with Mother over these exact issues. *You* were the one, *not me,* who insisted she was going to get married while she was still in school, even though Mother pleaded with you to wait. *You* were the one who fought with her all the time, who made her cry, who made her miserable. "Just wait till you've finished law school," she kept saying. "Don's a nice man, but he won't give you any room to grow. Just wait till you've finished school," she begged you. But you wouldn't listen. You knew everything then, just like you know everything now. So stop trying to assuage your own guilt by telling everyone else how to live their lives!'

'What do you mean, my own guilt?' Jess asked, almost breathless in her anger.

'You know what I mean.'

'What the hell are you talking about?'

'I'm talking about the fight you had with Mommy the day she

disappeared!' Maureen shot back. 'I'm talking about how I called home from the library that morning, I guess just after you stormed out of the house, and she was crying. And I asked her what was wrong, and she tried to tell me it was nothing, but finally she admitted that the two of you had been going at it again pretty good, and I asked her whether she wanted me to come home, and she said no, she'd be fine, she had to go out anyway. And that was the last time I spoke to her.' Maureen's features looked in danger of melting, her eyes, nose and mouth sliding across her face as she dissolved into a flood of frustrated tears.

Jess, who had risen to her feet at some point during the confrontation, sank back into her seat. She heard voices yelling, looked around, saw not her sister's living room but the kitchen of her mother's house on Burling Street, saw not her sister's tear-streaked face, but her mother's.

'You're all dressed up,' Jess observed, coming into the kitchen, and noting her mother's fresh white linen suit. 'Where are you going?'

'Nowhere.'

'Since when do you get so dressed up to go nowhere?'

'I just felt like putting on something pretty,' her mother said, then added casually, 'and I have a doctor's appointment later on this afternoon. What are your plans?'

'What kind of doctor's appointment?'

'Nothing special.'

'Come on, Mom. You know I can always tell when you're not telling me the truth.'

'Which is one of the reasons you'll make a great lawyer.'

'The law has nothing to do with the truth,' Jess told her.

'Sounds like something Don would say.'

Jess felt her shoulders tense. 'Are you going to start?'

'I wasn't trying to start anything, Jess. It was just an observation.'

'I'm not sure I appreciate your observations.'

Laura Koster shrugged, said nothing.

'So, what kind of doctor's appointment is it?'

'I'd rather not say until I know for sure whether I have anything to worry about.'

'You're worried already. I can see it in your face. What is it?'

'I found a little lump.'

'A lump?' Jess held her breath.

'I don't want you to worry. It's probably nothing. Most lumps are.'

'Where is this lump?'

'In my left breast.'

'Oh, God.'

'Don't worry.'

'When did you find it?'

'This morning, when I was taking a shower. I called the doctor and he's sure it's nothing. He just wants me to come down and let him have a look at it.'

'What if it's not nothing?'

'Then we'll cross that bridge when we come to it.'

'Are you scared?'

Her mother didn't answer for several seconds. Only her eyes moved.

'The truth, Mom.'

'Yes, I'm scared.'

'Would you like me to come to the doctor's with you?'

'Yes,' her mother said immediately. 'Yes, I would.'

And then the conversation had somehow veered off track, Jess recalled now, seeing her mother at the kitchen counter making a fresh pot of coffee, offering Jess some fresh blueberry buns she'd purchased from a nearby bakery.

'My appointment's not till four o'clock,' her mother said. 'Will that ruin your plans?'

'No,' Jess told her. 'I'll call Don. Tell him our plans will have to wait.'

'That would be wonderful,' her mother said, and Jess understood immediately that her mother wasn't simply referring to the plans they'd made for the afternoon.

'What is it you have against Don, Mother?' she asked.

'I have absolutely nothing against him.'

'Then why are you so against my marrying him?'

'I'm not saying you shouldn't marry the man, Jess,' her mother told her. 'I think Don is a lovely man. He's smart. He's thoughtful. He obviously adores you.'

'So, what's the problem?' Jess demanded.

'The problem is that he's eleven years older than you are. He's already done all the things you've yet to try.'

'Eleven years is hardly a major age difference,' Jess protested.

'It's eleven years. Eleven years that he's had to figure out what he wants from his life.'

'He wants me.'

'And what do you want?'

'I want him!'

'And your career?'

'I'll have my career. Don is very intent on my becoming a successful lawyer. He can help me. He's a wonderful teacher.'

'You want a partner, Jess. Not a teacher. He won't give you enough room to grow.'

'How can you say that?'

'Honey, I'm not saying you shouldn't marry him,' her mother repeated.

'Yes, you are. That's exactly what you're saying.'

'All I'm saying is wait a few years. You're only in first year law school. Wait till after you pass the bar exams. Wait till you've had a chance to find out who you are and what you want.'

'I know who I am. I know what I want. I want Don. And I'm going to marry him whether you like it or not.'

Her mother sighed, poured herself a cup of freshly brewed coffee. 'You want a cup?'

'I don't want anything from you,' Jess said stubbornly.

'Okay, let's just drop it.'

'I don't want to drop it. You think that you can raise all these issues, and then say, let's drop it just because you don't feel like discussing it anymore?'

'I shouldn't have said anything.'

'You're right. You shouldn't have.'

349

'Sometimes I forget you know it all.'

'Oh, that's rich, Mother. Really rich.'

'I'm sorry, honey. I shouldn't have said that. I guess I'm a little nervous today, and maybe more upset than I realized.'

'No, you can't use that excuse,' Jess said mercilessly. 'Don't start laying any guilt trips on me.'

'I'm not trying to lay any guilt trips.' Tears filled her mother's eyes.

'And don't you dare cry,' Jess warned. 'I'm not the bad guy here.'

'I never said you were the bad guy.'

'Stop trying to live my life.'

'That's the last thing I want, Jess,' her mother said, tears falling the length of her cheek. 'I want you to live your life.'

'Then stay out of it!'

Her mother shook her head, dislodging more tears. 'I don't need this, Jess,' she said. 'I don't need this from you.'

And then what? Jess wondered now, feeling like a large wind-up toy, unable to stop spinning until its battery ran out. More careless words. More angry protestations.

'You don't have to take me to the doctor's. I can get there on my own.'

'Have it your way.'

Storming out of the house.

The last time she saw her mother alive.

Jess jumped to her feet, raced toward the foyer, stumbling into the Jolly Jumpers, almost knocking them over, taking a few seconds to right them.

'I'm sorry, Jess,' Maureen was crying after her. 'Please don't go. I didn't mean to say those things.'

'Why not?' Jess asked, stopping abruptly, turning toward her sister, seeing her mother's face. 'They're all true. Everything you said is true.'

'It wasn't your fault,' Maureen told her. 'Whatever happened to our mother wasn't your fault.'

Jess shook her head in disbelief. 'How can you say that?' she asked. 'If I'd taken her to the doctor's like I promised, she would never have disappeared.'

'You can't know that.'

'Of course I know that. And you know it too. If I had gone with her to the doctor's, she'd still be here today.'

'Not if someone was stalking her,' her father said, crowding into the foyer, Barry by his side. 'Not if someone was determined to do her harm. You know as well as I do that it's next to impossible to stop someone if they're really out to get you.'

Jess thought immediately of Rick Ferguson.

The phone rang.

'I'll get it,' Barry said, crossing into the living room. No one else moved.

'Why don't we go back into the dining room and sit down?' Maureen offered.

'I really think I should leave,' Jess told her.

'We never talked about what happened,' Maureen said. 'I mean, we talked about the facts; we talked about the details. But we never really talked about how we felt. I think we have a lot to talk about. Don't you?'

'I want to,' Jess told her, her voice like a small child. 'I just don't think I can. Not tonight anyway. Maybe another day. I'm so tired. I just want to go home and crawl into bed.'

Barry appeared in the hallway. 'It's for you, Jess.'

'Me? But nobody knows I'm here.'

'Your ex-husband knows.'

'Don?' Jess vaguely recalled having told her ex-husband she was having dinner at her sister's.

'He says it's very important.'

'We'll be in the dining room,' Maureen said, allowing Jess her privacy as she walked, trancelike, toward the phone.

'Has something happened?' she asked instead of hello. 'Did Rick Ferguson confess?'

'Rick Ferguson is on his way to Los Angeles. I bought him a ticket and put him on the plane myself at seven o'clock this evening. It's not Rick Ferguson I'm concerned about.'

'What are you concerned about?' Jess asked.

'Are you seeing Adam tonight?'

'Adam? No, he's out of town.'

'Are you sure?'

'What do you mean, am I sure?'

'I want you to stay over at your sister's house tonight.'

'What?! Why? What are you talking about?'

'Jess, I had my office do some checking on this guy. They called the State Bar. They've never heard of any lawyer named Adam Stohn.'

'What?'

'You heard me, Jess. They never heard of the guy. And if he lied to you about who he is and what he does, then there's a good chance he's lying about being out of town. Now, do me a favor, and stay over at your sister's, at least for tonight.'

'I can't do that,' Jess whispered, thinking of everything that had happened tonight, the things that had been said.

'Why not, for God's sake?'

'I just can't. Please, Don, don't ask me to explain.'

'Then I'm coming over.'

'No! Please. I'm a big girl. I have to take care of myself.'

'You can start taking care of yourself when we know everything's okay.'

'Everything *is* okay,' Jess told him, feeling numb from head to toe, as if she had been injected with an overdose of Novocaine. 'Adam isn't going to hurt me,' she mumbled, speaking away from the receiver.

'Did you say something?'

'I said not to worry,' Jess told him. 'I'll call you in the morning.'

'Jess—'

'I'll speak to you tomorrow.' She hung up the phone.

Jess stood by the telephone for several seconds and tried to make sense of what Don had told her. No record of a lawyer named Adam Stohn? No one by that name registered to practice law in the state of Illinois? But why would he have lied? And did that make everything else he'd told her a lie as well? Was there nothing in her life that added up? Nothing that made any sense?

Jess stared at the bare Christmas tree waiting patiently for adornment, heard the quiet voices emanating from the dining room. 'I think we have a lot to talk about,' her sister had said. And she was right. There was a lot that needed to be said, a lot that needed to be dealt with. Together and alone. Maybe she'd call Stephanie Banack on Monday morning, see if the therapist might consider seeing her again. She had to stop acting as her own judge and jury, she realized, creeping quietly into the foyer. It was time to let go of the suffocating guilt that had coated her for the past eight years, like a second skin.

Grabbing her purse but abandoning her coat to the hall closet, Jess silently opened the front door and stepped into the bitter night air. In the next instant, she was behind the wheel of her rented car, speeding south along Sheridan Road, tears streaming down her cheeks, music blasting from the radio, wanting only to crawl into her bed, pull the covers up over her head, and disappear until morning.

Chapter Twenty-Seven

She was still crying when she arrived home.

'Stop crying,' she admonished herself, turning off the car's ignition, silencing Mick Jagger's misogynistic boasting. *Under my thumb*, he wailed after her as she raced through the cold toward her three-story brownstone. 'What are you still crying about?' she asked herself, pushing her key into the lock, feeling the front door give way, locking it again securely behind her. 'Just because you acted like a total idiot tonight, because you called your sister Donna Reed and your brother-in-law a pervert, because you made the impression of a lifetime on your father's new girlfriend, because you snuck out of the house like a thief in the night, because Adam Stohn isn't who he claims to be, because Rick Ferguson gets to go to California instead of the electric chair . . . No,' she reminded herself, taking the stairs two at a time, 'they don't fry people in Illinois any more. They put them to sleep. Like dogs,' she added, mindful of the last line from Kafka's *Trial*, crying even harder.

There were no trumpets or saxophones to accompany her up the final flight of stairs, no light creeping out from underneath Walt Fraser's door. Probably away for the weekend, she thought, thinking that maybe she'd call Don when she got inside her apartment, suggest a few days in Union Pier. Forget about Adam Stohn. Or whoever the hell he really was.

She unlocked the door to her apartment and stepped over the threshold, allowing the silence and the darkness to draw her in, like old friends at a party, warmly greeting the late arrival. No need anymore to leave the radio or the lights on all day. No more innocent, sweet melodies to welcome her home. She double locked her door.

The street lights filtered in through the antique ivory lace

355

curtains, casting an eerie glow on the empty bird cage. She hadn't had the courage to put it away, the will to consign it to the back of a closet, the strength to tote it down to the street, the good sense to give it to the Salvation Army. Poor Fred, she thought, giving in to a fresh onslaught of tears.

'Poor me,' she whispered, dropping her purse to the floor, slouching toward her bedroom.

He came at her from behind.

She didn't see him, didn't even hear him, until the wire was around her throat, and she was being rudely yanked backward into oblivion. Her hands automatically flew to her neck as she frantically sought to dig her fingers in between the wire and her flesh. The wire cut into her bandaged hand, and she felt the stickiness of fresh blood on her fingers, heard herself gagging, gasping for air. She couldn't breathe. The wire was cutting off her supply of oxygen, slicing into the flesh at her throat. She lost control of her legs, felt her toes being lifted off the floor. With everything in her, she fought to stay erect, to pull herself away from her attacker.

And then, somewhere inside the panic, she remembered — don't pull away; don't fight it; go with it. Use the image of circularity. If someone pulls you, rather than resist and pull back, use the attacker's force to be pulled into his body. Strike when you get there.

She stopped fighting. She stopped resisting, although it went against every instinct she had. Instead, she allowed her body to go limp, felt her back cave in against her assailant's chest as he pulled her toward him. Her neck throbbed in pain, like a giant pulse. For a terrifying instant, she thought it might be too late, that she was in danger of blacking out. She found the idea surprisingly seductive and was momentarily tempted to give in to the sensation. Why prolong what was clearly inevitable? Blackness was swirling around her. Why not dive into the thick of it? Why not simply disappear inside it forever?

But then suddenly, she was fighting back, fighting her way out of the darkness, using her assailant's weight against him, allowing the force of her body to knock her attacker to the ground. She fell with him, her hands shooting wildly into the air, knocking against the side of the bird cage, sending it crashing to the floor. Her assailant yelled as he lost his balance, and she quickly used her feet to kick at his legs, her nails to scratch at his arms, her elbows to jab at his ribs.

She felt the wire around her throat loosen just enough for her to break free. She scrambled to her feet, gasping for breath, her body on fire, trying desperately to suck air into her lungs, almost collapsing with the effort. She felt the indent of the wire still pressing into her throat, digging deeper into her flesh, as if it had become part of her, even though it was no longer there. She felt as if she were dangling from a hangman's noose, as if, at any minute, her neck might snap.

Suddenly, she heard him moan, turned, saw his dazed, muscular form sprawled across the floor, took quick note of the black pointed-toed boots, the tight jeans, the dark T-shirt, the brown leather racing gloves covering his large hands, the long dirty blond hair that was whipped across the side of his face, hiding all but his twisted grin.

I am Death, the grin said, even now. *I have come for you.*

Rick Ferguson.

A small cry escaped her throat. Had she actually thought he'd quietly board a plane to California and disappear from her life? Hadn't this night been a foregone conclusion from the moment of their first confrontation several months ago?

A million images flooded her brain as she saw him struggling to regain his footing — eagle claws and zipper punches and hammer fists. Then she remembered — getting away comes first. Forget the heroics and the theatrics. Running away is what works most often for most women.

But Rick Ferguson was already on his feet, lumbering toward her, blocking her way to the front door. Scream, her inner voice commanded. Yell, goddamn you! Roar! '*Hohh!*' she cried, watching him flinch, momentarily startled by the sound. '*Hohh!*' she yelled again, even louder the second time, thinking of the gun that lay in the drawer of the end table beside her bed, wondering if she could get to it, her eyes scanning the dark room for whatever weapon was at hand.

If anything, her outburst seemed to bring him new life. Rick Ferguson's evil grin burst into an outright laugh. 'I like a good fight,' he said.

'Stay away from me,' Jess warned.

'Connie wasn't much of a challenge. She just kind of crumpled up and died. No fun at all. Not like you,' he told her. 'Killing you is gonna be a pure pleasure.'

'Likewise, I'm sure,' Jess said, lunging to the floor and scooping the empty bird cage into her hands, hurling it at Rick Ferguson's head, watching it connect, seeing a thick line of blood race down his cheek from the gash in his forehead. She turned on her heels and ran from the room, her thoughts scrambling to catch up.

Where was she going? What was she going to do when she got there?

Her bedroom had never seemed so far away. She tore through the hall, hearing him only steps behind her. She had to get her gun. She had to get her gun before he was able to lay his hands on her again. She had to use it.

She threw herself at the small end table beside her bed, pulling open the top drawer, her desperate fingers searching for her gun. It wasn't there. 'Goddamn it, where are you?' she cried, throwing the contents of the drawer to the floor.

The mattress! she thought, falling to her knees, reaching under the mattress, though she distinctly remembered Don insisting she not keep it there. Still, what if she was mistaken? What if she hadn't moved it after all?

It wasn't there. Goddamn it, it wasn't there!

'Looking for this?' Rick Ferguson stood in the doorway, dangling the revolver from the end of his gloved fingers.

Jess rose slowly to her feet, her knees knocking painfully together, as he aimed the gun directly at her head. Her heart was pounding wildly; her ears were ringing; tears were falling the length of her cheeks. If only she could get her thoughts together; if only she could stop them from careening around directionless inside her brain, hammering on the inside of her skull, as if they were trying to escape; if she could only stop her legs from shaking . . .

'Nice of you to invite me into your bedroom,' he said, moving slowly toward her. 'Of course, I already know where you keep your panties.'

'Get the hell out of here,' Jess yelled, recalling her torn panties, seeing the blood from her neck smeared across the white of her duvet.

He laughed. 'You sure are a feisty little thing, aren't you? Yea, I gotta say I admire your nerve. Telling a man with a loaded gun to get the hell out. That's real cute. I suppose now you're gonna tell me I'll never get away with this.'

'You won't.'

'Sure I will. Don't forget — I've got a very good lawyer.'

Jess looked toward the window. The curtains were parted, the light from the street filling the room with ghosts and shadows. Maybe someone would see inside. Maybe someone was watching them now. Maybe if she could just keep Rick Ferguson talking, if she could somehow distract him long enough to get to the window . . . And then what? Jump? Scream? A scream could only travel so far against a loaded gun. She almost laughed — tomorrow was the day she was supposed to learn how to disarm a would-be assailant. Tomorrow — not much chance of that.

Her forehead grew wet with perspiration, the sweat dripping into her eyes, mingling with her tears. The light from the street lamps blurred, spinning out in all directions like a spotlight, blinding her, like the sun. She thought she heard voices from somewhere outside, but the voices were distorted, like a record being played on the wrong speed. Too slow. Everything too slow. A scene from a movie filmed in slow motion, happening to someone else. So, this was how Connie must have felt, Jess thought. This was what death felt like.

'I thought Don put you on a plane to California,' she heard herself say, as if she were an actress and her lines were being dubbed by someone else.

'Yea. Generous of him, wasn't it? But I decided California

could wait a few days. I knew how bad you wanted to see me. Take off your sweater.'

He said it so casually, the words didn't quite register. 'What?'

'Take off your sweater,' he repeated. 'And your pants too, while you're at it. The fun's about to start.'

Jess shook her head, feeling a word dislodge itself from her throat, tumble out of her mouth. It hit the air, barely audible. 'No.'

'No? Did you say no?' He laughed. 'Wrong answer, Jess.'

She felt as if she were already naked, standing exposed before him, and she shivered with the sudden cold. She imagined his hands pinching her flesh, his mouth biting her breasts, his body pounding cruelly into hers. He would hurt her, she knew, make sure she suffered before she died. 'I won't do it,' she heard herself say.

'Then I'll have to shoot you.' He shrugged, as if this were the only logical alternative.

Jess's heart was beating so furiously, it threatened to burst out of her chest. Like in *Alien*, she thought, amazed her mind could focus on such trivia. She felt as if she was burning up, then was suddenly ice cold again. How could he be so calm? What was going on behind the opaque brown eyes that gave away nothing. 'You'll shoot me anyway,' she said.

'Well, no. Actually, I was planning on using my hands to finish you off. But I'll shoot you if I have to.' His smile grew, his eyes slithering across her body, like an army of tiny snakes. 'In the shoulder. Or maybe the knee. Maybe in the soft part of your inner thigh. Yea, I kind of like that. Just enough to make you a little more cooperative.'

Jess felt the sting of the bullet pierce the flesh of her thigh, though she knew he hadn't fired. She could barely stand for the shaking in her legs. Her stomach cramped, threatened to humiliate her further. If she could just keep him talking, she thought. Isn't that what they always did in the movies? They talked, and then someone came along just in the nick of time to rescue them. She pushed words out of her mouth. 'You shoot, and it'll alert the neighbors.'

He was unimpressed. 'Think so? Didn't look like there was anybody home when I got here. Now, take off your clothes or I'm liable to get bored, and when I get bored, my lovemaking tends to get a bit rough.'

Oh God, Jess thought. Oh God, oh God, oh God.

'How did you get in here?' she asked, wondering where her voice was coming from. It felt detached, as if it had been disconnected and was now floating free form in the room.

'The lock hasn't been made that can keep me out.' He laughed again, clearly enjoying himself. 'I guess I can say the same thing about a woman.' He cocked the trigger of the gun. 'Now, you've got thirty seconds to get those clothes off and lie down on the bed.'

Jess said nothing, her throat suddenly too dry to form words. From somewhere beside her, her alarm clock loudly ticked off the seconds, like a bomb about to explode. So, this is how it ends, she thought, unable to swallow, to draw air into her lungs, terror gnawing at her extremities like a hungry rat.

What would it be like? she wondered. Would there be a white light, a long tunnel, a feeling of peace and well-being, as was often reported by those who claimed to have died and come back? Or would there be blackness? Nothingness? Would she simply cease to be? When it was all over, would she find herself alone, or would her loved ones be there to greet her? She thought of her mother. Would she finally get to see her again, to find out exactly what fate she had met? Had it been this way for her too? My God, Jess thought, her chest aching, as if it were splitting in two, had her mother experienced this same kind of terror and pain before she died? Was this what her mother had gone through?

And what would this do to her father, her sister?

When they didn't hear from her, when they couldn't reach her, Barry would probably assure them that Jess was just too embarrassed to contact them, that she'd merely taken off for a few days, that she was too self-centered to realize the pain she might be causing them, that perhaps, on some subconscious level, she was punishing them. It would be days before they took her disappearance seriously, before the police were called and her apartment searched. Her apartment would show obvious signs of struggle. The blood on her duvet would be analyzed, found to be hers. There would be no signs of forced entry. No revealing fingerprints. Don would point the finger of suspicion at Adam. By the time everything was sorted out, Rick Ferguson would be long gone.

'Don't make me tell you again,' Rick Ferguson was saying.

Jess took a deep breath and pulled her sweater over her head, the delicate hairs along her arms rising in protest. Her skin started to throb, as if she had pulled pieces of it off along with her sweater, as if she'd been skinned alive. The sweater dropped to the floor.

'Very nice,' he said. 'I always liked black lace.' He shook the gun in the direction of her pants. 'Now the rest.'

Jess watched the scene unfold as if from a great distance. Again she recalled the experiences of those who claimed to have died. Didn't they always report leaving their bodies and floating toward the ceiling, watching the events from the air? Maybe that was what was happening to her. Maybe she hadn't escaped from her living room after all. Maybe the wire had sliced through her throat and killed her. Maybe she was already dead.

Or maybe she still had time to save herself, she thought, a renewed surge of adrenaline interrupting her reveries, convincing her she was still alive, that there might be something she could do. Use whatever weapons are at hand, she heard Dominic instruct, as her fingers curled into the elastic waistband of her wool pants. Like what? she wondered, impulses colliding painfully in her brain, causing her head to throb. Her bra? Could she strangle the man with her lace brassiere? How about smothering him in cashmere?

How about her shoes? she wondered, slowly removing her hands from her waist. Rick Ferguson jabbed the gun impatiently into the air. 'I have to take my shoes off,' she stammered. 'I can't get my pants off if I don't take my shoes off first.'

'Hey,' he said, relaxing, 'the nakeder, the better. Just hurry up about it.'

She bent over, wondering what in God's name she was planning to do, slowly removing her left shoe and tossing it casually aside, thinking she was out of her mind, she didn't have a chance, he would kill her for sure, then moving to her right foot, knowing she only had seconds left, lifting the black flat off her foot, making a motion as if tossing the shoe aside, instead gripping it tightly, then hurling it with all her strength toward the gun in his hand.

She missed completely.

'Oh God,' she moaned. 'Oh my God.'

But the sudden action caught Rick Ferguson by surprise, and he jumped back in alarm. What the hell should she do now? Could she push past him toward the front door? Could she possibly survive a jump from a third-floor window? Did she have the strength to disarm him?

It was too late. Already, he'd recovered his equilibrium. Already, the gun was cocked and pointed at her heart. 'I think I'm going to enjoy killing you even more than I enjoyed roasting that damn canary,' he said, tracing an invisible line through the air with his gun, down past her breasts, past her ribs and stomach, stopping at the crotch of her pants.

There was no time left, no choices left. He was going to shoot her. Render her defenseless long enough to rape and sodomize her. Then finish her off with his hands. Oh God, Jess thought, picturing her dead canary, wishing she would faint, knowing he would only force her back to consciousness, make her suffer through every agonizing second. And then without thinking, without even knowing what she was doing until she was already doing it, Jess was leaping across her bed to the window, screaming at the top of her lungs.

The shot exploded into the air around her, and she knew she was as good as dead. It was so loud, she thought, louder than she had ever imagined it could be, like a burst of thunder at her ear. The room assumed an eerie glow, as if the contents had been hit by lightning, the colors newly magnified, the soft

363

peaches now a vivid orange, the greys and blues electric. Her body felt light, suspended in mid-air. She wondered where the bullet had struck her, how long it would take her to fall to the floor.

He'd be waiting to rip the remaining clothes off her near lifeless body, to force himself inside her, smothering her with his weight, overwhelming her with his odors. Already she could feel his fingers tearing at her, his tongue licking at her blood. His would be the last face she would see, his grin the sight she would take with her to her grave.

And suddenly, she was spinning around and Rick Ferguson was coming at her, his hands reaching toward her, his face white with fury, his smile gone. And then he was falling, tumbling toward her, and Jess realized that she was all right, that she hadn't been shot, that it was Rick Ferguson who was plunging to the floor, sprawling across her stockinged feet, that it was Rick Ferguson who was dead.

Darkness swirled around her, like a whirlpool in the middle of an ocean, threatening to pull her into its center, as her eyes absorbed the gaping hole in the middle of his back. The blood spurted from it, like oil from a geyser, soaking his black T-shirt, spilling onto the rug. Jess felt dizzy, faint. She clutched the side of her dresser for support.

And then she saw him in the doorway, the gun dangling from his hand. 'Don!' she gasped.

'I told you if that bastard ever tried to hurt you, I'd kill him myself,' he said quietly. The gun slipped from his fingers to the floor.

Jess rushed into his arms. Immediately they encircled her, pulling her tight against him. She pressed her head against his shoulder, absorbing his clean smell, clinging to the warmth of his body. He felt so good. He felt so safe.

'You're safe now,' he told her, as if reading her thoughts, kissing the side of her face over and over again. 'You're safe. I'm here. I won't ever leave you.'

'He was waiting for me inside the apartment,' Jess began after several minutes, trying to come to grips with everything that had happened. 'He had a wire. The kind he used to kill Connie. He tried to strangle me. But I got away. I ran for my gun, but it wasn't there. He had it. He must have searched the apartment before I got home. He said there wasn't a lock that had been made that could keep him out.'

'It's okay now,' Don said, his voice a salve. 'It's okay. You're safe now. He can't hurt you anymore.'

'I was so scared. I thought he was going to kill me.'

'He's dead, Jess.'

'I kept thinking about my mother.'

'Don't, sweetheart.'

'About what this would do to my father and my sister.'

'It's over now. You're safe.'

'Thank God you got here.'

'I couldn't let you stay alone.'

'He didn't get on the plane,' she said, then laughed, feeling giddy, light-headed. 'I guess that's pretty obvious.'

'I'm just glad I got here in time.' Don hugged her tighter against him.

'I can't believe you did. You're my Prince Charming,' Jess said, and thought that he was. How could she ever have hurt him the way she had? How could she have left him? How could she possibly survive without him? 'It's just like in the movies.' She laughed nervously, recalling all those movies where a monstrous killer erroneously presumed dead rises up to strike again. Her eyes drifted back to the body on the floor. 'Are you sure he's dead?'

'He's dead, Jess.' Don smiled indulgently. 'I can shoot him again if you'd like.'

Jess laughed, surprised at the sound. She'd been savagely attacked with a piece of wire rope, almost raped, almost murdered, and here she was laughing. Probably it was a nervous reaction, a way of coping with what had very nearly been. Her eyes travelled the length of Rick Ferguson's body, and she understood how easily that body could have been hers. If Rick Ferguson had been allowed a few more minutes. If Don hadn't shown up when he did, like a hero from a silent movie, riding in on horseback in the final seconds of the reel to rescue the unfortunate heroine from her fate.

It was uncanny how well Don knew her, Jess thought, burrowing in closer against his chest, how he always knew when she needed him, whatever her protestations to the contrary. She'd told him on the phone that she was all right, that she'd speak to him tomorrow, that she was in no danger tonight. And still he'd come. Still he'd charged in and taken control. Saved her from a gruesome death. Saved her from her own stubborn stupidity.

Was she really surprised? Hadn't he done the same thing throughout their marriage, ignoring her wishes to do what he thought best? She'd gotten angry, railed against him, fought for the freedom to make her own mistakes, demanded her right to be wrong. He'd tried to understand, given lip-service to her pleas, but in the end, he'd done things the way he'd always intended. More often than not, it had proved to be the right way. Like tonight.

As if watching a television rerun, Jess saw herself pushing open the downstairs door, locking it after her, racing up three flights of stairs, entering her apartment, once again locking the door after her, taking several steps inside, suddenly feeling the sharp tug of wire around her throat, struggling with her assailant, momentarily breaking free, seeing the door, wondering if she could get to it, open it, before Rick Ferguson could get to her.

Her mind's eye narrowed in on the locked door of her apartment, as if she were adjusting a kaleidoscope. What's wrong with this picture? a little voice asked, snapping her sharply back into the present. The door to her apartment had been locked, she realized, swallowing a gasp, as was the outside door. How then had Don gotten inside? 'How did you get in?' she heard herself ask.

'What?'

Jess pulled slightly away from his embrace. 'How did you get inside the house?'

'The door wasn't locked,' he said.

'Yes it was,' she insisted. 'I locked it after I came in.'

'Well, it was open when I got here,' he told her.

'And my apartment?' she asked. 'I double locked the door as soon as I got inside.'

'Jess, what is this?'

'A simple question.' She took several steps back, stopped when she felt Rick Ferguson's feet against the backs of her legs. 'How did you get inside my apartment?'

There was a moment's silence, a look of calm resignation, then, 'I used my keys.'

'Your keys? What do you mean? What keys?'

He swallowed, looked toward the floor. 'I had a second set made when you had your locks changed.'

Jess shook her head in disbelief. 'You had a second set made? Why?'

'Why? Because I was worried about you. Because I was afraid something like this might happen. Because you need me to look after you. That's why.'

Jess looked down, saw Rick Ferguson dead at her feet, her gun still inside his open hand. Don had saved her life, for God's sake. Why was she suddenly so angry with him? What difference did it make that he'd had a copy of her keys made? If he hadn't, she'd be a corpse, for God's sake. Was she really going to be angry at him for saving her life?

She felt an annoying tickle at her throat, tried to dismiss it as a byproduct of the injury to her neck, almost succeeded, until she felt the tickle creeping stealthily toward her chest, like a large spider. Picking up both strength and speed, it scurried across her arms and legs, depositing its poison, leaving everything it touched numb. Was she going to have an anxiety attack now? she wondered incredulously. Now when it was all over? When she was safe? When there was no reason for her to panic?

And then she heard Adam's voice. *Go with it*, he said. *Don't fight it. Go with it.*

Adam, she thought. Adam, whom Don distrusted and had tried to warn her against. Adam, whom Don had investigated, who wasn't who he said he was. What did Adam have to do with any of this? 'I don't understand,' she said out loud, staring at Don, wondering if there was more he hadn't told her.

'Don't worry about anything now, Jess. All that matters is that you're safe. Rick Ferguson is dead. He can't hurt you anymore.'

'But it wasn't Rick Ferguson you were worried about,' Jess persisted, remembering his phone call to her sister's, stubbornly trying to make sense of all that had happened. 'It was Adam you claimed was dangerous. You said you'd had him investigated; you said the State Bar had never heard of him.'

'Jess, what's this got to do with anything?'

'But Adam was never a threat to me. It was Rick Ferguson all along. So, why would Adam lie?' Once again the kaleidoscope shifted, its contents scrambling to present yet another picture. 'Unless he didn't lie. Unless it was you who lied to me,' she said, scarcely believing her own ears. Was she really saying these things? 'You didn't call the State Bar, did you? And if you did, then you found out that Adam Stohn is exactly who he says he is. Isn't he?'

There was a long silence. 'He isn't right for you, Jess,' Don said finally.

What was going on? What was Don saying? 'Isn't that for me to decide?'

'Not when it's the wrong decision. Not when it affects me, when it affects us, our future together,' he told her. 'And we *could* have a future together, if you'd only stop fighting me. You need me to take care of you, Jess. You always have. Tonight proved that.'

Jess looked from her ex-husband to the body lying on the floor, then back to her ex-husband, the kaleidoscope in her mind twisting and turning furiously, until the captive bright pieces of multi-colored plastic could no longer differentiate between up and down, right or left, and the kaleidoscope burst apart, scattering the delicate slivers of her reality into the air. 'Why did you come over here tonight?' she asked. 'I mean, you knew Adam was out of town, and you thought Rick Ferguson was on a plane to California, so what made you come over? How did you know to have a gun? How did you know I was in danger . . . unless you set this whole thing up?' she asked, her voice trailing into the air, the sudden realization of what she was saying slicing through her body as painfully, and as easily, as a piece of wire rope. 'You did, didn't you? You set this whole thing up!'

'Jess . . .'

'You coached him, told him what to say, what buttons to push. Right from the beginning.'

'I used him to bring us back together,' Don said simply. 'Was that so wrong?'

'He almost killed me, for God's sake!'

'I would never have let that happen.'

Jess shook her head in disbelief. 'You orchestrated everything. The way he was waiting for me when I got to work that first morning, the way he followed me up the stairs, like he'd stepped right out of my nightmares, nightmares you knew all about, goddamn you! It wasn't a coincidence that he used the word "disappear". You told him about what happened to my mother, didn't you? You knew exactly the effect it would have on me, the anxiety it would produce.'

'I love you, Jess,' Don told her. 'All I've ever wanted is for us to be together.'

'Tell me,' Jess said.

'Tell you what?'

'Everything.'

'Jess, what do details matter? The important thing is that we were meant to be together.'

'You did this so that we could be together?'

'Everything I've done since the day we met has been for that reason.'

'Tell me,' she repeated.

He took a deep breath, releasing it slowly into the space between them. 'What do you want to know?'

369

'What exactly was your relationship with Rick Ferguson?'

'You know my relationship with him. He was my client; I was his lawyer.'

'Did you know he'd killed Connie DeVuono?'

'I never asked him.'

'But you knew.'

'I suspected.'

'And you offered to get him off if he'd do you a favor in return.'

'Connie was still alive when I agreed to take his case. I had no idea at the time he was planning to kill her.'

'But you knew he'd broken into her apartment, knew he'd raped her, knew he'd beaten her, knew he was harassing her.'

'I knew the charges against him.'

'Don't be coy with me, Don.'

'I knew he was probably guilty.'

'So you suggested a deal?'

'I suggested we might be able to help each other out.'

'You told him all about me, coached him in what to say and do.' Jess's voice was a monotone, her questions flat, as if they'd already been answered.

'Something like that.'

'But why? Why now?'

Don shook his head. 'It was something I'd been thinking about it for a long time, a way to prove to you how much you needed me. And suddenly, there he was, opportunity knocking, as it were. And the idea sort of came together in my mind. Plus, there was something about the symmetry I found appealing – you know, four years together, four years apart. I knew I couldn't afford to wait much longer. And then along came Adam Stohn, and I knew I couldn't afford to wait at all.'

'What exactly did you tell Rick Ferguson to do?'

'Essentially what he did best. I gave him free rein, as long as he didn't hurt you.'

'Hurt me? He almost killed me!'

'I was right behind you, Jess. You were never in any real danger.'

Jess rubbed the front of her neck, felt the blood still damp. 'You told him to break into my apartment and slash my underwear! You told him to destroy my car!'

'I told him to frighten you. I left the details up to him.'

'He killed Fred!'

'A canary, for God's sake. I'll buy you a hundred canaries, if that's what you want.'

Jess felt the tickle of the spider's legs spreading from her arms and legs up toward her brain. Could she really be having this conversation? Could they really be saying these things to one another? Could she really be hearing them?

'And tonight?' she asked. 'What was he supposed to do tonight?'

'I told him that, considering your famous tenacity, you'd never rest until you saw him convicted of Connie's murder. I knew he couldn't resist coming after you, and I wanted to make sure I controlled the time and place, so I simply encouraged him to finish the job as quickly as possible.'

'You sent him here to kill me.'

'I sent him here to be killed!' Don said, and laughed. 'Hell, I even gave him a key.' He laughed again. 'I used him, Jess, to get what we both wanted.'

'What we *both* wanted?'

'Be honest, Jess. Wasn't the death penalty what you were after? The State wasn't going to do it. I did it for them. For you. For us,' he added, the laughter gone.

'So you set him up.'

'The man was an animal. Scum. Your words, remember? He killed Connie DeVuono. He fully intended to kill you.'

'But you called me at my sister's, urged me to spend the night. You begged me not to come home.'

Again Don laughed. 'Knowing you'd do just the opposite. Knowing your pride would send you scurrying back as fast as you could. God forbid you listen to what your husband tells you to do.'

'My *ex*-husband,' Jess quickly reminded him.

'Yes,' he acknowledged. 'Your ex-husband. The man who

loves you, who's always loved you, who never stopped loving you.'

Jess raised her hands to her head in order to stop the sudden spinning. None of this was real, she thought. None of this was actually happening. This was Don, for God's sake. The man who'd always been there for her, who'd been her teacher, her lover, her husband, her friend. The man who'd nursed her through her mother's death and years of crippling anxiety attacks. And now he was telling her that he'd deliberately engineered their return. He was telling her that he'd been behind Rick Ferguson's prolonged campaign of terror. He was telling her that he'd come here tonight to commit murder. All in the name of love. My God, what else was he capable of?

Jess's mind raced backwards through the last eight years. Her anxiety attacks had begun just after her mother's disappearance, had lasted throughout her marriage to Don, abated only after their divorce. Had they been trying to tell her something?

He won't give you room to grow, she heard her mother say.

Her beautiful mother, she thought, slowly approaching Rick Ferguson's body and kneeling over it, hearing her knees crack, wondering if her body was about to break apart. Her eyes quickly passed over the gaping wound in the middle of his back, as she tried to ignore the sickly sweet odor of death that was straining, like a mask soaked in ether, to cover her nose.

'I love you, Jess,' Don was saying. 'No one could ever love you the way I have all these years. I could never let anyone come between us.'

The kaleidoscope in Jess's mind refocused, the last of the pieces falling into place, arranging themselves in front of her eyes with startling clarity, and suddenly she knew exactly what else he was capable of.

Jess swivelled around on her haunches, found herself staring up at her ex-husband, whose brown eyes reflected only his love for her. 'It was you all along,' she said, her voice an alien force that had invaded her body, pushing out thoughts she didn't know she had. 'You killed my mother.' As soon as the words touched the air, Jess understood with absolute certainty they were true. Slowly, she rose to her feet. 'Tell me,' she said, as she had said earlier, the alien's voice low, barely audible.

'You won't understand,' he told her.

'Make me understand,' she said, forcing her voice into a gentle caress. 'Please, Don, I know you love me. I want so much to understand.

'She was trying to keep us apart,' Don said, as if this was all the explanation necessary. 'And she would have succeeded. You didn't know that. But I did. As she was always pointing out, I was a lot older than you. I had a lot more experience. You were so hooked into her, I knew she'd eventually wear you down, convince you that you should wait until you graduated. And I knew that if we waited, there was a chance I might lose you. It was a risk I couldn't take.'

'Because you loved me so much,' Jess said.

'Because I loved you more than anything in the world,' he qualified. 'I didn't want to have to kill her, Jess. Believe it or not, I actually liked the woman. I kept hoping she'd come around. But she never did, and I gradually came to understand that she never would.'

'So you decided to kill her.'

'I knew it had to be done,' he began, 'but I was waiting for the right moment, the right opportunity.' He shrugged, the gesture filled with ironic innocence, as if everything that had happened had been beyond his control. 'Sort of like what happened with Rick Ferguson, I guess.' He shrugged again, and the innocence fell away. 'And then one morning, you called and told me about the fight the two of you had had, about how you'd stormed out of the house, told your mother to find her own way to the doctor's. I could hear the guilt in your voice. I knew that you were already regretting the fight, that if the lump in her breast proved to be malignant, you'd agree to postpone the wedding. I recognized that if I didn't move quickly, it would be too late.

'So, I drove to your house, told your mother you'd called and told me what happened, explained how sorry you were, said I didn't want to be the source of any more problems between you, that I'd back off, talk you into postponing our wedding until after you graduated.'

He smiled, obviously caught up in the memory. 'She was so relieved. Really, she looked like the weight of the world had been lifted off her shoulders. She thanked me. She even kissed me. Said that, of course, she'd never had any objections to me personally, but that, well, you know . . .'

'So you offered to drive her to the doctor's.'

'I *insisted* on driving her to the doctor's,' Don elaborated. 'In fact, I said it was such a lovely day, why didn't we go for a nice drive first. She thought that was a lovely idea.' His smile grew wider. 'We drove to Union Pier.'

'What?'

'I had everything worked out. Once she got in the car, it was easy, really. I said that I wanted her opinion on some renovations I'd been thinking about for the cottage. She was happy to help, even flattered, I think. We walked around the house, she told me what she thought would look nice, then we went out back, stood looking at the Bluffs.'

'Oh, God.'

'She never saw it coming, Jess. One clean shot to the back of the head. And it was all over.'

Jess swayed, almost lost her balance, grasped the floor with her toes, managed to hang on. 'You killed her,' she whispered.

'She was a dying woman, Jess. In all likelihood, she'd have been dead of cancer within five years. Think of the pain I saved her, the years of agony for everyone concerned. Instead, she died on a beautiful sunny day, looking out over the Bluffs, not worrying about her daughter for the first time in months. I know this must be hard for you to understand, Jess, but she was happy. Can't you see? She died happy.'

Jess opened her mouth to speak, but it was several seconds before any sounds emerged. 'What did you do . . . afterward?'

'I gave her a proper burial,' he said. 'Out by the Bluffs. You were looking at her grave a few weeks ago.'

Jess pictured herself standing by the back window of Don's

cottage, staring through the swirling snow toward the Bluffs beyond.

'I thought of telling you the truth then,' he continued. 'To finally put your mind to rest, to let you know that you had nothing to feel guilty about anymore, that your fight with your mother had nothing to do with her death, that her death was a foregone conclusion from the moment she tried to interfere with our plans. But I knew the timing wasn't right.'

Jess recalled the feel of Don's arms around her, the touch of his lips on hers as they'd made love before the fireplace, the false comfort he'd provided. That he'd always provided. Had some deep part of her self-conscious always suspected as much? Surely that was what her anxiety attacks had been trying for years to tell her.

'What about my father? He was against our marriage too.'

'Your father was a pussycat. I knew once your mother was out of the picture, there'd be no problem with your dad.'

'And the gun?' Jess asked. 'What did you do with the gun?'

Again Don smiled, a smile more terrifying than Rick Ferguson's had ever been. 'I gave it to you as a present after you left me.'

Jess clutched at her stomach. She stared down at the small revolver in Rick Ferguson's outstretched hand, the gun Don had insisted she take to protect herself after their divorce, the same weapon he had used to end her mother's life.

'I liked the irony of it,' Don was saying, as if he were commenting on a point of law, not confessing to her mother's murder. When had his obsessiveness crossed the boundary into madness? How had she failed to recognize it for so long?

She had slept with her mother's killer, for God's sake. Was he the crazy one or was she? She felt dizzy, her head lolling backward, as if she might faint.

'Now you understand how much I love you,' he said, 'how all I've ever wanted was to take care of you.'

Jess's head swayed from side to side, her eyes unable to focus. Was he going to kill her too? 'And now what?' she asked.

'And now we'll call the police and tell them what happened. That Rick was waiting for you inside your apartment, that he tried to kill you, that I got here just in time, that I had to shoot him in order to save you.'

Jess's eyes rolled back in her head, her head snapping over her right shoulder.

'And then it'll all be over,' Don continued, reassuringly. 'And you'll come home with me. Back where you belong. Where you've always belonged. And we can be together. Like we were meant to be.'

Nausea swept across Jess's body like a giant wave. It rolled over her, knocking her feet out from under her, sending her crashing to her knees, carrying her out to sea, threatening to drown her. She reached out instinctively for something to grab onto, something to save her, to keep her from being swept away, from going under. Her fingers found a branch, grabbed hold, tightened their grip. The gun, she understood, curling her fingers around its handle, using it to pull herself back to safety, straightening her shoulders as she fought her way free of the deadly current. In one quick and fluid motion, Jess brought the gun up, pointed it directly at her ex-husband's heart, and pulled the trigger.

Don stared at her in surprise as the bullet ripped through his chest. Then he crumpled forward and fell to the floor.

Jess rose slowly to her feet and walked to his side. 'Bull's-eye,' she said calmly.

She wasn't sure how long she stood there, staring down at her ex-husband, the gun pointed at his head, ready to shoot again if he so much as twitched. She wasn't sure when she became aware of other sounds, of traffic outside her window, of laughter echoing down the street, of her phone ringing.

She looked over at the clock. Ten o'clock. It would be Adam, calling to check on how she was, to find out how her day had gone, to wish her a good night's sleep.

She almost laughed. She wouldn't get any sleep tonight, that much was sure. She'd have to deal with the police, contact her family. Tell them about Rick Ferguson, about Don, the truth about what had happened here tonight, the truth about what had happened eight years ago. The whole truth. Would they believe any of it?

Did she?

Jess walked to the phone and picked up the receiver. 'Adam?' she asked.

'I love you,' he answered.

'Could you come home?' Her voice was soft but in control, surprisingly anxiety-free. 'I think I'm going to need a good lawyer.'

THE LITTLE MADELEINE

Books by Mrs. Robert Henrey

THE LITTLE MADELEINE (*her girlhood*)

AN EXILE IN SOHO (*her adolescence*)

MADELEINE GROWN UP (*her love story and marriage*)

A FARM IN NORMANDY *and* THE RETURN (*the birth of her child*)

MATILDA AND THE CHICKENS (*a winter on her farm*)

A JOURNEY TO VIENNA (*the making of a film*)

PALOMA (*the strange story of a friend*)

MADELEINE'S JOURNAL (*her contemporary diary*)

LONDON (*with water-colours by Phyllis Ginger*)

THE
LITTLE MADELEINE

by

MRS ROBERT HENREY

LONDON: J. M. DENT & SONS LTD

B 25/5 m

This is the story of my girlhood.
No fact has been altered.
Each character bears his, or her, own name.

The frontispiece is from
a water-colour by
I. Le Tournier

I

WAS born on 13th August 1906 in Montmartre in a steep cobbled street of leaning houses, slate-coloured and old, under the shining loftiness of the Sacré-Cœur. Matilda, my mother, describing to me later this uncommodious but picturesque corner which we left soon after my birth, stressed the curious characters from the Aubergne and from Brittany who kept modest cafés with zinc bars. Behind these they toiled, storing in dark courtyards or in windowless rooms coal, charcoal, and firewood dipped in resin, which the inhabitants of our street, who never had any money to spare, bought in the smallest quantities such as a pailful at a time. The Auvergnat traders in particular formed a clan of their own, each knowing from which village the others came, all speaking patois, and so unaccustomed to French that they mangled it when speaking and could only write their names.

The woman who owned the café over which we lived had a sister called Mme Gaillard, a fine-looking person who had come from the rockiness of her native village to Paris to sell lace. Her stock-in-trade consisted of a large red umbrella with a cherry-wood handle rubbed to a shine, and two chests opening out fanways on leather hinges which she placed on a deal table supported by trestles. These contained the more valuable stock such as laced table linen, curtains, and lace blouses. The red umbrella, opened out and placed point downwards, formed a recipient for cheaper laces sold by the yard, or made-up articles which, whilst inexpensive, attracted knowledgeable customers by the excellence of their quality.

My father would take his aperitif every day at the café downstairs, and buy his litre of red wine for the table, my mother going there for a pail of coal or a bag of charcoal. When my mother was expecting my baby brother and was too advanced in pregnancy to fetch the piece goods on which she sewed buttons and

press-studs at home, Mme Gaillard, being at the café with her
sister, the owner, offered to teach Matilda how to work lace, an
art in which few were expert.   My mother accepted.   She was a
genius with the needle, as others are born with minds rich in
melody or with eyes receptive to colour, and her fingers took
naturally to the softness and prettiness of lace.   She started with
window curtains and house linen.   Then, carried forward on
wings of creation, put together her first lace blouse, which was
immediately sold by Mme Gaillard to a wealthy South American
woman.   Mme Gaillard now gave my mother Valenciennes laces
of increasing beauty which were turned into blouses as fine as
spiders' webs.   Unfortunately, alone in her room, bending over
her work, she earned hardly anything.   In winter she was cold.
In summer, the sun beating on the adjoining roofs sent red-hot
reverberations of lead and zinc through the attic window.

Her days passed slowly.   From time to time neighbours from
the Auvergne or from Lombardy quarrelled in the courtyard.   A
street singer with a baby in her shawl sang a romance, but before
it was finished the *concierge* would come out and noisily chase
her away with a broom.

My mother had a sister called Marie-Thérèse with whom she
was brought up at Blois where my aunt was seduced by a young
soldier who looked very fine dancing the polka and the mazurka
in his gaudy uniform.   The regiment crossed the Loire behind
flaming torches every Sunday evening so that the population
could dance in the main square to the sound of a brass band.
Marie-Thérèse and her soldier had loved each other passionately
for a while, but when Marie-Thérèse was pregnant the soldier
disappeared.

My aunt ran away to Paris where my mother was already
married to my father and was living with him in Montmartre.
As they were so poor and my mother was expecting my baby
brother I had been sent to a foster-mother at Soissons.   Marie-
Thérèse was not able to find work when she arrived, her pregnancy being too visible, and she therefore knocked at my mother's
door asking for hospitality.

She was pretty but irresponsible.   Her dream was to make
hats.   She was later to show a real gift for this, but the sort of
work my mother did, mounting lace, was too finicky for my aunt,
who passed a good deal of her time dreaming and cutting out the

romantic serials from the daily papers, which she eagerly discussed
with anybody who would listen to her. Her tireless chirruping
rather fatigued my mother who was serious and taciturn and just
now wondering how she would manage to make ends meet after
the birth of her second child.

Within a week Marie-Thérèse knew everybody in Montmartre.
It did not even seem to matter to her that the Italians and the
people from the Auvergne spoke hardly three words of French.
She was soon on the best of terms with all the parlourmaids and
cooks who borrowed her serials which she kept locked in a
barded trunk. Nobody was so happily unconscious of her
responsibilities. The expected child, the fact she had no home,
not a room, not a lodging of any kind, did not matter to her.
She was not even put out by the tumultuous scenes of my violent
father who could not stand seeing her lolling about his one-
roomed flat.

Towards Easter Marie-Thérèse, who could not remember how
long she had been pregnant and who had never consulted a midwife or a doctor, was taken with pains. She thought they were
due to indigestion, but my mother who was less sentimental and
more worldly wise had no doubt her sister was starting her
labour.

Drenching spring rain had been falling since morning and now
the ground was so wet that my father had been sent home from
work. He was laying bricks, and when the weather was bad the
workmen were dismissed without pay till the sun came out again.
When the men came home early in the morning they annoyed
their wives by sitting around doing nothing, and so they preferred
to stay amongst themselves, playing cards in a café. At night they
arrived drunk and penniless. On this particular day my father
had come straight home. He was sitting on a kitchen chair
with a plank across his knees mending his hobnailed boots.
Marie-Thérèse moaned and writhed as she turned the pages of
her serial. Matilda, in front of a small table, her feet on a stool,
her work pinned to her bosom, was passing her needle with ever-
increasing speed through the lace of a blouse, as if trying to
compensate for the two idle people in the room. Her thin lips
were sarcastically closed, for she was losing patience with her
sister's airy nonchalance. My mother had no illusions about her
own future, but she discussed it with nobody, for she was timid.

My mother listened to my father knocking nails into his boot. She was aware that in an hour or two he would feel thirsty and go to the café. Her sister's moaning put her nerves on edge. She was angrily puzzled that Marie-Thérèse had become so popular in the cobbled streets of Montmartre along which, in spite of her pregnancy, she tripped so carelessly, amusing the neighbours, helping them with a smile, recounting to each what the other did, and prodigiously interested in the unhappy things that happened to a great number of unimportant young women. Marie-Thérèse was by definition an onlooker. Her immense pity for others was never lessened by any consideration for herself. When, tearfully, she brought back news of some seduced servant girl, Matilda would remark scathingly: 'Why is she any worse off than you?'

'Oh, but it's not the same thing!' cried Marie-Thérèse. 'She hasn't a home or a penny in the world!'

My mother turned her head angrily. Marie-Thérèse was as naturally happy as my mother was, by experience and outlook, sad. If ever my aunt thought about herself it was in the light of a story-book heroine who, though having a spot of bad luck in the current chapter, would eventually, towards the end of the book, marry an earl for love. Matilda had no doubt that the morrow would be just as melancholy, if not more melancholy, than the other days. Was she not married to a man whose fate was to be always poor? Had she not a baby girl whose foster-mother kept on sending the bill? And how would she manage when the second child was born? Paris, beyond the slate roofs of Montmartre, glittered at the feet of happy Marie-Thérèse. Matilda saw no romance in it.

Marie-Thérèse continued to twist in her chair and suddenly the book fell on the floor. Seeing this, my mother lay the exquisite piece of tulle and lace on the small table, took off her thimble, unfastened the pins from her dress, and looked at her husband. Émile put down his hammer and taking his coat off a peg went to fetch a hackney coach. My mother made a bundle of what she supposed her sister would need in hospital and silently waited. They were not quite ready to have a good cry and make it up. My father came up the stairs and asked my aunt if she was ready. Hurt and puzzled, she looked at my mother, her eyes filling with tears. My mother gave a gulp and cried too. They flung themselves passionately into each other's arms and wept, and my father had some trouble in pulling my aunt away and leading her down to the waiting cab.

The matron of the Lariboisière, a thin bleak woman, who knew my father, having seen him prowling and anxious at the time of my birth, asked why he had not warned her at least a day in advance. She might have found a spare bed. As it was the hospital was full and Marie-Thérèse would have to go to the annexe. This would take them five minutes in a cab.

My father and a nurse helped Marie-Thérèse down the stone stairs. The hackney coach had gone, my father having paid it off as soon as he could. They would now have to wait till one passed along the street. The rain was still coming down hard, sheeting the pavements with steaming water which flowed turbulently along gutters. The first gaslights were going up outside buildings and in shops. There was a sudden cry, piercing, frightened, a muffled fall and skid on the wet asphalt, a streak of blood, and Marie-Thérèse, losing her blood, swooned in my father's wiry arms. The nurse, quickly bending, picked up from the pavement the ball of flesh, laying it tenderly in her upheld blue overall. The party returned now, commanding attention, to the busy hall where the matron gave orders to set up a camp bed. Gently taking from the nurse's blue apron the shapeless parcel, she said to my father 'It's a girl!' and quickly tied round the tiny wrist a ribbon with the number.

Émile hurried home to tell his wife the exciting news. The next day my mother went to hospital where she found her sister pale and weak and the baby so lifeless that she wondered if it would live. Marie-Thérèse had already built a dream future for her daughter who was to be called Rolande after the heroine of her latest serial.

My aunt remained nine days in hospital after which she bravely walked out through the gates, her baby against her breast, clutching a package with the layette given to each mother— swaddling bands, nappies, a brassière, and a small pink cloak. Rolande was sent to a foster-mother near Soissons where I was. Marie-Thérèse succeeded in finding a job, but my father, with this bad weather, spent most days at the café playing cards with his friends.

2

IN the sunniest part of the *midi*, among the vines, the olive-trees, the high-pitched cicadas, the blood-red tomatoes, and the poems of Mistral, there is a village called the Grand' Combe where men dig for coal. Here was my father born. The inhabitants are, on the whole, religious and law-abiding, but their tempers smoulder like volcanoes and are always ready to burst into flame. Wars of religion had once raged furiously. Catholics and Protestants massacred each other, and their bones now lie under rocky, parched earth. Though men of my father's time were placid and jovial when resting under their vine trellises, in the cool of the evening they would fight suddenly in the village because of a word construed as injurious to wife or daughter. A word was not even necessary. A look was sufficient or that smacking of the lips by which a man in the *midi* shows his appreciation of a pretty face, for is not appreciation tantamount to coveting? The honour of the family is carried high. Enthusiasm boils over also during political arguments, and at the time my father was growing up the first trade unions were cautiously taking shape in this district where underground, far below the warm sun and the sound of the thrush, the entire male population worked from dawn till evening.

My father was an only son and much cherished. Grandfathers, fathers, sons, are little gods in the *midi*, and my father's family, the Gals, the cocks, were well named. Fine-looking and proud, but appallingly quarrelsome, they strutted through life. Émile's father was an inspector in the mines who often took his son, quite little, into the long dark galleries where the boy learnt to crawl under the seams and advance, like a snake on his back, wriggling into places where nobody else could go. On his eleventh birthday he asked to work underground with the men, and his parents, proud of his strength and courage, gave him their blessing. His older companions praised him because he

6

could so easily have had a soft time at school and he, to show off a little, tried to match his output against that of the grown men, with the result that they began to treat him as one of themselves, patting him on the back and inviting him to drink with them. 'When you work like a man,' they said, 'you mustn't drink like a woman.' So they offered him absinthe, so cool to the lips, so cheap and easy to drink—the blue, the green, the *mominette*, pretty, tender appellations to hide the most virulent of poisons.

Life for Émile was an enchantment. Fortune seemed anxious to show her favours. When he reached call-up age he drew a lucky number which cut down his term of service to one year, and he was sent to Nice in the cavalry where, because his limbs had grown strong and supple in the mine, he learned to ride quicker than any of his draft. He was immediately posted to the private guard which the French Government gave Queen Victoria when, that winter, she went to Nice. Magnificent in his uniform, his pockets full of gold pieces sent by his proud parents to their brave 'Milou,' every young woman falling in love with him, but he merely casting quick glances at them, as admired by his new companions as he had been by those in the coal seams, the weeks passed joyously. Then suddenly a telegram informed him that his father and mother, his grandfather and grandmother, and a sister had died in appalling agony in the course of one night after eating a dish of poisoned mushrooms. An elder sister alone survived, for, being pregnant, she had never stopped being sick. Émile went sadly to live with this sister whose name was Augustine. Her husband, Ernest Agnel, which is patois for 'a lamb,' a man of infinite kindness and tenacity, worked in the mine. In the evenings Émile, unwilling to thrust himself on his sister's home life, went to the café. He was the last remaining Gal and, without doubt, the most aggressive.

The need for companionship, to feel in the centre of things, tempted him to join the clandestine meetings where burly fellows, having known him since he was a lad, put their big hands affectionately on his shoulder, saying: 'You, Milou, you are afraid of nothing! Tell the bosses what we think!' These words made him feel very proud, and he became more than ever anxious to live up to his reputation, to accomplish something for which these men whom he admired would be grateful, perhaps even choosing him as their leader. Nobody yet dared to ask openly for

better conditions in the mine. What they wanted were simple
things, long overdue. But they were still, like children, afraid,
their banding together not yet having an official character. The
less scrupulous recognized in this young orphan, ardent and quick
with his tongue, a tool whom they could push into making rash
demands, arguing that if things turned out badly they would
slink away, pretending not to know him, waiting for another
opportunity to achieve their ends. Milou was young. He had
no parents to shame, no family to support. If the owners
dismissed him he still had all the world at his feet. It was not,
therefore, being so very unscrupulous, thought these men, to
make use of his fiery ardour. They were not without admiration
for his physical strength, his exploits in the cavalry, guarding the
Queen of England, speaking both patois and French, and having,
which I forgot to tell you, several generations back, a school-
master and a beadle in his family.

Augustine's husband, M. Agnel, merely dreamt of a comfortable old age. He was not the man to start troubles with the
owners. Besides, he was starting to put a little money aside,
and just as a lamb grazes contentedly on the same piece of grass
day in day out, the lamb that was M. Agnel scratched uncom-
plainingly the coal from the bowels of this sun-drenched earth,
happy, when his day's work was finished, to wash himself clean
and smoke a pipe under the cool vine trellis of his own cottage.
He was, of course, the last person in the village to discover the
sort of name his young brother-in-law was making for himself,
and it was not therefore until most of the harm was done that
he learnt the truth by the ironical reflections of his friends.
After much heart-searching M. Agnel resolved to talk to Émile
strongly, fortifying himself for this unpleasant task by reflecting
that he was older and already the mainstay of a family. The
young Gal resented the Agnel's intervention and became so
aggressive in manner that the lamb feared for the safety of his
person. Soon everybody in the village whispered that the owners
had scribbled the words: 'Hothead and agitator' against Émile's
name on the card index at the mine offices. M. Agnel became
increasingly perturbed for the good name of his family and his
own future in the mine, but this time, instead of upbraiding his
brother-in-law, he confided in his wife the necessity to turn
Milou's thoughts in the direction of matrimony, certain that love

would damp the young man's political ardour; but though they both reviewed in Milou's hearing all the prettiest girls of marriageable age, Émile, being ambitious, was not to be influenced. As his zeal grew the marginal notes against his name took on a more ugly meaning, two of them, 'carboniarist' and 'anarchist,' being of a nature to alarm the police who detailed detectives to follow the unsuspecting Émile as he walked airily down the street.

Now it was too late to arrange matters, even by a marriage. Milou, seeing his friends turn their heads away when he walked into a café, lost his assurance. The cicadas sung to no avail. The sun merely warms those who are happy. One evening M. Agnel and his wife, using circumventions and stratagems, asked Milou to leave their house. And not only their house, but the village, and indeed the entire department of the Gard where his presence was everywhere suspect to the authorities. 'Think, my dear Milou,' said M. Agnel softly, 'how agreeable for a young man of your age to see something of the world, to spend a few weeks in Paris, exploring the many angles of the capital. Consider the fine people you would meet, you who have seen Queen Victoria at Nice and all those smart folks who gamble at Monte Carlo! Come, my little Milou, Augustine shall prepare your things, not forgetting the fine socks your poor mama knitted you before she died, and I warrant they will give you a grand air among the smart young men you'll soon be rubbing shoulders with!' Then kissing him, for she loved him still, Augustine would say: 'You'll make them gape, my fine Milou, when you arrive in Paris!'

The unfortunate innocent prepared to leave for ever carefree days in the hot sun, the shade of the vine, the comfort of being loved by those who had known him from childhood and remembered his parents, and could speak to him of his grandfather who taught in the school and wore the uniform of a beadle. Old women with wrinkled faces would not stop him to recount the brave deeds of even more distant Gals, adding with fervour: 'But you, little Milou, will be the strongest and bravest of all!' He would no longer watch on Sundays the entire village outside the church waiting to go in, hear the bells ring, and laugh when sly husbands under the great portals gave the slip to their wives, to run off, guilty as schoolboys, to other husbands waiting under the cool trees, winking, taking off their too warm clothes smelling of moth balls, saying with a nod in the direction of the church:

'Good enough for females, that's what I say!'

Milou, who was not one for mass, would watch them go arm in arm to the café, perhaps swagger up and join them for the fun of being patted on the back:

'Hallo, Milou, how about a game of billiards?'

Then an hour later, when the bells clanged out again, male voices would call out:

'Waiter! The bill quickly!'

Coats would be put on, and the guilty ones would edge into the church where, innocently, they would wait for their wives, pretending they had been there all the time. Some wives, of course, guessed, but the younger ones took a long time to discover the stratagem, not willing to believe their dark eyes could not chain up their husbands even at mass. Church parade was a fine thing under the hot *midi* sky, the women unaccustomed to their large hats, their noses white with powder they never used on weekdays, their white canvas shoes whitened specially, leaving powdery marks along the hems of their long skirts, thinking gluttonously of the cream cakes and strawberry tarts they would eat at the pastry-cook's where all the smartest people went after church. The husbands nudged each other again, not liking these sugary things that were female food. Men were men. Whilst the women stood in front of the counter to eat their cakes, their little fingers held on high, yapping, thrusting their faces under other hats to kiss their friends, the men went off to have an absinthe, perhaps two, before lunch. Milou in Paris, Milou banished, would think nostalgically of the Sunday lunch, invariably the same, rabbit, wild rabbit, steaming in a bubbling sauce of claret, garlic, and thyme. Then, in the cool of the evening, a game of bowls under the chestnut-trees in flower.

That was the *midi*, the native soil.

Milou took the evening train, the slow one that had third-class coaches of hard wood and that rumbled smokily on its long journey through the night. He carried a bundle containing his clothes, and a basket with some bottles of wine from the family cellar and a good satisfying meal prepared by Augustine and wrapped up in a linen napkin, and when he had eaten and drunk he turned his back on his fellow passengers and slept.

With daylight quite a new landscape stretched before his eyes, flat and unbelievably grey. He stared at monotonous cornfields for a long time in anxious surprise, then, suddenly, the thought having struck him that he might have taken the wrong train or gone past Paris without knowing it, he put on his straw hat, opened the window, and looked out. The telegraph poles rushed past, the cool air fanned his cheeks, a speck of dust lodged itself in an eye, and his straw hat blew off. Milou turned round furiously, bumping his head against the top of the window. He was convinced that one of his fellow passengers had knocked his straw hat off as a joke, and he was not a man to appreciate any joke that affected his dignity. He woke up the passenger nearest him, insulting him in patois, and when his anger was spent he scowled round the compartment and went to sleep again.

At last, late in the morning, after passing through miles of suburbs, the train steamed into Paris. He was obliged to make his first appearance in the capital without a hat which, in those days, would make people look at him. He said to himself: 'They'll think I've been following a funeral procession.' He clutched his bundle and stepped out on the platform, mixing with the crowd of passengers hurrying along in the direction of the barrier. Here two gentlemen stopped him asking to see his papers. They read the details, and looked him up and down. 'Tall, fair, blue eyes, grey suit, straw hat. . . . What have you done with the straw hat?' asked one of the plain-clothes men with scant politeness.

'I looked out of the window and it blew away,' said Émile.

The detective laughed sarcastically: 'It'll cool you down, you hothead!' he answered.

3

WHEN Émile had walked out of the station he stood still a moment, listening to the noise of Paris, wondering in what direction to go. Then, reflecting that he would be as well here as anywhere else, he crossed the street and took a room in the first lodging place whose modest sign met his eye. He was quick to make friends, and within a few days came up against a man who had served in his regiment. This man, from the *midi* like Émile, had been for some years in Paris where he worked as night porter in a luxury hotel. Milou, in the days of his splendour, guarding Queen Victoria at Nice, had been kind to him and now Jean Bonhomme was surprised to find the once swaggering cavalryman so timid and worried in the big city.

Bonhomme slept every day till lunch, after which he would take an airing in the streets till it was time for him to go to work. He invited Émile to a meal, suggesting that the next morning he should go to see the manager of the hotel where he worked who might find him something to do. Émile followed his friend's advice and was immediately engaged to polish the parquet floors, for Paris was just then preparing to welcome distinguished guests for a great exhibition.

Polishing floors proved even harder than the mine. He had to rub steel mesh over the surface of the wood, and then polish rooms and stairs and corridors, continually breathing minute particles of dust. He would become very hot and then be thrown into a bitter draught when called upon hurriedly to give a hand to the luggage porters. And yet Émile was never tired and when Bonhomme, who was not strong, needed help, Milou would stay with him a great part of the night.

He was gay and earned a lot of money. The luck of his boyhood and soldiering days had come back, and whenever he played cards he invariably won. There was one café he favoured particularly for a game of whist. The place was owned by a rich widow, rather a fine woman in her way, who was looking forward to taking life more easily in her native village in the *midi*. She liked to talk about the good things waiting for her in the sunshine, the big house with the vine growing against it, the linen and solid furniture, especially the beds with the wool mattresses and, of course, the regular dividends from well-chosen investments which were always necessary when one did not want to worry about the future. She only needed one thing to complete her happiness, and that was a husband, her first, an Auvergnat, having died from the strain of building up this fine Paris café of which she was now the owner.

She decided that Émile was her man and she set about giving him a foretaste of what their married happiness would be. Émile enjoyed Juliette's hospitality and liked to feel that she was always there, behind her cash-desk, important, dignified, showing to advantage a large, heaving bosom and a fine head of dark hair constellated by *diamanté* combs which shone like glow-worms. She had a court of admirers who formed too valuable an adjunct to her establishment to allow any of them altogether to despair of obtaining her hand, but now that Émile was her chosen one she used the others mostly to show off her gifts of repartee, that Émile should realize what a fortunate young man he was to have won the heart of such an accomplished lady. But Émile hesitated. Paris, for a young man who never felt tired, was much more fun than even Augustine had prophesied, and thanks to his luck at cards his pockets were always full of golden louis.

Jean Bonhomme was consumptive. He coughed, and his thin legs could hardly climb the stairs which led to the apartment where his wife, Charlotte, already contaminated by the malady, took in piecework for the multiple tailors. He left both his post of night porter and his apartment and moved to Montmartre where he hoped the clear air would be good for his lungs. Charlotte went on with her piecework, but as they were childless and had a little money put aside they could now take life easier, he occasionally staying in bed, she taking more care and time over the food. They got on well together, and had it not been for the illness they might have been happy. Their apartment was on a level with the street, and when the post of *concierge*, or hall porter, became vacant they were given it, which saved them the rent. Charlotte distributed the letters, took messages, and from her bed at night pressed a button to open the street door for the tenants. As her husband was supposed to polish the stairs Émile came along once a week to do this for him, and afterwards he would stay for lunch and a game of cards.

Every now and then the multiple tailors sent Charlotte Bonhomme a parcel of machine-cut men's suits which she distributed to a small band of seamstresses who were much poorer than she was.

Thus one morning a girl arrived with her bundle of waistcoats. Charlotte verified the seams. The waistcoats would now go to another woman who specialized in making the buttonholes and sewing on the buttons, but before this happened Charlotte herself liked to sew on the buckles and claws at the back.

On this particular day Charlotte was unusually tired. She cleared a place for the seamstress at the dining-room table, and fetching a great quantity of buckles offered the girl lunch and a little money if she would sew them on and take the waistcoats round to the buttonhole woman. This was not the first time that the young seamstress had relieved Charlotte of her work. Usually the girl's lunch consisted of fried potatoes, bought at the corner shop, and some cherries. Charlotte and her husband ate rather well, and an invitation to lunch pleased the pretty girl. So she immediately began to sew on the buckles, deftly, her head bent low, while Charlotte talked and prepared the food. An hour later the pile of metal clasps and the waistcoats smelling of new wool and dye were pushed to the far end of the table. Lunch was laid. There were to be four people— the seamstress, Charlotte, Jean Bonhomme, and Émile who was coming to polish the stairs. The two men arrived noisily and very hungry. They had called at several cafés for aperitifs and now they showed off a little by talking patois. Charlotte introduced the seamstress: 'This is Mlle Mathilde.' 'That's funny,' said Émile, looking sharply at her, 'Mathilde was the name of my poor young sister who was poisoned by a dish of mushrooms.' The seamstress, shy and sensitive, not sure whether Émile's remarks were a compliment or a reproach, coloured violently. She was only eighteen. Her skin was like milk and her head covered by red hair which burned like a bronze helmet caught by the rays of a hot sun. Every time she went out into the street people turned to look at her, and this made her horribly self-conscious. Moreover, in black, not from choice but out of economy, she made a contrast in colours that was breath-taking. She also had a waist so slim that she could encircle it with her tiny hands. Nobody had ever seen anything like it before. But what is the good of flaming bronze hair and a seventeen-inch waist when you are timidity itself? Instead of holding her head high in the street, she brushed against the wall, feeling her heart beat with shame because men looked so hard at her.

Émile, a travelled man, having seen things at Nice and at Monte Carlo, was suffocated by this golden top. The frailty of the schoolgirl brought out the man in him. Her fingers, as she took the crockery, appeared like butterflies poising for timeless moments on each thing, then fluttering away ethereal. Unconsciously he began to make comparisons between this delicate apparition and the imposing fatness of Juliette seated like a Teutonic goddess behind the cash-desk of her gilded café.

As soon as lunch was over Matilda began to sew again. The two men went off and Mme Bonhomme, washing up, said: 'Yes, as I tell you, that man Émile is as strong as ten men, but he is a bit hasty and drinks more than is good for him, though I reckon a wife would make all the difference'; and she went on to tell Matilda about Émile's good fortune in having a dignified and wealthy woman, even though a few years his senior, so anxious to make him financially independent for the rest of his life. Just after five, all the waistcoats having their buckles firmly attached, the two women totted up how many buttons it would be necessary to take to the woman whose business it was to sew them on. Charlotte treated her buttons with right regard to their cost, giving only two or three more than the total count in case of loss or breakage. The garments were then placed in a square of green serge, the ends of which were tied tightly. Matilda counted her earnings, placed the silver in the purse she carried hidden in an underskirt, and was taking up the green serge parcel when Émile, who had been secretly waiting, arrived, offering awkwardly to carry her waistcoats for a little way up the street.

When Émile lifted the parcel he did it with a great flourish to give her a picture of his strength. Together they climbed six storeys to the woman who was to sew on the buttons. Then Émile offered Matilda something to drink at the terrace of a café. As they sat out in the warm air he questioned her eagerly, but she,

having fresh in her ears the marvellous story of the rich widow
anxiously waiting for Émile to marry her, instead of realizing
that her companion had fallen in love with her at first sight,
imagined that he was merely being polite, in memory, doubtless,
of his sister poisoned by the mushrooms. They left each other
at the corner of the street. Émile felt himself quite a different
man. When, because he had nothing else to do, he sauntered
into the beautiful Juliette's café for his evening game of cards
she welcomed him with a round of abuse. This was his day off.
Even though he had gone to Jean Bonhomme's to polish the
stairs he had no business to have stayed so late. What was his
excuse this time? 'I suppose I can do what I like, can't I?'
retorted Émile angrily. 'After all, we 're not married!' The
unfortunate Juliette winced. Not yet being married was just
what rankled and she had been unwise to allow the quarrel to
take this dangerous turn. Her heart was full of forgiveness, but
Émile, now he had seen Matilda, was no longer touchable.
Instead of sitting down for cards, he walked back angrily to his
hotel. Juliette wondered if he had been drinking. She resolved
to make this quarrel an excuse for bringing the question of
marriage to a head on Sunday. As she was the one with money,
and was the eldest, it was up to her to propose. Everything for
her future happiness and tranquillity would thus be fixed.

Whenever Matilda went to the Bonhommes' she found Émile,
who was showing quite a passion for polishing the stairs. His
presence raised no flutter in her heart, for she was so convinced
of his attachment for the rich widow and so absolutely certain
that there was nothing about her person to arouse the affections
of men, that she neither saw nor understood anything. The
Bonhommes, on the other hand, quickly sensed what was
happening, but they could not understand how this insignificant seamstress with freckles and red hair, a young woman so
shy and awkward, quite incapable of saying two words without
blushing, could have knocked over this fine fellow from Nice
with whom all the richest women were madly in love, who during
carnival time on the Riviera was pelted with the largest and most
beautiful bouquets.

Charlotte felt a curious animosity towards her seamstress. A
natural compassion for the shy young woman was now replaced
by a feeling that Matilda was neither poor nor lonely any longer

but quite likely to outwit Juliette. She began to give her the hardest and longest work instead of the easiest, and Matilda had to drink black coffee at night not to fall asleep over her sewing.

Juliette now suspected a rival. She grew morbidly jealous, and decided to make a surprise call on the Bonhommes to discover why Émile remained with them so long on his days off. She arrived so early that Charlotte was alone in the kitchen. The two women, though each had heard so much about the other, had not met before. Within a few minutes they were fast friends. In a way they could both claim to have been successful in life, putting some money aside, able to look down a little on those who had to count every farthing. They were capable women and knew how to run a home. They drank several cups of mid-morning coffee, exchanging confidences, but not yet touching on that question which it would not have been wise to broach too soon. The important thing was first to establish a solid intimacy.

After about an hour Matilda arrived with her piece goods under her arm, and then Juliette, seeing a change in Charlotte's face, and the strange beauty that emanated from the pale features of this copper-haired seamstress, understood that here was her rival. Charlotte, having recovered from her momentary embarrassment, and silently allying herself with her new friend, took up each garment critically, biting her lips and examining the work with a hard look, trying to find fault. She took from her purse the money she owed Matilda after which, instead of giving her a new batch of work, she remained motionless and harsh, intent only on gaining Juliette's approval. To Matilda she said at last: 'I shall not need you any more. I have discovered a woman who works much faster and quite as well.'

Matilda hung her head, and went to the door as if she had done something wrong. When she had gone Charlotte looked up with expectation at her new friend, hoping for a bright smile of thanks, but Juliette had been going through the most painful emotions during this scene, and now burst out in an explosion of injured pride.

When Émile found that Matilda was not working any more for Charlotte, he went to wait for her at the street door of her lodging-house, in the evenings, as soon as he was free, but it was not till the following Sunday, in the morning, that she came down, paler and very thin. He asked her what she planned

to do and she answered that as Charlotte refused a reference
nobody would give her any sewing, and she was now anxious to
make enough money to pay her fare back to Blois where she was
born.   Émile's heart was touched and he invited her to lunch.
They spent the afternoon together, and the same evening he asked
her to marry him, saying he had loved her from the beginning,
and that it was the first time that such a thing had happened to
him.   'But then,' she queried, 'isn't it true about the rich widow
Charlotte said you were going to marry?'

'I 'm not in love with her,' answered Émile, 'and never have
been, and the proof is that if you were to refuse me I would be
the most unhappy man in the world.'   He implored her to accept
him in spite of the fact that he was older than she was, quite a lot
older, so that he was just as afraid of appearing ridiculous as
Juliette had been in wanting him to marry her.

There was no point in prolonging their engagement.   They
went to find the priest of the parish in which Matilda had her
room and their banns were published.   Émile chose an employee
of his hotel as witness.   He had asked his friend Jean Bonhomme
to attend their marriage but Jean, influenced by Charlotte, refused.
As long as the Bonhommes had believed that Émile might change
his mind and return obediently to Juliette, they had not altogether
put an end to their friendship, but when the banns were finally
published outside the town hall, and it was clear to everybody
that poor Émile had quite lost his wits, then Jean openly declared
himself against his former friend.

Émile and his young wife went to live in a tiny apartment in
the rue Lepic in Montmartre among the people from Brittany
and the Auvergne I have already described.   Émile had said they
would buy the furniture by degrees, nice things they could later
take with them to a larger place, but the gold pieces which
hitherto Émile had won with so little trouble ceased magically.
Anybody might have supposed that his luck had changed from
the very moment of his marriage.   Nostalgically he thought back
to the money he had made at the races, playing cards, and all of
which had been thrown away so light-heartedly.   Nothing seemed
to work any more.   He had less time to go to the races, and when
he laid a bet it was done so hurriedly and the horse never won.
He sometimes played cards but as he was afraid to lose the stakes
were small.   Jean having said something to the manager, Émile

lost his job at the hotel. They bought one or two cheap bits of furniture, but Matilda soon realized that she was not to have the bedroom suite, and especially the wardrobe with mirrors she had always dreamed about.

Now that Émile had lost his job, he realized he knew no trade. Matilda's prospects were perhaps a little brighter. The people in the warehouse were more inclined to trust her because she was a married woman and she could get practically all the work she liked. She continued to make seams and sew on buttons but still later into the night because, for some weeks at any rate, she would be obliged to keep Émile.

Émile started to take casual work and then drifted into the building trade, leaving his young wife early in the morning to go with a band of workmen to the outskirts of Paris, to St. Cloud or perhaps St. Germain, where new houses were being put up. Matilda stayed at home, bending over her sewing-machine.

The Bonhommes watched the newly married couple from a distance, and though it was they who had severed relations every little thing that happened to Matilda or to Émile, and especially every misfortune, was discussed from all possible angles as if their hatred had become a necessity at all costs to be nourished. Juliette had no happiness but to lament in the company of Charlotte, and from surprise and indignation they came at last to revenge, not so much on Émile, whom they feared for his physical strength and violent temper, but on Matilda who was the very picture of a weak, shy, and insignificant woman whom it would be a real pleasure to torture. The fact that she was alone nearly every day would increase any pain they could inflict on her, for she would brood over the poison they would begin to instil by a series of anonymous letters addressed to Émile. To make more certain of their arrival they would be registered. If the postman could not find Émile, the unfortunate man on his return from work would have to go to the post office to collect personally the injurious sheets. He was no match for the Bonhommes in this insidious warfare. Like Dumas's musketeers he liked to catch hold of a man and fight him in the open. As the Bonhommes had calculated Matilda was the one to suffer. When the postman knocked in the morning, asking for Émile, brandishing in front of her the registered letter that, by French law, could alone be handed to the addressee, she began to blush with shame, her heart beating with unknown fear. All day alone, bending over her sewing, not bothering even to eat, she waited in trepidation for his homecoming. The Bonhommes, seeing that their victims, even the redoubtable Émile, did nothing, became bolder and now sent their poisonous letters direct to Matilda who hid them from her husband fearing that at last he would lose patience and murder his former friend. Émile's immense strength gave her no sense of security. He was too unpredictable in his moods. Inebriated, he would not have known what he was doing. It was her constant fear that his chivalrous Quixotic nature would one day land him in a criminal adventure. She was already learning to suffer silently, but her anguish was so real that in the end she dared not even leave the house for fear of finding Juliette waiting for her in the street. Soon it was not sufficient, in her frenzied thought, to remain at home but she must barricade the door in case Juliette called on her. Sometimes, of course, she was obliged to deliver her work, and then she went down the stairs on tiptoe, and in the street clung to the walls like a fugitive from justice. One day, as she had feared, while sewing she heard footsteps climbing, stopping on the stair-head. Juliette, finding the door locked, insulted her for everybody to hear, laughed loudly, made fun of her red hair and her white skin which she said was that of a dead woman. After this Émile took a different apartment hoping that Juliette would lose trace of them. But Matilda, in these new rooms, suddenly discovered she was pregnant and now, strong in the hope of her child, she was no longer afraid of Juliette or the Bonhommes. She was only nineteen. Shaking off the nightmare of the last few months she worked even harder. Émile worked hard also, but there were days when it rained and the workmen were dismissed.

The anonymous letters began again. Matilda, needle in hand, turned over the cruellest tortures to punish her enemies. She thought about nothing else for hours, and her character, which had never been gay, now took on a sombre manner. The momentary feeling that she could conquer her fears did not last. The child was the important thing. Her pregnancy was visible and her adversaries must still be watching her, for soon the letters made mention of her state, and the maledictions which hitherto had been centred on Émile and on her, were directed against the child. He was to be a monster. His hair was to be the colour of fire. He was to be idiotic, the child of a witch and a drunkard. All these abominations weighed upon her tired mind, the mind of a young woman of nineteen, the loveliest age in a woman.

She spent the whole summer making all the money she could and, jealous of every minute of daylight, never went out. When her deliverance was at hand she went off stoically to hospital in the middle of a thunderstorm. Because of her long weeks of immobility she suffered cruelly from her kidneys, and complained so much that one of the nurses said to her roughly:

'That's enough! Anybody would think you were the first woman to have a child!'

Timorous, as always, she tried to stifle her moans, whereupon a doctor, standing near, went up to her bed and patting her on the cheek exclaimed:

'Go ahead, little girl, have a good cry. How old are you?'

'Nineteen, doctor.'

'Well, well, at nineteen you have the right to do anything!'

She had a little girl whose hair was not red, as the enemy had prophesied, but blonde. Émile was very proud, and when Matilda heard that her girl was fair, she went soundly to sleep. The date was 13th August which, some people said, would prove lucky for the baby.

4

THE little Madeleine was put out to nurse at Soissons with a countrywoman who had a baby boy, but as my parents allowed half the winter to pass without having me baptised, the village priest so worked upon the mind of my foster-mother, saying she must not continue to give the breast to a pagan, that she threatened to put me out of doors unless my parents came immediately to arrange for my christening. This priest had been annoyed that my mother had not called on him when she first brought me to Soissons, but she was probably too much affected to think of this detail, and in any case, shy as she was, she would never have dared call on a stranger.

My parents were thus obliged to undertake the expense of the journey, choosing two days at Christmas. The woman who looked after me agreed to be my godmother.

That winter was a hard one for Émile because the building trade was in the doldrums, but by this time my mother had made the acquaintance of Mme Gaillard and had quite given up working for the multiple shops. One day Émile, crossing the lower end of the rue Lepic, saw a funeral procession, and, asking the neighbours, learnt that his old friend and enemy, Jean Bonhomme, consumed by tuberculosis, had just died. When he informed my mother of this news, she said calmly: 'And so they shall all die who set out to hurt me, for what harm have I ever done to anybody?' There was not the slightest look of pity in her eyes, whereas my father, violent as he was, was quick to forgive. It was in his character to flare up one moment and to forgive the next. But Matilda, rancorous and weak, having suffered too deeply from the persecution of these wretches, had learned no other way to alleviate misery than by a long-kept-up vengeance.

It was Émile's practice each evening to go down to the café below our flat for an innocent game of cards. My mother accompanied him, not to play cards but to sit modestly in a corner, mending for Mme Berthier, the owner of the café. This woman occasionally did my mother the honour to sit beside her. She too had a baby daughter put out to nurse in the country, and she found in my mother a woman admirably suited to sympathize with her unhappiness in being robbed of the joy of watching her child grow up. At this hour Mme Berthier's elder sister, Mme Gaillard, would arrive with her umbrella and the boxes in which she kept her lace. Married to a useless man, aged by the many children she had brought with difficulty into the world (put out immediately in her native Auvergne), she was constantly making the journey to those parts either to carry a fresh baby to the wet nurse or to bury one who had died from want of care. Though she handled gold all day life was hard with her.

Her shop—by which I mean her umbrella and the boxes—was put up every morning in the carriage entrance of a fine apartment house in the Boulevard Haussmann, between two fashionable Parisian stores, the Galeries Lafayette and the Magasin du Printemps. Rich and poor passed in front. Foreigners visiting one or other of these magnificently gilded emporiums were dazzled by the whiteness and beauty of her rare lace. This woman, who at home was bruised and beaten by a brutal husband, had tucked at the bottom of her heart a shining passion for this luxury trade, and when she was behind her umbrella she was a matchless business woman, judging to a nicety her customer, knowing exactly by the manner of the stranger's dress and speech what would please, and never making a mistake in the change though she could not read.

She seldom reached her doorway till eleven had struck, having previously visited in all the finest hotels, the English, German, American, and Argentine women who were her most enthusiastic customers. To these she showed her latest discoveries, measuring them for blouses or taking their orders for table linen. As soon as she reached her place of business she unrolled a wide piece of scarlet material, hanging it against a panel of one of the two immense doors. In front of this she put out the umbrella and the trestled table, and from behind these she did not move till seven, not even for her lunch of fried potatoes and black coffee brought from across the street.

As if the martyrdom of her home life was not enough, Mme Gaillard was obliged to suffer the slings and irony of the door-keeper and the doorkeeper's wife from whom she rented that half of the carriage door which formed her shop. The door-keeper, wearing a striped waistcoat, a blue apron, and a black silk skull-cap, spent his afternoons seated on a low chair upholstered in red velvet, holding a walking-stick, on which he rested his chin, between his knees. Thus occupied he decorated, by his colourful presence, the second of the double doors. Keeping an eye on his tenants when they came in or went out, but scarcely removing his gaze from the unfortunate Mme Gaillard and her customers, he never spoke to her except to say something dis-agreeable about her lack of authority towards her husband and predicting that before long she would sink into poverty, a state which Mme Gaillard herself was only too well aware might befall her.

Sunny days were the best, but even though it rained Mme Gaillard was obliged to stay, sheltering against the door; for in addition to her customers she received here the many women who either made lace on a spindle at home or, like my mother, put together blouses. It was a fine sight indeed to see her measure the narrow laces. She would use a tape-measure with the customers but for the lacemakers it was the tip of her nose to the outstretched hand and, while asking news of the family in patois, gossiping about this and that, the lace was measured in swift flashes, and unhappy the passer-by who, during this operation, thought it safe to filch something quickly out of the open boxes! When the lace was measured and the price agreed upon, Mme Gaillard would pull out from under her apron of black pleated satinette an accordion shaped purse like those the cattle dealers use at market, a shiny, grubby thing that she opened cautiously and closed suspiciously, angry with herself for having revealed its existence to prying eyes. One heard it fall loudly to the bottom of the deep pocket in her skirt. Then diving behind her mer-chandise, yards of lace wound round blue cardboard, she would look for a black note-book on whose yellowed pages she made signs to remind her of the transaction she had just completed. Illiterate, her language on paper was after the Egyptian manner, a series of childlike pictures and signs by which each sort of lace was differently represented, each coin secretly remembered, the name of the work girl or woman memorized artistically by depicting some peculiarity of face, speech, or way of walking.

When Mme Gaillard came to join her sister, Mme Berthier,

and my mother in the café at night she would take advantage of this quiet place to tally her accounts before going home to her husband, and for this reason she would be obliged to bring out her note-book and, being long-sighted, would hold it at arm's length which allowed my mother to study the curious entries I have just described. Mme Berthier said these hieroglyphics were chiefly to confuse her husband, but she was no judge, not being able to write herself, and no night passed without Mme Gaillard announcing to the two women in the café: 'There, my dears, another dreadful day!' And she would put two fingers in her purse and draw out some small silver, being careful not to open the compartments which held the larger silver and the gold.

She had been in Paris for a great number of years. In their native Auvergne her husband had followed the picturesque profession of pit-sawing by which, before the invention of mechanical saws, laths and floor boards were hewn from the tree. This age-old craft gives a man a great thirst and Gaillard had succeeded in drinking as many as thirty pints of wine a day. The whole of his salary was employed in this manner and their penury became such that they decided to begin life again in Paris. I presume that by this time planks were being cut by electricity. Gaillard, like Émile, looked to the building trade for employment. His speciality was to dig the trenches in which the bricklayers laid their walls. His features were scarlet and puffed out horribly, and his nose so large and pitted that it resembled a pincushion. Mme Gaillard, unable to admire this unlovely husband, showed a growing affection for her eldest son, a delicate lad of fifteen who was still in the Auvergne. He was like his mother both in appearance and courage and wrote her long letters which she brought to my mother, to Émile, or to the *concierge* to read to her.

My poor mother had now fresh reasons for unhappiness. Though Émile, when the weather was fine, worked hard, as hard as even she could have wished, he earned little and spent far too much at the café. I think he had not ceased to love my mother, but absinthe made a tiger of him, and when he became violent the sight of my mother, pale and silent, increased the devil in him, so that in an attempt to make her speak or cry he would shatter whatever object was nearest his hand, whereupon her misery was doubled, for, as you can imagine, she had not the wherewithal to replace the most common utensils in the house. Marie-Thérèse

chose this moment to make a second appearance, and as she was
again without work my parents laid a mattress on the floor and
rather unwillingly offered her hospitality.   She was not altogether
cheerless about the future, having paid a countrywoman a month
in advance for looking after her daughter Rolande.   She spent
the days looking for work and the nights dancing at the Moulin
de la Galette and Bullier's.   Émile, who quickly repented his
generosity in having Marie-Thérèse in the house, but not being
brave enough to send her away, made her presence the excuse of
new and more terrible quarrels which my aunt, as gay as ever,
seemed not to notice.   At least, my mother had a companion with
whom from time to time she could gossip, recalling their childhood at Blois, discussing the eldest sister Margaret with whom
momentarily neither was on speaking terms, and rediscovering
some of the fragrance of girlhood affection which had united them
at school and during apprentice days.   Matilda blamed Marie-
Thérèse for her frivolity whilst Marie-Thérèse blamed her sister
for her want of spirits and energy, not perceiving in these faults
an infinite capacity for hard work.   Consider that my mother at
this period even busied herself on Sunday mornings washing the
linen and the sheets.   She had never been inside a theatre and
had only danced as a little girl with the soldiers in the open air
at Blois, being dressed in a very short skirt and wearing her hair
long in the back, that golden hair which streamed down like a
river on fire.   She was much too young, too blushing, too
delicate a flower to be married to a man who would have needed
a sturdy fishwife to stand up to him, to counter his choleric
outbursts with a fine flow of words.   She was infinitely too young
to have one child already and to be expecting a second.   Nevertheless it was my mother who with her needle and agile fingers
built a wall against misery on those days of rain, sleet, and snow
when Émile was unable to make houses.   Marie-Thérèse, herself,
just now was also taking advantage of my mother's magic
needle.   Mme Berthier was perhaps the only person who appreciated my mother's stoic answer to her destiny.   She occasionally
let fly at Émile about it, and my father, who was good-natured
at heart, hurried up to my mother with immediate offers of
forgiveness as if she, and not he, were the offending person.
She met his advances without enthusiasm, being convinced that
life reserved for her the hard lot of a Russian peasant woman—

work, children, and, by way of diversity, an occasional thrashing.
Up to now Émile had not beaten her, but she feared him.
Her delivery being near, she made a parcel of her things and,
accompanied by Marie-Thérèse, walked to the Lariboisière
hospital. Émile, on his return that night, was surprised to find
the house empty. He was annoyed, thinking his womenfolk had
gone shopping, and began to work himself up into a fine temper
because supper would be late. When Marie-Thérèse came back
alone he became nervous, and hearing what had happened ran
off to the hospital in great commotion. On his return, very late,
extremely in need of a person to talk things over with, aware like
all men of his inability to be of any use on these occasions,
fretting, looking forward to questioning Marie-Thérèse and to
confiding in her, he found nobody at home again. She had gone
out dancing! Put out, quite torn with anxiety, he went dismally
to bed.

As early as he dare in the morning he went to the Lariboisière
where he learnt that he had a son. He now flew back home
where Marie-Thérèse, who had arrived during his absence, was
fast asleep on her mattress. He woke her with the great news,
saying that he was going straight back to see her sister, that he
would not go to work that morning, and wanted her to make
lunch early. She clapped her hands joyfully, congratulated him,
and fell asleep again.

When Émile arrived at my mother's bedside and saw his son,
he was moved like all powerful men looking at the tiny, helpless thing which is theirs and requires protection. At this
moment he would have done anything for my mother. He had
missed her terribly during the night, and he was now very proud
that she had given him a son. She asked him what was happening
at home and he told her that Marie-Thérèse had gone out dancing
all night. At the thought of it, anger rose in his throat, but she
refused to say anything, knowing how easily she could add to
his wrath. Besides, she was worried about a big pile of his dirty
socks which she had put to soak before going to hospital. She
thought they might spoil, in addition to which they all needed
mending. She liked her husband to have a clean pair every
morning. He needed them, and this necessity had become a rite
which would be broken unless Marie-Thérèse could be persuaded
to go on with it. She also thought that if Émile did not have

his clean socks there would be quarrels she would not be there to appease.

My mother's short stay at the hospital proved a holiday for her. She ate well and read lazily in bed. On the Sunday morning Émile arrived. My mother saw immediately from the whiteness of his cheeks that he was bringing her bad news. He covered with wide steps the few yards between the door and her bed, and at his first words she knew that her fears had not been idle. Not once, since her confinement, had he found the evening soup waiting for him! Not once had he found a clean pair of socks! And last night a dreadful smell had revealed, in a dark corner, the basin in which the dirty socks had been rotting in soapy water for the last week! What else could he have done but to throw Marie-Thérèse with her baggage and her silly novelettes out into the street? He had told her never to set foot in his house again. If ever she came to the hospital to complain about him, he would smack her in front of all the nurses!

Matilda winced. The holiday was over. These sudden worries turned her milk. Her baby son began to cry from hunger. She left hospital in a sad state, and after a few days at home took the train to Soissons where she would put her son out to nurse and visit her daughter. I was then eleven months old, and when my mother saw me she was jealous because I treated her as a stranger, calling out 'Mama!' to the woman she paid to look after me.

Back in Paris life became more and more difficult for my mother. Before long, also, the woman with whom my little brother was put out sent alarming news about his health. He was always hungry. The doctor had come. Then, one day, came a telegram. My brother was dead. The wet nurse, having seen him so hungry, had given him an egg beaten up in milk. Diarrhoea had begun and within twenty-four hours there was one more angel in heaven. Émile and my mother took the train for Soissons, close to each other in their misery, and my mother has told me that her son, in death, looked so much like his father that it startled her. After the funeral they took the train back to Paris, my mother holding a parcel containing her child's baby-clothes, tight to her heart. They had no time to visit me, nor the money, I think, for my mother had been obliged to borrow some money from Mme Berthier for the coffin, and to pay off the woman.

My mother was not the sort of person to bear a debt lightly,
and she took on an increasing amount of work which, added to
her grief, finally gave that stamp of sombreness to her character
which had been only too ready to assert itself in her more tender
years. As, during these joyless days, she sewed alone in her
room she set herself the further task, after repaying the money
to Mme Berthier, of putting enough aside to bring me back from
Soissons, partly to lessen her loneliness, partly because having
lost one child she was afraid to lose the other. Though in
appearance she was like some tender flower whose bright but
delicate head seemed always on the point of drooping, she had
the nervous resistance of many apparently weak women, and
when her mind was set on a thing, she was able to go forward,
resisting the longest hours and the worst storms of her marital
unhappiness. It was at this period of lonely contemplation that
she learnt of the death of Charlotte Bonhomme. Later came
news that the comely Juliette, so flourishing but yesterday, had
cancer and was in hospital for an operation from which she was
not likely to make more than temporary recovery. I am not sure
to what extent these terrible facts satisfied my mother's inborn
desire for vengeance. Death had touched her too closely and
too recently for her to get much enjoyment out of a sensation
which is necessarily more virulent in youth than when experience
begins to soften us. At any rate, a phase in her married life was
over, and though she still had no illusions about her future she
could go out into the street without fear of being insulted.

One evening in the extreme heat of a Montmartre summer my
mother was serving an omelet and a fresh salad to Émile by the
open window when she heard what she thought for a moment
was a voice calling her faintly in the yard. Almost at the same
time her husband spoke to her, and she did not dare pay any
further attention to the voice, about which she might so easily
have made a mistake. Later, however, another voice, strong and
unmistakable, that of Mme Berthier, calling 'Matilda!' came up
into the room. This time my mother took it that Mme Gaillard
had sent her sister with some message about a lace blouse and
she ran quickly down. In the shadow of the courtyard, against
the damp stone wall, trembling, Marie-Thérèse stood with her
baby Rolande wrapped in a woollen shawl and clasped tightly
in her thin arms. She explained in short, breathless sentences

that having been without work since Émile had thrown her out
into the street, she had been unable to pay the woman with
whom the baby had been deposited, that neighbouring countrywomen had written to say the infant was being left to starve, and
that she had spent all the money she possessed to go to fetch her
unfortunate daughter. The wet nurse had refused to give her
the baby's clothes until the debt was settled with the result that
Marie-Thérèse had brought her back in her own shawl. 'Now
there is nothing left for us,' she exclaimed, clutching the child
nearer to her, 'than to jump into the Seine!'

How changed was this pretty frivolous sister! No happy turn
had yet come in the novel of Marie-Thérèse's existence and indeed
it seemed that the story might that same evening end in a suicide.

'Is he up there?' queried Marie-Thérèse in a whisper.

'Yes,' answered Matilda.

'I know,' said Marie-Thérèse. 'Mme Berthier came out of
the café to warn me. It was she who called out to you.'

Matilda looked round, and in spite of the stifling night she was
as nervous, as trembling, as her sister.

'Wait!' she exclaimed. 'I'll go and see what I can do!'

My mother came back very white, her lips twitching, and as
she stood in the doorway, not yet brave enough to speak, Émile
said sharply, looking up from his paper:

'What a time you've been! Gossiping again?'

'Émile, listen to me! Marie-Thérèse is downstairs.'

'I told you I never wanted to see her again!' said Émile, throwing down his paper and getting ready to roll up his sleeves.

'She has the baby with her,' my mother objected softly, 'and
they haven't eaten for three days.' She went very close to her
husband and went on: 'What am I to do? Shall I send them
away?'

My father's good nature immediately welled up and, remembering how only a few weeks back he had walked behind the tiny
coffin along the powdery road outside Soissons, he said huskily,
trying to hide his emotion in a manly way:

'Let them come up then!'

Matilda flew down the narrow, uneven stairs, into the yard
where, seeing her sister so weak, so terrified at the thought of
meeting Émile, she took the baby and led her by the hand.
Émile said nothing and Marie-Thérèse, cringing, did not

recognize the look of pity in his eyes. She went past him and wept, stupid with fatigue and hunger.

My mother cleared the table, and taking a pillow from her bed laid the baby on it, removing the soaked swaddling cloths.

'Hold her a moment, Émile,' she said quietly, and he, obediently, placed his strong, hairy hand under the baby's soft chest whilst my mother took from the bottom of a drawer the package of poignantly evocative garments she had brought back with her from her baby son's funeral at Soissons.

'Everything is just as the woman gave it me,' she whispered to Émile. 'It's all we have left of *him*. At least they will come in useful, useful to some other little innocent.'

Émile was crying. Whilst Marie-Thérèse sobbed helplessly in her corner, my father and mother washed the inanimate Rolande, thin and white-cheeked. My mother began to think that she was really dressing her little niece for the coffin. She sent Émile down to find some milk. After this hot summer's day there was not any to be had. He went to Mme Berthier, thinking that she, at least, would help.

'I've none,' she answered, 'but as the baby has had nothing for several days you would only kill it.' Then pouring out some boiled water from a kettle: 'Give the child some of this with a little sugar.'

When Émile saw Rolande washed and in clean things but even whiter than at first he began to lose his head, but my mother put some of the sugared water in the baby's mouth and they both saw the blood run up to the cheeks, colouring them like rose petals. Small blue eyes opened, lids closed, and sleep came. Though Marie-Thérèse was still sobbing, the tears which streamed down her cheeks seemed at last to be doing her good and she accepted a few leaves of lettuce and a glass of wine which Émile put out at the end of the table. My mother, seeing her husband so moved, fetched the mattress which had always been her sister's bed on these occasions and laid it on the floor. Marie-Thérèse cried herself to sleep and the baby was put on a pillow beside her.

Émile had quietly disappeared to play cards with his friends at the café, and soon my mother went to join him, thinking that Mme Berthier might be of further counsel. This excellent woman wisely suggested that Rolande be sent back to the country as soon as she was well enough to travel. She knew too much about

Émile's character to think his present docility would last, and his violence would not only make life impossible for the two women but might kill the child.

It was wonderful next morning to see how anxious Marie-Thérèse appeared to repay my parents' hospitality by going off to find work. Rolande, also, who remained in my mother's care, made one of those rapid recoveries which so often snatch babies from the very shadow of death, and give them, almost as one is ready to despair, fine pink cheeks and healthy, kicking limbs. Marie-Thérèse, whose great interest in life, apart from reading novels and dancing, was to make gay hats, had been introduced by the doorkeeper's wife to a modiste who lived on a higher floor and this modiste had engaged my aunt for the equivalent of thirty shillings a week and her keep which arrangement promised to supply her with a home and enough money to send Rolande back to the country.

Mme Pauline was the name of this modiste and a great number of the smartest *demi-mondaines* climbed the five storeys leading to her apartment for the honour of acquiring her airy creations. Circus riders also came to Mme Pauline, and all these ladies drove up in their smart carriages. Marie-Thérèse was at last certain that the novel of her life was taking a better turn and that the preliminary difficulties had been merely put in her way to give greater splendour to the next chapters. Mme Pauline, friendly, talkative, hard-working, was so clever at building up on her fist one of those magnificent hats of which she alone had the secret, that Marie-Thérèse was quite faint with admiration. Here was the Parisian woman in all the wealth of her inborn taste! The admiration of the apprentice was most agreeable to the expert. They were both about the same age and often, in the evening, Mme Pauline would take Marie-Thérèse to the Cirque de Paris or to Médrano for which she had, of course, from her many equestrian customers a great number of free tickets. The smell of the sawdust, the lights, the beating of the drums, opened the way to fresh dreams. Diana de Poitiers and Laure de Valenciennes in shimmering white or hope-spelling green, spangled with tinsel, a top-hat worn swaggeringly over golden locks, stood on their white horses in the blinding arc-lamps, whilst from every part of the arena moustached admirers in evening dress with black capes, cigars between lips, clapped enthusiastically, their gold-topped canes under their arms. These finely dressed men, these women so artistically made up, these splashes of colour and prancing horses, gave comforting reality to my aunt's dreams, and when the circus was over Mme Pauline and she would have a liqueur on the crowded terrace of the Café de la Paix.

Our doorkeeper's wife had a young maid-of-all-work called Ermeline, and my aunt, having made the acquaintance of this serious and excellent person, decided to utilize the skill she had recently acquired from Mme Pauline to make her a hat. Ermeline, who had come from her native village of Marais in the Cher, in the hopes of earning enough money to find a husband on her return, had not worn a hat before, having travelled to Paris in a lace bonnet; and when she saw the beautiful thing Marie-Thérèse had created gratitude surged up and she was struck with the same burning admiration as my aunt had so recently felt for Mme Pauline.

Marie-Thérèse was delighted to have made her first hat and to see in Ermeline's happy features the proof that it was really liked. They became quite friendly, and soon Ermeline was told all about Rolande whose nurse in the country was now asking thirty shillings a week which left Marie-Thérèse no money at all for herself. Ermeline was a little put out to learn that her friend, though unmarried, had a child, but being goodness itself offered to take Rolande to her mother at Marais who, being widowed, lived with a deaf sister in a thatched cottage on the fringe of a wheatfield and had a little girl from the poor-law administration to look after. Marie-Thérèse was delighted and Rolande was transferred to Ermeline's mother and the orphan girl.

At about this time Émile was called up for a second course of military training at Nice, and it was decided that on his return he would call first on his sister Mme Agnel who, with her husband, was living in a fine new house all done up in white, with vines and tomatoes in the garden, at the Grand' Combe, and then go to Soissons to collect me from my foster-mother and bring me back to Paris.

The dark, narrow streets of Montmartre seemed very airless to Émile when he arrived at the café below the damp, stone house, with the unaccustomed burden of an eighteen-month-old daughter and a canary in a cage which last he had bought on the journey. His lungs were still full of mountain air and his skin burnt by a Mediterranean sun. Montmartre suddenly appeared repellent to him. During his absence Juliette had died from the inevitable recurrence of her grievous illness. Mme Berthier had suddenly decided to sell her café and go to live in her beloved Auvergne before it was too late. The unhealthy air, the fetid water of the open drains running crookedly over cobble-stones, the coal dust in the yard, were leading her slowly towards tuberculosis. Others also were preparing to go, either to spend what they had amassed in Paris in the villages where they were born or merely trying to find a cure for their restlessness by exchanging one part of the city for another.

One Sunday morning Émile borrowed a hand-cart and, with the help of a companion, started to remove the furniture. We were to follow the Avenue de Clichy as far as the old fortified walls of the city and, from there, go down to the bank of the Seine where new apartment houses had recently gone up. We would have purer air, the sight of some leaves and grass, and a less costly neighbourhood than Montmartre.

The two men made several journeys, Émile in front, strapped between the shafts, his friend behind, one hand placed with a protective air against a piece of bruised furniture. Other Parisian families were also on the move, and every now and again the men would leave their possessions, together with the women and the children, at the side of the road whilst they went to refresh themselves in a café. At the end of the day, fatigue and too many libations would lead inevitably to quarrels and blows.

5

THE year 1909 ended for my mother with the birth of a son who was to be her last child. He came into the world in the new apartment at Clichy and his arrival that Christmas constitutes my earliest memory. My maternal grandmother had come specially from Blois, dressed entirely in black and carrying an immense umbrella and a wicker basket in which a dozen pots of home-made gooseberry jam were wrapped up in a linen napkin smelling of lavender. As soon as the cover was removed from one of these jars, all the delicious evocations of a sunny garden in the Loire filled the room. The colour and taste of the fruit charmed the little girl that I was.

My baby brother had red hair, my mother's rather sad beauty, and was quite adorable when being bathed in the washtub. I recall equally the gentle hours we spent watching him asleep in his cot, my mother with a lace blouse between her delicate fingers and I, sitting on a low stool beside her with fragments of lace I had picked up from the floor trying to sew without pricking my fingers, not daring to cry when I did so for fear of waking my brother. Occasionally my mother would sing softly, with a little catch in her voice in the sentimental parts, the romances she had learnt at Blois from the seamstresses in her apprentice days. There were passages which the little girl found passionately unintelligible but which she interpreted as she could, helped by an already strong imagination, unhappy love, children without fathers, patriotic songs of the war of 1870 in which figured the tricolour, lilac in bloom, and the woods of Meudon. I learnt early to play without making a noise, most often at being haber-dasher with my mother as the customer who bought everything, paying with buttons, patiently lending me her scissors to cut out tiny designs from her lace. These were indeed gentle hours! The baby would wake up, whereupon my mother would lift him up out of the cot addressing him in a language of her own. Then taking the pins from her corsage she would proudly give him the breast.   All was calm.   One listened to the tiny creature feeding, and kneading with plump fingers the milk-heavy bosom.

I remember also Émile coming home one evening with a young fox-terrier which had followed him in the street.   Dogs and children were attracted by the loud authority in his voice and they alone, perhaps, perceived his deep hidden goodness.   He called the terrier Follette.   Knocking me over, she showed her friendliness and gratitude at being given a home by pawing and barking, but my mother was resentful, saying that there was no place for a dog in an apartment of one room and a kitchen and in which there were two children.   No dog could have kept quieter in the daytime than Follette who intelligently sensed my mother's antagonism.   She was anxious, in these circumstances, to remain unnoticed and scarcely emerged from her hiding-place even for food, but at night, hearing Émile's footsteps long before my mother did, she would run to the door, sniff and yelp, and when Émile arrived her happiness would have touched any woman less embittered by life than my mother.   She, I think, saw in the animal's joy merely the waking of her son in the cot, and often her husband caressed the dog before he spoke to her.   I have a clear picture of him at these times putting down the heavy sack in which he brought back for our stove wood salvaged from some demolished house or picked up from under the carpenter's bench. When we had all been kissed he would go out again, with the dog at his heels, and for long we would hear the animal's delirious barking as they went along the street.

My mother laid supper on the round table covered with an oil-cloth and in the centre of which she placed, on winter evenings, the lamp with its yellow flame that I likened to a mermaid in a mysterious sea.   This mermaid became, at my will, a fairy, a sleeping princess, a fair damsel imprisoned in a glass tower. Then came the evening soup after which Émile would take the wood out of his sack and a pleasant odour of resin and tar would fill the room.   When a piece was too large for the stove he would split it with a hatchet against a plank balanced on his knees, and when a splinter flew across the carpet Follette, her tail wagging, would bring it back in her mouth and drop it at the feet of her master, certain that she would be petted and sometimes, even, given a lump of sugar.   After this ceremony Émile took a foot-bath, which would be removed by my mother, holding it by the two handles, her young body and narrow waist bent under the weight, obedient and lovely like a Roman slave, whilst I knelt down with the slippers. He went to bed almost immediately, and within a minute or two was fast asleep, for his day began at five. His snoring was echoed by that of his dog. My mother put out a clean pair of socks, a clean shirt, the money for the subway train, and a thick slice of bread spread with dripping or hard pork sausage which he carried in his haversack to eat at midday. The remains of the evening soup she poured into a saucepan for him to heat it up before going to work. He liked to dip a piece of bread in it and always shared this early meal with the dog.

After a hard winter the Seine, in 1910, began suddenly to overflow its banks and everybody watched the stone figure of the zouave which, with its back against the central arch of the Alma bridge, is invariably used as a yardstick on such occasions. The water quickly covered the zouave's feet, rose above his gaiters, and in a few days reached his chin. Then panic took hold of those who lived nearest the river. These are my first clear-cut memories of the outside world.

Our street had become a tributary of the Seine during the night and the water continued to rise. The doorkeepers left their lodges and arranged new quarters for themselves on the first floor. As the cellars were flooded there was no coal for heating, and in ours Émile had put a cask of wine which somebody had sent him from the south of France, and this cask, half empty, had been raised by the water, and thus floating on the summit of the waves bumped so loudly and continuously against the roof of the cellar, which was also the floor of our room, that we had the impression all night of a visitation by a ghost.

Every fifty yards along the street barrels filled with stones had been laid down with ladders stretched across them to form piers on which the inhabitants waited for a service of row-boats to take them to work. A wine merchant, having sawn two vats in half, took three of these to build himself a triangular craft. Sitting in the middle one, navigating with a home-made paddle, he had filled the half-vat on his right with beer and wine bottles, and the one on his left with coal. Thus equipped, he cried: 'Beer, wine, and coal for sale!' My parents were in great fear the water would come in through the window or that our cask would end by bumping away our floor. Émile had begun by letting down a pail at the end of a string to fetch up enough water for my mother to wash my brother's nappies, but it was so muddy that he was obliged to abandon this expedient and take a jug to the top of the street, a journey which necessitated waiting for the row-boat. Matilda, who was still breast-feeding my little brother, did not sleep at night, fearing our house would collapse as many others in the neighbourhood did. Follette disappeared and Émile never found out whether she had come across her original master, run off with another dog, or been drowned. My mother did not hide her relief, and Follette herself, I think, had understood in the end that it is not enough to be loved only by the master of the house. The doorkeepers, from their lodge, had also taken unkindly to Follette because she spoilt with muddy paws their parquet stairs. They had even threatened to complain to the landlords—two children and a dog made any tenants undesirable.

Still the Seine rose; sewer rats swam along the streets. People started to talk about a plague. A house not far from ours caught fire and firemen arrived in a punt, their shining hats reflected in the muddy water.

Then, as happened to Noah, the water suddenly fell. Émile found his cask of wine dented but in tolerable condition. His potatoes had become mixed up with his coal, and the subsiding waters had left three dead rats on the infamous heap. Our neighbours turned their attention to the coming carnival. Re-opened shops decorated their windows with masks, false noses, and confetti. A new picture is now printed on my mind—the queen of the carnival on a throne surrounded by her princesses. A monkey dressed as a zouave played tricks at the end of a string. The brass bands made me cry with soldier-loving emotion. Clowns rode on elephants. Thousands of people threw confetti.

That summer little girls, older than I, played diabolo in the street; others spun coloured tops under the very wheels of the drays and horse-cabs. The cry of the creamy cheese vendor came, through the open window, into our stifling room. Her earthenware jar full of fresh cream was wrapped up in a damp napkin of the purest linen, and when, at the request of a customer, she ladled the cream on a heart-shaped cheese, the whiteness of the cream contrasted with the whiteness of the cheese, the whole handed for freshness on a leaf in an osier heart. My mother, putting a few halfpence in one tiny hand and a salad bowl in the other, sent me with much trepidation to buy two for her lunch and mine. Soon I accompanied her to the baker, often hiding in the cages in which the long French loaves were placed. I remember the bakeress pulling me out, giving me a kiss on my forehead, and placing in my hand a *croissant* still warm from the oven.

My first remembered sight of Marie-Thérèse was on a Sunday morning in this tiny apartment which was much too small for us. My aunt wore a hat which, for a while, occupied all my attention, so marvellous and extraordinary were the size and design. Having examined it at fascinating length, I looked with no less wonder at the gentleman who had come up with her and who, exceptionally for those days, wore no moustache. Marie-Thérèse kissed my mother and me, took my baby brother in her arms, shaking him good-naturedly, and smiled affectionately at the clean-shaven gentleman who ran downstairs, returning a few moments later with a bottle of sparkling Saumur wine and some finger biscuits, which collation made everybody even merrier than before. Émile, under the influence of the health-giving wine, took strongly to the purveyor of it whilst Marie-Thérèse won me over by the gift of a doll dressed in a white cambric chemise and a hat as ornamental and enormous as her own. Moreover, with the doll, she had brought me some pieces of soft, differently coloured materials, some Italian straw, and some hat veiling, all of which being a delightful change from my mother's lace which hitherto had been my only means of amusement, filled me with such surprise and gratitude that I exclaimed piercingly: 'Oh, thank you, madame!'

'But, silly girl,' cried Émile indulgently, 'the lady is your aunt.'

Marie-Thérèse had come to invite her sister to her wedding with the clean-shaven gentleman. She had at last become a modiste with a business of her own. The small parcel of Italian straw, soft materials, and veiling were the snippings from her masterpieces, and the magnificent hat she wore and which, on more mature reflection, looked like a piece of piping set on a nest of curly, brown hair, was her proudest creation. She had remained with Mme Pauline until one night, going off to dance at Magic City, she had fallen in love with Louis Soilly and he with her.

The stream of their love had, of course, been hindered by her

*B

secret.   Her airy inconsequence, her Berrichon accent which lent
a strange, perplexing colour to Parisian slang, her tiny head, not
pretty, but decorated irresistibly with fun and sparkling blue eyes,
had grown on him and he was all ready to declare his honourable
intentions when one Sunday, she, knowing that the moment her
secret was out their romance would end, decided not to meet
him at the usual place and hour.

Louis Soilly waited, became impatient, working himself up into
such a state that he promised to seek revenge in the arms of
another woman.   Gradually, however, fear assailed him that she
might be ill or have slipped on account of her high heels under a
hackney cab.   He passed a miserable night, paid no attention to
his work the next day, and in the evening, jealousy having once
more gained supremacy in his mind, went to wait for her outside
the establishment where she made her hats.   She came out pretty
and apparently unconcerned.   His fury exploded all of a piece.
She was unfaithful!   She had spent Sunday with another man!
Why couldn't she say something?   Her silence condemned her!
A slight colour rose to her cheeks.   She looked down awkwardly,
eyelashes quivering with emotion.   How could she say anything
whilst he continued to shout so angrily?   But she must try.   She
began timidly to explain that there was nobody else, that she had
thought of him all the time, but a moment later her gentle voice
was lost in the thunder of his accusations and she became aware
that people were turning round to look at them.   Impotent, her
cause lost, ashamed to be the centre of a crowd, anxious above
all to stem this inexhaustible flow of words, she said in real
despair:

'All right!   Have it your own way!   I shall tell you what I
was doing yesterday.   I was in the country with my baby girl!'

'Your baby girl?' he repeated unbelievingly.

'Yes,' she answered, taking advantage of his silence to raise
her voice.   'It's the truth!   I swear it!   Now, you can go!
I'm used to men dropping me.   I'm quite able to get along by
myself.'

There was a long silence whilst he tried to understand the full
meaning of her words, but his anger had quite subsided, and the
flow of people round them had resumed its normal course.   Then
he asked:

'When will you go to see her again?'

'Oh,' she replied, trying to mask her happiness with a show
of sarcasm, 'from now on I shall be free to go every Sunday.'

He was holding her arm. She pulled herself free and queried
as a last fling:

'I suppose it *is* finished between us?'

As she looked up her interrogating blue eyes drew him nearer,
and he answered boldly:

'No, it isn't. When you go to your baby again, I shall come
with you.'

The following Sunday they went together to see Rolande who
was growing sturdy in the care of Ermeline's mother. The
little girl, from a vague desire to please, set out to charm Louis
Soilly and succeeded. That evening, back in Paris after the long
train journey, Louis asked my aunt to marry him. He did more.
He promised that Rolande should never know he was not her
father. The first volume of my aunt's life was ending, as all good
novels should, with a wedding.

They were married within a week of their visit to us. Louis
Soilly was a sort of majordomo, or chief butler, to a fabulously
wealthy store-owner and wanted everything just right. He
quickly found himself a mews flat behind a magnificent block of
apartment houses in the aristocratic rue de Longchamps. The
mews were entirely inhabited by the servants of the wealthy who
appreciated the high-sounding address and who formed a society
of their own, taking the cool air on summer evenings under the
trees in the Bois de Boulogne. Almost immediately Marie-Thérèse
and her husband brought Rolande to Paris, and as there were only
eight months between us we were considered ideal companions.

Every alternate Sunday we lunched with the Soillys in the
rue de Longchamps where my uncle kept a fine table for his
friends, the men clean-shaven like himself, some of them tall,
blond, extremely good-looking like Raoul the footman, who,
during the week, in livery with gold buttons, wearing white
gloves, sat very erect beside the coachman, breaking the heart of
many a *midinette*. Raoul used to come with Hélène the doorkeeper's wife, with whom he was in love, and well he might be,
for she was dark with romantic eyes and an ochrous, unpolished
skin. The doorkeeper was an old man who had taken advantage
of her lack of money to make her his wife. He was as jealous
as a Spaniard, but his position of *concierge* was too important for

him to leave it long enough to follow his young wife who was clever, by long experience, and never went shopping or walking without her eight-year-old daughter, Françoise, whom she passed off as her sister. It was a curious thing to hear Françoise addressing her mother as Hélène. Her complicated existence, the double dealing, the transitory attachments, the lies, stratagems, and many pleasures had made of her an astute little person and she was admirably versed in the art of making capital out of her mother's duplicity. For all that one could not altogether blame the pretty young mother for making the best of her twenty-seven years. I remember her mostly in a long black skirt and a cherry-coloured blouse, the collar gracefully encircling her white, chubby neck. She sang delightfully all the tunes she picked up at the café concerts, ditties by Dranem full of allusions which made the women blush and the men puff out their cheeks and cough, and Françoise, who had a good memory, chimed in with the choruses, singing as gracefully as her mother, winking at the right moment, but probably not understanding much more than little Rolande and I.

At my uncle's also we made the acquaintance of Rose, poor fat Rose, not very young, but an excellent person who had been cook in the same house for so many years that everybody said she must have quite a little fortune. She owned a modest apartment which she went to on her days off or when her employers were travelling abroad, and nobody had quite understood why Rose, so industrious and economical, should have gone to this expense, till it became known that she had a lover. Rose the virtuous, Rose the far-from-pretty, had made the conquest of a very eligible young man. She was invited by my uncle to bring him along, and the next Sunday she arrived behind a large bunch of lilac and introduced Frederick who bowed to Marie-Thérèse and kissed her hand like a lady.

Rose was delighted to discover what a good impression Frederick had made on the company. He was gentle, knew a great many languages, and seemed not at all of our world. At Christmas he brought the most expensive toys for Rolande and me. I had a magnificent doll and a pure china tea service. Afterwards he took us all to visit the Eiffel Tower.

We now moved into another part of Clichy, a three-storeyed house of dull grey aspect but facing a large garden which, at this

moment of spring, was filled with lilac. Émile was taken by the
smaller rent, the larger rooms, the possibility of storing firewood
in the garden, and the idea of sitting out to smoke his pipe in the
evening among the grass and trees, our apartment being on the
ground floor. In the autumn the dampness of the house became
alarmingly apparent, the wall-paper peeling off in our bedroom.

The lilac in the garden had momentarily hidden other aspects
besides the greyness of the house. The rue Kloch, so called
after a revolutionary in the Commune, paved with large, uneven
stones, made grim by houses in which animals would have been
less resistant than man, was the *repaire* of rag-and-bone men,
ambulating fruit vendors who kept their barrows in the narrow
passages of their houses, and other strange people. Mme
Choblais, the owner of our house, kept ducks which dabbled about
in the pestiferous water of the gutters and followed me, quacking
loudly, when I went to the fountain to fill my pitcher. Their
eagerness to refresh themselves was such that they gathered round
me and bit my bare legs with their flat bills.

Mme Choblais was a fine-looking woman with that throaty,
warm, vicious voice typical of the apache world which grew,
like a dangerous moss, round the Paris fortifications, and indeed
her husband was so wiry and muscled, with such an air about him,
that we all called him in secret the apache. He used to disappear for weeks. On his return Mme Choblais and her children
would display themselves in the market-place, she in a red or
apple-green blouse with long earrings and a necklace of coloured
glass, the children in frilly aprons, and whilst these acquisitions
were still new nobody would do any work, and the apartment
would remain unswept and the beds unmade. The husband
lorded it, recounting his adventures but, strong drinker of
absinthe, he would suddenly turn white and with the violence of
a man in a strait jacket would set upon his family. The
children, in tears, ran to their grandfather who, arming himself
with a cudgel would hide behind the door, waiting for his son-
in-law, determined to break his skull before he reached the
children, and the apache, as afraid of the old man's club as the
old man was afraid of him, spent his energy against his wife,
catching her by the hair, tearing the earrings away from her
bleeding ears and the satin blouse from her bosom, and finally,
when his anger was spent and the vapours diminished in his

brain, hurling her like a bundle of dirty linen into a corner.
Then, tired and satisfied, he would go to bed, or rather throw
himself upon it, fully dressed, and sleep heavily for five or six
hours. Soon after our arrival the grandfather died and the
apache arrived from a long absence for his funeral. All the
son-in-law's companions gathered in the room to wake the corpse,
and when the lid of the coffin had been nailed on they brought
absinthe and used the lid of the coffin as the zinc bar of a café,
placing their glasses on it. The more honest people in the house
were shocked but were too afraid to do anything. My mother,
aware that Émile was the only one not to fear the devil, was in
a great state lest he should seek out the apache who would have
met his fists with a concealed knife and possibly murdered him,
but nothing happened, and when the funeral was over Mme
Choblais and her children paraded in the market-place in
mourning clothes.

As I was five my mother decided I should go to school. There
was a stone and wood building at the end of our road on which
she had read: 'Protestant School for Girls, Infants' School, School
for Boys.' On 1st October my mother, having plaited my long
hair, led me by the hand to the infants' school. I was crying and
she also was near to it. A large woman came to speak to my
mother, put an arm round my waist, and led me to a schoolroom
with a pine-board floor in the middle of which there was a black
stove surrounded by a tall railing. The mistress began by
teaching us a prayer, but I had no comprehension of the sense,
never having heard until then the name of Jesus. We were then
taught how to sing a hymn. I continued to sob quietly. A
young woman came to inquire why I was unhappy. I answered
that I was not unhappy but I was alone. 'Alone?' she queried.
'But what about all these other children?' At midday I handed
the penny my mother had given me to the mistress for lunch.
We had soup and rice pudding. Afterwards we played in the
courtyard till four.

When I came home I made straight for my toys, having the
idea that during my short absence everything would have changed,
all that I cared for would have disappeared. My treasures
appeared at first much as I had left them but when, running to my
doll's bed, I discovered that in the place of my doll my small
brother had deposited his white rabbit with the red eyes, I

imagined myself dispossessed and became so angry and injurious
that my mother, having noticed nothing unusual, was wide-eyed.
I explained as clearly as possible, because of the tears running down
to my lips, what had happened, and she took my side, scolding
my brother; but this in turn so affected me that I put his rabbit
back in my doll's bed though insisting that the doll should lie
with it.

I had little time to accustom myself to the infants' school. I
learnt by heart the hymn beginning:

> Gentle Jesus, meek and mild,
> Look upon a little child.

Matilda sang it while she sewed. My baby brother also learnt to
lisp it. I was on the point of being taught the Christmas hymns
when I was taken with a sore throat, and then a headache and
a fever. Émile went in the middle of the night to fetch a four-
wheeler beyond the gate in the fortifications, and when I had
been wrapped up in a blanket I was taken to the Hérald Hospital
suffering from diphtheria.

For several days I was in danger. I used to see the whiteness
of my mother's face through the glass partition, her eyes red with
crying, her brave but unconvincing smile. Émile also had a
whiteness about his skin, and his long moustaches could not keep
still. He was made to put on a surgeon's white coat and this
new manner of dressing intrigued me. My small brother on
these visits was left in the care of the hospital porter. After a
few moments my parents blew me a last kiss and departed, leaving
some small gifts which a nurse would later bring and put on my
bed, and the fun of opening these things repressed the tears
which usually started to well up at the sight of their emotion and
sad going away.

I was later moved to a room which faced the kitchens, and as
I was better and consequently thought only of food I had the
satisfaction of watching the cooks, dressed in blue blouses,
stacking the red copper cauldrons full of hot soup on the trolleys
for distribution in the wards. Our meals were arranged in this
way. Our usual nurse would place an empty plate in front of
each patient. One of the blue-coated cooks would then put into
it a full ladle of raw horse-flesh, minced fine, upon which a second
cook would pour the soup. There were mashed potatoes also
which, if I remember accurately, came later as a separate course.

On what was to be my last night in hospital I was unable to sleep, and in my restlessness listened for the first time to the noise of the street, the rumbling carts, and the tired tread of the cab horses. When, next morning, my mother arrived with my clothes the ward sister told her that I had scarlet fever. She came to see me the next day but I was far too ill to recognize her. Later she came on Thursday alone, and on Sundays with Émile. In due course I was again ready to leave hospital but so enfeebled by these two serious illnesses that the doctors were for sending me to a convalescent home in the country, being of the opinion that lack of proper care at this stage might permanently affect me; but my parents wanted their daughter back at home immediately, and so, wan and much taller, I returned to Clichy.

The Sunday after my return, Marie-Thérèse, her husband, and Rolande came to lunch and I was much petted. Life appeared to me new and wonderful, and during the ensuing week my mother, laying aside her blouses, occasionally took us for a walk which she had never done up to now. Another Sunday had not passed, however, before my small brother, feeling listless and not inclined to play, became at the approach of night feverish, and my parents, leaving me asleep in bed, hurried him to the Bretonneau Hospital where they learned that the serum he had been given at the time of my first illness not having taken, he now had diphtheria with complications.

There followed a series of pitiful visits to see him behind his glass partition. Meningitis set in and the ward sister exclaimed to my mother: 'Ah, madame, he is very young for two such serious illnesses!' But soon pneumonia arrived also. When, after this, my mother came back from seeing him, she said tearfully that his forehead was full of bleeding wounds from throwing his poor head against the iron bars of the cot.

We were in December. My mother's birthday was on the twelfth and with her still beautiful waist and magnificent red hair she was only twenty-six. That morning she hurried up the stairs of the hospital, anxious, hoping. A hand was placed gently on her arm and she was led to a bare room where her son lay dead on a marble slab. He had died in the night far from her.

My grandmother from Blois came for the funeral, and as my little brother had died at the Bretonneau he was buried in the vast cemetery of St. Ouen.

My mother's resignation had been strained beyond her capacity to bear, and when she left the service her revolt was immense. Her suffering was so acute that it is a wonder she did not die. I became a silent witness of it when for entire afternoons she would howl with pain, like a she-wolf barking, or again, her head in her hands, her whole frail body would shake with heaving sobs. Every day we found something fresh to increase her misery. My brother's grey cat, the stray he had befriended, miauling for him, not knowing he was dead. There were nails, stolen from Émile, he had clumsily but strongly hammered into chairs or furniture, pieces of clothing, tiny trousers whose pockets revealed pebbles and bits of string, a purse with a halfpenny in it, and, of course, worst of all, the rabbit with the red eyes.

My mother burned the rabbit but devoutly put away the sailor's cap with the red tuft which he had so often worn. How dreadful for the little girl who remained, who neither dared to cry nor to play but was obliged to look on silently at all this early sorrow. Things became less strained when Émile arrived. There was supper. People spoke. Émile worked too hard, did not have the time to be so occupied with the one thought, and yet he felt it cruelly. The tears women shed appear natural. Those of a man are too terrible to be renewed. Émile did not cry after the funeral but he grew old. My mother would have ended by killing herself if it had not been for me. My parents could not have brought me back after my illness to a more destructive atmosphere, and I now began to show signs of the grievous deterioration in health which the doctors at Hérald had feared, so that my mother was torn from her grief to combat the violent fevers which took hold of me after the slightest cold.

Every Thursday afternoon my mother took me to the Boulevard Haussmann to deliver her blouses to Mme Gaillard who was also very unhappy; for though her business continued to go well and her husband was in the Auvergne, her eldest son was in the worst stage of tuberculosis and she could not even say to herself: 'It will all be for him.' The cruel doorkeeper had just lost his wife and sat sadly on his low chair not daring to go into the lodge, and Mme Gaillard, touched by pity, had taken the habit of putting out her stock a little earlier each morning to have time to tidy up his lodge and put a stew on the fire. He saw his wife everywhere. Seated on his chair, a rug round his thin legs, he looked like a cab driver who had mislaid his horses. Anxious not to lose his situation of *concierge*, he would get up after the postman had brought the letters and he had examined them all carefully back and front, to deliver them to his various tenants.

For me the Boulevard Haussmann was an enchantment. The Magasin du Printemps gave away coloured balloons and similar toys to the children of their customers every Thursday afternoon. It was for this reason, I think, that my mother chose this particular day to deliver her work to Mme Gaillard and she was able to qualify as a customer by buying at this magnificent store the many yards of fine net which she needed to line her blouses as well as the mother-of-pearl buttons with which to finish them.

The following Thursday we were informed by our friend the porter that Mme Gaillard had gone to bury her husband in the Auvergne. The next Thursday she was not yet back, and as my mother had finished all the work in hand she decided to take advantage of this lull in her sewing to wash a great many things, and on the Saturday night, having tied up all the dirty linen in the largest bedsheet, we went together, for by now I accompanied her everywhere, to the famous public wash-house in the Boulevard Victor-Hugo.

A number was attached to the bundle, its counterpart being given to the owner, and the attendant, armed like a halberdier with a tall pole, then threw the bundle into the centre of an immense copper in which the linen bubbled and boiled. The next day the bundle, plainly numbered, would be found on an iron trolley, and then my mother would take her place in the long line of kneeling women who, their sleeves rolled up, their bodies moving rhythmically, scrubbed and soaked in the limpid water.

I loved this wash-house because we walked on planks under which the water lapped and gurgled. Women of all worlds came here, from the most vulgar to the most respectable, who quickly struck up wash-house acquaintanceship. Waiters from the neighbouring cafés moved deftly amongst us selling buttered rolls, *croissants*, hot coffee, and glasses of rum, but those who did the briskest business were the fortune-tellers who interpreted the future in the lines of wet palms that smelt agreeably of soap and disinfectant. These fortune-tellers were never for a moment idle. Even those women who pretended not to believe in them soon gave way. One would see them getting up from the water with loud laughs or nervous tittering, wiping their hands on their rough aprons before going over to the gipsies, and then believing everything they were told. There were other ambulating vendors who passed through this picturesque crowd giving the place the colour and movement of an Eastern bazaar, dark-skinned men who sold scrubbing brushes, iron handles, beeswax, and even toilet soap and cheap perfumes. When the linen was rinsed one would make up the clean bundle, pushing it on the iron trolley to the drying-machine, where for a penny one could get rid of the water, or at least a good deal of it, which made the bundle much lighter to carry home. Later when the linen was hung up in our yard I would love to run between the sheets, playing at being the little girl lost or pursued in an imaginary city of white towers.

My mother had met in the wash-house an Italian woman called Francesca who invited my mother to call on her the next day. Still young and extremely pretty, Francesca lodged with her jealous husband and her three children over a courtyard near the Boulevard Victor-Hugo where, from morning till night, she made pleated skirts. She was so quick and clever that money came easily. Her husband, Julio, Italian also, was a roadmaker which at that time, at any rate in France, was a highly skilled and excellently paid profession. Francesca and Julio had come separately from Italy, he to work on the roads, she as a waitress. They had met and married in Paris, and with their joint economies had bought a little café-bar in Montmartre where they would have prospered had it not been for Julio's fits of dark jealousy which made him accuse her of being light-hearted with the customers. For long she endured these melancholy quarrels, but at last, driven almost mad herself, she left him, pregnant of her second child. He, distraught with love, finding her again after days and nights of searching, successfully obtained her pardon for the abominable scenes he had made, but as he could not stand the thought of her returning behind the café-bar, and of being racked himself by doubts and sufferings, he obliged her to sell their business at a low price and look for accommodation elsewhere. Another child was born and poverty came in at the door. Francesca started to do a little housework for the neighbours, but as soon as a place suited her Julio imagined some fresh lover, and at night the walls of their lodging shook with his threats. She accordingly decided that only a cloistered life could save her from this persecution. Thus, young and pretty, surrounded by her children, she pedalled all day on her sewing-machine without ever an opportunity to see a new face or to exchange an intelligent thought. She gave my mother a few lessons in skirt-making, and henceforth we went to her lodging every afternoon, my mother to sew on hooks, to stop seams, and verify the work before it was delivered, and I, at last, to play with the two little girls, Maria and Francine, of my own age. The third child, a boy, was still in his cot.

One evening Julio brought home with him a young paviour newly arrived from Italy and who could not yet speak any French. The next day Julio introduced him to the foreman of his gang who gave him a week's wages in advance so that he could find a room in one of those many small hotels which at that time abounded at Clichy. Giovanni loved children, and was delighted, having left his brothers and sisters in Piedmont, to renew the calm satisfaction of family life by frequenting Julio's crowded lodging. A few days later, Julio coming home earlier than usual, saw Giovanni's good-looking features bent over the lips of his wife. He closed the door quietly and said nothing, but henceforth there was such an ugly look about him that Francesca had no more peace. The next evening Julio, returning home drunk, threatened her with a revolver. That night, as soon as he was asleep, she made a parcel of her things and, leaving husband and children, went to a cheap hotel, hired a sewing-machine, and continued to make her pleated skirts.

We had been warned by Francesca of these happenings in a letter, and my mother and I went to the new address where we found Francesca entirely occupied with her romance, Giovanni having followed her. She showed no sorrow at being parted from her children, but mightily afraid that her husband might discover her whereabouts, for which reason she never left her room, persuading my mother to deliver her skirts to the wholesaler. We even bought her thread and the daily provisions.

One morning when we had arrived very early at Francesca's, my mother, having given me a hot *croissant* she had bought on the way at the baker's for my breakfast, left me alone with her friend whilst she went off to collect a new bundle of skirts. I remember looking up from the enjoyment of my warm pastry to see Francesca, who had a long, sharp knife in her hand apparently engaged in cutting a slice of bread, turn round on her heels, throw up her arms, and collapse on the floor, the knife clattering on the boards. I was terrified and remained helplessly pinned to my place. Francesca did not move and nor could I. At last the door opened and my mother arrived. I threw myself into her arms, sobbing. My mother, who on such occasions kept admirably calm, gently lifted up Francesca who lay in a pool of blood, and arranged for her to be taken in a cab to the Beaujon Hospital. As her condition was extremely serious, Julio was sent for. He tore to her bedside, again asking forgiveness of this too young wife who had nearly died of a miscarriage.

She returned in a very weak state to her husband and children in their lodging near the boulevard and resumed her occupations as if nothing unusual had happened; and as Mme Gaillard was now back at her stand in the Boulevard Haussmann, my mother was glad to exchange skirt-making for the creation of her lovely blouses. We continued on Saturdays to see Francesca at the wash-house. Her accident had aged her and she was beginning to lose her beauty. One day Julio said to her: 'I 've put some money aside. What do you think? Shall we take another café-bar?'

'Not with a jealous fellow like you. It wouldn't be possible!' she answered.

Julio looked through her with the sharpness of a dagger and answered: 'See yourself as I see you, Francesca. I 've no longer any need to be jealous!'

6

THERE was a little old woman from the Auvergne who brought Mme Gaillard the lace she made on a spindle. This Mme Valentin would attend the various markets round Paris, selling exclusively the laces of her native province, and it was during her idle moments, sitting by her wares, that she made the lace she sold Mme Gaillard.

More in width than in height, toothless, and wearing a black woollen shawl over her sparse grey hair, she had been introduced to my mother by Mme Gaillard thus: 'Mme Valentin also lives at Clichy. You ought to go to see her. She has all the lace you need to make your blouses, and if you had known each other when I was in the Auvergne burying my husband you could have gone on working, and I shouldn't be without a blouse in my box. It's a wonder my customers haven't gone somewhere else.'

These last two words were accompanied by a dramatic pointing to the opposite side of the street and a mysterious drop in the voice, alluding to the resplendant Ville du Puy, the prettiest lace shop in Paris which Mme Gaillard liked to consider her only rival.

Giving up our usual visit to the store where I was given a coloured balloon, we went back to Clichy with Mme Valentin, who said to my mother as we neared home: 'Suppose you come to my place a moment? I would show you my lace, and you would know where I live, and sometimes you could take my work to Mme Gaillard, for I'm getting old and tired.'

We followed Mme Valentin, delighted to find she was leading us so much in our own direction, but this was only part of our surprise, for soon she entered the garden where our lilac grew, and we discovered she lived only one house away from ours.

She had an immense bed with red curtains which came from the Auvergne and in which she had had thirteen children! On the table, covered with a red carpet, was a great quantity of lace in the various stages of its making, reels of cotton, spindles, and pins with different coloured heads as well as a sheaf of designs on pink cardboard. Quite a number of different laces were begun, emerging from the 'cushions,' and she explained that she would change from one to the other, according to the urgency of the order, with the same ease; but never did she waste her time, and I noticed that she never looked at the work she was doing except, occasionally, when she altered the arrangement of the pins, and in this way there came out from between her delicate fingers, browned, veined, and bent with age, yards upon yards of snow-white lace of pure design.

She was Mme Gaillard's most treasured lacemaker and, quite unable to read or write, had apparently been born with the gift of lacemaking in her fingers, exercising them, making them nimble, whilst she watched the geese or the sheep in her native Auvergne, and looking at me with her kind, tired eyes, she said: 'Little girl, when I was your age, I had already made enough purl to go all round my village!' This purl being the first and easiest lace one is given to do. Then turning to Mme Gaillard's shop and our introduction, she continued: 'I am very glad that you live so near to me. I had already noticed you, Mme Gal, on Thursday afternoons in the Boulevard Haussmann. Your beautiful hair and the little girl made me want to know you. I must teach Madeleine to use her fingers.'

Of the thirteen children Mme Valentin had in the red-curtained bed only four survived, three married daughters and a son. Her daughter Augustine, dark-haired, lazy, often drunk, was married to a paviour and lived in the house opposite our own from which she seldom emerged, the effort of going down the stairs being too much for her. The children slept, dressed, ate, went to school, and came back from it by a series of miracles as if they belonged to nobody. They played in the street and were supremely happy.

Léa, the second daughter, lived with her children in a shack built by her husband on a piece of waste ground. This house, shaped like a mushroom, had a tall chimney surmounted by what looked like a mandarin's hat. The children were as happy as the day was long, having a large field to play in, no neighbours, and no *concierge* to worry them. The parents worked hard and were fond of each other. I used to discover Léa, a towel round her head like a turban, sorting out rags thrown away by the textile factories. She arranged these marvels in separate piles—cotton, silk, and wool for her husband to pack tightly into box-shaped bundles and deliver to the papermakers at Levallois. We would go with him, he so gentle and kind, harnessed to his hand-cart like a scraggy horse, we either in it or trotting beside him.

Léa knew that I loved bits of silk and satin, and put aside for me the prettiest and brightest which I excitedly took home to turn into dresses and hats for my dolls. Her eldest daughter helped us as soon as she came home from school and was already very clever at knowing the different materials at a touch.

Mme Valentin's third daughter, Léontine, was married to a terrible drunkard she simply adored. Her lovely eyes were sunk in a face studded with deep smallpox holes. My mother, recognizing her goodness and courage, admired her, and Léontine tried to comfort her, pointing out that there is always somebody more miserable than oneself.

Every other Sunday we lunched with Marie-Thérèse and her husband at their flat in the rue de Longchamps. The guests were the same, and if the conversation was apt to become more political as the weeks passed it invariably ended on dresses, hats, veils, and love. Hélène, still wholly attached to Raoul, told us with satisfaction that her husband, the doorkeeper, growing older, was becoming more reasonable, his jealousy taking on a less violent character, and he even granted her a little liberty, with the result that she was just now making the most delightful plans to go to Algiers, in appearance to visit her sister Germaine, but actually, of course, to take a sea trip with Raoul who, if he took a liking to the North African coast, could stay there for ever with his adoring mistress.

As the winter had been disastrous to my health, and because Marie-Thérèse was anxious also for her daughter Rolande to have a change of air, though she never had a cold and grew like a young oak, she suggested to my parents that she should take us both to Marais to stay with Ermeline's mother, Mme Brossier, who had looked after Rolande during that critical moment in her babyhood. She extended a similar invitation to Françoise, Hélène's astute eight-year-old daughter, who was no longer so necessary to her mother now that Hélène, less watched, could do without an alibi. Ermeline, having earned enough money in Paris to make of herself an attractive match, had returned to Marais, and we three little girls were promised the fun of attending her marriage to a young farm worker who hoped, before long, to have some land of his own.

When Rolande, Françoise, and I set off with my aunt in the train not one of us children, I think, had a very clear idea of what a wheatfield looked like. And what a golden field was the one facing Mme Brossier's house! And what magnificent country! To find myself that evening in a fairy-tale house was an enchantment. My two companions, however, were too clever and wide awake for my simplicity. Françoise especially terrified me by her cunning, whilst Rolande, admired by her parents who applauded all she did, had developed an assurance that disconcerted me and obliged me in everything to acknowledge her supremacy.

My only ally was Yvonne, the bashful little thing from the poorlaw administration, but though we spent many hours trying to hide behind haystacks and in long grass to enjoy the peace of our own thoughts, our tormentors always found us and bent us to their will.

Soon the wedding preparations began. The guests arrived in gigs and traps, grandmothers all in black with white bonnets and fat blue umbrellas, the men in farm blouses. Two bakers from the village came to make a three days' provision of bread and buns, kneading the flour on trestled tables on the grass, and as the cottage was much too small to accommodate so many people, white linen sheets with red roses pinned to them were stretched against the walls of the barn, and the roof disappeared under garlands of sweet-smelling flowers. The long tables were never cleared, the meal continuing for the three days and nights, with intervals merely for dancing and sleep. There was the wedding procession led by the fiddler, we four little girls holding up the bride's train all along the powdery road, the men wearing white flowers in their buttonholes and white cockades in their black hats, the women wearing their loveliest lace bonnets. Then, after three days of eating and dancing, the guests went off in their traps and gigs. Ermeline and her husband, Laurent, became the owners of the cottage. Esther, Mme Brossier's deaf and crippled sister, went off each morning, wound up in her grey cape whose greyness seemed to reflect the colours of the sky, leaning on her stick, taking with her for pasture the goat, the turkeys, and the one cow Blanchette. When it was fine she made lingerie for the shops at Vierzon. When it rained she knitted long black stockings. Coming back to the cottage at night she put away her stick, and sitting in the huge fire-place merged with the blackness of the smoke-stained bricks. There, while we gathered round the large table, she would remain, her soup bowl on her knees, smacking her tongue as she drank, for being deaf she was unaware of the noise she made. She was goodness itself to us, but we, hiding in the hedges of the fields where she kept her animals, suddenly rushed out and surrounded her, obliging her to leave off what she was doing to follow us. She laughed toothlessly, exclaiming: 'Ah, ces pôques!' which meant: 'Ah, those little girls!' I was not very taken with this game, knowing how much it put her out, but I was obliged to follow suit.

On Sundays we went to mass at Menneton, Mme Brossier sitting out in the market-place beforehand to sell her butter and goat's cheese. She would then buy some cotton and a packet of salt and we would go into the old church, closing ourselves up in a seat with a door, and looking forward to the moment when, after mass, the priest and the uniformed beadle would pass down the aisle with a platter of bread or cake, offered every Sunday by a different parishioner, and which, before passing it round cut up into little squares, the priest would bless. Then we would go home along the white road, passing fields of corn and wheat or clover.

One Sunday afternoon, just like this, we found Marie-Thérèse wafting for us, and as we were to go back to Paris the same evening she put a tub of hot water on a chair in front of the cottage door and washed our heads. At the sight of the soap and water and at the idea we might lose our fleas, Mme Brossier, Esther, and Ermeline gesticulated like three witches, crying out that we should become deaf, if not lose our health altogether, and while they implored us, making the sign of the cross, my little friend Yvonne sought refuge under Mme Brossier's skirts.

We dried our long hair, playing for the last time in the wheat-field, picking marguerites, cornflowers, and poppies which have remained my favourite flowers, reminding me of that sweet summer of 1913 when I became conscious, for the briefest moment, that there were other destinies than the sort of servitude my mother bowed down to with a mixture of bitterness and submission, never able to leave our miserable flat and the burning streets. Paris swallowed me up again. Almost immediately I caught an eruption on my gums. I could not eat but remained sobbing with pain. When I was cured my mother caught this strange disease and took to her bed for three days.

My father, having been invited to attend a banquet organized by his trade union, decided, because of my mother's indisposition, to take me. We set out very proudly, he in a grey alpaca suit and a straw hat, shaven close and wearing a tie, I in a white dress, white linen shoes, and an adorable hat of Italian straw, soft and full of graceful curves, and decorated with field flowers which splashed it with colour.

He held me by the hand. I buried mine in his. For a little girl to walk out with her father is an exquisite thing. She does not fear to tell him she is tired, or hungry, or thirsty, or even to suggest, when passing in front of a shop, that it is high time she had a hand-bag; he is sure to believe her. The little woman who sleeps in every little girl tries out her charm and persuasion first on her father. My mother would have been too well aware that I was almost bound, if she gave me a hand-bag, to lose it the first day in the underground; that so short a walk for me, who played in the streets all day, was insufficient to make me tired; and that hunger and thirst were sensations that had no business to be felt outside meal times and must, at all costs, be discouraged.

My mother was very quickly forgotten. The banquet was a fine sight with the long tables, the tricolour flags grouped together, four differently shaped glasses at the side of each plate, and what a magnificent thing it was to be seated next to my father, to see him happy, not haunted, expecting some withering remark, but at ease, expectant, greedy for the meal and the companionship of men who were friendly and sometimes admiring. Soon I heard him speaking in patois, warming up, emptying his glasses and mine. I took my pleasure silently, eating abundantly to make up for the days when, at home, there was not enough food or, if enough, the wrong kind for a little girl. I thought everything delicious. There were cakes and coffee, and a fat, flushed individual climbed on a platform and, having made a speech, began to call out the names of people who were to come up for medals and prizes.

After a time my father's name broke upon us stridently. I felt him start with surprise, look round a trifle lost, and then bend under the table in an effort to put on his shoes which he had thrown off at the height of the repast, not normally accustomed to having them on at meals. All the company took a lively interest in poor Émile's predicament, but he, laughing, and still unable to get his shoes on, took me by the hand, and in his socks led me brazenly to the platform while the company applauded and his special friends urged him on in patois. He was given a medal, though for what reason I am not clear, and I a savings book with a five-franc piece. When we were back at our places my father succeeded in putting on his shoes and we left the banquet. Half-way along the boulevard he bought a pair of linen shoes, tying his heavy ones by the laces and throwing them over a shoulder, and thus, his straw hat thrown well back on his forehead, he took me home in happy mood.

My mother who had had a haemorrhage during our absence was very pale. As in my case the illness was coming to an end most painfully. My father told her all about our exploits. She could see by his bright cheeks that he had drunk abundantly. He told her how much I had enjoyed myself. My mother answered acidly that whilst we had been having such a good time the people in the flat above had also had a banquet in honour of a baptism, and that, of course, nobody had given a thought to her, though she had been unable to eat a morsel all day!

7

ON the first floor of our house lived Marguerite Rosiers, her husband, Hyacinthe, and their little girl, Lucienne. My mother's friendship with Marguerite started by her watching this woman going off in the morning, a scarf round her hair and a black osier basket, presumably containing her lunch, under an arm. My mother wondered who she was and where she was going. Occasionally Marguerite would come back in the evening with Mme Maillard, her mother, but more often Mme Maillard would arrive first and, not having the key, would wait on the landing. After several occasions when my mother would have invited her in if she had dared, Mme Maillard knocked at our door and, introducing herself, asked to sit down till her daughter came home.

Mme Maillard had followed the picturesque profession of baker's delivery woman, or bread-carrier, as the French say, which was so cruelly hard that only the most miserable women in Paris would consent to such abasement. Curled up in a corner with my doll I liked to hear her say how she was up at four weighing the long loaves and placing them in the panniered carriage which she wheeled over the cobbled roads, pushing with all her might when she climbed towards Montmartre, retaining the vehicle against her flanks during the descent. The light, crisp French loaves were ranged like little soldiers standing up. One saw but their golden heads. The heavy loaves, especially the four-pounders, were stacked horizontally, and each had the little extra piece to make up the exact weight, attached to the top with a steel pin so that they looked like sleeping humpty-dumpties with top-hats.

Though the work was grossly underpaid, bread-carriers could take home what bread they needed for their own families, and often a few stale *croissants* if any were left unsold from the previous day. At the New Year their customers gave them sixpence or a piece of worn clothing.

The work finished at eleven after which most of the women did something else. A few made mattresses, others, like Mme Maillard, ironed for a laundry. Mme Maillard had been so much on her tired legs that she could no longer stand for more than a few minutes at a time. That is why she had knocked at our door.

My mother was delighted to have somebody to talk to, and Mme Maillard seemed happy to recount the details of her life. She had been a widow for a long time; indeed her daughter Marguerite was born just after her husband's death. My mother, who always liked to compare husbands, asked what hers had been like, and Mme Maillard answered that he had been a cruel and dissolute drunkard who went away every few months, came back to give her a thrashing, and then disappeared again.

One day whilst she was pregnant with Marguerite, but still working at the bread because she needed the money, she was told that her husband was in hospital. After finishing her rounds she went to see him. He was terribly ill and his mistress was there sitting on the edge of his bed. Maillard was furious to see his wife; the mistress insulted her. She left under a hail of language.

Her bosom heaving with indignation, she recounted the scene to her friends at the bakery. Mme Malgras, the owner, a person of strong will who kept both her business and her husband on a tight rein, exclaimed: 'My poor Adèle, do you know what I would do? I 'd throw a bottle of vitriol in his face.' The other women gave similar advice. They offered to procure pepper or vitriol according to her choice. In the end it was decided to give her a bag of finely ground pepper.

Mme Maillard again found her husband in the company of his mistress. The mistress laughed at Mme Maillard's pregnancy, asking who in the world might be the father. At this Mme Maillard took the pepper bag out of her pocket and threw the contents at the woman, who filled the hospital with her yells.

Mme Maillard did not wait for the consequences. She fled. Two days later her husband died. Marguerite was born a sickly child, having inherited her mother's tired blood and her father's unhealthiness. She grew up neither much stronger nor at all pretty, but she had a little money which, at the death of an uncle, a market gardener at Argentan, was divided equally between her and her sisters. Lucie, one of the sisters, married an officer in the regular army. Marguerite used her dowry to marry an extremely good-looking young man who worked at a hosier's. Beautifully dressed, he looked like a wax figure in his shop. Unknown to Marguerite he was violently in love with another woman, and she discovered too late that he had simply married her for her dowry. She inspired him with such physical repulsion that he never consummated the marriage. He fell ill, raved deliriously about the other woman, and died within two months from galloping consumption, leaving Marguerite a widow, a virgin, and modestly rich.

She lived alone in her tiny flat. She worked on weekdays, but on Sunday she dreamed behind the geranium pots on her window-sill.

She had no particular aspirations, just wanting to live for herself, selfishly. Meanwhile Mme Maillard had become the cashier at her bakery.

One Sunday, after Marguerite had washed her hair and was doing a little mending, feeling satisfied, gently wondering if her mother would come to see her that afternoon so that they could go for a little walk to see the new buildings being erected along the Seine, as was their custom on Sunday afternoons, she looked up and saw a young man staring at her from the opposite window. She was annoyed because her long hair was streaming down her back and she had not put on her corset. The idea that she was being watched upset the contentment of doing just as she pleased in her little room behind the barrier of bright geraniums. The next Sunday he looked at her again and even smiled. Offended, she closed the windows, but an hour later, the room becoming too warm, she was obliged to reopen them.

For a few days her opposite neighbour, who was very shy, suffering from this window virtually banged in his face, did not dare show himself, but soon, in the evenings, she began to hear love songs scratched on a violin; and as he became braver his fiddling figure became discernible behind the curtains, and though she could not see his eyes she guessed they must be turned in her direction. Languid and romantic tunes now crossed the frontier of geraniums each time she came home and, in due

course, the doorkeeper who, like all doorkeepers, knew everything, began to let drop the nicest things about young M. Rosier
who was so serious and economical, and worked in a bank. Then
one day Marguerite met him on the stairs and they went for a
walk under the flowering chestnut-trees in the Avenue des Fêtes.
They were married and two years later Lucienne was born.

The many visits which Mme Maillard made us naturally led
to us being introduced to Marguerite who, in turn, confided a
good deal in my mother, saying with a wry smile that she had
not been lucky in love, her first husband not wanting to have
anything to do with her, and Hyacinthe, her second, being so
awkward in this art that she often wondered if Lucienne's arrival
was not due to a miracle. After this confidence my mother and
she laughed, forgetting my silent presence.

Marguerite had had a milk-fever after the birth of her daughter.
Too run down to feed the baby, unable to get rid of her milk,
she was still the victim of severe bouts of neurasthenia which
quite changed her normally gentle disposition. She no longer
went out to work as she had done at the beginning when my
mother and I used to watch her setting forth in the morning
with a scarf round her hair and a basket under her arm, but we so
often began to hear little Lucienne crying in the flat, sometimes
for many hours, if not the whole day, that in the end my mother
decided to investigate. She found the door ajar, the baby
screaming in her cot, but otherwise nobody in the flat, and
thinking that Marguerite must have been called away suddenly,
my mother took little Lucienne in her arms and brought her to
our place.

Some days passed before we discovered what happened to
Marguerite when she so mysteriously disappeared, but as my
mother and she became closer friends the tragedy of her broken
health and hallucinations became our everyday preoccupation.

Marguerite, torn at intervals by cerebral anaemia, became mad
with fear at the sight or sound of horses. When through her
window she saw the brewery cart coming down our street, she was
convinced that it was not a brewery cart but a van from the mad-
house, and that jailers were arriving to lock her up. Her instinct
was immediately to hide, anywhere, in a cupboard, under the bed.
She must have been hidden in this way when my mother, hearing
the baby cry, had first entered her flat, but now having complete

confidence in us, she would, at the first sound of the brewery cart, rush down to deposit Lucienne in our care, and then throw herself into the most convenient hiding-place. A van drawn by four horses used to draw up on certain days outside the grocer's, and as long as it was there poor Marguerite, her teeth chattering, would not emerge from behind our curtains. The trouble was that the driver of this particular van had a habit, after discharging his merchandise, of going off to lunch, leaving the van where it stood, the horses enjoying their nosebags. One heard the hoofs beating against the cobble-stones, the bells on the harness ringing, the horses neighing quietly, friendly, familiar sounds which normally merged into the other noises of the street. Eventually the driver would come out of the café, climb into his high seat, take his whip, making it sing in the air, and urge off his horses. The heavy cart would shudder over the cobbles, shaking the houses, then gradually die away. Then our curtains would move, and Marguerite, serene again, quite normal, would exclaim with pitiful relief: 'They must have spent the best part of three hours looking for me, what do you say, Mme Gal?' After which, gathering up her baby, she would leave us to make her husband's supper.

My mother, wise and experienced, had much pity for her friend, and aware that Marguerite's attacks of madness might if talked about by the neighbours do her a great deal of harm, encouraged her always to come to us when she was afraid.

8

MY father had discovered, during the course of the banquet we had attended together, that his friends from the *midi* travelled regularly between Paris and the place of their birth on cheap railway tickets obtained for them by their member of parliament. This information came back to his mind when his sister, Mme Agnel, wrote saying that as my health appeared so poorly he should send me for at least part of the winter to their cottage at the Grand' Combe where I could regain my strength in the sunshine.

The Comte de Ramel, our deputy, having given us the necessary railway tickets, my father decided to take me there, and my mother, not without tears, packed my clothes in a basket together with my dolls, my bits of material, my scissors, blunt at the ends, my coloured silks, and some Italian straw which Marie-Thérèse brought me from her workshop.

We took the night train from the Gare de Lyon. My father and I each ate a hard-boiled egg after which he put his legs up and went to sleep. I remember nothing else about the journey except arriving at Nîmes where we took a slow train for the Grand' Combe.

Mme Agnel, or my Aunt Eugénie as I learnt to call her, and her husband, Ernest, had built their pretty house on the flank of a rocky cliff, and the road up to it was so precipitous that the roofs of the houses looked as if they had been made to fit into each other. At this hour of the morning when my father and I, hand in hand, climbed it together, all the women of the street were on their doorsteps, each holding a large bowl of black coffee, talking from door to door in the sonorous, golden patois of those parts. I had not thought it possible that an entire village could speak just like my father. I told him my surprise. He laughed, happy to understand everything the women said, and put out his chest with pride.

At the top of the road the last house was built crossways. Above that the mountain rose toweringly. What a house! A little gate, half hidden under a vine bower, led to it up ascending steps of garden in which tomatoes splashed their red, and grapes, ripe for picking, filled the warm air with their sweet perfume. One did not come immediately upon the house, new delights keeping one, at every fresh climb, in suspense. There was a sylvan antechamber, for instance, with russet tiles and walls of vine, walls that curved upwards to form a dome from which hung the fruit tantalizingly so that those who sat round the table on which, as we approached, a big cat was asleep, could raise their arms and pick their dessert warmed by the sun.

At this moment a rather portly woman appeared and at the sight of my father threw her arms up, exclaiming: 'Ah, my own Milou! It's you!' Then, smiling so happily that all her face seemed bathed in sunshine: 'How happy I am! And this is your *pitchounette*, your little girl! How pale she is, but real *poulide*!' (This word, I discovered later, means pretty in patois.) 'Take off your coat, my Milou. Make yourself comfortable and taste a glass of our wine. It's not too bad, I think. Ernestine! Ernestine! Your Uncle Milou is here! Come quickly and see him!'

A beautiful girl of eighteen, dark, and a real pleasure to look at, came out swinging her hips, and having kissed my father, looked at me unbelievingly because of my fair hair, remarking upon it rather sarcastically to her mother in patois which I easily understood, having picked up many of the words at home, and even more importantly, the intonation, so that I read clearly into her thoughts. As a peace offering, and to make up for the misfortune of being so blonde, I immediately opened my osier basket and produced the magnificent lace blouse which my mother, at great cost, had made for her niece, intending thus to repay at least part of their hospitality. The blouse was much admired but my aunt still had it in her hands, complimenting my mother on her skill, when the most curious sound, hollow and rhythmical, caused my father to look inquiringly in the direction of the house, upon which Ernestine remarked: 'Té! But that's only your Aunt Marie, the doddering thing, who claps her hands all day to keep warm. We don't take any more notice.'

'Aunt Marie!' exclaimed my father, rushing indoors.

He came out, holding the frail creature in his wiry arms, smothering her with kisses, she, thin, wrinkled like a dried fruit, clothed dismally in black. Last link for my father and Eugénie with their paternal family, she was being looked after by Eugénie in return for her fortune when she was dead.   Not that Aunt Marie had much money, doubtless not more than a few pieces of gold, but she owned four great cupboards, made of walnut and barded, filled with sweet-smelling linen which the old lady kept locked up, determined not to part with it until she had to.   She was taking a most unconscionable time leaving this earth, forgotten by death, unheeded by the family in whose house she had become merely a piece of creaking furniture.   Her food was taken to her, and she spent the day dragging herself backwards and forwards between her arm-chair and her close-stool; in the evening Eugénie came to help her undress and go to bed.

Now, hot and happy tears were rolling down her withered cheeks, and one would have said that his kisses were making her live again.   His immense tenderness in talking to her, his gentleness in putting her down, filled me with wonderment, and I looked at my father almost as if I had never seen him before.

Ernestine took me indoors to show me round the house and to take me up to her room which I was to share with her.   The transition from the arbour was so sudden that my eyes, blinded with strong light, could scarcely distinguish anything in the shuttered rooms and cool obscurity.   In Ernestine's room, for instance, I noticed little but the comfortable softness of the large bed.   Peeping into my Aunt Eugénie's the beds had curtains. My great surprise was the abundance of linen, of a quality I had never seen, which gave the rooms a cosy richness, an odoriferous well-being, like bees in a flower garden.   In this house were gathered all the treasures owned by the many victims of the mushroom feast.   Half the inheritance had been my father's who proudly abandoned his share, a fact which, when my mother was led to speak of it, choked her with indignation.

We lunched in the arbour, under the cool vine, on fried aubergines, an admirable dish of tomatoes, and beans which all the morning had simmered in earthenware pots over a charcoal fire and which were served to us in those same pots, blackened by the fire.   The meal was flavoured throughout by the olive oil in which the aubergines were fried, garlic, and pepper.   We picked the grapes from our verdant walls and drank hot black coffee. My aunt tried to make me conform to the usual siesta, but I was too excited, too anxious to push my inquiring nose along the narrow steps of this precipitous garden burning in an undimmed sun, and soon I came upon the kitchen garden and all its attendant wonders, lettuces, peas, tomatoes, rabbit hutches, a hen house, and a dovecot, all against a magnificent stone wall not built to protect this little kingdom from thieves but from the face of the mountain, lest it should crumble and carry away the house and garden. My Uncle Ernest kept the closest watch on this wall for a possible crack, for I learnt afterwards that it was his constant fear to find the mountain coming in through the drawing-room window. The vines fought to cover up the wall, for they were everywhere and the grapes so profuse that before I was there long I learnt to give succulent bunches to the rabbits and to the hens who enjoyed the pips. Beyond the wall the mountain towered omnipotent, studded with pines and tufts of heather which gave a special aroma to the honey. Occasionally some old woman, wearing a wide black straw hat, would climb up the mountain, her steps silent on the carpet of dead pine-needles. First one would merely see the cone of her hat and hear the sound of her mumbling voice. Then one would see her brown, veined hand, her stick, and the goat she was leading by a string and with whom she did not cease to converse.

At the other end of the garden there was a deep water tank let into the rock and covered with a slab of cement over which, when one walked, one's steps echoed deliciously. An old-fashioned pump with a creaking handle brought up the cool, clear water. Two pails filled with it hung in the sun to warm. My Aunt Eugénie, I discovered later, was convinced that the slab would give way under her weight and precipitate her into the echoing cavern, and it became my joy to watch her skirting round it like a large and cautious cat.

I played in this garden happily till past six when the gate opened and a little man, black from his cap to his boots, arrived, and at the sound of his steps on the gravel everybody in the house flew out to meet him. His teeth, sparklingly white, shone when he smiled. He shook hands with us all, threw his cap on the table, and sitting down in the arbour began to take his boots off. This was my Uncle Ernest. He proceeded to strip to the waist whilst his wife and daughter filled a tub with the two pails of warm water I had seen hanging out in the sun. He plunged his head and shoulders in the water, scrubbed himself energetically with a large cake of Marseilles soap, and finally emerged as clean as clean. His wife stood by holding a large towel in her hands. My uncle put his head a second time into the tub and bringing it out all running with water received the towel from my aunt. The tub was lifted from the two chairs on which it had reposed and placed gently on the ground. Then my uncle sat on one of the chairs and put his feet into the tub. Finally, having dried himself, slipped on a pair of white linen shoes and a clean shirt, and combed his hair, he kissed his wife, his daughter, and then me. The brothers-in-law now gave each other the accolade and went off, arm in arm, to the village to take an apéritif. My father was eager to meet the men he had known in the mine. My uncle and he came home rather late that evening, and rather gay. The next morning my father went back to Paris.

I was immensely happy in my new family, being accustomed to play by myself. My favourite corner was in the kitchen garden, beside the rabbit hutches, where the vines and beans climbed up the wall whose russet brick divided us from the mountain flank. Here, shaded from the fierce sun, I stayed for hours, my aunt respecting the laws of hospitality, never obliging me to do any-thing in the house, not requiring me to go to the village, the bread being delivered every morning.

The baker's man harnessed himself to a little cart full of warm, country loaves and made his passage known by blowing into an old hunting horn. When the notes became increasingly loud I would run down to meet him where the road came to an end. Besides bringing the bread, he disseminated the day's news in patois so that there was always a great crowd of women round his cart which, as the loaves diminished, he filled up with tomatoes, grapes, and lettuces. The first days he spoke to me in French, but soon, taking me under his protection, calling me 'Milou's little girl,' he addressed me in patois which by then I understood perfectly, though I had trouble in speaking it.

My beautiful cousin, Ernestine, was unbelievably spoilt. When my Aunt Eugénie came to wake us in the morning she would help her daughter to dress, putting on her stockings. Ernestine's great trial was not living in the heart of the little town where her loveliness could have shone with more effect. She was always reproaching her parents for building a house so far from everything. What made the house so lovable to the parents caused the despair of their daughter.

Lazy and complaining, always in the shade to keep her skin white, she did not know what to do. She had not learnt enough at school to work in the offices of the mine, and a young person of her importance could not, without loss of face, accept anything less important. The shops in the Grand' Combe were tiny and mostly in family hands. My Uncle Ernest had a sister who was married to the owner of a café in the main square, and every Sunday after lunch Ernestine hurried off to spend the afternoon with her cousin Irma; not that she had any affection for her, but the café was the meeting-place of all the beaux in town. The Agnels were disappointed at their daughter going off on her own and they would have liked to go with her, but to do that they would have been obliged to leave their cool arbour and their much-loved house, and on Sunday afternoons my Aunt Eugénie knitted and my Uncle Ernest enjoyed wearing his linen shoes and smoking his pipe.

The first Sunday I was there Aunt Eugénie, having kissed us both good morning, prepared her daughter for church. When we finally set out my cousin was wearing a white pleated skirt, the lace blouse I had brought her from my mother, and a hat that made me laugh so rudely that my cheeks were wet with tears. Marie-Thérèse had not wasted her creations on my childish intelligence. At least I knew what a hat should look like and that, to be pretty, it must be light, and be, in the main, of a sober colour, that the flowers or feathers with which it is decked may have their vividness heightened. It was not my Parisian taste that was at fault but my politeness, or, to be exact, the lack of it. One can merely, as a child, pick up the faults and qualities of the home, and my mother's life was too raw and bitter to breed the niceties of speech and behaviour. There was also, at that moment, within me a pent-up resentment about what my cousin had said concerning my blonde hair. At any rate a demoniac gaiety rocked me at the sight of this apple-green basin, topped by a gigantic bow of cherry-coloured taffeta which needed, to keep it at all straight, a dozen hatpins, some, in this case, being decorated with imitation pearls, others with the heads of animals in cut glass, that stuck out in all directions like the arms of a windmill. As we went solemnly down the steep road, women, drinking their black coffee on their doorsteps, bade us good morning and then gaped with admiration at Ernestine's coloured pyramid.

The hat I wore that Sunday did not prove any more acceptable to Ernestine than hers was pleasing to me. One of three that Marie-Thérèse had made specially for my journey of pale blue linen (the others were white and rose), there was nothing to make people look at it but the freshness of the linen and its tender colour which harmonized with the pearly texture of my blonde skin. In Ernestine's estimation a hat without trimmings was a sign of poverty. She knew we were poor. The satin, the ribbons, and the pins of her edifice represented cash in the bank and the undeniable proof that her family was one of the most important and looked up to in the Grand' Combe. If I was ashamed of her country bumpkin taste she resented what she considered an outward sign of my poverty.

We all arrived outside the church in rather irritable mood, Ernestine specially, pulled about in her Sunday clothes, her hair tightly tied under her hat, her fingers sticky in gloves, and her black leather bag with the silver clasp overfilled with an enormous handkerchief. In her other hand she held her prayer book and rosary. We stayed a few minutes talking outside the porch, Ernestine looking for her cousin Irma and other particular friends, and becoming, on their arrival, suddenly gayer, more smiling, discussing the hats of the other girls, turning slowly from one side to the other to let everybody admire hers. When the bell rang and we went in the young men of the town, wearing white trousers, white linen shoes, and holding straw hats in awkward fingers, adroitly manœuvred themselves into the right position where they could offer the holy water to their loved ones.

This was the third occasion on which Ernestine had received the holy water from the moistened fingers of Louis Verdier, a blond young man, pale, distinguished-looking, but rather lacking in colour amongst so many turbulent, gesticulating companions, speaking in the street in high tones, boiling over with vigorous enthusiasms.

Some of Ernestine's friends made fun of her ascetic young man, but in a kindly way, for he was rich and of a much considered family, and the other girls would have been delighted to become the object of his attentions. He was particularly bold on this Sunday morning and sat beside us. After the service, probably to court Ernestine in a roundabout way, he said the nicest things to me, and in such a calm, gentle voice that I was quite overcome.

We were to lunch with Irma's parents and Ernestine was smiling, for not only would she be spared the climb home up the mountain during the hottest part of the day, but she would spend an animated afternoon. On the way from the church to the café Ernestine and Irma walked in front. Louis Verdier, who had stayed a little behind with me, questioned me adroitly on our plans, and when he learnt that we were all to lunch in the town he showed his lover's joy by inviting us all to the pastry-cook's where the fashionable crowd would be gathered.

The café which belonged to Irma's parents was the prettiest in the town, having a long terrace, and tables of cool marble behind little trees and green tubs gay with geraniums. We went in by the large swing doors and at the far end of the room, by the leather *canapé* against the wall, two tables were laid end to end. The girls were put on the leather *canapé* which stuck to my bare legs. Aunt Jeanne was at one end of the table on a chair, her husband at the other end, ready to jump up at a moment's notice and look after a customer or to put some money in the till. The waiter lunched with us, his napkin over his shoulder. We ate very happily but discreetly, being obliged every time a customer of importance passed to say good morning even though our mouths were full.

When lunch was over Ernestine went up to Irma's room. They looked very fine as they walked away, Irma being no less tall and good-looking. Before they had made many steps they turned and invited me to join them which I did with alacrity. Irma had a young man who was doing his military service on the Riviera and who sent her magnificently coloured picture postcards of mimosa and blue skies which she stuck in an album. The two young women, after admiring these cards, tried on each other's hats, measured their waists, spoke of the novels they had read, and at three o'clock returned to the café which by now was full of people; some, the young ones, their sleeves rolled up, playing billiards, the older ones drinking cool glasses of beer as they watched the activity under the trees.

At a table, all alone, his straw hat placed carefully on the unoccupied chair, a bottle of lemonade untouched, Louis Verdier was waiting. I went over to sit with him and he gave me a cardboard doll to cut out, and this gift enchanted me, for I was not particularly spoilt by the Agnel family, and I was touched by this

*c

mark of kindliness. We talked merrily, I entirely absorbed, he merely waiting for Ernestine, but she, knowing that he was pining for her, laughed with the billiard players till, more interested in their play than in her, they turned their backs on her, leaving her unattended. Gracefully, and not showing her vexation, she went over to Irma who was washing glasses behind the counter, lifting them against the light to judge of their specklessness, and then plunging others under the tap and arranging them upside-down and still dripping on the counter so that the water ran off from them in rivulets. She made me a sign as I watched her, inviting me to come over and dry them with a fine linen cloth, and leaving Ernestine's unfortunate lover all alone I ran to the counter.

When evening came it was no longer possible to put off our return home where my uncle and aunt would be waiting for us, having hurried to their beloved arbour immediately after lunch. This was the moment Louis had been so patiently waiting for, and his eyes were moist with grateful tears as Ernestine slipped her arm in his to wend her way back. In her spare hand she carried her monumental hat wrapped up in a square of white linen, for at this hour all the women in the streets would be bareheaded.

Up the mountain path I ran behind or in front of them picking camomile flowers, there being no other flowers at this season, the earth being pitilessly burnt by the sun. We passed over a bridge under which flowed a river of tar which one could gather up and mould into pretty shapes, such as cups and saucers for my dolls, but they were sad to look at because of their blackness. After this we came upon a street in which there were a few shops. Louis gave me a halfpenny to buy a bag of toffee. Then, when we were in sight of our house, I heard Ernestine forbidding Louis to come any further, saying that she would not have all the women round about knowing she had a young man. They talked a little longer. On Thursday evening there was to be a cinematograph performance under the trees in front of Irma's café. Louis Verdier wanted us both to go with him, and Ernestine promised that if her parents were agreeable she would bring me to this same spot after supper where he could meet us as if by accident.

During the next few days Ernestine did little but sigh, and when her mother asked her if she were ill she answered: 'No, I'm just bored!' Then a moment later she would exclaim: 'I wish I were in Irma's shoes, living in the middle of the town!

She at least has a good time!' Poor Aunt Eugénie was terribly
upset, and not knowing how to take her daughter's mind off this
painful subject would say coaxingly: 'Come! A big girl like you
must not cry!'

'That's the point!' exclaimed Ernestine, flaring up. 'I am a
big girl, and look at the way you treat me. I never go out except
on Sundays, and that's only to go to church!'

On the Wednesday she refused to get up, saying there was
nothing to get up for. Nobody called except the postman, and the
young one had been replaced, whilst he did his military service,
by an old fellow who puffed in your face and smelled of garlic and
red wine. This time Aunt Eugénie was seriously alarmed. The
baker's man was at the gate, loudly blowing his hunting horn,
for Aunt Eugénie came down herself on Wednesdays to pay the
bill. We tore down the path together, she and I, and as soon
as he saw us he gave me, with a little pout, a sheaf of handbills
with all the details of the cinematograph performance, saying:
'There you are, Milou's little girl, you can make paper boats with
these, for nobody in this part of the town wants to bother about
such fantasies!'

The handbills smelled of fresh ink, and as we went back to the
house my aunt held the bread in one hand and a printed notice
in the other, reading aloud the headlines: 'Great cinematograph
performance to-morrow night, Thursday, in the open air.'
Suddenly she lifted her head and shouted excitedly in the direction
of our bedroom window: 'Ernestine! Ernestine! This is a real
coincidence! As you're so frightfully bored, how would you
like to go to the cinematograph to-morrow night?'

Slowly Ernestine put her pretty head out of the window and
answered, yawning: 'You know quite well that papa would never
let me go alone!'

Mme Agnel, willing to do anything to bring back a smile to
her daughter's face, said: 'We will ask your father this evening
while he is washing himself under the vine, and I'll prepare the
tomatoes for supper the way he likes them best so that he can't
help being in a good temper.'

Ernestine made no answer but decided that she would get up,
and when her mother had made her bed and tidied her room we
sat down to lunch: a salad, a piece of goat's cheese, and a bowl
of coffee. The long afternoon dragged on, implacably hot,

whilst Mme Agnel knitted, her ball of wool reposing in a long osier basket which had been Ernestine's cot, and in which many generations of the family were rocked when babies.

I loved the heat, the sound of my aunt's knitting-needles, and the monotonous singing of the cicadas. Putting my fingers through the treasures in the osier basket, I sought inspiration from the various coloured wools and pieces of material for the fine dresses I would wear when I was grown up and married. I thought I would also have a cherry-coloured blouse like the one Hélène wore at my uncle's place in the rue de Longchamps, so very becoming with a black skirt. I thought of something languid and frilly, in pale blue, to wear in the morning when I got up, with vaporous flounces and a train of aerial lightness. Ernestine chose apple greens, pinks, and yellowish golds, but her imagination, less capable of high flights, could not picture the dresses of her future wardrobe cut and sewn. Mine were clear to me to the last fold and hook. They rustled as I walked, and in numbers would have exceeded those of Sarah Bernhardt. The design of my hats I left to Rolande who was already acquiring her mother's cleverness in this direction. My occupation was so engrossing in the cool of the vine arbour that I even forgot the existence of my dolls, a serious omission, proving that I was unconsciously neglecting my maternal responsibilities to become a vain and flippant woman.

Ernestine began to yawn. Her new attack of boredom momentarily checked my contentment, but I was soon off again on another line of thought. I would open a store full of electric globes and soft materials, having a gilt lift and coloured balloons like the Galeries Lafayette, and it would be fun to see Ernestine's face when I showed it to her, for she had never seen anything of this sort in her small-town life. She shrugged her shoulders when I told her of my plan and said to her mother grumpily: 'This child never seems to languish as I do. She's for ever inventing things.'

When my Uncle Ernest arrived back from the mine we welcomed him with an even greater show of affection than normally. There was quite a scuffle to bring his slippers. Ernestine held up the towel while her mother ran off to see how her baked tomatoes were progressing in the oven. The smell was delicious. They must be cooked to perfection. The poor man was delighted but a tiny bit anxious. He was suspicious. We could all see that. Ernestine was beautiful, but nobody had taught her how to be gracious, and when she tried to please there was something unnatural in her behaviour. At any rate, when my uncle was clean and had been kissed by us all in turn, he sniffed the tomatoes and smiled as he walked towards the supper table. There was the tenderest expression on his face. Nevertheless, my Aunt Eugénie was nervously fussing about and talking about a dozen different things, mixing them all up together. She was not exactly afraid of her husband but she knew that when he said 'No' it was impossible to make him change his mind. He was calm but obstinate. My Aunt Eugénie was rather ostentatiously preparing something on a tray to take up to poor Aunt Marie who had already been put to bed, when she began:

'Ernest, my love, did you pass by the main square on your way from the mine?'

He looked up at her inquiringly. 'Why, yes,' he answered. 'What makes you ask?'

The tray shook a little in her hands. She continued:

'You didn't see anything extraordinary?'

'Perhaps I didn't look very carefully. Has somebody opened a new shop?'

'Oh, no, not that.'

'Well,' he answered, 'I give it up. Everything appeared as usual.'

Ernestine's cheeks had become the colour of her mother's tomatoes. My Aunt Eugénie broke out, all in a breath, desperately:

'It's that our little Ernestine would like us to take her to the cinematograph show under the chestnut-trees to-morrow night!'

The words had flown out of her mouth. We all looked anxiously at Uncle Ernest. My aunt, a little bolder now that the elements had not come down from heaven to strike her dead, went on:

'Of course, we would come straight home and you would not be in bed too late.'

My uncle turned the matter over in his mind, and then pouring himself out a glass of wine, said slowly:

'I could never do it. I'm far too tired after a day in the mine. Take the girl yourself. I'll be happy enough by myself, for once.'

My aunt, who had not the slightest desire to go to the cinema, exclaimed, looking at me: 'Why, when I come to think of it, my little *pitchounette*, how would you like to go?'

I became, with this, the centre of their conversation. Everybody, mindful of the laws of hospitality, politely offered to take me, but Ernestine's voice at last dominated the others with these words: 'I really do think I am old enough to take a little girl to the cinema!'

Her mother, relieved at the thought that she would be able to stay at home with her husband, answered quickly:

'Of course you are!'

Uncle Ernest said protectively: 'Wouldn't you be afraid, Ernestine?' Then, noticing the resentment in her features: 'No, I suppose not. After all, you are eighteen.'

'Then can I go?'

'Yes, you can go.'

Ernestine gave a little yell of joy. She kissed her father, her mother, and me, and gave me, in recognition of my usefulness in this affair, a beautiful ribbon of striped taffeta which shone like the wings of a butterfly. The meal, in these circumstances, was a magnificent success, and afterwards, when they played dominoes, I marking the points, Ernestine, losing, forgot to be angry.

The next morning the postman brought two letters, one for me from my mother, and the other for Ernestine who, never having received a letter before, took it into the house to ask her mother from whom she thought it might be. The three of us gathered round to open it, pulling out from the envelope a large sheet of pale blue paper, bordered with doves, butterflies, and lilies and in the centre of which were some verses signed by Louis Verdier. Ernestine thought the border pretty but said the poem was silly. Her mother and I, on the other hand, were very touched by this expression of Louis Verdier's love.

The day passed quickly enough. Ernestine kept her curlers on till evening, applied young lettuce leaves to her cheeks to give them a suitable pallor, and tried on all her skirts.

We were ready immediately after supper, Ernestine in a white skirt and her lace blouse. A long muslin scarf rested gently on her dark hair, making her look like some magnificent oriental flower in a *sari*. Never had I seen her so simply dressed or so utterly beautiful, or her eyes so large with expectation and pleasure. 'You are beautiful!' I exclaimed, looking at her, and she blushed.

My aunt and uncle bade us good-bye, and my uncle specially showed his admiration for so lovely a daughter. Her dark eyes and fine-grained skin were his, her mother's qualities being exclusively in the gentleness of her character and her usefulness as a housewife. My aunt gave a little money to Ernestine and I was given sixpence.

A short way down the road Louis Verdier was waiting for us, a white silk handkerchief hanging out of the breast pocket of his blue yachting jacket with the silver buttons. Ernestine, the ends of her muslin scarf floating behind her, had an amazing effect upon him. He looked at her, subjugated, speechless. She teased him, saying:

'Well, what's the matter with you? Have you lost your tongue? I suppose I am not to your liking?'

He answered finally: 'Oh, yes, but I would have liked to find other words with which to say it.'

'Don't worry,' she answered callously, 'for if they were anything like those verses you sent me I wouldn't understand a thing!'

He silently took her by the arm, wincing under the failure of his sonnet, but in a few moments he pressed her more tightly to him, and walked with his head leaning against her breast like a wounded bird. Though not saying anything, he enjoyed to the full the possession of this moment. Falling night enveloped them both. Their silhouettes appeared, his dark, hers white. They were charming. Soon night fell altogether, but from the direction of the town came the sound of laughter and chairs being dragged. Louis Verdier sighed.

'I wish it were already time to go home,' he whispered. 'I could walk like this, next to you, for ever. Oh, how I love you!' He was quite broken with emotion and went on: 'What shall I become? What shall I become?'

Suddenly, at this late moment, he became aware of my presence, and, making me a little bow, exclaimed: 'My most profound respects, little Madeleine. I had forgotten all about you!'

He smiled sadly, affectionately. Ernestine, who was a good deal moved by his declaration, put in softly: 'We mustn't forget about her. She made our meeting possible.'

We arrived in the main square.

A white screen had been made taut by ropes stretched to the branches of the chestnut-trees, and in front of it all the benches from the boys' school and the girls' school, on which a great many people were amorously or noisily seated, had been arranged, the girls and boys of school age huddled in front. The mayor, a former miner, talked importantly with the two doctors: the general practitioner who, though the sun had long since been replaced by a bright moon, wore a panama, and the doctor of the mine. Louis Verdier had taken us to the terrace of the café from where we could see all that was happening whilst enjoying a cooling drink. Suddenly the lights went out, and the performance began.

The film was a comic. A coal-heaver with a sack of coals on his back met a miller with a sack of flour, and the two men fell upon each other. It did one good to hear the peals of laughter, or at least, I think in retrospect, it would have done; but for me who, having followed Ernestine and Louis through the dark streets, had transformed them into a prince and princess touched by the fairy wand of love, the coarse jokes on the screen jarred my romantic sense. Louis did not laugh either, but in his case he had certainly no idea of what the picture was about, for he was looking only at Ernestine, and one had the impression he was breathing in her very soul. Clearly from hour to hour his love was surging up more powerful.

There was an interval.

A man and a woman came over to our table, and Louis, seeing them, blushed deeply. Rising, he went towards them, whispering in the woman's ear: 'Mother, it 's her!' These words, hushed but near me, were the only ones he uttered. The 'her' sounded like a reference to some goddess of the mountain, and after it had left his lips he was too moved to do anything but limply make room for his parents at our table. I do not believe the father took in what was happening, but both sat down a moment and the mother scrutinized Ernestine closely. Then the performance began again and they went away. Louis replunged himself, with even greater content, into the contemplation of his loved one, whilst I, exhausted by the heat, the noise, and the effect made upon me by Ernestine's romance, fell fast asleep.

On the way back the lovers, very close to each other, would stop to kiss. They were continually bidding each other good-bye and then continuing their slow climb. I was sleepy, and felt suddenly horribly alone in the warm air under the bright stars. The road was quiet, and the housewives we had seen earlier drinking their coffee on their doorsteps had been replaced by big cats enjoying the beauties of the night. One was surprised not to hear them talking with human voices, gossiping about their owners. Some got up at our approach and ran in front of us, the black ones reputedly of ill omen.

When we reached home my Aunt Eugénie, fatigue and anxiety lining her face, was waiting up for us. I hurried into bed and had just time before closing my eyes to see her undressing her daughter.

Plans were made for me to attend a day-school kept by the nuns. I was to leave early every morning and go to an old lady who took her granddaughter to the same school and would now take us both down. Under my arm, as in the pictures of Little Red Riding Hood, was to be a basket with my lunch, bread, goat's cheese, and some grapes. At four Ernestine would come to fetch me, and as a return courtesy see safely home the little girl whose grandmother had taken me to school in the morning.

I was a good deal worried about this important change in my life. I spoke of it to the rabbits and the hens. The big cat who liked to sleep on my pretty materials blinked as if he understood.

The school proved adorable— a sandy courtyard, tall trees with thick leaves, benches set out in their shade, and a table at which sat a sister of St. Vincent in blue, the lower part of her veil resting starchily on her shoulders, the upper part flapping like the wings of a great white bird. When the sun was at its hottest she would lift the tips of these wings with extreme delicacy till they touched above the crown of her head, and then secure them in this upright position with a clothes-peg. One saw her then in quite a different light. She was very old and tiny, her body withered, her cheeks brick red, her black eyes swift to notice and full of kindness. When she learnt that I was Milou's little girl she kissed me, saying that she had taught him to read. There were little boys in this school. We sang hymns and were never punished.

Twice a week we used to put flowers on the church altar. A nun went to the altar, prostrated herself, took a silver vase in both hands, prostrated herself again, and brought it to us. We would fill it with white roses or lilies. This rite was carried out for every vase. The flowers filled the church with their heavy scent, and once, overcome by it, I fainted.

On Saturday mornings we were brought a great quantity of

freshly cut roses from which we had to pull the petals for a religious procession. We sat on the floor round a white linen sheet, throwing the petals into baskets. The very open flowers shed their white dresses easily, but when my fingers closed on the buds I felt so sad, imagining them to be princesses in disguise, that I was overcome, and I would stuff them in the pockets of my dress. There they would remain forgotten till, a day or so later, I would find them more sadly withered, more surely touched by death, than if I had not been moved by a desire to save their lives.

Ernestine was delighted to have an excuse to come to town every afternoon. She would lunch at home with my Aunt Eugénie, take her siesta, and then walk down to Irma's café where she would stay till four. We would go back with her to Irma's, and after a while take the road home by the mountain; and every day, as if by accident, Louis would suddenly appear from behind a bush or a tree. Once, instead of going as usual to Irma's, we went to call on Mme Verdier. Louis's parents liked solid furniture. The dining-room was in French Henry II style, a massive black sideboard, and sculptured chairs done up in Cordova leather which stuck to my little bare legs disagreeably. The table was covered by a horrible rug on which minute tongues of black felt bordered with a buttonhole stitch in brightly coloured wool were superimposed like the scales of a fish. Young married women made these rugs on winter evenings, or even in the afternoons as they sat behind half-closed doors watching the people passing in the street. They were ugly but touched one's heart by the amount of work they represented. My Aunt Eugénie had a magnificent one, but it was carefully put away in naphtha balls for Ernestine when she married. Mme Verdier, excellent and severe, placed a chair against the table. I had the impression of being seated on a Spanish saddle with my legs wrapped up in a long cloak. She brought me the family album, bound in red velvet and fitted with a bright copper clasp, to look at while she talked to Ernestine. She spoke interminably of her son who, not strong enough to be called up for military service, but extremely clever, was on the point of becoming a mining engineer, a magnificent and enviable situation. The parents and grandparents were comfortably off and Louis would have a fine house the day he was married.

From time to time good Mme Verdier would look up and I

would plunge my blonde head over the faded photographs of little girls in their first communion dresses, married couples, young men in uniforms, mostly wearing the pretty beret of the *chasseurs* at an individual angle, babies on the knees of their grandmothers. I was too small to see the top of the book. Only the bottom row came within my line of vision. I have an idea I missed the most intriguing pictures. When I came to the last page I would turn back each leaf, and, after a time, Mme Verdier rose, opened the massive sideboard, and brought me some quince jelly which was excellent. Ernestine was very lucky to be loved by this woman's son who was the richest and cleverest young man in the Grand' Combe.

As a result of this visit, Louis came to lunch with us every Sunday under the vine. My Uncle Ernest had a great affection for him, but my aunt considered him too effeminate, too pale, his wrists too delicate, and his hands too white. She said she was afraid to touch him. They did not speak at all the same language. He only sipped the wine in his glass and never smoked. His one interest was to design motifs for the embroidery of Ernestine's trousseau. After he had made the drawing we would reproduce it with a carbon on the fine linen. Mme Verdier embroidered some of it, and the rest was done by an expert. The engagement was openly talked about and the young people, Louis especially, were radiant. Ernestine became prettier than ever, and there was not a young woman in the neighbourhood who was not jealous of her.

One day, when she had come to fetch me after school, passing through the centre of the little town, we kept close in to the shops where the sun was less intense. A small hairdresser's, newly opened, attracted our attention. In the window there was a wax model with a beautiful head of real hair, and round her, on black velvet, were undulating plaits of dark, brown, and blonde hair, tortoiseshell hairpins studded with imitation diamonds, and some bottles of fragrant perfume from the hot, beflowered city of Grasse. While we were enjoying the sight of all these wonderful things, a young man who, unnoticed by us, had been leaning against the door frame, exclaimed boldly to Ernestine: 'It would certainly be no good trying to sell *you* a plait of false hair!' He laughed, and Ernestine, looking up, blushed violently. We went off hurriedly, and, as Irma's café was at the end of the street,

Ernestine went in to question her friend about the young owner
of this newly opened saloon.

Irma knew all about him. His name was Henri Toulouse.
He had just finished his military training and, though not of the
Grand' Combe, was of a neighbouring town. He was apparently
charming, had already made friends with the youth of the
billiard saloon, and, being both generous and gay, had been put
down by Irma's parents as an excellent customer.

The following Sunday Louis Verdier came to lunch again.
While waiting for my Aunt Eugénie to lay the table the lovers,
holding each other by the waist, walked backwards and forwards
along the length of the terrace. When they came in front of the
vine they stopped, turned round, kissed each other virtuously
on the cheeks, and then resumed their promenade. They repeated
this charming comedy quite twenty times. Ernestine had become
a much more kindly person of late. Louis's love was so ardent
that one felt its rays all about one like those of the sun. I
watched them both, my heart filled with childish devotion. When
at last, exhausted by the heat, they could walk no longer, they
sat breathless at the table, laughing, delightfully happy. My
Uncle Ernest looked benevolently at these young lovers so different
from his own memories, the timid miner courting Eugénie,
but he was proud to think his daughter was benefiting by his
hard, sober years. My Aunt Eugénie arrived from indoors
behind an enormous, round, earthenware dish, holding it by the
single handle, sniffing proudly the steaming odour of jugged rabbit
which, with a sauce of black olives and red wine, had been simmering on the charcoal since seven in the morning. The fat tabby
passed ceaselessly between my aunt's legs, affectionate and hungry.

Louis was so quietly joyful that I loved him for being so much
in love. He would have been delighted to spend the entire day
with us in the family. He was already fond of my uncle and aunt,
and he felt that Ernestine was by now really his, but Ernestine's
nature demanded swiftly changing scenes and interests. She
must see different people and be herself seen by them. In order
to please her we were obliged immediately after lunch to go
down to the main square, to spend a few moments looking at
the townsmen playing bowls: middle-aged miners, shopkeepers,
and dignitaries in their shirt-sleeves, their Sunday waistcoats
unbuttoned, their straw hats placed at an angle or perched at the

back, revealing shining bald heads, sweating because of the torrid
heat, repeating the same old jokes as, from time to time, they
slapped a thigh with a fat, red hand, and gave a coarse, throaty laugh.
We went to drink coffee with Louis's parents. Mme Verdier,
who had certainly hoped for this visit, had bought a magnificent
cake, as light as a pair of lovers could wish, topped with freshly
beaten cream. But Ernestine's mind was restless, thinking of
the crowd which by now must have gathered at Aunt Jeanne's
café. She was burning to see her cousin Irma.

The café, as she had supposed, was at its most colourful with
not a table empty, but we, of course, having our private ways,
walked superbly through the crowd to where Aunt Jeanne and
her husband, at opposing ends of the family table, with Irma and
the little waiter whose napkin was always under his arm, were
avidly listening, in the company of many others I did not know,
to an orator whose back was turned to us but who, obviously,
was proving both witty and undividedly popular. Irma, seeing
us, waved affectionately to Ernestine, and then rose to make room
for us, all of which naturally disturbed the orator's discourse.
He turned angrily, not liking the idea of anybody stealing his
thunder, but as soon as he recognized Ernestine his features
turned from threatening to gay, and he called out: 'Hallo, my
proud young lady! Thus we meet again!' Afterwards, addressing me, he inquired if I were not even more stuck up than my big
sister. The last query took on in his mouth a rather broad tone,
for he was checked by a fear of having made too easy with us;
but everybody found his joke excellent, everybody, I quickly own,
but Louis and I whose happiness was shattered. We found each
other's gaze and detected we were both near to tears.

Henri Toulouse was overcome by the presence of Ernestine,
who was blushing as hotly as on the previous occasion in front
of the shop. The two young people looked acutely at each other.
Then Toulouse, making a circular gesture to embrace his
audience, set about to recapture its attention and sympathy with
coarse jokes and bombast. His stories had all to do with his
military training, and one could not help being sorry for Louis
who had been prevented by his health from proving himself
equally a man. The hairdresser described encounters with his
officers. One heard such phrases as: 'I told him this,' or 'I soon
put him in his place,' or 'I paid for drinks all round.' The first

person singular was invariably predominant. This man was the ideal café orator, a splendid-looking creature with dark moustaches, bright amorous eyes, the sort of fellow to make himself loved by any girl and to get round older women with wheedling compliments.

Ernestine, swept out of her languor, looked at him with large melting eyes. She must have been burning inside. His voice thickened as he cast exploit after exploit, like bouquets, at her feet. His softest smiles and most knowing winks were for her. When Aunt Jeanne brought tall glasses of golden beer for her guests Louis pathetically declined. His feeble but only too marked answer brought stillness to the entire table. Henri Toulouse looked at him sharply and, warned of the truth by a lover's second sense, read into this refusal a personal affront. The two men glared at each other like antagonists armed with steel. Then somebody spoke, and for the moment this was all.

In the evening, when Ernestine and Louis walked slowly up the mountain road and Louis, as usual, slipped his arm round Ernestine's waist, she appeared restive, complained of a headache, said her feet hurt, that the flies were annoying, and that I either jumped too near her or lagged too far behind. It was no longer the return of the goddess touched by love, unheedful of the stones on the road.

We took leave of Louis at the last house, and without a word went up to bed. From the next day Ernestine took me to school and spent as many hours as she could at the café. Henri Toulouse was always popping out of his shop to refresh himself with a lemonade and amuse her with his coarse wit and his heavy compliments, and he would repeat, for all to hear, that now, unlike some shirkers he could name if he cared to, now that he, Henri Toulouse, had done his military service, his one, ever-present thought was to find a pretty girl and settle down to the happiness of married life; and at this point, if he had an audience, he would wave his arm in the direction of Ernestine and add: 'A girl like that. That's the sort of girl who would look a real picture in a nice, smart-looking shop!'

Ernestine was becoming more and more restless. She could not live away from the sight of Henri Toulouse. He occupied her every thought. He, meanwhile, was falling increasingly in love with the same theatrical excitement which took hold of him when he was going forward with a barrack-room story.   He was just as noisy a lover as an orator.   Even his silences were ostentatious.   When his drinking friends asked him suddenly: 'Eh, Toulouse, what's up?' he would look at them wild-eyed, put his hands to his heart, and exclaim:

'Honestly, I'm all changed. Something has happened inside me.'
Then somebody would pipe up:
'You're in love, Toulouse, that's what it is.'
'You think so?'
'Why, yes, Toulouse, it's obvious.   You must marry.'
'Ah!' he would sigh.   'Getting married is easy.   What's difficult is when the girl one loves isn't free.'

When this had gone on for some time all the regulars at the café knew that Henri's meridional heart was on fire, and as he was such a good fellow and quite a hand at billiards they sided with him against the sentimental Louis, and when the poor young man came into the café there would rise, from every table, tittering and whispered allusions to faint-hearted men who, instead of doing their military service, wore out their pants on office stools and earned more than they should because they had influential parents to speak up for them.   Louis held his head with dignity.   He was not intimidated by Henri Toulouse as a man, and as for the café whisperers, he took them for what they were, a fine set of cowards; but he knew he had lost Ernestine, at least for the moment, and was too gentle and sensitive to arm himself with loud words and flattery.

Ernestine was always writing to my mother for lace to make her trousseau, and after my mother had sent her what she was able to save from the blouses she still put together for Mme Gaillard, she was obliged, in view of the hospitality I was receiving from my Aunt Eugénie, to buy lace by the yard which soon became too onerous for her small means.   When my mother came to the end of her savings she sent a final parcel of lace to Ernestine with a letter addressed to my aunt saying that as she could not afford such high terms Milou was coming to bring me home.   The two women were appallingly vexed, neither having probably realized what a strain they were putting on my mother's purse.   I heard some rather hard things said about my parents and I ceased going to school, but on the whole nobody treated me with any less kindness.   Old Aunt Marie was told all about it but she sided with us, perhaps because of the love she bore my father. After siesta my Aunt Eugénie took me down to see another cousin, Catherine Nègre, who was also much attached to my father and to whom I should have paid a visit earlier. The news that Milou was arriving was certainly the reason we went so suddenly to see her, and Catherine Nègre may even have written to my aunt, for as soon as we entered the low house where she lived all by herself she told us that my father had asked her to take charge of me till he came, being so angry with his sister about her requests for lace that he refused even to see the Agnels. Catherine Nègre had the reputation of being a saint, which was increased by her solitary life and the fact that her son was a priest. She made a big fuss of me, and said to Aunt Eugénie: 'This is what happens when one is too greedy. God gave you the opportunity of doing a kindly act in taking your brother's little girl who needed our sunshine, but you merely thought of it as a chance to get something out of the poor mother who has just lost her *pitchoun*. If my dear son were here he would make you see the shame of it, though to be sure with a heart like his he forgives everybody. You must become kinder, my good Eugénie, otherwise your daughter will go wrong for want of a good example.'

My aunt tried to justify herself, but Cousin Catherine went on: 'And do you suppose, my dear Eugénie, that it's right for your daughter always to be with her cousin in a public café? A daughter's place is with her mother. And besides, I hear she has a nice young man. Why have they not come to see me?'

My aunt looked down on the tiled floor. Her admiration for Cousin Catherine prevented her from speaking.

'And now that I have scolded you enough,' Cousin Catherine went on, 'go back home with little Madeleine, and when Milou arrives I will climb up to your place to fetch her. She will be better on the mountain than down here in the stuffy town with me. Now that Milou is taking her back to Paris the poor little girl will need every breath of air.'

When we reached home my aunt was obliged to tell her husband that Milou was going straight to Cousin Catherine. My uncle, who never understood anything about petticoat machinations, was puzzled and hurt, but it was old Aunt Marie's grief that was pitiful to see, for the poor woman took it into her head that in these circumstances she would never see her Milou again, and that night she cried herself to sleep.

Our placid existence began to lose some of its charm, but the next Saturday Cousin Catherine came to take me to her house, my father having arrived. I saw him framed in the doorway, waiting for us, and when he heard me speaking patois, he laughed so happily that I was vexed.

Aunt Marie, having heard that Milou was in the town, made my aunt a scene that showed the violence of her character. She would not die without seeing her Milou again. He must come to her or she would go to him. My father decided that it would constitute no loss of face to go to his sister's house on the condition it was to call on Aunt Marie and not on the Agnels. Accordingly, on Sunday morning we climbed the road leading up the mountain and, reaching my aunt's house, went straight to Aunt Marie who was sobbing. Eugénie and Ernestine, hiding in a corner, looked rather silly, but as soon as my father saw them his big heart melted and he kissed them with such immense joy that everything was forgiven. My Uncle Ernest was delighted at this unexpected happening. To celebrate the event it was decided to spend the afternoon all together with Aunt Jeanne and Irma at the café.

On the way down Ernestine gave her arm to my father, and when we arrived she introduced him first to Henri Toulouse, then to Louis Verdier. I must confess that the unhappy Louis looked very out of sorts, my father giving it as his opinion that he was rather a fragile young man. Henri Toulouse, on the other hand, had scarcely time to finish his first barrack-room story before my father discovered that they had been in the same regiment and that Henri Toulouse had done his service, like Émile, at Nice. They immediately became fast friends, and Toulouse was wise enough to make full use of his new ally, for officially Louis Verdier was still betrothed to Ernestine.

Ernestine, at every joke, laughed very loud, throwing her head back in a movement full of sensuality. She was a slave of this hairdresser's slightest remark. One felt almost sorry for her. She knew now that she had never been in love with Louis. What she had taken for love was merely the satisfaction of being courted by a youth of good family and being engaged before her Cousin Irma. But this was love, love at first sight, love so blinding that she could not even see what an inferior match she was making. She laughed and laughed again, triumphantly, full-throatedly, after the manner of a courtesan, and suddenly I saw Louis turn white and leave his chair. He appeared anxious to make himself as inconspicuous as possible as he stole past the fresh marble tables to a door at the back which led to a courtyard and an iron staircase built against the wall. I followed him. He climbed a few steps and then sat down, and burying his face in his hands cried. He cried so hard, with all his heart, that his shoulders rose and fell with each convulsive sob. I climbed the staircase and sat beside him, crying also. I cried over the sad end of my beautiful love story. I cried angrily to see Ernestine such a slave to this vulgar hairdresser. I cried over myself who the next day would be leaving the hot sun, my garden, the mountain we were always so afraid to see on fire, the cat which had taught me patois, Uncle Ernest whom I would no longer see plunging his black face into the cool water and come out all clean, the basket full of coloured wools, and the vine. Oh, how I cried! Suddenly he raised his head from the palms of his hands and saw that I was with him. He put his arms round me and said: 'My little Madeleine, how I would have learnt to love you if . . .' The rest of his sentence was lost in hot tears. I heard my father calling me, and running down the iron staircase I broke into the lighted café, my cheeks wet and my eyes red. Everybody wanted to know where I had been. I was anxiously questioned and I told them I had been with Louis Verdier, but even as I spoke I saw that Henri Toulouse had slipped his arm round Ernestine's waist and it was clear that the irremediable had happened, that poor Louis was forgotten, and that Ernestine had not a single regret to throw, as an act of charity, in his direction. Cousin Catherine was right. My Aunt Eugénie had set a bad example. Her daughter was not kind.

The next morning I woke up at the station in Paris. As we hurried down the platform I was so afraid to be separated from my father that I seized his strong hand. Several months in the country had made me unaccustomed to all the noise. I was horribly aware of my coat and dress being too small, and my hat, after a night spent in a third-class compartment, being crushed. My arrival in Paris was not exactly a glorious one. I felt a sudden desire to see my mother.

When we arrived home my mother had only just got up. She had been working very late at night during my father's absence. I was overjoyed to see her. She marvelled at my pink cheeks and my arms browned by the sun. But when, in reply to her questions, I spoke like Ernestine spoke, in a strong accent and half in patois, a look of horror spread over her pale features. The children in the courtyard, having seen us arrive, were calling me and I was longing to join them. My accent surprised them and soon became an object of derision. My mother, anxious to deliver me from their jibes, called me and together we went to market.

Our open-air market was at its busiest at this hour of the morning. The colour and rich variety of the stalls set out under gay canvas on the pavement were delightful. My mother was gradually shedding her mourning and now wore white or mauve. We discovered Mme Valentin sitting on a folding stool, her fingers busily engaged in lacemaking, her eyes scanning the passing crowd, picking out potential buyers or welcoming with a glint those who had purchased from her in the past. She knew a great number of people, enumerating them for her benefit, not by their names but by their blemishes or idiosyncrasies—the little brunette who limps, the tall woman with the false hair, the nice little thing who spits in your face without realizing it. We would bid her good morning; she would answer amicably, but to see her thus at market made of her, in my eyes, quite a different person.

I thought it must be a wonderful thing to have a stall in the open air. A little further along, for instance, my mother called on a woman known as the 'fat brunette' whose dress-lengths and pieces of silk and satin were put out in the bowl of a black umbrella. Most of her materials were just too long for the rag merchants, but not quite long enough to make anything useful. Nevertheless my mother, who appeared to plunge herself bodily into the cavernous umbrella, managed with dexterity to bring up each piece in turn, calculating with an experienced eye its length, its possibilities, and suitability for me, to make an apron or a dress. When, after due thought, the length, the width, and the colour combined to give her satisfaction, she would ask in a

small voice, timidly: 'How much is this little piece, madam?'
Then the 'fat brunette' would proclaim the measurements which
my mother already knew, proceed to an appreciation of its quality,
whether it was wool or silk or cotton, and, continuing for
several more seconds to expatiate upon its merits, so that mentally
she could fix the price at a safe figure, she would end by exclaiming: 'Well, my good lady, let us say eight sous, and I assure
you it 's a gift!' This declaration would seldom satisfy my
mother who, throwing down the piece, would answer: 'Oh, dear
me, no. That is much too expensive, and as it 's a trifle on the
short side I may as well keep my money to buy just what I need!'
The 'fat brunette' would then say: 'Have it your way, little lady.
You can have it for six sous, but if you were clever you would
take this piece also which would cost twenty sous in the Avenue
de Clichy but which I 'll give you for twelve! Shall we call it a
bargain? Twelve sous and six sous make eighteen, and here are two
sous change out of your franc. I shall look out for you next week.'

My mother would be delighted with the piece that had cost
her six sous, but she would be much less sure about the other.
Her thoughts would go round and round upon this painful matter
whilst we hurried past the butcher's on whose stall were lamb
cutlets in paper frills and delectable steaks. My mother would continue, unseeing, until at last she reached some fishwife from whom
she would buy two herrings in a newspaper, the only food which
could compensate by its cheapness for her folly in buying that
extra piece of material for twelve sous.

All the way home I would smell those acrid herrings, but my
imagination would be coloured by the prettily flowered muslin
which, fashioned by my mother, would turn itself into something
adorable for me, something light, of a cut quite her own. Not
till after my marriage in London were we ever able to buy a piece
of material of the right length, but I believe this merely increased
my mother's genius, causing her to invent subtle masterpieces.

I now noticed that we had some new tenants in our house or,
to be exact, on the ground floor of the house next to ours, under
Mme Valentin's flat. There was a tall girl of fourteen with a

tail of yellow hair down her back, uncouth, dirty, and quite straight. This Germaine Séguin had just arrived with her parents from Brittany. The mother was in a factory where they made men's collars out of celluloid, work which was both dangerous and unhealthy, but tolerably well paid. The father was employed by the Magasin du Printemps as a carpet-beater, which employment quickly ruins the lungs. When this man came home in the evening he put the soup on the hob, and then slipped his tired feet in bright red or blue slippers made out of the carpets he beat or mended, and thus shod he gave the impression of sliding across the floor on immense coloured rafts. When the soup began to sing he would push a short chair across the uneven paving-stones of the little courtyard till it stuck conveniently between the stones. He would then get astride of it and take out of his pocket a newspaper so minutely and tightly folded that the creases formed little squares as on a chess-board. From another pocket he pulled out a pair of spectacles which he placed across his forehead like an aviator. He would then read his newspaper, the print so near his eyes that a fly would only just have had room to pass between the paper and his nose. In this position he absorbed politics, crimes, scandals, and financial intelligence, keeping only the serial for after his supper.

This good man was an excellent citizen till Saturday which was pay-day. He would then go with his wife to the cafés and grocers which had given them credit during the week, pay these debts, eat pork-pies, and drink red wine till, having no more money left, he would follow her back to the flat where he slept thickly. On Sunday evenings he got up for a game of cards. On Monday morning he returned to work. By Tuesday he was again in debt.

The mother found a job for Germaine in the celluloid collar factory. The girl's tail of hair was put up in a bun which sat importantly above her not indelicate neck. When, in the evening, father and daughter sat out in the yard, the father with his large feet and the daughter with her oversize bun of hair looked like freaks on a fairground. But I was not to see them often together. Germaine began to wear high heels, knot a velvet ribbon round her thin neck, and speck her hair with *diamanté*. The martyrdom of walking with high heels over the paving-stones was compensated for by the impression she made on the bad lads round

the fortifications.   When we came out of the underground
station and followed the boulevard where the wash-house stood
we would see her.   Then she would hide under a railway arch
or in a gateway, deserting momentarily the apache and the fire-
eyed girls with whom she now passed all her spare time.   The
apaches were frightened of her because she was still a minor.
From time to time they made her show up at the factory, not
only for their own safety but to keep her parents ignorant of her
nocturnal occupation.   She knew that neither my mother nor I
would talk, but occasionally she would say to me: 'The girl or
the boy who lets on to my people what I do won't be long to
get a knife in the small of the back when he or she leaves the
Métro at night.'

We ended, my mother and I, by being very frightened.   Every
evening we saw youths moving swiftly, silently, over the uneven
ground in linen shoes, their long trousers tight over the hips,
wide at the bottom, a red kerchief round their necks, a cap with
squares or of black satinette, their long white fingers juggling
with the blade of a knife.   They had the art of flattening themselves against a wall, stickily, like slugs, darting out of a hiding-
place to run swiftly after some man walking home alone, late,
perhaps a trifle drunk.   They were not killers yet, learning the
business till they were of age to move into Paris, but as they were
many, without being brave they were insolent.   To look in their
direction was enough to bring insults on one's head.   They were
vulgar but often witty.   When the police cycled past two by
two, as they did once or twice a night, one heard catcalls and
barking all along the boulevard which was the apache way of
sending forth a warning.   Then those who had no time to disappear would seize a barrow and pretend to be going quietly
home.   As soon as the police were gone, the youths would re-
group, emit streams of contemptuous saliva, and then whistle or
sing the most tender love-songs.

Germaine came to us one day.   Her parents, as usual, were at
work.   She was upset and ended by confiding in my mother
that she was in the middle of a miscarriage.   A woman we knew
at the public wash-house was apparently the expert, and the
apaches and the girls, worried because of Germaine's age, would
have nothing more to do with Germaine till it was all over.
Germaine, though vicious, was still at heart a poor little girl, and

she would bury her face in her hands and cry. One night she was taken by pains and the whole house was awakened by her pitiful, unending yells. Afraid of her dangerous companions, she would not say anything to her parents, and we, being as frightened as she was, were equally silent. My mother said to Mme Séguin: 'It must be appendicitis.' She was taken to hospital weak from loss of blood, and the police came to make some inquiries. Germaine was too ill to talk the next day, but a search was made for the woman of the wash-house.

We were now in the last days of July 1914.

My Aunt Marie-Thérèse had invited me to stay for a week at the rue de Longchamps. Rolande went to quite a good school in the wealthy parish of St. Pierre de Chaillot. While she was there I spent the day with my aunt, mostly out and about, delivering hats to her customers or buying ribbons and veils in the stores. In the evening we had lots of visitors. When, at the end of this short holiday, I returned home I found that nothing seemed to be going right. My father had struck a moment of unemployment in the building trade, and was very depressed. Suddenly my Uncle Louis also lost his job, his wealthy employers having given him notice before going off on a trip to Scotland.

Mme Gaillard, when we went to see her in the Boulevard Haussmann, complained that all her rich customers from South America had already gone back. One of them, a tremendously wealthy woman from the Argentine, took all that was finest from her most expensive box, saying: 'Good-bye, Mme Gaillard. How I pity you! It will be a long time before we see any more lace from Belgium and France!' Mme Gaillard put her gold coins away carefully. Business was bad, her son's health had become alarming, and she felt guilty about having brought him to Paris. He might have been better in their native Auvergne but she had felt the need of him so much!

The doorkeeper watched her with humid eyes from his chair. They had been secretly married, and this old man who had once taken a delight in persecuting her was now a tender husband.

I found it very hard to believe that our good Mme. Gaillard, as we continued to call her, now shared without fear the door-keeper's lodge which my imagination pictured hung with whips and instruments of torture. They invited us in, and I was surprised to see a large rectangular table drawn up against the curtained window, upon which there stood a veritable forest of rare plants in their pots. Each pot stood on a white saucer. Some of the pots were tied round with satin ribbon, pink or blue or tricolour. A little palm-tree grew out of a cask barded with shining copper. There were also many rare birds of pretty plumage in cages, rich cages with coloured bars. A large cat, content and well fed, blinked sleepily between the flowers and the birds. The air was scented and tuneful. On the chimney-piece, between two ferns, was a marriage wreath of orange blossom under a glass globe. A photograph tied with a ribbon of faded tulle showed the doorkeeper in the uniform of a cavalry regiment with shining cuirass and helmet streaked with horse-hair, standing proudly beside his first wife in her wedding gown. Other relics attracted my childish eyes—a military medal in a leather case, a piece of shrapnel, a woman's gold watch with amethysts at the end of a long chain. I think I was looking at these things mostly to bolster up my courage, for at that moment I was alone with the doorkeeper and I was still a good deal afraid of him. He came up softly behind me and took in his rugged hands the shrapnel and the medal.

'There, little girl,' he said, 'to win the medal I had to have the shrapnel in my thigh. Do you remember my first wife?'

'Yes, a little,' I answered.

'Well,' he continued, 'we made a fine couple, and we waltzed all the night of our marriage. As a matter of fact, I waltzed that night all the waltzes of a lifetime, for soon afterwards, during the war of 1870, I was taken prisoner at Sédan and it was trying to escape over a bridge that I got that piece of shrapnel in my thigh. So you see, that put an end to my waltzing days!'

He played with one or two other small objects on the mantel-piece and added:

'When I came back to my wife, dragging a wooden leg, and nothing to keep us but a small pension, things looked pretty bad till one spring morning, as I was sitting on a bench in the avenue of the Bois de Boulogne, warming my stump in the sun,

who should I see coming along but my officer? The excellent
gentleman had escaped over the bridge at Sédan at the same
time as I had, and later it was he who got me the medal. He
asked me how things were going, and when I told him it was
not easy for a man with a wooden leg to live on a small pension
he gave me the job of doorkeeper here. That was in 1873.
My first wife died here, and I shall too, I hope. As for my
officer, the brave gentleman lives on the second floor, and the
palm-tree in the cask you were admiring just now is his. He
brought it back from Tunis after a campaign. The poor gentleman is getting old, but as you see, I still serve him when he's
in town.'

He turned awkwardly on his stump and went on:

'The tall fern with the red ribbon belongs to a lady who sang
in opera. She is retired and spends six months of the year at
Evian. That is when the plant comes down to me and this is
the tenth summer I've been looking after it.'

He waved his arm possessively and said:

'You can be sure, little girl, that I know all there is to be known
about these plants and they know me. The birds, too, they
belong to the tenants, for the tenants in this house all have a
place in the country. Retired people they are, whose children
have families of their own, mostly in smarter parts of Paris, for
the younger folk want lifts and big windows that let in the air.'

He laughed gruffly to show that he was not the sort of man
to be taken in by the youngsters, and went on:

'Would you think, by looking at those plants, that the air
about here was no good? That tall young lady, the fern over
in the corner, has grown a whole new storey this spring. See
how the leaves are of a tender green! And the cactus and the
hydrangea and my officer's palm-tree. I would say they were
nearly all as old as you. By the way, how old are you, little girl?'

'I shall be eight next month,' I answered.

'That's as I thought,' he said, 'and if you ask me my opinion,
I look after my plants a deal better than your parents look after
you. I give them good clear water to drink. I protect them
from slugs and flies. I put them, each in turn, in the sun, and
when the barometer is set fine I put them outside on a bench I
made specially so that the dogs cannot sully them. Tell me,
little girl, do you like my plants?'

D

'Oh, yes,' I answered, 'but I like the ribbons best.'

'Is that so? I 'm glad, for it is I who dress them. Come and peep into this drawer.'

Raising myself on my toes I saw to my delight yards upon yards of different coloured ribbons. Some were red, white, and blue. Others were of the tenderest blues and pinks. He gave me some pieces which had already been used. They struck me as sumptuous. I thanked him, my joy overflowing, and I said: 'Does Mme Gaillard like your plants?'

'Very much, but the trouble is,' he exclaimed, laughing, 'that she would like to put lace flounces under their ribbons!'

This idea quite went to my heart, and I said:

'Oh, but it would be much prettier!'

What surprised me most was my former enemy's double life. I had imagined him for so long an ogre that to see him laughing, playing with his ribbons, was too absurd. I thought his plants pretty, but I liked them less than the lilac in our garden and the wild flowers at Marais.

On the last Sunday in July we went for lunch to the rue de Longchamps where Rose arrived in tears. Her good-looking lover had suddenly disappeared. The German nurse who looked after the children in the house where she was cook had also gone without even waiting to collect her wages for July. My Uncle Louis's Austrian friends had all left. Some did not trouble to take any luggage, saying that they were merely going for a walk. Nobody knew what to make of it. Rose was in a piteous state. How could he have been so cruel? She muttered his undoubted qualities like prayers between sobs—so honest, so distinguished, so immensely clever, of such an excellent family! Alas, we learnt far too quickly the reason for all these happenings. Rolande and I watched the bill-stickers pasting up the orders for mobilization on the walls of Paris, black writing on white sheets with two flags in colour at the top. We would run from one placard to the other hoping to discover they were not exactly alike. Crowds gathered in front of them. Then we would slip in front of the grown-ups to read all over again the same fateful word. Mobilization! Mobilization!

9

AS my Uncle Louis was ten years younger than my father, he was the first to receive his call-up papers. That morning I saw Marie-Thérèse huddled on a doll's chair in a corner of the room where Rolande kept her toys. Her face was covered by her hands and she was crying. My uncle was pacing up and down behind her, but soon he put his large hands on her quaking frail shoulders and said:

'Come, little wife, there's nothing definite yet. There's still time for something to happen. There may not be a war after all.'

Rolande and I were also sad, though our sadness was a pose more than a state of mind. We were already tired of pretending to be sad when suddenly from the far end of the rue de Longchamps a trumpet call broke across the warm air. Rolande and I darted to the window, but as we could see nothing we climbed on the sill. Two strong hands gripped us and drew us into the room again. We were then, rightly, smacked. I think that if my uncle had not been there we would have both fallen from this sixth-floor window into the street. My aunt was much too busy crying on her doll's chair to have taken any notice of us.

My father and my mother had gone to the savings bank to draw out their savings. Long queues had formed outside all the banks, and my father had taken his stand at four in the morning. My mother went as often as she could to relieve him or take him something to eat.

That evening we walked all across Paris from the rue de Longchamps to our flat in Clichy. A few people were gathered round the Arc de Triomphe. People fought each other. Insults were thrown. Other people embraced each other or wept. No quarter was given to any unfortunate Alsatian whose guttural accent suggested he might be a German. People jumped to the conclusion he was a spy. He would be hit, and the police would have to rescue him from a quickly forming, nervous

97

crowd. Our apaches crossed the fortifications, descended upon Paris, and taking advantage of these disorders forced their way into shops, making the onlookers believe they were doing so out of patriotism because the owners were German. The dairy next to our house had a German name. Broken eggs made splashes on the pretty, clean walls. Milk which I would have been glad to drink was spilt uselessly on the floor. The factory where Mme Séguin made celluloid collars was smashed because the Dutch owner was thought to have German sympathies. Across the street flames were going up from a gramophone factory, threatening nearby houses. The main gates in the fortifications were closed as in medieval days, only the side-doors, guarded by two gendarmes, being open. The fine houses in the leafy avenues had their shutters up. The underground had ceased to work, but a few buses went by and there were taxis with luggage on the roofs hurrying from one station to the other. Everybody who could left Paris. Mme Valentin, quite terrified, had gone with her daughter Augustine and the children into the mountains of the Auvergne. Augustine, for this journey, had apparently put on a corset and shoes for the first time in seven years. The Séguins hurried away. Two days later my father left to join his regiment on the Italian frontier. He was neither proud nor brave. England had just declared war. My father cried. I cried. My mother cried.

As soon as my father had gone we went to live with Marie Thérèse, thinking it would be cheaper to combine the feminine members of the two homes. Marie-Thérèse was genuinely grieved to lose her husband. My mother merely considered this phase as a possible holiday. She had worked hard all the summer, and in addition to her blouses had made two suits for my father and turned his overcoat, and it was annoying to think she had done it all for nothing. There was no longer any question of making blouses. Mme Gaillard had taken her dying son to the Auvergne, leaving her new husband in his porter's lodge with his beribboned plants and singing birds. Marie-Thérèse was also without work. Her customers had all gone to the country and were not yet back.

My aunt and her daughter were accustomed, when alone, to dispense with the complicated business of cooking. For instance, they would merely eat a piece of bread and a few grapes or nibble a bar of chocolate. If the urge to cook ever did overcome Marie-Thérèse it would be to spend the whole morning making something horribly difficult but quite flippant, like meringues and whipped cream. Of course, this would be served as the only dish so that afterwards we would be as hungry as ever.

During the first days of our association Marie-Thérèse would say to her sister: 'You must admit, Matilda, that we can quite well do without your heavy meals. To-day, for instance, we have only spent eight sous.'

My mother would answer: 'Do you suppose that in winter we shall eat peaches and grapes?'

'Of course,' Marie-Thérèse would insist. 'You 'll see. It 's such fun. We shall be able to look at the shops instead.'

After a fortnight the colour had gone from my cheeks and I did nothing but sleep. My mother quickly saw the danger, and insisted that Marie-Thérèse should provide us with something more substantial, but my aunt accused her sister of having the vulgar gluttony of a workman's wife. She said the mere thought of steak and fried potatoes made her swoon. It was time we shook the atmosphere of apaches and rag-and-bone men out of our system, she contended. My mother sulked. Marie-Thérèse also sulked and took her daughter out for a walk. My mother took a piece of paper, wrote half a dozen lines on it, placed it on the long, crisp bread, and having packed our belongings in two of her sister's hat-boxes, took me by the hand and slammed the door behind us.

It was a long way home. From time to time we sat down on a bench under the trees. The weather was magnificent, but Paris was so empty that we hardly met anybody. The flags of the Allies flew from the windows. There were thousands upon thousands of them. One saw them waving through the leafy greenness of the chestnut-trees, and some of them were strange and until recently unknown to us, like the flags of Montenegro and Serbia. One seemed to hear the strains of the *Merry Widow* distantly rising, echoes of Balkan princes in musical comedies. The flag that impressed us more than any was that of the Czar Nicholas with the eagle. The Russian steam-roller was said to be crushing the German troops already. As we left the fine avenues of the centre there were fewer flags and they were smaller, but, already tired of the rue de Longchamps and what in the eyes of Marie-Thérèse were the smart folk, I thirsted for a sight of the marshy land beyond the fortifications and the sound of our own people. My mother had reasons of her own for being pleased. She was free. Freedom, in her mind, was the right to eat what she pleased at the hour which suited her best, to read in bed until midnight or longer, not to get up early in the morning, to dirty so little linen that she could deal with it at home without going to the wash-house, not to be obliged to buy wine, but with the money she saved buy face powder and various other feminities for herself and for me.

When we came within sight of our house many familiar flats had their shutters closed—those of the Valentins, the Séguins, of Mme Choblais and her children—but as we reached the entrance we saw a perambulator, and looking into it we discovered that the pillow still had the warmth of a little head. The pram belonged to Lucienne Rosier.

Our apartment smelt horribly of damp. My mother threw back the shutters, filling the uninhabited room with light and air. She took me to the pump to draw water. I followed her everywhere. We would look at one another and break out laughing. We were so happy to be home again.

After we had done the housework and put away the things we had brought back in my aunt's bandboxes, my mother took down her string bag and we went to market, walking light-heartedly and swiftly over the hot paving-stones. To celebrate our return my mother fried some potatoes. It was quite a feast.

Now that my father was in the army we no longer had any rent to pay. Our allocation was small, but as there was no wine, no alcohol, and no tobacco to upset our budget we could at last look after ourselves. Accordingly my mother invested in fifty yards of white calico with which to set us both up, and from that moment our living-room was strewn with flounced petticoats and night-dresses which were to be garnished with lace. Any pieces of lace left over from Mme Gaillard's blouses did us excellently. As the weather remained hot we used to leave our door wide open, and Mme Rosier would come with Lucienne to watch us admiringly.

I do not remember ever having learnt to sew, but I think it must have been then that I started seriously to make my own things, leaving my doll's wardrobe to my play hours. It was much more difficult to make flounced petticoats and night-dresses for myself than for my doll. If the stitches showed my mother made me start all over again. I was trained in a hard school. She would not tolerate the erring needle, the slovenly seam, or a thimbleless middle finger. There is no better way to learn than under the sharp, unforgiving eyes of the maternal seamstress. My first petticoat, with the flounces edged with purl which Mme Valentin had given me, was really very pretty. My mother worked at a tremendous speed. When I went into raptures at the sight of her nimbleness she would answer: 'You see, I have the satisfaction of knowing in advance that my young customer will be pleased!'

Mme Rosier felt a great longing for all this beautiful lingerie, and one day she told my mother that if we would agree to make some garments for her and for her daughter, Lucienne, she would bring some material and do what she could to help. She made the admission she could not sew, and added that it made her even more ashamed than if she had not known how to read.

The next morning she came down with little Lucienne in one arm and an enormous bundle of bits and pieces under the other. She had bought a big stock of linen and silk and cotton from the rag-and-bone dealers for next to nothing during the first days of the war, and it took us nearly a week to sort them out for petticoats, aprons, blouses, and the like. Our far-sighted neighbour, not knowing how to sew, had lived practically in rags, unable to make use of these treasures.

Marguerite Rosier was at home all day. Her husband went out early and came back late. Hyacinthe's father and mother were peasants who owned a little farm on the plateau of Langres, modest farmers who worked desperately hard and who had ill spared Hyacinthe when he had been forced to leave them to seek a livelihood in Paris. The younger of two sons, he was born with an inflammation of the spine and one leg shorter than the other. This deformity was so pronounced that every time he made a step he gave the appearance of stooping to pick something off the ground. As a lad he was taught to milk and look after the cows, but being unable, because of the way he was made, to take a sudden step backwards, a cow one summer night flicked its tail into his right eye and blinded it. He was therefore, with only one eye and one valid leg, less fitted than ever to work on a farm. The village priest, moved by the boy's miserable condition, advised the parents to have him educated in Langres where his physical deformity and his close-to-the-earth accent made him a grim joke. Of no natural intelligence, slow to learn and to memorize, Hyacinthe needed immense courage to pass what examinations were needed to serve as a junior clerk in a bank; but his perseverance was such that gradually he rose and was sent to headquarters in Paris. He had been there only a few months, lodging outside the city walls to save each penny, when he had first seen Marguerite at the window opposite, and had ended by courting her with romantic tunes on his violin.

The bank in Paris had been no easier than the bank in Langres or his school, for though his colleagues were less brutal, a trifle less coarse, they were cunning and underhand. He would find the door of his office locked just as he was due to see a customer; when a director crossed the floor the door would open mysteriously to humiliate him. He would find his pens stuck to his desk with glue, his drawers would conceal rotten eggs. When his colleagues heard that he was to marry a widow who was not only young but a virgin they sent him anonymous letters offering to replace him on the wedding night. He was neither bitter nor revengeful, for his life was now so governed by a greed for money that he was eternally plunged in deep calculations, working out hypothetical savings at compound interest, so that even when his shoes were quite worn out he would defer indefinitely the purchase of another pair.

His superiors were quick to see his value. He did not know what it was to be tired and had no desire whatever for anybody's money but his own. The bank was his spiritual mother. His proudest moments were crossing the threshold in the morning, entering the marble hall, cool in summer, overheated in the winter. His colleagues, most of whom were young, complained that the day was too long. They formed groups to talk about theatres, dances and *midinettes*, songs, and love. Their work was neither good nor bad. Hyacinthe's work was immutably excellent. He was never ill, never late. He would have preferred not to take any holidays.

The declaration of war was Hyacinthe's magnificent opportunity. All his colleagues, those fine dancers, those inveterate theatre-goers, those good-looking lovers, those alert walkers and sportsmen, were carried off on the tide of war. Those who remained were very old. Hyacinthe became a manager. His salary was doubled. They needed him so badly that he slept for a week at the bank.

For Marguerite, for Lucienne, for my mother, and for me that week was a real joy. We did everything forbidden by husbands. We drank coffee with cream in it and ate caramels and cake. We made omelets with so much rum that the flames nearly set our hair on fire. We were deliciously frightened. My mother and Marguerite laughed like schoolgirls. We lived according to the impulse of the moment, as *demi-mondaines* are supposed to live, taking a long walk one day, the next day not going out at all. We broke into our landlady's kitchen garden one night, but we could just as well have gone there by day, for she was away in the country. One afternoon, when Mme Maillard, Marguerite's mother, called on us she found all of us disguised, Marguerite wearing Hyacinthe's top-hat, my mother with a toque decorated with a feather broom, and I with one of my mother's hats. We were seated round the kitchen table, drinking coffee and eating an enormous omelet. Mme Maillard, knowing that her daughter was subject to fits, imagined she must have communicated to us a share of her madness. We laughed so much that little Lucienne began to cry.

Mme Maillard had come to tell us that her baker had sold his shop and that she was going to marry him. They were going to live on a bit of land he owned at Nogent. She wanted to know if her daughter would come to the wedding. Mme Maillard was then sixty, wrinkled as a winter apple. Marguerite thought the idea of her mother being married was so funny that she ripped the cloth from the table and draped it round the old lady's head to see how she looked as a bride. Mme Maillard herself was so gay that it struck us as just possible that she was already married and that they were in the midst of celebrating at the bakery, but we soon dismissed this thought and decided we would rehearse for a picturesque country wedding. Marguerite struck up a very old favourite for such occasions about a farmer who 'loved dearly his wife Jeanne, but would prefer to see her die than lose his precious cattle.' Marguerite carried off this song very well, with her hand on her heart. My mother gave us a sermon with the accent of the Berry, which she had not forgotten from her

*D

childhood. Mme Maillard, a little nervous at the idea of being
taken a second time to the altar, gave us a fresh account of how
she had thrown the pepper into the eyes of her first husband's
mistress.

The proceedings were likely to continue for some time, there
being no husbands present (though, in truth, all the conversation
turned on them) so I quietly slipped out into the courtyard to
play ball. Suddenly, looking over the low wall which divided
me from the street, I saw a familiar head, rising, falling, like a
ship dropping from the crest of one wave to be taken up again
on the next. I rushed with such eagerness to announce the news
that I slipped on a mat outside our door and, landing on my
posterior, shot across the room on my improvised toboggan.
The three women at the imagined wedding feast laughed so
hilariously that my words of warning were drowned. Though
my pride was hurt I nevertheless continued to shout: 'M. Hyacinthe has arrived!' Suddenly I saw Marguerite throw off her
hat, pick up her daughter, and rush upstairs with such speed that
my mother, Mme Maillard, and even I remained wide-eyed.

A moment later Hyacinthe's uneven step tapped over the floor
boards. We heard his wooden leg on the stairs. We listened to
him pause and put the key into the lock. He was above us now.
He stumped about a moment, took off a boot that fell noisily.
We guessed he was changing his striped trousers, the ones he
kept for the bank, and putting on others too frayed for public
view. He would button up his alpaca waistcoat, light the spirit
lamp and soon go down to the cellar to weigh the provisions
he would give his wife for the next day or two.

All the tenants had private cellars in which they kept their wine
and potatoes. Hyacinthe, since his recent advancement at the
bank, had not had a chance to give his usual care to this matter
with the result that Marguerite had gone without or borrowed
from us. Every month Hyacinthe's parents sent him from their
farm a tightly sewn sack and a barrel of wine. The railway people
would have to leave these things in the passage because Hyacinthe
would not trust the cellar key to his wife. As soon as he came
home Hyacinthe, limping, sweating, cursing, wiping the sweat off
his forehead with a pocket handkerchief, would force himself by
an indomitable will to pull the sack and roll the barrel along the
corridor, send them bumping down the stairs and into the damp

darkness of the cellar where he would light a candle stub and measure, with a mercer's wooden yard, how much wine the new barrel contained and what there was left in the old one. He was always afraid some tenant might bid him good evening whilst he was occupied in this way. In the passage or on the stairs, for instance, he never accepted an offer of help in bringing down his merchandise for fear it would cost him a glass of the wine. One felt it might have saved a lot of trouble not to drink any himself, but the miser had been brought up to it at meals. Besides, it was his due. He paid his parents' income tax which in those days was not considerable. His mother sent him hams and salted bacon, sausages, lard, butter, and quite a pyramid of potatoes. Everything had to be measured up and weighed, but as he was awkward, having only one leg and one eye, he was always having accidents. The wine would escape from the barrel. The candle, without protection, amidst so much grease and oil, would nearly set fire to the house, or else it would blow out and leave him sitting on a heap of coal in the dark.

We used to hear all about his adventures from Marguerite. He once turned the key in the padlock without having fastened the bolt. Anybody could have entered his precious cellar. He was three days before going back. Marguerite told us that when he returned to the flat after discovering this tragedy he was so white that she thought he must have seen a ghost behind one of the wine barrels. He told her in a shaking voice what had happened. 'Oh! If only I had known!' she exclaimed. On another occasion he came back smelling appallingly of rum, having broken a five-litre glass jar. Furious to see her care so little, he started a long speech about the savings they would have to make in consequence, and as he became more and more excited he raged round the room gesticulating. Marguerite, revengefully unsympathetic, laughed till she cried. Every first of April he would consign the oil lamp to a high cupboard, and from that day till winter his family would have to go to bed with the last light of evening. It was their custom to go to bed early. Hyacinthe rose at dawn and walked all the way to his bank in Paris to save the fare. Marguerite got up early too. What was wonderful about her was her capacity for fun. One evening, in a mood of devilry, she stole her husband's famous violin, the one on which he had played those love tunes to charm her, and she arrived in our flat with the black case under her arm. We all went out into the passage and with the help of Mme Séguin, who had come back with her family to Paris, tried to pass the bow across the strings. Our laughter must have echoed through the house, especially when Marguerite, having put the fiddle in the right position under her chin, began to imitate her husband, limping about as he always did on these occasions. An upper window was thrown up and we heard Hyacinthe asking in an anxious tone what was happening. Of course he could not see us or we him, but he exclaimed: 'There's something funny going on. Oh, all those plaguy females!'

He closed the window and we heard him go back to bed. After giving him a minute or two to sleep we started up again with more gusto still. The window was flung open a second time and on this occasion Hyacinthe had discovered that his wife was missing from her accustomed place in the double bed. We heard him roar: 'That's enough, Marguerite. I can see you.' Of course, that was nonsense. He could not possibly have seen any of us. Mme Séguin called out: 'That's a lie, M. Hyacinthe. She's much too far from your one eye!'

Hyacinthe closed the window and our jesting ceased.

Germaine was now in a nursing home, a rather sinister place where they tried to reform girls. So many serious complications had followed her miscarriage that she had lost the use of her legs. The police had not discovered the woman who had done it for her. The war had broken in on their investigations. Mme Séguin was more concerned about herself than about her daughter whom she considered as a nuisance, a vague possible cause of trouble, she and her husband preparing to do factory work and not wanting the police about their tracks.

Mme Séguin sang well with a deep, throaty voice which the common people have. No woman could sing with more passionate warmth a song which then was sweeping Paris: *Sous les ponts de Paris.*

We had really no idea how the war was getting on. There had been a card, a highly coloured affair with mimosa and tangerines on it, that my father had sent us addressed to the rue de Longchamps and which Marie-Thérèse had forwarded. He was at Sospel, a fort on the Italian frontier, and I don't think he liked it at all, the manœuvres being extremely hard and the food indifferent. He said he was looking forward to leave.

One evening, after a particularly hot day, Mme Séguin, Marguerite, my mother, and I were all sitting on our cane-chairs in the courtyard when we heard the sound of horses along the road. Marguerite began to shudder. Horses' hoofs! We looked at her anxiously, wondering whether she would have an attack. The horses came nearer. Then we heard the big gates of the board schools being opened. Such a great commotion followed, hoofs on the gravel, people running, that we all four got up together and tore out into the street. What a sight! The school playing-ground was full of soldiers in bright red trousers. They were unshaven. Their dark blue cloaks were filthy. They looked as if they had neither slept nor eaten for a week. An army of beggars would not have made a more pitiful sight. Some limped in front of their horses. Others dropped the bridles and lay down on the gravel refusing to move. Two gendarmes stood at the gates and told us to go away. Obviously they had orders not to talk. We skirted the outside of the boys' school and after a while from an upper window we saw a curl of tobacco smoke, then a pipe. We crossed to the opposite pavement, looking up, and saw a soldier. He told us that the regiment had been in full retreat since 6th August, that Belgium had been invaded, and that the Germans were quite near Paris. We stayed looking up at him, our mouths open, our eyes glassy. We could not understand it. We had taken it so much for granted that the war was going on in a proper way, distantly. The soldier with the pipe was getting used to the idea of things going badly. His main interest was to have a loaf of bread. He asked us to go and get him one. Of course we promised. Marguerite, who was more moved than any of us, went to her flat and crept into the kitchen on tiptoe so that her husband would not hear her. She came down again with some provisions and four litres of wine which was what Hyacinthe had given her for the whole week. She whispered: 'I'm lucky. He was asleep.' We went to our place and put everything in a basket. It was so heavy that we could hardly lift it. The man with the pipe was waiting for us. My mother and Marguerite hoisted me on Mme Séguin's shoulders, and whilst I was thus not very securely balanced I started to hand up each thing, first the bread, then the bottles of wine. We all slept badly that night. Only Hyacinthe slept well.

These soldiers remained in the school for over a week, cut off

from the civilian population.   This was perhaps a good thing for
us, for they were covered with lice and mange.   Apart from this
we soon got tired of looking up at them, and we were not rich
enough to feed them and take them wine.   Hyacinthe had made
us a little speech saying that as he was not personally responsible
for the war, those who had started it might as well get on with
it, that it was definitely no business of his.   Of course, it was a
nuisance about the Germans being so near Paris.   The bank
might have to close or be evacuated.

Queues began to form outside the grocers' shops.   There
were women who hoarded sugar and flour.   As soon as the
soldiers had gone, we saw the first refugees from Belgium and
the north-east provinces.   Marguerite was suddenly confronted
by her aunt from Rheims.

We had often heard about this aunt from Rheims whom Marguerite, in her conversation, trotted out as being a cut above the
others.   There are many families who like to refer with pride
to a member who has done better than the rest, just as in
times past an Englishwoman might refer with pride to some
distant cousin who had married the nephew of an earl.   The aunt
from Rheims lived in a house that belonged to her.   Marguerite
had met her at her sister Lucy's marriage, for I am not sure if I
have mentioned that Marguerite's sister Lucy used a little money
she inherited to get herself married to a professional soldier.
This professional officer was a nephew of the aunt from Rheims.
If these relationships are at all clear you will readily understand
that though Marguerite and the aunt were poles apart our friend
found it pleasant occasionally to bandy about a rich relation who,
in our ears, had a fortune as inaccessible as that of the Rocke-
fellers.   My mother and I had always been very impressed.
Whenever we had a new hat or a roast for lunch, it was a suitable
occasion to exclaim: 'Why, it's good enough for Marguerite's
aunt from Rheims!'

With all this in mind we saw a little old woman in black with
a lot of ungainly packages done up with rope.   She was covered
with dust and her eyes were haggard with fear and fatigue, for
her house had been transpierced by a shell.   You can imagine
what we felt like to see this legendary figure in such a terrible state.
Could it really be that the aunt from Rheims was so insignificant,
so dusty, and nervous.   That she was now as poor as we were.

Even poorer. Her house was gone. She had nothing left but what she carried with her.

Seated very stiffly on a high-backed chair, her little hands joined pathetically on her black skirt, she remained silently in a dark corner, as, I suppose, she was used to sitting by her window overlooking some narrow and busy street in Rheims. When I saw her thus I thought she was dreaming of what she had lost. We made her a cup of coffee. She drank it eagerly and the bitter, familiar taste must have touched a chord, for she suddenly burst into tears. I fancy she did not see us through those tears which were shed for herself only. We stood in front of her like figures turned by fear into marble. We could not hope to understand what was taking place in her mind.

As Marguerite was unable to lodge her aunt we decided to give her hospitality for a night and the next day to take her to her niece Lucie who lived at St. Cloud. The old lady, accordingly, did not unpack any of her parcels. She took her shoes off, undid the ribbons of her black straw bonnet, and proceeded to remove from her hair dozens of tiny steel pins. Two plaits fell down her back like long, thin serpents. Now she unplaited them and one could see that they were speckled with white. She plaited them again and fastened them with all the little steel pins which she had just taken out, but she did not put her bonnet back. She washed her hands, took from a pocket of her petticoat a black rosary, and started to pray silently. One merely saw the lips moving rhythmically. This silent, pious presence in our room made us feel more uncomfortable than if she had talked all night. Instinctively we moved about the flat on tiptoe. My mother did not dare interrupt her prayers. As it was very late I was falling asleep in spite of the many black coffees which my mother, put out by the strange visitor, had made us drink.

I slept in my mother's bed. My own, with clean sheets, was left to the aunt; we found her stretched out on it the next morning, her hands joined under her breasts in the attitude of a corpse. Her eyes opened, however, and followed our every movement. Then she spoke. Hyacinthe could be heard coming down the stairs cloppety-clop, through the front door, and off to the bank. Marguerite arrived, all ready to go out, her hat on, and when she had gathered the aunt's parcels together they set off for St. Cloud, leaving us Lucienne. We watched them going, and when they were quite a distance off, their heads bobbing up and down, we took Lucienne in our arms and danced for joy. The unfortunate lady in black had quite taken the spirits out of us.

Everywhere we went now the accent of the north filled the streets. Our most dreadful lodgings were snapped up by these refugees. The Belgians sorted old rags in the courtyards. There were Serbians also. The battle of the Marne was going on.

Lucienne was now old enough to play with me, though in games like those we organized on the burning asphalt of the street I would let her win. Then she would clap her hands delightedly. Suddenly we would hear the parish bells. The bells were rung to announce something out of the ordinary, but even if it was only a baptism we were glad of the fun. At the sound of the bells, therefore, Lucienne and I, hand in hand, would run down to the bottom of the street which, on one side, was bordered by a high wall surmounted by broken bottles. Above the wall and the glass one could see the higher branches of magnificent chestnut-trees and, farther, the buildings of the Gouin Hospital, a private institution where the nurses were nuns. We would watch their pretty caps with the triangular white sails floating in the breeze.

On arrival here we became aware of a funeral coming in our direction, but of an obviously special kind. The coffin was covered with flags and at one end a military cap and dark blue cape. Immediately behind the hearse wounded soldiers, helped by nurses, limped along. Some had their arms in slings; others had bandages across their heads. They looked like the coloured pictures of the war of 1870, for they still had gilt buttons on their capes and vivid red trousers. Their caps also were of the old kind. The procession, with wheels creaking on the paving-stones, went very slowly. When it reached the church the soldiers formed two rows and remained at the salute whilst the sisters, praying in low voices, their white wings floating, took down the coffin. There were so many wreaths that many were left on the pavement after the people had gone into the church. We read 'Mort pour la France' in golden letters. From others we gathered that the soldier who had thus bravely died for his country was twenty years old. This was the first one, nursed, fussed over, loved, who had died at this hospital. He was the parish hero. The bells started to ring again and the people

came out. The more seriously wounded, unable to accompany
their dead comrade to his last resting-place, were taken back by
the nurses to hospital. Lucienne and I watched all this sadly.
We were gradually becoming cognizant of the war. The funeral
we had seen that day was the first of many, but subsequently the
red trousers of the mourners disappeared. Khaki or French blue
replaced the gayer colours. The cap was shaped differently.
Instead of the many flags on the coffin the parish supplied a
large sheet dyed in the three colours which was used over and
over again, and the processions moved along at a much quicker
pace. Then came the first air raids. *Taubes* glittered unmolested
over Paris and we were told they dropped poisoned sweets for
the children. We looked up at them with much interest and I
do not remember feeling afraid. In October the schools started
a new term and once more my mother, in tears, led me off by
the hand. I asked her why she cried so, thinking, of course, that
it was entirely because of me, but she answered with a touch of
annoyance that she was thinking of her son, remembering that
occasion in 1912. Several mistresses were in the room when we
arrived. The headmistress would have a few words with the
mother and then introduce her to the mistress in whose class her
daughter would be. When it was my mother's turn to be
introduced she was so upset that, after murmuring a phrase that
nobody understood, she fled from the building, leaving me
amongst my young companions who seemed just as lost as I was.
One of the mistresses sounded a bell. We were formed into two
rows and led off to our respective classes in rooms which had
been sprinkled with water from a gardening can and then
swept.

This was certainly the poorest of poor schools. Two classes
were taught by the same mistress who sat at a desk midway
between them. The little girls were on one side, the older girls
on the other. I was put at a tiny desk. The furniture had been
given piecemeal by various charitable ladies with the result that
the pupils' desks were all of varying sizes. Mine, besides being
small, was low. The girl next to me had an unusually tall one
so that her feet, against the bar of her desk, were level with my
eyes. She amused herself by dropping all sorts of things on
my head.

However diligently I applied myself to my work, bending over

my copy-book, my companion's ill-shod feet burst into my line
of vision, giving me eye-ache, headache, and stomach-ache.
Mlle Allard, our mistress, was a Huguenot from the Savoy, and
accordingly more fervently protestant than those in countries
where this religion is not in the minority. She began lessons
with a prayer after which two senior pupils handed round the
hymn-books. We sang a great deal. My childish intelligence
judged these hymns to be admirable. We picked ears of corn
with Jesus in immense golden cornfields, we fought shattering
battles against evil hordes, we walked miraculously over the sea
holding Jesus' hand. Our Lord became such a real Person for
me that I saw Him everywhere. He was a Shepherd, a School-
master. He liked children and held His classes in the open air.
What gentle hours I spent listening to Mlle Allard reading the
Scriptures to us, explaining them with such simplicity! Her
great and good soul overflowed into ours. She filled with contentment daughters of rag-and-bone men, stone-breakers, apaches,
thieves, and drunkards whose tenderer feelings had been taken
right out of them by misery and illness. I cried over the Passion.
My sensitivity was beginning to make itself apparent. Mlle
Allard scolded me, saying: 'He died but He rose again.'

I was tolerably happy at school but my throat gave me a lot
of trouble. I ended by running such a high fever that I had to
remain at home, and Dr. Lehman, a picturesque old Alsatian
doctor, told me that I should have to have my tonsils out.

We went to the out-patients department of the Gouin Hospital
where they still dealt with a few civilians in spite of the fact that
they were so short of space that many seriously wounded soldiers
were left to lie on the floor. I arrived with my mother in a dark
room where a doctor took me on his knees and proceeded,
without an anaesthetic or any sort of drug, savagely to hack at
my throat. I howled with pain and scratched. A nurse scolded
me. I kept on seeing this brutal wretch, a lamp attached to his
forehead, thrusting curved scissors into my throat and then with-
drawing them. At last, mastering me, he got to work properly.
I could hear, though mad with pain, the snipping of tissues cut.
This unbelievable torture lasted a matter of minutes or seconds.
A nurse tied a towel round my neck and tipped me over a basin
as if I had been a bundle of dirty washing. The blood gushed
out. When they were tired of watching it flow they put a piece

of ice in my mouth, and giving me back to my mother told us to go home.

I groped my way out of the hospital, clinging close to my mother, my head bent into the towel. I could see nothing. I think my mother would have carried me but I was too big a girl now. Fortunately I slept till the next morning. When our old Alsatian doctor arrived my mother let fly at him, telling the poor old man what she thought of his cruelty in sending me to such a place. He said it cost money to have an anaesthetic and that we could never have paid for it. The operation had been appallingly done. I had fought bitterly. My throat had been torn in all directions. All my life I have suffered from it.

When I went back to school another little girl had taken my low desk and I was given the very tall one, inflicting on my neighbour the same vexation as I had previously suffered. One day Mlle Allard asked me if it was true that my mother was a dressmaker. My mother made her several blouses with which she was delighted.

In the middle of our school, which had the form of a tiny feudal city, was a structure made partly of planks and partly of stone. This was the church or, to be more exact, it had been the church, for it was now more or less in ruins, quite impossible to heat in winter, and had been abandoned at the beginning of the war in favour of a new church in the rue Gobert. The tumbledown structure was used by the pastor's wife on Mondays for her mothers' meetings.

Mothers and grandmothers arrived from the most curious places. Some were in weeds, all were in black. They were very poor, lame, blind, furrowed, horrible to look at like beggars on the steps of a cathedral. When they sang one heard their thin voices quaking on upper notes. They listened, some of them knitting, to a little talk. A few old clothes were handed round. At five those of us who had been specially good at our class work were chosen to help the woman in the canteen prepare the hot chocolate and cut the bread and butter. We served these poor wrecks proudly, happy to feel ourselves young, and quite certain that never, never would we become old and ugly women. When they had all eaten and drunk we would finish up the hot chocolate, whilst the pupils who had not been counted good enough to assist looked greedily at us through the dusty window.

The big girls in the class next to ours were taught by the headmistress, Mlle Zélie. Mlle Zélie was the daughter of a pastor of Montauban which is in the hot and sunny south. Excellently brought up, very trim about her person, a pretty waist, a boned lace collar holding erect her delicate neck, she had a fine air. Her blend of piety and coquetry was very charming. She was of violent temper like everybody from the *midi*, and resolutely led her girls forward to a love for God and their country which with her was so deep that she would have gladly become a martyr for the one or the other. We used to join her pupils at a certain hour every morning to sing, for she was an excellent musician. We sang hymns and patriotic songs, fervently, in quick succession, until one was tempted to wonder whether one would be required in womanhood to do anything else but sing. Examinations had no sort of importance for little girls in the middle of the war.

One morning I was wakened up by two loud kisses on my cheeks. My father was home on leave. He let me off school that day and we went together to market. I was very proud to have my soldier but he looked changed. In dark blue uniform, an old artillery cap as they wore in 1870, long upcurling moustaches, he appeared older and thinner. He was very unhappy in his fort and cursed the Italians who refused to make up their minds on whose side they would fight. After he had been at home a day or two he got tired of having nothing to do. In the afternoons we would see him slink off to the café for a game of cards. My mother was not pleased. Then he went back to Sospel and we went on as before.

About a month later my Uncle Louis came to see us. He had done rather well for himself, having been drafted, by the help of friends, to a safe job in a military hospital near Le Creusot. He brought Rolande with him as a sort of peace-offering because my Aunt Marie-Thérèse was anxious to make things up with my mother. He invited us to lunch at rue de Longchamps the following Sunday and my mother accepted.

Many of our old friends arrived in different circumstances. I mean, the war made them look tired and disillusioned. Rose was patiently waiting for news of her German lover. She could still not believe anything bad of him. Before others, at any rate, she would not admit the possibility of his having been a spy.

Her wounded heart longed for his polite affection and it was a sad sight to see her withering away. Hélène was there but her Raoul was at the front. Marie-Thérèse had received information from Marais that Laurent, Ermeline's husband, after having been on the list of missing for several weeks, had been discovered seriously wounded in a military hospital. My aunt and my mother were delighted to be together again and poured news into each other's ears.

From the Grand' Combe we had received a letter saying that Aunt Marie was dead and that Henri Toulouse and Ernestine were married. The wedding had been very simple because of Aunt Marie and the war. Henri Toulouse had closed his shop and gone off with his regiment. Ernestine was living with her parents. Uncle Ernest was working very hard in the mine which had become of much greater importance since so many had been overrun in the Pas-de-Calais. Indeed, miners from the north had been sent there.

These things, of course, I had known when my mother first received the letter. What had saddened me was to hear that nobody mentioned Louis Verdier.

10

THERE arrived one day at home a little man who took me on his knees and kissed me on both cheeks. He spent the whole day with us. He was Cousin Prosper Nègre, related to us on my father's side, who had left the Grand' Combe many years earlier to settle in Paris where he had bought 1 small hotel with a wine and café-bar.

Cousin Prosper was a very pious man, his church-going having been inculcated into him, I fancy, by Cousin Catherine whose son, you will remember, was a priest. Prosper's hotel quickly made money. On the first floor women of a certain world slept throughout the day; then at night, looking very pretty, went out into the streets. The rooms on the higher floors were occupied by male shop assistants and bank clerks. Cousin Prosper, his pockets full of money, was on the point of returning to his native Grand' Combe when the devil took hold of him. He fell in love with his servant-girl who was delighted to see this man of fifty suddenly starting to sow his wild oats. She quickly gave him a child. His fortune began to run through her fingers and her conduct was so bad that he was not even certain that the child was his. She had persuaded him to make over a great deal of his money at the time of the marriage. He was imposed upon, deceived, ruined, and cheated in love. Worst of all, for a man so religious, he was obliged to institute proceedings for divorce. He had come to see us before returning penniless to his sunny birthplace. Sadly to my mother and to me, a little girl, he made a *mea culpa*. He had earned a small fortune by closing his eyes to prostitution and encouraging men to drink in his wine shop, and these two vices had taken revenge on him in the person of his wife. He had perished from their sharp arrows.

Cousin Prosper was going home that night, travelling as my father and I had done, third class. We watched him as he went down the street, his back bent with sorrow and remorse.

We were at the beginning of a hard winter and my mother feared the dampness of our apartment for my frail health.

One afternoon Marguerite Rosier called on us with her sister Lucie, the one with whom the aunt from Rheims had gone to live, but the aunt had decided to accept a position as house-keeper to a priest where she felt more useful, living at nobody's expense. Lucie, having four children and a husband who was in the regular army, had been given the enviable post of *concierge* at a magnificent villa at St. Cloud. She lived in the grounds in a gay lodge and her only duties were to keep an eye on the villa which was not lived in. Just now she was expecting her husband to arrive on leave and she was anxious for my mother to make her a blouse.

She was a big woman, dark, with blue eyes, pretty but with no waist, and short. She was terribly quick, could sweep and clean a room in no time, giving the furniture a polished appearance which was very pleasant in a house. She was dreadfully in love with her husband. She believed he loved nobody but her. He, the wicked man, was naturally inconstant. He would only arrive at home after most of his leave had been spent with a mistress. He would give his wife one magnificent day, spend all her savings, beat his eldest daughter Alice whom he considered ugly and useless, put his wife pregnant, and then hurry back to his regiment.

Whilst Lucie was singing the praises of her husband and laughing at Hyacinthe whom she could not stand my mother was cutting and sewing her blouse, trying it on, or serving coffee to go with the biscuits that Lucie had specially brought.

Lucie talked about the war expertly, conscious that she was the wife of a regular soldier. She wanted to make herself look important and well informed, but when she boasted rather too much about her military knowledge Marguerite said to her:

'My dear Lucie, instead of worrying about your husband's regi-ment you would do better to buy a new corset. You 're getting as round as a barrel, and when Maurice comes on leave he won't want to make you that fifth child!'

Lucie, dear soul, laughed, but taking up the tape-measure rolled like a snail on the table she measured her young elephant's waist. That started us all off. We measured our waists. Lucie was genuinely unhappy, but when my mother had finished the blouse, seeing it so fresh, so pretty, so delicate, her blue eyes became bluer still and we all forgot her waist in the sweetness of her expression.

It was decided that after Maurice's leave my mother and I would spend a few weeks with Lucie and her children at St.Cloud. Mother would do a lot of sewing to pay for our keep. My school could wait till winter was over.

That evening, after saying good-bye to our guests, I had to tell my mother that I was not feeling well. All the afternoon, contrary to her nature, she had been so full of laughter and happiness that finding me so flushed and hot she blamed herself for not keeping a better eye on me. She began to call me her 'little rabbit,' and whenever I heard her use that appellation I knew I was in for a serious illness. I tossed in my bed; I scratched; then exhausted I fell into a troubled sleep. In the morning I felt well, but in the evening the same thing happened. My mother, curiously enough, was not well herself and she began to scratch. Then it was Lucienne. Then Marguerite.

As I was the worst my mother sent for Dr. Lehman, the Alsatian doctor. He arrived in a black gig drawn by a very old horse that was so accustomed to waiting for its master that it automatically put its forelegs on the pavement and kept off the flies by lazy flicks of its tail. When it felt it had waited long enough it would give gentle taps of its hoofs like a ballerina. If the doctor still did not come his horse would change its tactics and behave itself like an angry, petulant little boy. Dr. Lehman would hear it, even if he had his ear against the chest or the back of a patient. One would see him rise slowly and, taking his note-book, his pen, and a tiny phial of ink which he kept clipped to a pocket of his pale grey satin waistcoat, write out the prescription in a deliberate, slow, slanting hand which, in spite of the care he took, was always quite unreadable. Then he would sign the prescription. My mother would hand him a five-franc piece, or cartwheel, large as the obsolete English crown. This was his fee. We would bend out of the window to see him drive off. As he emerged from our house he would call out: 'Well, Coco, have I really been as long as all that? Very well, Coco, let's go home!' He would climb up painfully, gripping with a veined hand the edge of the black hood which, folded back during the air alarms, showed the threadbareness of the moleskin and looked like the black bonnet of a beggar woman. He sat down, took the reins, passed the whip through his fingers, and then laid it against his shoulder in which position it rose amusingly above his bowler hat in the form of a very thin feather. They would then set off, the horse as old as the master. This war was giving them the evening of their lives. The doctor had been spared for his patients; the horse for his master.

Dr. Lehman told us we had a horrible disease but one which was not serious. We had scabies or the itch. There was an epidemic amongst the soldiers at the front and the refugees who continued to crowd into Paris. We would not be ill long but we would have to go to the skin diseases hospital, the famous St. Louis, for we needed to have a certain ointment put all over us.

A long queue of women and children had been waiting for hours when we arrived. They all had the itch. There were women of all conditions, women wearing hats, bread-carriers, middle - class women, and beggar women, all itching and scratching.

The woman next to us had already come for treatment. 'This is what happens,' she said. 'The department we go to there are only women. We all have to be naked—as naked as the back of the hand. Then a nurse comes along with a scrubbing brush and yellow soap. After that she puts sulphur ointment on you and when you 're all sticky and stink like a cheap match, you try to put your clothes on again.' Other women in the queue had turned round, listening. She went on: 'Wait till you hear the kids yell and the women who have it on the breasts! I 'm all right. I 've only got it on the stomach and the arms.'

My mother, that model of bashfulness and modesty, waited to hear no more. She took me by the hand and hurried home.

She had learnt exactly what to do. We bought a soft hair-brush and a large quantity of ointment. In the evening she made me stand in the washtub and she started to pass the brush over my body. I shrieked with pain and she cried to hurt me so. In the end I realized she was suffering more than I was and I bit my lips to keep quieter. My eyes were filled with tears. I could not see out of them. The ointment was another martyrdom. My mother wrapped me up in an old sheet, but as I then looked as if I were all ready to be put in my coffin she took it off and gave me a night-dress. She painfully went through the same treatment, but I was asleep by the time she had finished.

Dr. Lehman came back to see us. He was not pleased to have to treat this malady at home. We were very unhappy, for we could not visit Marguerite and Lucienne Rosier. We had to talk to them through the window. Lucienne was already well again, having had it very lightly.

In due course, when we were getting better, Dr. Lehman advised us to go to the public baths where we could take a sulphur bath. We set off with a change of clothing. The attendant ran the bath, gave us a clean towel, and left us to ourselves after my mother had slipped her a penny for herself.

I undressed first, and bathed in yellow water smelling of rotten eggs; then my mother, having taken her clothes off discreetly in a corner, came forward to step in after me. But even in front of me she would have been ashamed to show herself naked. She arrived, therefore, in a chemise which, as soon as she touched the warm water, rose like a balloon. I laughed shamelessly to see her try to bring it down with both hands. Later we took starch baths. The water was white and soft and smelt good. My mother, having become modern, made herself a sort of bathing dress, but not covering her breasts which she said I had seen often enough when she was feeding my small brother. At last we were cured, but as nearly always happens in epidemics the children suffer most, and in this case I remained extremely weak.

Hyacinthe was working at the bank on Sundays now for which he received double pay. His savings were growing; he computed what they would be in so many years at compound interest. He had become insatiable. He had rolls of golden louis which he refused to give up to war savings but he was terrified that they would be stolen. He started by keeping them at the bank, but having taken fright at a remark which in reality had nothing to do with him, he brought them back to Clichy, not sleeping for fear that our apaches might get to know about his treasure.

Occasionally when the secret was too much for him alone he would confide in his wife, but immediately afterwards he would be sorry he had told her and would be obliged to change the hiding-place. One day she threw away a box of pills she had found at the top of a dusty cupboard. When Hyacinthe came home he made an atrocious scene and spent the evening going through the garbage cans until he remembered that he had recently taken the gold from the box she had thrown away and put it in another hidden under the wash-stand. Marguerite was even more afraid of his joy than she had been of his despair. On the first Sunday that I was well again, Hyacinthe being at his bank, Marguerite brought Lucienne to spend the day with us. My Aunt Marie-Thérèse and Rolande also came to lunch. My mother had told them how amusing Marguerite could be, how full of fun, and they were looking forward to meeting her. Unfortunately Marguerite was not at her best. Hyacinthe had exhausted her the previous evening with a terrible quarrel about his gold. Lunch was not particularly successful for the women, therefore. For us children it was a success. Rolande and I had dressed Lucienne up. We then borrowed my mother's high heels and each in turn pretended that we were on a visit with our daughter. The daughter was Lucienne. While my mother was serving coffee Mme Maillard, Marguerite's mother, arrived accompanied by her new husband, M. Malgras, the former baker. We were all delighted to see a new face. M. Malgras had fresh, pink cheeks which looked as if they had been lately scrubbed. His eyes were full of life, and when he discovered that he was the only man amongst so many females he set out to charm us all. His politest shop manners came forward. One might have supposed a fairy had taken ten years off his age. He smiled and beamed and distributed compliments, and gallantly suggested that we should allow him to take us all for a stroll in the avenue.

We went off in great style, women and girls tripping along in the wake of this rejuvenated old gentleman who was bursting with joy and vanity. We drank some beer at the terrace of a café and M. Malgras gave us, the children, money to buy *croissants* at the baker's. The outing brought Marguerite back to her jolly self. Suddenly we saw coming towards us a young English soldier, fair-haired, fresh shaven, beautifully clean-looking in his khaki uniform. He was accompanied by a young Frenchwoman and the efforts he made to speak French made him still more irresistibly attractive. We all thought he was as handsome as a young god. Our eyes followed him as he passed. Our hearts beat for the love of him. Our tongues let forth a melody of praise. M. Malgras tried hard to interest us in the amazing happenings of his former bakery; we ceased to listen to him.

He let slip the expression 'when I was young.' That did it. The spell departed. His shoulders drooped, his mouth sagged, his eyes lost their brightness. He became rather a silly old man. He looked round in despair. He was beaten and should never have taken out all these females. We saw him yawn. Mme Maillard, now Mme Malgras, paid for the beer, and we got up with no more poetry in our hearts.

This was the first time I had seen an English soldier. I made a queer resolution, to marry an Englishman. I confided this to my mother the same evening as I was going to bed. 'The point is,' she queried, 'are they any better than ours? Men promise so much and give so little.' I did not pay great attention to her and when I dreamed that night I believe I dreamed in English!

During the second week in October we took the tram-car as far as Asnières, and another one from there to St. Cloud. The little estate where Lucie was *concierge* was quite a way from the centre of St. Cloud, along the towing-path. Our parcels were very heavy and all the houses facing the lazy, wide river seemed alike, magnificent iron gates, tall trees browned by autumn, curled-up leaves smelling damp, eddying at our feet. I picked up some leaves and filled my lungs with the autumnal odour. The Seine was beautiful and deserted, barges idle along the muddy bank. At last we arrived. There was a bell in the gate. We pulled it and it tinkled amongst the distant trees. Young steps ran over hidden gravel and then we saw a little boy who opened to us with both hands saying:

'We 've been waiting for you. How old is your little girl?'

Lucie arrived, very fat, with her youngest child in her arms.

'You 're late,' she said affectionately. 'Dédé was impatient.'

Dédé was, of course, the little boy. My mother followed Lucie into the lodge and Dédé and I were given permission to run away.

Dédé, more properly André, was ten, fair, pale, slender, but quick. As he only went to school from time to time he was as ignorant as I, but we were both extremely inventive when it came to playing. Gentle and patient, mostly playing by himself, he was overjoyed to have me.

The garden was enormous with curving lawns whose grass, not mown, was turning brown at the tip, gravel-walks that crunched underfoot, tall trees, and a stone wall round the lodge.

This wall was full of secrets. There grew against it ivy, climbing roses, and other plants. Birds and snails lived in the crevices. By following it we came upon another which divided the estate from the towing-path, a tower built upon it in which there was a spiral staircase, a room on the upper floor containing rustic chairs, and a table and from which, when we were sitting there. we could see the Seine flowing past.

This belvedere soon became our castle. We hid all our treasures in it and nobody ever came to disturb us. From early morning we were there, whatever the weather, and only when we heard the tinkling bell of the great iron gate did anybody see us, and then we tumbled and ran, out of breath and terribly curious. This same bell, rung by Lucie in a manner we recognized, brought us turbulent and hungry to our meals.

The lodge reminded me of a transfer picture, but so small that Lucie and her husband might in normal times have found it rather difficult to pack their family inside. A dining-room, a kitchen, and a bedroom comprised the ground floor above which there was nothing but a sweetly sloping roof. The dining-room table was round and covered with an oilcloth upon which a full pack of cards in colour was designed. We ate in turn upon the king of diamonds, the knave of clubs, or the ten of hearts. Lucie refused to have her meal upon the queen of spades, who was bad news, or the queen of diamonds—the flippant woman, the woman of bad character, the traditional enemy. The knave of spades, whom she called the 'dog of spades,' was malevolent and underhand. Alice, the eldest daughter, aged fifteen, planned manœuvres worthy of a great general to find herself in front of the knave of hearts—a beautiful young man, dignified and clever, about whom she dreamt and who, one day, would marry her, taking her miles away from her parents and the brothers and sisters she was obliged to look after. She was in the ungraceful age and was conscious of her awkwardness. Though small she already had breasts that rose to her chin and a large posterior. As soon as she tried to draw one in the other became more apparent. She was unhappy, but her mind was crammed with dreams, hopes, and desires. Lucie, who was only sixteen when she had given birth to her, now found her slightly embarrassing, seeing in her many of her own defects, and was worried this girl would go wrong.

My mother and I had immediately set to work to make a dormitory of a large room above the stables. A steep and quaint ladder led to it. My mother, Alice, Dédé, and I slept in this delightful remove. Dédé and I were not long in going to sleep but often, beforehand, I would hear Alice asking my mother:

'Tell me, Matilda, do you suppose I shall remain as ugly as this for long?'

My mother would gently pass in review all the young women she had known as young girls and she would end like this:

'You know, it's always the same. At fifteen you would see them without a waist, the nose askew, pimples on the face, and then, two years later, hey presto! you would meet them again and they had waists so thin you could span them in your two hands, a skin like peach bloom, and a Greek nose!'

Alice would sigh and answer:

'But fancy having to wait two years!'

My mother sewed. She remade entirely her friend Lucie's wardrobe and did what she could with Alice's misshapen form. The lady of the house, before going to the *midi* where her husband, a celebrated aeroplane designer, was working in a factory, had left Lucie many clothes for herself and the girls. These my mother also arranged.

Every two or three days we all went together into the big house to open the windows. We skated along the parquet floors and sat in the arm-chairs. We slid down the banisters and crept wide-eyed into the cellars where the central heating was built, machines that we pretended were the turbines of a great liner.

Just before Christmas Lucie had a telegram to say her husband was wounded. She left with the baby she was breast-feeding. Alice was delighted to find herself at last at the head of the family.

The forest of St. Cloud was full of soldiers, and we had discovered a door in the wall through which we could reach their tents. They would give us hunks of army bread which we thought excellent, and it was Alice who always led these expeditions. I suspect that her main motive was to ascertain if her ungainliness was passing sufficiently for her to make any impression on the soldiers, for she began to laugh less wildly and to make fewer efforts to hide her posterior and her breasts. For André and me these walks in the forest were magnificent. Hand in hand we would press forward, imagining all sorts of things. Then when we came home we would find that my mother had made a great bowl of apple fritters sprayed with sugar. In a moment the table was arranged. Alice would have her plate on the knave of hearts; my mother would take the king of hearts, a gentleman of middle age, excellent situation, probably a business man; and we would leave the queen of spades at a safe distance. Without saying as much we probably thought that it had a message for Lucie who would become a war widow. After the feast I would sew for my doll, but not for long. Dédé and I, drunk with the air of our long walk, would soon find our little heads drooping over the cards on the oilcloth.

Lucie came back to us for Christmas. Maurice had only been slightly wounded but had told her the most dreadful stories of trench warfare. Christmas was delightful, a few toys and some real snow. The garden, the park, the forest, looked quite different.

When winter was over how marvellous the arrival of spring! With April all the lilac came out in flower; the air was heavily alive with it. Over every wall gently waved billowing clouds of white and mauve. André and I had an idea. We picked as much as we could carry and then let ourselves out by the door in the wall. After a little while I began to say: 'Oh, the lovely lilac, freshly picked!' The more distant we were from home, the louder I spoke. A workman going home on his bicycle stopped, took several branches which he tied to his handlebars, gave me a few sous, and went off to beflower his house. A man hurrying past hesitated, took André's entire armful, and left him with three sous in his little hand. Soon we had no lilac left. We slipped home unseen, but at supper our two mothers had little trouble, seeing us so elated, to draw our secret out of us. They were amazed but not angry. They took six sous from us, left us two, and we were happy. The following Sunday my mother and Alice made us up some fine branches and sent us into the town. I sold all mine to various women outside the military hospital. I thought I had found my vocation—to be a flower-girl. Alas, the lilac was soon over. Rain fell, and the room where we slept above the stables was requisitioned. A soldier, a real peasant in uniform, arrived with a large white horse. The white horse broke its tether, and having wandered into the

passage where the steep ladder led to our bedroom was unable
either to proceed or to turn back. My mother and I had been
upstairs. We could not get down because of the horse. Lucie
arrived, caught sight of us, and broke into laughter. She tried
to tell the soldier what had happened, but every time she opened
her mouth she laughed louder. The unfortunate peasant thought
she was bedevilled, but when he noticed that his horse was stuck
in the passage his features took on such an expression of alarm
that Lucie's hilarity increased. In the end he went off to find
six other soldiers who released the horse and us.

Italy was now in the war. The forts on the Alps were accordingly vacated. My father was sent to the front from which he
sent us the most poignant letters. For the first time he was
unable to use his fists. He complained of being attacked without
seeing the aggressor. He managed—I am not quite sure how—
to get himself transferred to a field kitchen; then one day whilst he
and some other men were sweeping the floors they began to
fence with their broom handles. My father received one of the
sticks in an eye. He was sent to the field hospital, from the field
hospital to the base, where they told him his eye was lost. As a
result he was sent home.

We had left St. Cloud. My health had much improved and
during the long winter I had not had a single cold. Paris was
very busy, full of English soldiers and extremely gay. War
factories were expanding. The Séguins were both in work, one
on the night shift, the other on the day. Their daughter
Germaine came home on her eighteenth birthday and went to
work with her mother. Taller than when we had seen her last,
very pretty, she wore a long black overall with red buttons and
had high-heeled shoes. She earned a great deal of money, refused
to discuss her operation, and was waiting to be twenty-one to be
free. She would often visit us, especially when Marguerite
Rosier was there, and to see her so gay, so easily amused, such a
charming companion, it was hard to realize that she had been
the centre of such a sombre story. Mme Séguin seldom left
her; if Germaine was indisposed or for some other reason did
not go to work her mother would stay at home to look after her.
On Sunday evenings my mother, Germaine, and I used to take
a stroll along the Avenue de Clichy to watch the picturesque
crowds. We would have something to drink at the terrace of a

café, and then Germaine could not help looking enviously at the women walking up and down or waiting at street corners, to whom in thought and desire she was still bound by malevolent and powerful ties.

My father worked in a shell factory on the banks of the Seine. One day after he had been there several months I came back to lunch and found the apartment empty. Marguerite Rosier gave me lunch with Lucienne and told me that my father, injured by the snapping of a taut cable, had been placed on some straw and brought back to my mother in a horse-drawn cart. They had first tried to take him to the Gouin Hospital, but as he had a fractured leg they would not admit him, this being apparently out of their sphere. He had now been taken to Beaujon in Paris. I was in a sad state. My mother came back during the afternoon with my father's clothes which she folded. There fell out two small pieces of flat, highly polished wood which had served to support my father's leg and which I turned that same evening into shelves for my doll's cupboard.

We visited my father twice a week, on Thursdays and Sundays, setting forth very early, burdened with a basket of food but mostly wine, and waiting for the big gates to open. Unless we were the first to enter the ward when it was thrown open to visitors my father, tied down to his bed, worked himself up into a towering rage, saying that we were abandoning him. He suffered a lot of pain and passed it off on us with the result that our visits to the hospital became veritable nightmares. We stood at the side of his bed feeling very uncomfortable, my mother tidying his provision cupboard, putting away the wine she so hated the sight of. When the bell rang for us to go we ran gaily down the stairs, elated at the thought of having three clear days before us. We used to go home by the Avenue des Ternes, skirting the fortifications, my mother advancing with tiny quick steps, I running in circles or playing with a hoop.

Sometimes Marie-Thérèse and Rolande came to see us on Sundays and then we would drag them to the hospital. On one such occasion a beautiful woman wearing a long tight skirt walked gracefully towards a very young man whose legs had been crushed by a tram-car. This woman made a tremendous impression on me. I saw in her all the elegance of a world outside mine. The first time, a wide velvet hat of a warm red was poised at the most graceful angle over her peroxide hair. I dreamed about her. My visits to the hospital now had a purpose, to see this magnificent creature who had a new hat or a new dress on each occasion. Her face, much made up for those days, haunted me. Standing by my father's bed, my eyes fixed on the door, I awaited her arrival. Once she smiled at me and I felt myself swaying with emotion. It was a wonder I did not faint. When Rolande and I walked home we pretended we were the beautiful lady.

At last my father began to walk on crutches but the leg was to take a long time to mend. My mother wondered anxiously if he would ever work again. Our reserves were dangerously low.

MME Gaillard had written asking us to come and see her, and as it looked as if my mother would have to start working again we went as soon as possible to the Boulevard Haussmann.

We found her at the stand again set up, a few blouses and some lace in the best box, but she herself in deep mourning, her son having died. She had begun to work again to console herself, but she had found already that money was not in the same hands. Fashion also had changed. I did not see her husband, the doorkeeper. He was ill in bed.

That afternoon it was raining and Mme Gaillard was closing early. She invited us to the little café-bar where for thirty years she had carried out all her transactions. She told us that she was just now doing the rounds of the old curiosity shops looking for lace, and she showed us some from Russia which was delicate and pretty, so full of minute detail that she was continually bringing it out from a pocket in an underskirt to admire it at leisure and discover new angles of its beauty. She said that she would not sell this piece until she had learnt all about it and made it as familiar to her eye and hand as Valenciennes. She had also found some lace bonnet crowns worn by the peasants of Nohant where Mme George Sand lived, the scene of so many of her finest country books like *The Little Fadette*. She had great patience, looking into every shop, walking sometimes miles through the streets, and though it exhausted her physically this was what she wanted to keep her mind off the loss of her son. Of course, no other woman in all Paris could have told so accurately, at a glance, exactly where a strange lace came from and what it was called. She kept on saying that it was a terrible thing to have worked so hard for her son and to think that now he was dead. Her husband, the doorkeeper, also was dying like his poor plants. For so many years she had yearned to buy a house in her native Auvergne where she could retire, and now that she had the money, just see what had happened! She was too old to enjoy it.

Mme Valentin also, it appeared, was in a bad way. She missed the Paris open-air markets, and worried to distraction about her son Louis who was in the front line. Mme Gaillard told us many other details about Mme Valentin, but they were also of the most depressing nature. We left her and tried to brighten our afternoon by looking at all the pretty things in the Galeries Lafayette.

As my father remained in bed all day mother and I lived in the kitchen. I had a passion for ironing and I was given the handkerchiefs to do. Mme Maillard, Marguerite's mother, having ironed for a laundrywoman, would give me lessons when she looked in. You should have seen her take a handkerchief, stretch the corners, fold it, hit it with the iron. For a handkerchief to be ironed perfectly it had to remain rigid, in its folds, when one took it up. I think the art of ironing as it was done in Paris in those days has quite disappeared. Nobody to-day realizes what sorcery these women had in their fingers, how their irons ran and beat and curved with a speed and a deftness that came from secrets handed down and hours and hours of practice. What miracles one can do with heavy old-fashioned irons heated on coals or on the gas-ring! Pleats form themselves magically all down night-gowns or lingerie; blouses stand up like living things! To sew quickly and deftly (with a thimble) and to iron like these Paris women used to are the loveliest gifts that a woman can have.

My father liked to have Lucienne in the room with him, and she liked him also, calling him 'father Mimile.' Though she was normally impatient she would play contentedly by the side of his bed. My father's strength was still enormous and he could take Lucienne in his powerful arms and, the lower part of him tied down to the bed because of the plaster, make her do what he called the 'trapeze' act. The child, having in Hyacinthe a father who was lame, sickly, always engrossed in dreams of avarice, much admired my father who could throw her so easily from hand to hand. He also taught her to sing in the patois of the *midi*. My mother and I took advantage of their friendliness to run off to market where the Belgian refugees, selling their specialities, gave it a new charm. These people were so tireless and pushing that they quickly captured the trade. There were moments when we forgot the growing difficulties at home. On a fringe of the market there were street singers, a woman sang and a child played the accordion. We would hear the latest songs of love and war, and there would be an appreciative audience, for the woman had a deep, sensuous voice. When she finished an air the child went round selling the words and music which we bought and learned on the way home. If Marguerite was with us we would each try to memorize a verse. At home, making the lunch, we would hum the tune. Later in the day, anxious to bring it out again, we would discover that it had escaped our memory. Marguerite would be just as silly. A couple of days later when we were engaged on something quite different she would hurtle down the stairs, two at a time, crying out: 'I 've got it! I 've got it!' and she would sing us our ditty which we would take up for the rest of the week while washing, ironing, or sewing.

Hyacinthe now wore a tailcoat at the bank. He went to the hairdresser at regular intervals and put on a clean shirt. He was becoming more and more important. His former colleagues who went back to the bank during their leaves from the front could not believe their eyes. Of course, they were young and very good-looking and had enormous success with the girls, but all this did not somehow compensate for seeing Hyacinthe climbing to success. Nevertheless they went humbly to pay their respects to him, for it would not have been wise to forget the coming back to the bank after the war. Marguerite was longing to move to a better flat. There were some very modern ones further along the avenue which we often admired during our walks, and one day when we were all out together she took us to the building she liked best and asked the *concierge* to show us a vacant apartment.

We were taken to the fifth floor. The staircase was wide and clean. The entrance to the flat was very pretty, with a bell. The dining-room had a balcony wide enough for a whole family to sit out on warm evenings and look down upon what was happening in the street. There was also a private w.c. instead of having to use a general one at the bottom of the house. We were all in a state of wonderment, and Marguerite, dizzy with emotion, not even waiting for her husband's permission, gave some money to the *concierge*, saying she would take the flat. On the way home her courage sank.

She was helped by the most singular good fortune.

Quite a serious affray took place during the night between a band of apaches and a tenant. A revolver shot was fired.

Hyacinthe, terrified, already imagined himself wounded and unable to go to his beloved bank. At breakfast he was white. Marguerite said to him:

'You see, Hyacinthe, that it's not worth being so successful at your bank if you end by being shot in your own home like a rabbit. We simply must move to another building. This one is no longer safe. The police have been called in. There are deserters in the house. I wouldn't be surprised if next time several people were shot. Oh, my poor Hyacinthe, I pity you! Having a chance to become director of the bank and to end with a bullet in your head! It's too sad!'

Hyacinthe was trembling. He said in a low voice:

'How do you expect me to go flat hunting, I who work every moment of my life? Women are all the same. They leave everything to the men!'

Then Marguerite, magnanimously:

'Listen, Hyacinthe, if you think it's my duty, I could try. That would be the only way. Your life depends on it.'

Hyacinthe went off, limping even more because of the exhaustion of his poor body due to a sleepless night and mental agitation. Marguerite smiled. Like a great general she had won her battle. She would have a dining-room, a parquet floor, and a w.c.

My mother was in despair. Marguerite was moving resolutely towards a life of greater ease and sunshine. Her future and that of Lucienne were being guaranteed by a husband who, however ridiculous in certain ways, was a hard worker, a serious man in his private life, not a drunkard. Marguerite would go to her better life leaving us in despair with no savings and no money coming in for the moment except what my mother was able to earn with her needle. And then there was the loneliness of it! My mother would no longer have a friend to talk to while she was ironing or sewing. The days would be unending again, as in her early married life. The Séguins were always in the factory.

The great removal took place the following Sunday. Hyacinthe hired a donkey-cart and put himself between the shafts, a leather strap round his waist, limping, limping, but a model of courage. Behind the cart my father, limping, pushed and talked. They did the trip a number of times—to the church and then round the board schools to the rue Souchal. That was the name of the street where they were to live. Marguerite, my mother, and I put

the crockery in Lucienne's pram and made the journey several
times too.   Later the men turned their attention to the cellar and
took the wine cask.   My father complained that it was heavy.
He did not like to see it leave the house and thought that if it
must go, it would be easier to drain the best part of it.

My father went back to work, just a few hours a week at first
and then gradually more till he did a full shift.   My mother and
I spent many hours with Marguerite who was a little lost in her
beautiful apartment.   Lucienne and I would sit on the balcony
trying to peep into the neighbours' windows.   When my mother
and I went home in the evening we had fits of depression.   The
walls were damp.   The paper was peeling off.   The rooms were
so small.   My mother began to talk over supper about the
desirability of moving into a modern flat.   My father said he
was quite happy where he was.   He liked the garden on the
opposite side of the road where he could sit in the summer, but
he liked better his favourite café where he played cards with the
regulars.   Since his accident he had made new friends.   He
therefore went more frequently to the café.   Often he came home
very late, and when my mother reproached him he picked
quarrels that day by day became more violent.   He would take
what happened to be on the table, the stew or the soup, and hurl
it into the courtyard.   When his anger subsided he would go to
bed, but we, shaking with fear, sat at the table in front of empty
plates.   My mother sobbed without noise.   She has always wept
silently.   I would try to sleep, but often I woke up with nightmares, my forehead bathed with perspiration.

One Sunday when Marie-Thérèse and Rolande were there my
father became so violent that they left the house, refusing to
come again to see us.   My father was forty-three.   My mother
was not yet thirty.   My father could drink little now without
losing control of himself.   My mother spent the whole of that
night on a chair, crying and turning things over in her mind.
When my father got up to go to work he saw her shivering with
cold in the cruel, pale, early hours before dawn.   He probably
felt ashamed of himself but he did not know how to make
excuses.   His language was not sufficiently rich in words or
suppleness.   I don't think strong men ever make excuses to a
woman.   He came to kiss me, a thing he never failed to do, and
then went off.

My mother then went to bed and slept till eleven. She began making parcels of her things and of mine. After lunch we went to Marguerite's flat taking some of the parcels with us. We then went back for more. My mother sat on the chair where she had spent the night, looking round her. There were things which still reminded her of her baby son, a watch, for instance, hanging up by a silver chain which he had taken to pieces one day, sitting with his legs crossed under him, a very serious expression on his face. My mother was passing the last years in review. There was the cretonne of the hanging cupboard behind which Marguerite hid when she heard the horses' hoofs. There were some toys of mine, a portrait of the actress Réjane and one of Sarah Bernhardt in the role of Aiglon. Poor little mean room in which, since we had taken away our personal things, so little seemed to be left. My mother got up, cried, rummaged, and finally taking my school exercise book wrote on a page:

'Émile, as you continue to make life impossible for us by your anger, I shall take my daughter away. She is all I have left. We are leaving you for ever. Do not try to find us.

MATILDA.'

She put this white page in the middle of the oilcloth on the kitchen table, read it over in a sobbing voice, and led me out by the hand.

We had arranged to spend the night with the Rosiers. The next day we would go to my grandmother at Blois.

I had quite a nice afternoon playing with Lucienne who was only five and very sweet. We had a great deal of trouble making her understand that if my father came she was not to tell him that we were hiding in the flat. At seven we saw my father coming down the street, his bad leg still rather stiff, but he was moving quickly as if in a hurry. From my place on the balcony I could only see his back. It was his back that gradually, moving up and down, full of sad expression, reached the end of the street, then turned out of sight in the avenue. My heart thumped. Something stuck in my throat and I silently wept.

My mother was anxious. Both of us started to imagine each thing my father would do. First he would go by the little garden opposite our house, then cross the road. He always wiped his boots before coming in. At our door he would knock. This evening as nobody would answer he would have to take the key out of his pocket and let himself in. That is when he would see the page out of my copy-book. Tears would roll down his manly cheeks. I knew he would cry and cry. After that he would rush off to Marie-Thérèse.

I was wrong. He came to Marguerite. My mother and I, hiding in a clothes cupboard, heard Marguerite tell him that she had not seen us all day. We kept very still not to give Lucienne an excuse for piping out that we were there all the time, in the dark, playing hide and seek. Lucienne said nothing, so my father went away. His *midi* accent was loaded picturesquely with sorrow. He limped down the five storeys. That was all.

I was miserable. Though I knew in my heart that my mother was right, I pitied my father, being already sufficiently a woman to feel my sentiments go out to the less strong. The day before I had seen my father, strong as Samson, in all his fury, but this evening he was weak and quite lost without his two women.

Hyacinthe was surprised to find us in his house, but he asked no questions and went straight down to the cellar where he spent most of the evening.

We went off very early in the morning and Hyacinthe carried our bags to the underground, for we had to cross Paris to take our train from the Quai D'Orsay. My mother was not only tired but anxious about the reception we would have at my grandmother's, and she would have warned her of our coming if she had not feared my grandmother would, if telegraphed to, have revealed our intentions to my father. We were doing a very serious thing. By law my father could make us both come back because of me. The law was very particular on this point. My mother would have been quite in the wrong. My father could even have demanded the custody of his child. He could have separated my mother and me.

The beginning of our journey was not very gay, therefore, but at Orleans I had forgotten most of our troubles and my nose was firmly fixed to the window pane—cornfields, poppies, and cornflowers. We were in the middle of flaming summer. Life looked tempting. We were going to the country at last. Clichy seemed a long way off and even my father was a little spot on the horizon which grew less and less important at every mile.

We reached Blois at about midday.

*E

My grandmother at that time lived on the far bank of the Loire, in the rue Pontchartrain, a very old house, half town, half country, with a large main room having several beds, and a dark kitchen beyond which was a courtyard full of small cellars in which the tenants kept their wood, their coal, and the rabbits.

As she was not expecting us my grandmother was not at home, but the owner of the house gave us her key and we went in. The apartment smelt of dried earth, thyme, and mint. My mother began by taking off her large hat and sighing profoundly at the sight of this untidy room, the room of an old woman living all by herself, eating bits and pieces on the edge of the table, and who, never expecting anybody, never did anything to make the place look nice. We had bought some peaches and a French loaf on the way from the station and we now ate in silence. I hazarded a few questions but my mother was thinking of something else. I was anxious to open the wicker basket in which I had brought a celluloid baby doll called Bambino, feeling, I think, that if I could rock somebody to sleep I should be less lonely. Bambino appeared as abandoned as I was in this strange house. I looked at the basket longingly but did not dare ask my mother to let me undo it, aware, in spite of my ten years, that my request would sound futile compared to the important problems which my mother was just now turning round in her head.

She was seated by the window, and the sun's rays entering the room set fire to her golden hair, giving her a wild, unnatural look. She emitted a deep sigh. Then undoing the hooks and eyes on the deep wristbands of her sleeves she turned them up with thoughtful care, not at all hurrying. She took a coarse blue linen apron from where it hung on a hook and placed it round her waist, after which she set about quickly doing the room. Suddenly, as if seeing me for the first time, she exclaimed rather harshly: 'Don't you think you could help?' I can still picture myself turning in circles, making great exertions, without knowing where to start. Provoked, my mother cried out: 'Run into the yard and look at the rabbits. You're useless here.'

She was undoing my grandmother's bed, having put two chairs side by side in front of the open window to air the sheets. With a jerk she raised the mattress at arm's length when there rolled out a large-size cocoa tin which seemed very heavy as it bumped on the uncarpeted floor. My mother took it up, opened it, and saw that my grandmother had hidden her savings and a few jewels inside. Alarmed at having thus innocently violated my grandmother's secret she put back the box, remade the bed in a hurry, and sat down to wait.

The hours passed monotonously, but little by little a few neighbours went to their cellars in the courtyard, pretending to fetch wood or give food to the rabbits, but in reality to examine us and perhaps ask a few questions. My mother went out, exchanged a few words, and at last we heard a wheel grinding against gravel and saw my grandmother arriving behind her wheelbarrow full of herbs. She was very surprised to see us, kissed her daughter, and appeared enchanted at my apparition. 'How tall you are and pretty!' These words made me her slave for ever. In a way she also became mine.

My mother went close to her to say what was on her mind but the poor thing was appallingly deaf. One was obliged to take her by the neck and shout into the right ear, this one being the least deaf, and in this way she heard. My mother explained that she had brought me on a visit, but said nothing about my father, fearing my grandmother would send us back. After these few necessary words my grandmother, pushing her wheelbarrow into the courtyard, said: 'Come, we'll give some grass to the rabbits.' She proceeded to empty the wheelbarrow, bringing out from it many different kinds of grasses and herbs, an enamel saucepan full of holes, a lettuce, and a goat's cheese. She then hung the wheelbarrow up by the handles, fed the rabbits, and led me back into the big room where my mother was waiting for us. Here she opened a huge cupboard, brought out some sheets and pillow-cases, giving them to my mother to make up a bed for us on a very large, old-fashioned one in a corner, covered with a red eiderdown. My mother took the eiderdown and shook it out of the window. My grandmother went from one piece of furniture to another showing us where everything was, for being deaf she was suspicious and hid her belongings in nooks and corners she was not always able to remember herself. Going to a chest of drawers of heavy, ancient design, she drew out the top drawer which was rather high up, stood on her toes, plunged her hands inside, making mysterious faces, and suddenly out ran a fat mother mouse and her family of little ones. I let out a yell but my grandmother took on the same sort of expression as Don

Quixote probably did when he found himself in the presence of a wrinkled peasant woman instead of his imagined Dulcinea, and thereby believed that his enemies, the enchanters, had played him a new trick.   Once my fright was over I think I was nearly as indignant as she was, though for an unconsidered reason except that having taken a liking to my grandmother I meant to defend her.   My mother, curling her lips, did not hide her disgust.

After the goat's cheese and the red wine, my grandmother let us into the secret of her vast projects.

Mme Collinet, whose linen she washed in the Loire, helping her also to look after a house on the castle moat, was going to Paris to look after the affairs of her husband and her son who were in the army.   The house which had many tenants would need somebody to keep an eye on it.   Mme Collinet had chosen my grandmother for this position of trust suggesting that she should go and live there.   Our arrival coincided almost exactly with the taking over of her functions.   My mother would help with the moving in and do all the listening when people had something to say.   We would have a pleasant apartment in the centre of the town, instead of being on the outskirts as now, and there was the market, one of the finest in all the Loire.   My mother made no great comment.   She had no choice in the matter and anything was preferable to going back to my father.

During the next few days my mother and I started to make packages once more, not only for ourselves but for my grandmother.   Granny went off behind her wheelbarrow looking for things along the banks of the Loire.   Occasionally also she went to wash on the planks in the middle of the shallow river.

I have already said that my grandmother's furniture was queer and old, but the things she kept in them were even stranger. Little shoes, tiny clogs, thimbles, medals, charms, pieces of coloured glass that she put close to an eye so that they coloured the objects seen through them.   Her delight on these occasions was immense as if she had discovered a way of making all about her gayer, prettier, less monotonous.   The rabbits became blue or violet.   The grass we gave them to nibble took on equally absurd colours.   Life appeared charmingly upside-down.   I was enchanted.   When we had spent enough time with these varying treasures we put them back in a silk handkerchief full of holes. Then Granny, who had a low voice in spite of her deafness, would say in the most mysterious tone: 'I am going into the garden to cut some leeks for supper.' You would have thought she was going off on a secret mission.

My mother, because of so many things round us which reminded her of the days when she was little, began to speak about her father whose photograph, very faded, stood on a table in the picturesque 1870 uniform of a zouave. We were also led to talking about him owing to a discovery we made after Granny had gone to cut her leeks. My mother was poking about, rummaging, when she suddenly came on a long and wide red sash, holed by moth till it scarce held together, and a braided short jacket which together constituted her father's sash and bolero, the same as the zouave was wearing in the photograph.

My zouave grandfather, brought back to life by my mother's memories, came into my existence for the first time. He had died full of rheumatics and had been unlucky from childhood, just like her, she said. Nothing had ever worked out right for him.

Born in Colmar, miserably, he had twice sold himself for the wars. Military service in those days was by lottery. The youth who drew the unlucky number had seven years in the army, but if he was rich he could pay another man to take his place. My grandfather had obliged first one young man and then another. Fourteen years he battled, in the Crimea, with Faidherbe in Algeria, and during the campaigns in Italy, and lastly, of course, in the war of 1870 after which, returning to Colmar, he discovered that the city of his birth had become German by annexation. Deprived of his nationality he returned to the banks of the Loire where he had spent the later months of the doomed campaign. He fell in love with Juliette Lacoudrette, my grandmother, married her, and bought a grocery shop in the tiny village of Selles-sur-Cher where my mother was born.

Juliette was a trifle unbalanced, full of strange dreams, believing herself to be the love daughter of the village seigneur who would one day set her up in her proper station, invite her, dressed as Diana with a floating veil, to follow the chase with him, she mounted on a white horse, he on a black one. The tinkle of a little bell would bring her mind back to the pepper and the eucalyptus on the shelves of the tiny grocery store. A little woman all in black or a grubby child would come asking for a halfpennyworth of salt. She would give them too much change or forget to take the money altogether, be led to give them twice the weight, and as soon as the door was closed go off dreaming again.

Three little girls were born of the marriage, Marguerite the eldest who had not yet come into my existence, Marie-Thérèse, and my mother Matilda. They were brought up in pretty frocks to lend substance to Juliette's dream. They had a pony and trap, but the trap soon broke up from want of care and the horse died. The grocer's shop was sold. Malevolent tongues drove the family out of the village, and Juliette, the rheumatic zouave, and the three little girls took refuge in the anonymity of Blois.

The zouave, old and tired by his campaigns, was hounded from place to place, people taking him for a German. My mother discovered in herself increasingly traits of his character. She had his honesty and hard work but in neither case did they lead anywhere. He gardened a little, broke stones on the road, and ended by choosing solitude. The three little girls had a sad childhood between a deaf and dreamy mother and a father embittered by ill fortune. Juliette alone was happy. At the break of each summer's day she would set off happily to look for hidden treasure, pushing her wheelbarrow for miles along the water bank or in the forest of Russy. She felt sure there was gold wrapped up in a pair of leather trousers buried in this forest. The great thing was to find it. One day she took Marie-Thérèse with her, Matilda remaining at home with the zouave, the eldest sister, though only twelve, being apprenticed to a dressmaker in the distant town of Vierzon. Juliette, searching the sweet-smelling ground for the leather trousers, left Marie-Thérèse sleeping at the foot of a tree in the forest and then quite forgot her. When she came home in the evening she was surprised not to find her daughter. They beat the forest for her all night but not till the next day did they find her, kneeling in prayer, her eyes glazed with terror. Nights of fever, delirium, convulsions, followed this appalling adventure, the little girl crying out that she could see the wolves. After being on the point of death for eight days she recovered. One eye was smaller than the other, a cheek slightly paralysed. Her lovely hats were always designed to cast a shadow over these defects.

When the two youngest went to school Marie-Thérèse was just old enough to lead Matilda by the hand and look the big sister. My mother, who had never talked much about her child-hood, gave me for the first time glimpses of the Ursuline convent where she received her education, the religious bodies having not yet been expelled from France. The whole thing was just as in the days of the French kings. The convent was divided into three distinct layers of human status—the nobility, the bourgeoisie, and the *tiers état*, or commonalty. Behind its high walls the convent was a city with its own laws, the cloistered nuns making their own bread, owning and milking their own cows, growing their vegetables and their flowers, and possessing their own burial ground. The young ladies of noble birth from the provinces or from Paris came here for their education. The chapel was divided into three parts, the titled young women praying on the right, the daughters of professional men or of those enriched by commerce in the centre, and poor girls, like my mother, on the left. The poor girls finished off the copy-books of the young ladies of quality and fell in love with the beautifully romantic names of those whose forbears made French history. My mother remembered specially Sophie de Cantre and Athenaïs de Grandchamps, about whom she later told me many stories. Occasionally, when the poor girls were playing in their miserable courtyard, the young ladies who lived in threw from upper windows texts and pious pictures which, thus released from white hands, fluttered to the feet of the poor girls who fought one another for these pious mementoes.

The Mother Superior went to Rome once a year, returning for Easter. She travelled in a Berlin, a four-wheeled carriage with a hood behind, comfortable, well sprung, and with curtains always closed. She had a thick veil over her features, was not allowed to get down even for requirements of hygiene, and her departure was accompanied by much picturesque ceremonial. All the pupils gathered in the main courtyard and knelt as the carriage went by. She blessed them, blessed the nuns, and very solemnly handed over the keys of the convent to her deputy. On her return she distributed relics blessed by the pope. She appeared in the splendour of a queen returning into her kingdom. The convent, the nuns, the divisions of classes, echoed monarchist France with its privileges, its fine sides also. Most little girls were too young to appreciate the historical interest of this strict community. My mother was merely aware of the discipline, the long litanies, the prayers in a half-understood Latin, the hours kneeling on stone, arms in the form of a cross, draughts under doors, chill winter blasts from the Loire.

Holy Week was a long fast for children who, like Marie-Thérèse and my mother, were already underfed, seldom eating more than an apple and a handful of nuts. The nuns remained kneeling in ecstasy for several hours, would faint, and then, as soon as they were revived, take up again their rapturous attitude. Marie-Thérèse, much affected by what she saw, superimposed her growing religious feeling on what remained in her mind of the happenings in the forest. She claimed to have seen the Virgin Mary, either in the convent or at night when deliriously searching for Juliette. The wolves were temptation and the devil. She carried in her apron or the pockets of her dress many pious pictures, and soon the nuns began to consider her in the light of a potential recruit, for the poor girls could eventually be turned into excellent servants. As soon as school was over in the evening the little girls flew out of the convent and Marie-Thérèse and Matilda crossed the Loire, their empty luncheon baskets passed under their arms as in the pictures of Little Red Riding Hood. The brightly lit shops held them up all the way. They clattered down the steps of the rue Denis Papin, lost their hearts to a box of chalks, a doll, or a shuttlecock, admired a hat or a parasol, envied grown-ups who drank at the café terrace, read the play-bill outside the theatre, and did not go back to their sombre home till the very last moment. The beds were never made, the floors never swept, cups from the last meal remained unwashed on the edge of the table. Juliette left at dawn and was seldom home till late. The two little girls would light a lamp and tidy the house. Then Marie-Thérèse, being the elder, would try to make a soup, but more often they would have to go to bed with nothing more satisfying than a piece of bread, a walnut, and an apple.

When Juliette arrived and found her daughters in bed she also would eat an apple and a nut. This light collation became in her imagination the richest repast. Taking up the only lamp she would retire to her room where her daughters listened to her talking to herself, shuffling about, putting things in secret drawers, and muttering, muttering.

Finally the oil lamp was put out and night fell, dark and silent.

Marie-Thérèse would now begin to toss in her bed, afraid of the unseen things hovering in her imagination. The darkness, the quietness, their mother who would not even hear them if they called, made the night fantastic and terrifying. The nuns, graceful in their robes, entered into her feverish mind, moving slowly towards her. There was no sound but the turning of their rosaries. The stone figures in the candle-lit chapel stepped down from their pedestals, moving like phantoms across the room. The child Jesus with His father, the good St. Joseph, just as Marie-Thérèse dusted them every morning. Then the dog with St. Roch, but the dog was suddenly turned into a wolf, the wolf of the forest of Roussy. Sweat would form on her brow. The saints were all devils and the gentle nuns became witches. Prayers gushed out through hot lips, became alarmingly audible, and ended by frightening her. She would wake Matilda out of a peaceful sleep and pinching her little arms begin:

'Mater Dolorosa.'

Matilda, the sandman refilling her eyes, repeated, yawning:

'Ora pro nobis—Turris eburnea—Ora pro nobis,' she whispered and sank back into sleep.

Marie-Thérèse, furious, pulled her hair, beat her, pinched her.

'Mater Dolorosa. Go on! Go on!' she cried.

My mother remembered having seen her father, the zouave, leave the house for ever. He had obtained a bed in an almshouse. He left early just as his daughters were going to school. He wore a scarf and carried his stout stick and made off along the empty road in the direction of the forest. He would have to cross it. There was a tall brick wall with a small door. Through this he would have gone. When in 1908 he died in the hospice for old soldiers, my grandmother was the only person to follow the coffin.

During the daytime when my mother and I were alone in the house we tried to tidy up the big room. Wherever we turned new secrets came dustily to the surface. We discovered the accounts that Juliette kept just after her marriage at the grocer's shop. There was a dark chest that we forced open, removing yellowed newspapers dated 1889 before coming to a little taffeta dress of the sort of grey which changes colour according to the varying light.

'What an adorable dress!' I cried. 'Just look at the leg-of-mutton sleeves! It reminds me of the *Malheurs de Sophie*!'

'Why, it's my pigeon-breasted dress!' exclaimed my mother.

Alas, the taffeta, on contact with the air, disintegrated. The beauty and colour of the apparition vanished almost as soon as we had spoken. The dress had been known as the princess's dress because all three little girls had worn it—Marguerite first, Marie-Thérèse next, and Matilda whose wearing of it coincided with the last happy days of the grocer's shop before the pony and trap disappeared and the family was obliged to leave the whispering village. My mother was very affected. Unwilling to throw away the remains of the dress, she put it into the fire. The pigeon-breasted taffeta gave a last sparkle and soon there was nothing but a powdery form which broke up, dancing above the embers, as my mother touched it with the poker. The silkworms had become butterflies chasing each other lightly up the chimney.

A few days later we left the rue Pontchartrain.

We crossed the Loire by the long bridge and putting down our parcels in front of the Hôtel d'Angleterre rested a moment out of the hot sun. It was market-day. The milkmaids with their lovely lace caps hurried in every direction. I watched with wondering eyes the battles of the pony chaises, each driver trying to be first to cross the bridge. The centre of the town so full of colour and people, rich merchandise, flowers, vegetables and magnificent fruit, the farmers in their blouses, the wagons full of hay, the shouting, the blowing of horns—all these things were no less wonderful than my mother remembered from her own childhood days. I had mostly heard from her about the rue Denis Papin with its wide stairs leading up steeply to the statue of the great seventeenth-century physicist who had something to do with inventing steam power. Everything that mattered in Blois took place in this street or on these steps. We began to climb them, but instead of going to the top we turned left and found ourselves on cobble-stones between tall, very old, grey houses. There was a fork and we then entered the rue des Violettes.

Here, in the oldest house of all, crazy and picturesque, with its unevenly flagstoned courtyard against the château wall, my mother and I were to lodge.

12

THE house was very still, and as we did not hear or
see anybody we put our parcels at the foot of a steep
iron staircase which we climbed as far as the first floor
where we knocked.

My mother explained our business to a lovely girl who said
she had been sleeping whilst waiting for us to come. As it was
midday we were rather surprised that she should sleep so late,
surprised to find her with her hair in a long plait hanging down
her back, and herself draped in a dressing-gown of faded flannelette which in its better days had been sky-blue. She led us into
a large room, a little dark, with curtains and arm-chairs of red
velvet. I saw my mother look at the antimacassars, which were
not of real lace, and her lips tightened and curled downwards as
they did when she was critical. At the far end of the room a
large bed had red curtains round it. There was a massive round
table covered with a thick felt embroidered with differently
coloured wool. By the window stood an extremely large fern
decorated with a red satin bow and standing in a shiny copper pan.

The young woman spoke to us pleasantly. She told my mother
that she could see at once they were going to be friends. She
added: 'My name is Berthe. If you like I'll call you Matilda.
I expect we are just about the same age in spite of your having
such a big girl.' She had looked at me whilst saying these words
and now kissed me.

My mother, having removed her wide hat, was holding it on
her knees, trying to push the long hatpins through the usual
holes in the crown. She must have found this occupation
unsatisfactory, for she suddenly rose and with a slight movement
of enervation placed her hat on a bust of the Venus of Milo. A
gilt clock showed that it was a few minutes past midday. My
mother looked at me, glanced back at the clock, and said:

'I think we ought to lunch.'

'So we ought,' agreed Berthe. 'If you run out and buy some bread, a cream cheese, and some fruit, Matilda, I 'll lay the table. There 's plenty of wine.'

She spoke very gaily. My mother and I hurried down the iron staircase, our steps echoing sonorously, quickly bought our provisions, and on our return found that Berthe had used our short absence to wind her plait hurriedly round her head, lace her corset, and put on a pleated skirt. She had forgotten, however, to do up the back of her lace blouse, and as my mother did it for her Berthe said:

'If you don't mind I 'll wait till after lunch to do my hair properly.'

We had an excellent lunch. The two young women then began to exchange confidences and I, restless, unable to bear this atmosphere of red velvet and cream cheese heated by the hot sun, crept out of the room. As a matter of fact my mother had quite forgotten me. At the bottom of the stairs, turning away from the street, I found myself in a narrow, rectangular courtyard into which the sun came obliquely, warming alternately our house and the house next to it. Under the iron stairs was a narrow glass-panelled door leading to my grandmother's lodging. She had chosen this one, the most modest, because of the staircase which filled her with terror and also to be nearer the courtyard where she could put her precious wheelbarrow.

At the far end of the courtyard was an arch which, stretching away deeply, became cavernous and damp. One could follow it for a few yards; one then came up against railings of forged iron surmounted by arrows in the form of fleurs-de-lis. A man in the courtyard said that this iron gate led straight to the secret dungeons of the Château de Blois of which these houses formed the base. He was carrying a package roughly tied with string. It was full of humps which seemed to move and he said to me: 'Come along if you want to see what I 've got in my parcel.'

He untied it and took out seven new-born puppies, still blind, which he took one by one, throwing them with all his strength against the wall. They fell like smooth balls at our feet, white with black markings. When he came to the last, he looked at it a moment, appeared to hesitate, and then raised his arm and threw it, like its brothers and sisters, against the wall. I was overwhelmed and, I fear, intensely interested, surprised to see how these tiny things had passed so rapidly from life to death. The man left their sad little forms lying in the earthy dust of the cave and asked me a lot of questions. I answered him guardedly. Suddenly a little bitch came in sight, her tail wagging anxiously, criss-crossing in the courtyard, seeking the scent of her little ones, and when she reached the mouth of the cavern she gave a pitiful yell and threw herself on one of the lifeless forms which she took up between her teeth, growling and crying. I watched her with a thumping heart. The puppy's head hung loosely from her mouth. Then the man started to pick up his other victims whilst I, nearly out of my mind, noisily ran up the iron staircase, breaking in on my mother and Berthe, tears gushing down my cheeks.

They were just as I had left them, still gossiping, but a huge coffee-pot had arrived on the table, seemingly dominating the situation, and I could see, through my tears, that they had sunk so comfortably into their red velvet arm-chairs that they must both have unlaced their corsets. Berthe's curiously arranged plait crowned her head as before. My mother, looking up, supposed I had fallen down and cut my knee. I tried to explain the horrible scene I had just witnessed, but I was put out by Berthe's presence and furious that my mother should be gossiping so comfortably with a friend. It struck me that as she had so recently left my father she should have kept a more dignified attitude, cried often, and spoken only to me.

Instead of this she gave me two sous to buy a flute of bread and a bar of chocolate. I bought some by the name of Poulain made at a factory in Blois that employed many hundreds of people, and whose gay orange posters covered the walls of the town.

I was walking back from the grocer's nibbling at the chocolate and the bread when I heard the sound of a wooden wheel creaking on the cobbles. Granny was coming home with her wheelbarrow. I rushed at her, stifled her with kisses, and trotted beside her till we came to the glass-panelled door under the iron stairs. We put the wheelbarrow in the courtyard and entered her apartment. I was quite happy again now. Mother could go on gossiping with her new friend. I was no longer alone.

A very large room was the first we came to with barred windows looking out on the narrow rue des Violettes. In front of Granny's bed were all the bundles she had brought from her other flat. Everything was deliciously untidy. Granny took down an apron which she put round her narrow waist. I wanted one also. She gave me one, knotting it for me at the back. It was lovely to feel it round my legs just as if I had already been a grown-up woman. Alas, examining myself in a mirror I saw that my apron did not join behind but left an expanse of white leg and sock! My deception was great. Granny, who was indulgent, took down a second apron which she fixed up behind me so that the two together formed a dress with a long skirt. They were of different colours, but that did not spoil my make-believe.

We now started to pull the bundles about and open the cases and drawers. I shouted myself hoarse.

'Grand'mère,' cried I, 'here's a set of liqueur glasses!'

'My little Madeleine,' she said, looking round suspiciously, 'it's the set your great-grandfather, the marquis, left me.' She put her finger to her lips and whispered: 'I can't tell you his name because of the family, who would kill me. But patience! Have no fear! The usurpers shall pay, and you, my little Madeleine, shall become a marquise!'

Her flights of fancy changed every day. One had to learn the new ones. It was delicious!

After we had rummaged and upset everything in the room we went up the iron staircase. Berthe and my mother were still gossiping in their arm-chairs but Berthe had done her hair and powdered herself. Her powder was now added to the other smells of the room all baked by the sun. When Granny entered, my mother and Berthe stopped talking; afterwards the conversation restarted fitfully. The two young women shouted trivialities whilst my grandmother stretched her neck trying to hear. She looked on these occasions like a rare bird out of the fables of La Fontaine. When she thought she had understood she shortened her neck in the funniest way, only to shoot it out again a moment later. She laughed, wondered if she had done the right thing, looked angrily puzzled, tried to catch a fresh phrase, and then because she was tired her expression hardened. Imagining that they were muttering unpleasant things about her she fixed first one, then the other, with sullen eyes. At last, cold and dignified, she rose and left the room. I followed her and we went back to our rummaging and fairy-tales. I slept with her that night and the following night. She seemed to hear and understand me and her deafness did not inconvenience my prattling.

One afternoon after a succession of visits by cattle-dealers in their long blue pinafores, my mother suddenly understood what Berthe had so carefully hidden from her. Berthe and several other women in the house used the red velvet drawing-room to receive farmers and butter merchants coming into town. A regular customer finding my mother alone asked her if she was a new girl in the house. He said he was used to Mlle Berthe and, in principle, did not like changing, but if Mlle Berthe was busy he was willing to try my mother.

Berthe, who had become free, noticing through the half-open door that her regular customer was talking to my mother, did not dare come in. Instead she returned silently into her bedroom, anxiously waiting. The man, puzzled by my mother's lack of enthusiasm, ceased turning his straw hat between his fingers and got up. As he reached the stairs another girl whose room was on the corridor whistled to him. Delighted, he darted into her room whilst the girl broke out, for Berthe's benefit, into a triumphant laugh.

My mother, feeling the need of air, pushed the green plant to one side, and went to sit by the open window. As it was so hot she leaned out. At that moment a man dressed in black and wearing a boater came into the narrow street, looked up, took a golden coin from his waistcoat pocket and placed it in his eye like a monocle so that the sun played on the gold. With his other eye he winked at my mother.

She, thoroughly upset, withdrew into the room which the man took as a sign of acquiescence. Double footsteps now sounded on the iron stairs as the man in the blue blouse, having finished with the girl opposite, going down to the street by the stairs crossed the man with the gold coin who was coming up to my mother.

After this adventure my mother and I chose a little room on the second floor. This part of the house was inhabited by modest employees and my mother decided to start sewing again for a living. She bitterly reproached my grandmother for bringing us to live in such a disreputable place, and my grandmother took this outburst ill. Mother and daughter were no longer on good terms, and again, as in Paris, I was to witness bitter quarrels.

Berthe had got to know a Belgian called Adrien who had something to do with delivering mail to German prisoners. He had fallen desperately in love with Berthe and was anxious they should live like husband and wife. For this reason, being herself fond of him, she used to lock herself up in her room on market-days so as not to have to satisfy the farmers and merchants who came to see her.

One day Berthe announced her intention of giving up her old ways, but she wanted Adrien to marry her in church. She began to make a great fuss of my mother with the intention of purifying herself, so to speak, by contact with a married woman, the mother of a little girl, and a person in every way above suspicion.

Berthe undertook to introduce my mother to many women in need of a good dressmaker. She would even help her to sew. They would turn the room with the red velvet curtains and the tall fern into a sewing-room where the two women would be at home to a very different clientèle. My mother accepted this arrangement, and Berthe told her friends that the most famous dressmaker in Paris had come to live in the house. Customers began to call. Adrien was so delighted that he sent the wives of his superiors to my mother who now had so many orders that she could not deal with them.

Berthe was overjoyed by her new life: for my mother, alas, it was the continuation of her old one. During the day I wandered from the sewing-room to the courtyard, from the courtyard to the mouth of the cavern, fascinated by the iron gate leading to the castle dungeons. I waited impatiently for my grandmother to come home, remaining with her till the following morning. Never have I been so spoilt; it was her opinion that all I said and did were perfect.

Emboldened I played in the street and soon discovered the most picturesque cutler's stall built into the wall of an old leaning house. Though the window was small the scissors and blades made it scintillate; it looked like something out of the *Arabian Nights*. The rays of the sun caught steel and mother-of-pearl, painting them with changing colours. Large scissors for cutting out dresses and coats, murderously pointed knives, sweet little scissors for cutting round lace after embroidering. . . . I spent enchanted moments in front of this window. Soon the cutler's daughter, a Madeleine like myself, took a liking to me and invited

me into her darling shop, giving me permission to put my fingers
on the ivory handles of the pocket-knives and sculptured wooden
handles of the big knives. There was a dirk or dagger drawn
a little way out of its leather sheath. There were also swords
unsheathed but which, at night, were placed back in them.

Madeleine Béant was sixteen, large and awkward with a shapeless waist, big hands, big feet, but agreeable features and a warm
heart. As happy as a lark she sang all sorts of love-songs, new
ones, old ones, with an accent of the Loire, and the Parisian slang
in the country girl's mouth seemed quite a different language.
She was making her trousseau and we put our heads together
about it, but in the morning she helped her mother in the shop,
polishing the knives and swords with a huge chamois leather
whilst singing: 'Viens poupoule,' counting those which remained
in the drawers, and, especially on market-days, making everything
shine in the window. Many of the cattle-dealers and farmers in
their blue blouses after a visit to the drawing-room with the red
velvet chairs and the tall fern, light-hearted and satisfied, had, as
they turned from the iron staircase into the narrow street, noticed
the cutler's shop; conversely a goodly number of Mme Béant's
customers, after buying a good strong pocket-knife, had looked
up at Berthe's comely figure and smiling face in the opposite
window and decided to spend a few moments in her gentle
presence. The two establishments accordingly held each other
in mutual esteem. Madeleine Béant had merely kept away from
our house because she discreetly felt that her presence might have
made Berthe and the other ladies feel uncomfortable.

We used to go to market together, this fabulous market in the
garden of France, with its luscious pears, ripe and yellowed by
the sun, sold in small boxes, transparent raisins, mountains of
butter, pyramids of goat's cheese, set out in front of country
women in black with white lace bonnets When we had time to
spare Madeleine and I went as far as the rue Denis Papin, climbing
like two silly girls the wide steps leading to the fair-ground.
We would come home laden with purchases, pink cheeked.

After lunch we had a different meeting-place.

Where the rue des Violettes forked there was a pretty, curved
pavement round a jutting-out house the base of which was
occupied by a seed merchant, but as the merchant's entrance was
in another street, Mme Béant, the seed merchant's wife, Madeleine

Béant, and I brought out our chairs and sewed on the curved pavement from where we could see everything that was happening in both streets.   We cut out our petticoats and embroidered them, or hemmed the napkins and sheets for Madeleine Béant's trousseau.   We sang love-songs; when a passer-by came towards our raised platform we would gradually stop singing out of curiosity to inspect him.   One day we heard people shouting and running.   A German prisoner had escaped from the castle and was being chased by a crowd of children and shouting men. He passed us, miserably red in the face, his hair shorn, his thick neck pearled with sweat.   He held a tiny attaché case in his immense hand.   He was caught and led back by those who had pursued him.   We could see his face this time: tears fell from his blue eyes, wetting his cheeks.   He still held tightly to his attaché case.   The whole thing had passed so quickly that I still held my petticoat in the air, my needle poised above the embroidery.

There lived in the house opposite the seed merchant's a little boy called George whom I first saw looking intently at us through an upstairs window.   He smiled, and Madeleine Béant who knew him both vexed me and made me blush with pleasure by saying that his gracious little ways were all put on for me.   We met him one morning in the market held in the Place Louis XII.   He followed us and Madeleine Béant asked him to come to us while we sewed during the afternoon.

George's parents were deaf and dumb.   They only spoke to each other by signs and George knew their language perfectly; sometimes forgetting, he would address us in this way.   He was a pitiful little object, suffering from weak eyes and an excessive timidity.   Few people called him George; they referred to him as the deaf and dumb couple's boy, and this increased his misery. My young heart was full of sympathy.   I took him under my wing and often left my lingerie on my chair to play with him in the courtyard.

Granny had some tenants, M. and Mme Garnier and their daughter Fernande, who lived in a large room facing the rue des Violettes with a door into the street.   It was probably converted from a shop.   These people owned a large covered barrow which they kept near the rabbit hutches and George and I liked to play round it.

M. Garnier was the least interested in the barrow. He mostly went out to work at the chocolate place or at a factory where they made heavy boots for soldiers. He was taciturn and elusive. Mme Garnier was dark, fine-looking and powerful, in the thirties. She dominated: when one saw her behind her barrow all done up in red with the jewellery, the rings, and the brooches sparkling on sawdust, at these times Mme Garnier had the authority and poise of a Roman empress. She would place in advantageous positions the minute little boxes in which the finest pieces of her collection reposed on cotton wool. There were gold brooches with the names of the various saints — Sainte Marie, Sainte Jeanne; pious effigies and metal hearts that opened out and in which one placed a wisp of one's lover's hair, charms made like four-leaved clover, others with the figure 13, and horns of plenty.

Fernande Garnier was so small and slight for her fifteen years that she seemed to have nothing in common with her mother. The barrow was really hers. She pushed it to market and brought it home, and by long association with it she had come to resemble it, her poor thin arms sticking out like shafts. At dawn she was up making the coffee, cutting sandwiches for the man's lunch, whilst the empress continued to sleep in a vast bed with red curtains at the far end of their one-roomed apartment. Three of these beds elbowed up against one another for space. The members of the family retired to their closed-in beds like Mme de Maintenon withdrew to her apartments. Once behind their red curtains they saw nothing, heard nothing, dressed, undressed, and when they opened their curtains you might be certain they would be all ready to go out of doors.

Fernande, having served breakfast, swept the floor, and collecting the chamber-pots under each canopied bed, emptied the contents into the gutter whose foetid water flowed unhygienically down the picturesque rue des Violettes. She then took the wash-basins with their soapy water and emptied those also at the street door. A moment later you would see her leave with a tall pitcher to draw clear water at the pump. She was always so busy I think she often forgot to drink the bowl of coffee getting cold on the edge of the table. Soon she would be in the courtyard, uncovering the heavy barrow, harnessing herself to it, drawing its iron-rimmed wheels over the uneven cobbles, clattering out into the rue des

Violettes, then down the rue du Commerce on her way to the fairground above the statue of Denis Papin, or perhaps bound for the bridge across the Loire, to set up her barrow in some distant village.

A few hours later Mme Garnier, cool, rested, magnificent, would emerge from between her bed curtains and pass along the rue des Violettes on the way to join her daughter. If the market were at Blois, and we went there, we would see her enthroned beside the yawning Fernande. She had a knowledge of magic, so people said, and could sell one a locket that was certain to make a man amorous if only one could steal a bristling hair from his moustache and imprison it in the charm. Then somebody would arrive, whisper a few words in her ear, and wait. Mme Garnier, leaving her august throne to Fernande, would follow the stranger. Fernande, now in charge of the stall, huddled herself up on her mother's chair and soon fell fast asleep. Sometimes Mme Garnier, on her return, woke her daughter with a tremendous smack, but often Fernande was amicably warned by a neighbour of her mother's coming.

Madeleine Béant and I used to love going to see Fernande at market. Mme Garnier, though hard on her daughter, was always glad to see us. Then there was a morning in the week when neither Fernande nor her mother sold trinkets. They remained at home, Mme Garnier in the privacy of her bed, Fernande airing the mattresses of the other two beds in front of the open window. The mattresses, being large, choked up the window, keeping out the light. Fernande accordingly opened the street door, and taking up her broom swept away the dust in eddies which met similar eddies emerging from the house opposite where Madeleine Béant was sweeping out the cutler's shop. At this moment, having nothing to do, I would rush out into the middle of the road, stopping at an equal distance between the two brooms, and soon I would have both young women in cascades of happy laughter.

A quarter of an hour later, like three frolicking children, we set off for the local market. The joy Fernande experienced to go to market with a basket under her arm instead of professionally behind a heavy barrow was quite delirious. She bought her lunch on these occasions, a steak and potatoes to fry, for she must have it piping hot to make up for the cold collations, the fruit,

the cheese, and the bread, eaten quickly all the rest of the week
in the open air behind the ambulating jewellery shop.

She adored her mother and served her with a face garlanded
with love. Nothing her mother wanted was tiring or difficult,
and if Mme Garnier smiled at her, calling her 'my little goat,'
then Fernande's expression was beatific.

One afternoon she came to join our sewing class outside the
seed merchant's shop. She had started a petticoat which was
taking so long to finish that the silk was shiny by contact with
her rough, benumbed fingers more accustomed to handling the
polished shafts of her barrow. The needle kept on dropping
from the slippery folds of her creased lingerie. The scissors rolled
off her lap. Her thimble became unstuck and danced lightly over
the paving-stones. We laughed joyously as she kept on stooping
to pick something up. Her mind was not on what she was
supposed to be making. Her eyes darted in the direction of her
house and every now and then a man or a woman, walking or
driving a pony trap, would stop at the door and be swiftly let in.

We did not wonder overmuch about all these comings and
goings. The rue des Violettes had many a secret. One felt that
it had grown wise and tolerant with centuries and that we probably
elbowed the ghosts of Catherine de Médicis and Nostradamus.

I had not been long in this street before I discovered nearly
opposite our house a long, dark tunnel which led to a transversal
street. The taking of it saved those of us who were in the secret
several minutes' walk when going to another part of the town,
and though I was at first terrified by its darkness, its echoes, and
the fear of being chased by rats, I learnt to keep my eyes firmly
fixed on the distant circle of light and walk bravely through.

We had been sewing all the afternoon when Fernande, looking
up, saw her mother leave the house and take this passage. Mme
Garnier's eyes, plunged too quickly into darkness, did not distinguish, straight across her path, an open trap leading into a deep
cellar. She fell through it and remained for a time unconscious.

Fernande went on embroidering, but as it was late George
returned home, his mother having made signs that the soup was
ready, and Madeleine Béant slowly folded her smartest petticoat.
My mother sent me a message to go to the baker. Fernande
stayed on, apparently, another half-hour and then went home to

prepare supper. When her father arrived but her mother still did not come back Fernande, suddenly anxious, hurried across the road, ran into the tunnel, and half-way through saw the open trap. Kneeling down she heard her mother, who had just recovered consciousness, groaning, and, terrified, went to fetch her father. They managed to let themselves down into the cellar, but it was not till the fire brigade arrived that Mme Garnier could be brought up and safely laid on her four-poster bed.

‹ When the street had become reasonably quiet again, the firemen gone, and the crowd scattered, Mme Garnier told her family that she had broken her leg, that it was a simple fracture, and that whatever happened nobody must fetch a doctor. She asked her husband to give her a glass of rum and sent Fernande to fetch my grandmother. Granny undressed her and then Granny and Fernande, guided by Mme Garnier grimly clutching the bed-posts, tugged and pushed the broken leg. The husband, who was also pulling under his wife's direction, fainted, rolling gently on the floor. Granny and Fernande, and I looking on, continued to do just what Mme Garnier told them. Suddenly she let go of the bed-posts and as she sank down into the bed the broken ends of bone fitted into each other.

Mme Garnier then massaged herself, helped Granny to wind a bed sheet round the leg, and quietly went to sleep. We simply could not believe what we had seen. The husband was brought back to life with a jug of cold water and Granny and I went back full of wonder.

The next morning Fernande went off with her barrow as if nothing had happened. For a week she attended all the usual markets after which she stayed at home and nursed her mother with touching devotion. Soon crowds of people knocked at her door. Some went in limping and came our cured. She was the most celebrated bone-setter on the whole of the Loire. She had effected the most extraordinary cures in addition to which she was gifted with second sight. Naturally the doctors waged on her an unending war. Her ambulating stall was merely a blind. She got better very quickly. We used to go to see her in bed and she told us our fortune; mine was so unlikely that my mother would never believe in it. She told my mother that she would soon be a widow. She said we would both go to England and that eventually I should become famous. When I laughed, she said:

'Laugh, little girl: it isn't with you that I shall begin making mistakes. Your destiny is as clear to me as black coffee is black.' She told Berthe she would marry the man she wanted to marry and that she would have two children. Berthe was delighted. She was not a person to doubt good news.

As soon as she was able to get about again Mme Garnier went to lodge in another part of the town. She doubtless felt that her many visitors had created too much attention. The barrow remained in our courtyard and we continued from time to time to see Fernande.

My mother received a letter from Marguerite Rosier who told her that my father was so miserable that everybody was sorry for him. He had found out where we were and wanted us to come back. Soon he began to write himself and my mother read his letters to Berthe. Then Berthe left us. She was going to marry her Belgian.

Besides looking after the house in which we lodged my grandmother was the keeper of a garden which was a veritable paradise. A lovely road of yellow earth led to it beside a high wall at the end of which was an ogival door, thick, sculptured with medieval designs, and barded with decorative ironwork. When we stopped in front of this door we were overcome, Granny and I, by the silence we had made for ourselves, for all along the road the wheelbarrow had creaked and now its noisy wheel was stilled at our feet. Impressed and a little frightened, Granny would lift up her black apron and fetch out a key from a pocket in her underskirts. My heart beat at the sight of this, so eager was I to penetrate into the garden, but Granny would first stoop down and, nodding her old head, examine with great suspicion the state of the lock to see if anybody had tampered with it since her last coming. Then making some incomprehensible remark she would insert the key into the hole and try to turn it with both hands. The rusty lock resisted, a spider came running out, and just as I was certain that we were going to be kept out for ever the lock turned, the door opened scratchily against the gravel, just a few inches before sticking, and a great wave of sweet smells rushed into our nostrils.

We pushed against the door with all our might. Since the previous week the herbs, the flowers, and the weeds had sprung

up in the path and made a luxuriant barrier. We now went back
to fetch the wheelbarrow. All round us the bees and insects
buzzed and sang in the hot, dry air. Purple irises, tall, thick, and
beautiful, reaching to the level of my eyes, headily scented arum
lilies, red currant bushes from which hung strings of rubies,
peaches resting their velvet cheeks against the hot wall, greeted
me, causing me to run from one to the other. At every new
discovery I would call Granny and she, hurrying up, would screw
up her face, purse her lips, and exclaim 'Heu!' as if she were just
as surprised as I. Indeed, that is why Granny and I got on
so well together. She was always expressing the most candid
surprise. The magnificent strawberries and peaches, red currants,
and greengages all about us seemingly filled her with perplexity
as if she were trying to decide how to turn them all into jam.
She said: 'We would need a magic cauldron for all this. I have
an idea. Let 's first have something to eat.'

A small tool-house stood against the garden wall. The window
panes were broken, and inside the table and chairs were covered
with spiders' webs; but we had it clean in no time and my grandmother, plunging her wrinkled hands into a black basket which
she carried about with her on all important occasions (she had
brought it to Paris when she came to see us), brought out a
beautiful white napkin, smelling of soapy wash being dried
in the sun, and laying it on the table placed on it a long French
bread, into which she stuck her pointed knife, a goat's cheese,
and a bottle of black coffee.

I was longing for the bread: Granny was thinking about the
coffee. Like a witch in a fairy-story she was soon gathering dry
sticks to make a fire, and now I understood why there were always
so many saucepans in her wheelbarrow. When the coffee was
hot she brought it into the summer-house. Then she took the
bread, removed the knife from it, and holding the golden crust
against her black dress made the sign of the cross upon it. She
cut several large slices. Then it was the turn of the goat's
cheese, hard and blue. I was deliriously happy, but soon, finding
that I was tired of sitting down, I took a final slice of bread and
ran out into the garden where I picked some greengages and
strawberries for dessert.

I hid in the hollow of a tree and soon I heard Granny calling me.
She passed by without discovering my hiding-place; then I ran

behind her, catching hold of her apron strings. She laughed, called me a little she-devil, and by flattery and vague promises to tell me stories and to show me 'certain objects which she possessed but that nobody had yet seen,' she brought me in front of the large basket we were to fill with gooseberries to make a jelly.

At four o'clock we had to leave this paradise. The wheel-barrow was full of fruit and dry wood. Its wooden wheel sang over the yellow road. The black basket was strung round me and was so large I could hardly see where I was going, but I never felt under my feet the cobbles of the bridge across the Loire. I moved ethereally, my mouth daubed in the juice of sun-ripened fruit.

The rue des Violettes seemed narrow and dark after this day amongst the butterflies and bees, but though I was tired I deter-mined immediately to go in search of George to tell him every-thing we had done. As soon as I discovered him I gave him a handful of greengages picked in the enchanted garden. 'Take me one day,' he implored, but firmly I answered: 'Only if you first let me see where you live. I want to go inside it.' Then he looked down at his shoes and said nothing. Nobody in the street had ever been to call on the unfortunate deaf and dumb parents. When did the mother sweep out the room? How did she cook? These were questions that we were for ever discussing. I was just dying to go and see, but nothing could tempt George. Was he obeying his parents' orders or was he ashamed of them? I do not know. During my absence he had cut out with his clever hands a tiny cupboard to put my doll's clothes in, and seeing this treasure I forgave him for being so stubborn about not showing me his home. I even invited him to come and see Granny making her jelly the next day.

While waiting for the evening meal I used to establish myself on the two bottom steps of the iron staircase. It was the hour of the day when, feeling maternal, I rocked or undressed my doll Bambino. Our stay at Blois had not improved his looks. Too frequently washed he had lost the blueness of his eyes and most of his hair which had been inadequately stuck on with glue. My doll, therefore, was bald. His cheeks were pale and because his eyes had no more colour he looked blind. After each new infirmity he became dearer to me, and I saw to it that his clothes

F

became increasingly elegant to compensate for the fast disappearance of his physical charms.   His intelligence was beyond discussion.   George who at first had thought him horrible now claimed that he was magnificent.   Secretly George and I were husband and wife and Bambino was our child.

On this particular evening my mother had gone across to see Berthe.   My mother and Granny were keeping away from each other and just now were hardly on speaking terms, with the result that my mother was making all the more fuss of Berthe whose lodging was in the house above the tunnel where Mme Garnier had had her accident.   Granny was preparing supper.   I thought it would be fun to go to the top of the iron staircase and see how fast I could run down.   Putting this project into immediate execution I missed my foothold and rolled down to the bottom of the flight where, like a turtle on my back, I shouted with all my force.

I was picked up by a ravishing figure, lips as fresh and red as raspberries, a perfume which went to my head deliciously.   The curiosity of examining further this new face put a stop to my tears.   The lady helped me up, placed Bambino gently in my arms, and asked me where my mother was.

'With Berthe,' I answered.

At this she showed her gums, as pink and strong as those of a young wolf ready to bite, and asked again:

'And that old witch of a grandmother, where 's she?'

'Underneath.'

'Then, come.   I 'll take you to her.'

She opened the door.   Granny, seeing the bump on my forehead and my bleeding nose, immediately concluded that somebody had tried to kidnap and murder me, and, gesticulating like a windmill, warmly thanked the young woman, who exclaimed:

'Well, if you ask my opinion it 's a real pity to see a little girl like that with nobody to look after her.   Her mother won't speak to me because I 'm not an honest woman, and there she goes spending her afternoon with Berthe who was no better than me till she hitched up with her Belgian.   There 's no reason for this little girl's mother and Berthe to put on airs.   Anybody would think they were princesses!'

She turned to go up the iron staircase.

I ran after her because she had promised me some cotton wool for my nose. We went into her flat which smelt deliciously of make-up and perfume.

I looked round full of wonderment, a sombre little room with postcards of aviators pinned to the wall, a photograph of the King of the Belgians, bowls of imitation crystal like the ones you can win at fun fairs, and oh, most beautiful of all, a pink bedspread with tulips of all colours! She went to a small table with a marble top, pulled a tiny piece of cotton wool from a roll, and dipping it in her wash-basin jug handed it to me.

While I washed my wound she pushed the bidet under her commode with her foot, tidied up a little, and then smiled at me, glad to have enticed me into her room and anxious to keep me a few moments by any subterfuge.

She showed me the postcards on her mantelpiece thus:

'That is the King of the Belgians, a jolly fellow, and here's the Prince of Wales, not a bad sort at all! Oh, it isn't that I know them personally but there are things that one gets to hear about. Nobody can hide what they've done. Remember that. Some try, but it all comes out in the end. Take Berthe, for instance, she may *think* I don't know about her, but I do. We all know about her. Even if she went to the other side of America, and that's far enough, isn't it, well, they would find out. There's no point in a woman putting on airs because, for the moment, one man happens to be paying her as much as it took several to pay her before.'

She went to the door and listened, danced about her room like a butterfly, opened and closed a drawer, asked me suddenly what I thought, broke into a pretty rage, showed her lovely teeth, and then smiled angelically. She took off her jacket, tapped her hair to bring back the waves, powdered her face with a swan's-down puff, passed the rouge unnecessarily over her painted lips. 'As a matter of fact, I was just going out into the street. You understand?'

'Of course I understand,' I answered innocently. 'It's funny your only going out at night. Do you work at the chocolate place?'

She threw back her pretty head and laughed so much that tears fell down her freshly made-up cheeks, making warm rivulets across the powder.

'How old are you?'

'I shall be ten on the 13th.'

'Ah! You were born on a 13th! You'll be lucky, lucky all
the way, lucky with men, lucky in everything. It's written all
over your face. I was born on a 31st. To get my luck I have
to reverse the figures—13th, do you see?'

She showed me a brooch with a 13. It had a long chain with
a silver watch at the other end and was attached by a safety-pin
to the belt of her skirt.

'I have a little luck from time to time,' she said, smiling prettily,
'as much as I can expect, having cheated on the date!'

She was making good the damage on her cheeks from laughing,
and looking at me coyly in the mirror asked:

'Frankly, do you think I'm pretty?'

'Oh, very! Very!' I shouted enthusiastically.

She kissed me.

'Your mother is pretty in a sort of way but she never smiles.
In our profession one needs to smile all the time.'

Suddenly we heard steps on the iron staircase and looking out
we saw my mother's flaming hair. Then my new friend pushed
me roughly out of her room, crying out to my mother:

'Here, you silly bitch, take a look at your daughter. I had to
pick her up and look after her while you were gossiping with
that tart of a Berthe!'

My mother remained gaping at this unexpected sally whilst
the door was slammed behind me, the same door through which
the man in the blue blouse had been enticed when Berthe was
afraid to meet him in the *salon* with the red velvet chairs. My
mother sniffed as I came near her, smelt the woman's perfume,
and angrily passed a damp towel over my face as much to remove
all trace of bad companionship as to clean the blood from my
nose. Her frigid disapproval saved me from being smacked for
playing on the iron staircase. We went to supper. Granny was
laying the table and had quite forgotten what she had witnessed
of the incident.

The next morning my mother kept me by her; she had hired
a sewing-machine and spent most of her time with Berthe, but as
this was Adrien the Belgian's day off he insisted on taking us
all to visit the castle of Blois. Berthe wore her check coat and
skirt with a shiny leather belt; my mother's costume was black,
but both had been made by themselves, and Berthe was terribly
proud to show her lover what she had learnt to do.

We climbed a lot of stone stairs and joined a group of sightseers
who were being taken round by a guide. The guide recognized
Adrien who must have been quartered in the château, I think,
and he hailed us with familiarity and importance. We saw where
the Duc de Guise was assassinated by Henry III; we were even
shown the blood. I was enchanted but terribly eager to get
home to Granny who would be making the gooseberry jelly
at any moment. The duke's blood and the jelly got so mixed up
in my mind that I made a thorough nuisance of myself. It was
decided to take me home. My mother would spend the evening
with Berthe and Adrien.

I arrived home out of breath and very red in the face and found
George and Granny, each gripping the end of a napkin, squeezing
the juice of the gooseberries. The copper pan was there, shining
like a hot sun, and mountains of castor sugar, and the scales with
their various-sized copper weights in wooden sheaths, a treasure
saved from the grocery shop at Selles. I was put out to think
that Granny had dared to start without me. The clean pots stood
in a line like little soldiers, and I was set to work cutting out
circles of transparent paper which had to soak in a saucer of rum.
I quickly noticed that Granny was not her talkative, happy self,
and I recalled hearing my mother tell Adrien and Berthe, during
our visit to the castle, that we would soon be returning to Paris.
Granny was delighted to see the back of her daughter but broken-
hearted to lose me. She was a real mother hen when her children
were small, but as soon as the chicks grew into hens themselves
she lost all interest. When the jelly began to boil Granny put
twenty pots on one side. She wrote with a shaking hand on
the sides: 'August 1916.' These were the ones we were to take
away.

As it was still quite early Granny took her wheelbarrow full of
linen as far as the washing boat in the middle of the Loire.
Having nodded to the other washerwomen she knelt at her usual
place, the water running lazily under the planks, the smell of
disinfectant mingling coolly and pleasantly with the mire and
grasses of the shallow river. On our way back to the town we
picked roses through the fences of pretty villas, and these small
thefts delighted me. Granny put her wheelbarrow in a friend's
yard and took us to the finest pastry-cook's in Blois, ordering
expensive cakes with the most noble air. The waitress looking

at Granny's shabby clothes, still damp round the sleeves from
washing in the Loire, hesitated to part with such very expensive
merchandise, whereupon Granny, delicately lifting up her apron,
pulled out a fifty-franc note from her underskirt. She gave the
impression of unhurriedly preparing to pay; in reality she had
guessed what was in the waitress's mind. At the sight of so
much money the girl became all smiles, but Granny became
haughtier than a marquise, looking down at her with withering
disdain.

On our return home I saw Granny putting the twenty pots of
gooseberry jelly in a basket with straw: then she sat down and
wept. I came up behind her and kissed her. She gave me a
golden coin of twenty francs, some blue liqueur glasses, and a
saucepan of blood-red enamel which I had always admired in
her kitchen. This saucepan gave me such intense joy that I
became quite happy to leave my grandmother. I ran to our own
room where I found my mother kneeling on the floor packing.
I had no longer any doubt. We were leaving. My mother
looked at me sideways and said: 'Well, here's my little girl!' I
burst out crying. I was eternally between mother and daughter,
father and mother.

Granny cried herself to sleep, then, as soon as it was light, came
to kiss me and went off. A few moments later I heard her
wheelbarrow dancing over the cobble-stones.

13

AS soon as we arrived at the Quay D'Orsay I saw my father eagerly looking out for us. In the first moment of recognition, from a distance, I noticed with surprise more than with pain how much older he had become, but as I ran to him he lifted me off my feet and kissed me so tenderly that a wonderful warmth flowed over my body. He put me down and looking at my mother said in a low, loving voice:
'I was *so* afraid you would not come!'

They walked in front of me to the barrier. I was carrying a small wicker basket with Bambino, the liqueur glasses, and the chest of drawers which George had made me to put Bambino's trousseau in. Suddenly, thinking of George, I imagined that, like mother, I had left home, left George my husband, taking our child away, leaving a curt note on the kitchen table. I therefore composed my features to the severe and sharp expression of a woman who had recently taken an important decision.

This occupation with variants lasted till we reached the fortifications at Clichy. The grass along the wall had grown tall and hard, yellowed by the heat of a nearly finished summer; forgotten smells greeted me, the flowers in pots from the nearby cemetery, the distant river smell of the Seine, and the dusty putrefaction of the streets.

My father explained that he had taken a new flat, his peace-offering to my mother. Clearly he was very anxious to know whether she would approve of it and there was a touching desire in his explanations to see her smile and say 'Thank you' which she pretended not to notice, keeping her thin lips closed, reserving anything she had to say till she was aware of as yet unknown but suspected difficulties.

Marguerite Rosier and her daughter Lucienne were waiting to show us round by which it was clear that they had helped my father choose our new home. The flat was on the ground floor with hardly any light, two hours of sunshine every day at the most, but it had what our neighbours in those times called *le confort moderne*, which meant gas, a tap with running water over the sink, and a w.c. of our own!

My father, before coming to the station, had put a stew to simmer on the range, and as he was very good at putting in the right herbs the apartment smelt already lived in. Moreover, he had laid the table in the kitchen; there was a new American oil-cloth with red and white squares that I thought magnificent. My mother noticed it also and my father, who was watching her every movement, said quickly: 'I couldn't stand the other any longer. You remember, it was on it that you left the note?' My mother answered dryly: 'There was no reason to throw it away. It would have come in useful.' Her answer made me wince and I saw my father look down discomforted.

We went to the Rosiers' for coffee. I was delighted to be back with Lucienne. Hyacinthe, terribly busy at the bank, puffing with importance, made a few judicious remarks about the High Command, and then suddenly gave us his views on why gas was becoming so bad for cooking and lighting. Like most shy men he allowed himself to become heated in an argument, hoping to be judged by his intelligence. I think he really must have been very clever and Marguerite was lucky to have a husband who was almost bound to push his way to some degree of success, but though we admired him in the abstract his learned arguments made us yawn or laugh. He repeated a great number of times:

'Containers, containers, that 's what we need. We need containers and more containers!'

Marguerite made joyous signs behind his back as if to say: 'You see! He 's just the same!' Then said to her husband: 'Come, Hyacinthe, hand me over your container and I 'll pour you out some more coffee!'

Hyacinthe who, in the full fever of his speech, was stumping up and down the room, looked at his wife frowningly and asked: 'What do you mean? A container for coffee?'

He brushed a wisp of hair back from his forehead and went on angrier:

'You 're mad! You 're not capable of understanding anything. Can't you see that a container for gas is a huge affair?'

He suddenly remained open-mouthed in front of the hilarious tears of his wife. She was laughing at him! Making a fool of him! He looked round savagely to see on whose side we were. Then furiously he limped out of the room and down the stairs to count the provisions in the cellar. Unwisely he had left a bottle of rum on the table which Marguerite and my father and mother cruelly emptied.

My father was helping to make a new airfield just outside Paris. They were being built everywhere and labour was short so that he could be reasonably certain of work. His courage was still immense; he would do so much overtime that he occasionally remained away half the night.

A few days after our return my mother and I who now went to the Lorraine market, being the nearest to our new home, met Germaine Séguin perched on very high heels. She invited us to come to their flat which we did the same afternoon, bringing Marguerite Rosier with us. M. Séguin, even more short-sighted than we had last seen him, had just inherited twenty thousand francs from a distant uncle. This sum was so considerable for a family who had never come to the end of the week without having to ask for credit that M. Séguin had immediately resigned from his job of beating carpets for the Magasin du Printemps, and there remained nothing to remind him of his past but a pair of rose-coloured carpet slippers. Mme Séguin and Germaine, taking their cue from the man of the family, immediately left the factory where they worked, and for a full month, newly clothed, they paraded the avenue and went to the theatre every night. At the end of this period, fearing to be penniless again, they invested their remaining money in buying knitting-machines, preferring to stay at home making knitted goods, which were then rapidly coming into fashion, than to go back to factory life. Each had a machine. The kitchen table was covered with apparatus over which hung a smell of warm wool, machine oil, and M. Séguin's pipe tobacco. Germaine went to fetch the wool and delivered the work when it was finished. Mme Séguin was looking for a little girl to help her wind the wool on the bobbins. My mother offered to loan me to them for a few hours in the afternoon, at any rate till the end of the summer holidays.

At first the different coloured wools delighted me, but I have never been any good at doing the same thing for more than a few minutes. Happily Germaine took me with her to deliver the finished garments. We would hurry to get rid of the parcel

*F

and then walk slowly up and down the Boulevard Victor-Hugo, an avenue of ill repute. Germaine would stop, roll her hips, and show off her high heels in front of the apprentice apaches who, hidden just inside dark doorways, were learning the business whilst waiting for the call-up. I became somewhat frightened of these faces, so good-looking but false, youths with sticky dark hair who whistled like nightingales without moving their lips, or who played such pretty love-songs on the mouth-organ that stones would have wept. I was afraid, I know not of what. I would press Germaine's arm and whisper for her to come away. She would scold me. Then I would say: 'Come, Germaine, or I shall go home by myself and tell your mother where you are!' Suddenly she would straighten her hips and run after me on her high heels. The fear of getting into trouble before she was twenty-one checked her natural aspirations. Occasionally after long wanderings we would return after dark, holding each other tightly by the arm, Germaine sniffing the night air, dreaming of love-songs, idleness, and the excitement of being a prostitute.

My mother had started to sew again. She could never leave it. She used to say that she was tied to it as the galley-slaves were chained to the heavy iron ball. We met Mme Gaillard who now centred her attention on table linen, deploring machine-made lace and all this knitting that was becoming increasingly in the fashion. Only a few old-fashioned ladies wore lace jabots and fronts which Mme Gaillard would send to their country homes. Then, too, crape was increasing its ugly head. The mourning departments of the big stores were the busiest—in the streets the crowds, though made picturesque by men's uniforms, were streaked with black.

Marie-Thérèse and Rolande were still in their apartment, rue de Longchamps. My aunt could not stand being left so long without her husband and her character was showing bitterness and revolt. He was not in danger but she was afraid he would be sent to the front. Fear kept her awake at night. She thought of her husband incessantly, working very hard so that when the war was over he would find a little money at home. She and Rolande went without what was necessary for their health. I went to stay with them for a while; in the evenings we used to call on my aunt's customers, parlourmaids for the most part, or ladies' maids for whom she made the prettiest hats. A sister of

Raoul, the footman, a girl called Louise, had managed to keep an excellent situation as cook. She was lovely and had what modistes call *une tête à chapeaux*: a person on whom any hat looks its best, a quality that has nothing to do with beauty as such. Hats fit some heads magically. There is no explaining these things. They depend on line or colour which the eye does not always perceive in advance. At all events the ugliest hat in the world would have looked pretty on Louise's head. This girl served her mistress with the utmost devotion. In the evening she would bid her good night and then, running up to her sixth-floor attic, would dress with extraordinary taste and elegance, put her gloves on, and, of course, one of my aunt's hats, and then run off to Magic City or Luna Park where she would roller-skate or dance with officers, French or allied, till dawn. She would then sleep for two hours, step softly into her employer's room, draw the curtains, serve her breakfast in bed, looking as fresh and happy as somebody who had slept the whole night through.

In the evening she would make the most succulent dishes for her young mistress whose husband was at the front, putting all her heart into the cooking of them out of genuine affection and sympathy. When the meal had gone up to the dining-room, she would receive my aunt who would bring her a new hat or one of her old ones made to look different with a fresh ribbon. These fittings would take place in the clean, bright kitchen with Rolande and me shyly standing in a corner. Afterwards, when supper was brought down again and there was part of what Louise had so lovingly made left over, she would quickly bundle a peach or an ice into a paper bag and give it to us. To my aunt who always carried about a large bag of American oilcloth she would give a few pieces of coal. Then, sweetly, she would shoo us off the premises, go to put her young mistress to bed, flying off to her night's pleasure, figures of eight and dreamy waltzes on the roller-skating floor, or languid tangos with good-looking foreigners. Charming Louise! How adorable you could look in those hats, one I remember, in particular, with a bunch of forget-me-nots next to your young cheek!

We ran down the service stairs and out into the streets where the lamps were shaded. My aunt, since the departure of her husband, wore the strangest clothes—some of his tweeds, for instance, curiously re-cut and adapted to her use. With these rather mannish costumes she put on a black taffeta hat made out of a piece of material left over from a customer, and so narrow in the brim that it looked like a bowler hat sat upon and squashed: however, it had in the front a rectangular buckle in mother-of-pearl which, in conjunction with the tweeds, gave my aunt a curious resemblance to an eighteenth-century postilion. This unusual costume caused amusement in the rue de Longchamps, but my aunt was so proud that the suits her husband wore, given to him by the baron his master, emanated from Savile Row, that whenever any of her friends passed a remark she took on a knowing and superior air and said: 'The material is English.'

Thus dressed, my aunt, carrying with both hands the shiny bag with the coal in it, Rolande and I trotting beside her, was preparing to cross the road when, her view partly obstructed by the bag, her legs curved by the tallness of her Louis XV heels, tripped over the edge of the pavement and fell on her knees in the gutter, in which ludicrous position she remained with her arms folded over the bag, her heels caught up on the edge of the pavement. Rolande and I regarded her with the utmost surprise. The moon cast a glow on the mother-of-pearl buckle on the front of her hat and made it appear phosphorescent. Rolande started cruelly to laugh. Marie-Thérèse called us furiously to order and obediently we began to lift her up, helped by a passing gendarme. The presence of the policeman, smiling, had covered her cheeks with pink confusion. We walked silently and more carefully home.

The next day when we went to call on Louise, the doorkeeper told us that her latest nocturnal adventure had ended in hospital where she now lay on the danger list. Her young mistress, accustomed to be wakened by Louise every morning, had slept till midday; then fearing an accident had run up to the room on the sixth floor where she found that Louise's bed had not been slept in. She had sent to the doorkeeper's lodge for news. Towards lunch time a police sergeant came to report that a young woman of her name, having fractured her thigh while skating at the Palace of Ice, had been taken unconscious to hospital where pleurisy had set in.

Louise's young mistress had hurried to her pretty maid's bedside, but three days later Louise died.

My aunt took me back to Clichy where this appalling tragedy

was much talked about. During my stay at the rue de Long-champs Marie-Thérèse had taken me to the hairdresser who cut my hair short. My father was not at all pleased, disliking any change of feminine fashion, and whether on account of this or simply on old scores he became increasingly disagreeable to Marie-Thérèse whom he accused of having a thoroughly bad influence over my mother, making her believe that her lot was worse than it really was and exciting her to revolt. After lunch on Sundays he would not stay with us at home, and to escape what he called our 'insipid feminine talk' would go to play cards at his favourite café. He would come home late and joyful, but his gaiety would be quick to turn at the least provocation to violence, and then, in spite of his tenderness at the Quay D'Orsay station and his many solemn promises, the angry scenes would start all over again just as in the old days. Marguerite Rosier, wise in her manner and of excellent counsel, advised my mother not to see Marie-Thérèse any more; this my mother agreed to. Our visits became fewer and soon we broke off relations altogether.

Marie-Thérèse, perhaps out of revenge but also from curiosity, started to write to their sister Marguerite who had married an Armenian and now lived in a London suburb. Marguerite, you will recall, was the eldest of the three sisters who at the age of twelve had been apprenticed to a dressmaker at Vierzon. Anxious for news of Granny and what was happening at Blois, Marguerite, informed of our visit by Marie-Thérèse, sent dolls to Rolande and to me, and asked my mother to write to her; but here again my father intervened. Though he had a soft spot for his own sister he wanted to estrange my mother entirely from hers.

When my Aunt Marguerite continued to send me presents, my father could not well prevent me from writing to say thank you. We therefore started a correspondence which later was to have important results. Her husband, a good deal older than she was, was in the Levantine trade. The fact that we knew practically nothing of her married life was typical of my mother's family, who were always not seeing one another for long periods at a time. We now learnt that Aunt Marguerite and her husband owned a little house at Beckenham, Kent. Obviously the eldest sister had become the most successful of the three, and from now on we spoke of her as 'the aunt from England.'

On 1st October I went back to the Protestant school which I

had left a year earlier, before going to St. Cloud, and I was automatically placed with the older girls in Mlle Zélie's class. Mlle Zélie was delightful, but I made no scholastic progress, having been outdistanced during my year of idleness and being unable to catch up in a class where there were so many pupils. We spent too much time also, I expect, singing hymns and reading the New Testament, though both these occupations delighted me.

Meanwhile we again changed our apartment, leaving the ground-floor flat, which was really too dark, for one on the first floor on the opposite side of the street from which my mother, hidden behind a muslin curtain, could see everything taking place in the busy avenue. This amusement partly restored her composure. So many things happened: a horse that stumbled, bringing to the scene of the accident waves of women and urchins, or possibly an ambulance clanging along to the Gouin Hospital, or, most interesting of all, a funeral. The war was becoming interminable. Men were going away every day, and though my father limped and only had one eye he was placed in a labour corps to guard the railway. Soon America came in; he was then directed to factory work.

The Americans put up a camp overlooking the Seine, and though the English had surprised us by their clean appearance and smart uniforms the Americans surprised us even more. Their hats made a devastating impression, and Paris immediately invented a feminine adaptation. The women all went to work wearing these fantastic shapes in red, mauve, blue, and green. Any woman who neglected this important innovation was laughed at. Thus began the wearing of a felt hat at any time of the year; previously hats were exclusively of straw in spring and summer. The American hat vogue, as such, did not, of course, last long. Only in Paris can a fashion descend upon the population overnight, become a sort of madness, and then disappear as suddenly as it came.

Bread was now rationed; sugar, coffee, chocolate, and oil were rare. Rough table wine was no longer to be had. We were obliged to queue for hours. Mother and I left the house very early and began to queue for a so-called superior wine which alone was obtainable. Not only was it more expensive, but the bottles were sealed with coloured metal paper, with the result that we could no longer add tap water to my father's wine as we normally did. We would come home soaked, chilled, thoroughly miserable. My mother would go back to bed for an hour; I would run off to school, not knowing my lessons, having no time for homework. On my way home I would look round to see if there were likely queues in the shops. I became an expert, and my mother, delighted, used to give me five francs with which to buy anything we needed. I learned how to slip unnoticed towards the top of a queue and then glide in again after I had been served to obtain two portions of coffee or sugar. Twice a week there were tobacco queues in which soldiers on leave had priority. Soldiers would lend their military cloaks to civilians to take advantage of this privilege in which we, the women, queuing up for husbands or fathers, had no possibility of joining. My mother would become very bitter spending so much time getting cold and wet for tobacco and wine for my father. It made her hate him at times, I think. For me it became a sport. I would even seize a soldier's hand as he was going up the queue and take advantage of his preferred treatment. On such mornings I was let off going to school. When it was very cold my mother and I would try to warm ourselves with a sharp walk, and on these occasions we went to call on Mme Gaillard, knocking with an umbrella handle on the window of her lodge, being asked to go in for a cup of coffee while she was dressing.

Her husband was now bedridden, immobile beside his still lovingly tended plants. She herself, who once knew every corner of Paris, no longer moved from her doorkeeper's lodge and was growing fat. The last of her private customers had disappeared. Her business had disintegrated. She told us that Mme Valentin, worn out by work, was dead. We would leave her, promising to come again, but secretly resolved to find a gayer way of getting warm, and if we were lucky we might chance on another pound of coffee or tea on the way home.

Amongst our new neighbours there was a family from the Auvergne called Alexis. Jules, the father, was red-haired and a drunkard, his nose horribly tumefied: Mme Alexis, though not much more than forty, was so exhausted by putting children into the world that she looked an old woman. If anybody questioned Mme Alexis about the number of her children she would begin to count them on her fingers thus:

'There was Marie, she makes one; there is Jules, two; there was Valentine, three; and then Paul, four; oh, and there were the twins, Berthe and Jeanne, they would make six; then the imbecile who died, he made seven; there's Blanche who is married, she makes eight; my little Louis, nine; the red-haired girl Maimaine, ten; Henriette, eleven; and Maurice, the youngest, makes twelve.'

The fun of seeing Mme Alexis enumerating her children, finger by finger, was such that we never failed to ask innocently:

'How many children have you in all, Mme Alexis?'

Then she would begin:

'There was Marie, she makes one . . .' At the town hall, where she often sought relief, this unusual way of counting her children annoyed the employees. Poor Mme Alexis could never remember that the enumeration totalled twelve. Each time the figure came to her as a surprise. We would say to her:

'But, Mme Alexis, why don't you think of a dozen eggs? A dozen! It's easy.'

Then she would become very angry and shout out that we were insulting her, comparing her to a hen.

Nearly every night the sirens wailed to tell us there was a German aeroplane over Paris. Then Mme Alexis would become crazy with fear, and gathering up her youngest child she would hide with him at the bottom of a dark cupboard. Crouching, like a stone figure, this normally noisy woman would not make a sound. She became a mere bundle of rags, her eyes looking up at one with pitiful supplication. To try to calm her we went to her place as soon as the warning sounded. She liked to have a great crowd of people round her, or, more accurately, in front of her, for their presence would not prevent her from seeking the comfort of the cupboard, the door of which, as a concession when we were about, she would leave open. Germaine, called Maimaine, her tenth child, the red-haired one, had a pale milky skin; Henriette, the eleventh, dark, with gentle blue eyes, warm and full of perversity, was my age. Maimaine was already the housewife; she prepared the soup for the evening meal, washed up mountains of crockery, cleverly, without a sound, without a glimmer of revolt! She put the younger ones to bed in beds which unfolded like cages all along the wall, and would then slip into hers with Henriette. There was one bed in this strange dormitory which was seldom slept in. It belonged to the boy

Louis, sixteen years old, his mother's favourite child, dark as she was with blue eyes which looked at you deliciously under long black lashes, a mouth like a ripe cherry, an angelic face with no sign yet of hair on the chin, and a delicate white neck emerging from a dirty, creased collar. Little Louis was the prettiest child in the world. He was a pleasure to look at, though, of course, he filled one with apprehension. These candid charms hid a store of wickedness. He would only work in fits and starts, for instance, after a gendarme had called or after a quarrel with his father. The other days and nights he ran off to companions on the fortifications wearing the traditional red scarf. He cajoled his mother, knew to a nicety how to kiss every woman, and all, irrespective of age, fell willingly under his spell. Mme Alexis opened her purse: he would sleep at home for a night or two, then, after tenderly kissing her, would disappear. Just before dawn, during an air raid, he hurried in, took off his cap, his red scarf, and his linen shoes, and went to bed. In the morning the police came, but he found all the house to witness that he had been home since the previous evening.

Jules, the eldest, was at the front where he was not brave. At home he was the apache Louis would soon become, the formed man who, to tame women, made use of his strength, whereas Louis was still in the stage of charming them. On leave he looked wonderful in his blue uniform, but black revolt lurked behind his smooth forehead. Paul, the next, was monstrously ugly, like his father, but his nerves were magnificent. He deserted and hid in our cellar. Maimaine used to bring his food. He might have remained there longer if a tenant had not heard him snore. He was taken hurriedly to another cellar, but he must have found this life monotonous, for he was soon with his companions on the fortifications, stealing their women, holding them to ransom, and leading a joyous life till he was denounced and shot by a firing squad at Vincennes. Mme Alexis was broken-hearted to think that her son had ended in this way: Jules, while on leave, had volunteered to work in a munition factory, and just as he was due to go back to the army he managed to upset a carboy of chemicals on his leg. He was rushed to hospital with severe burns and escaped being sent to Verdun, but now, with what had happened to Paul, Mme Alexis trembled to think what her little Louis would do.

Jules grew fat and well in hospital, where his sister Blanche, a superb girl with flaming red hair like mother's, used to come and see him, and turn the heads of all the patients. Now, suddenly, Mme Alexis was going to have another baby, though suddenly is not the right word. She was several months pregnant, but her body was so misshapen that we had none of us noticed that she had grown fatter. She said it made up for losing Paul—one had been shot as a deserter, a thirteenth was on the way. Blanche was also going to have a baby, with the result that Mme Alexis would be simultaneously mother and grandmother. Poor Mme Alexis suffered a great deal from her condition, continued to work hard, and worried about her children from morning till night, whilst her husband, quite oblivious to anything that was not a glass of wine or a tot of rum, took no notice either of his wife or his children. Money was plentiful in the family, though nobody knew where it came from. Maimaine was making the layette for the new arrivals. Henriette went to school with me. She was a terrible little liar, but had the queer charm of pretty Louis and knew too well that school could teach her nothing about life, that all she had to do was to exercise patience. She said to me: 'You understand, Madeleine, at fifteen and three months I shall get myself married by an old man. I shall leave him. That will make me free and of age. I shall be able to do what I like. Goodbye to mother Alexis and all the family! Not so silly, am I?'

During the early spring a generous and wealthy woman invited a number of girls from our school to spend a fortnight in a property she owned at Vauancourt in the Oise. I was a member of the chosen group. We were lodged in a grange, but were well fed and were out all day. I came back with pink cheeks and my clothes full of lice.

I immediately started queuing up again with Henriette and Maimaine, who had grown more expert than I. Unfortunately their methods brought them into such ill repute that I thought it wiser to operate on my own. This, too, had disadvantages. We waged a war of opposing gangs. My mother had a new friend called Mme Maurer, whom she had met at the Alexis flat, and I used to queue up for her as well as for my mother and Marguerite Rosier.

This Mme Maurer had a well-brought-up aspect which seemed quite out of place in our hard, bitter world. She spoke a French

as pure as ours was deficient and slangy, but though everything
we did should have shocked her, her eyes twinkled with amusement each time she spent an evening with the Alexis family.
About sixty, corpulent, continually in physical pain, a noted
atheist, she lived modestly with her son, who was about thirty.
Their flat was the one next to that occupied by Mme Alexis.
I heard her complain one day, but not bitterly, that having run
out of oil and coffee she could get no more because she was not
strong enough to stand in a queue.   I repeated this to my mother,
who sent me next day with some coffee, oil, and chocolate, the
exact value being discreetly marked in pencil on the wrapping
paper.

Mme Maurer asked me to come in; our flats were exactly alike,
but I was very surprised to see the out-of-date furniture which
seemed to be grouped in front of a portrait of Napoleon III.
Another portrait showed a gentleman of the same period with
the Legion of Honour across his chest.   This was Mme Maurer's
father, a famous actor of the Imperial Theatre who had received
his medal from the emperor in person.   There was another
portrait of a bearded man, clearly of more recent date.   He reminded me in a general way of M. Poincaré, the then president
of France.   This was M. Maurer, her late husband.

This strange woman moved with dignity amongst her Second
Empire furniture, under the gaze of these three unsmiling men.
There was no portrait of a woman, not even a photograph, but
Mme Maurer, now that she was old, was becoming so masculine
in her features that she seemed to make a fourth with the portraits
on the wall.   Her high, powerful forehead had no hair falling on
it, her nose was straight and large of the type known as *bour-
bonien*, her double chin gave her an expression of will power, and
her voice was deep and manly.   This first glimpse of her might
easily have put us off had she not quickly displayed a kinder, more
sensitive side, and even these qualities would not, I fancy, have
been enough.   What drew us towards her was her love of
beautiful things.   My mother, in spite of her ill fortune, sensed
what was beautiful.   Her genius for working blouses of rich lace
and of instinctively putting together the loveliest dress, was proof
of inborn gifts.   You should have seen her handle a material
and judge it.   She read voraciously, like Marie-Thérèse, but
managed in some curious way to read books that were excellently

written. Being poor she had taste, whereas many, being rich, do not have it. I also was at an age when I may have been starving for an appreciation of the beautiful. This Mme Maurer imperceptibly took my literary education in hand and excited my imagination to the highest degree. On Thursday when I took her the coffee, the oil, and the other little things, she would do the accounts with me, treating me not like a child, but like a grown responsible woman, and would afterwards take me to the room she shared with her son and show me miniatures hidden in drawers. She lent me books which precipitated me into a world I knew nothing about.

She had known personally the Comtesse de Ségur, whose books for little girls form the jewels of the *Bibliothèque Rose*. She was scrupulously tide, which we at home never were. Everything was put away, ticketed, dusted, laid lovingly in little boxes. I think it was her son who did this when he came home in the evening. They had spent so many years moving from one apartment to another, each fresh one meaner and more cramped than the last, that being tidy was their only way of keeping anything. As we saw more of each other she would come on a visit to our apartment on the opposite side of the street. I would do my lessons or sew by the window. Mme Maurer sat between the table and the cooking stove. Mother, of course, would be sewing. Mme Maurer would begin to tell us whatever might have happened during the morning or in the course of the night, it being rare that the whole house was not wakened by a violent quarrel between Jules Alexis and one or other of his children, and, starting to reminisce in her deep voice, she would take us back into her past. Then we would hear the sound of galloping horses. She had travelled from Paris to Chartres in a stage-coach; she had kept rendezvous with famous men in closed carriages, the blinds drawn; she adored de Musset and his *grisettes*; spoke of Mimi Pinson as of a sweet friend; had lived and loved in Paris when people said of it: Paris —the paradise for women. 'How many gold pieces! How much misery!' was her frequent comment. Love still beat in her heart. Like Marie-Thérèse she had cut out a vast number of serials from the newspapers, binding them together, putting them away to read and to lend, the first novels of George Sand, Jules Sandeau, Balzac, Victor Hugo, and Dumas *père et fils*. These

dead giants had been alive in her day. She had known Théophile
Gautier, adored Zola. Her enthusiasm set us upon a phrenetic
course of reading. When she was sad or depressed, as women
so often are for no reason, or perhaps because we are happy, she
would not say: 'I have the *cafard*,' as the women in our street
said, but 'I have the *spleen*,' which is Baudelairian. This word
came strangely to us, but soon mother began to have the *spleen*
and, of course, so did I. Mme Maurer sang adorably the airs of
Offenbach, and had danced the can-can. She had seen the czar,
the czarina, the grand duchesses, the kings and queens who still
sat on their thrones, for Russia was still 'the steam-roller,' and
the Balkans had their states—and yet she had been in Paris
during the Commune, living with her parents and her three sisters
in a magnificent house in the ancient rue des Saints-Pères on the
left bank where her father, the great actor, received the writers
of the day. She took me once to see it, for she cultivated her
memories like flowers in a garden. On anniversaries such as
the death of her father or of her mother, instead of visiting their
graves, she went to see the places where they had been happy.
Thus she and I stood in front of the house in the rue des Saints-
Pères, feeling rather scared that the doorkeeper would come out
to shoo us away. There was a beautiful door with glass and
wrought iron, through which we could see the inner courtyard.
'There,' she said, 'when I was four, having just returned from
Chartres by coach, I hid in a corner and started to sing, oh, but
with all my soul! My father came down those steps and told
my mother in his deep actor's voice that it was a scandal to lèt
a street singer come into the courtyard of a house like his.'

She loved the streets of Paris, and on some trivial excuse, like
wanting a piece of ribbon, she would walk interminably. She
took us to the Bon Marché, and thus taught us the left bank.
My love of walking interminably through a great city comes
from her.

Her mother was from Chartres, her father was Parisian. The
three daughters had almost immediately been marked by fate as
if the wrong fairies had attended their births. The eldest at the
age of sixteen had an intestinal obstruction which for five months
prevented her from clearing her bowels. No laxative was of
any use. She was given pints of oil and large quantities of milk;
the Paris faculty, interested in this strange case, prescribed liquids

and completely starved her. The parents did not know how to take their meals without increasing the misery of this young girl who was dying of hunger. She would ask them in a beseeching voice for a crust of bread, just a crust of bread, but her parents, having been told by the most learned doctors that the slightest morsel of solid food would prove fatal, energetically refused, and hid everything in locked cupboards. She became enormous and was hardly able to walk, but her legs and arms were terribly thin. Her cheerfulness was extraordinary, and being a born actress she would ask for her little piece of bread dramatically after the manner of Rachel, or in the droll way of a character out of Molière, and she would make her family laugh till they wept, though in secret, knowing that she must die, their tears were real. One day at supper during a severe thunderstorm, she as usual eating nothing, the thunder shaking the old house in the rue des Saints-Pères, the young girl suddenly rose, as pale as if she had seen a ghost, and cried out: 'Quickly the pan! Bring me the pan!' Her weakness, this hallucination in the middle of a storm, her wild eyes convinced everybody that the end, foretold by the doctors, had arrived; her mother hurriedly fetched the pan, put it down in a corner of the room, and tenderly arranged her daughter on it. An explosion like another clap of thunder, followed by an appalling smell of sulphur, made them wonder if their house had not been hit; then they saw their daughter, bent in two, laughing as if she had lost her mind. The parents' joy, when they understood, was immense, but their daughter remained in this posture till several doctors interested in this terrible case arrived, and eventually announced that the great amount of liquid the patient had absorbed had ended by forcing down a cancer complete with its adhesions.

I am not surprised that my homework made little progress. School books lay pushed aside; I preferred to sew. Little girls in poor families, in Paris at any rate, become quickly aware of the fundamentals of life and death. Things are not hidden from them, and they accordingly grow more sensitive to the pain and sorrow of others. Tragedy does alight on certain families like a great black bird on its victims. If this had not happened in the case of Mme Maurer's family she might still have been living in a lovely house on the left bank of the Seine. In fact the eldest sister, delivered of her cancer, recovered, and marrying had lovely children, but one would have said that fate, having made this experiment, was anxious to try its hand again. The next thing told by Mme Maurer in her slow, beautiful, but rather out-of-date French concerned the second sister, and happened when Annette was fifteen.

Their father was rehearsing a new play, in which his important scene was with a young actor, discovered by him in the provinces, who was to stay at the rue des Saints-Pères till he could find a suitable lodging of his own. Every morning in the drawing-room the father and his protégé would rehearse the difficult passage. The young man became almost a member of the family, but though he was charming to look at neither the mother nor the daughters liked him; indeed Annette had such a dislike of him that she had great difficulty in not showing it, and her father made several angry scenes, saying that by this piece of girlish stupidity she risked antagonizing the young man and causing a quarrel before the opening night. All this made little difference. When Annette looked at the young actor anybody could see how she hated him.

Mme Maurer was then ten, and the two little girls slept in the same bed. Their mother came to kiss them good night; the youngest was soon asleep, but Annette, after some hours, crept out and went to join the young actor whom she loathed, but who each night took advantage of her.

She became pregnant, and soon the parents were convinced that she was going to have the same cancer as the eldest girl. One night she began her labour and gave birth to a little girl in the bed which the two young sisters still shared. The young man had disappeared, having left Paris as soon as the play had finished. Annette was sent to a convent till she was twenty; the parents, unforgiving, never allowed Annette back in the house. Mme Maurer could not tell what had happened to Annette or to the child.

The story made us shudder, whereupon Mme Maurer, turning to my mother, said: 'When I told you, Mme Gal, that nothing ordinary ever happened to us! My parents viewed their lovely house in the rue des Saints-Pères in disgust—or perhaps they were ashamed; at all events they sold it, and went to live in Chartres, where my mother started a little business in men's shirts. Two or three girls were engaged. I also was put to work cutting and sewing.   My mother was much older than my father.   What had happened to Annette had turned her from a good-looking woman of middle age to an old woman.   Her shirt business in her native town was a gentle employment in which she could nurse her infirmities, but my father, rested, his nerves recovered, his fine personality admired and fêted in this small provincial town, became such a youthful and popular figure that my mother was made miserable by a sudden, burning jealousy.   Soon her life became intolerable.   For all the rest of us it became a purgatory.   My father, who was very good, very serious, would never have been unfaithful to my mother, but he had a charm when speaking to anybody that he could no more hide than the nose in the middle of his face.   He hated to see his wife so unhappy, but the nicer he was with her the more convinced was she that he was trying to buy her pardon.

'Soon my father's happiness was sapped by the life my mother led him.   He lost his colour, had the spleen, refused to eat, and soon fell ill.   My mother, delighted to have him exclusively in her care, nursed him like a she-wolf with her young.   She left the little factory entirely in my hands and would not move from my father's room.   He, as good as ever, recited his roles to her as he had done when they were first married.   My mother's joy was immense.   Her happiness increased as my father's physical break-up became more apparent, but it did not last long.   My father died in his sleep one morning; my mother, discovering a phial of laudanum, swallowed it, and fell in agonizing pain beside her dead husband.'

Mme Maurer looked up and added simply:

'I was nineteen.   When everything was sold I came to Paris and found work as a seamstress in a men's shirt factory.'

Now, because she was young, began for her that life in Paris which could be so wonderful for a pretty woman.   There was, of course, no question of a rich marriage.   She had to do what any young woman did in those days who wanted to succeed— she became the mistress of a diplomat, a married man and famous, distinguished, much older, rich, and selfish.   He understood nothing of her difficulties.   When coming to see her in her little flat he would express surprise at her frugality; she had not the courage to tell him that she had nothing to eat.   A clever woman would have known how to excite pity.   She was always butting up against her pride. 'Boldness, that 's what was missing in me!' she would cry. 'Without daring a woman gets nowhere!' She paused a moment to give full effect to this exposure of a failing which she believed had ruined her life. She went on: 'I was pretty. I had a magnificent voice. I ought to have been a big success in the theatre, or just in life itself, but no, this damnable timidity prevented me from doing anything, and now that I 've conquered it it 's too late. Some people say one shouldn't talk before little girls, but I 'm telling you this, Madeleine, so that you shall remember that what you want in life you must ask for. It 's all very well being proud and waiting for destiny to bring it along on a silver dish, but that 's merely romanticism. If you have read Grimm you will know that fairies always asked little girls what they wanted.'

'Oh, yes,' exclaimed my mother, putting down her needle and looking wistfully out of the window. 'I who have always blushed, always been timid. You see what has happened to me!'

Not anxious for my mother to break into the story I said to Mme Maurer impatiently:

'What happened after that?'

'With the diplomat, you mean? Oh, well, in spite of all the care he took, his diplomatic caution, one might say, I became pregnant.' She turned to my mother, knowingly. 'I let myself slip from a hackney coach in the Bois de Boulogne, I washed down the walls, I did things I wasn't used to doing, nothing was any help. My friend left me. They always do when you want them most. He was a coward, afraid of scandal, afraid of what his wife might discover.'

She had a son, who was difficult to bring up, probably because she was not rich enough to give him the things he needed. There was also the fall from the hackney coach which might have done him harm. She met Louis Maurer, who was employed at one of the toll-houses which, until quite recently, were set up all round the Paris fortifications. He married her, took a great liking to her son, to whom he was anxious to give his name, but she refused. Louis Maurer had not made her happy, but she spoke of him tenderly and with gratitude. He had a stroke, partially recovered, but became mad in a harmless, quite amusing way. He would accuse the king of England of stealing his razor, and then go out for long walks forgetting who he was and where he

lived. Finally he was taken to Villejuif where he died shortly before
the war.   Her son was now draughtsman in an aeroplane factory.

One Sunday when my parents were still at table, I, looking
out of the window waiting for a sign from my mother to go with
Maimaine and Henriette Alexis to play in the street, I saw a
chasseur alpin going into the house on the opposite side of the
road where we had lodged on our return from Blois.   A few
moments later he came out and crossed to our side.   Steps
climbed the stairs.   Our door bell rang, and when I opened I
found myself looking up into the dark eyes of Henri Toulouse,
the husband of the lovely Ernestine.   All the warmth of the
midi came with him into the room.   A little stockier, wider in
the shoulders, his dark blue beret over one eye, he was still very
good-looking.   He had an arm in a sling.   Poor Henri!   At last
we felt sorry for him!   My father greeted him in patois, sat him
down at table, and my mother poured him out some freshly
made coffee.

My father's deep voice broke out:

'Tell us all about your campaigns, Henri!'

Well, he had come from Nice.   He had been in Italy, and now
they were probably going to send him to the eastern front.   He
and his companions had spent a long time in the train.   He had
leant out of the window, and a train coming in the opposite
direction had grazed his arm, and so he had gone to hospital to
have it put in a sling.   My father exclaimed:

'Just like me and my hat!'

So that was Henri Toulouse's glorious wound!   Mother and
I broke into peals of laughter.   He seemed puzzled by this
hilarity, and turning to my father asked him in patois what had
happened to his hat.

'Oh!' exclaimed my father, 'I was looking out of the window
too.   I was afraid the train had passed Paris without my knowing it.'

My mother, who was tired of the story of the hat, said to
Toulouse:

'Please, M. Toulouse, give us some more details about the
accident.'

He looked reassured by her change of tone and answered:

'That's all about the accident, but thanks to this sling I've
had a wonderful time in Paris.   The young women offer me

their seats in the underground.   Of course, I don't dare tell them how it happened.   In fact I just let them understand it was on the battle-field.   *Péchère!*   They don't know me, and they'll never see me again, but I'm sorry Ernestine wasn't there to see my success in the capital!'

'Yes,' agreed my mother dryly, 'it is a pity.'

Henri Toulouse drank his coffee, stretched out his legs, and answered:

'Oh, but I shall have to stay in Paris several weeks because of my wound.   Ernestine who has never been here yet will have a permit to come.'

She arrived two days later, and we were obliged to put her up. She was still a fine-looking girl, but her sparkle was less brilliant than at the Grand' Combe.   She was very much the matured woman, more so than one would have expected for her twenty-two years, and her love for Toulouse was undimmed.   The war had prevented her from setting up a home of her own.   She was still living with her parents on the mountain, and was delighted to come to Paris, but though she spoke up very boldly in patois when she was with us she was terrified when she had to cross the road alone.

One day when Ernestine and I had gone to spend the day with an aunt of Henri Toulouse who lived in Paris, Place des Vosges, I took advantage of our being together in a corner of the kitchen to ask her what had happened to her first fiancé, my friend Louis Verdier, whose sad face still haunted me.

'Oh, that one!' she exclaimed.   'Well, would you believe it? Though he had never done his military service he volunteered on the 3rd August, and was immediately killed in the front line. The poor boy!   His mother is still bitter with me because they found a photograph of me next to his heart, and she accuses me of having killed him!   Between you and me I don't believe a word of it: I don't say he wasn't fond of me, but a man doesn't die for the love of a girl.'

She had raised her voice.   Her aunt was peeling the potatoes by the sink.   This woman had a son on leave who had been wandering through the flat in his sky-blue soldier's trousers, and with his shirt-sleeves rolled up.   He looked at Ernestine and asked:

'How can you say that a man doesn't die for the love of a girl? Haven't you ever read the *Arlésienne*?'

'No,' she answered, uninterested. 'I don't know any Arlé-sienne. I 've never been that way.'

He shrugged his shoulders and started to whistle *La Madelon* without even deigning to look at her again.

That evening, while we were all having supper in a little restaurant in the avenue de Clichy, Ernestine said over the dessert:

'By the way, Toulouse, you have been about a bit, do you know a story about an Arlésienne—some young man who died for the love of her?'

'No,' answered Henri Toulouse. 'Why?'

'Little Madeleine wanted to know what had happened to Louis Verdier, and when I told her that Mme Verdier accused me of having been the cause of his death that young cousin of yours asked me if I knew the story of the Arlésienne. Your young cousin is awfully good-looking, isn't he? I notice you never told me anything about him. He knows Paris very well, and practically invited me to go to the theatre with him. You wouldn't mind, would you, Toulouse? He would take little Madeleine too.' She turned her large eyes on me and added: 'Honestly, you bring me luck. Every time we go around together I find a new gallant!'

Henri Toulouse looked down at his plate. I was not sorry for this small revenge.

My father was delighted to have his niece in the house; but he never could keep awake in the evening, and when Ernestine said to him: 'Come now, Uncle Milou, surely you 're not going to sleep during the whole of my stay?' the name of Milou struck a chord in his heart. Milou! He was forty-three and nobody ever called him that any more. It was the name his mother and grandmother had called him. Yes, that was right. Milou was the name of the young miner so much admired by his elders, the little boy who caught frogs in the Gardon, the lad who would shout at the top of his voice under the Roman arches of the Pont du Gard. All the lads would call after him. Milou! Milou! Milou! But however hard he tried to keep awake, sleep would come. He fell back in his chair and closed his eyes like the little Milou who would come home so tired after running after thrushes and cutting his knee on a sharp stone. My mother would look down at him and say: 'He 's up at dawn. It 's a long day. And he 's not so young as he was.'

14

APART from the hymns that Mlle Zélie made us sing, and her delightful readings of the New Testament, my religious instruction was neglected. I never saw my father or my mother in prayer. Marie-Thérèse was equally neglectful of Rolande. My mother and my aunt had no memory of the beautiful convent of the Ursulines at Blois but the sweeping out of the class-rooms. Of the litanies they recited in their beds at home next to their deaf and sleeping mother, nothing remained but bitterness and irony.

In our street the separation of church and state was clearly successful. Hardly anybody went to church, and the few who did were immediately put down as being bigoted: they became objects of scorn, not of veneration. When a person died in our street he went directly from his mean apartment to his last resting-place without passing by the church. There were few baptisms. If little girls received their first communion it was to wear the dress and give the parents an excuse to feast at home.

Mme Maurer, who by now was exerting a considerable influence on my mother, both for good and for ill, found no difficulty in making her renounce what was left of her religious beliefs. Life had plunged this embittered woman in a bath of steel. Her eyes had been opened wide, from childhood, on the more ghastly aspects of our mortal existence, and she would say: 'At my age, Mme Gal, one becomes a mere looker-on at life. I fill my lungs with air, I drink and eat, but I cease to feel anything, even pain. I ought to be grateful for the fun I get out of watching others. The Alexis family, for instance, with all their pointless fussing about, give me a tremendous amount of amusement.'

My mother saw nothing funny about the Alexis family. She judged them harshly, blaming their loose living, but insensibly I began under Mme Maurer's tuition to be more indulgent, to see the unusual and picturesque in people, to become in short an onlooker. A sudden bout of reading, also under this woman's guidance, began to form, though curiously, my young intelligence. After playing wildly in the traffic or under the fortifications with Maimaine and Henriette, I would return dishevelled, dirty, unrecognizable, and discover in some novel by Gyp a whole existence of châteaux and rich people which seemed to me of another planet. I wept over George Sand's *Indiana,* but sunshine filled my day when François le Champi married the girl he loved. The Montmartre cemetery became a place of pilgrimage after reading the *Dame aux Camélias*; nightmares broke my sleep; waking I would see my mother looking like an icon, a tiny, shaded, flickering lamp beside her golden hair, for it had become a habit with her also to read nearly all night.

On half-holidays Henriette and I and another little girl with immense dark eyes called Hélène, played while poor Maimaine was finishing the washing-up. Then, as soon as she was free, we would go off and look for snails under the fortifications or rush across the public gardens under the nose of the scandalized keeper.

One afternoon, when our gang was complete, I exclaimed:

'Maimaine, mustn't it be wonderful, a real drawing-room with arm-chairs and tables and flowers all over the place?'

'Like at the theatre?' she asked.

'Yes, but in a theatre it isn't real. Nobody really lives in it.'

'I suppose it must be beautiful,' said Maimaine. 'A room where you don't sleep and you don't eat.'

'Well, what's the point of it?' asked little Hélène.

'You talk, you play the piano, and gentlemen ask you to marry them.'

'Then let's go and find a drawing-room!' said Henriette.

In the Avenue des Fêtes there were some pretty villas owned by engineers of the great aeroplane factories. One of these villas had a balconied window, fat and rounded, at which we had often watched a maid shaking her feather broom, beating cushions of coloured silk, and generally occupying herself with much more flippant material than any of us were accustomed to see in our own homes. This balcony became our rallying place. As we took counsel underneath it formed a sort of crown over our heads. When it rained we would seek its shelter. Just

now, being summer, the window was always open, and one
afternoon, having seen the maid go off with a shopping basket
under her arm, we determined to clamber up and see for ourselves
what a drawing-room really looked like.

We hoisted Hélène, the smallest, up first. She resisted, but
we were anxious to compromise her so that she would keep quiet
about what we had done. As soon as Hélène was inside Maimaine, Henriette, and I gently let ourselves through the half-
open window, and shaking with emotion and fear entered the
little drawing-room with its red and gold arm-chairs, its nice
thick carpet, and bright cream walls. We were longing, of course,
to sit in the chairs, but we clambered out into the street almost
as fast as we had come in. I then discovered that I had left my
woollen scarf in the drawing-room. We were all much too
frightened to go back and fetch it; on the other hand, I was equally
afraid of my mother, who was not forgiving when it came to
lost clothing.

Maimaine and Henriette had gone off to make the evening soup,
little Hélène was back with her mother, I stood scarfless and very
undecided on the threshold of our house when Mme Maurer,
seeing me from her window, beckoned me to come in. She
asked me what I had on my mind, and when I told her she said:

'It's a nuisance that you left your scarf in the drawing-room
of those bourgeois—it might get you into trouble—but you were
right to go in. You must always do what you want, only next
time don't drag that gang of girls round the place with you.
They will lie, swear they were not with you, and probably de-
nounce you. Their kind are not brave. You know that! Go
home, don't say a word to your mother, and begin reading
Eugénie Grandet. That ought to cure you of Gyp's drawing-
rooms!'

During the holidays of 1918 a list of girls was drawn up at our
school to attend a camp in Normandy. Mme Maurer strongly
advised my mother to let me go. We were to meet at the Gare
Saint-Lazare, each wearing a blue ribbon in the lapel of our coat.
One of the mistresses would be waiting under the clock.

As soon as the train started to move we became so excited that
our mistress, anxious to calm us, suggested that we should look
what our mothers had packed for us in the small wicker baskets

which each girl had been asked to bring. We accordingly unpacked our hard-boiled eggs, our fruit, our chocolate, exchanging
these delicacies with our neighbours. After what seemed to us
an interminable journey we reached Caen, and from there we
took a tiny train, through rich orchards, to Ver-sur-Mer, where
I saw the sea for the first time.

We were to lodge in a large house with a big garden overlooking the wide stretch of golden sand. Our dormitories were
cool and agreeable; the refectory was composed of a long table
with straw-backed chairs; at the head of the table we found a pile
of New Testaments, hymn books, and a long sharp bread knife.
Every day we took turns to help in the kitchen, lay the table, cut
the bread into even slices. For breakfast we had bowls of milk
and coffee, and after prayers we were free to go to the sands.

We would come back when the churches of Ver, of Asnelles,
and of Arromanches sounded the angelus. Their deep tones
were impressive in the calm of the fields. The sea grumbled
distantly.

The farm was pretty, and when the woman was not there we
used to play with her little boy of three, who waited for us, and
whom we covered with kisses. One evening as we were crossing
the cornfield with our milk-pails we heard, instead of the angelus,
a lugubrious tolling, and we became sad, so near seemed death
in the quiet of the country. When we reached the farm we discovered that the bell was tolling for the little boy who that afternoon had been drowned in a cattle pool. We filed past his bed.
His colourless face was unlike the happy features we had learnt
to love. His poor body seemed taller under the white sheet.
Sadly we went back to our dormitory, but none of us slept. We
cried. We called for our parents. We longed to go back to
Paris where there was noise and life.

As the holidays lasted two months I had the whole of September
to play in the street. The waste land under the fortifications was
becoming powdery, the grass was tough and yellow, there were
thistles, but no flowers. Occasionally, if it had been raining,
my father and I left very early on Sunday morning to look for
snails. We would follow the river bank as far as a poor little
café (we call them *guinguettes*) by the Seine, where my father would
order a glass of wine and fried potatoes. He always claimed

that the wine was served in too thick glasses and that he was being cheated, this remark being in the form of an aside to me in patois. Though these expeditions were charming I missed Sunday school, and this affected me more than I dared tell my father.

Our clergyman was a chaplain to the Forces; the headmaster of the boys' school accordingly took the service on Sundays. He was a rough-spoken Alsatian with a very strong accent. He would climb into the pulpit with a menacing look, as if aware of the sad fact that once there he could no longer pull the ears of his pupils. M. Brandt was the most ardent Protestant. Once he had ceased to worry about his tiresome little boys he reached heights of ecstasy, speaking of the Saviour as of a personal friend. When he prayed, asking protection for our clergyman, who was in the front line, imploring for victory, his voice, in spite of its accent, moved us. Then, as if for a moment taking leave of heaven, he would descend from the pulpit mumbling, seize upon a couple of his boys, whom he would march off to the sacristy, and then very quietly mount his stall and announce the number of the next hymn.

He knew excellently how to interpret the Scriptures. The wife of our clergyman, surrounded by her five children, all of rare beauty, helped and encouraged him. Before the end of the service he would go to the door, of which only one side was opened, and await our passing. He would extend a large, dry hand, inquire about our parents, their work and their health, and when it came to the turn of the boys he would squeeze their hands, bless them, if possible with even more goodness, and then, having closed the church door, would return into the choir stalls, where he would bend his head in fervent personal prayer. We were asked to do all we could to bring our parents to church. On Monday they would promise to come; on Tuesday they would still come, but as the week went on they became increasingly tired, and by Sunday all their good resolutions were gone. I tried desperately to bring my father and mother. I would have liked to show them the place where I discovered my most intense happiness. My father was the chief stumbling-block, not from any hardness of heart, but merely from bashfulness and an inability to pray. When we began lunch my father would say to me with affectionate mockery: 'Well, Madelon, what did your

G

shepherd say to you to-day?' I immediately began to repeat the sermon to the best of my understanding and memory. My father would listen with interest, show surprise that we were taught in such clear language, and end by being rather moved. This Sunday school language destined for children suited him admirably, was just enough, and filled him with gentle thoughts, but when I had finished he would say: 'You see, Madelon, you speak so well, you make all their ideas so clear to me that why should I put on my shoes, the ones that are so painful, to go to listen to M. Brandt? You must tell me the rest next Sunday.'

One evening when we were still at supper our clergyman, who had just arrived on leave, looked in. In his beautiful dark blue uniform, with the chaplain's chain and cross, he looked like a crusader returning from the Holy Land. He sat at our table and spoke little. My father admired and respected him. He knew that every moment of his leave would be given to his parishioners; that he liked to call in the evening when the head of the house would be at home. He avoided speaking of religion, but told us about his children, discussed his personal problems, the course of the war, and my coming first communion. Then he shook hands, saying:

'Well, M. Gal, I shan't see you on Sunday. I'm going back to the front. The boys out there need me pretty badly.'

We heard him going down the stairs, passing out into the dark night. My father went to bed, saying:

'That's a saintly man.'

My mother began to sew for the women in the factories. Some of them worked in the same place as my father. They dressed gaily: light-coloured stockings, shoes with very high heels. We would see them step carefully on the paving-stones so as not to sprain their ankles. Their hair would be waved in the new Marcel fashion, tied down in a net. They found it difficult to spend the money they earned, and smelt of perfume and machine oil. They came in droves from Paris for the night shift, made up, full of energy, meeting others on the way back to Montmartre wearing high boots of coloured leather laced on the calf as was then the fashion. As both lots, those going to work and those returning home, came face to face with young prostitutes they would good-naturedly throw them coarse sallies, asking if they were not in need of a screwdriver or a little grease. Often the prostitutes, amused by the spontaneous wit of the factory women, broke out in swift replies and merry laughter.

My companions and I had a friend who exercised this profession that so many of us, prettier girls, grew up to. Her name was Didine, and she was fine looking and gentle hearted. Dark, made like a mare, broad hips and thin legs, she was the tender mistress of an Italian shoemaker of the rue Fontaine, a shoemaker who worked exclusively for these ladies. Didine had the most magnificent high boots, heels and ends shiny black, the rest in supple red leather of a kind only the Italians know how to make. Didine Garcia, whose invented name matched her Spanish beauty, lodged on the sixth floor of the house in which Mme Maurer and Mme Alexis lived. She arrived in the morning, slept till four, visited the baker and the dairy, smiled graciously at the *concierge*, climbed up to the sixth, and cooked her steak over a spirit-lamp. As she loved children she would say to us: 'Now, girls, come up in a quarter of an hour. I shall have a surprise for you!' We would run up as fast as we could just in time to see Didine put a match to a magnificent rum omelet, which gave a blue tint to her lovely features, and brought out all the sparkle of her splendid white teeth. She served us, and we would take our plates and sit on her bed, which she had not yet made, and on which her orange lingerie, garnished with black velvet, made us stare with surprise and envy. At six she would send us away. Then she would dress, and an hour later we would see her come out, painted, wearing her lovely boots, smelling good, hardly looking at us, thinking only of what the night would bring her, weighing her chances, possible success, and pleasure.

On these evenings I would sulk in front of my soup. My father would scold; my mother, thinking I was ill, would worry. I dared not say I had been with Didine, and I was afraid Maimaine or Henriette would tell. I knew that out of principle my mother would not approve of these feasts in Didine's flat though actually she rather liked her. Even my father had a certain regard for Didine. She was not proud, was herself the daughter of a workman, and in fact was at home in all spheres. She would disappear for several days; then one morning we would see her newly dressed from head to foot. New boots, new coat or tailor-made, according to the season, exquisite new hat, all proving she had been with an American officer during his leave, that she had lived

with him, loved him, and certainly made him forget his blood
bath over in the trenches. She always put his photograph with
a pin on the wall. Would she ever see him again? It was unlikely. She did not even know his name. I used to count all
these fine officers, American, French, English. She would say:
'They are my brothers!' Even Maimaine, who knew something about large families, thought this was a poor excuse.

Maimaine was worried about her mother. Air-raid alarms
were becoming more frequent, and the poor woman, tortured
by her pregnancy, was obviously overtired. She was becoming
enormous, and one morning Maimaine went off to warn the
midwife that her mother was starting labour pains. Maimaine,
like a general, arranged the flat: she brought Henriette to us, left
Maurice with Mme Maurer, and another with the *concierge*. Little
Louis, who had returned in the middle of the night after having
disappeared for eight days, was left on his iron bedstead in a
corner of the dining-room. The midwife came. The doctor
came. There were consultation and arguments and cries of pain
from the mother and yells from the new-born. Little Louis,
exhausted with adventure and love, slept like an innocent on his
iron bedstead. The thirteenth child was a male. His name was
George or Jo-Jo, and he was magnificent. He shattered every
prediction, every theory. Child of a drunkard, child of a worn-
out mother, born in the heat of September, Jo-Jo was simply
glorious. We saw him in Maimaine's arms, in Henriette's arms,
and whenever I had a chance I took him in my arms. Mme
Alexis was not doing well. She was so feeble that she wept, and
the doctor was anxious. 'The mother of a large family is the most
precious thing on earth,' he used to say to my mother and to Mme
Maurer, 'but the poor woman is quite worn out. The baby has
taken everything out of her.'

Mme Alexis became stronger. She left her sombre bed and
took her favourite place by the window in the dining-room. She
was as gay as ever, but if she went downstairs she could not climb
up again. One day, when Didine had just come back from one of
her long adventures, we all went up to show her Jo-Jo, putting
the baby in her bed next to her orange lingerie, she the lovely
woman and we the little girls all paying our court to the smiling
child. Suddenly we heard a far-away voice in the street crying
out for Maimaine, and hurrying to the balcony we saw Blanche,

her own child in her arms, crying at her loudest. Maimaine
snatched the baby from Didine's bed and rushed down the six
storeys followed by us all. Mme Alexis had just had a heart
attack and wanted Jo-Jo. Again she recovered, but the doctor
insisted that she must return to her native province, and a few
days later she went off with Henriette, Maurice, and Jo-Jo to the
Auvergne. Maimaine stayed to look after the father and little
Louis. The house seemed empty, and we missed Jo-Jo cruelly.
Henriette wrote once, Mme Alexis not knowing how to write or
read, and then M. Alexis received a letter from his sister asking
him to come quickly. He took the train, but while he was still
travelling Maimaine received a telegram to say her mother was
dead. She howled like a wild animal, and her magnificent red hair,
gay and sparkling, seemed to mock her face streaming with tears.
She had to wear mourning. My mother adjusted one of Mme
Alexis's own black dresses, and little Maimaine became suddenly
a grown woman. Her hair, rolled up, revealed an adorable neck,
and the red girl, so often laughed at because of her golden helmet,
became so beautiful that we held our breath. Her black dress
suited her magnificently. She looked like a pearl in a case of
black velvet. M. Alexis came home with Henriette, Maurice, and
little Jo-Jo, and Maimaine became the mother of the family.

My mother met Marguerite Rosier in the market. We had
been seeing less of her. She would spend several weeks at a
time with her mother, now Mme Malgras, in the cottage she and
the former baker owned in the country. Hyacinthe was becoming
increasingly morose. Terrified by the nightly bombardments of
Big Bertha he feared for his life and his situation at the bank.
His wife and daughter had a miserable existence; the more money
the husband earned the less fun they got out of it.
Marguerite Rosier had met Léontine, the daughter of the late
Mme Valentin, the lacemaker. Léontine wanted us all to go
and see her. She was still living at St. Ouen, but as her husband was at the front she had found a job in a munitions factory
and had become the overseer: one of her daughters was working
with her.
We decided that as soon as my father was asleep we would
steal out of the house. St. Ouen was not far. All we need do
was to follow the Boulevard Victor-Hugo.

When Léontine saw us her lovely dark eyes lit up her face, and though she was pitted by smallpox she appeared almost pretty. The truth is that at last she was happy. Yaya, her daughter, once so thin and disfigured by want, had become grown up and good-looking. Léontine had been lucky. Her husband was at the front, she paid no rent, had the allocation of a soldier's wife, and she and Yaya earned a great deal of money. She said to my mother: 'I 've been made to suffer so much from wine that I can't stand it on the table any more. When my husband comes on leave I can see he hasn't changed, that he 'll never change, and so I 'm broken-hearted to think that my happiness will end with the war; and yet believe me, Mme Gal, I *do* want the war to finish.'

Léontine would not change her flat. She said she was superstitious and feared that by going elsewhere her luck might alter. After coffee Léontine brought out a pack of cards. She had an amazing gift for telling the future. Marguerite Rosier was the first to hear her fate. Her husband would earn more money. In a few years' time they might even have enough to take a little place in the country. When it was my mother's turn there was no sign of money, just illness and death. 'My poor Matilda,' said Léontine, 'you will soon be a widow. Then you 'll cross the sea and your daughter will marry and have the loveliest clothes, and travel. Her life will be quite different to yours.' My mother turned white. Léontine had repeated in the most curious way what my mother had been told by the bone-setter at Blois!

It was late and we had rather a long walk home in the dark. We were all sad, Lucienne and I holding our mother's hands, the two women discussing what Léontine had foretold. My mother said: 'You see what it is! Léontine has a little happiness at last. You, Marguerite, will have money. But I, nothing good ever comes my way. What do you think I 've done to deserve all this? Of course, I would be glad for my daughter to have a better life, but it will be for her. I don't see how it can benefit me.'

Suddenly we heard a terrible cry, followed by others even more dreadful, and we saw a man with a long knife, like the one the ogre held when he was going to cut Tom Thumb's throat. The man ran towards us and we, petrified, remained where we were. Marguerite was the first to recover. Catching hold of Lucienne she ran and ran and ran. The man, surprised by their sudden flight, hesitated a moment, then brandishing his knife, went off in the opposite direction. My mother, very pale but calm, whispered: 'It 's all over. There 's no more danger.' However, instead of continuing along the pavement we walked in the middle of the boulevard, the big uneven paving-stones causing us to twist our ankles at every step.

My mother, describing this scene the next day to Mme Maurer said, laughing, that she had thought for a moment that Léontine had made a mistake in her fortune-telling. 'It looked,' she said, 'as if I were the one who was going to die!' Mme Maurer made no comment. She believed neither in God nor in the devil and, in consequence, fortune-tellers left her quite indifferent. My mother was extremely vexed by Marguerite's panic-stricken flight, and I could see that relations might be strained.

The next evening my father came home looking drawn and ill. He refused his soup, and his hand trembled as he shaved. During the afternoon he had been testing an aeroplane engine when his companion was struck by the propeller and killed. This accident had made a deep impression on him. I was asleep when he left in the morning, but all day I kept on thinking of his sad face, so changed and shaken, and in the evening as it was fine I went to wait for him at the factory gates. A crowd had gathered and there were several gendarmes, a fire having broken out in the place where the engines were tested. Nervously I ran through the crowd looking for a known face, and when I recognized some people who lived in our street I exclaimed: 'But what a lot of accidents there must be in this factory! Why, only yesterday my father had his best friend killed by a propeller in front of his eyes.' A strong hand closed in on my arm and an ear was gently twigged. I looked up and saw a gendarme who said to me: 'Little girl, you are much too talkative. We shall have to find a way of curing you. Suppose you come along with me.'

I was terrified, but the day shift was now pouring out and in the distance I joyfully recognized my father. I ran towards him, and buried my hand in his; as together we passed through the gate, the gendarme raised a finger to his lips and winked at me, but I had already learnt my lesson.

Now came the first days of September, rain falling continuously, turning the street into a grey corridor. One hardly saw anybody about. The women who always had so much to discuss remained on the different landings, gossiping, broom in hand, or gathered outside the doorkeeper's lodge. Mme Guillet, the doorkeeper of the house in which Mme Maurer and the Alexis family lived, was the wife of a railway driver. This stupid, spendthrift Auvergnat had two daughters, Marie and Louise, and did her dusting in a large white overall with a coloured scarf bound round her head like a dark woman from the East Indies. The turban protected the deep waves that ran across her hair like the tracks on which her husband drove his trains. She brushed the carpets, polished the stairs, cleaned the brass, and at two o'clock removed the coloured scarf and took up a position in front of the house seated on a low chair upholstered in red velvet. The postman arrived, handed her the tenants' letters, which one then saw her examine in detail as if she were the chief censor. When she had satisfied her curiosity she would raise a buttock and slip the letters underneath her. If a tenant came in or out, and there was something for him, she would pass a hand between her posterior and the red velvet chair and bring out the letter which by then was warm and convex.

She adored her husband, who in the course of his train driving was constantly unfaithful, but she hid her jealousy and Marie was her favourite daughter because she most closely resembled her engine driver. Towards the end of this rainy month Mme Guillet inherited some money from a relation in the Auvergne, and decided to give up her position of doorkeeper. They would rent an apartment like everybody else. Louise and Marie were sent to a paying school, where shopkeepers put their daughters to keep them away from the daughters of workmen and rag-and-bone dealers. Both were to learn music. Every morning Marie Guillet went off to school with a violin case and a bundle of music, her sister trotting beside her. Mme Guillet, bursting with pride, peeped through her window curtains. Marie kept close to the wall, her eyes on the ground for fear she would slip and break her precious violin. She held the case pointing downwards, so that from a distance she looked as if she had three feet. Mme Guillet had so little to do that at ten she was ready to take off her coloured turban; instead of sitting on the pavement in front of the porter's lodge, she sat by her fourth-floor window. She soon became intolerably bored. Happily Sunday compensated for the rest of the week. Marie and Louise, in their ready-made clothes, went to mass, and after lunch Marie, in front of a music stand by the window, played the first bars of the *Berceuse de Jocelyn*, indeed played them over and over again until the whole street began to cat-call.   Little Louise, younger and there-fore more reasonable, would escape from her family and join us, but she was so frightened to be seen with such common children that she would only play immediately under her parents' balcony where she knew they could not see her.   We who considered the whole of Clichy our playground, soon tired of this restricted space, and left her to play alone.   She would watch us, forget to remain properly hidden, and be noticed by Mme Guillet, who would cry out: 'Aren't you ashamed of playing with those horrible little girls?'   Then all together we would parody the first bars of the *Berceuse de Jocelyn*, and Marie would blush with hurt pride.

We froze in our lodging that autumn.

Coal was rationed.   Our Protestant school had practically none, but every now and again a horse-drawn cart rumbled over the paving-stones, taking a consignment to the state schools.   As soon as we heard it we flew into the street to pick up what might drop from behind.   We quarrelled and fought like a cloud of starlings—those of us who had no sacks held up our aprons like a sower going out to sow.   This was the grandest fun of the week, and then when I came home it was lovely to see my mother's smile when I filled her oven with beautiful coal which had cost her nothing.   This matter became more important as the season advanced.   Our ration was a hundredweight every so often, but we had to fetch it ourselves.   The first thing to do was to hire a wheelbarrow and a sack with which we would take our place in a queue, watching the wheelbarrow with one eye and the mound of coal with the other, for it often happened that the coal ran out before our turn came to be served.   When we were lucky a man with a red-flannel belt would fill our sack and help us to hoist it on the barrow.   We then clattered down the avenue.   We made this journey twice, once for ourselves and once for Mme Maurer, and my mother was in constant alarm that my father would dis-cover that the coal could be fetched on a Sunday, for he would then have wanted to relieve us of this heavy work.   He would, of course, have done it admirably, but with so many visits to the café that it would have doubled the price of our coal.

Mme Maurer, grateful and generous, found a charming way to say thank you.   Immediately after lunch on my half-holiday

*G

she, my mother, and I would go to the cinema in the Avenue de Clichy, where the programme included a film in several episodes, with Pearl White, and a Max Linder comedy. The programme started at two, and as soon as I heard the bell announcing the approach of the great moment my excitement was immense. Pathé Journal began with a flickering news-reel. Weary soldiers in long files marched down the lines. Lloyd George and Clemenceau danced across the screen with unbelievable speed. King George V and his good-looking son, the Prince of Wales, shook hands with soldiers and climbed over trenches and barbed wire. The cinema seemed to soak all these famous men and incidents with an oblique and incessant rain.

My mother found in these visits to the cinema her first moments of genuine pleasure. We would discuss what we had seen, thinking all the week about the next episode. A little later the great Gaumont Palace was opened in the Place Clichy. Then it was a different matter. The most famous cabaret singers in Paris were engaged to appear in the intervals, and the auditorium, full of soldiers and officers of every nation, made our hearts beat with patriotism.

One fine autumn Sunday the children in the various schools were asked by the mayor to take part in a flag day. Our flags had the effigies of Washington and La Fayette, and were mounted on coloured pins. Another girl and I were given osier baskets fastened round our necks with wide tricolour ribbon and collecting boxes with handles, so that we could shake them under the chins of passers-by. Clichy not being a suitable terrain for our activities my companion and I passed through the gate of the fortifications into Paris proper to offer our flags on the terraces of the great cafés. We came at last to the Café Wepler, with its magnificent orchestra and wide terrace crowded at this hour with allied officers, accompanied by the smartest women in Paris whose wide hats of black velvet waved and fluttered over gay faces prettily made up. All these people spoke loudly, laughed, made jokes. Their momentary pleasure was profound, visible, noisy, and generous. Silver coins poured into our boxes, and we learnt to say thank you to the English and Americans. An extremely good-looking young officer was deep in conversation with a woman who was listening to him, her elbows on the marble-topped table, her ravishing face resting between open palms, the tips of her pointed nails lightly touching the pink lobes of her ears. I went up fascinated, shaking my box. The young officer, annoyed, fumbled in his trouser pocket, then removing his eyes unwillingly from his companion, looked for the orifice of my collecting box. The young woman, amused and curious, raised her features, tiny under the very wide hat, slowly, with an oblique movement, then cried out: 'Well, there's my little Madeleine!' and to the officer: 'Be generous, darling. This is a friend. Give her something for herself. Come, my little Madeleine, it's for you, just for you!'

The young officer amused by this soliloquy handed me a five-franc piece. Innocently I lifted my dress and slipped the coin in the pocket of the white cotton petticoat with its lace flounce, which I had begun making at Blois with Madeleine Béant, and which I was now wearing for the first time. Never had I seen Didine looking so perfectly lovely. She was in her element, a jewel in her case. Oh, how I envied her! With what ambition she filled my breast!

Tired, our baskets empty, having talked a great deal, often said thank you, my little companion and I sat down on a bench like two lovers who had walked too far through the woods on a Sunday afternoon. Our heads buzzed with life and noise. We were terribly thirsty. The way home was long and dusty. I decided to go into a café and ask the imposing wife of the owner, seated behind her high zinc counter, to give us a glass of water. She was embroidering a baby's brassière. She gave no answer to my shy request, but laying her work beside her, got up, took two glasses, and filled them with water and crème de menthe, handed them to us, and picked up her brassière again. In spite of our thirst this woman's generosity overcame us; we remained wide eyed. She now said: 'Come along, my children, drink it up and run along home. You look dead tired. And whatever you do hold tightly to your collecting boxes. They seem to me pretty full!' Refreshed we ran off, and when we reached the town hall and our boxes were opened, our takings proved the largest of any. We were given a picture of Washington and La Fayette, which I took proudly home.

I slept till lunch the next day. My mother looked rather severe when I woke up, having noticed that I had worn out my shoes. Quite apart from this she had been anxious all day, imagining that I would be raped, strangled, or robbed.   She told me that this was the last time I would go gallivanting about the place, and as she spoke she brushed my dress, folded my linen, and prepared my everyday clothes.   When she took up my petticoat she discovered the five-franc piece.   I had been much too tired the previous evening to talk, but now I broke into all the details, describing Didine's hat, the hats the other women wore, and at last, sighing very deeply, I asked:

'Mother, do you suppose that when I 'm grown up those wide velvet hats will still be in fashion, and that they will suit me?'

My mother answered:

'Oh, a hat always ends by suiting one.   It 's just a question of cheating a bit—the way you do your hair, the colour of your lipstick.   No, the important thing is to *have* the hat, and when one has the hat to make the men lose their heads while keeping one's own tightly fixed on one's shoulders!'

At this time of year all the children had to have their kites. We used to make them at home, and then run with them as fast as we could over the waste land under the fortifications.   The boys used to arrive wearing their fathers' *képis*.   A few were nice, but most of the boys had the gestures and the words of their fathers.   Anybody could see they would continue in the tradition. As soon as they were married they would drink too much and pick quarrels with their wives in one-room flats with the children looking on, not understanding, afraid.   Yet some girls already ran after them, resigned after marriage to serve them, and probably get a beating when the pay was spent on drink.

One could tell fairly easily what most of the boys would become —modest employees, truck drivers, or mechanics.   I was gladder than ever to be a girl.   It gave me a feeling of superiority.   I knew in some secret way that I would have a big velvet hat like Didine's and sit one day to my heart's content on the terrace at Wepler.

Mme Maurer's son was thirty, and would have given anything to be married, but he was so timid with women that it had become a malady.   As soon as a woman spoke to him he stammered and looked idiotic.   But by himself at night he believed himself capable of the most atrocious things.   He would have dragged a woman by the hair from her husband and cynically raped her. His bed became a veritable battle-field.   His night was broken

by vivid dreams and nightmares.   One wonders that by morning
he was not all bumps and wounds.   But once this Don Juan of
dreamland stepped again into the ordinary world he would look
idiotic again.

Mme Maurer, being an atheist, had refused to give him the
name of a saint in the calendar.   She had resorted to Homer,
and called him Ulysses.   This name made him suffer all through
life.   When he was a boy at school and was obliged to call out
his surname and Christian name in front of the whole class the
room went into an uproar.

Quick and muscular he might, with an English education, have
overcome his troubles by being good at games.   The aeroplane
factory where he worked as a draughtsman mostly employed
female labour, and Ulysses' purgatory was having to cross shop
after shop full of women who stared at him with mockery,
perversity, or fierce provocation.   He felt as if he were being
undressed and made to run naked before them, and when the
factory became even busier, and his table was put in the middle
of the assembly shop, eyes converged on him incessantly.   Every
morning his drawing-board was covered with notes, letters, and
pictures—offers to meet him in the evening, to marry him, ribald
jokes, and suggestive pictures.   He would have been delighted
to accept one of the rendezvous but he was afraid it might prove
a joke.   One woman, bolder than the others, having sworn she
would get him at any price, slipped a note into his hand as he
came to inspect her machine.   This time he was obliged to
understand.   He waited for her, and she became his mistress.
She was coarse and vulgar, but she gave him the happiness he
needed.   Meanwhile Mme Maurer, seeing him so thin, so dazed
with passion, became alarmed; she had gone without things to
give him a chance; she now fancied that his romance with an
uneducated factory hand would end in misery.   Had she not
planned for him a better life than her own?   Ulysses' mistress
became pregnant, slipped from a ladder at the factory, and
miscarried.   Under pressure from his mother Ulysses abandoned
his mistress but was soon unhappier than ever, for he had come
under the spell of love and could no longer do without it.   His
nights were appalling.   Soon the sight of his mother became un-
bearable, reminding him of his weakness in giving up the woman
he needed.   His filial love turned to loathing.

When my father was on a night shift my mother, Marguerite Rosier (we had now forgiven her for running away from the man with the knife), and I went to a cheap cinema in the Boulevard National, arriving half an hour before the performance started, to be sure of having the best seats.

Our cinema smelt of garlic and peppermint drops. Palm-trees stood on either side of the stage, their branches casting uneven shadows on the white screen like giant spiders. Excitedly we waited. In spite of our love for Pearl White we had not quite cured ourselves of thinking of the cinema in terms of the age-old theatre, and we had gone instinctively to the front of the stalls where, after a while, we would see appear from behind a curtain a little hunchback woman with a big white head surmounted by a number of *diamanté* spangled combs. She would slip her rheumatic knees under an upright piano and begin a Strauss waltz. The apache boys from the fortifications who were here in large numbers whistled the accompaniment, while putting an arm round the shoulder of a girl, getting into position to unbutton the blouse and fondle her breasts. These were the girls who worked for them as prostitutes on the outer zone, drawing men with alluring gestures, like Circes, near to the wall where the apache lay in waiting with his knife. All the boys wore their caps and sometimes their red scarves. A few moments later came a small dark man holding a violin case tightly under his arm, and as he made his way towards the hunchback his journey was followed by loud whistles and exclamations of 'Hurry up, maestro! You're late, brother! Let's go and sleep with his wife while he scratches a tune on his fiddle!' The fiddler, pale and without any sign of fluster, removed a black hat, placing it carefully on the edge of a chair, folded his overcoat, took up the hat which he would then place on top of the folded overcoat, and delicately brush the dandruff from his narrow shoulders. At last he opened the case, holding the violin under an arm whilst he put a handkerchief under his chin. The audience invariably cried out: 'The little old man is going to weep!' Then dolefully: 'Don't worry, daddy, you'll see her again, your girl friend!' Now at last, with a sign of his bow to the hunchback, he would begin to play. The lights would go out. The screen flickered.

By the time the big film started this chaffing audience was

settling down to the charms of Mary Pickford with her blonde curls. The love-story was getting the better of these boys and girls from the fortifications who, for all their naughtiness, were just sentimental children. At this magnificent moment, after all the fatigues of the long day, after school, after queueing, after playing in the street, exhausted, I fell fast asleep on my mother's shoulder! This happened every time we went to the cinema. Before setting out in the evening I would say: 'If I go to sleep you *will* wake me up, won't you, mother?' She promised. Indeed she did wake me, but after rubbing the sand out of my eyes and trying to unravel the plot, I fell asleep again, and my mother, transported to a land of make-believe, was far too interested in the romance to keep on pinching my arm. I would sulk on the way home, and childishly threaten to tell my father where we had been. My mother answered patiently: 'To-morrow I will describe the whole episode to you while you are sewing, and next time you really must try to keep awake!'

The 11th November: the church bells rang and Mlle Zélie, weeping with emotion, took a large flag out of a cupboard and reverently kissed it. We sang the *Marseillaise* and some hymns. A factory on the opposite side of the street let out all its workers who thronged the avenue, kissing strangers on the way, being kissed, singing, shouting. By evening the cabarets were full.

The armistice did not make any immediate difference to our lives. Women waited anxiously for the return of their husbands. Jules Alexis, who had burnt himself so cruelly so as not to be sent back to the front, was drafted to Russia. Little Louis was packed off to occupy the Rhineland. Both were relatively safe, but they were being deprived of liberty and their beloved fortifications. They would not be able to roam all night and sleep like cats all day. They did not dare complain since the eldest son had been shot as a deserter. Maimaine, matriarch, had left school. M. Alexis *père*, tired of being a widower, had found a dark woman in the early fifties, who little by little began to chastine the children, and drive Maimaine out of her position of housewife and female head of the family. We then saw these children, brought up first in the most tender love of a mother and then in the affectionate respect of an elder sister, beaten and imprisoned in the flat. My mother and I and Mme Maurer were kept away from them.   We did not even dare speak to them in the street.

By the middle of winter Mme Maurer was afraid that her son would lose his fine situation.   The munition and aeroplane factories were either closing down or changing over to peace-time products.   My father was fortunate enough, when his own factory closed, to be taken on by another, but night work and double pay had finished.   My mother, as provident as an ant, had saved enormously, foreseeing this moment, preferring to stint us when things were easy than find herself penniless when things became difficult.   Other families, less wise, were now leaving their flats to take smaller ones.   Women went less often to the hairdresser.

After the Christmas holidays my mother decided to send me to the state schools.   I was twelve and terribly backward, and the drastic change was at first very upsetting, but I was so very conscious of my apparent ignorance, so determined to do better than the other girls, that I began to climb higher in the class by sheer hard work.   I was helped by having read enormously under Mme Maurer's guidance and having learnt closely to observe what was happening round me.   Unconsciously I was being given the training of a newspaper woman.   The female writer was learning her craft.

Having started fortieth out of forty girls I was eighth by the beginning of the third term.   I wrote French without a mistake, which was rare even amongst highly educated women, and my reading made me so enthusiastic that by Christmas I was the second of the class.   I never became the head girl.   This honour, which I coveted, went to the daughter of a Spanish fruiterer, Carmen Fernandez, not at all like the Carmen of the opera, but pale, having had infantile paralysis, and still dragging one of her poor legs in a heavy apparatus.   We were good enough friends out of school hours, but in the class-room we fought bitterly, she to keep her place, I trying with all my might to wrest it from her.

In February my father fell ill, coming home one evening with a burning temperature and a stitch in his side.   The next morning he was unable to get out of bed.   My mother and I were seized by the same malady.   Not one of us could get as far as the kitchen to make a cup of coffee.   We remained in this condition for three days, at the end of which Mme Maurer, becoming anxious, crossed the road, found us in bed, and sent for the doctor. My father had congestion of the lungs; my mother and I were merely victims of the Spanish influenza then sweeping Europe. My father suffered a good deal. Spring was already visible in the warmer weather and the budding of plants and certain trees. The doctor advised my mother to take me into the little garden up the street. We would come back with cleaner air in our lungs, our eyes brighter, better able to nurse my father. After several weeks, very thin and weak, his blue army cloak over his shoulders, he walked slowly from his bed to the kitchen, his forehead cold with perspiration. He recovered, and immediately went back to work.

We had been unable during the war to obtain one of the modest allotments that had been made out of waste ground near the river. Now, suddenly, one of these became vacant. My father was deliriously happy to have his garden. He felt in a pathetic way that he was being given all the wealth of his beloved *midi*. On the first Sunday he could walk a little we crossed the Seine to visit a market gardener at Asnières, and brought back seeds and young plants. Then, as soon as my father came back from work, he hurried to his garden. He grew the finest vegetables, watered them for hours, and was so happy that our hearts melted. He built a little summer-house for his tools, and we bought a rabbit, for which he made a hutch. In front of the summer-house my father put down paving-stones and when, in the warm weather, he sat under a veranda of climbing beans, he smoked his pipe in perfect contentment. I never heard him desire another man's house or somebody else's land. The golden fleece would not have pleased him better than the tender lettuce or the green peas he brought home in the evening.

I was now desperately anxious to pass school certificate. Every month our mistress, Mlle Foucher, gave us increasingly difficult tests. Mathematics gave me serious trouble, and so, in some ways, did geography. Distant countries did not interest me. I could not imagine the English and the Americans any-where else but at Wepler's or on the roundabouts in the Place Clichy. I do not believe it struck me that there could be Ameri-can *women*, except, of course, Mary Pickford and Mabel Normand.

I was up at five to go over my homework, and at this hour the kitchen table was my own. At eight I made my own breakfast, and went to school. Mlle Foucher encouraged me. Of Alsatian descent, she was ardently patriotic, of rare intelligence and humanity. Her lessons acquired polish and extreme simplicity. Young, pretty, elegant, always beautifully shod, she seemed to dress for us. This combination of beauty and intelligence has ever seemed to me the most desirable thing on earth. When on arrival she took off her coat or her jacket, according to the time of year, and stood before us in her blouse—rose or blue or white—we would glance at one another with appreciative winks; then during recreation we would say: 'Personally I like to see her in pink!' 'Oh, no, she's far better in blue!' She was ours. We loved her. Her hair prettily done, her cheeks slightly pale but with dark, deep eyes contrasting with their pallor, she had a personality of her own. Her smile was shrewd and a trifle surprised when one of us passed a clever remark or one that came from the very depths of our childish experience. She loved to draw and make us illustrate our prose: I used to make tiny pen and ink sketches that delighted her.

The school certificate was in July and took place in another school at the far end of Clichy, a large cool room whose windows, wide open, overlooked a courtyard. As we were on the first floor the higher branches of the chestnut-trees were level with our faces. Starlings and sparrows hopped from green branch to green branch as if to mock us, we who were locked up in our big cage smelling of disinfectant and ink. Sheets of paper were handed round. Dictation, parsing, French history, and then off we went without appetite to lunch. The afternoon passed heavily, the sun being very hot. Even the sparrows had lost some of their energy. We were with girls from other schools. Marie Guillet, more than a year my senior, was almost next to me, pale, lips tightly closed, looking quite miserable. At the far end of the room sat Carmen Fernandez, magnificently cool and unmoved. A curious jealousy rose within me, a desire to become a woman of importance. Pride and ambition took hold of me. Even if I failed in my examination, yet would I outshine with my prose. Heroines flared my path. George Sand, for instance. If only I could be a famous woman writer; but even as this idea took shape, I decided that it must not interfere with my having a wide velvet hat like Didine, or of being pretty like her, or of being clever with my needle or with the iron. All these were perhaps quite normal dreams for a little girl; only in my case poverty became the driving power to give them substance. I fought like a she-wolf to make them come true. At four we were let out, and the next day we went to school as usual while waiting to be examined orally. We repeated feverishly historical dates, the rivers of France, and the capitals of Europe which politicians were just then so busy meddling with for no better reason than to confuse children who were due to sit for their examinations the following year. We would soon be bidding farewell to Montenegro—capital Montenegro; Turkey —capital Constantinople. Good-bye brave little Serbia and glorious Petrograd of the Russia of the czars, of the czarina, and of those grand duchesses so much admired by Mme Maurer. The tragedy of Ekaterinburg was slipping into history with that of Louis XVI and of my dear Marie-Antoinette, and with the martyrdom of Charles I of England. We crammed dates. Tragedies, battles, and glorious happenings were marshalled to satisfy an examiner who would probably be thinking merely of the heat and the tiresomeness of little girls.

My mother was worried about my health. The strain of the last months was bringing new paleness to my cheeks, my eyes were not good, I was insufficiently fed, and my lungs were in need of pure air. Neither she nor my father emitted any great desire to have their daughter distinguish herself academically. For my part I had not worked to please anybody but myself, being by nature suspicious of compliments, just as later my head was seldom turned when men said that I was pretty. The force to succeed grew within me, beyond my control, and often my gaiety was tempered with envy and discontent so that, never satisfied, I was thrust further and further forward.

One Monday morning our headmistress entered the class-room. We all got up, and Mlle Foucher, rising also, offered her seat. The headmistress opened her spectacle case, and before putting on her pince-nez held them between forefinger and thumb whilst examining our ranks, her eyes occasionally resting with particular interest on one or other of us. When she had made us suffer several moments of this torture she adjusted her pince-nez, coughed like Sarah Bernhardt, and unfolded her list. Only eight of us had passed. When I heard my name a great inward satisfaction made me blush. Many who had failed wept, some

with their faces hidden in their arms, bent over their desks. I
did not hurry to go home and announce the news to my parents,
being first anxious to savour it myself. To my surprise my
mother was peeping behind the curtains, waiting to see me come
along the street. She must have guessed from my face that I
had passed, for she opened the door, kissed me, and that was
all. My father's pleasure was touchingly meridional. He wept!
Marie Guillet's name was not on the list. Her mother said she
must now concentrate on her music, and a woman came to teach
her the violin.

In Marguerite Rosier's house, on the second floor in a small
flat like ours, lived Mme Gontrel, a tall woman with a big head,
ugly, and yet so amiable that one quickly forgot her ungainliness,
charmed by her voice. Mme Gontrel had a daughter of six
called Dédée, dark and little, like an ant, jumping up and down,
fast on her legs—one saw her everywhere at almost the same
moment, in a queue outside the milk shop, buying a loaf of
freshly baked bread. Mme Gontrel's second child was a boy
aged two, whose over-sized head leaned to one side, an abnormal
child, who never spoke and hardly moved. Henri, or Riri, was
always in his mother's arms. Her body was quite deformed from
carrying him, and she looked like a lanky tree with an extra
branch grafted to it. She went to market, returned laden with
provisions (and, of course, Riri), always in excellent good humour.
My mother used to see her talking to Marguerite Rosier and
another neighbour whom we used to call 'Mother Newspaper'
because she never stopped talking. As Mother Newspaper's
husband worked in a bank like Hyacinthe she was alone all day.
Her gossiping had to be done in the open air. The market was
her favourite tribune, and when she could catch hold of one of
these ladies she did not let them go in a hurry, having limitless
stories to tell. Tall and pale, leaning slightly as if bent by the
wind, she must have been sixty. She was dressed in greyish black
and nobody had ever been to her flat.
I see her very clearly even now, her elongated features shining
like wax, a great many tortoiseshell combs stuck fanwise in her
bun, a high-necked collar garnished with jade, and a cameo
representing a beautiful gazelle encircled with small pearls, of
which quite a number were missing. One day, when I was

examining the cameo instead of listening to what she was telling
my mother, she said:
'I see that you are interested in my cameo, little girl. It is
quite a favourite, and I want to be buried with it. That 's what
I told my husband,' she continued, turning from me to my
mother. 'You understand, Mme Gal, that I have made all
my arrangements, and taken the necessary precautions, for my
husband being twenty years younger I must be ready to leave
him at any moment. We often talk about it, and I practically
live from day to day. For instance, what I wash in the morning I iron the same evening. I do the mending and tidy the
house as if I were on the point of leaving for a journey.' Then
looking down at me again with a twist of her neck, which
made her resemble a giraffe moving from leaf to leaf, she continued: 'This cameo is the only jewel, other than my wedding
ring, that I have ever owned. I bought it in London, in the
French quarter of Soho, during the reign of Edward VII. I had
gone to England with my first husband, and as he was busy all
day I wandered alone through the streets of London, for hours
on end, never tired. A magnificent town, Mme Gal! And how
wonderfully paved! A real pleasure to the feet! Oh, and
another thing! Nobody ever asks any questions. You have
your key in your bag, and there 's no *concierge*, no doorkeeper.
I lived three years in London. My husband and I used to go to
the theatre; never have I seen such lovely diamonds and pearls!
Quite the finest in the world. And some of the ladies had dia-
mond buckles on their shoes worn with the most natural grace,
as if it were no surprise to them to have such elegance and wealth;
and indeed, is it not true that they have been accustomed for
generations to their fortunes? They are not nearly so placid as
they are supposed to be. They laugh loudly at the theatre, and
are quickly enthusiastic. My husband and I were very quiet in
comparison. Of course I was sometimes jealous of the jewellery,
and it was after one of these evenings at the theatre that I took
it into my head to have something really fine. This was the
result. My cameo was really most beautiful. The pearls were
all of the same size, and if ever I lost one it was immediately
replaced; but now when I take it off I look to see if there is not a
new hole, and that is very easy to tell, for when a pearl is newly
fallen out it leaves a bright cavity which soon grows dim like the

others.   There are only two or three left now, and I have a feeling that when I am down to my last pearl I shall do my last wash, iron my last sheets, and mend my clothes for the last time.   Little Madeleine, I am merely a sentimental old gossip, as ugly as a scarecrow, who ought to disappear, but who would like to remain invisible, helping with what remains of her strength the man she loves with a heart that never grows old.   Good-bye, little Madeleine; good-bye, Mme Gal.   I am jugging a hare for supper to-night.   Good-bye!'

We were very intrigued by these confidences, for Mother News-paper had never told us that she had been twice married or that she had lived so long in London.   What she told us was never dull, but this time, instead of us leaving her, she had left us, and we would have liked some more.

Once a week we received a letter from my Aunt Marguerite. She sent us some lengths of pretty cotton out of which my mother made me dresses and aprons.   At Christmas we had a plum pudding, but as we did not know that it had to be cooked we found it indigestible and threw it away in my father's allotment, where all the birds in Clichy were soon enjoying an English Christmas dinner.   They had been quicker than we to realize its potentialities!

This summer my mother sent me again to Ver-sur-Mer.   In fact I had become so thin and anaemic that I was sent before the end of term, which was disappointing.   My schooldays were now over.   In October I would have to find work.

For a few weeks, however, on my return from the country, I took possession again of the street.   Maimaine and Henriette had grown-up work to do.   Hélène, though younger than I, came occasionally, but she also was required at home.   The boys already wore long trousers and followed their elders to the various factories.   There remained Louise and Marie Guillet, and Dédée Gontrel, who hopped from pavement to pavement like a canary in a cage.   Dédée was great fun, her twittering was bright and clever: she came to us and I went to her.   Mme Gontrel continued to carry Riri, who was very good, but so ugly that nobody but his mother would kiss him.   Dédée, who in spite of this loved him dearly, would occasionally rub his poor slobbering cheek with hers, pretending to kiss him.   As for me, I kissed him in the name of Jesus, inspired by these words written in large letters on a wall of our Sunday school: 'Jesus loves little children.' I kissed Riri with all my heart, and I was sorry that our Saviour was not amongst us in the flesh so that I could have taken Riri to Him to be cured. One day, more than usually moved by this desire, I mentioned it to his mother, who looked at me with such immense surprise that I was quite disconcerted. Very occasionally Mme Gontrel would put down her little son. Dédée and I would then play at the lost child. Riri was placed at the foot of a chair. Dédée and I, two ladies out walking, would find him, give him another name, and bring him up. At this point Mme Gontrel would arrive, clasp him to her bosom, cover him with kisses, and give a little tap to his overgrown head so that it took the right angle against her shoulder. Riri, happy, would suck his thumb.

Towards six the family went to the windows of the flat to look up the street. The kitchen window was occupied by Mme Gontrel and Riri; the one in the bedroom by Dédée and, if I happened to be with them, by me. Sometimes we waited for as long as an hour, and then suddenly Riri would show signs of life, making the strangest contortions, and there would appear from the corner of the rue Souchal a dark little man wearing a frock coat with a magpie tail, a soiled white waistcoat, and a black hat. This curious little man held a black violin case, as black as his coat and hat, in one hand, and in the other, by the string, a toy balloon, which would float a yard or two above his hat, or sometimes, in the place of this, he would carry a coloured windmill in celluloid.

This was M. Gontrel.

As soon as he had turned the corner of the rue Souchal he planted himself firmly on both feet, raised his head so that one could see the Adam's apple floating in his thin neck, and began:

'Good day to the prettiest woman, to Riri the cleverest child, to Dédée the famous dancer, and'—this was addressed to me—'to the little blonde girl!'

Having finished this welcome he advanced a few yards, looking sharply to right and to left, and if by chance a *concierge* or a tenant leaning out of a window dared to laugh at him, he would emit like fire from his mouth the most foul invectives and menaces it is possible to imagine. Those who received these burning addresses, as if scorched, withdrew their heads into their houses like snails. Then he, victorious, his coloured balloon bobbing up and down above the crown of his black hat, or the windmill turning in the breeze, would continue his way. As he passed the doorkeeper's lodge one would hear him cry: 'Good day, Mme Machin, are you still cuckold?' The poor woman retreated into the depths of her kitchen, not daring to show her head till he was on the stairs. At last he arrived, having bumped up against several steps which he insulted as if they had been responsible people, entered, kissed his wife, saying: 'Heavens! How awful you look, even worse than yesterday!' He kissed Riri. 'Well, there you are, poor brat, take your balloon!' Looking at Dédée, a curious tone of affection would creep into his voice: 'You're as ugly as an ant, but you'll turn into something good. I know it. I know it. You'll be everything I haven't been.' Riri laughed almost intelligently. M. Gontrel sat in the kitchen, took off his boots, plunged his thin feet into a tub of cold water, and, fully dressed, laid himself on the bed, where he was soon fast asleep. His wife waited, listened, smacked Dédée to keep her quiet, then crept to the bed where, with the expertness of a professional, she picked his pockets, taking the larger silver and a few notes. Crossing the room on tiptoe she placed these in an enamel box marked 'Kitchen Salt,' and putting Dédée and Riri to bed, went back to her place at the window, where she would remain till night fell and the lamplighter lit the street lamps. She would now wake her husband and prepare some black coffee, which they would both drink. She knelt to lace his shoes. He fumbled in his pockets and gave her the small change. Then putting a white scarf round his neck he would take his violin case from where it reposed on the kitchen table and bump down the stairs. Before turning into the rue Souchal he would stop, take off his hat, bow like a Spanish grandee, and exclaim: 'Good night to the woman I love, and may all those who are peeping at me behind their curtains be bitten by fleas!' He would be gone the next moment, and the street would again become silent.

M. Gontrel played the violin in front of the terraces of the Montmartre cafés. When dawn whitened the fortifications he would be on the way home, but often, stupid with absinthe and fatigue, he lay on a bench, and there he would sleep clutching his black violin case against his poor narrow chest like a girl mother with the baby she cannot abandon, till wakened by cold or rain.

15

THE weather had been very hot and Riri looked more pitiful than ever. Mme Gontrel suggested going to the Bois de Boulogne and eating sandwiches on the grass. My mother gave me permission to accompany her, and we took the underground to the Étoile, where I thought of Marie-Thérèse and Rolande, wondering what had become of them since my father had sent them away from the house. Mme Gontrel led us up a fine avenue full of rich modern apartment houses, and stopping in front of one of these she knocked at the *concierge's* glass door and whispered something I did not catch. We passed into the pretty gravelled courtyard, Dédée making me a sign that I must hide with her behind a shrub. Suddenly Mme Gontrel began to sing, first rather timidly, but soon her voice, warmed by the love-theme of the waltz, became natural, and swelling out revealed all its purity and strength. Windows were opened, heads put out. The singer with the child in her arms became focused like an actress on a stage. The heads were withdrawn, and a moment later, as the song ended on a last tender note of love, pieces of silver rained on the gravel. Dédée sprang from our hiding-place, ran from coin to coin, lightly plucked those which had fallen behind a piece of netting, into a pail, or behind the shrubbery, filling her apron like a sprightly elf. Mme Gontrel meanwhile bowed, thanked her audience, kissed Riri as a gesture of maternal love, and plunging a hand into Dédée's outstretched apron, withdrew the silver, which she weighed expertly, selecting half a dozen coins which she dropped on the *concierge's* doormat as we passed, crying out: 'Good-bye, madame, I shall look forward to seeing you next week.'

We repeated this profitable experience in another block further along the avenue, but Mme Gontrel again left the place hurriedly for fear of the police, street singing not being allowed by law. On the grass overlooking the lake in the Bois de Boulogne we ate like happy people. Riri crawled over the daisies, while Mme Gontrel counted her money and made plans for the future.

As these were my last holidays my mother thought I should make myself useful. She had built up quite a fine dressmaking business, and now sent me into the heart of Paris, to the Magasin du Printemps, or to the Galeries Lafayette, to match a material or to buy trimmings or buttons.

I set off proudly all alone, extremely frightened. I had made the journey many times with my parents, especially my mother, but on this occasion it seemed longer. In the dim openings of carriage doors, leaning flat against walls, young apaches, their eyes mocking, their teeth white, gave me the uncomfortable feeling of resembling Red Riding Hood watched by the wolf. I walked briskly, then in a sudden panic ran, but a moment later, ashamed of my cowardice, walked again. Turning into the boulevard I now had to pass in front of a long line of women drawn up gossiping, knitting on kitchen chairs, taking the air, commenting on passers-by. Turning sharply left there was a street with a high wall. Behind this wall was the cemetery of the Batignolles, one of the richest in Paris, where families owned the land for ever. My childish person cast an elongated shadow across the stone wall preceding me fantastically. Suddenly a long funeral procession came into view, and passed through the great double doors, the wheels of the hearse grating against the fine gravel of well-tended path wending ahead between graves. Quickly I tried to look into this jealously kept city of the dead. The doors closed in my face. Even now I could hear, though less loudly, the grind of the wheels and the tread of the mourners walking behind. Then silence. From here I turned into a street exclusively occupied by florists, admiring magnificent flowers in warm earthenware pots arranged on shelves like spectators on the tiers of a circus. At the far end tall stelae of rose, grey, and black marble, not yet carved, virginal, patiently waited for the customer who was bound to come, some leaning casually against vaults so beflowered, cool, and well polished that they appeared almost desirable to inhabit. The street smelt of wet flowers, flowers cut down in the full vigour of living— death, in short. I shuddered, but nothing would have persuaded me to take another route. In the evening on my way home the shops were closed by open-mesh steel gates so that the flowers would have air. The employees, having lived in the proximity of a cemetery all day, had doubtless returned to the heart of Paris seeking nocturnal gaiety. Paul Verlaine, sad and tormented poet, is buried here.

My mother remained during the time of my absence in great agitation. My only adventures were to be chased from counter to counter by vicious old gentlemen, to be pinched and fingered rather too often in the crowds of the underground. I became used to this, and the nausea brought on the first few times by these sneaking and not altogether flattering attacks quickly subsided. Paris is thus. Life was beginning. A young woman develops her own defences, but clearly the days of playing on the pavements were finished. I was to know the joys of growing up, the satisfaction of seeing men turn round in the street to take a second look at me.

Mother Newspaper had not been to market for several days. Marguerite Rosier thought this curious, and went to knock on the door of her flat, but there was no answer. The husband came in from his bank in the evening, but as Marguerite had never spoken to him she lacked the courage to ask him for news of his wife. The next morning the husband went off as usual, but in the evening he came back with another man, and the next day, just as Marguerite was going off to market, she heard heavy footsteps and a banging on the stairs, and leaning over the banisters she saw two men bringing up a coffin. They came right up to her landing and then stopped. Mother Newspaper's door opened, and the husband, coming out, made a sign to the men to come in. During the afternoon a hearse arrived at the house. The coffin was brought down, and the street, to its stupefaction, saw the husband emerge all in black and follow the hearse quite alone. Nobody had been told—there were no mourners, no flowers. Burying somebody in such a secret, unneighbourly way had no precedent. Mother Newspaper had told us she had taken her precautions, but these were of a nature to shock us profoundly. I did not sleep all night, dreaming of the cameo brooch, wondering if the last pearl had fallen out, if the poor gazelle was now under the earth. Had she done her last washing, her last ironing, her final mending? Her waxen face haunted me for many days in the market. I kept on seeing her in imagination with her long grey-black clothes, her bun with the tortoiseshell combs. We had laughed a good deal at her expense; but we missed her now, and as I hurried along the pavement, keeping close in to the houses, I would seemingly recognize the peculiar smell of her black clothes when the sun used to scorch them.

My clergyman, back from the war, found me my first job.

Two Protestant Dutchmen owned a new white factory on the Boulevard de la Révolte, where they made imitation pearls which were just then coming so much into fashion.

This boulevard encircled Paris on its outer perimeter, was paved with great stones as in the days of the French kings, and along the side of it, on slightly higher ground, ran a little tram-car which made a tremendous noise as it went slowly along. I could catch this tram-car opposite the public wash-house, and it took me almost to the door of the factory.

I learnt to classify correspondence, and to run quickly on errands through the ranks of women dipping the pearls, bending over tiny cauldrons in which the pearls bubbled in fish scales to make them smooth and rosy as the dawn. In the private office of the Dutch partners there was a picture of Saskia, Rembrandt's wife, after whom our factory was named. I looked at it with interest and pleasure. The idea of luxury entered my mind and I was soon dreaming of real pearls (not artificial ones) to wear against my blonde skin.

The main office was full of cashiers, who came from Paris. My mother packed my lunch in a napkin, and a young cashier and I lunched together, and with the hour left to us climbed the fortifications in the hope of finding some flowers. We never found any. The grass grew tough and high, always inclined to the east or to the north according to the prevailing wind. When the breeze came from across Paris we liked to feel it against our cheeks, blowing through our hair as if bringing us the million sensations of a great city. We heard the hooter of our factory and the hooters of other factories. We would get up like two children from our seats on the grass and return rather sadly to work.

In the evening I would say good night to my companion of the lunch hour and join Mlle Augustine and Mlle Pannier. Mlle Augustine lived in a block of flats behind the Gouin Hospital. I used to wait for her in the morning. She was a religious girl

with a pretty skin, fresh and rosy, and eyes of such a shallow blue
that they gave one the impression of having been washed. A
huge bun, the colour of a cow's tail, respectfully plaited, spoiled
by its too great size the effect of her wide-brimmed hats. Her
hats were of an honest grey in winter, of light straw in summer.
Both her parents worked in a chocolate factory. She was
eighteen, dispassionate, went to church, and represented her
family's ambition to make of their daughter an educated girl
employed in an office.

Mlle Pannier was thirty. Small brunette with large black eyes,
sallow cheeks, a skin that was losing its freshness because of a
too long virginity, half consumed by envy and rancour because
she was still without a husband, she waited but had less and less
hope. Dressed in a tailor-made with a long jacket and a cherry-
coloured velvet toque, the collars of her white blouses always
speckless and of pretty form, she was still a most desirable
person—eyes full of promise, burning with sensuality, but over-
brimming with scruples and honesty, quite determined not to do
what she shouldn't till the ring was on her finger. She lived in
the Place de la Mairie with a brother, who, like her, was longing
to marry, but could not find a worthy enough partner. On
summer evenings they walked together like husband and wife, or
leant out of their balcony, elbow to elbow, looking at the people
in the square. She stayed at home on Saturdays and told us on
Mondays how many marriages she had counted at the town hall,
and she described exactly what each bride wore as she angrily
hit the keys of her typewriter: 'Sir, we thank you for your letter
of the 16th inst. . . .' Then, tearing out the paper with a quick,
dry movement, she would say to Mlle Augustine:

'You see little Madeleine there? Well, she's just the type to
get easily married. Gay! That's what she is! And as she doesn't
give marriage a thought she'll get it offered to her all day long.'

A new sheet of paper went into the typewriter, and she continued:

'I think of nothing else. I dream marriage, breathe marriage,
and when a man talks to me, it doesn't matter what I answer, he
sees right off that I'm thinking of marriage, and he drops me like
a hot brick. I suppose it shows.'

When she had done a paragraph or two at great speed she
would stop, rest her elbows on the desk, and say:

'For two years I 've been in this office, and next door'—she nodded in the direction of a glass partition dividing the typists from the accountants—'next door, I tell you, Mlle Augustine, except for M. Binche, who is not at all young, not a single one of those men was married when I first came here. Since then every Monday morning or Friday evening, one by one, they have come here to say: " To-morrow, Mlle Pannier, I am going to be married," or "You know, Mlle Pannier, I was married on Saturday." And yet I was here, right next door to them, just as pretty as the women they married. Not one, not a single lone one who ever thought I might make him happy! Mlle Pannier is my name, and it 's only too clear that Mlle Edith Pannier I shall remain. Consider that even during the war, when everybody found a husband, I was left high and dry. Yet they say I 'm pretty, that there 's life in my eyes. The other women are envious of my hair, but they would not want it!' She turned to me. 'Quick, Madeleine, give me the file of the *Printemps* at Marseilles! And you see, Mlle Augustine, with my brother it 's the same thing. Unlucky! That 's what we are! If only we could find another flat, one where we don't have to watch the marriages!'

I was in my fifteenth year, slim, almost dangerously, my magnificent blonde hair, according to the rules, caught up in a bun, so that I looked all head. A boy of seventeen, draughtsman in the gas company which the Dutch brothers owned further along the boulevard, was already courting me. He lunched quickly in the canteen, and came to walk with my friend Georgette and me along the fortifications. On our return, his good-bye drowned in the noise of the hooter, he would blow me, without shame, without fear of what anybody might say or think, a kiss with the tips of his fingers to which I would reply in the same way, laughing hilariously. One day when the noise of the hooter subsided I heard Mlle Pannier's voice in the office: 'Just look at that, Mlle Augustine, the very boy I had my eyes on! I wouldn't be surprised if he didn't come to me on Friday and say he 's going to marry our little Madeleine.'

At the end of the month I brought home one hundred francs, and I once again witnessed my father in his more touching moments. He cried with happiness, saying that we were as lucky as millionaires. A few days later, in a tombola, I won a very large coffee-pot, made of some light metal, presumably tin.

My mother to please me immediately made some coffee in it. We all found it excellent, but my father, looking enviously at the pot, said: 'It would make a magnificent watering-can for my allotment; the filter would produce a fine rain! I wouldn't dare buy anything half so good. Do please give it me, Madelon.'

To celebrate the event we shuffled the cards for bezique, my father, after each game, marking the scores on the wall, and my mother pouring out a fresh round, the supply of coffee seemingly endless. My mother played cards indifferently, and she and I nearly always lost, but later in the evening I improved so much that I beat my father, and he said:

'It 's funny the way one's children always catch up with one, and then seem to do better; but what good does that do them? In the end they come back to where their parents left off.'

'You 're not where *your* parents left off!' cut in my mother bitterly. 'At least *they* had a house of their own, whilst we are still in this miserable lodging!'

My father, the joy driven out of him, shook his head and went off to undress. Our evening ended sadly, and the disenchantment that never left my mother enveloped us like a damp fog.

After a few months at the pearl factory I began to have serious indigestion. There were too many things against me. I was in the middle of growing up, I did not eat nearly enough, and the journey was tiring. One morning, when it was raining, the little tram-car which clanged forward on its own elevated path along the boulevard went beyond my pearl factory before I emerged from my usual day-dream. Almost as soon as I had made this tiresome discovery the factory hooters all began going, and I was filled with that absurd panic which young people have when they realize they are late for work. I jumped off the tram while it was still rattling along. I did not of course take into account the difference in level between the track and the paved highway. Rolling over, my bag and my small parcel of sandwiches scattered, I remained unconscious for a moment or two in the ditch.

This accident, which shook me considerably, brought on new attacks of indigestion. That morning I was not at all well, and Mlle Augustine brought me home, where my mother put me to bed. I became delirious, battled with an imaginary tram-car, and ran a high temperature. Two days later, however, I was back at work, though I refused to take the tram.

Mlle Pannier advised me to learn shorthand. She and Mlle Augustine liked to argue about the merits of their different systems. My mother agreed that I had no hope of becoming a secretary without an adequate training, and I therefore, at my own expense, attended night classes in the Place de la Mairie.

Mme Duville, a former shorthand-typist, had opened this little school to take advantage of a sudden desire on the part of factory girls and even seamstresses to 'better themselves' by working in an office. After a quick supper at home I attended night class till ten, and the next day, instead of climbing over the fortifications with Georgette and our young man from the gas company, alone in the office I practised assiduously.

Meanwhile the business recession was gathering momentum and turning into the short but vicious slump which followed the spending of war bonuses. Factories everywhere were closing down. The Dutch brothers dismissed a large part of their staff, and after only five months with them I found myself again at home. Accordingly I went more often to Mme Duville, where, at last, I was making a little progress.

In a large room full of chairs and tiny tables women and men of every age wrote hieroglyphics, typed on large machines, read aloud, or grouped themselves round Mme Duville, who, a great silver watch in her hand, rolling her r's with a thick Bourguignon accent, dictated acts of sale from some notary's office, leading articles from the newspapers, or the incomprehensible speeches of members of Parliament. When Mme Duville had finished she would cry out theatrically: 'How many of you have followed without missing a word?' Few put up their hands. Then she would announce with a doctoral air: 'That was seventy to the minute. Go to your machines now and start typing.'

M. Duville was employed at the town hall, where he kept the register of deaths. He was gentle, dressed entirely in black as befitted his occupation, and helped his wife in the evenings. One would then see, and hear, two opposing groups, that of M. Duville: 'Those of you who have followed me without missing a single word have done sixty to the minute,' and his wife, beautifully marcelled, her large head seemingly neckless, so solidly was it fixed upon her shoulders, dictating with obvious relish a peroration of M. Herriot.

Spring was coming along. On Saturdays I also would watch

the wedding parties driving up to the town hall, many of them in open carts with long benches facing each other which, in France, are called *tapissières*, the bride, all in white with her veil, being helped down by gentlemen with well-oiled hair and white buttonholes. Often after leaving the town hall the procession would walk to the adjoining church of St. Vincent-de-Paul for the religious ceremony. The decorated carts waited, drawn up in rows, in the square. The various parties often fraternized and went together for a drive round the Bois de Boulogne before the wedding breakfast and the ball.

Up against the railway embankment of the *ceinture*, the line which encircles Paris like the fortifications, was a little café where my father went to play cards on Saturday night. This café was owned by Louis Duparc, whose wife, Louise, my mother and I had got to know at the public wash-house when we lived in the rue Kloch. Daughter of honest folk, of very poor health, she had a son of six and tenderly loved her husband. A few months earlier she had nearly died from a miscarriage, and my mother had got into the habit of helping her with the housework. From her first-floor bedroom window one could see the trains go by. Innumerable goods trains, night and day, shook her bed and prevented her from getting to sleep. She was in despair, saying that she would never be strong again. Louis filled his bottles of wine, served his customers behind the zinc counter, tried to cook something appetizing for his wife, bringing it up to her when he had a moment to spare. When she saw him come in she would say: 'My poor Louis, I shall never recover. These trains are killing me.' They were obliged to send their son to a grandmother at Angers, and it broke their hearts, for they all loved each other. Thus the boy was at Angers, Louis was in his cellar or serving his customers, and she, shaken by the goods trains and their strident whistles, shaken also by a dry cough that never left her, was alone in her room. The doctor moved his head in a way which left no doubt, and spoke about the chest being weak. He would then look at Louis and say: 'As for you, you 're more seriously ill than she is. You ought both to throw all this up and go to live in the country! Soon it will be too late. But you won't understand.' Louis looked at the doctor and answered:

'Understand? But that is what is going to make us die, understanding that it 's too late!'

H

'Come now!' said the doctor in a kindly tone. 'You are both still young and, I may say, both intelligent and reasonable. Only, I must warn you, no more miscarriages or it will be the end.'

Thus on Saturday nights I would go to fetch my father here after his game of cards. If he was not quite ready I would go up to see Louise, talking to her a little, watching the heavy trains go past. She would remain motionless, her thin arms stretched out beside her enfeebled body, her eyes looking at me sadly.

My father and I would return home together, and the next morning, being Sunday and in March, he would go off to his garden, having bought some manure in anticipation of a good morning's digging. He did not come back till I was leaving for Sunday school, and exclaimed: 'How lovely you've become, Madelon! But oh my, what a hat!'

'For all *you* know about hats!' I exclaimed, holding this one in both hands to prevent it from being blown off my head. Besides, now that my hair was done up like a lady I was not against giving myself a few airs. In the evening my father went round to play cards with his friends and to 'help poor Louis.' My mother and I sewed and then made supper.

On this particular Sunday the table was laid and the soup was gently simmering. My father was very late. Eight struck at the state schools, then the quarter and the half. We were anxious. In a few moments my mother would send me to look for him. I would have to leave my favourite corner between the laid table and the sideboard, vacating the broken chair on which I was so comfortable. The sideboard had followed us everywhere, originally painted white, now battered and scratched. My little brother had once hidden in it with the grey cat, finishing between them a stolen leg of mutton. My mother and I used to stand on the broken chair to put pennies in the gas meter.

I was slipping on my shoes when I heard a noise on the stairs, and after a moment of apparent hesitation the bell rang. I was already there, and opened quickly. My father, supported by Louis Duparc, had obviously had trouble in getting up the stairs. Louis Duparc explained in the nicest way that as my father had not felt well in the café he had not wanted to let him come home alone. 'But I must run,' he added, shaking my mother by the hand, 'for I've left the café with nobody to look after it. I told the customers I wouldn't be long. They won't take advantage of me.' Then, in a confidential tone to my mother: 'Louise isn't at all well. She seems to be getting weaker all the time and calls out for our son. It 's no good the mother-in-law going to see her. She comes to the café, does her best to be brave, but when she hears Louise coughing she cries and cries. She cries so much she puts us both in a worse state. As a matter of fact my wife doesn't know her mother is here this time. Only when I take her meals up on a tray she 's surprised to find all sorts of little dishes she used to like when she was a child. She wonders how I 've the time or the patience to make them. She says: "How you must love me, Louis! And how I love you!" '

Poor Louis, as he stood in the doorway speaking, cried gently, as a man cries, not being accustomed to tears.

My mother said to him: 'Poor Louis, be brave. I 'll come and see Louise to-morrow. Go back quickly, and thank you for what you 've just done!'

He ran down the stairs and was gone.

My father was sitting on a chair laughing gently to himself. His thoughts were far away, his knees were wide apart; on one of them rested an elbow, a clenched fist supported the chin. Suddenly realizing where he was, he said: 'You know, Matilda, it beats me. I 'll swear I had the ace of clubs!'

'You 've a tidy bit more than the ace of clubs!' answered my mother. 'You ought to be ashamed of yourself!'

'Oh, please, Matilda, don't be angry! I hardly had anything to drink.'

'Well, have something to eat,' answered my mother.

'No,' he objected wearily, 'it would be no good. I 'm not hungry.'

Emerging from my seat between the table and the sideboard I said: 'Mother, why don't you give father some warm water? It 's so horrible it would make him sick and he might feel better.'

At the thought of warm water my father broke into peals of laughter. He brought his hands loudly to his knees, crying: 'Warm water for me, for *me*! What do you know about that ? My own daughter telling me I ought to drink warm water! Matilda, did you hear that? *Peccavi*, warm water for Milou! Well, if that doesn't beat everything!'

'But, father, it was to do you good!'

'Keep quiet, naughty girl!' he exclaimed, his eyes now full of tears. He had laughed so much that he had difficulty in speaking. 'Are you really my daughter that you can offer me water—and warm water at that?'

We could do nothing with him that evening. He would drink nothing, not even the soup that was filling the kitchen with its homely smell. My mother put him to bed, and he was soon asleep. Then she came into the kitchen, and we ate silently, but after a while she said, as if in continuation of her own thoughts: 'The trouble is that to-morrow he will be really ill. Every holiday now is followed by a day of illness. His strength is leaving him, and the day will come when he won't be able to work any more, and then where shall we be?'

She continued thinking by herself, I expect, for soon she said:

'You don't really know how to do anything, do you? And as for me, my dressmaking scarcely does more than pay for the rent and the shoes.'

She pushed her plate away, and suddenly asked me for a page of my shorthand note-book and a pen. Then in her neat hand she wrote to her sister Marguerite in England, imploring her to do something for me.

'Probably,' she wrote, 'I shall have to look after my husband for years to come. I would do anything for my daughter not to share this martyrdom.'

My mother must have been in real despair to go to her sister for help. It must have hurt her pride terribly. She was pale. Her golden helmet shone under the electric light bulb. She sealed the envelope, and fetching one of Marguerite's letters, copied the address, spelling out each word, drawing such a heavy line underneath that she scratched the paper. She gave me the impression of having signed her death warrant. She opened her purse, took out a blue stamp, and stuck it on the letter, saying:

'Keep your slippers on. Run and post this in the box at the corner of the Place de la République. I'll be looking out for you at the window. Don't make a sound on the stairs. We must post this letter immediately, for if I found it to-morrow morning I'd be ashamed to ask the help of your Aunt Marguerite and her husband, whom I don't even know, and I should tear it up.

Run along quickly, and as soon as you 're back we 'll go to bed.'

I tore down as lightly as on wings, and running as far as the square, raised myself on tiptoe to slip the letter into the box. Then I took one foot off the ground, thinking it must be wonderful to dance in a ballet. I heard the letter drop amongst the others. The sound made me smile, not guessing that what my mother had just done would change my destiny.

My father went to work as usual but, as my mother had feared, he was ill, and when he came home in the evening we were overcome with pity for his pale cheeks and his worn-out features, which seemed to beg our forgiveness and affection. He went to bed very early and read a newspaper. To our immense surprise he even started a serial. He would buy the *Excelsior* on his way to work, and bring it back to us, having read it during his lunch hour, folded neatly to fit into his pocket. My mother used to dictate the short story so that I could practise my shorthand. There were some magnificent ones by Fréderic Boutet, Pierre Mille, and Lucie Delarue-Mardrus, whose stories of her beloved Normandy rank to-day amongst the finest in French literature. *L'Enfant au coq* and *Graine au vent* are novels that sit always in the bookshelf at my elbow.

We went to see Louise.

Spring was tormenting her, filling her alternatively with hope and despair. Sparrows chirruped on the railway lines, joyfully, lungs clear and free, supple and alert. I sat at a marble-topped table in the café, against a leather-upholstered bench. Louis was cleaning his zinc counter, wiping and setting down bottles of varied drink which he kept close at hand to tempt his customers. Yellow, green, and red aperitifs glistened. Louis, between rumblings of the trains which set all the glasses chattering, the bottles quivering, listened to Louise and my mother, whose voices came down from the bedroom softly. When Louise coughed Louis's fingers tightened over the damp cloth with which he was wiping the water from the sink.

On the first floor of our house lodged a family called Neveu. The man was about forty-five, the woman slightly older, and their son, Lucien, was twenty-two. Father and son had fought in the war. Mme Neveu and the daughter Jeanne, who now was married and lived elsewhere, had worked in a factory. M. Neveu had an allotment next to ours, and my father and he exchanged plants and seeds, and occasionally, when they had watered during the hot weather, they would have a drink together.

It was unfortunate that M. Neveu, taciturn and hard working, should have a wife who frittered away all the money he made. With the bonus the men had been given after the war she had taken this flat, which was a good deal larger than the others, but as there was no money left to buy any new furniture the rooms looked absurdly bare with only three beds, two chairs, and a table. They owned a large red cat, that often walked along the parapet to our windows and sometimes, when I woke in the morning, it was asleep at the foot of my bed.

Lucien, the son, was a giant. The father had probably been powerful in his day, but hard work had given him a heaped-up appearance like sand tightly packed in a bag. Lucien had hands like sledge-hammers. He wore a red neckerchief, a grey cap, and his carter's whip was thrown over his left shoulder. Lately he had been bringing his heavy tumbrel to our door, leaving it there for several hours while he went upstairs for a good sleep. His business just now was to deliver paving-stones to a gang of Italians mending the boulevard five minutes from where we lived. His horse, an enormous animal, whose harness was decorated with red topknots, pawing the asphalt under the hot sun, driven mad with flies, fought a lonely battle against thirst and the indifference of a Parisian street. Awakened suddenly, perhaps by his mother, more probably by some noise outside, Lucien, looking furious, would hurry down the stairs, run out to his horse, punch it in the neck with tremendous force, jump up on his load of stones, and crack his whip like a Roman charioteer. The heavy tumbrel quickly took off. One saw the horse's hoofs throw up sparks. An appalling noise shook the windows.

A day or two after our visit to Louis and Louise Duparc, Lucien Neveu, having repeated this episode, was sending his whip whistling over his horse's flanks when the animal must have slipped over the burning surface of the street or found the load too heavy. At any rate it fell right over, its four hoofs uppermost, and the shock was such that Lucien was thrown from his tumbrel, receiving a load of stones on his legs. He picked himself up, swearing like the traditional carter, and hung on to the ends of the shafts, trying to bring them down by the weight of his huge body. We could see the veins of his neck standing out and becoming blue, and the muscles of his arms resembled those of a boxer. He succeeded without help in bringing down the shafts. A great crowd had gathered. Puffing and panting, straining and slipping, he did not cease to insult the onlookers and his horse, with whom he was now having a veritable battle trying to put it on its feet. He succeeded after kicking it cruelly for a full five minutes. From our first-floor window I was so sickened by the sight of his brutality that I covered him with shrill girlish insults. He looked up like a toreador facing a hostile crowd, and sent his whip cracking in my direction. The crowd protested. He then turned with lightning speed and cracked it half a dozen times over their cowering heads. On the advice of a passer-by, however, he unharnessed his horse, and with the help of this man he made it more comfortable, the stranger coaxing it and flattering it. Soon he was able to drive off and everything became quiet again.

The next day Mme Neveu came to ask if we had any milk. She told us that Lucien was in bed with a stitch in his side and that she was going to fetch a doctor. My mother had no milk, but offered to take the young man some coffee which we had just brewed. 'That will do just as well,' said Mme Neveu. 'Here is the key. Would you mind taking it to him while I go to the doctor?'

My mother, bearing in mind the scene of yesterday, was a little nervous about her reception. 'But there was no need to be afraid,' she told me on her return. 'He was in bed, pale, shaking with fever, as weak as yesterday we saw him strong.' The doctor came, made his auscultation, and told Mme Neveu that he would have him taken to hospital immediately in an ambulance. The mother, blinded by her tears, was helped by mine to wash him, change his shirt, and put on his Sunday clothes. When the ambulance arrived two men lifted Lucien with infinite care, placed him beautifully dressed on a stretcher, went down the stairs almost on tiptoe, and placing him in the ambulance drove off as smoothly and as silently as twenty-four hours earlier Lucien had gone violently on his way. This big man practically without sign of life had surprised us more than anything else. We

hardly dared speak about it, for we none of us doubted that
heaven had sent down a swift and terrible vengeance. We had
admired the Herculean force of a giant who had been abased
with the ruthlessness of biblical law.

The red cat came in through the window, and spent the rest
of the day with us. Towards nightfall Mme Neveu came in to
tell us that Lucien had double pneumonia and a lesion of the
heart. The doctors had said that the powerful frame hid a
multitude of weaknesses. The poor woman went every morning
to visit her son; then one day returned earlier than usual, saying:
'He was still warm, but it 's finished. The funeral will be Saturday at eleven.' She went across the corridor to her own flat, and
we heard her howl like a she-wolf. M. Neveu became more
heaped up than ever. On the Saturday morning they went to
the hospital. It was pouring. They had to wait more than an
hour for the procession, which they then followed on foot to St.
Ouen. When they came back in the evening M. Neveu was
scarcely recognizable. The next morning he stayed in bed,
coughing, and it was not till the following Sunday that he put
his soldier's cape over his shoulders and tried to dig a little in the
garden. My father was shocked by his drawn features, by his
pallor and his thin body. The two men planted a few seeds,
walked home together, and as M. Neveu was in a cold perspiration, his wife put him to bed and called the doctor. Pneumonia having set in it was too late to take him to hospital. A
week later he was dead.

Two men, our neighbours, having died within three weeks of
each other, the street began to murmur: 'Never two in a house
but it 's three. You 'll see, there 'll be a third!' And all the
men in our house were passed in review, to discover who it
would be.

Mme Neveu, heart-broken, went off with the red cat to live at
her married daughter's house, and we felt a little better thinking
she had taken away the bad luck.

Summer was starting, and the people in the street lived at open
windows. After lunch the doorkeepers put their red velvet
chairs on the pavement and nodded to the postman, remarking
on the heat, as he came along with piles of catalogues from the
great stores. One's thoughts instinctively turned to straw hats
and pretty light dresses.

I was hoping soon to pass my shorthand examination, after which I could be certain of a reasonable salary, but though I worked very hard I was not good at it. The speed refused to come. When Mme Duville made her little speech about 'those who have not missed a word will have done seventy to the minute' I felt like throwing pad and pencil out of the window. My father, since his homecoming with Louis Duparc, had become very reasonable, working on Sundays in his garden from dawn till almost nightfall. One evening, after taking some lettuces to Louis at the café, my father told us that their little boy had arrived with his grandmother. Louise had just not been able to do without him, but the poor little boy, unaccustomed now to his parents, tripping up against the marble-topped tables, not knowing where to play, deafened by the noise of the trains, could not make out why he had been brought back from his grandmother's wide fields and lovely garden. Louise quickly noticed her son's indifference. She had thought about him night and day; he would not even look at her—a quick glance out of the window and he would slip out of the bedroom. The boy's callousness sunk into her heart like a knife. From that moment she became weaker and, quite gently, died in her sleep. Louis's tears, those of the mother, and the whistle of the goods trains filled the room horribly. The little boy went back to the country with his grandmother, and Louis made arrangements to sell the miserable café.

*H

16

AT the bottom of our house, exactly below our windows, was a newly opened bicycle shop. A good-looking young man, with very dark hair, who spoke with a strong Spanish accent, worked from dawn till dusk mending punctures, blowing up inner tubes, and arranging handlebars. On summer evenings and on Sunday mornings his tiny shop and all the street outside was crowded with French, Spanish, Belgian, and Italian racing cyclists and their backers and enthusiasts. Bicycle racing was the most popular national sport. The dream of every youth was to bend over the lowest possible handlebars, a spare inner tube slung from shoulder to waist, and pedal, pedal, pedal round France, from Brittany to Biarritz and from Nice to the Belgian frontier, up mountain roads, along powdery miles of poplar-shaded ribbon, snatching their food and drink from comrades as they passed.

These young men, arguing, elbowing, gesticulating round a machine or a tyre, dressed in orange or violet sweaters, or both colours together, filled our street with their vociferous presence. None of them lived in the neighbourhood. They arrived like a company of starlings at six o'clock on a Sunday morning, and whilst the Spanish owner noisily threw up the steel curtain of his shop, commenting on the races of the previous day, his followers would make figures of eight and sudden spurts in the still rather milky dawn. Former soldiers, aviators, and tank designers soon came to encourage the young generation, tapping them amicably on the shoulders, cracking an obscene army joke, feeling younger by this contact with youth, and then suddenly the whole company of sportsmen, with a last ringing of bells, their supple bodies arched over their specially constructed machines, would go off in one long tightly packed line for a distant destination. The owner brought down the steel curtain of his shop as noisily as he had thrown it up, and went home to breakfast. The entire company would return at five exhausted but happy, flowers tied to their handlebars, anxious to spend the next hour or two discussing the labours of the day.

At this moment Marie Guillet, as if by mere chance, would go to her window and play her violin, whereupon the youths would look up and cheer, and making a trumpet of their hands cry out: 'Play something else!' Marie blushed, made signs to suggest that her modesty forbade it, and then suddenly ran down into the street with the air of a person who has suddenly remembered an urgent errand. Emerging amongst all these boys, flustered and self-conscious, swinging her hips and casting down her eyes, she would go as far as the first turning on the left, down which she would disappear. Ten minutes later, having walked round the block, she reappeared from the opposite end of the street, became flustered again, and looked for the face of a timely neighbour with whom she could talk for a few moments before going back to her flat. The boys, at the sight of her, stopped arguing. A curious stillness fell. Some of them had sensed the trick; but Marie was fifteen, chubby, with a big posterior, large breasts, and a pretty pair of legs. Meeting nobody she knew, she slowly crossed the road, wiped her shoes lengthily and unnecessarily on the threshold to gain another minute or two, and then, head lowered, looking round archly at a slant to intrigue them, dived into the corridor. One heard her running up the stairs, the door of the flat opening and closing. Then the boys in the street, like sparrows to whom you throw crumbs, all lifted their heads at the same time to catch a glimpse of Marie at her window. A moment later, ashamed to have been subjugated by this girl, they became self-conscious, and broke out as one voice: 'Well, she has got a nerve, hasn't she?'

The spell was over. Their sporting instincts again took possession of them, and their exclamations and arguments reverted to the subject of bicycles.

On Monday morning the postman brought us a letter from England.

Aunt Marguerite said that just now she had a little girl staying with her, but that in a few weeks she would be delighted to have me. My uncle was already looking round for a firm who would be glad to employ a young French typist. Would my mother be sure to make me go on with my shorthand? It would be of the greatest use.

This friendly letter gave my mother some relief. She began to make inquiries about a passport, but as I was under age I needed my father's permission to leave the country. The letter was hidden under some shelf paper in the dresser. Meanwhile she and I had both taken to knitting. We each made a sock for my father; mine had a square toe, my mother's was pointed like the hat of a Chinese mandarin. When my father put them on one Sunday morning we laughed happily, listening to his merry talk in patois. He put on his heavy boots and went to the allotment, where he was sowing a great diversity of seeds, the weather being fine. He came home that evening tired, in excellent humour, but anxious to go quickly to bed. 'I 've nothing more to worry about,' he said. 'I 've planted everything but the runner beans.'

The next evening my father complained that his breathing was painful. Instead of going off to sleep as soon as his head touched the pillow he tossed feverishly. My mother made an infusion, and as he was drinking it he said:

'Matilda, I 'm afraid I 've got what I had last time. You remember, when we were all three ill?'

She took his hand and found it warm, but she answered:

'I expect it 's only a chill.'

In the morning he was so much worse that on my way to shorthand school I called on the doctor, asking him to hurry across, and when I came back for lunch my mother said he had been but could say nothing definite till the evening. He had wanted my father to be taken to hospital, but unfortunately my father had overheard the conversation, and his anxious face had assumed the most miserable expression. For my father hospital was the last extremity. He had left my little brother there. Young Neveu had died there. My mother, in the doctor's presence, had said firmly to my father:

'You won't go to hospital. I promise you that. I 'll nurse you here.'

The doctor came back before supper and spoke very jovially to my father. He said:

'I often see you crossing the square with some of the lettuces from your garden. One day you 'll be winning a prize for them.'

'Ah, doctor!' answered my father. 'Get me out of this and the first, the largest, will be for you!'

'But that's just what I'm going to do!' answered Dr. Ravaud. 'Now try to sleep and I'll go and write out a prescription on the kitchen table.'

Dr. Ravaud closed the door behind him, and going over to the open window said in a whisper to my mother:

'Your husband has double pneumonia. You know what it is. In nine days he will be out of danger—or dead. A great deal depends on the fight he puts up. You would have done better to send him to hospital, but there's no teaching some people. Still, if you insist on nursing him, though you'll have a lot of trouble, it *can* be done. You must be brave and patient, and learn to economize your strength to go right through with a job you should never have undertaken.'

He looked at me and said:

'Go to your father, and if he asks what I've said tell him I'm writing out a long prescription and that I'm explaining things to your mother. You'll have to help, you know.'

I was surprised at the way he spoke to me. When I was down with influenza he had treated me as a child. Now I sensed that he took me to be a young woman. I went in to my father to calm him, and as soon as the doctor had gone went to the chemist for a thermometer, a bed-pan, a hot-water bottle, and some little bags of linseed and mustard for the compresses the doctor had ordered.

The patient had to drink a great deal. To find milk became a necessity. My mother went from the bedroom to the kitchen all day, and my father's eyes used to follow her pitifully like those of an affectionate dog. The compresses were extremely tiring to make. He was like a little child to nurse. We could do what we liked with him. The important thing was to keep him propped up in bed, and as we were short of pillows my mother sent me to a corn chandler to buy a bundle of straw, which she covered with a bed sheet to make a pillow for his back. When my father saw this arrangement he said:

'You see, Matilda, you were right. You always said I would come down to sleeping on straw. I've made a rotten failure of life.'

'Don't be silly,' my mother answered. 'You're not going to lie on it. It's simply to rest your back against.'

'I'm worried about the money,' he went on. 'All these things must cost a fortune.'

'Yes, they do,' agreed my mother. 'That 's why I 've always pinched to have something aside for a time like this. And I expect the health insurance will give us something.'

He was very quick to reassure himself, looking at her affectionately and commenting: 'How good you are!' He had never seen his wife so gentle and loving. Unwilling to spoil the effect by too much hard thinking he asked:

'Where 's the little girl?'

'At her shorthand class.'

'My! Isn't she becoming clever!'

'She 's jolly well got to!' exclaimed my mother with emphasis. 'Perhaps she 'll be the one to get us out of all this mess, especially if'—she looked quickly at my father—'if she could go to England. I feel sure that Marguerite and her husband would look after her. While you and I were quietly here, not worrying, she would be forging ahead.'

'Do you really think so? But it 's such a long way off!'

'My poor Émile!' snapped my mother. 'You don't really suppose that a girl like Madeleine will spend her life between the Place Clichy and the Place de la République! We 've walked up and down the avenue often enough, you and I, and a fat lot of good it has done us! No! Madeleine will have to try her luck somewhere else, beginning all on her own.'

My father was too weak to say anything. Matilda, having sown the seed, went over to the window, which the doctor insisted must always be half open, and looking down into the street said:

'There 's M. Gontrel going off with his violin. The poor man doesn't look too steady on his legs. Listen to him insulting the *concierge*, saying that he hopes she 'll find a bushel of fleas in her bed!'

My father laughed and said:

'He 's lucky to be on his feet at all. I envy him!'

'Come!' exclaimed my mother indignantly. 'You who never envy anybody! Surely you don't envy that miserable old man? Hallo! There 's Mme Luche, who is going to have a baby, and M. Campion driving his taxi home. That means it is seven. I must take your temperature.'

When she had removed the thermometer she would say brightly:

'Excellent! Quite a bit better this evening. The doctor will be delighted.'

She lied. His temperature rose every day. The doctor shook his head and tried to reassure her.

'But that 's the way it always is, Mme Gal. Now I told you the other day. You must keep calm.'

I took to getting up at five, having discovered a dairy in front of a shed in which there were four or five cows. This vestige of country life was in the rue Martre, quite a long way off. The animals, of course, were never put on grass. Their fodder was piled to the roof of this grey wooden edifice, outside which, every morning and evening, a queue of women formed, each holding a jug. If I was lucky I came away with half a pint. I would run home, put this down on the kitchen table, take hold of an empty jug, and go off in search of a little more, for milk was the only nourishment that seemed to do my father much good.

I would then do the shopping and go out and buy a paper, which my mother would read to him while waiting for the doctor. I don't think my father was interested in the news. His thoughts were continually in his garden, wondering if the seeds he had planted needed watering. In the end he worried so much that one morning, after the doctor had been, my mother and I set off with a watering-can and came back exhausted with a bunch of parsley and a salad. When my father saw these trophies he took the parsley in his feverish hand and smelt it. A smile broke out on his drawn features. 'Are the seeds coming up?' he asked in a whisper.

'Not yet, but we watered them.'

'The salad 's a beauty!'

'Yes, it 's the first.'

'Oh, and the radishes?'

'Yes, they 're coming up, and the strawberries are in bud!' I exclaimed. 'Only I 'm afraid the slugs will be at them!'

'And now listen to this,' said my mother. 'There 's a piece of news. Mme Gontrel is in a terrible state. She thinks her husband has gone off with another woman. She hasn't seen him for two days. Riri keeps on asking for his balloon, and there 's not a penny left in the house.'

'Gone off with another woman!' repeated my father. Then winking: 'You see, Matilda, I was right to envy him!'

My mother looked shocked.

'A man with two children who still thinks of that sort of thing! It 's horrible!'

M. Gontrel's disappearance was the chief news in our street. Some were sorry for Mme Gontrel. Others claimed she richly deserved it. Didine, whose rum omelets I had not tasted for a long time, took M. Gontrel's side. She said he had probably gone off to be fiddler to a wedding in the country. Mme Maurer felt certain he had fallen in love. M. Campion, who drove a taxi, thought he had recognized M. Gontrel talking to a foreigner. Poor little Dédée Gontrel was ashamed to show herself in the street. She was obliged to go off with her mother to collect the sixpences when she sang in the courtyards of rich houses.

As each important day slipped by my father, emerging from his long periods of semi-consciousness, asked:

'And Gontrel, the rascal, has he come home yet?'

'No,' my mother answered with compressed lips, 'I doubt if he 'll have the face to show himself.'

My mother and I went to my father's factory to tell them about his illness and to draw his pay. Down by the Seine where the Americans had camped during the last years of the war were wide fields of beetroot. The many factories which had turned Clichy into a state of activity were now idle and falling to pieces. Those that by some accident were still working dismissed a few men every week. One felt that paralysis had touched this low ground watered by the majestic river. At my father's factory the foreman broke us the news that even if my father got better there would be no work for him. We crossed rather a big yard. Two or three men came to ask us news about my father, and then went about their business.

At the end of the fourth day the doctor prescribed bleeding by cupping glasses. It was to be done by a professional whose wife was a midwife. I went to call him. He lived next to the public wash-house. Two hours later he arrived with a wicker basket full of tiny bell-glasses shaped like the ones market gardeners use to grow their lettuces under. He went in to my father with all this clinking apparatus, lit a candle by the bedside, and with dexterity and gentleness placed the bells on my father's back, each with a piece of burning cotton wool inside. The skin rose and turned red. When there were about forty in position and my father's breathing made these ghastly things with their lurid lights dance one against the other, the man swept them away, and with a small instrument drew blood where each had been. The operation was horrible to watch. In the kitchen, as he was going, the man said:

'Tell the doctor it's hardly worth doing them again. They weren't very successful. We shall hurt him for nothing.'

My mother wrote to the Agnels at the Grand' Combe, to cousin Prosper Nègre, and to my Aunt Marguerite in London to say my father was very ill, though I do not think we expected any answer. His only relations were too far away. The doctor now told my mother that she was doing too much and must try and rest. She had put a mattress on the kitchen floor for me. This evening she would sleep till midnight and I would watch my father.

We were in the middle of a heat-wave. I was writing at a table. Up through the open window came the young voices of the bicycle enthusiasts, who had come in force. They were laughing, ringing their bells, making figures of eight, shouting to distant friends. The evening dragged oppressively. I looked across to my father. His face was getting a pinched look, his nose seemed to be growing more important, and I found it difficult, looking at him, to remember his everyday appearance. His hair, stuck together with perspiration, made him a skull-cap like a cardinal, and his hands, normally so large and red, had turned white and almost thin. His heavy breathing cut into the joyful cries of the youths in the street. Eventually the cyclists went off in a cloud of dust. The Spaniard let down his steel shutter. My father opened his eyes and asked:

'Where's Matilda?'

'Asleep next door. Do you want her?'

'No, it isn't that. Only it's the first time I've woken up and not seen her next to me.'

I gave him something to drink and he turned his face to the wall. His neck was terribly thin. He murmured:

'Oh, the heat! The heat!'

One now heard the lamp-lighter treading past, shutters being closed, doorkeepers taking in their chairs. A certain Mme Camille, one of our tenants, was playing the piano with two fingers. She would begin:

'C'est mon homme——'

Her mother, leaning out of the window to catch the last breezes of the night, continued the words of the famous song:

'Ce n'est pas qu'il soit beau, mais je l'aime. C'est idiot!'

Her voice brought other housewives to their not yet shuttered windows, and one heard:

'Good night, Mme Jeanne. What heat!'

Camille, louder with two fingers and trying to drown her mother's conversation, went on:

'Mon seul bonheur, sur cette terre, c'est mon homme!'

Finally they also, beaten by a desire to sleep, closed their shutters, and the clock on the state schools struck midnight. Distantly one heard the Sacré Cœur booming over Montmartre, which would now be waking up to tangos and fox-trots. The terrace at Wepler's would be full. Grooms would be crying out for taxis. The roundabouts would be turning in the avenue. I felt very little, and very afraid alone with my father. Only fifteen years old was the little Madeleine, but already she had lost her two brothers, been through a long war, and was now meeting the spectres of illness and unemployment. . . . My father was asleep, but his breathing was raucous.

Fairly early in the morning two policemen on bicycles stopped in front of the house where Marguerite Rosier lived and asked for Mme Gontrel. This news was quickly disseminated. There had been a rumour since yesterday that Mme Gontrel had gone to the police. She had spent a whole night in Montmartre, prowling round the cafés outside which he generally played his violin, questioning waiters, street singers, flower sellers, and taxi-cab drivers in the hope of getting to know something. He had not been seen since the night he failed to return home. Mme Gontrel thought it better to confide in the police. If he had gone off with another woman, at least she would know the truth. The police had begun their inquiry. Everybody became interested in this miserable man whom they used to chase from café to café, from street bench to street bench when he sank down on them in the early hours exhausted.

The two policemen remained about an hour with Mme Gontrel. One of them went to fetch a red taxi-cab from the Porte Clichy. We next saw Mme Gontrel, without Riri in her arms, coming down with the policemen and getting into the taxi. She was

very white, and refused to say anything to anybody.   Riri and
Dédée were entrusted to a neighbour.

About an hour later she came back.

The police had driven her to the morgue where, among tramps
and unfortunates thrown up by the muddy waters of the Seine,
she saw behind glass a poor wizened figure, green and black, his
head bashed in, a celluloid windmill peeping out of his torn jacket.

He had been attacked and robbed by apaches on the fortifications.   Knowing his habits they had lain in wait for him during
the cold dawn as he was coming back from the rue Blanche,
where the night clubs had thrown out their hot jazz melodies.
His body had been found in a lonely spot where thistles and tall
tough grass, blown by a sweeping wind, had hidden him for
four days.   His violin was discovered half a mile away, in a ditch
by the railway that ran past Louis Duparc's fateful café.

This story swept through the street.   My father, as he always
did, turned to my mother and asked:

'And Gontrel, the rascal, has he come home yet?'

My mother told him what had happened.   He turned to me
and said:

'Madelon, you must be very careful at night near those fortifications.   Matilda, don't let the little girl go to Paris any more alone.'

He thought things over a minute and added:

'Poor fellow, and fancy everybody accusing him of going off
with another woman!   How will the children get on now?
And poor Riri?   How sorry I am for them!'

The next morning my father, opening his eyes, looked at my
mother, who was bending over him, and took her hand.   He
looked at her with a gentleness and affection which touched her
and said:

'You're still there, Matilda?'

'Why, yes, of course, Émile.'

Now he was at the point of death.   It was still very early,
and we were in our night-gowns, not quite understanding.   Later
he became conscious again, looked round him, stretched out a
hand and shook with extreme violence the chair we normally
used by his bedside, called my mother's name, and sank back for
the last time.

Émile—Milou, the strong, the strongest of all the Gals, was
dead.

17

MY mother had gone out. I was alone and rather afraid of the recumbent white form, so very tall and still, which I could see on the bed through the open door. The heat-wave continued, but we only had the kitchen now. I was impatient for my mother to come back. 'Mother!' I called out. She would be the only one to hear me from now on. Why was she so long? I wanted to escape, to run into the street, to hear some noise, to see people. At last, my mother returning, I threw myself into her arms in such a fever that she thought something must have happened. She could not believe that merely to see her alive could give me such immense joy.

I had been writing some addresses on envelopes with wide black edges. I pictured one of them being delivered at the house half-way up the mountain at the Grand' Combe, and I let fall a tear at the thought of Aunt Eugénie exclaiming 'That must be our poor Milou who is dead!' I had addressed one to my Aunt Marguerite in England, but my mother had not wanted me to send one to Marie-Thérèse, saying it would be bad taste after not being on speaking terms for so long.

She now told me to go to the post office at the corner of the street, a sub-post office where the woman spent all her time threading pearls on brass wire to make garlands of flowers and leaves to decorate funeral wreaths. I was to post the letters and order a wreath on which there was to be a message in gold letters on white ribbon.

Our funds were now very low. The doctor and the chemist had delved deeply into the savings of the provident ant that was my mother.

Mme Maurer, pointing out that I was still very young, and that we had no family to help us, advised my mother to ask the parish to bury my father. This suggestion shocked my mother profoundly. She hated to think that my father would lie in a coffin of white wood instead of one made of oak. Mme Maurer said

that the second-class funeral we could afford for my father would
in no way help him, whereas the money we saved might make
all the difference to the continuation of our lives.   This hard logic
convinced my mother, who was obliged to ask two neighbours
to go with her to the town hall and swear that we were paupers.
She had been doing this when, alone in the kitchen, seeing my
father stretched out under the white sheet in the adjoining room,
I had been so frightened.   At all events the town hall accepted
my mother's request, and the funeral was fixed for 9th April in
the afternoon.

On my return from posting the letters and ordering the wreath
a young man called at our flat and handed my mother her identity
papers, in which she had put my father's death certificate and
almost all her money.   She gave a cry of relief, not yet having
discovered this important loss.   The young man then told her
how unwise she had been to put her money in her private papers,
'for if I had been dishonest,' he said, 'I would have thrown away
the documents to hide the theft of the money.'

Abashed by this sensible remark made in a strong male voice
my mother and I glanced at each other, conscious of what our
future was going to be without a man's protection and advice.
The young stranger, before we could thank him, doffed his cap
and was gone down the stairs.   We hurried into the kitchen to
comment on the news, but almost immediately the door bell
rang a second time.

A young workman stood before us cap in hand.   He had come
in the name of all my father's companions at the factory.   My
mother said to him: 'Would you like to see him,' and then
in a whisper, as if my father might be listening: 'He's
in there.'

I could not accustom myself to the tallness of the white figure
whose presence so entirely filled the room.   The young workman looked at my father a moment, then, going close to him,
tapped him amicably on the shoulder.   He then turned and
taking a long envelope from his coat pocket handed it to my
mother, who discovered one hundred francs and a long list of
names.   With tears in her eyes she read: 'Giraud, five francs;
Dupis, five francs; M. Dumay, foreman, ten francs.'   The young
workman said:

'We didn't know at the time, but we thought you might be in

trouble. The factory is closing down on Saturday. We shall all be out of work. For me, being young, it doesn't matter so much. I 'll find something. But for those'—he turned and nodded in the direction of my father under the white sheet—'of his age it will be pretty tough. He went just in time, madam, I promise you.'

Then going to the door, after a last salutation to my father, a movement full of dignity, he shook us by the hand and took his leave.

As soon as we were alone my mother carefully closed the kitchen door. I did not leave her shadow and she guessed the fear in me. She spoke loudly, put the lamp close to me, and gave me the hem of my black dress to sew. She said:

'All the men of the family have gone, your two brothers and now—him.'

We slept on the mattress on the kitchen floor, I very close to my mother; but soon she, alarmed by the strength and vividness of my nightmares, got up and lit a lamp, giving me a sleeping draught.

The next day the sun came out hotter than on any day.

Mme Maurer crossed the street to see us, and my mother told her about my night. I think my mother was seriously worried about me. She could sense that with my father having been so long in the adjoining room, the heat increasing, she and I imprisoned in this tiny foetid kitchen, I would soon lose my nerve.

'Let her be!' exclaimed Mme Maurer in her deep incisive voice. 'It 's only in watching death that she 'll learn to live. She 's sensitive, has a vivid imagination—don't give her sleeping draughts! There are so many people in this world who are as callous as paving-stones. Your little Madeleine will make her own life. Let her cry, and fear, and go through all the range of emotions. That 's life. Crying and laughing. Then, when she 's my age, she will have a range of experiences and emotions to draw on. She will be sorry for people who suffer. She will cry when they cry, and perhaps comfort them. Hide nothing from your little Madeleine, and if later her luck changes, she 'll know something about both worlds.'

The day dragged on.

Towards evening the coffin was brought. My mother made me stay in the kitchen, where the noise of furniture being moved hammered at my heart. Then, towards eight, two little men, all in black, arrived. We were so surprised neither my mother nor I could speak. They were my Uncle Ernest and Henri Toulouse, who had travelled half through the night and all through the hot day to guard my father during his last night. Uncle Ernest said:

'My wife Eugénie didn't want her Milou, full of sunshine, to be put into the cold earth of Paris without somebody from his family being there.'

He was so upset that he sat down, and he was so tired with the journey and the different air that his head drooped like an ill bird. My mother took pity on them both. She said:

'I 'll watch my husband. Go and have a good sleep and come back to-morrow.'

The next day M. Gontrel came home, also in a pauper's coffin.

It was the usual thing, on the last day, for the coffin to be put out in the entrance hall of the house, with the wreaths placed on it and some crape on either side of the front door with a notice edged in black giving the details. The neighbours, even those who were indifferent, uncovered their heads, the women made the sign of the cross, and thus paid a last tribute to the tenant who was about to leave the house, the street, and even that part of Paris where he had been a familiar figure.

M. Gontrel lay in the entrance hall opposite ours. The tenants collected some money and bought a wreath, which they put on the coffin. It was the only one. Mme Gontrel, dressed in weeds that had been lent to her, wandered about with Riri clasped to her breast. Dédée, blacker than black, recalling her father, recounted the details to anybody who liked to listen. The doorkeeper, so often insulted by the violinist, devotedly arranged the material round the coffin, not daring to polish the stairs or to use her broom.

My father, resting on two chairs opposite, thus faced the man whose lot he had momentarily envied. The hearse which came to fetch M. Gontrel at two returned for my father at four. Uncle Ernest and Toulouse, Marguerite Rosier and Louis Duparc, my mother and I, walked behind. When I imagined my father bringing home his lettuces, my heart broke, but my mother, hidden behind her long black veil, remained dry eyed. The sun burned into our dyed clothes. As my father was being lowered into the grave a goods train, passing by Louis's café, let out its strident whistle. Louise was here now. Her grave was a month old, and she had begun the alley which the violinist and my father were finishing. In the middle was M. Neveu, whose son had died from so fiercely beating his horse. All these neighbours continued to be neighbours in death as perhaps they would be on the day of judgment.

When we returned home, the fresh air in a great draught now sweeping through the little flat, my Uncle Ernest, looking very small in his Sunday clothes, could hardly wait to unbutton his pointed boots. He put more comfortable ones on, and, as he and Toulouse were going to take the night train, we all had dinner in a little restaurant of the Boulevard Victor-Hugo.

In front of the bottle of red wine and the steak and fried potatoes set out on white paper, we began to talk of the Grand' Combes. Ernestine had a little girl, Henriette, just a few months old. Toulouse was very proud. Luck, too, was coming his way. Irma had lost her fiancé during the war, and her parents, wishing to retire, had let their beautiful café to Toulouse, who for ever had abandoned the trade of hairdresser for that of café owner. Ernestine sat like a queen at the cash-desk, and soon her little Henriette would be playing round her skirts. Oh, how happy they were! Uncle Ernest intended to work four more years down the mine and then retire to his mountain fastness, half-way to heaven, with a grand-daughter to cherish.

Uncle Ernest asked my mother for a walking-stick with an ivory handle which my father had used when he broke his leg. My mother opened a drawer of the sideboard. Here were my father's razors and half a dozen square packets of tobacco. She gave them to my uncle, who opened a little black bag and slipped them in. They both kissed my mother and gave her a final word of consolation. I watched them going down the street, my uncle wearing a curious round-shaped hat, leaning on his stick, not quite used to the feel of it, turning round for a last good-bye, and then he and Toulouse suddenly hurrying to catch the train that would take them back to their eternal sunshine.

18

MME DUVILLE'S pupils were taking part in a state examination which, if they passed it, would give them a recognized diploma. I had missed so many classes that I had no chance of success, but Mme Duville advised me to compete for the experience. She said it would give me greater confidence next time.

Girls from all over Paris gathered in the big examination hall overlooking La Nation, a very large grey square near the Gare de Lyon, which just now was preparing for a gay and noisy spring fair. The weather had changed. The heat-wave, breaking up violently, had been followed by intense cold. Anybody would have thought it was mid winter. In the morning, during our first hour, snow fell thickly on the booths of the fortune-tellers and the coco-nut shies.

We all filed out for lunch together and, of course, few of us knew this distant part of Paris. Gipsies were tugging at ropes, hammering, and putting the machinery in order. It seemed to me the coldest, most miserable place I had ever seen. The gipsies, seeing us, decided it was time for lunch, and hurried into nice warmed caravans, where babies yelled and from which smoke rose in homely spirals. We, the future shorthand typists, thought of our hard-boiled eggs and sandwiches, wondering where we could shelter from the snow to eat them. A piece of tarpaulin, beating in the wind, revealed a covered-up roundabout. Ostriches, piglets, and various other animals which on bank holiday would turn swiftly to music, shone with gay paint. We looked at each other knowingly, and squeezed through, clambering on the backs of animals and birds. We laughed, I the loudest of any. I was deliriously happy with girls of my own age. All the horrors of the last three weeks rushed out of my system. Perched on the back of a giraffe I must have looked like a scarecrow in my black clothes.

Going home in the evening the snow seeped through my shoes. I was soaked, and when I took my jacket off my arms were stained with cheap dye, but nothing seemed to matter quite so much. I told my mother that half-way through the dictation I had given up. She sympathized and said that for the next few days the important thing was to eat and sleep.

The sun came back on Sunday, and we went to the allotment. Between the various rows of newly planted vegetables we could not help imagining my father, his yachting cap at an angle, watering. His spade, the handle made smooth by the sweat of his hands, was carefully put away in the tool-house. The most recently bought packet of seeds was just as he had left it on the rickety table. The peas were coming up nicely. He would have been delighted. But how could we be expected to tear up the weeds which were already stifling the vegetables? A new man had taken over M. Neveu's garden. He welcomed us in a polite way and started to talk, leaning over the hedge which separated the two gardens. He said he was a bachelor, living with an unmarried sister and his mother, and that he was quite willing to advise us, and even help with the digging. My mother, though touched, was vexed at his insistence, but fortunately, as he was trying to climb over the fence, somebody else came along.

Mme Maurer advised us to sell my father's tools and his clothes to give us a better start in our new life. His tool-box was of iron and very heavy, and he used to keep it at the bottom of our only wardrobe, so we were rather glad to get rid of it. There were hammers and pliers which we took to the merchants in the Boulevard Victor-Hugo, who handled them disdainfully, and gave us a few pence for treasures which my father considered amongst his most valuable possessions. His hats were in a bandbox given him by Marie-Thérèse—a strange collection consisting of a bowler, a panama, a straw boater with a black ribbon clipped to the brim and which could be fastened to the buttonhole on windy days, and a tall silk hat doubtless emanating from my Uncle Louis's rich employer. At the bottom was a tiny beret with a red topknot belonging to my baby brother. My mother, at the sight of this, cried. She would not sell it, preferring to burn something which might have made strangers laugh. She then went through my father's shoes and his suits which we laid out on the bed, where they looked like men without heads.

My mother's conversation, meanwhile, showed a marked change of tone. She did not mention my father's bad habits any more, but said briskly:

'Your Uncle Louis gave us this piece of grey suiting. I think it came from one of the smart tailors in London. You know, a man needs to be tall and slim to wear a suit well. Your Uncle Louis, for instance, though he is supposed to be a terror with the women, never had your father's distinction!'

I looked up surprised at the gay, proud air, and answered:

'Oh, yes, my father had something.'

The next day we went to pay Dr. Ravaud. He looked at me and said:

'The little girl has become an almost too good-looking young woman. What are you going to do with yourself?' Then, remembering that I had attended shorthand school: 'Why, yes, of course, a shorthand typist. A more difficult profession than most people believe.'

He put the money in his waistcoat pocket, and took us to the door with a mixture of goodness and indifference.

We now turned seriously to the future.

My mother had lost all her customers. They had gone elsewhere when my father fell ill, though we might have lost them anyway because of the slump. As usual Mme Maurer made a suggestion. This woman had become a great influence in our lives for good and bad. She was a careful reader of small advertisements in the newspapers, chiefly for her son who was looking for something different, and had noticed that a lot of women were asking for a person to sew and mend at their homes. My mother answered one of these and was engaged by a regular officer's wife in the military district of the Motte-Piquet, from eight in the morning to eight at night, for lunch and ten shillings a day. She was on the point of setting out one day when a telegram came. I remember her standing by the door, wearing her large hat. She exclaimed:

'Aunt Marguerite's husband is dead!'

The paper fell from her hands.

'Think of it!' she whispered, turning quite white. 'We are both widows within twelve days!'

'Then I shall have to start all over again!' I said dismally.

She looked at me quickly and answered:

'This isn't the morning for me to get the sack. I must go.
We'll talk about it to-night.' She ran to the window, pulled
back the curtain, and continued: 'If it isn't raining! First one
thing and then another. I did want this hat to last six months.
We might have a bit more money then.' She fingered the brim
angrily. 'This cheap stuff simply melts in the rain!'

The next day there was a letter. My uncle had died very
suddenly. He had complained of feeling tired. His heart was
thumping. He stretched out a hand to pick up a book, and that
was the end. My aunt said I must be patient. As soon as she
had put her affairs in order she was coming to Paris and would
talk it over.

I therefore looked round for another job, and found one in a
factory in the Boulevard Victor-Hugo.

In a huge office sat a great quantity of women of every age and
quality, some from Paris, some from Clichy, all unbelievably gay.
We used to arrive at 8.15, and from then till 8.30 the entire company, in a deafening chatter, talked about their love affairs; and
when the head of the department arrived, breaking through these
waves of femininity, some hurried to their typewriters, others
to the accounts department, and the rest to other duties like
the telephone exchange. It was just a riot of cool white or
coloured blouses. The fashion or *bon ton* of the place was ruled
by the four sisters Maréchal. The eldest, Mlle Arlette, of the
accounts department, sat in front of M. Piétry, the chief accountant, whose beautiful white hands passed through his fine black
beard in a series of slow and amorous caresses. M. Piétry came
from Paris, and had the dignity of a doctor or a notary. Though
he was slightly affected in his speech and manners he was always
gracious, especially with the eldest Maréchal who, emboldened
by her situation of favourite, had successively brought her sisters
Edith, Adrienne, and Gabrielle each to rule a section of the office.

Arlette was a lovely girl who, extremely aware of her importance, treated the rest of us with the slightly condescending
goodness of the morganatic wife of a grand duke. Her three
sisters were lumped together under the respectful title of the
'young ladies Maréchal.' All dressed as Arlette dressed. Arlette
gave the tone, first to her sisters, then to the office as a whole.
When, on Monday morning, Mlle Arlette and her three sisters
arrived, marching very close together, everybody jumped up to

see what they were wearing. They must have spent the whole
of every Sunday recasting a hat or making a new blouse. The
fashion in hats that spring was for immense bows of tulle against
a dark crown. There was nothing easier than to make oneself a
pretty model—one chose a frame of light *sparterie*, covered it
with dark-coloured silk, then brightened up the whole thing
with a great blob of vivid tulle. The first Monday I was there
the Maréchal sisters, all four of them, turned up in black hats
with masses of coral tulle, airy, crisp, full of life and sweetness.
The eldest, tall in any circumstances, seemed a giantess with this
extra height. Edith, less tall, was sheltered from the arrows of
the waiting multitude by the fact that she kept her hierarchical
position of one step behind her sister, covered by her wing, so to
speak. The two young ones immensely enjoyed the obvious
commotion they were making. These extraordinary hats, after
leaving the heads of their wearers, were hung up on hat-stands,
where they entirely covered up a great quantity of sombre male
headgear. Their flashing airiness brought coral flames to the dull
brown walls. One was for ever looking up from one's typewriter
to admire them.

The Maréchals lived near the café which Louis and Louise
Duparc once owned. The four young women crossed the whole
of Clichy four times a day—in the morning and the evening, and
back and forth for lunch. Dominating the crowd by their tallness as they dominated the office by their importance, one saw
their hats waving up and down like pink sails on a choppy sea.
Their rhythm was perfect. I think they even kept in step. I
used to go with them as far as the Place de la République. From
here I ran home for lunch. Afterwards I waited for them on the
kerb. Unfortunately I could not rival their gay hats and blouses,
being immutably in black. I was obliged to make up for it by
being the happiest and lightest hearted of all, and my laughter
rose in ripples even higher than their tulle.

Once or twice a week my mother stayed at home. On one of
these mornings as I was coming back for lunch I saw her leaning
out of the window, smiling, making signs for me to hurry. I
raced up the stairs and as soon as I arrived she pointed to the bed,
where she had laid out a delicious white blouse with the slightest
but prettiest black markings. She said she was revolted to see
my youth drowned in this cruel mourning, and she did not mind

what the neighbours thought.   I put the blouse on immediately.
My heart truly beat with joy, and I rushed back to the Maréchals
to be suitably admired.

On the days my mother was not at home I could not stand
being in the house.   I used to go anywhere to escape from my
thoughts.   There were some people called Breton, who had
bought many of my father's clothes.   I told them during the
lunch hour how impossible it would be for us to go on with the
garden.   M. Breton, his little boy on his knees, put in: 'But it's
very difficult to get allotments just now.   All the spare land is
being built on.   You're really very lucky.'

'We would be glad to get rid of it,' I answered, 'but there's
my father's little summer-house.   I would want a hundred francs
for that.'

'A hundred francs,' repeated M. Breton.   'Yes, it is a lot of
money.   What do you think, Jeanne and Simon?'

Jeanne was his wife, and Simon the little boy on his knee.
His wife said nothing, but the husband, putting his son down,
opened a drawer and brought out a note.   'Really, Madeleine,
would you sell me the garden for a hundred francs?'

'Certainly!' I answered.

'Oh, how happy I am!' he exclaimed.   'Here's the money.
I shall go right away.'

Thus fell the last link with my father.

That evening I went to fetch my mother at the underground
station.   She looked very glad to see me, even proud, as if she
liked people to know I was her daughter.   I said I had sold the
garden and the summer-house.   She looked at me with admiration and exclaimed: 'Perhaps you'll have a good head for business?   Who knows?'   As soon as we arrived home my mother
took off her mourning clothes and put on a lilac dressing-gown,
in which rather old-fashioned colour she was still amazingly
pretty.   She seemed very pleased with her day's work, saying
that her employer, Mme Laparge, had great quantities of silk and
satin put by since before the war, which she was now anxious to
utilize.   They had spent hours inventing models for blouses and
dresses, the rich materials massed on the dining-room table,
Mme Laparge's two children doing their lessons in a corner.
During the afternoon Mme Laparge's sister Yvonne had arrived.
Yvonne, said my mother, was so beautiful that when she came

into a room one could hardly believe one's eyes. She had started life as a mannequin, now had a house, almost a palace, of her own, with cabinet ministers, millionaires, and maharajahs at her feet. My mother had been introduced to her, and Yvonne had asked her to spend the next few days at her house helping the maid to remake some curtains. To celebrate the event my mother had brought me back some cakes which Mme Laparge's cook had given her at tea time, and some snippets of material to make dresses for my doll, for in spite of being so nearly grown up I still played with the doll I had taken to Marais, to the Grand' Combe, and to Blois.

The next evening, eager to hear about the beautiful Yvonne, I went again to meet my mother at the underground. She arrived up the steps with Ulysses, Mme Maurer's son, who appeared even more sombre than usual. When we reached the street bordered by the cemetery wall Ulysses, pointing to the tops of the tombs, said in a deep voice: 'That 's where I ought to be, Mme Gal. I can't go on living like this!' My mother was about to comfort him when we came upon a fine big woman cleaning the street with long rhythmic movements of a birch broom.

This was Mme Gaillard's sister!

We had passed her quite often without knowing who she was till one day we had heard her talking in Auvergnat with Léontine Valentin, and Léontine had introduced us. She wielded the birch broom as old Mme Valentin wielded the spindle or my mother the needle—expertly. Her semicircles were each of the same size to the fraction of an inch, and she produced a sort of lace fringe on either side of the road, using the water from the gutter to dampen her broom. She was affable. Her skirts were folded up against her wide hips, and there hung from her belt an enormous key in the form of the letter T with which she turned the water main to wash down the streets. She looked like a magnificent Flemish portrait, her blue eyes sparkling with fun and cleverness.

My mother's first day with Mme Laparge's sister had been quite astonishing—a magnificent private house behind the Étoile, where a butler had taken her into an immense linen-room. Here she had met Gracieuse, madame's maid from the Basque country, dark, with large black eyes and a lilting accent. My mother and Gracieuse were soon busy sewing. Madame was having all her curtains redone, and for this purpose had bought several hundred yards of white tulle. Gracieuse measured, cut, and ran up the seams, and when each curtain was ready the footman came to hang it up. The walls of the linen-room were composed, from floor to ceiling, of glass cupboards, in which one could see madame's dresses, coats, furs, and *négligés*—all these masterpieces from the most famous houses in Paris.

After they had been working all the morning like two busy bees, a bell rang. Madame had decided to get up. Gracieuse glided from glass case to glass case, deftly lifting finely pleated lingerie, a dress, shoes, a hat, ran in to madame, hurried back, went off again with something else. Punch, a little dog with bells round its neck, arrived, looked at my mother, wagged its tail, and hesitated to come further. The servants hated it for the extra work it gave them, its silly paws making marks on the polished floors which madame never considered sufficiently shiny.

Gracieuse came in and whispered:

'She's in her bath, Mme Gal. We've a clear hour. I'll show you her bedroom!'

The bedroom was all white, with enormous mirrors, a pink carpet, and a wide low bed covered with hand-made lace. Everything smelt delicious, was heady like the heart of a beautiful red rose.

Gracieuse made the bed, then expertly started to tidy, looking closely at each new thing. In front of the dressing-table she exclaimed:

'That's funny! She had her pearls and her emeralds on last night—with that blue dress! Personally I'd have worn my sapphires. Well, I suppose, she can do what she likes!'

Gracieuse flew lightly from object to object, talking all the while, delighted to feel that my mother was watching her wide-eyed, listening surprised and full of wonderment at her chatter. 'Now give me a hand with the white bearskin rug. Madame rubs her feet into it, right as far as the animal's skin. Apparently it gives her a sensation!' She had one ear cocked in the direction of the bathroom just in case madame might be needing her. It was 'she' and 'her' all the time, and my mother was never quite sure whether it was from admiration or sarcasm. 'Now, Mme Gal, run into the little *salon* behind you and fetch her fur coat. You must take it down to the linen-room. It's a lovely coat, you

know, and so soft, though she has even better ones. But I must
say I look beautiful in this one. Ah! It's heavy, isn't it?
But wait till you try it on and you'll be surprised how light it
feels!'

My mother had taken up the mink in both hands. It smelt of
amber, of wild beast, and of a woman who is happy and loved.
My mother drew the skin close to her face and, shutting her eyes,
breathing deeply, seemed to inhale a whole world that surprised
her. Curiously she stroked the skin with its soft, dark, shining
fur, which lay down obediently under her caress, but quickly
sprang back with pride as soon as she removed her hand. It
was as fine as her lace. The putting together of the many skins
to make this sumptuous object had required the same sort of
skill as had gone into her blouses. My mother had the admiration of one craftsman for the work of another. Gracieuse arrived,
and seeing her in this trance exclaimed: 'My poor Mme Gal, if
you go into raptures so easily we'll never get anything done!'
She took the mink from my mother, bundled it on the table, and
opening one of the glass cupboards brought out a squirrel cape.
'There!' she said. 'This is my favourite, and look at the adorable
muff that goes with it!' She threw the cape over her shoulders,
and asked: 'Don't you think it suits me?'

My mother said, with compressed lips: 'It's certainly a lovely
cape.' She was never a person to pay compliments unnecessarily,
and she thought Gracieuse merely pretentious. They went back
to their sewing, and about an hour later madame arrived asking
for a pair of shoes. She said good morning pleasantly to my
mother, who remained once more overcome with admiration for
this woman's strange beauty. Not a word could my mother
utter. While Gracieuse was finding the shoes madame plunged
her hands into the mountains of tulle, and my mother watched
her white fingers, heavily ringed, playing in the soft whiteness
of the billowing material.

'I'm going dancing at Ermenonville,' she said. 'I shall be
back at three. I shall only just have time to dress. Please see
that everything is ready. And, by the way, if M. X telephones
tell him that I'm lunching with Mme d'Antin. Good-bye,
Gracieuse. Thank you for coming, Mme Gal.'

She was gone in an instant, leaving a trail of perfume right
through the house.

I

Gracieuse sighed deeply.

'Well, that does give us a breathing space. Let's go and see if the cook has got lunch ready.'

In a light and spacious kitchen Maria, the cook, a Basque like Gracieuse, was rattling pans on the range whilst talking to 'fat John,' the footman, a lumbering Bourguignon peasant. He had been chosen by madame because he looked so honest, but nothing cured him of his heavy gait and thick accent. He rubbed, polished, swept, and generally did the heavy work, and was occasionally sent to the front door when the butler was anxious to get rid of an unwanted caller. They had just sat down when the good-looking Marius, madame's chauffeur, arrived back from Ermenonville. Olive-skinned, big eyes, and a dazzling smile, he looked magnificent in his black uniform. Maria and Gracieuse dreamt of winning his heart—Maria made him special dishes which she served him herself, bending over his shoulder so that her face brushed his cheek. The conversation, which had creaked somewhat when 'fat John' was the only man, now became a duel between Maria and Gracieuse, stories about madame to excite his interest, intimate details which made my mother blush, about madame and her lovers.

Over coffee Marius said nonchalantly:

'Oh, you know, if I were willing . . . but I never have liked these over-washed and over-scented women. There's such a thing as exaggerating cleanliness. A female should have a female smell. Do you get me?'

Gracieuse and Maria, momentarily allied, smiled at each other. They were each a point up. My poor mother, very flushed, looking down at her cup, thought: 'Is it possible? Could any man not want *her*?' To hear a woman so magnificently beautiful discussed, undressed, sullied, trodden under foot by a chauffeur revolted my mother who, by class solidarity, should have been on his side; but my mother was never proud of being poor. Her one idea was to climb out of the trough.

Maria was saying disdainfully:

'When I was cook at the Comtesse de —— that was another matter, but of course with people like *her*'—and she jerked her head in the vague direction of madame's bed—'it's different, isn't it? Any man who is rich enough can have her. She's really only a prostitute. And there's another thing. With real ladies you don't need to worry so much about the tradesmen's bills. One can make a sauce with two dozen eggs. They 're not a bit surprised. They 've known that sort of thing all their lives; but with these ex-officers' daughters, who five years ago had to save every penny . . . do you get my meaning, Mme Gal?'

'The same here,' said Gracieuse. 'Do you suppose anything ever comes my way with all her poor relations? She gives all her dresses to her sister's little girl. The family has no money at all. You can't have any admiration, can you, for somebody who was as poor as yourself?'

'Poorer,' said Maria.

'And doing what she does!' exclaimed Marius. 'Why, I reckon there 's not much difference between that and walking the streets——'

'Filthy!' said Maria. 'Some more coffee, Mme Gal?'

'Still, in September we go to Biarritz,' exclaimed Maria, pushing back her chair. 'That 's something.'

Back in the linen-room Gracieuse unhooked madame's dress and ironed it. A parcel had just come from the dressmaker Jenny. She undid the paper, opened the long white box, and drew out from folds of tissue-paper an afternoon dress made of cherry-coloured satin. Her critical eye examined it and she said: 'She 'll look stunning in that! Now I wonder who it 's in honour of?' She was starting to put it away when the front door bell rang. John could be heard opening, and a moment later madame called for Gracieuse. In less than half an hour madame, dressed differently from head to foot, went off, driven by the good-looking Marius, to a *thé dansant*. From this amazing day my mother brought me a pair of silk stockings which Gracieuse gave her, pearl-grey as the fashion then was. They were the first I had seen, and I wore them on Sundays.

At last I had something to talk about at the office. The four Maréchal sisters almost fainted with envy. Their favoured position seemed to them ridiculously trivial. Disenchantment stole into the heart of Arlette, the beautiful eldest, who began to treat M. Piétry with less regard.

My mother gradually recovered from her first surprise, and when she went back to the Motte-Piquet Mme Laparge, measuring and cutting the *crêpe de Chine* on the dining-room table, talked freely about her sister.

'She's happy enough for the moment, but when she was a young married woman her husband chose the ugliest women in Paris to be unfaithful to her with, and gave her such thrashings! She has certainly got her own back on men since then!'

'And is the husband dead?' asked my mother.

'No, alas, very much alive!' answered Mme Laparge. 'He goes to see her sometimes, and we are all so very afraid she will go back to him. People are so curious, aren't they? Luckily we have a grand ally. She's quite crazy about dancing, and I think that keeps her mind off her husband. It serves our purpose in other ways. She looks in here occasionally between a tango and a fox-trot. Then on Sunday nights she comes for dinner. She simply adores a stew but, of course, she couldn't ask Maria to serve her one because the servants would think she was being stingy. Stews are absolutely not possible when one has servants and a situation to keep up. None of her friends would dare admit they like anything so cheap. So here, every Sunday evening, we have the family stew and my sister Yvonne is as happy as a little girl, and we are just as glad to have her with us.'

My mother and Mme Laparge talked endlessly in this way. M. Laparge, of very humble stock, had passed all the hardest examinations, and now occupied a very high post in the senior naval college. He was one of those French technicians who think merely in terms of examinations, and was tutoring his eight-year-old son to follow in his difficult steps. Their little girl was not pretty, but her ambition was to become a *demimondaine* like her aunt. As she was exclusively dressed in her aunt's lovely things, which my mother soon learnt to arrange, it was presumably difficult for her not to think along these lines.

Mme Laparge had a slight limp. The family had been coming home by underground from a circus one evening when Mme Laparge, imagining that her son had been left on the platform, rushed out after the train had started, and broke an ankle and an arm. Her children had, of course, been quietly sitting with their father in the compartment. This accident had tired her heart. Though only thirty she was beginning to feel the first pangs of disenchantment. Her middle-class existence with a husband who was affectionate but neither good-looking nor rich and, in her opinion, a bore, made her increasingly envious of her sister

Yvonne. In fact we all began to consider Yvonne as the one person in the world we would like to be.

There were apparently lots of cousins with places in the country who invited the two sisters for week-ends, and as M. Laparge urged his wife to go in the hope of seeing her get better, my mother's chief business was to make a wardrobe for these country visits. Even when Mme Laparge was away my mother went to the house to sew and look after the linen. When M. Laparge was there my mother would make his lunch. He would say: 'A steak without sauce, if you please, Mme Gal. Why do people put rich sauces over their food? Animals would not thank you for a *Béarnaise* with their pieces.'

On these occasions he would often arrive reading a letter from his wife.

'My poor Mme Gal,' he would exclaim, 'do listen to this.' He read a few lines from the letter. 'To think that at her age she cannot even make her participles agree! A mistake in spelling makes me ill for the whole day. It's so easy to write correctly, and yet it's extraordinary how few women can write a letter in French. Do they think that the rules of grammar should be changed twice a day like their hats and their dresses? Women will never know how to write. A female is a female, Mme Gal, and nothing will ever change that. And all this slang! The word *chic*, for instance, and silly phrases like the *dernier cri*! There, my poor Mme Gal, my wife has made me all upset!'

My mother, afraid to say a wrong word, served the steak and kept silent. But she watched him with interest. Fair, insipid, blue eyes with a slight squint, his features lit up when he spoke, and yet he bored his wife. Now that she was away all his conversation was about her. He must have loved his wife very much—yes, in spite of her spelling and the fact that he thought all women rather silly. My mother, who perhaps would have been happy with such a husband, was touched by his eagerness to please.

When Mme Laparge came home he was overjoyed, but she, on the contrary, dreaming of pretty things, feminine things, was sullen. She said it tired her to climb the stairs, to order the meals, and to look after the children. 'Mme Gal,' she would say, 'you do it for me.'

M. Laparge blamed much of this on his sister-in-law, the lovely

Yvonne. He remembered that when Yvonne had been un-
happily married it had been he and his wife who had appeared
the happy ones, whereas now . . .

'Oh!' he would exclaim, 'how I hate these odious comparisons! Why are women never satisfied?'

One day when my mother was queueing for a ticket on the
underground a young woman wearing a plain but impeccably
cut tailor-made edged up and asked if she would buy hers at the
same time. They met several times after this, and my mother
and she would do part of their journey together.

The holidays were beginning. M. and Mme Laparge and the
two children were to spend a month in the château of an old
aunt. Mme Yvonne was preparing to close her Paris house
for the usual stay in Biarritz. Gracieuse having gone for a week
to her parents just outside Bordeaux, my mother took her place.
She came home quite miserable. My mother, with me continually in her mind, had certainly become as jealous as everybody
else of Yvonne's brilliant life. At the end of the week, when
Gracieuse came back, my mother gave her notice, and she was
walking rather dejectedly to the tube when she met the friend
for whom she had taken the ticket.

'What are you doing?' asked the young woman in the grey coat
and skirt.

My mother told her all about Mme Yvonne, and how depressed
she was at the thought of finding a new job in August.

'I'm just back from New York,' said her friend. 'I was
manicurist at the Ritz-Carlton, and now I'm doing the same
thing at the Hotel Crillon. Lots of my New York customers
come to ask for me here, and as they don't know their way about
Paris they take my advice on almost everything. One never can
tell. I might be able to help you. Come to the ladies' hairdressing at the Crillon to-morrow, and ask for Mlle Joubert. If
I don't turn up immediately you'll know I'm with a customer,
but I won't keep you waiting long. Good-bye, Mme Gal.'

When my mother arrived home that evening she found me in
bed with a high temperature. I had not lunched properly since
my mother started work, eating all the things that are bad for a
delicate digestion, like gherkins and cold ham. For a few days
I was seriously ill, the doctor warning me that I must take care;

but as he knew in saying it that I was too young and flippant to be reasonable when my mother was at work, he ended by patting me on the shoulder and adding: 'Thank goodness, you're young. You'll quickly get over it.'

My illness did not prevent my mother from going to her appointment. She had brushed her clothes with great care, and left me in bed with Émile Zola's *Bonheur des dames,* and my imagination quickly turned our room into a vast store full of rich brocades and ladies in Second Empire crinolines. I forgot all about lunching in this exquisite dream.

When my mother came home that night she told me that Mlle Joubert had introduced her to two American women who were looking for somebody to alter their dresses. In those days Paris fashions were much slower to cross the Atlantic or even the Channel. These two young American women had arrived with lots of dresses which were charming in New York but ridiculously out of date in Paris. They were heart-broken, saying that the shortness of their dresses made people look at their strange clothes and not at their faces. They were so pretty that normally they should have received many compliments.

The two young Americans and Mlle Joubert had an animated discussion in English. Then Mlle Joubert, acting as interpreter, explained all the details to my mother. Several trunks of dresses were to be urgently altered. Some would be cut to pieces to lengthen the others. Occasionally my mother would suggest something by signs, and then there would be cries of enthusiasm.

The two women had a large room and bathroom on the fifth floor. My mother would sew alternately in the bathroom or the bedroom, both rooms full of dresses.

One of the women was tall and fair, the other was small, chestnut, extremely quick in her movements. Miss Sarah was the tall one. She seldom spoke to my mother. She smiled a welcome, smiled through all her numerous fittings, smiled her pleasure and approbation, and jumping into the nearest of the twin beds was soon fast asleep like a child. My mother had been very shocked at first to see this beautiful creature walking completely naked about the apartment, but gradually she became accustomed to the pure lines of this living statue whose voice she seldom heard. Miss Amy would come in almost hidden by the boxes and parcels she had bought. She talked incessantly to anybody about anything, with the result that every hour she added new words to her French vocabulary. She would be quite worn out after these long shopping expeditions, but her eyes would glisten. Paris had got into her system. She breathed it, felt it, adored it. She would hurl all her packages on the bed on which Sarah was sleeping, and then give her a fierce shaking.

'Hi! Sarah! Wake up, it's wonderful!'

Sarah yawned, stretched her lovely limbs, and sitting up in bed would stroke the things Amy had brought back. Then Amy would run to my mother and say:

'Mme Gal, you simply must have Miss Sarah's blue dress ready for to-morrow night. Come early in the morning. Don't worry if we're asleep. Just make yourself at home and start to sew.'

Her French was not always of the best, but the words gushed out. Women have a sort of Esperanto when it comes to dresses and hats. The dictionary is quite inadequate. A ribbon or a length of muslin was to make a flounce, a piece of pink satin was to line a skirt, a lovely lace would become a tunic. Everything was clear, and the three women understood one another perfectly.

Towards five the languorous Sarah began to wake up. She took a bath, then sat quite naked at her dressing-table to do her hair. Putting the curling iron on an electric heater, she would proceed, wisp by wisp, till it seemed that her entire head was covered with tiny snails. She now made herself up and dressed with the slow deliberation of a woman at ease with her beauty. When she had put on her necklace, her rings, and her shoes, which she did with remarkable velocity, these things having been timed and calculated in advance, she would take a comb, and with short, quick, almost brutal movements shake out her little snails till her hair stood out in rays above her head like a golden sun.

Miss Amy put on an evening dress, and soon the two young women went off to dine and to dance in the Parisian night. The valet and the maids came to do the apartment, arrange the bed, put clean towels in the bathroom, and exchange a few words with my mother, who was tidying her needles, the cotton, and thread. Then finally my mother would go to the mirror where an hour earlier Miss Sarah had made herself so beautiful, and put on her black hat with the long black veil, comparing her tired, sad, and anxious features with those of the young and pretty American.

Now she left the hotel with a Paquin bandbox containing one

of Miss Sarah's dresses to be run up on the sewing-machine at home. I always waited for her at the underground. The light, gay hat-box made a curious contrast against the blackness of her widow's weeds. As soon as we were home I used to plunge my head into this cardboard box, knowing there would be some snippets for me. We would have something light to eat, and I would oblige her to come with me to the circus which, at this time of year, took possession of the Place de la République.

The next morning my mother went back to the Crillon. The maid let her in with a pass key. She went silently into the bathroom, took off her hat, which she hung next to the white bath wrap, and stole on tiptoe into the bedroom to fetch her work. Miss Amy murmured from under the sheets: 'Good morning, Mme Gal!' turned, and went back to sleep.

At midday my mother went to the little market behind the Faubourg Saint-Honoré, bought some fried potatoes and a few cherries, and, retracing her steps along the rue Boissy d'Anglais, turned right, and sat on a bench under the chestnut-trees of the Champs-Élysées, to share her lunch with the sparrows. An hour later she hurried along the thick carpeted corridor of the Crillon to the apartment, where the two young Americans were just starting to take an interest in life. They were drinking orange juice, followed by black coffee, and offered my mother a cup. Miss Amy dressed and went off in search of a ribbon or a piece of material. Miss Sarah dozed, tried on a dress, and dozed again till it was time to have her bath and curl her hair. After which, if the new dress was to her liking and she found herself pretty in it, she would blow a kiss to my mother like a little girl proud of her Sunday frock.

My illness had been quite serious. The doctor said that I must stay at home for a while. Accordingly my mother brought me home work in the Paquin bandbox. Once, when she was busy elsewhere, I was obliged to take a finished dress to the Crillon. The rue Royale seemed truly regal that evening, and the small page boy who took me up to the fifth floor in the lift, seeing me so wonder-struck, told me, to increase my surprise, that the gentleman with the white hair I had bumped up against was Mr. Lloyd George. Secretly I was hoping to find Miss Sarah and Miss Amy naked. They were both dressed, ready to go out, happy, extremely friendly. I hurried back into the street, paused to look

*I

at Maxim's. Night was falling, an elderly man spoke to me, frightened me, and made me run. My joyful expedition was rather spoilt, for like a rabbit I dived underground. Yet I was proud, very proud to be a young woman and to have been spoken to in the street.

That evening we received a letter from my Aunt Marguerite. She was coming to see us, arriving at Saint-Lazare the very next day. As my mother was working she told me to meet her. The only indication she gave me was that my aunt was very dark with blue eyes. My mother appeared to think that this combination was so rare that I should be able to pick my aunt out in the largest crowd. I arrived at the station feeling very uneasy. Most of the women wore wide grey coats and large comfortable shoes. Searching amongst the seemingly unattached women I saw one, still young, dressed entirely in black, with blue eyes. I advanced and queried: 'Aunt Marguerite?'

'Ah! My little Madeleine,' she answered. 'The last time I saw you you were three days old. It's thanks to me you're called Madeleine. I was so indignant when your mother wanted to call you Matilda that I thought, anything but that.'

'In that case why specially Madeleine?'

'A cousin with whom I was in love jilted me for a Madeleine.' She smiled.

'Where's your mother?'

'She's working. She couldn't come in time to meet the train, but she said that if we waited a moment she would do her best.'

'Then let's sit on a bench and wait.'

My Aunt Marguerite intrigued me. I rather liked her confidences. She went on, referring to the cousin who jilted her:

'Yes, it was a bit because of that I went to England, feeling like crying and not speaking a word of the language. The funny thing is that now, after fifteen years over there, I feel a stranger here. Do you think I've an accent?'

'I think you have, Aunt Marguerite. Perhaps it's the way you say things?'

'Possibly. Ah! there's your mother!'

19

THEY really were very much alike. The same height, extremely slim, pretty legs, but with that sad anxious look which gave them a not very amiable expression. One felt with my Aunt Marguerite, as with my mother, that the quick sarcasm was never far behind.

They kissed each other with pursed lips, still somewhat on the defensive, called a porter, and off we went after him in search of a taxi. I was enchanted by this unusual form of travel. We climbed to the Place Clichy, sped along the avenue, and passing through the toll-gate at the fortifications, bumped over the paving stones of Boulevard Victor-Hugo.

All the women of our street were leaning out of their windows to see Mme Gal's sister from England. There was a murmur of excitement as we drove up in the taxi. My poor aunt looked a trifle disconcerted, but her surprise turned to consternation when we took her up to our apartment. The scantily furnished room and kitchenette must have seemed a terrible come-down after her semi-detached villa in Beckenham. She looked round and said softly:

'My poor Matilda, I never imagined you were as poor as this!'

My mother was vexed and said proudly:

'There are lots of people much poorer than we are. There's Mme Gontrel, for instance, who even when she goes with Riri to Paris doesn't wear a hat. Besides, we haven't any debts!'

The two widows put their identical black hats with the black veils on my mother's bed. My aunt's luggage took up most of the bedroom. She was looking round, wondering what to say next, when Didine arrived with the most elegant leather bootees between finger and thumb.

'My friend of the rue Fontaine has made them a tiny bit on the short side,' she said to my mother, after a neighbourly smile to my aunt. 'I thought Madeleine would like them.'

265

My mother saw my enthusiasm.

'Try them on,' she said.

They were magnificent! The suppleness of the brightly coloured leather was a real joy. I blushed with contentment. Here I was half-way to the wide velvet hat. Just think of it! I was going to wear smart leather bootees like Didine, and my feet were smaller than hers. My heart thumped with happiness.

'Thank you! Thank you, Didine!' I said.

Her gesture struck me as even more magnanimous than the rum omelet feasts when I was younger. She laughed and said to my mother:

'Madeleine has always admired my bootees even before she was grown up. I wouldn't have liked anybody else to have them. By the way, Mme Gal, could you possibly let down the hem of a coat for me? I bought it from a friend. It's a very pretty model, but a trifle short.'

'Of course, Didine.'

'And you know, Mme Gal, I expect things are a bit hard for you just now. I'd love to help. I know lots of young women who need a good dressmaker. Well! It's getting dark. I must go off to work. It's a shame to think summer is nearly over, isn't it? I see there are oyster booths outside the cafés already.'

She looked round, obviously put out by my aunt's iciness. Then to me, still in the heaven of delight:

'The coat's with the doorkeeper. You'll go and fetch it, won't you, my little Madeleine? It's really so sweet of your mother to do it. Well, I must rush. Good night, Mme Gal, good night, madame. So long, Madeleine!'

As soon as she was gone my aunt looked up from a portmanteau she was unpacking and asked rather dryly:

'And what does *she* do for a living?'

'Oh,' said my mother, 'she's one of those awfully nice girls that do a bit of everything. You know what I mean?'

'I'm afraid I do. I notice you move in the most curious circles. I hardly think they can have a very good influence on your daughter unless, of course, you want her to do a bit of everything.'

'Don't be such a prude!' snapped my mother. 'Since Émile died life has been pretty tough, and it's a good deal thanks to a woman who is kept in a big way that Madeleine and I haven't starved. Oh, I'm not saying I've done marvels, but if it hadn't been for making dresses for *demi-mondaines* I just wonder where the rent would have come from! The trouble is that Madeleine is still too young and I'm not young enough. That's why my needle is at the service of anybody who appreciates it and can pay for it!'

My aunt was a bit shaken.

'I didn't know it was as bad as that,' she said in a less antagonistic voice, and not daring to look my mother in the eyes. 'You should have told me.'

'Some people have their pride,' said my mother. 'With you I went as far as I dared.'

The next day, on her way to work, my mother met Mlle Joubert in the tube. The two young Americans were apparently delighted with what she had done for them. Miss Sarah was a Hollywood starlet; Miss Amy was a trapeze artist. As they both had many friends in Paris they were having a gay holiday.

Mlle Joubert was the daughter of a former member of the Clichy fire brigade, who had been pensioned following an accident; he had, I think, fallen from the top of a ladder when a wall collapsed. The family lived in a tiny house with a garden near the Seine, and Mlle Joubert invited my mother, my aunt, and me to take coffee with them on Sunday.

The place proved delightful—pretty, clean, and well furnished. Mlle Joubert had obviously contributed most of it, and it was nice to see how she loved her parents. The fireman's leg was amputated below the knee, the trouser leg being fastened back with a safety-pin and the stump fitting into a piece of wood which narrowed off into an iron circle that echoed when it touched the floor boards. Mme Joubert was large and perfectly happy. Her only fear was that her daughter might go back to America. My Aunt Marguerite and Mlle Joubert discussed life in London and New York, and M. Joubert, tired by female conversation, stumped off to plant his cabbages.

As soon as he was gone Mme Joubert began to talk about fortune-tellers, saying that her daughter's journey to New York had been clearly foretold. My mother described how Mme Garnier, the bone-setter at Blois, and Léontine, Mme Valentin's daughter at St. Ouen, had both predicted that she would soon be a widow, and that I should go to England and become famous.

While she spoke Mlle Joubert, sitting by the window, would peep through the net curtain at her father going about the garden on his steel ring, and her eyes were full of affection. Suddenly she said:

'Yes, mother, you 're quite right. They told you I would go to America; but though I 've lived in New York and now work in the heart of Paris not a single man has ever asked me to marry him!'

Mme Joubert looked at her daughter who, at thirty, was still pretty and fresh, and answered:

'On the very next Friday 13th I 'll go and consult Mme Speller.'

'How very strange!' cried my mother. 'Mme Speller lives in our street. I didn't know she was as good as all that though, I do remember she told me I would soon be a widow.'

Actually this Mme Speller was married to an assistant at the Magasin du Printemps, and lived on the same floor as Didine. Quite a number of women used to visit her on Friday the 13th.

My Aunt Marguerite, who had remained quietly in a corner, now said:

'I had a niece staying with me at Beckenham who used to tell my fortune with a pack of cards. I 've never seen so many spades. It was spades every evening. When Matilda wrote to tell me that Émile was seriously ill I thought: "Well, that explains it. My brother-in-law is going to die!" Every evening the cards looked worse. Then one night my young niece, Matilda of Graçay, said: "What 's certain is that Matilda of Clichy is a widow by now!" Two days later we received the letter with the black border. It sounds cruel, but we gave a sigh of relief. We expected after that to see plenty of diamonds and hearts in the pack. Not a bit of it! There were as many spades as ever, night after night. My poor little niece hurried back to Graçay, thinking her parents were ill, but no, it wasn't that. On 21st April, six days after she had gone, my husband had his stroke and asked me for a bottle of ether screwed up in a heavy container to prevent evaporation, but though it was always in the same place, I simply couldn't find it. Seconds were going by. I lost my nerve and panicked. While I was still looking—in reality I had my eyes on him all the time—he stretched out a hand to pick up a book and died. Well, the other day when I was packing up to leave the house that ether bottle fell from its shelf and, hitting me on the head, knocked me unconscious. I 'm wondering if it was trying to kill me for not having found it in time. I must go and consult that Speller woman. There 'll be no more spades, that 's certain. I 've lost the only man I loved, but I 'd like to find a journey in the cards. I want to see new faces, new places.'

20

MY aunt returned to England in the autumn and almost immediately wrote for me to join her. She was selling the house at Beckenham and winding up the estate, but some Armenian friends had offered to put me up. Mr. X, the husband, was staying in an hotel in the Champs-Élysées, and he was to take me to London by the Dieppe–Newhaven night service. I left my mother in tears. Only now do I realize how cruel this parting must have been for her.

I was extremely intimidated by Mr. X, but on the boat I met another girl, and we went on deck together. The night was magnificent. The moon was reflected in the inky water, and English seamen sang *Tipperary* and *Whispering*, which we all knew in Paris.

When at last we reached Newhaven, after showing our passports and passing through the customs, and were going forward, tightly packed, towards the waiting train, a little grey cat demurely sitting on its tail looked at us from between railings. Mr. X put his suit-case down and stroked it. Several other people did the same thing. The little cat stretched its neck out as if expecting and enjoying these marks of friendship. Mr. X said:

'Now, my little Madeleine, anybody can see that we're in England. The English love animals.'

I was touched and charmed. Then when we were in the train, which seemed so very small, we drank tea which was excellent. We reached Victoria soon after five in a thick fog, which made the night even denser. Mr. X put me in a taxi. We crossed the Thames, and suddenly I remembered a song we used to sing during the war:

> Tout le long de la Tamise
> Il faut aller tous les deux
> Goûter l'heure exquise
> Du printemps qui grise.

The fog leered at us, hanging over interminable streets of low houses.   After about twenty minutes our tall black taxi stopped in front of a semi-detached villa similar to hundreds of others we had passed.   Though it was not yet six Mr. X's children, Tatiana and Boris, were already dressed, waiting for their father.

Tatiana, all black stockings and child's short dress, was a few months younger than I.   Boris was twelve, with the prettiest face and deep grey eyes.   They kissed their father deliriously, and helped us to take the luggage down a narrow dark staircase to a basement.

Here, by a gay fire, sat a woman no longer young, but quite beautiful, turning the handle of a coffee-mill.   She would give it a dozen rhythmical turns, pause without removing her fingers from the handle, take part in the conversation, then, having said what she wanted to say, give a little laugh and begin turning again, her nostrils sensuously inhaling the aroma of the ground beans.

This was Mr. X's sister.   Everybody called her Aunt Pia. She kissed her brother, exchanged a few words with him in Armenian, and went on grinding.   The children prepared some coffee for their father in a tiny copper pan and then, at the top of their voices, called out for their mother.

Minoche, as her husband and her children called her, was a small Parisian woman who had been so long in England that there remained nothing French about her but the language, into which she put a great number of English words and expressions.   Quick in her movements, dark, and with the same deep grey eyes I had noticed in Boris, thick lips, and small head, she was the best of women.

I quickly settled down in this strange family.

Minoche adored her husband, who was always disappearing on long business trips.   Aunt Pia thought Minoche stupid for letting her husband so often out of her sight, but she told her this in the most affectionate way, and when her brother went off on an expedition she comforted Minoche by talking about him, especially of their childhood in Armenia.   At last Minoche would sigh and object:

'That's all very well, but it doesn't alter the fact that he's gone off on another business trip!'

Aunt Pia would answer testily:

'Listen, Minoche! You're frightfully lucky to have him at all.
I can't tell you how many times we were nearly all massacred by
the Turks. Then you *would* have had something to cry about!'

'Perhaps,' agreed Minoche, who had heard this argument a
hundred times and was always touched. 'It really is dreadful
—about the massacres, I mean. How could people?'

Aunt Pia went on turning the handle of her coffee-mill, or if it
was tea time she would make toast at the end of a long fork of
twisted wire. She only went out of the house to go for a
journey, to the Pyrenees, for instance, where she had an adored
nephew, the son of a dead sister. When she had been there long
enough, or quarrelled with her brother-in-law, she came back
to Brixton, resuming the tenancy of the wicker arm-chair which
the cat occupied in her absence. In the evening, taking as many
hot-water bottles as she could lay her hands on, she went to her
room on the second floor, where she carefully brushed her long
grey hair and, calling the cat, wound herself up in a thick blanket
like a mummy. The cat jumped up on the bed, chose the place
he liked best, and soon both would be fast asleep.

The children went to school. They were up early, rushed to
the front door, where the milk bottles were lined up like little
soldiers, and fought for the *Daily Mirror* to follow the adventures
of Pip, Squeak, and Wilfred. Then Tatiana made the tea and
cooked the porridge.

I saw little of my aunt, who was still busy selling her house.
My new life was charming. We all did exactly as we pleased.
Tatiana practised her drawing when she was supposed to be
peeling the potatoes; little Boris, who was musical, composed a
symphony long after he was supposed to be in bed. Minoche
and Aunt Pia and my Aunt Marguerite, when she was there,
gossiped endlessly in the basement, whose warmth and soft gas-
light, its smell of coffee and toast, and its large table which took
up nearly all the room, made it charmingly cosy. We each had
our place at the table. Aunt Pia's was nearest her wicker chair.
She kept a large box of coffee grains on it. Tatiana had a box of
paints; her brother a book. Minoche and my Aunt Marguerite
had piles of mending, into which they dived at random. I sat
demurely making one of the embroidered petticoats which my
aunt seemed to think I should possess by the dozen, being hopelessly out of date in her ideas. These petticoats oppressed me.

They were so different from those my mother garnished with Mme Gaillard's precious lace or from the orange *crêpe de Chine* and black net favoured by my good and pretty Didine. None of us ever wanted to go to bed, our bedrooms, which were quite at the top of the house, being cold and damp. When at last we went up my head was deliciously full of stories I should not have listened to—confidences exchanged between the three women, sometimes enlivened by some massacres by the Turks and, if her husband happened to be gone away, by fresh tears from the unfortunate Minoche.

My Aunt Marguerite sold her house, and told us she was going back to France to live with a branch of my mother's family at Tours. As she did not want me to go with her I was to be put in a convent at Tooting.

The morning before my departure I went with Tatiana as far as her school, but on the way back I lost myself amongst streets which all looked exactly alike, and was obliged to ask the help of a policeman. He ended by finding the right house, where my Aunt Marguerite, Minoche, and even Aunt Pia were on the threshold in much alarm, thinking I must have been run over or kidnapped. The policeman was warmly thanked, and my aunt laughed at me, but Minoche said:

'There's nothing to laugh about, Marguerite. The same thing often happens to me. When one isn't tidy, tidy things like streets that look all alike put one off.'

I nodded approvingly, knowing exactly what she meant.

21

AUNT MARGUERITE and I waited in the parlour, where the parquet floor was polished to such a shine that two pieces of felt matting for the feet lay in front of each cane-chair. At the end of the room there was a grated partition with tiny windows. A veiled sister arrived. One of the windows opened with a metallic click. After a few words my aunt went off through the door by which we had come and I followed the sister into the unknown.

As it was five o'clock I was taken straight into the refectory, where I was placed between two young English girls, who were kind to me, but finding I spoke so little English they soon left me to myself. The big room with its many long tables was gay and noisy. Then suddenly Sister Aimée de Jésus, standing by the fire-place knitting long white stockings, called for silence by a sharp rap with the clapper. After grace we went silently and in tightly packed rows to a study where we again had the right to talk, but after a while a sister came to fetch me. I followed through many airy passages to a box-room where my trunk, which had preceded me by Carter Paterson, lay open and emptied of its contents. Sister Odile—it was she who had come to fetch me—had made neat piles of my linen. She showed me where to hang the dress I would wear on Sundays, and I was given a number for my dressing-gown. Then returning to my trunk, Sister Odile said in quite a kindly voice:

'You may now take your personal things—your sewing-case and your photographs—but I must warn you that in this house we do not tolerate your Bible. I am sorry that your aunt did not think it necessary to tell us you were a heretic. That we should be established in a heretical country is not our fault. It pains us to find this in a French girl. That, I must admit, was most unexpected.'

The Bible, in which our clergyman at Clichy had written, after

274

my first communion, when he had kissed me paternally in memory of my father, was put by Sister Odile at the bottom of the empty trunk. The lid was closed, and I was marched out of the room, shown my bed, and taken back to my companions.

Several girls had arrived earlier in the week from France and Belgium, and we immediately exchanged confidences. Most of them had already earned a living, fought morning and evening for room in the underground, brought up younger brothers and sisters, and been introduced rather too early into the mysteries of life. There was a tall girl who spoke French with the strong Parisian accent which is the counterpart of cockney in an English girl. A Polish girl of weird brilliance, who was later to become famous as a painter, said that she was accustomed to discipline, the Poles being alternatively dominated by the Germans and the Russians. A Greek girl laughed innocently, not yet under-standing a word of French or English. I did not share the initial revolt against obedience and discipline, and I foresaw the possi-bility of learning more than one modern language at the same time as Latin and Greek.

Sister Joseph, banging the clapper, sent us back to the re-fectory, where we were given twenty minutes to eat supper in silence—three plates grouped in front of each chair. The first generally contained a stew, the second apricots or prunes, and the third a slice of bread with margarine. After this meal and Sister Aimée's prayer, we got ready for bed, first kneeling in a vast circle round a dust-sheet cleaning our shoes under the critical eyes of Sister Odile, who stood in the doorway telling her rosary.

There was no time to dawdle. Our shoes finished, we put on slippers, washed, and undressed in the required way, slipping our night-gowns over our petticoats, without putting our arms in the sleeves, so that under this tent-like protection of stiff calico, fumbling and perspiring, we could modestly pull away the rest of our clothes. Sister Odile, meanwhile, would be reciting:

'Saint Joseph.'

Whereupon we, heads covered up by night-gowns, would answer:

'Pray for us.'

Then when everything was put away, the taps turned off, and the light switched off, we would go to bed, Sister Odile retiring to her cubicle surrounded by tall white curtains. She would continue to recite her prayers a little while until gradually the dormitory fell asleep. The heavy tram-cars clanging across Tooting Broadway threw splashes of coloured light against the little white beds. From time to time one of the sleepers in the middle of a nightmare would sit up in her bed and call for her mother. Then Sister Odile, looking like a ghost in her long white garments, would calm the child, and all was quiet again. I cried a little the first night, but chiefly I sent up a feverish prayer asking to learn English as soon as possible.

This order, expelled like the rest from France, had brought its own beds, and not till I had a house of my own did I ever find their equal. The mattresses were stuffed with wool from sheep in the Auvergne, for the nuns nearly all came from the province of Mme Gaillard and Mme Valentin. In the morning Sister Odile emerged from her cubicle, clapped her hands, switched on the light, and began the first prayers. We dressed under our night-dresses, made our beds, and went down to mass.

The sisters attended holy communion every morning. One saw them in two files, one on the right and the other on the left of the nave, led by the mother superior. Hands together, thumbs joined, their black veils drawn level with their eyes, they arrived in front of the tall latticed screen separating the altar from the rest of the chapel. Then in twos, one from each file, they knelt to receive the sacrament, after which, eyes closed, in ecstasy, they returned silently and in perfect order to their stools. One of the sisters then gave us the order to leave. As we marched out I would look back for a last picture of these black veiled figures bent low in prayer. Then joyously, because we were cold and hungry, we would rush to the refectory, where milk and coffee was already served.

Our class-rooms were speckless and smelt of beeswax. The desks and the floor were polished till they shone like glass. We knelt on the long benches for prayer. During our religious instruction we had a right to sew or to knit. Sister Edwina taught us in English and French with equal grace. Another sister arrived, intoned a prayer, and gave us a lesson in mathematics. This went on all day. Every time a new teacher came into the room we began with prayer, but the sisters taught with remarkable clarity, and I made swift and delightful progress. At the end of a month the most stubborn began to feel the advantages of this regular, cloistered life with its superb teaching. We were too closely watched for the pupils to inflict the small miseries on each other that are inseparable from secular education. All our energies were put into learning and prayer. The tall Parisian girl with the strong accent, who on our first meeting had sworn she would get the better of the nuns, now dreamt of taking the veil; and though, personally, I remained true to the Protestant faith, I felt as my mind expanded that I was at last building up a personality of my own.

My mother wrote to me occasionally. She had gone back to Mme Laparge and Mme Yvonne, to Mme Yvonne especially, where she had been obliged to bend to the minuteness of the work, learning under the direction of Gracieuse. She had not perhaps realized, when my aunt sent for me, that I should be away for a number of years. She could not realize that the time which seemed so long to her was providing me with a rehabilitation and a profound, unhurried education which later would set me along quite different paths. I think she was even sorry for me, thinking back to her own sad experience with the Ursulines at Blois, an experience which, at heart, I envied.

Mme Yvonne had a new lover, not, of course, an exclusive lover, but just an extra laurel to her wreath. He was a tremendously rich business man, a factory owner from Lyons, who gave her sumptuous presents but broke everything in the house. She was quite panicky each time he announced his arrival, and always tried to drag him quickly out of the house into restaurants and hotels, where what he broke was less important. He claimed that by these spells of violence he got out of his system a nagging wife, tiresome relations, and the appalling stiffness of provincial life. Generally he came once a month, spent a fortune, then when his nerves were quietened went back to Lyons. He broke one of Mme Yvonne's rarest pieces of Sèvres, for which he gave her a cheque for twice its value. Gracieuse thought him charming, and so did Maria, the cook, but the lovely chauffeur Marius said he was no gentleman.

Marie Guillet, tired of learning music, had gone to work in a factory, and the neighbours said she had a young man. They had been seen kissing under the shadow of the fortifications. Dédée Gontrel had been accepted by the ballet school at the Paris Opera, but poor Riri had gone to the hospital for incurables, and

Mme Gontrel, obliged to work, was employed in a newly opened
cinema in the Place des Fêtes.

Marguerite Rosier and Hyacinthe had left the street. Mme
Malgras and her husband, the former baker, were finding it impossible, owing to all these devaluations in the franc, to live on
their savings in the little country house to which they had retired.
Hyacinthe had thought about the matter carefully. He would
not give them money. This would have jeopardized his own
little hoard. To give up the apartment at Clichy and go and live
with the old people in their cottage might help M. and Mme
Malgras, and even save Hyacinthe some money, if the fare up and
down every day wasn't too expensive. He worked it out on
paper and decided to leave Clichy. After all, the cottage would
go to Marguerite when the parents died. Keeping it in running
order was really money in the bank, money like gold, which would
not become less valuable after each new devaluation. So they
went. Marguerite Rosier disappeared out of my mother's life.
Hyacinthe went clop, clop, clop, down the street for the last
time. It was all rather sad.

There was a lady near the convent who once a week invited two
French girls to take tea with her. To go there was considered a
great honour, a reward for having been particularly good.

We went without a sister, and this charming person welcomed
us in the prettiest drawing-room, where tea was served by a very
smart little maid. We tried very hard to make suitable conversation, but very soon the lady, seeing our distress, opened a drawer
and showed us the table-cloths and napkins she had embroidered
at different times during her life. They were quite magnificent,
and Mme Gaillard would have loved them; but the important
thing about them was that each cloth or napkin represented a
journey in some distant part of the world, or a phase in her
amazing existence. This one, for instance, had been begun in
Italy and finished in Madrid. This other one had been made while
sailing round the Cape. The last stitch was done at Cape Town.
As she showed them to us fascinating stories came to her mind.
She described a hot afternoon when seated elegantly on a long
chair she threaded her needle with this pretty blue silk while listening to a distant orchestra playing a waltz. She described palm-
trees, a veranda overlooking a blue lake, a house in Japan with

a snow-capped mountain in the distance.   I began to have that taste for geography which had been so long in coming.   She would send us back full of dreams and a home-made cake.

As my time at the convent came to an end I began suggesting to my mother that as life was so hard for her in Paris she should come to London.   A particular friend of mine, a girl of my own age, invited me to spend Sunday with her mother, a very success-ful dressmaker in Soho.   This Mme Monnier promised to look after my mother and give her enough work to keep her busy till she could build up a business of her own.

Towards the end of my last term my mother wrote to say that she was coming to explore the idea, and that as she was to lodge in Old Compton Street I was to ask for three days' leave to be with her.

These three days proved a real dream.   We ate buns in the park and watched the people in evening dress going into the theatres in Charing Cross Road and Shaftesbury Avenue.   This was my first view of the West End.   My mother and I both fell in love with it at first sight.   The Soho street market with the bananas, oranges, and pineapples filled us with wonder.   She said:

'You 're quite right.   Let 's live here permanently.   It 's not even taking a risk as we 've got nothing to lose.'

She quickly went back to Paris, sold everything she could, and arrived a month later with two trunks full of clothes and all that was left of Mme Gaillard's precious lace.

22

MY mother worked for a short while with Mme Monnier, gradually adapting herself to life in London. She had found a single room on the second floor of a house in Stacey Street, some fifty yards from where the Phoenix Theatre now stands. She was thus on the fringe of Soho, merely separated from Old Compton Street by the width of Charing Cross Road. Here the traffic flowed fast like a river with the lights of the Palace Theatre scintillating with musical romance.

At the end of my term at the convent I was longing for the picturesqueness and excitement of the West End. My mother and I were both convinced that we had left our cares behind us. I thought our room delightfully furnished. Titiche gave us a bed. We bought a divan for me on the instalment plan, which we put up against the window. During the day I sat on it to sew, to read, and to day-dream. The mattress was very hard compared to those at the convent. With its dark wood frame it looked rather like a cage for a wild animal, but it was my domain and I loved it. Grey linoleum covered the floor. A common deal table took up nearly all the middle of the room. My mother used it for her sewing, to iron on, and to cut materials. At meal times we pushed her work away from one of the corners and set out the crockery on a dish cloth. She still looked amazingly young, and for the first time had a happy confidence in the future. Everything was so deliciously new and we were starting our new existence with £40 in the bank, my mother's savings whilst she had worked alone in Paris.

I did the shopping in Seven Dials. There were so many sausages that one might have supposed that Londoners ate nothing else. I heard myself for the first time called 'dearie' by costerwomen wearing black satin hats strongly attached to hair yet unbobbed with great hatpins topped with coloured glass. Vegetables and fruit on barrows splashed the grey streets with

280

greens and reds. Canterbury lamb hung outside the butchers' shops lit up at night by acetylene flares. There were tomatoes and oranges out of season. Provisions in Paris were not so easily within the reach of people with little to spend.

My mother not working on Saturday afternoon, we would then do our shopping in Soho, where one heard every language, especially French and Italian, finding the specialities of the various countries, even smelling them as one passed such restaurants as Le Petit Riche, Le Restaurant d'Italic, Molinari, Genaro, and the Rendezvous. In the shops long-necked bottles of Chianti hung in dark cool corners over barrels of black olives and gherkins. Foreign newsagents, café-bars where coffee was made in the French way, cutlers where the kitchen knives came from Nogent, shops that specialized in aprons and tall white hats for chefs, having a wax model in the window dressed up and with black upcurling moustaches and pink cheeks, Italian hairdressers, a coffee merchant from Le Havre, Belgian pastry-cooks—these gave Old Compton Street a dashing cosmopolitan air. Groups of women holding shopping baskets laden heavily with food, as if they were going home to a siege, gossiped on the kerb, young men in bright pullovers discussed boxing and bicycle racing as at Clichy, dressmakers from Baker Street and Paddington came to fetch the Paris fashion magazines.

We bought our coffee from Mme Sandret, who had a curiously picturesque shop at the end of a dark and narrow passage. Heavily built, her hair done up tightly and neatly in a bun, her dress always made bright with beautifully white collars, pearls, or a coral necklace round her thick neck, she roasted the coffee while one waited, and tied up the bag with amazing speed and dexterity. We used to say to her: 'Don't bother to put any string round, Mme Sandret. We 've only a few yards to go.'

'It 's on account of the name,' she answered. 'I couldn't have it not looking neat while you carry it.'

The name SANDRET printed obliquely across the bag was a cult with her. She looked after her husband, who spent all the profits, with equal devotion. This excellent woman became my mother's first customer, and soon she began to speak so highly of my mother's talents that many of her customers became customers of my mother who, leaving Mme Monnier, bought a sewing-machine at Selfridge's and set up on her own. We also, because

of the mice that overran our room, acquired a black cat called
Nanny, who slept on my bed and became a most affectionate
companion.

It was now that my mother, who bought her fashion papers
from a Frenchman called M. Marcel, who owned a tiny but
famous newspaper shop in Old Compton Street, heard that he
was looking for an assistant. M. Marcel told her he wanted a
girl, lively and pretty and sufficiently inexperienced to accept a
small wage for long hours. His wife had her eyes on me, and
stressed the advantages of working in a shop where the door
was open all the time—indeed there was no door at all, the
premises being closed at night by a steel curtain. She pointed
out how good this would be for my health, and what a satisfaction it would be to my mother to talk to me each time she
passed along the street. I started work the following Monday,
being paid fifteen shillings a week, and for several months had
enormous fun selling the *Vie Parisienne* and *Le Matin* to the curious
crowds who came in from Old Compton Street.

Not long after this a friend sent my mother a new customer
called Mme Néroda, a manicurist, who visited in their flats
the French girls who at night grouped themselves on the
pavement in Bond Street and Jermyn Street plying their age-old
profession. Mme Néroda's husband, who was a hairdresser,
specialized in the same clientele, and between them they made
a great deal of money. She quickly persuaded my mother to
make dresses for these women, many of whom were of amazing
beauty, and one day when I was complaining how little I earned,
she said:

'Why don't you do something else? Take up my profession,
for instance? To begin with it's such fun for a young girl to
talk! You'll meet a great many different people. That's
wonderfully useful. Look at me, for instance! With my little
manicurist's box I've been to Shanghai and to New York and
to Rome. I've made plenty of money. It was as a manicurist
that I met my first husband, a very wealthy business man. When
he died I took my little manicurist's box again and found a second
husband, not so young, less important, but that will come in
time, for every year we are getting richer. It's quite simple
really. The great thing is to keep a little book, and take care
that at the end of each day you have spent less than you have

earned. Besides, it's amusing. One ends by turning it into a
sort of game.'

I left M. Marcel's paper shop to work at the Galeries Lafayette
in Regent Street. My mother and I began to make money.
We had practically no expenses except food, stockings, shoes,
and materials. Everything that could be sewn, lingerie, dresses,
coats, and hats, we made ourselves during the long winter evenings under our gas lamp. Her new and specialized clientele paid
well, and to supplement our income I did some translations. I
continued to read widely both in French and English, and hearing
so much Italian spoken round us in Soho, and being angry with
myself for not understanding it, I began to learn that.

The franc had been devalued three times since my mother's
arrival, but instead of being sorry about the financial straits
our poor country was in we used joyously to work out what our
savings were now worth in French money. We had never been
so rich. We replaced the linoleum by a carpet, which we ordered
from the Magasin du Printemps' warehouse at Clichy, where M.
Séguin had worked; and as in those days one could trade freely
between the two countries, our carpet cost us less than if we had
bought it in London.

I had been rather impressed by Mme Néroda's advice, and as
I was to have a fortnight's holiday in August I suggested to my
mother that we should go to Paris, where I could take a course
at a beauty institute. We had a money box, in which every week
we put something towards the journey. My mother was all the
more anxious to go because for the first time in eight years she
had received news of her sister Marie-Thérèse and Rolande.
Rolande had written me a short, awkward letter, not quite sure
if my mother was yet ready to forget the far-off quarrel which had
kept us so stupidly apart; but though the information was of the
vaguest, my mother, who really loved her sister, was alarmed.
Marie-Thérèse had apparently twice been to hospital for a serious
operation. Rolande herself was not well.

A week later my mother who, though extremely happy had
been very tired, fell ill. I was then with Gaumont. Without
daring to ask for leave I nursed my mother, and did a great part
of her work in addition to my own. I shopped during the lunch
hour, made her lunch, ran up the hems of her dresses on the
machine, and in the evening when there was anything to deliver

to a customer I would take it round. Several times a week I went to flats in Jermyn Street and Bond Street, where the walls were decorated with pictures from *La Vie Parisienne* and *Le Sourire*. Coming out into the dark streets groups of women under lamp-posts, nearly all knowing me now, whispered good night sympathetically. I thought them pretty but cruel, and I envied their large painted eyes under bright felt hats, their slim figures draped in mink, and their very high heels.

At the end of six weeks my mother could walk round our room. The first strawberries were being sold on the barrows in Old Compton Street. The bookmaker who ran his business from the dead end of our narrow street was busier than ever. Any stranger put him immediately to flight, but when he had seen a person once he always remembered the next time who it was. Our neighbour, the wife of a cook, backed two or three horses every day, and put her winnings in a box towards the trousseau of her daughter Adrienne. She slammed the front door, looked quickly to right and left, and hurried to the bookmaker to collect her money. Just before the Derby a strong man, whose companion tied him up in chains, began to operate in our street. This performance embarrassed the bookmaker, who used to retire dejectedly into the pub till his rival had gone.

My mother was much better, and though she was not yet strong enough to go up and down the stairs, we were still determined to spend our holidays in Paris. Mme Néroda, meanwhile, sent us two new customers, who arrived one day when, in spite of the heat, I was in bed with a heavy cold. Of these two women one was clearly more important than the other. Putting down her Pekinese, who immediately made friends with Nanny, our cat, Mlle Thémiers walked round the room, explaining her requirements to my mother in a strong Bourguignon accent, whilst her friend sat rather stiffly on a chair. Mlle Thémiers, from beginnings no less humble than Didine, had been fortunate enough, soon after her arrival in London, to find a rich banker, who had given her a house near Park Lane, a small farm in the country, and a large white motor-car, which had sent our bookmaker scurrying away. My mother soon discovered that she thought of little else but putting enough money aside for her old age. Her idea was to buy some cheap models in the stores, have my mother alter them, and then, when her banker had a party, pretend she needed £60 to buy a dress at Patou or Worth. My mother pointed out that it took a great deal of time to adjust a dress, and that it was too ill paid to be worth her while. I suppose my mother's eyes turned to me while she said this, because Mlle Thémiers, to win her heart and mine at the same time, promised to send round a suit-case full of brocades and satins, which had been sent from Lyons to her friend the banker to show to English and American buyers. Some very lovely materials had arrived for the same purpose. Would my mother be willing to turn these into dresses?

This was quite a different proposition. My mother relented, and we watched the two women through the window leaving the house. By this time a crowd had formed round the white car with the uniformed chauffeur at the wheel. The car and the chauffeur returned later with the promised suit-case, and my mother showed the same skill in turning these beautiful satins and brocades into dresses as she had shown with the lace for Mme Gaillard's blouses. Mlle Thémiers, delighted, brought me several rolls of superb blue and orange ribbon, knowing that the best way to please my mother was to please me. All this contributed to my mother's convalescence. July was half over, our plans for Paris were becoming more definite, and my mother made me a lovely dress with Mlle Thémiers's gift of ribbon— a wide skirt of pleated *crêpe de Chine* finished off most prettily at the bottom with a length of the ribbon. More of this same ribbon went to make the corsage, which had short sleeves and a little bow under the chin. Nothing in the world could have been more graceful for dancing, for running about, for taking to Paris for a fortnight's holiday! This was my dress for important occasions. I had others which my mother made from the bits and pieces left over from the dresses of her Bond Street and Jermyn Street customers. I was very dissatisfied with office life. My head was full of Rudolf Valentino, Pola Negri, Mae Murrey, Norman and Constance Talmadge. I was all for taking Mme Néroda's advice.

All the young women at the office were having their hair cut short. First it was one department, then another. On a Monday morning we would see them arriving with hats no longer poised on rolled-up buns, but stupidly, amusingly bumping over a void. The slightest movement would turn these rudderless hats round.   The bit of fur on the coat collar rubbed against freshly shaved necks full of hard bristles and not yet toned down by air and sun.   Each new victim was taken to the ladies' cloak-room to be examined.   We were not sure whether we liked it but we knew that our turn would come.   My mother kept on saying: 'It's really too great a shame!'

One evening my mother's friend Emma arrived gaily at our second-floor room with a box of cream buns from Valérie.   She was of about the same age as my mother, freshly made up on this occasion, a new hat of the prettiest kind from under which two curls emerged, clinging to her cheeks like question marks.   She looked younger, her head moved gracefully as if lighter, more airy now that it was freed from the usual multitude of hairpins. She let us admire her, turn her this way and that whilst she stood at the table undoing the box of cream buns, Nanny playing with the string, waiting to catch the crumbs full of sugar.   My mother was quite won over, and we were all very happy.   Emma, who was waitress at the 'Pop,' always informed of the latest gossip, brought me some money for several handkerchiefs in *crêpe de Chine* I had made to her order.   They were of gay colours with a girl with bobbed hair wearing a *cloche* painted in a corner.   A swan's-down powder-puff was sewn to the middle of the hand-kerchief, and Emma disposed of them with ninepence profit on pay day when the waitresses were changing from their uniforms into their own clothes before going off duty.   Every kind of important transaction took place at this well-chosen moment, and when Emma told me about it I used to think of our adventures in the public wash-house at Clichy.

On the next Saturday, having lunched quickly, my mother and I went to a hairdresser's in Wardour Street, where we sat at the end of a long queue of women who, like us, were patiently waiting to let down their beautiful long hair and have it murderously cut off with a few cruel snips of the scissors. When it was my turn my mother lost heart.   She raised her voice, spoke with unaccustomed loudness, and kept on opening her bag to look inside, as if wishing to remain blind to the crime.

An hour later, with hats far too large for diminished heads, feeling very self-conscious, anxious to be home where we could make a minute, pitiless examination of our changed appearance, we went down the narrow, steep staircase into Wardour Street where, across Shaftesbury Avenue, the Saturday afternoon street market in Soho was at its busiest and most picturesque.

Celestine was a curious little woman who, though French, had lived so long in London that she could not speak three words of her own language without adding two of English. She was small, sprightly, and of no known age. I had seen her for the first time when selling newspapers at M. Marcel's shop. Both in summer and winter she wore the same black plush coat, turning a horrible shade of green from long wear, not unlike those favoured by the last of the flower-girls in Piccadilly Circus. Her hat, equally discoloured by age and weather, fitted her head in a way that made one suppose she never took it off—the front was smooth like her forehead, the back protruded, covering her bun, forming an excrescence like an oak-apple. She lived in a small room at the very top of a sordid house facing Middlesex Hospital. The women of Bond Street and Jermyn Street would send for her if their maids fell ill or had to go away to Switzerland or Belgium, for she was admirably versed in their difficult and specialized work. She also kept *en pension* these ladies' Pekinese, and was occasionally invited to supper by them in return for telling their fortunes. As all her front teeth were missing she used to lisp like a little girl, with the result that her most awful predictions, the blackest calamities, fell from her lips in an absurdly childish voice. Her short arms, imprisoned in the plush coat which she refused to take off because of the filth of the clothes she wore underneath, moved so awkwardly that when shuffling the cards one or two generally fell face upwards on the table, whereupon she would exclaim in a tone of surprise as if she had seen a butterfly flying upside-down: 'Why, yes, it fell, but you know the saying, don't you, everything that falls on the ground comes true!'

Placing the fallen card, or cards, on the right heaps, she would continue:

'One, two, zee, ze widow. One, two, zee, ze dark zung man. One, two, zee, I zee ze postman. Of course I can make a meestake, but zat's what I zee!'

Celestine often came to our place, and when my mother was ill she had told me how to deliver the dresses to my mother's

K

customers. There was never anything very sensational about her predictions concerning me. They ran like this:

'One, two, zee, un zeune homme. One, two, zee, a nouveau zob. One, two, zee, a voyaze.'

As she spoke she would fondle Nanny, who loved her. Everybody confided in Celestine. She listened to what one told her with sympathy and emotion. There were moments when she looked on the verge of tears, but as soon as she left one's presence everything was forgotten. Secrets just flew out of her head. She was thus incapable of an indiscretion. This system had only one disadvantage, for occasionally when somebody poured out into her ear some story of unrequited love or money not paid back, she would exclaim:

'Zen I tell you what to do! Zere ees nothing like a good smack to calm ze nerves!'

'You really think so, Mme Celestine?'

'Yes, of course. It calms ze one zat gives as well as ze one zat receives!'

A moment later she had forgotten all about the incident, and would be quite surprised when her customer would stop her in the market and say:

'You know that smack you told me to give her, Mme Celestine? Well, it didn't calm her nerves a bit. Look what she did to me!'

Now at last my mother and I were off to Paris. We were to cross by the night service on a Saturday. During the afternoon, having put our dear Nanny in a basket, I set off for Mme Celestine's attic flat opposite the Middlesex Hospital, where Nanny was to lodge during our absence. Sleek and black, with a white front which made her look like a young woman barrister, I could see her through the osiers, hear her heart beating every time the omnibus came to a noisy stop. The journey seemed very long. At last, having carefully carried the basket up the narrow stairs and cautiously opened Mme Celestine's door, I came upon a hovel the floor of which was strewn with saucers of milk of varying freshness. Through a wide-open window stretched a vista of roofs. Cats came and went, and could be seen stalking on the sky-line. As soon as Mme Celestine crumpled a piece of grease-paper scores of them, their tails up, galloped over the tiles, jumped lightly through the window, purred, and arched their backs as they rubbed against her legs. Nanny, released from her

basket, appeared full of surprise, and then darted under Mme
Celestine's bed. Lifting up the flounce we could see eyes shining
in the dust and darkness against the wall. Mme Celestine called
out wheedlingly:

'Come, my petit cat chéri, zere ees some poisson fried. Viens,
pussy dear, zere ees also some bonne cat's-meat!'

Nanny, being herself bilingual, was not slow to emerge from
her hiding-place and taste the fried fish and cat's-meat. I gave
Mme Celestine five shillings for Nanny's lodging, left her the
basket, and hurried down the stairs, my nostrils filled with the
terrible smell of fried fish and curdled milk.

My mother, having finished packing, was now emptying all
the cupboards while her friend Emma sat on my couch.

'Give me a hand with the carpet,' exclaimed my mother as I
opened the door. 'It will be safer to roll it up.'

'Safer because of what?' asked Emma, swinging her short
legs over the side of the couch.

'The mice,' explained my mother. 'On account of Nanny
not being here.'

'So you really think,' asked Emma, 'that the mice will eat up
your carpet in a fortnight's holiday? Anybody would think
you were going to your château for the season!'

'The carpet came from Clichy,' said my mother reflectively.
'It's rather a special one.' But she was struck with the truth of
Emma's remark, and said: 'Yes, I suppose we can leave the carpet,
and in any case it's time we fetched a taxi.'

Emma offered to fetch the taxi, which could drop her at the
'Popular' on its way to Victoria. She went ahead of us while
we drew the curtains, made sure the gas was turned off, and had
a last look round. We took down our suit-cases and, finding no
sign of Emma or the taxi, began to be impatient, and then increasingly flustered as all our neighbours, putting their heads out,
passed loud remarks. As it was Saturday night our bookie was
there with a long queue of punters. A very old taxi wheezed its
way down Phoenix Street. The door opened, swung on its
hinges, and Emma made frantic signs at us, crying out that unless
we hurried she would be late to 'clock in.' She had to be at the
restaurant in time for the dinner shift. We retorted angrily that
we had supposed that the idea of fetching a cab was primarily to

allow us to catch a train. The bookie was annoyed at the commotion in his street, and the taxi driver was rattling his vehicle backwards and forwards in jerks to turn into Shaftesbury Avenue, where the theatre traffic was at its busiest. We got in and pulled the door, closing it with such a bang that the glass shook in its frame. Our driver, to avoid the congestion in front of the Palace Theatre, tried to turn left for Trafalgar Square and the Mall, whereupon Emma, rising from her seat like a termagant, brought down her knuckles on the glass partition between driver and passengers, shouting out in a mixture of English, French, and her native German-Swiss:

'Mais, donnerwetter, silly fool, I must pass au Pop for clock in!'

We all started to talk at the same time; the cab driver, suddenly understanding, swerved in the right direction. Then my mother and I, amused by the outraged expression on Emma's face, broke into laughter. Our cab had no sooner turned round the statue of Eros in Piccadilly Circus than Emma, kissing us good-bye, rose in the still moving taxi to struggle with the door in her eagerness not to waste a moment. The driver put on the brakes, and our poor Emma was thrown into the arms of the magnificently uniformed commissionaire of the Pop. Her chubby Swiss cheeks pink with confusion, she slipped past him, and we saw her rushing round to the employees' entrance.

Now we were relieved, though almost surprised, by the stillness in our taxi. Quietly, in plenty of time, we turned down St. James's Street, past the wooden-looking soldiers in their bearskins and crimson coats, and a quarter of an hour later, not quite recovered from so many emotions, we took our places in the night mail for Paris.

It was five in the morning when we emerged from the Gare Saint-Lazare. We had been given the name of a tiny hotel in the rue Vivienne, between the vegetable market and the bourse, where for sixteen francs we could have an attic with a clean bed and running water. Leaving my mother in the taxi with the suitcases, I ran up several flights of private flats to the top of the building where, at the end of a corridor, I found a glass door with some keys hanging from a board. A woman, having thrown a dressing-gown over her night-dress, came in answer to my ringing, and asked me disagreeably what I meant by waking her so early in the morning, but noticing my youth and confusion she became much more friendly, and gave me a key which I hurriedly took down to my mother. We washed and tidied our hair and my mother unpacked our dresses, which she hung up in the wardrobe. I persuaded my mother to go out again. A church clock struck six. 'Oh!' she cried, suddenly vexed, 'that's just like you! We could have had a good sleep!' I began to hang my head down when suddenly a fine smell of coffee and buttery *croissants* greeted us, and after an excellent breakfast in a café-bar we saw the steel shutters being thrown up in front of all the small shops. Housewives hurried past with newly baked bread. Church bells rang gently, and a bright sun warmed the suddenly busy street. We promised ourselves a complete rest all day, no cooking, no washing up, no *crêpe de Chine* handkerchiefs for Emma, no opening and closing the door for Nanny, no dresses to be hurriedly finished and taken round to flats in Bond Street and Jermyn Street. At midday we lunched in one of those small restaurants where evergreens line the pavement—*hors-d'œuvres*, leg of lamb and French beans, a Camembert and ripe peaches from southern vineyards, with a carafe of *vin rosé*, all served on crinkly paper on which, after coffee, the waitress pencilled the bill.

We followed the crowds moving slowly along the boulevards. The men with black suits and black hats seemed fatter and smaller. We thought the women amusing, but the streets less imposing than when we used to come up from Clichy and gape at the Boulevard Haussmann. Oxford Street with its throngs was still in our eyes. In the evening we went to the Casino de Paris, and on our return at midnight we quickly went to sleep.

The next morning the sun came out again, and Paris, with its thousands of foreigners, scintillated. I had left Clichy in a depression. I had returned to France in the middle of a boom. The first thing was to find a school where I could learn hairdressing and manicuring, and about this we had no trouble. We came across just what I wanted near the Pont Neuf, a wide, dark staircase leading to an office where a young woman in a white blouse assured us that in twelve days I would know enough to be employed in the most exclusive establishments, as hairdresser or manicurist, in Paris, London, or New York. We left the place full of hope, and went joyously to the perfumery department of the Magasin du Printemps where my mother, still so very young, examined lipstick and powder-box, scent and eau-de-Cologne, with an enthusiasm no less than mine. All these things were displayed in the prettiest manner. How good they smelt! How attractive to the eye! One took up quite the most charming object, looked at it a moment, then quickly put it down for another that seemed even more desirable or more original. Women on these occasions are as fickle as men who, seeing a woman, fall in love with her, are proud to be seen with her, then lay her aside to pass on to the next. Curiosity, a fear of having missed something good or of making a wrong choice, sent us hurrying from counter to counter. We had no sooner made our purchases here than we ran to the artificial flowers, and from there to the gloves whose minute stitches are not sufficiently appreciated by their wearers, and off again to the handkerchiefs, poised like butterflies ready for flight. Glass lifts ran up and down. One could see right through them. Delicately shaped they looked like flowers with a golden stem, the calyx full of women whose coloured hats emerged like pistils. English, Americans, and Scandinavians were everywhere.

We took a taxi to go back to the rue Vivienne, discussing what we had seen, saying over and over how wonderful it was to have just enough money to buy frivolous, useless, pretty things, and when in our hotel bedroom we undid our parcels my mother was quite changed by a happiness out of all proportion to our real situation; for, after all, we were not yet so brilliantly set up, but since we had gone to live in London she had a complete and touching faith in the future. She was convinced that she had left the bad times behind her. Clichy was synonymous with illness and poverty. She watched me growing up much better in health, animated, very gay, and with an assurance that she had lacked at my age. She believed I was capable of conquering the world. And at that time I may have thought so myself.

After lunch we took a taxi and told the driver to take us to the rue de Longchamps. My mother was anxious to see her sister Marie-Thérèse alone, and she knew that Louis would be working in the afternoon.

23

QUICKLY passing the doorkeeper's lodge, the long narrow corridor seized us with its sudden cold after the sunshine in the street. We climbed flight after flight of backstairs till at last, at the sixth, my mother timidly knocked with bent finger at her sister's door, then, placing her ear against the panel, listened. After a while, hearing footsteps, she drew herself up and knocked more loudly.

A slim woman appeared, and was beginning to ask us what we wanted when she suddenly exclaimed:

'Oh, Matilda, fancy, it's you! It's dark in the passage, and I was sitting by the window sewing some white material, so I didn't recognize you immediately. And there's Madeleine! Come in, both of you, do. Nothing has changed in the flat except the people who live in it.'

She went swiftly ahead, and we followed. No, nothing had really changed since that August in 1914 when I stayed here; only in a room through which we passed with two doors but no window, lit merely by a skylight, which was Rolande's bedroom; her bed, which I had shared on many occasions, she sleeping with her head at one end and I with mine at the other, was now pushed into a dark corner, obviously not for the moment in use, and quite covered over with dusty bandboxes.

My aunt, going to her own room, sat by the open window, the same window through which I so nearly fell trying to see the soldiers with their band on the declaration of war, and arranging her skirt round her skinny ankles took up the white hat she had been making when my mother rang. My mother was terribly affected to be in the presence of this sister from whom she had been alienated for so many years. We had last seen her so very young and frivolous. Now she was unbelievably thin; her beautiful brown hair had turned grey, her sweet irregular face, that used to be so full of charm when she was happy, was rutted with deep, tragic lines.

She put a ribbon round the crown of the white hat, made a stitch or two, broke the cotton, and placing the hat on her fist twirled it round.

'There!' she exclaimed. 'Thank goodness this one 's finished. You 'd never believe the trouble it 's given me. Oh, these rich, mean women! I was supposed to copy exactly the model from Maria Guy—the one on the table—but to do that I should have needed to match up the materials, and it simply isn't possible. All the famous modistes stick tight to their own materials. I have to run round the shops and get second best. Then when I 'm home I close my eyes and hope that having opened them I shan't see the difference between the original and the copy. I may as well tell you right away, it 's no good. One can't compete with firms like Maria Guy. The manufacturers pander to them, make materials exclusively for them. Oh, the lovely models I 've made in my imagination! I, Marie-Thérèse! Well, I 've never made those masterpieces and never shall. My hats have been a mess. My whole life has been a mess. Of all the hundreds of hats I 've made there 's not been one outstanding enough to get itself talked about. No newspaper has even photographed one of my hats at the Grand Prix. It 's terrible to be a failure.'

My mother, who was gradually mastering her emotion, put in:

'Come, Marie-Thérèse, what 's the matter with you? Your hats have always been quite charming. You never took yourself so seriously before the war.'

'That 's true,' answered my aunt sadly, 'but things were very different.' She laid the hat on the table next to the one from which it was copied, and said more gaily, turning to me: 'Suppose you run down and buy some *croissants* and some *brioches*. Your mother and I will get coffee ready in the kitchen.'

When I came back I found them talking round the kitchen table. Marie-Thérèse took a *croissant*, ate a few crumbs, and said:

'There, that 's all I can manage, and yet I assure you, Matilda, I was ravenous. It 's such a wonderful thing to feel hungry. To think there are women who, to keep slim, refuse to eat. The poor fools! To feel hungry is to be healthy. Fancy wanting to fight good health! Supposing they were like me! Supposing they were afraid to die at any moment!'

My mother began to look a bit serious, and said:

'What 's come over you, talking about dying at your age?

You're as bad as when we were children at Blois. Do you remember how you used to wake me up to recite prayers in the middle of the night?'

'When I wake up now,' answered Marie-Thérèse, 'it's to exclaim: "Heavens, what pain I'm in!" and to take half a dozen aspirins.'

'I think you exaggerate,' said my mother. 'Lots of people have operations and get quite well again afterwards. I expect it's the after effects.'

My aunt, having rinsed the coffee cups under the hot-water tap, was not putting them away very carefully. She said affectionately:

'Let's go next door. Louis will be back at any moment and I wouldn't like him to see me looking sad. He has enough troubles, what with my being ill and Rolande in a sanatorium.'

'In a sanatorium?' queried my mother, not quite expecting that. 'Tell me everything. She gave us no details in the letter, merely that she herself was not well.'

'Rolande,' began Marie-Thérèse, but as she spoke a key turned in the front door and Louis came into the passage. He was followed by a young woman who turned out to be a lady's-maid come to call for the hat Marie-Thérèse had just finished making. She said she would bring another to be copied in the morning, and went off. Louis welcomed us and then, kissing his wife with the greatest tenderness, asked:

'How is my darling to-day? I swear she's looking a great deal better!'

He pinched one of her cheeks as if she had been twenty, and was altogether so loving that one felt a lump in the throat. He asked us about London, and then said:

'Go ahead! Gossip to your hearts' content! I'll go and fetch something good for dinner and an old bottle of Burgundy.'

As soon as he was gone Marie-Thérèse said to my mother:

'You see, Matilda, he hasn't changed a bit. He's just as loving as the day he married me. His goodness, that's what makes me less brave to face another operation. Can you understand?'

'I understand that you're so happy you want it to go on for ever,' answered my mother. 'Not having been very happy with Émile I suppose I suffered less than those who were happy. It's a tiny consolation!'

*K

I was rather shocked to hear my mother say she had not been happy with my father. Since we had lost him he had taken a more important place in my heart. I only remembered his kindness, the sunny part of his character, and I much preferred his southern brusqueness, even his moments of violence, to the sugary talk of Uncle Louis when he was with women. The conversation turned for a few moments to my father's death, and to all the other people in the family who had died during the last ten years, to my granny, for instance, who, after living as a recluse in the old district of Blois, had died all alone in 1922, probably dreaming to the end of adventure and pieces of gold. Then Marie-Thérèse, who had the gift of turning abruptly from one subject to the other, looked at me and exclaimed:

'It's amazing how your daughter still has her straight hair and her fat cheeks!'

My mother, springing to my defence, answered:

'How can you talk such trash, Marie-Thérèse. She has the cheeks of any healthy girl of twenty. I certainly wouldn't have them any other way. As for her hair being straight, I don't see how that can matter with this new permanent wave.'

Were the sisters so soon to have a new quarrel? Happily the conversation turned on dress, and then to my aunt's illness. She was to have yet another operation.

'You mustn't mind too much what I say,' put in Marie-Thérèse hastily after another sharp volley inspired by something my mother said about my aunt exaggerating the seriousness of her condition. 'It was yesterday at the hospital. I came back quite shaken.'

My mother, sitting very primly on her chair, arched her eyebrows inquiringly.

'I was on the couch being examined. A very famous woman doctor turned round suddenly to the medical students round her, and asked: "Well? What have you got to say?" I couldn't see their faces. I'm so tired of being pommelled in public. I hate them. I bit my lips and closed my eyes. The woman doctor's voice rang out again. "I say it's a waste of radium," she said, and went off and left me, followed by her disciples. You laugh at my prayers, Matilda, but He would not have left me without putting His hands on me and healing me. What did the woman mean? Did she think my tumour had grown so much smaller that it wasn't worth while wasting radium on it? That it would go down by itself? Or with this other operation? You know how famous doctors aren't really interested in a case unless it's out of the way or frightfully serious? And she obviously wasn't interested any more, was she? Otherwise she wouldn't have gone off so quickly with her disciples?'

There was a pleading in my aunt's voice. My mother looked down at her shoes. She did not really understand. In our world people went to hospital and either came back or died there, but people knew less than they know now. Suddenly my aunt broke out:

'You don't believe I'm exaggerating any more, do you, Matilda? Not now, you don't? You don't think the tumour is any better? They give one radium to heal one. Why didn't she want to heal me? Aren't I worth healing? When I came home I threw myself on the bed and cried and cried and cried! I'm surprised at the amount of tears I can well up. I cry when I'm alone, but as soon as Louis comes home I smile and make plans for our future. I almost believe all the nonsense I talk. He's so very kind is Louis. But at night, when the pain gets the better of the aspirin, I turn away from Louis, with my face to the wall, and cry again till I fall asleep.'

She went on:

'I dream mostly of Blois. The military bands and our mother whose apron, when she came home, was full of nuts and apples. You remember the stories she used to tell us about washing linen on the Loire? Then I dream of Rolande playing with the goat at Marais, and of Rose, who was always waiting for her distinguished German lover to come back. Once I dreamt of our convent at Blois. I was sliding on the parquet floor. But it's funny, I never dream of you or of Louis. It's specially funny about Louis, isn't it? In the morning, when I'm having breakfast, I wonder how I can have been so happy in my dreams without him. I don't think I could really be happy without Louis.

'I've got to go to hospital again to-morrow. I really don't know what they do to me or even why I have to go. I wait there with a crowd of women of all sorts of ages. I know they've got what I've got, just as they know I've got the same as they have. Some of us are quite friendly. We've known one another for at least six months, and we try to see if we look any different—I mean, if the illness shows at all on our faces. Sometimes one or other of us doesn't turn up, and then we guess. We have such a long time to talk. Think of it, it's nothing to wait for two hours! The amount of secrets I know! Some go to church a great deal, or even go to Lourdes. Others go to fortune-tellers, hoping to be told things like: "Next year you and your husband will retire in the country," or "You are going to start a new life. I see a legacy coming your way." Obviously the deduction is that we have more years in front of us. And really, Matilda, between you and me, I don't think my tumour is of the serious kind. They say that when one has been loved very much the body is so much healthier. It's understandable, isn't it? It's wonderful to be loved like I'm loved by Louis. Well, I don't need to tell you that. You saw it just now with your own eyes, didn't you?'

I twisted on my chair, wondering how much longer this horrible conversation would go on. A pigeon came down on the window-sill and looked at us curiously. My aunt, picking up a piece of straw from the carpet, frightened the bird away, and soon a sparrow flew down and took its place. I went across to the window, remembering the declaration of war in 1914 and all the women who cried, but they cried differently to the way my aunt was crying now.

Suddenly my Uncle Louis arrived, telling us about his adventures and all the wonderful things he had bought for dinner. Saucepans soon sizzled on the fire. My uncle and I laid the table. He pulled the cork out of the Burgundy bottle with a bang. He was very gay.

24

ROLANDE was not happy at school. My Uncle Louis, who would have given her anything in the world, quickly saw that her real interest was plaiting and twisting bits of Italian straw and garnishing hats with vaporous tulle. He therefore called on all the great modistes in Paris and was successful in placing her as an apprentice, at the age of fourteen, with the great house of Lewis in the rue Royale.

She was delighted. She hoped, of course, to start making hats immediately, and was disappointed to discover that apprentices were used mostly to run errands, being sent out to match up materials in the shops or simply to fetch aspirins or *croissants* for the workwomen. When she was breathless from running up and down tall flights of stairs she was told to pick up the pins on the carpet. Occasionally, on busy days, she would be allowed to finish a lining or sew on the tab with the name 'Lewis' to the inside brim, but all the time she was looking at what the others were doing, and when they forgot her for a few moments she would make something on her own. Her very first attempts caused surprise. She was unconsciously creating. Lewis at that time made hats for the stage. Many of the greatest actresses in the world went there. Unusual ideas were therefore acceptable. A fancy, a whim, a caprice, could help the success of a revue or a musical comedy. What more staid houses might have frowned on made money for Lewis. At the age of fourteen and a half Rolande, after only a few weeks with Lewis, had the immense joy of making a hat which Mistinguette fell in love with and immediately put on her head! When, at the close of this amazing day, she ran up the six storeys of the rue de Longchamps to tell her parents the news, Marie-Thérèse exclaimed:

'I knew it! I always knew it! I 've given birth to an artist!'

Soon the hats the mother made with such difficulty and with misgivings, would be replaced by the masterpieces Rolande would create. The name 'Rolande Soilly' would glitter in the

rue de la Paix.   The veilings, the artificial flowers, the supple
straws, the birds of paradise, the egrets, the tulle, and the sumptuous tufts and plumes of the celebrated house of Lewis would
have to compete against the young genius.   This was exactly
what Marie-Thérèse had dreamt of when reading those serials
cut out from the newspapers—a glittering future.   What a
splendid marriage Rolande, the modiste, would make!

A few months later Rolande became a young woman.   Serious
disorders followed the young apprentice's maturity, and her
health, which in girlhood had seemed rather better than mine,
was violently shaken after each of her periods.   She had several
frightening haemorrhages.   The family doctor told Marie-
Thérèse not to worry too much, that if her daughter was losing
so much blood it probably meant that she had a lot to lose.   Her
condition was therefore normal.

Reassured, mother and daughter continued to make plans for
the future.   Rolande went on running up and down stairs,
fetching and carrying for the workwomen, rushing from store
to store searching for ribbons or artificial flowers, but she was
always quite stupidly tired, and soon every flight she climbed
quite exhausted her, and she would remain panting on the last
step, often having to sit down a moment before she could go on.

To celebrate her fifteenth birthday her parents were to take
her to see *Cyrano de Bergerac* at the Comédie Française.   Marie-
Thérèse adored this play, and knew the most important lines by
heart, claiming that it was the most magnificent of all love
stories.   Love stories were still her passion, she who was so
loved and loved so tenderly.   Rolande hurried home knowing
that Louis would return early from work, probably with a
present, anxious to help with the dinner, lay the table, and open
the wine.   She had not been well all day, but with the theatre
to look forward to, the fuss everybody had made of her at Lewis's,
the workwomen giving her bouquets of violets and lilies of the
valley, according to custom when a *midinette* had a birthday, prevented her from thinking too much about moments of giddiness
and suffocation.   When she reached the rue de Longchamps she
threw out a happy good night to the doorkeeper, started to run
up the stairs, and found them interminable.   At the top, quite
out of breath, she rang at the door, felt her head turn, and
cried out:

'Oh, mother, I think I'm going to be sick.'

Marie-Thérèse quickly fetched an enamel basin, held it in front of her daughter, then suddenly saw it fill with blood.

Rolande was not more than puzzled. My aunt had turned white. Her legs were shaking. She put her daughter to bed and sent for the doctor. A moment later Louis arrived with tall branches of white lilac, boxes of chocolate, and all sorts of presents for his dear little girl. When he saw her in bed he imagined that Marie-Thérèse was making her rest to be fresh for the theatre, but when, going into the kitchen, he saw the basin full of blood, and Marie-Thérèse, a finger on her lips, so white and shaken, he began also to be horribly afraid.

It was the same doctor who had come some months earlier. He fully reassured them, saying that as the accident coincided with her period he did not attach undue importance to it, but that it might be a good idea for her to take a tonic and that once a month she should spend the day in bed. Unfortunately other haemorrhages quickly followed. My uncle took her to a specialist, who immediately had her X-rayed. The negatives confirmed what the specialist already knew, that Rolande had been consumptive since attaining maturity. The dreadful illness was making swift progress. She must leave Paris as soon as possible and have a long rest in the country.

Marie-Thérèse turned to Ermeline. Ermeline was lucky to her. The first hat she ever made professionally was for Ermeline. Ermeline's mother, Mme Brossier, had been Rolande's second mother, her foster-mother. The house on the edge of the golden cornfield was a sunny memory. That Sunday, after she had taken Louis there to see Rolande who was then three, Louis had asked her to marry him. Miracles happened at Marais.

Marie-Thérèse and Rolande arrived at Mennetout on a hot July afternoon, and drove in a pony trap to Marais, where they lodged in the room where Rolande and I had stayed in 1912, the year Ermeline was so picturesquely married to Laurent.

Ermeline had changed terrifyingly. She had a charming little girl of seven, and Mme Brossier was still alive, but the tragedy of Laurent, still quite recent, hung darkly over the family.

Laurent had lost his right arm in the war. They had given him an artificial one, and sent him for a time to a place where he was taught to use the metal hand; but the peasant in him revolted at

the discovery that holding down horses, trussing hay, cutting
down trees, and digging the earth were no longer within his
possibilities.   His powerlessness gave him such bouts of fury
that he would remain for days with the most dark looks.   Ermeline, who loved him dearly, thinking herself lucky to have him
back at all, served him touchingly.   She tried, by working out
of his sight, to spare his humiliation, for what he hated most was
to see the things he would normally have done being done by
Mme Brossier, poor old Esther, and herself.   The idea that three
women, two of them very old, were doing his work—that was
what made him furious!   And yet he didn't spare himself.   He
led the cows to pasturage, the sheep to the shearer, and was never
too tired to bring up water from the well.

'There, my Laurent,' Ermeline would say, 'it 's a real pleasure
for us to do the washing when you give us all the water we need.'

'What 's so wonderful about bringing up water from a well?'
Laurent would grumble.   'Any fool can do that.   Woman's
work, that 's what I call it.'

Ermeline, rebuffed, would add her tears to the soapy water.
She loved him.   She tried to show it.   This sarcasm cut her
heart terribly.

The winters at Marais were hard, and Laurent became increasingly taciturn.   Other peasants swung the axe and the sledge-
hammer in the woods, put new handles to spades and forks beside
the fire in the low room during the long evenings.   Dispirited,
he sat back in his chair reading the paper, that is if anybody went
into Mennetout to buy one, for a newspaper was quite a rare
thing in the village.   When he had read all the news several
times over in a well-thumbed one he would look up and see the
four women knitting, sewing, or making cheese, laughing and
almost forgetting his presence—old Esther, Mme Brossier, his
wife, and his little girl, who was growing up so prettily, already
clever with her hands.   He had taken to raising his metal hand
on these occasions, and staring at it in such despair that the
women were moved by pity and fear.   In the spring Ermeline
and her mother turned the heavy, damp earth in the kitchen
garden, throwing out the weeds, planting the first rows of potatoes.   The sun began to warm the lovely country, buds burst
open, swallows made their nests, and robins left the eaves of the
houses where they had stayed all the winter for food and warmth

to seek adventure further away. It was a magnificent day, the
sort of spring weather that makes one glad to be alive. Ermeline's little girl was dancing round her skirts. Granny Brossier
was talking to her goat. Laurent just looked sadder than ever,
and his wife, vexed to see him so stubbornly insensitive to all the
happiness round him, teased him a good deal and ended by
putting a pail in his good hand, saying:

'Come on, Laurent, stop making a long face, and fetch me some
water to cook the dinner with. We 're all terribly hungry this
evening. Think of it, the first real day of spring. Mother and
I have dug twenty rows of potatoes, and to-morrow we shall have
to do just as many!'

He went off without a word. Then Ermeline, looking back
over her shoulder as she hurried towards the house, shouted:

'You will be quick, won't you, Laurent? And don't slouch
so! I 'll swear you 're getting lazy!'

She waited a long time for her water, doing a score of other
things about the house to keep busy. Then tired of waiting,
and anxious, she went to see what Laurent was doing. The
pail, still empty, was on the edge of the well, but the rope was
unwound, and when she caught hold of it to see why it had
slipped she felt a weight at the bottom. Hastily bending over
the aperture she saw, deep down, a dark shadow, and then,
understanding, gave a yell and ran to fetch her mother. The
neighbours arrived and brought up the unfortunate Laurent,
who had hanged himself from the rope. Ermeline continued
to be haunted by that spring evening and the unfortunate words
she had shouted to her husband on the way back to the house.

When Marie-Thérèse and Rolande arrived all this had turned
Ermeline into a very sad person. Nobody used the well any
more, with the result that the family had to make do with the
rain water that fell from the gutters into a big barrel at the end
of the house. Just then there was a heat-wave and the barrel
was almost dry. For my aunt and my cousin, who were both in
continual need of water to wash their things in, being scrupulously tidy, the situation was intolerable, especially as only ten
yards away cool water bubbled up in the well which, since the
tragedy, had become as inviolable as a tomb. Two fields away
they discovered a stream, and soon had great fun taking their
things there, but as it was in a valley the climb home was tiring.

The specialist in Paris had said that Rolande must eat as much beef as possible, but the inhabitants of the cottage, since Laurent's death, lived very frugally, existing entirely on the produce of their cow, the old lady's goat, and what they grew in their garden. Marie-Thérèse was obliged to go to Mennetout twice a week, on foot, of course. The amusement of visiting this little town, staring into the shop windows, especially that of the dark, curiously arranged haberdasher's, gave Rolande such childish happiness that her mother could not resist taking her; but the way home was so long and hot that they were both exhausted, and the meat they had bought for supper was so full of maggots that they would end by giving it to the chickens. So they had goat's cheese for supper—delicious, but not sufficiently nourishing for Rolande.

Rolande had discovered a great quantity of sedge which grew by the stream, and she plaited it into the most beautiful wide-brimmed summer hats which suited her admirably and which she could renew almost every day. It was wonderful to see how this talented young woman made models which would have delighted the great actresses who went to Lewis's. She decorated them with wild flowers, oxy-daisies, poppies, and cornflowers, and occasionally with ears of corn. One afternoon when she was fast asleep on a shady bank old Mme Brossier's goat came along and ate up her beflowered straw hat, and it must have been so much to the animal's taste that wherever Rolande went the goat was sure to follow.

The days went past very pleasantly—visits to Mennetout, long walks in the sun, evenings washing by the stream—and then one night, suddenly, Rolande had such a dreadful haemorrhage that the countrywomen, seeing her vomit, made the sign of the cross, tears falling down their faces, terrified, convinced she was dying. Rolande went to bed, staying there all the next day, but as she got no better the cottage, the wheatfields, the poppies, and marguerites became as hateful to her as once they had been dear. She entreated her mother to take her back to Paris. Esther, Mme Brossier, and Ermeline, meanwhile, were terrified by this illness which, because they were strong and healthy, filled them not with pity but repulsion. They turned their eyes away from the young woman whom they had brought up, edging away from her, treating her a little like an ill animal put in a dark corner to get better or die, and they seemed so terribly sorry for Marie-Thérèse that their exaggerated compassion frightened her. As soon as Rolande was able to travel my aunt took her back to Paris.

Louis was waiting at the station, and though he had not been told anything about the new haemorrhage he noticed immediately that for once Marais had done no good to Rolande; but mother and daughter were so delighted to see him again, having felt alone and helpless, that the mere idea of putting themselves under his protection was as if they were half out of danger. Louis had prepared the most charming supper, after which they told him what had happened. He tried to reassure them, but said they must see the specialist next day.

The holiday in the country had made my cousin much worse. Long walks under a scorching sun through cornfields had aggravated the illness, and she was now in a condition where she must remain in bed by a wide-open window by day as well as by night. The autumn was mild, and the cure in the apartment in the rue de Longchamps was not too complicated, but when the cold and fogs of winter came Marie-Thérèse shivered as she made her hats beside her daughter, who was in bed kept warm by thick blankets and hot-water bottles. The sitting-room was the only room with a window of any size, and Marie-Thérèse needed the light. She would wrap herself up in a big coat and blow on her fingers to keep them alive, for her needle kept falling. The window was only closed for supper. Gradually Rolande began to have a better appetite. Hope swept through the family, and they even made plans.

Rolande was sixteen that spring. A year had passed since the terrible evening when they had hoped to go to the theatre. Marie-Thérèse worked very hard, but tired quickly, and when the pains in her stomach became aggressive she went to a doctor who sent her to the Laennec Hospital, where she had the first of her serious operations. Louis now hurried back to Rolande every day to make her lunch, and then ran to see Marie-Thérèse in hospital, and he was always smiling and full of hope, bringing little presents and encouraging news.

Marie-Thérèse was very pale and feeble when she came out of hospital, but almost gay, saying how lucky she was to have Louis and Rolande and a lovely home. She had seen such horrible things in hospital. People had told her miserable stories. She sang now while she made her hats, feeling certain that next year things would be better, but when next year came Rolande, a few days after her seventeenth birthday, caught double pneumonia.

The little family was now in despair, waiting for the passing of each important day. A sister of mercy from St. Pierre de Chaillot, who had known Rolande when she was little, came every morning to pray with her, and finally suggested bringing a priest. Marie-Thérèse looked at the doctor, who nodded assent, whereupon the parents knew that the doctor had no more hope of curing her.

The priest administered the last sacraments, but when he had gone, though Rolande was very weak, she asked Marie-Thérèse for her curling-pins. She never went to bed without putting her hair in curls, and on this occasion she said, laughing, that at least she would die prettily, though in her heart she did not think she was going to die. After this show of bravery she relapsed, and the night proved very terrible, Marie-Thérèse and Louis watching her in turn. The next morning the sister of mercy arrived on tiptoe and asked in a whisper:

'The dear little angel is certainly in heaven by now, is she not, my friends?'

'No,' answered Marie-Thérèse, weeping, 'but I am afraid it will not be long now.'

Rolande was asleep, and that evening did not ask for her curling-pins. Then Marie-Thérèse threw herself on the bed unable any longer to hide her emotion. Both the parents remained up all night. Marie-Thérèse thought several times that her daughter was dead, so imperceptible was her breathing, and in the morning they hardly dared to move about the room. Suddenly Marie-Thérèse heard a faint voice:

'Are you still there, mother darling?'

Marie-Thérèse and her husband hurried to the bedside. Rolande went on:

'I've had such a beautiful sleep! I feel much better!'

The sister of mercy, who arrived a few minutes later, shook her head doubtfully. She had seen so many of these cases. Hope ran high, she said, only to be dashed down a few hours afterwards. This improvement was what she called the *mieux de la mort*—the better moment before death. They all prayed anxiously, but when the doctor arrived and felt Rolande's pulse he exclaimed with authority:

'She will live.'

Youth had temporarily won against the terrible illness. Rolande gradually recovered a little strength, but soon came the inevitable parting from her family—the always dreaded sanatorium. Marie-Thérèse was heart-broken. She and her daughter were such friends. They got on so well together, were both so gay and frivolous!

My mother and I, of course, were in tears by now. The supper which Louis had done his best to enliven with the bottle of Burgundy had turned poignantly sad. The window was wide open. The birds continued to hop on the sill, and from other flats one heard plates being rattled and children laughing. My mother looked at me in an anxious way as if she thought I might suddenly have been struck with the same ruthless malady. Then she and Marie-Thérèse got up and went into the room next door. I was left alone with my Uncle Louis, who said:

'My poor little Madeleine, all this isn't very amusing for you, is it? Paris is such a lovely city, and you're only twenty. Besides, you've become so pretty.'

He put a hand on my shoulder and looked at me, but he was really thinking of Rolande and how she could have been. We went to join my mother and Marie-Thérèse. The two sisters were in front of a big mirror trying on each other's hats and laughing.

25

ARLY next morning, leaving my mother in bed, I went into a café-bar for a French breakfast, very hot coffee and milk in a slender-stemmed glass, and three warm *croissants*, and set off gaily to begin my course of hairdressing and manicuring in the rue de Rivoli.

Several other young women arrived at about the same time as I did, and we were taken into a long, bare room in which there were a great many deal tables on each of which was a plaster head, some almost bald, others with a few wisps, and so on, through degrees, until at the far end of the room there were models with luxuriant hair which the more advanced pupils could skilfully wave and curl. In the centre of the room stood a large basin of water with sponges, a row of gas jets, and several dozen spirit-lamps to heat the curling tongs. I was given a white apron and led to the table with the most miserable of the plaster heads, my unfortunate mannequin having a single wisp of hair not more than three inches wide. Standing behind my model I was first taught to gauge the temperature of my heated tongs by placing them under my nose, and then to cool them by opening them and twirling them round, holding one of the branches between finger and thumb.

With the curling-tongs at the correct heat and a specially bought comb one was expected to execute that deft and pretty movement of pinching the hair, first on one side, then on the other, with the warm tongs. After each failure one went to fetch a damp sponge from the basin in the middle of the room. The ugly lines were removed, the hair dried with the tongs, and then all was ready to begin again. An instructress passed slowly between the tables, explaining patiently, taking up tongs and comb herself, then moving on to the next pupil.

After the first few days one knew everybody in this large, overheated room. *Midinettes*, tired of sewing, tried their hand at this new profession which, since the Marcelle wave and the vogue of short hair, was tempting people into it like a gold rush on the Yukon. Some of the sewing girls came after their own work was finished. They tried very hard, but were not always very successful, and then became heart-broken. Other pupils were on holiday, and others were out of work because it was August, and so many dressmaking houses, for instance, were closed whilst the customers were at Deauville. There were shorthand typists who had decided they would never be able to spell, sales girls from the big shops who could not get on with their buyers, and a few young women with money of their own. The chief difference between this and my school of short-hand was that we were as free to talk and sing as seamstresses. Serenades and tangos filled the air. As we became more expert we moved from quarter heads to half heads, and soon we were making partings, to the left or in the centre, and joining the waves to the tune of *Valencia*. This song continued to rise from every part of the city, from the errand boys on their tricycles, the ticket collectors on the underground, children playing ball in the Tuileries gardens. Paris, crowded with foreigners, hummed and sang and whistled this Spanish *paso doble*, marking an age, *Valencia, Valencia*.

My mother came to fetch me, and would lend her head to the more advanced students, who would give her a shampoo and a wave which cost her nothing. Factory girls and charwomen came with such sweet smiles, and the idea of being beautified free of cost made them indifferent to our awkwardness and the occasional wisp we burnt with the too hot iron. They also entrusted their hands into our care: poor, tired hands, red with work, stained by acids; swollen hands of washerwomen and ironers; bleeding fingers of seamstresses, pricked by the needle. We filed them and cut them and polished them, and gave them back unrecognizable even to ourselves. The instructress, to lessen our pride at this transformation, would say to us:

'That's nothing, my children. Wait till rich customers bring you hands that have never scrubbed a floor or washed a pair of bed sheets; soft, white hands that have always been perfectly cared for, and over which you will have to bend, my children, for thirty minutes perfecting their perfection, feeling hot and frightened, and when you've done wondering whether you've

done anything worth while.   Unfortunately you won't be able
to practise beforehand on hands like that.   They don't come
here to be done for nothing.'

Our teachers were so gentle and patient that one felt almost
sorry so much skill was not employed to more useful ends.   All
day long they trod the alleys between us, advising, encouraging,
smiling.   I began to be rather good, and then suddenly everything was tremendously interesting.   My waves became curved
and supple, joining in the middle, as they were supposed to,
forming pretty designs.   Speed was sought as well as one's
slowly improving cleverness.   We were given just under an
hour to trim, wash, and wave, and though by the end of the course
many of us acquitted ourselves honourably, especially with the
curling-tongs, the art of the scissors is far too subtle to be taught
entirely at school, even be it in the rue de Rivoli.   Nevertheless
our instructors did not tell us that, and our customers being invariably satisfied we were full of chimera and daring.

Though we did not necessarily talk about it, the idea of visiting
Clichy was always at the back of our minds.

Mme Maurer was our last remaining friend, and we decided to
go and have dinner with her; but as we were anxious to make an
impression walking down our street both my mother and I were
shampooed and waved at the school to look our very best, after
which we dressed in our Sunday clothes and took the underground to the Porte Clichy.

From here we went along the road bordered by the high
cemetery wall where we used to meet Mme Gaillard's sister with
her broom, past the big doors which opened on creaking hinges
for funerals, and thence beyond the fortifications to the Boulevard
Victor-Hugo, narrower and dirtier than I remembered it, narrower
especially in comparison to our busy Charing Cross Road.   The
rag-and-bone men and shadowy apaches were still there, but they
did not impress me, and I was rather disappointed not to feel
myself quaking for my life and—I must admit it—for my virtue.
The apaches were in small groups, so close to the grimy grey
walls that they gave the impression of holding them up, spitting
from time to time, a cigarette stub behind an ear, their check
caps pulled over one eye, a wisp of hair showing, red necker-
chiefs revealing the absence of collar and tie.   As we hurried
along the avenue memories came back thicker.   There was the

public wash-house from which women emerged stumbling under the weight of enormous bundles of damp linen. How I would have loved to go and rediscover that smell of soap and disinfectant, to see again the washerwomen with their naked, rosy arms, their wide aprons, skirts pinned up, and ample hair decorated with shiny combs! But no, these women had doubtless all cut their hair and shaved their necks. Though still in my teens what I had seen but yesterday had already passed into history.

When at last we reached the rue Souchal I was struck not with the smallness of the houses, but by their height. They were taller than I remembered them, their six storeys dwarfing our low dwellings in Soho. Children were playing in the street, and I was vexed at this sentimental moment not to recognize a single one. New faces also looked down at us from familiar balconies. Even the doorkeepers had changed. The Alexis, the Bretons (to whom I had sold our garden), and the Guillets had gone without trace. The bicycle shop was now a wine merchant's and our haberdasher's had become a garage.

Here was Mme Maurer's house.

The new *concierge*, not knowing us, asked where we were going. We told her.

'Mme Maurer? You'll find her on the sixth floor, facing the stairs.'

We thanked her and went up. On each landing we were greeted by the smell of leek soup, grilled steak, and fried potatoes. Doors opened and children came out with an empty bottle under the arm, on the way to fetch a litre of red wine from the corner shop or from a keg in the cellar. They looked at us with curiosity, halting a moment to discover at what landing we would ring. I had done the same myself, and could read their thoughts. Tenants changed, but the peculiar smells of French cooking and the curiosity of children with wine bottles remained constant. Men's deep voices could be heard above other sounds like the cries of babies and crockery being laid on oilcloth-covered tables. My mother continued to climb the stairs silently, her lips rather tight, not a spark of nostalgia for the old life in her breast, seeming not to notice the little girls with their dark wine bottles, hair in plaits as mine had been not so very long ago. At last, on the sixth floor, opposite the top of the stairs, just as the *concierge* had said, was a door which, gently pushed,

led into a room narrow like a corridor with a bed at the far
end. In this bed sat Mme Maurer wearing a white linen night-
gown with red edgings and puckered sleeves. Her eyes scanned
us as the door slowly opened, casting a shadow across our faces.
She remained inquiringly motionless, a piece of wire and a paper
flower in her hands, then suddenly exclaimed:

'Mme Gal! Madeleine! What a wonderful surprise! As
you see, I'm bedridden, but my heart leaps with joy! Madeleine
is magnificent, and as for you, Mme Gal, I swear you've grown
younger since I saw you last. Anybody might mistake you for
sisters.'

My mother blushed. She really did look very young. Life
in London had this effect on her. She mumbled something to
repay the compliment, but Mme Maurer exclaimed:

'No, please don't try to tell me I'm looking better. I know
too well, alas, how I am. Just half alive, my dear Mme Gal, a
poor wreck with nothing to live for. I ate my bread white when
I was young. Since then, year by year, it's been getting blacker
till soon, in the eternal night, I shan't even see it, and thank goodness for that! Madeleine, here, who ate her bread black when
she was little may, I hope, eat it white as she grows older. Both
of you are still very young. Your youthfulness warms my old
bones. You would scarcely believe the good it does me to feel
myself loved by a couple of strangers, for what are we but good
neighbours? I certainly never thought when first we met how
precious our friendship would prove to me.'

Mme Maurer spoke slowly in her excellent, rather stilted
French. She was obviously returning in mind to her childhood
in the historic house on the left bank of the Seine where her
father, the actor, must have declaimed in much the same deep
voice. Even I, who had little experience in these things, could
see that she was near the grave, horribly conscious of her loneliness, paying the price of her atheism. I looked at her with a
mixture of pity and horror. Was I to meet with nothing but
sadness in this gay city? Marie-Thérèse, Rolande, Mme Maurer.
I felt a desire to cry, and then to run out and prove to myself that
I was young and alive. Had I been a man I would perhaps have
smoked a cigarette, walked across to a café, and drank something
strong like brandy. Being a young woman I left the talking to
my mother and quietly went to the open window, peering over

the balcony. The street, seen from so high, appeared narrow, the children tiny. The doorkeepers were all sitting on their velvet chairs. The only difference was that I knew none of them. My eyes quickly sought the windows of our old apartment. There were bright curtains in both the bedroom and the kitchen, and where my father had died a young couple laughed amorously on the balcony, looking deeply into each other's eyes. At what used to be the Neveus' window a young woman with a baby in arms was talking to a little boy playing in the gutter. Mme Maurer said to me in her deep, solemn voice:

'Don't fall out of that window, Madeleine. The higher you are the more it hurts. I know a thing or two about falling from high up!' She laughed in a hollow sort of way. 'Sixty-eight! That's what I am! I've had a pretty long fall.'

She took a piece of copper wire from a bundle on her eiderdown and twisted some green paper round it to make the stem of a rose. She then made the petals of pink and red, saying as she worked:

'To-day it has really been far too hot. The sun just beats down through that window. The coloured paper tears and curls up between my sticky fingers, but I'll get up at four in the morning and make up for it. One practically needs no sleep at my age, and I rather like working at dawn. It's so quiet and cool.'

She turned to my mother and added:

'When I used to see these paper flowers on cheap stalls in the market I always thought them positively frightful! You must have seen them yourself. The factory hands love them. They buy them to put in those horrible vases they get for breaking clay pipes with an air-gun at the fairs. Still, believe me, now I make them myself I think they're rather nice. It just shows, doesn't it? One's tastes go down in the world!'

'I don't dislike them,' I said quite honestly. 'They look so fresh!'

'You really think so?' she asked, flattered. 'In that case you shall have the next dozen, but I'll make them deep red, red for love, and the green of the leaves will stand for hope. It will be rather exciting. This will be the first time I shall know what my customer looks like!'

The conversation was becoming a little brighter, and my

mother, finding that Mme Maurer's provision cupboard was empty, sent me down with a shopping basket to buy our supper. I ran down the stairs and made for the Place de la République.

I bought a loaf of bread and some cakes, passing the house where our doctor lived, the one who had looked after my father during his last illness. The brass plate had been pulled down. I remembered suddenly the way he had pocketed the fee and asked me what I planned to do, how he had said it was not so easy to become a good shorthand typist, and then, taking us to the door, appeared quite to lose interest in us. The wine merchant where my mother had bought a bottle of champagne for my father when he was dying was still there. I went in and chose a sparkling muscatel for our supper, and at the shop next door I bought half a dozen slices of ham, some hard-boiled eggs, a potato salad, and a few gherkins to remind me of my solitary lunches when my mother was out sewing. Further on there was a smart new hairdresser's, with a wax model in the window, a real peroxide blonde, scarlet lips, the bust draped in black velvet. I thought her quite magnificent, and was beginning to daydream, forgetting I was grown up, making the street again my playground. Suddenly I smelt fried potatoes which, exciting my hunger, made me hurry back holding tightly to my provisions. My mother had laid the table; Mme Maurer had finished eight red roses. The sparkling muscatel was voted excellent, and so were the ham and the hard-boiled eggs. Mme Maurer asked me if I had found the street very changed.

'There's a magnificent new hairdresser's,' I answered, 'and I suppose Dr. Ravaud must have made his fortune, for he's gone.'

'I know nothing about the hairdresser,' said Mme Maurer. 'Since I came to live up here on the sixth floor from the first where I used to face your flat, I haven't once been out, and I don't suppose I shall till I'm ready to make my last journey, but if it's any interest to you I can tell you about Dr. Ravaud.'

'I never liked him much,' put in my mother. 'He was so caustic because I wouldn't let him send Émile to hospital.'

'He came to see me here once or twice,' Mme Maurer went on, 'about my ulcer in the stomach. He said I didn't need to tell him how much it hurt because he had the same thing. A few days later he locked himself up in his consulting-room and opened a vein. He had cancer.'

'But he was quite young!' exclaimed my mother.

'Forty,' answered Mme Maurer. She lifted her glass and looked reflectively at the wine, then went on: 'Has anybody told you that Dédé Gontrel is quite a celebrated dancer at the Opéra, that her mother had her hair bobbed at the new hairdresser's, became an usher at the local cinema, and turned the head of the manager, and that poor Riri is in a home for incurables? Oh, yes, and that Didine, the lovely Didine, is married with two children, and lives in a house at Asnières, where she keeps hens and rabbits in the back garden?'

'And Marie Guillet, the girl who used to drive us mad with her violin?' asked my mother.

'She eloped on her twentieth birthday with an Italian pianist who was only sixteen,' said Mme Maurer. 'There was quite a scandal about it.'

We guessed that Ulysses must have told her all these things, but she never once mentioned her son's name. Before we left she handed me my bouquet of red roses, and my mother put an envelope on her pillow with what, for us, was quite a large sum of money. We felt somehow that we would never see her again.

26

THE next day was wonderfully warm and the streets sparkled, gay with people. Marie and her sister Betty, two girls I had made friends with in London when I was at the Galeries Lafayette in Regent Street, had now returned to their widowed mother in Paris, and my mother and I invited them to lunch. Both now worked on a fashion paper called *Au Jardin des Modes*, whose offices were then in the rue Édouard VII, and we arranged to meet by the equestrian statue of the good English king in the quiet square just off the Boulevard de la Madeleine.

We lunched in an excellent little restaurant. My mother, looking only a few years older than us, laughed at our jokes. I had never seen her in better humour.

Betty, the elder of the sisters, had been cashier at Raoul, the shoe shop, while Marie and I had been sales girls at the Galeries Lafayette opposite. Betty was our model. Extremely pretty, sweet tempered, and capable, she earned enough to keep her mother and two younger brothers very comfortably in their apartment on the outskirts of Paris. She was unofficially engaged to a boy called Jacques, who was madly in love with her, but not quite strong willed enough to marry her in the face of strong maternal opposition, for he came of rather a rich and famous family and his widowed mother had set her mind on a more suitable match. The romance had been going on for nearly two years, Jacques becoming more and more in love, but too fond of his mother to break with her, hoping that one day something would happen to make both women happy. Betty never blamed her fiancé for his evasiveness. When, after Christmas, he left her for the winter sports, or in summer for a holiday at his mother's villa at Deauville, she simply said it was the privilege of a young man of his world. She spent her own holidays at home with a pair of scissors and some patterns from the fashion paper on which she worked, cutting out dresses in which she hoped later to please her Jacques.

Marie was in violent contrast to her sister, small, dark, calm in appearance, but in reality torn by a sensuality that was in continual ebullition. Though we who loved her thought her pretty, she was less courted by men than Betty. Her features were gentle and her dark eyes full of promise. She was free, alas, too free, and though a first adventure had been catastrophic, she was now waiting with a young and loving heart for what she hoped would be the real thing.

I remember that our talk at lunch had mostly been about those pretty young Russian refugees who were just then filling Paris, having escaped from revolutionary Russia with a few jewels, their Slavonic charm, and large amorous eyes. Betty was in full cry against them, for they were apparently stealing all the best places in her magazine, prattling amongst themselves in their native tongue, affecting in French a quite delicious accent which made the men fall in love with them, and being so fresh in the morning after dancing till dawn in the night clubs of Montmartre.

'No, really,' she exclaimed, 'you have never seen such women! All night they dance, sing, drink vodka, and smoke like railway trains, and in the morning they turn up with ochre face powder, ravishing eyes, redolent of all that can be done in a night, mouths like ripe cherries, a tiny hat perched at an angle, and ready at a moment's notice to start work at their adding machines or draw a model from Lanvin. You should see them, Mme Gal, entirely absorbed in what they happen to be doing, quite oblivious to what has happened before, what is likely to take place in the future, and then suddenly a man comes into the room and immediately their nonchalant eyelids are raised, their eyes glisten behind lashes black and heavy with mascara, and now nothing matters but to capture his attention. I tremble to think what might happen if one of these creatures were to walk into my fiancé's office! They are irresistible, and the trouble is one can't even steal one of the men of their race, out of revenge, for all these Russians seem to be driving taxis or singing the Volga boat song in night clubs. It isn't fair, is it?'

We laughed as one does at that age, and Marie then said:

'I wouldn't blame anybody for dancing all night. This evening I'm going to the Rotonde in Montparnasse. You've no idea how gay it is, and everybody's dancing the Charleston. Oh, it's wonderful! You ought to come with me, Madeleine. Betty's going to the theatre.'

I looked inquiringly at my mother, not daring to answer.

'I don't see why you shouldn't,' she said.   'I shall spend the evening with Marie-Thérèse, and it's about time you should be with people of your own age.   Will you promise to be back by midnight?'

Marie and I gave a solemn promise.

Marie came to fetch me at the hairdressing school, and took me home with her.   It was quite a distance, in one of those broad avenues named after revolutionary leaders, on the fourth floor in a light, airy, modern building.   The table was already laid, and Mme Jourdain, small and dark like Marie, talked and talked her head off in the gayest manner, asking questions she never gave us time to answer, starting a phrase as she put a dish down on the table, finishing it when returning from the kitchen with another.   The two boys were here, both having just started to earn their living, very gay, listening to their talkative mother with affectionate irony, winking at us, not attempting themselves to put in a word.   One felt that dinner time was Mme Jourdain's scene, her play, her theatre, and that it was up to us merely to be the spectators, acquiescing from time to time, enjoying her magnificent cooking.

The younger of the two boys, however, thinking perhaps that his mother was surpassing herself this evening, began to laugh behind his serviette, giving me friendly kicks under the table, whereupon Mme Jourdain, not supposing for a moment that his hilarity had anything to do with her, said to him:

'Oh, and you, laughing over there, I shall never forgive you if you get me into trouble with the doorkeeper's husband!'

'What do you mean, mother?' asked the young man, colouring.

'I should be quite broken-hearted if I had to leave this apartment.   We are all so happy here like bees in a hive, just enough room for all of us.   And the piece of waste ground with the green grass I can see from the window gives me the illusion of living in the country.   Look for yourself, my little Madeleine!   Isn't it pretty, and you can't imagine how sweet it smells at night. You know, I'm always so sorry for the people who live in the centre of Paris.   The only way they can tell the seasons is by the oranges in December, the cherries and strawberries in summer, and the oysters outside the cafés in autumn; but as I say, I'm

privileged. I have my field. When one or other of you doesn't
come home till after midnight and I get too anxious I open the
window, listening for footsteps or the sound of a taxi, and look
at my field with the thistles and grass all covered with dew. And
the dandelions in spring, my little Madeleine! They make the
most excellent salads. The doorkeeper's wife knows about the
dandelions, but she's tied to her lodge like a dog to its kennel,
so I often give her some of mine, but that's no reason, you young
scoundrel, to make love to her. She belongs to the doorkeeper,
do you understand?'

'Oh, mother, what nonsense! She's thirty at least!'

'Nonsense? This morning you didn't know it, but I came in
behind you and with these eyes I saw you turn towards her lodge,
and then I saw the curtain move and one geranium being pushed
away from another so that madame could have a good look at
my son. Yes, my children, that's what I saw and if I had been
the doorkeeper instead of Mme Jourdain, there would have been
an immediate explanation with the wife and a month's notice to
the Jourdain family. That's why, young man, you will cease
making eyes at the lady, and all the more so because she's very
nice to look at!'

'I swear, mother, that if it hadn't been for Victor I wouldn't
even have noticed her.'

Mme Jourdain turned on her eldest son.

'Oh, so you're in it too, are you? How right I was to bring the
matter up. Now who wants some more of this Camembert cheese?'

The meal had been really delicious. Through the wide-open
window a slight breeze after the heat of this August day fanned
the tall grass of the field. Mme Jourdain served us coffee, took
some herself, holding the cup in both hands, sensually inhaling
the good smell, her nostrils quivering, her eyelids blinking. A
widow, very young, with these four children, too rigid in her
principles to think of remarrying, though she could have done
so easily, she was being inwardly consumed. She and her
daughter Marie had the same terrible sensuality, a need of
reciprocated kindness, a burning desire for male companionship.
All these things she tried to drive out of her system by an unending flow of words.

Suddenly dinner ended. Each took a dirty plate, knives, and
forks, and went off with them into the kitchen. The table-cloth

L

was shaken out of the open window, carefully folded, and put back in the dresser. We went into Mme Jourdain's bedroom where our coats and hats were stacked, and crowding in front of the tall mirror with which the wardrobe was faced we combed our short hair, powdered our faces, put on lipstick. The boys, after loudly kissing their mother and waving to us, had gone. The noise of their steps could be heard dying away on the stairs. We were longing to do the same, but because we were young women a stronger self-control made us impatiently retard the moment of saying good-bye to Mme Jourdain, who suddenly had become silent, as if her play was over, looking out of the window, holding a basket with socks and shirts to mend. As soon as we had gone she would go into her bedroom where she would sit under the portrait of her husband, dark, with moustaches, rather serious.

Marie's voice broke out:

'Good night, mother, don't worry, don't sit up. I 've promised Madeleine's mother to take her home before midnight. So you see I shan't be late myself!'

'Good night, Mme Jourdain. Thank you for the excellent dinner.'

'Good night, my little girls.'

We tore downstairs.

Outside on the pavement the doorkeeper's wife was sitting on her red velvet chair next to her doorkeeper, who was astride of his. He looked a very honest fellow with his flannel shirt open at the neck, revealing a hairy chest. His honest cap was pulled at an honest angle over his unimaginative head. I felt certain he must be quietly digesting leek soup and a rabbit pie left over from lunch and hotted up. One was not surprised his wife had moved her geraniums to see a good-looking young man, and she really was rather pretty for her age. She had the married happiness that poor Mme Jourdain so badly needed. Unfortunately none of us is ever quite satisfied with what is within reach.

Montparnasse was tremendously exciting. The Rotonde threw out its sparkle like a queen's diadem, and there rose from its crowded interior the sounds of a mad jazz. Crossing the terrace, elbowing our way past the customers sipping their multi-coloured drinks through straws, we went straight into the dance-room where enthusiasts were executing the newest steps. We had not been there a moment before I was carried off by an unknown dancer into the midst of the cacophony. After several turns on the floor I came back to Marie, who had ordered glasses of complicated liquid, of which I remember neither the name nor the taste, so entirely was I possessed by the frenzy of the dance. A moment later another partner arrived and I was led off again. I danced with Swedes, Norwegians, Americans, and Englishmen. The Rotonde had people of every land and, unlike the delegates at Geneva, they were only too anxious to get down to business without a word more than was necessary. I was delighted, heady with this instantaneous success which was due more to my gaiety and immense vitality than to my prettiness. I felt capable of going on all night, and yet my heels were bleeding and my toes throbbing in patent-leather shoes with short ends which were far too small. I would be complaining about them to Marie, then suddenly a new partner would arrive, bowing and beckoning, and I would fly off. At midnight Marie was obliged to use her authority to take me away from this delightful place so packed with Prince Charmings. I found my mother in bed with rather a severe face, trying to read, but she said nothing, and before I was undressed she had put out the light and turned over as tired with waiting and anxiety as I with dancing. My feet beat like drums, the contact of the sheets when I jumped into bed being painful in the extreme. How on earth had I managed to go on so long laughing, turning, gesticulating, with my feet in such a state? No wonder jazz was considered so diabolical by the older generation!

On Sunday we were to lunch at the rue de Longchamps, and then take the train to Groslay to see Rolande in her sanatorium.

Marie-Thérèse was alone when we arrived, very gay, warmed by the sunshine and the thought of seeing her daughter. She was in Rolande's former room, the one in which I had noticed all the hat-boxes on our first visit, laying things out on the bed, like clean linen and provisions, which she was going to pack and take to the sanatorium. My mother had brought several small parcels which were presumably also for Rolande, for she put them on the bed. We went into the sitting-room, where the window, as usual, was open. I leant out of it, looking up and down this wide, leafy avenue with magnificent houses, of which only the top floors were lived in during August. Lower down blinds were drawn and shutters closed, the rich tenants being in their country houses, at spas, or by the sea. The sparkling white houses had lost their expressiveness like people with their eyes shut.

Marie-Thérèse was doing her hair, and my mother was saying to her:

'Even though you don't like bobbed hair you must admit it saves a lot of trouble?'

'I'm beginning to think you're right,' answered Marie-Thérèse. 'If Rolande decides to cut hers I might do the same, only we're so united in the family that I think we ought to put it to the vote. If we wanted it enough—that is, Rolande and I—Louis would be sure to agree. He's so sweet about that sort of thing. The trouble is that with all this illness we've lost touch with what people are doing. Most of our friends have left off coming. I suppose they think we're not interesting enough.'

When my uncle arrived we had a cold lunch, and then hurried to the station, where we climbed into a third-class compartment, which we were fortunate in keeping to ourselves, Marie-Thérèse and my mother having corner seats by the open window. Marie-Thérèse was soon in agony, claiming that the hard wooden seat grated against her bones. Louis took off his coat to make a cushion for her, and for a few minutes she seemed better, but soon she began to wriggle and to complain again, and asked me to change places with her, saying:

'It's amazing how this poor tummy, which has hardly anything left in it, can make me suffer!'

She pushed her husband's coat aside, and sat on her folded hands as a pregnant woman sometimes does when she is alone. Louis opened a string bag and pulled out a bottle of water, a glass, and some aspirins. Then he skinned her a ripe pear with the patience of a man humouring a difficult child.

Conversation was not very brilliant, and I am ashamed to say that I was beginning to find the journey wearisome. Marie had told me she was going to a *thé dansant*, and I was jealous. The train was now clear of the outskirts and passing through the fresh country of the Oise.

Louis was talking to my mother about what he called his

business. He had left service, and had gone into a furniture shop near the Opéra, owned by a very old man who, having lost his only son in the war, had ceased to take much interest in the concern. My uncle was virtually in charge and dreamt of owning it one day. Marie-Thérèse listened to him in wide-eyed admiration and exclaimed:

'Really and truly Louis is magnificent! Oh, if only we had better health I don't know where he'd lead us to.'

A touch of colour was creeping back to her cheeks, and she began to prattle again under the influence of the aspirin. I had rather a pretty tie made of two marten skins which Mme Néroda had sold me, and which I had taken six months to pay for. I was extremely proud of it, and my aunt kept on stroking it and saying how pretty it was. She was herself wearing round her neck the most curious piece of fur without head or tail. My mother asked her what it was, having never seen it before.

'But of course you've seen it before,' exclaimed Marie-Thérèse, 'but not quite like this! Don't you remember that beautiful fur-lined coat which Louis's gentleman gave him before the war? I made myself a tweed coat with the outside, and I turned the fur into a three-quarters winter coat for myself and a collar and a muff for Rolande, and after all these years this is all that's left of it, and so I wear it round the neck with a costume in the form of a tie!'

'The colour is not very pretty,' said my mother, who never succeeded in hiding her contempt for what was not becoming. 'I'm surprised you can wear it.'

'Oh,' said Marie-Thérèse, biting her lips, 'after seeing it about the house for fifteen years I'm getting used to the colour. The important thing is that it cost nothing and keeps me warm.'

'Well,' put in Louis quickly, 'I think it's rather nice, and it looks so soft against her skin. She has such a fine complexion.'

Marie-Thérèse's complexion was, at this moment, extremely red under the strain of defending her pride without starting another quarrel with my mother. Hurriedly changing the subject she began:

'Last Sunday we were in the train like this with Rose——'

'What?' queried my mother. 'Is Rose still alive?'

'Of course,' answered Marie-Thérèse, 'and why shouldn't she be? She's only a few years older than I. And energetic! She has inherited the prettiest house in Burgundy, but insists on keeping on with her job in Paris. Of course, really she is still waiting for her German lover. Have you ever heard of such patience?'

'Call it what you like,' said my mother, 'but it's love. Yet I wonder what he would think of her if he came back now, for when I saw her last she was almost pretty, but that's ten years ago.'

'Pretty in her way,' said Marie-Thérèse, 'which didn't prevent her from looking like the cook she was. Only now she's different. She has become fatter and more prosperous with rings on her fingers and that necklace which we all thought so pretty, and which she has promised to leave to Rolande in her will. She's a good soul is Rose, and quite devoted to us, but when she comes with us to the sanatorium it's not really to see Rolande, but to spend the whole of the journey, there and back, talking about her German. If she saw you she would be delighted to have somebody new to discuss him with. She has developed a cult for everybody who ever met him. With all that she's my last friend. I'll never have time to get to know any new people. It takes too long.'

Louis sprang up, fussing with the parcels, for the train was pulling into Groslay, a pretty little town in the Seine-et-Oise, and as we walked down the platform my uncle and aunt appeared to know nearly all the other passengers making their way to the barrier. A tired little man doffed his hat, shook my uncle by the hand, and said:

'I'm so anxious, wondering how I shall find her to-day. I've had a terrible week. Something tells me she's worse.'

He doffed his hat again and slid through the crowd to the barrier.

'Poor devil!' exclaimed Louis, turning to my mother. 'His wife has just died from *it*, and now his daughter has *it*.'

We crossed the station yard, and were soon in the prettiest lane. Marie-Thérèse ran ahead of us and picked some wild flowers, exclaiming:

'Madeleine, doesn't it remind you of Marais? Here are some cornflowers and poppies!'

But almost immediately her high spirits drooped and she sat down on a grassy bank to rest, saying again that she could not understand why her tummy should go on being so painful after

all these operations.   She got up of her own accord after a few
minutes, and walked more quickly, trying to recapture her gaiety,
till we reached some gates where we found all the people who
had left the train at Groslay.   They were talking in groups with
the familiarity of *habitués* who arrived by the same train every
Sunday, waited for the gates to open at two, and came out together
when the bell rang in the evening.   Most of them had put down
their parcels and were fanning themselves with folded newspapers because of the heat.   A rather fat woman with her back
to the gates waved to my uncle and aunt and shouted in a shrill
voice:

'I got here first again!   The same as last Sunday, do you
remember?   This time I 've brought her a sirloin I cooked
myself before leaving!'   She pointed to an osier basket, and
went on: 'I shan't kiss her till she has eaten some.   Ah!   But
you 'll see!'

My aunt smiled at her in a friendly way, but while she was doing
so I noticed a curious twitch on the right side of her mouth.
All her lower muscles seemed to be dancing.   When she saw
that I had become aware of this state of affairs she quickly put
her hand to her face and the twitching ceased, but she blushed
violently.   I wondered at the time what her thoughts had been,
what had gone on inside her.   Later I knew it was physical pain
making more noticeable the effects of that terrible night when, as
a child, she was lost by my grandmother in the forest of Roussy.
She had been afraid, you remember, of being eaten by the wolves.
The muscles on one side of her face had never quite recovered.

Marie-Thérèse turned to my mother and said:

'We call the fat woman over there the Vierzonnaise.   She
comes from Vierzon.   She 's sorry for me because I 'm so thin
and I 'm sorry for her because she 's so fat.   Besides, look at that
ridiculous little *cloche* with the mauve feathers she 's wearing!
What dreadful taste!'

I looked back at the woman she called the Vierzonnaise, and
became aware of a tiny man beside her, dark, neatly dressed,
timid, looking terribly worried.   Whenever his wife spoke to
anybody in the crowd he smiled and bowed automatically, but
his thoughts were obviously on the other side of the gates which
now, suddenly on the striking of the clock, opened.

A wide lawn stretched in front of a large country house, 1900 style. We went up immediately to the main room, containing about forty beds facing one another, as in a hospital ward, with tables decorated with flowers. A few young women were in bed, but most of the patients were up, waiting for their relatives. The end of the room overlooking the park had sliding glass doors, which were always open so that we were virtually in the open air. Marie-Thérèse went straight to the second bed on the left, beside which stood a blonde young woman who threw herself into her arms before I had time to pay much attention to her features. A moment later my aunt, turning round, happiness written all over her face, said to my mother:

'Here she is, Matilda, here's my darling girl!'

'How do you do?' asked Rolande, as if she were being presented to my mother for the first time.

It was then my turn: two young women, quite unknown to each other, who might already be married. We were rather embarrassed, and looked for guidance to our mothers. Mine was very moved to be in the presence of her niece. Her blue eyes were filled with tears she was most anxious to hide. She bent over the parcels I had noticed in the morning, undoing the string, revealing all sorts of presents for Rolande, a pair of blue satin slippers with high heels, some lingerie silks, handkerchiefs, stockings, and some knitting wool. Rolande was delighted and kept on saying:

'Really, Matilda, you are too kind!'

I stayed a few paces away, being too healthy to feel the same emotion as my mother, and my eyes wandered towards a pale young woman in the bed next to Rolande's, frail as a child, her head resting on two pillows. Beside her knelt a man who was rummaging in a little food chest under the table, and as he looked up I recognized the man at the station who had said to my uncle: 'I've had a terrible week. Something tells me she's worse.'

He now said to the girl in bed:

'Oh, Laurette, how naughty of you. You haven't eaten anything I brought you last week, none of those lovely biscuits, or even the chocolates from the Marquise de Sévigné. Oh, my Laurette, how you grieve your poor father! To think I've brought you more biscuits and more chocolates! But, Laurette, why don't you tell me what you want? You know I'd go to the other end of the world to satisfy your desires.'

'Oh, I know, father,' she answered, coughing, 'but the only thing I want any more is not to cough.'

She stretched out a hand, and taking a small box from the table removed the cover and spat into it.   Then she went on:

'Oh, father, do stop rummaging in that cupboard.   You get on my nerves.   Sit on the edge of my bed and tell me about the *concierge* and our neighbours, and all the people I want to know about.'

He became agitated, making more noise than was necessary, rose from his kneeling position, and, after straightening his tie, changed the position of his hat, which looked like a puddle of ink on his daughter's white bed.   Drawing up a chair he took her hot hands in his and began to talk softly.   All my sympathy was for Laurette and her unfortunate father whose name I did not even know.   Suddenly I heard Rolande asking:

'Shall we go and walk in the park?   It's full of birds.'

She showed her new slippers to Laurette in passing, and smiled at the father.   Then, taking her mother's arm, she led us to the garden.

The lawn was covered with long wicker chairs, with mattresses and rugs on which the patients rested morning and afternoon, neither talking nor reading, merely listening to the birds singing and the leaves rustling.   Before dinner most of them walked a little in the park.   Afterwards they had to eat even though they were not hungry, but most important of all was to remain gay, to want to get well, to be full of hope.   For some it was very difficult; for Laurette, for example, who, unless a miracle happened, was very near her end.   That thought was clearly on her father's face.

Rolande really believed she would get well and said:

'In two or three years when I get out of here my daddy will have to buy me a little cottage in the country—oh, a very simple one with a thatched roof—with two bright bedrooms, one for you two and one for me, and in order to give me plenty of fresh air daddy and I will knock down a wall so that the birds can fly right in and nest above my bed!'

We laughed and I exclaimed:

'But what will happen when you're married?   Perhaps your husband won't like the idea of sleeping under a bird's nest.'

She answered superbly:

'If he loves me he'll like everything I like.'   Then more

*L

seriously: 'You wouldn't understand, Madeleine, what it means
not to be able to breathe. If I had to go back to the rue de
Longchamps I would stifle.'

Louis broke in:

'No, no, I promise. You'll never go back there. You
couldn't climb the stairs. I'll buy you a cottage in the country.'

The park was really very pretty. We passed other young
women with their relations, and every time, of course, we asked
Rolande who they were and for how long they were here. A
young woman arrived on the arm of her young husband. She
had been struck down immediately after the birth of her first
child, who was not yet a year old. All the week she worried
about her baby, about her good-looking husband, afraid to lose
him. As soon as she saw him she asked him cunningly a great
number of questions to discover what he had been doing all the
week, and as soon as he had gone she was so miserably jealous
and fearful of the future that she buried her face in the pillow and
sobbed. Then there was Laurette, also crying, pushing away
all the good things her father had brought her, and at the other
end of the room the daughter of the woman from Vierzon, tiny,
frail, worn out by her mother's insistence that she should eat the
lunch she had so lovingly prepared. Rolande told us these
things with such a mocking laughing air that one quite forgot
that she also had the dread malady.

She was beginning to look at me critically, admiring my
healthy cheeks, but blaming me for having had my hair cut short.
Hers—long, blonde, and silky—was magnificent, like that of a
child. We had escaped a moment from our parents, and compared our legs, deciding that in this respect there was nothing to
choose between us, that we had just the right legs for short skirts.
Then, without meaning to make her jealous, I described my
evening at the Rotonde and similar evenings in London, the flirts
I had to my credit, and my dreams for the future, which were
much vaster than a cottage in the country, more like the house
full of furs and dresses belonging to Mme Lapage's sister, who
remained a sort of heroine. Rolande did not laugh at me. On
the contrary, she seemed impressed and said:

'If that happens you might help daddy buy that cottage in the
country, for, between ourselves, I haven't much hope of the
poor dear doing it by himself.'

'Of course I will!' I exclaimed.

She pressed my arm by way of thanks. We had rediscovered one another.

Our parents rejoined us, and we went back into the house where Marie-Thérèse, exhausted, her face very red, sat down. Louis looked miserable to see his wife doubled up in pain. My mother was terribly moved, her eyes wandering round the room from bed to bed. If I had begun to cough at that moment I think she would have let out a cry.

These last few minutes before the bell were cruel. Marie-Thérèse drew her daughter towards her and kissed her greedily, while Rolande, to give herself courage, spoke to her mother as she used to do when she was little. Then she would turn to Louis and bring him childishly into the conversation. Laurette's father edged clumsily nearer the young woman whose life was ebbing away, closed her eyes as if by premonition, stroked her dark hair, clasped her clammy hands, and said pitifully:

'Really I find you much better this week.'

Furtively he looked at the clock, anxious to escape, and yet fearing to leave. My uncle, whose kind heart understood what was going on, said to the poor man:

'I've brought my niece this week. She no longer has a father, and she and her mother have found life pretty hard.'

Laurette looked at me with sudden interest, pitying me because I had no father. Louis went on:

'One can't have everything, can one?'

Laurette's father was grateful for this interlude. I heard my uncle whisper to him:

'Let's all go back to the station together, try to cheer one another up a bit, eh?'

'Yes,' agreed Laurette's father. 'We can talk of *them*.'

On the opposite side of the room the woman from Vierzon, whose mauve-feathered *cloche* was slightly askew, looked at her daughter, who for the last three hours had been reclining against the father's numbed arm. The little man's eyes were filled with tears. To make his daughter's position more comfortable he was trying to synchronize his breathing with hers.

One heard hurried kisses. A nurse had arrived, and was tidying up paper and string thrown down by the visitors. She said it was time for temperatures to be taken. A bell rang.

Laurette's father was the last to leave. We were waiting for him by the gates, but when he arrived he merely doffed his hat and said to my uncle:

'Ah, my good sir, my daughter is lost. Good-bye, my dear sir.'

He hurried off; then suddenly turned and exclaimed:

'*Your* daughter is much better. I am happy for your sake.'

He raised his hat for the last time and disappeared, leaving us all rather shaken.

When we reached Groslay the woman from Vierzon and her husband were sitting on a station seat, he silent and thoughtful, she dazed to the point of stupidity. Every Sunday, according to Louis, the unfortunate woman was struck in the same way. She owned a laundry, and worked so hard during the week that she had little time for reflection; then on Saturday night she would buy all sorts of robust food for her daughter, imagining that the slender girl could be bullied into having her own large appetite. 'She's just tired,' she would say to herself. 'A good piece of beef will put her right again.' Louis and Marie-Thérèse saw them arrive every Sunday full of energy, the woman speaking in a loud, rough voice, bustling her poor creature of a husband, but their return was very different. Faced with the full measure of the illness she would suddenly collapse into this dazed state. My aunt went up to her as she sat with her husband on the platform seat, and said compassionately:

'You mustn't worry too much. How could you expect any of them to look very well in this dreadful heat?'

'Do you really think it was the heat?' asked the Vierzonnaise. Then turning to her husband: 'Do you believe that?'

He sighed but said nothing.

The train came in, and we made a rush for the third-class compartments which were full of young people who had spent the day in the country, eating in arboured restaurants by the river, sleeping arm in arm in the freshly mown hay, happy, sunburnt, dishevelled, the women with wild flowers in their *cloche* hats which were pulled down over their young foreheads. Several squeezed to make room for us. We smiled and brushed past their short skirts. The train went off again and conversation began.

Marie-Thérèse had been offered a corner seat, and she sat,

exhausted, with her ridiculous piece of fur on her lap. She looked up at my mother and said:

'I heard you telling Rolande that everything had gone wrong in your life. I can't understand you saying that. Just now, for instance, you 're much luckier than we are. The past doesn't hurt as much as the present. It 's what happens now that matters and you won't know what health means till you lose it.'

'You can lose your health momentarily and get it back,' said my mother. 'People fall ill every day, but they don't all die. You and Rolande, for instance, are sure to get well again, and then you 'll find yourself in a nice home with a husband who loves you. That 's why I think you 're lucky. I 've never been loved like that.'

'That 's just a question of finding the right man,' said Marie-Thérèse, looking in the direction of Louis, who was standing at the other end of the crowded compartment.

'Luck, I say,' repeated my mother.

The train stopped at another station.

'By the way,' asked my mother, as the train moved off again, 'did you ever hear what happened to Raoul, the good-looking footman, and the beautiful Hélène, the old doorkeeper's wife?'

'Raoul lost an arm in the war. Perhaps you knew that?'

'Yes, I think I did,' answered my mother.

'He was no longer so pretty when he came back,' my aunt went on. 'He had a stubby beard, and was rather stout, and with only one arm . . . But then, of course, things had changed so, hadn't they? I mean, there were no more liveried footmen or smart carriages. All that had vanished as completely as Raoul's good looks. Well, at any rate, he and his rather faded mistress set up together and started to sell silk stockings on the boulevards or anywhere else where they could put up a trestle-table and an acetylene lamp.'

'Hélène's husband, the *concierge*, was dead, wasn't he?'

'Of course, quite a long time back.'

'Go on,' said my mother.

'You remember that when Hélène and Raoul were young they had wanted to elope to North Africa, where Hélène had a sister?'

'That 's right, but the war came and they couldn't go.'

'Exactly. But after the war Germaine, the sister, who was a prostitute in a brothel in Algiers, came back to Paris without any money, and turned up at Hélène's and Raoul's flat, where she installed herself, claiming that Hélène owed her hospitality. She used to stay at home all day smoking Raoul's cigarettes and reading novels. In the evening she made herself look nice and went to meet Raoul and Hélène on the boulevards. One evening, caught by a downpour, she ran across the road on her high heels to shelter in a doorway. She had the tiniest feet and was always particular about her shoes. An elderly man who was sheltering in the same doorway began to talk to her. She knew how to amuse men, and they got on so well that he offered to take her to the boulevards in a taxi. As they were getting in he said something to the effect that her shoes would be ruined by the rain. She agreed, and added that it was a pity because shoes were her one luxury. From that moment he never left her. It turned out he was a millionaire shoe manufacturer. There was a very smart wedding, and she was married in white!'

'Oh!' exclaimed my mother, biting her lips.

'Of course it didn't help Hélène and Raoul,' my aunt went on, 'because Germaine said they had tried to snub her when she had arrived from Algiers, and so she slammed the door and left them without a thank you.'

'Do *you* ever see Germaine now?' I asked, interested.

'Oh, no,' answered Marie-Thérèse, laughing, 'she's too smart for us. Fancy! jewels, furs, a motor-car, and a chauffeur!'

In the taxi from the station to the rue de Longchamps we were almost happy. When we drew up outside the house my mother nudged me to get out first and pay. The driver was a Russian *emigré*, the husband perhaps of one of those bewitching ladies who made my poor Betty so angry at the *Jardin des Modes*! I gave him a generous tip, very proud to show off a little, and the driver, making me the most comical bow, exclaimed in his Slavonic accent:

'Thank you, blonde and beautiful young lady. You are as generous and gay as the princesses in my country!'

He let in his clutch and very gravely drove off, looking straight in front of him.

27

FOR our passing out at the school of hairdressing each of us was to make beautiful some brave but impecunious young woman who had agreed to this free metamorphosis. Mine still had her eyes full of sleep, for she worked in a Montmartre night club and had only just got up. The heat-wave continued, and we had taken off our dresses and put our white linen coats over our petticoats. The very pretty dress which my mother had made out of Mme Thémiers's ribbon hung on a peg behind me above a chair on which I had put my bag and my hat. In the evening, whilst my mother was at the rue de Longchamps, I was to go dancing for the second time with Marie at the Rotonde, and I wanted to look my best.

I worked extremely hard, cutting, washing, and waving the hair of my young model. I then did her hands, and as she was pretty the effect was rather good. An instructress showed me what I had done wrong, improved several waves, and having done the same thing to the other pupils gave us to understand that we could now count on our diplomas.

When, at seven, elated, all talking at the same time, we started to take off our white coats and announce the good news to our parents, I could not find my bag. I looked everywhere, my heart thumping with emotion, childish tears pouring down my cheeks. My bag was full of newly acquired treasures, a powder compact, a lipstick, a comb, a note-book with some addresses, and all my savings in a pretty wallet. Between sobs I gave my companions a minute description of these objects. When I saw them powdering their faces and putting on lipstick my tears redoubled.

In a few minutes my companions had gone and the room was bare. The instructress with her hat and coat on was coldly impatient, anxious to lock up. She put the curling-tongues away noisily, gave a last tight turn to the taps, and looked at me inquiringly. Fear of what my mother would say was growing,

and then a new cause for panic. My passport! My nose
shining, my eyes red with tears, I went down the black staircase
into the rue de Rivoli, crowded, noisy, still bathed in hot sun.
Quite lost with nothing to hold, my arms and hands feeling
stupid, I was so conscious of looking ridiculous that I did not
dare hold my head at its proper angle, but hung it shamefully,
quickening my pace to almost a run, gradually conscious of a
fresh disaster, that I was penniless, and would have to cross half
Paris to confess myself to my mother at the rue de Longchamps.
My evening with Marie at the Rotonde was off.

While hurrying thus, blind to everything around me, I bumped
into a passer-by, a total stranger, who stopped me half angrily,
saying:

'Why on earth don't you look where you 're going, my poor
child?'

Furious at what I considered an unwarranted freedom, I said in
English:

'Leave me alone!'

'Oh,' he exclaimed in the same language, but with an accent
that was clearly French, 'I see we speak English, but even that
isn't a reason why you should run into me!'

I looked at him, still angry and even afraid, but his self-posses-
sion and grey temples reassured me. I said:

'I 'm sorry. I didn't do it on purpose. I was upset about
my bag.'

'Yes,' he answered, 'I see you haven't one, and that you 've
been crying. You don't need to be afraid of me. I won't eat
you. Let 's have a drink at the terrace of the Régence. It will
do you good to tell me your story, and as I 've parked my car
opposite I 'll drive you to wherever you happen to be going.'

The Régence, facing the Comédie Française, meeting-place of
writers and actors, had always struck me as one of the most
beautiful cafés in Paris. I saw immediately that my companion
was genuinely sorry for me, that the gaiety which replaced my
tears after a glass of sherry amused him, and that I need have no
fear for my virtue. The wine warmed me deliciously. I was
soon describing my aspirations, what I hoped to do in London,
how I lived with my mother in Soho. Nothing could stop this
flow of words which I could feel doing me good, calming my
nerves. He paid the bill and led me to his little open car drawn

up a few yards away, and as we drove to the rue de Longchamps I was almost happy, but as soon as we arrived the fear of what my mother would say again gripped me, and I climbed the stairs with a throbbing heart.

She was, of course, extremely surprised to see me and, after I had followed her through Rolande's former room and stood in the light by the open window of the sitting-room, she saw by my embarrassed look that something serious had taken place, and she said:

'I suppose you didn't pass your examination.'

'Much worse than that.'

'Worse than not passing your examination? What on earth do you mean?'

Marie-Thérèse was sitting on a low chair in her usual corner, her feet on a stool, an unfinished hat on her pointed knees, and she looked at me in such a funny way that I burst out crying and exclaimed:

'Listen, mother, while I was passing my examination somebody stole my bag, and I had all my savings and my passport in it.'

'It 's a nuisance about the bag,' said my mother calmly, 'and it 's a pity about the money, but you don't need to worry about the passport because this morning when you were still asleep I took it out of your bag for fear you would lose it. Here it is with mine.'

I was astonished at the unexpected turn in my affairs. Marie-Thérèse said:

'I can't understand you, Matilda. Aren't you going to punish the big silly?'

'What good would that do?' answered my mother. 'It wouldn't bring her bag back. She 's punished enough by having to stay with us this evening instead of going to Montparnasse to dance with her friend. All one can say is that it 's probably better for her health.'

When Louis arrived he was told the details, and during supper I was a good deal laughed at, especially about the small Citroën in which I had been driven back from the Régence. My uncle said he would have been more impressed if it had been an His-pano-Suiza. 'My poor Madeleine,' exclaimed Marie-Thérèse, 'anybody can see you were not born lucky!' My mother nodded as if approving.

At the end of what for me was a miserable evening we walked home, my mother, with her usual tiny steps, rolling her hips, I hard put to it not to sulk.

The next morning I went back to the school of hairdressing till lunch time. Then, hurrying out into the rue de Rivoli, I came upon my companion of the previous evening waiting for me. 'I couldn't resist coming to ask you if you had got into hot water last night!' he said, laughing. 'I see you 're still without a bag. Let 's have a drink. If you 're worried about going back to London quickly I might be able to help you at the passport office.'

I told him that my mother had taken my passport away in the morning while I was asleep, and that my only punishment would be to have no bag till we were back in London.

'Oh!' he answered. 'Now I really am sorry for you! What will you do with your hands for two whole days without a bag when you go out? Suppose you let me buy you one? Giving pleasure is the fun a man gets at my age. I 've kept my lunch time free. At three I shall have to say good-bye. What do you say to letting me entertain you till then?'

I hesitated.

We were passing at that very moment one of the many delight-ful shops in this famous Paris street where the prettiest bags abound. He took me by the arm and bought me one. Two doors further on a compact, a lipstick, and a tiny comb were quickly chosen. At the corner of the next street a window was full of delicate cambric handkerchiefs. He bought me one of these, saying that I was to have everything I had lost. I was delighted. We lunched in a small restaurant—a steak and fried potatoes, apricot tart and cream, cheese, and strong black coffee.

'I 've another half-hour,' he said, looking at his watch. 'Where would you like to go?'

'Anywhere.'

'How about Montmartre?'

'Oh, yes.'

We found the Citroën in a side street, and he drove me to the Sacré-Cœur, glistening in the hot sun.

'Come!' he said, jumping out.

The wide terrace in front of the church was crowded with

sightseers. We hurried up the steps, entered the cool nave, where my companion knelt and crossed himself. After a moment he whispered:

'The Sacré-Cœur is the vision I had during four years in the trenches. It was my comfort. It was all Paris. I come to pray here as often as I can. You'll often see my little car drawn up outside.'

'I was born a few yards away,' I said, 'and yet I 've never been inside!'

We went to the Place du Tertre, where a man with an accordion was singing:

> 'Comme il était beau mon village,
> Mon Paris, mon Paris.
> On y parlait qu'un seul langage,
> Ça suffisait pour être compris!'

Our little walk in Montmartre was magnificent. What a restful feeling to amble through these steep and crooked streets after the terrible emotions of the last ten days! I saw with eyes full of curiosity the house where I was born, the dingy café below, the firewood and charcoal in the yard.

A few minutes later my companion drove me back to the rue Vivienne, where my mother was waiting at our hotel.

The next morning I went for the last time to the school of hairdressing to receive my diploma, an illuminated scroll announcing that I, Mlle Madeleine Gal, had passed with honours an examination in hairdressing and manicuring. The parchment was addressed to prospective employers and signed by a member of the guild. I rolled it up carefully and held it tightly with my bag, which never left me now, and walked across to the Régence to say good-bye to my friend.

My mother and I were to lunch with Marie-Thérèse, and spend the afternoon with her before leaving on the Dieppe–Newhaven service for London. As it was too early to go to the rue de Longchamps my companion drove me round the Bois de Boulogne and then, returning to the Étoile, took me to a street off one of the radiating avenues where a shining new building was going up in terraces so that each storey should have the full strength of the sun. As soon as we parked the car the foreman came to show us round. I was very moved to find myself with men who reminded me of my father. I was not afraid of

the dust, and the smell of plaster was familiar. I would have
liked to embrace these men whose faces were lined deeply with
fatigue, long hours, and the sparse comforts of lodgings like
those we had lived in at Clichy.

My companion told me that he was so nervous of seeing his
entire fortune dwindle in successive devaluations of the franc that
he was building this hotel which would be ready in a few months'
time. There would be a beauty parlour which I could take over
if I wished. Meanwhile he had written me a letter of introduction to a friend in London who might engage me as a manicurist at the Savoy.

He then drove me to the rue de Longchamps, where we parted,
bringing to an end a strange acquaintanceship which was to have
quite an important bearing on the future course of my professional life.

Marie-Thérèse was in agony that day. The weather was
turning stormy, and the many aspirins she had taken during the
morning did not appear to be giving her the usual relief. She
was just back from hospital and my mother's departure made
her very sad.

The two sisters were sitting side by side.

My mother, to keep herself busy during the long hours she had
spent with Marie-Thérèse, had made a dress for Rolande. As
she said, it did not represent a great deal of work—a long corsage,
hardly any skirt, and no sleeves! Marie-Thérèse was making
me a jade-green hat. She laughed at me for my love of bright
colours, a taste I had picked up in London where brilliant hues
compensate for days of fog and damp. My aunt claimed that
one could only be smart in black or dark blue with a little white
in the right places.

Rummaging in her hat-boxes she had discovered this piece of
jade taffeta spun so tight that her needle had trouble in going
through the material. From time to time she would try it on
my head, making me step back to the window to judge the effect.
She would then have an idea and make me come forward again
so quickly that I hardly had time to catch sight of myself in the
big gilt mirror which the mother of my Uncle Louis had given
her in 1913 before leaving for the Argentine.

At six my uncle came back from his furniture shop and we got
ready to go. My aunt promised to write twice a week. Then

putting the finished hat in a bandbox with the name of Lewis on it, she kissed me tenderly and accompanied us to the door. My uncle took us some of the way home. He also promised to write to my mother, but asked her, if she mentioned my aunt's health, not to write to the rue de Longchamps but to his office. He left us reluctantly as if his responsibilities were too great for his tired shoulders.

28

WE reached Victoria at half-past five on Sunday morning. The milkman was at the top of the street, and we heard bottles being banged together and the cry of 'Milko' as he went from door to door. Our taxi driver helped us with the luggage, his heavy steps making a dreadful noise on the stairs. My mother clearly was nervous, fearing that our neighbours, suddenly awakened, would put their heads out and insult us.

Our room smelt of pepper and mice. Flowers in a jug on our wash-basin had withered horribly. I had refused to throw them away before leaving London—they were so fresh, so colourful, so pretty, that I could not believe they would die. My mother, whose nerves were already on edge because of the noise the taxi driver had made coming up the stairs, was angry because the water in the jug was rank, and now while it was still dark we would have to run down into the yard to throw the dead flowers in the dustbin and then wash the jug and draw clear water on the landing. Meanwhile, looking for matches, we hit our shins against the table legs. The foul air in this room, the window of which had not been opened for three weeks, caught our throats. Our return from holidays was certainly a sad business.

My mother took off her hat and turned on the gas. I watched her stupidly and half asleep.

'Run down and find that milkman,' she said. 'We'll feel better after breakfast, but see to it you don't make a noise going downstairs.'

Day breaking gave a little more colour to the street, and the air had a nice fresh tang. The milkman had gone, but I could hear the wheels of his cart in New Compton Street, and I ran in his direction. A real London Sunday morning was beginning. The old smells came back: cold fat from the Soho restaurants, banana skins rotting in the gutter remindful of nail varnish.

Paper flew from one pavement to the other, newspaper, betting slips. There must have been an important race the day before.

The milkman came towards me and queried:

'Bonne holidays in gay Paree, mamzelle? You aren't half lucky! I went to Moulin Rouge on leave during the war.'

In his enthusiasm he gave me good measure, and on my return to our room my mother had opened the window, made the coffee, and laid the breakfast at one end of the table. She had even thought of bringing a loaf of French bread and some *croissants* from Paris. I admired her thoughtfulness, and was extremely hungry. Afterwards she made me undress and go to sleep, for my lids kept on falling.

I was wakened by a fierce clanging of our old-fashioned door bell. I sat up in bed and leaned out of the window, whereupon I saw Emma, our Swiss-German friend who worked at the 'Pop,' in her Sunday clothes, a light grey coat and skirt and a vivid red hat, obviously all ready to go to the Swiss church in Endell Street. She gave me to understand that she first wanted to know how we had enjoyed our holidays. My mother gave me the key of the downstairs door, which we wrapped up in a piece of newspaper, throwing it down to Emma in the street.

She sat at the end of my bed and listened to everything. My jade green hat was about the only thing that met with her approval, but she pointed out that it was not practical to have a green hat at the beginning of autumn. 'When the summer holidays are over,' she said, 'you must think about winter.' She said she had already thought about hers, that while we had been running about in Paris wasting our time she had been having a very good season, by which she meant that tips had been good, especially from American visitors, and that she had bought not only a winter hat, but also a fine piece of material and a colleague's silver fox ('The silly girl sold it to pay for her holidays!') which would make a coat with fur on the collar and sleeves.

'So you see I'm all fixed for the winter. I don't need to be afraid of it, and there's no question of my not being elegant, but I must say that neither of you is very inquisitive. You haven't even asked me the colour of the material. Lucky I'm a good sort. You don't need to die of impatience. Bottle green, that's what it is! With bottle green *crêpe de Chine* for the lining.

If you close your eyes you can see right away what sort of effect that will make!'

'Why, yes, I think it will make an effect,' said my mother curiously. Emma looked up quickly, not liking the tone of my mother's voice, but my mother went on innocently: 'Would you like a cup of coffee?'

'Oh, no, not now. Thank you all the same. I would be afraid of having to go out in the middle of the sermon. Our dear, good pastor does so let himself go, and when I feel a need there's no holding me back. You know what I mean? I'd be interested to learn what you have for lunch. People of your sort never think of anything in advance. In Switzerland it's different, especially in German Switzerland. Nobody can accuse us of improvidence. Lucky you've got me! I thought it all out yesterday. Madeleine must go into my room and take the carrier from the arm-chair. There's an Ostend chicken which will taste pretty good, some tomatoes, a loaf of bread, and a bottle of Chianti. I hope you'll at least invite me to lunch. There! I've just time to open the door for Madeleine and then I must hurry to church.'

When I came back with the provisions my mother was looking very thoughtful, pouring boiling water on the coffee in the percolator. I know by experience she had moods when it was better not to disturb her, and so I simply started to unpack my crushed clothes.

After a few moments my mother said:

'I suppose it's time I thought about making you a winter coat. What a pest that Emma is! She's nice enough in her way, but she's always spoiling our fun. There's nothing more hateful than having a person around who is so jolly right. Her tidiness, her cleanliness, all those qualities—what's the use of them except to show up our faults? Yet I thought there was a saying about nothing venture, nothing have?'

Eleven struck at the church of St. Giles. Doors slammed as cooks, waiters, and *maître d'hôtels*, for whom Sunday was a day of work, hurried out fastening the belts of their blue overcoats. I needed fresh air. This return home was quite horrible, and I could see written all over my mother's face her regret we had spent so much money, her fear we might not easily find new work. I exclaimed suddenly:

'I'd feel better if Nanny were here. I think I'll run and fetch her.'

'Yes, do,' said my mother.

I ran downstairs and threw myself into the street. All the bells in London seemed to be ringing. St. Patrick's in Soho Square was busy answering St. Anne's in Old Compton Street. Charing Cross Road was littered with shiny cigarette cards showing famous boxers, butterflies, and animals from the zoo.

Celestine was already up when I reached her attic flat. She had her hat on. I wondered if she had slept in it. As she did not offer me a seat and all her chairs were filthy, we remained facing each other, cats passing between our legs, arching their backs against our stockings. I could not see Nanny anywhere. Celestine said very seriously:

'I'm afraid your cat is a leetle fière, proud, no? I cannot say she is happy. I cannot say she is unhappy. But independent, pas affectueuse. She know you pay her pension. Zat is what makes her fière. When my cats want zeir food, zey make me politesses; not yours. She come, like a lady, to table. You want know where she is? She is on ze roof. If she had been nicer, I would have wanted keep her, so it's lucky for you. I have spent all ze holidays here. My ladies are all at Biarritz or at Deauville and zeir maids at Ostend. I shall have to wait till Christmas to make money. The maids will catch ze influenza and I shall be asked to take zeir places.

'Don't *you* ever catch flu?'

'I? Zamais! To catch ze influenza, you must see peoples, and I only see cats, and when I take the place of a maid who is ill she is at her own flat looking after herself, and I am alone.'

'And the maid's lady? Don't you see her?'

'Zose sort of ladies don't count. One doesn't vraiment see them. They get up. They go to bed. They work, what? They have no time to lose. Sometimes, ze first day, zey go out of their way a leetle. One has to read the cards. C'est sûr, I talk more when I am here. One is always having to talk to the cats. Would you like me to call your Nanny?'

She took a knife and whetstone and put herself in front of the open window. Nanny arrived in the wake of a large tabby. Though I covered her with kisses she was not particularly pleased to see me, and made strenuous efforts to return to the slates.

Emma was sitting on my bed listening to my mother telling her about our adventures in Paris. Seeing Nanny in my arms she exclaimed:

'Haven't you got rid of that animal yet? How on earth do you suppose you can be tidy—two people and a cat in a one-room flat, and the cat always having kittens. I tell you, it isn't reasonable.'

Nanny went to my mother, then inspected everything in the room, sneezing because of the pepper on the carpet, jumping up on the table where she curled up on a piece of material, closing her golden eyes, dropping her head between her paws.

Lunch was very gay. The woman in the room next to ours was doing her autumn cleaning. Her broom would crash against the dividing wall and make us jump. Nanny turned her head disdainfully, though this was a neighbour our cat should have been fond of, recognizing her step; for twice a week, on Wednesdays and Saturdays, we used to find a tiny package of succulent morsels, pheasant, jugged hare, or shoulder of lamb, outside our door, left there by our neighbour for Nanny.

My mother decided I should lose no time in taking the letter of introduction to the Savoy Hotel.

On Monday morning, simply dressed, I left our house at exactly ten. The air was crisp. Autumn daisies with tall branches of coppery leaves were bunched in rusty tins on stalls in Seven Dials. Canaries in cages and second-hand clothing suspended from hangers decorated the fronts of low, soot-sullied brick houses. Strange cockney faces peered at one in this once dangerous piece of London. My love for this mighty, unhurried town was treacherously driving away memories of our holiday in Paris. My steps were surer here, my affection personal. The vegetable smells and encumbered streets of Covent Garden had become synonymous with my ideas of home. The market porters, a dozen round wicker baskets piled one above the other on their capped heads, bawling out a hopeful winner to their friends, picked a sure-footed way amongst wooden cases of black plums and over-ripe tomatoes some of which, escaping from their boxes, streaked the road, between the legs of the ponies, like blood. Loving the picturesqueness of the scene, childish in spite of my years, the woman in me shuddered at the thought of slipping with high heels, receiving from the top of some rumbling cart something to stain my carefully brushed costume or new hat worn to impress a potential employer. I crossed the Strand with the smell of onions and pears in my quivering nostrils. Now, in the courtyard of the famous hotel, with the tall, good-looking porters dressed in sky-blue uniforms, the perfumed American women impeccably turned out, their menfolk, spectacled, in light suits, as romantic as in a film, limousines parked outside the florist's shop, my heart thumped. A revolving door admitted me into an atmosphere of central heating and cigar smoke, thick carpets difficult to walk on, and black studded trunks with colourful labels collected during world tours. There was a glass door on my right. Here was the hairdressing shop with its bottles of costly French perfume, electric globes burning with the warmth of amber. The various perfumes escaped from their bottles, mixing headily. My eyes swept the shelves—the 'Quelques Fleurs' of Houbigant in its corpulent, healthy-looking bottle, the 'Heure Bleue' of Guerlain, safe under a little roof, the 'No. 90' of Guerlain, elegantly standing on one leg and a glass stopper in the form of Napoleon's hat, Coty's 'L'Or,' beside their 'Emeraude,' 'L'Origan,' and 'Paris'; the magnificent 'Nuit de Noël' of Caron, and Mme Chanel's precious 'Number Five.' Many others were there also, which I was to note in more detail at a later date. A little higher up I remember admiring the lavender waters and the eaux de Cologne.

The cashier took my letter and like a queen beat her hands for a tiny page dressed in grey with gold buttons who arrived and flew off with the letter as lightly as a butterfly. I had time to examine other things, the powder-puffs of swan's-down, hairbrushes with ivory backs, lipsticks, and eyeblack.

The small page came back and beckoned me to follow him. We passed silently along the thick carpet. A man with rather fine delicate features, grey hair, and a Belgian accent explained that I would have to wait, but not very long because one of the girls was leaving to get married. He gave me a copy of the *Hairdressers' Journal*, telling me to find something else till he was ready for me. He said he would walk with me as far as the Strand.

'So you went to Paris to learn the whole business in a fortnight? Some girls don't even do that. The important thing is to be young and pretty.' He smiled at the cashier, passed a finger over the scent bottles to see if they had been dusted, and gently lifting a curtain pulled out a bowler hat which he kept hidden so that the staff should not know when he went out.

In the Strand he repeated his promise to engage me within the next few weeks, shook me almost affectionately by the hand, and after a quick look over his shoulder, dived down some steps into a tavern.

I hurried delightedly past the Adelphi Theatre to Trafalgar Square, where a professional pigeon charmer had collected a crowd round his untidy person. The misty sun gave a pale wash to the crystal globe above the Coliseum. Great names in music hall were written large. My mother and I occasionally went here to see Little Tich and Lily Morris. In the middle of the traffic rose proudly the Edith Cavell memorial with its stark inscription: 'DAWN 1915,' which sent a warmth of pride up the spines of English people remembering. Flowers were strewn on the stone floor. The noise of the German firing squad was muffled by the continual roar of traffic.

I went on unhurried, full of my youth and belief in the future.

By the first week in October I had already started at the Savoy. Being the youngest I went there very early, putting in two hours at the cash-desk, where I used to browse amongst the perfumes and sew my lingerie. I continued to sleep on my couch under the window, with Nanny or one of her kittens rolled up in the hollow of my neck, and as soon as coffee was ready my mother used to wake me up. I had to dislodge the cat or her kitten and start immediately to put on my stockings, whereupon my furry companion would jump into the couch where it was even warmer and curl up, purring. Soon ears would twitch, nostrils dilate, paws lazily stretch out. My mother, having placed a saucer under the table, the smell of warm milk would come up alluringly. The cats jumped down, and I was free to make the bed.

The postman acted as my clock.

He began at the end of the street, giving a double knock at each door all the way down. When he reached the house before ours I put my hat on, kissed mother and the cats, and pulled open the door at the very moment he was putting out his hand for the knocker. Thus, instead of pushing the letters between the bottom of the door and the white step he handed them to me, a letter for the cook on the top floor and another in my mother's hand written to Mme Maurer at the Beaujon Hospital in Paris, and returned to sender.

I gave a shout to my mother, so that she should know there was something for her, and ran up. She was bending over the banisters to save me coming right up to our landing. As I handed her the letter I said:

'It looks as if Mme Maurer has left hospital without leaving an address. Obviously she hasn't gone back to Clichy.'

'I don't understand,' said my mother, turning the letter up and down, back and front. Then, peering at a strange hand: 'What 's it say here?'

I ran up the last few stairs, took the much-marked envelope, and read:

'Widow Maurer, deceased.'

The next Saturday at one my girl friend, Scotty, and I came home for lunch. We were to go to Richmond that afternoon on top of a bus. As soon as my mother leant out of the window to throw us the front-door key I could see she was upset, but as, during the meal, she said nothing, I did not dare question her in the presence of a third person. She had been making a dress for my companion, who tried it on, but though we both admired it, played with Nanny, and did our best to appear light-hearted, my mother remained sad. I thought she might still be upset about Mme Maurer's death, for this strange woman had been of great influence in our lives. I took Scotty down to Stacey Street, telling her she must go to Richmond by herself, as I could not leave my mother alone in the state she was in.

When I returned to our room I found her ironing. A large tear dropped from her cheek and hit the hot iron, where it was absorbed with a tiny crackling noise. Then another fell, and the same thing happened.

'What *is* the matter, mother?'

'Just a letter from Marie-Thérèse.'

She tossed her head sideways, indicating a large sheet folded in four.

'Does that mean Rolande is worse?'

'No. You can read the letter.'

I took the paper covered with my aunt's childish hand, and read:

'MY DEAR MATILDA,

'I am in despair. The last few days have been really disheartening. The latest operation is to take place on Saturday, the day you will probably receive this letter. Oh, these first days of October when the leaves fall and the children go back to school! Do you remember them at Blois, the shops full of school books and coloured crayons, and the boys and girls wearing their black aprons? Everything smelt so good. The wine shops sold the first wine of the autumn, and then there were bags of fresh walnuts outside the grocers' shops. What an October I shall have this year! The pain has become intolerable. It's not worth while taking aspirin any longer. Nothing makes the slightest difference. I dragged myself as far as Groslay on Sunday to tell Rolande that Louis would be coming alone for a week or two. I've already packed my bag to go to hospital. That will leave me clear to work. I simply must finish all the hats I've started. Have you heard about hats this winter? There'll be lots of feathers, I think, and thick felts in brown and grey, and the cutest dark red. Rolande has become the cleverest needlewoman. She has already made herself a set of lingerie, and her needles are so fine one can hardly believe they are for human hands. She has also made me a nightie in the silk you gave her. I found her very gay, and though she coughed quite a bit she joked all the time with Louis. What weather we are having! But the leaves were falling fast and the gardens were full of chrysanthemums. When we were little girls I remember we did not like chrysanthemums. I went to buy a few things at market this morning, but by the time I came home I was so done in that I had to rest in the porter's lodge. The dear woman helped me up the stairs, pretending she was obliged to go round with the letters. There was nobody in the flat, of course, not at that hour. I drew up a chair by the open window and cried. Yes, I cried because I'm sad and it hurts so. Honestly, Louis is so good. He doesn't deserve a wife with cancer and a daughter with consumption. It's too much for him. I know everything now. I know, for instance, that nothing will ever do me any good. I wouldn't go through with this new operation if it were not for Rolande and Louis.

'Tell Madeleine to take care of her health. We never take sufficient care of ourselves when we are young women. I shall be at the Laennec Hospital.

'MARIE-THÉRÈSE.'

My mother did not suggest going to Paris. Though the idea may have passed through her mind she was too economical to spend so much money on a new journey. Mme Maurer's philosophy was not to allow sentiment to put one into debt. We had not forgotten the lesson of my father's coffin.

My mother was also of the opinion that just now my future was taking shape. She wanted to be with me. The Savoy Hotel, with its glittering mirrors, heady perfumes, and American millionaires had an unreal, Arabian night's atmosphere, exciting, but not without danger for a young, exuberant girl. A magic name in the motion picture world offered to groom me in Hollywood. I was to be the star in an important picture. My name would glitter on Broadway. I hesitated; then refused, unwilling to leave London. A distinguished New York publisher, whilst confiding his hands into my care, talked seriously about books. I did not hide my ardent desire to become an authoress. These great men, world-famous figures, were full of interest in the unknown person who sat so humbly at their feet. I began to have a new conception of the American people. Their simple kindly manners and immense generosity and, even more, their eagerness to help somebody else along the path to success found immediate response in my young heart. My mother was quick to sense that herein might lie the explanation of those words so often used by fortune-tellers—that I would become famous. With my pen? It was not yet possible to tell. Our lives were taking a sudden turn like the bend of a river, changing its whole course. Clichy, Mme Maurer, and my Aunt Marguerite, who had once again quarrelled with my mother, belonged to that part of the river we were leaving behind.

My mother went on ironing. By now there were three piles of warm, clean, freshly ironed linen. Nanny sat on each in turn. We stroked her with tears in our eyes.

On Thursday evening I came home rather depressed, having been scolded by M. Adolphe, my Belgian friend, for having misunderstood an order on the telephone. I had not yet realized he was too kind ever to hurt a member of his staff.

I again found my mother in tears. This time she had received a letter from my Uncle Louis, which she silently handed me.

'MY DEAR MATILDA,

'As you know, Marie-Thérèse was to go to the Laennec Hospital on Saturday for another operation. On Friday evening, when I came back from work, I found her sitting up in bed, her face all drawn, holding a hat so tightly that I had trouble in taking it away from her. She seemed frozen in this attitude, not lifeless but rigid. I ran out for our doctor. He said it was a stroke. She had gone mad with fear about the operation. We took her immediately to the Laennec, where she died the next morning without ever recovering consciousness. We buried her on Monday, my dear Matilda. I had no time to let you know. You know what it is with cancer. My darling Rolande was too ill to come. The only other person besides myself was dear Rose.

'I am so very unhappy. Fancy going mad with pain and fear! Each time I shut my eyes I see her with the unfinished hat in her hands. She was a brave little woman. Now, only Rolande is left. . . .'